The Chronicles of Arax
Book Seven

Restoration

Benjamin Sanford

Copyright © 2024 Benjamin Sanford

All rights reserved

STENOX PUBLISHING
Clarksburg, MD

Cover Art by Karl Moline

ISBN 979-8-9890221-6-8 (paperback)
ISBN 979-8-9890221-7-5 (ebook)

Printed in the United States of America

ACKNOWLEDGEMENTS

I decided to wait until this last book of the Araxan Saga to list the many people who have influenced this work and provided helpful feedback. Without their insight and encouragement this work would never have been completed, and I wish to take these pages to express my deepest gratitude.

I want to first say, that without the love and influence of my parents, nothing I accomplished in life would have come to fruition. As my brother Harv often said, "There are no one like Mom and Dad, no one. They are the finest people I have ever known, and no one else is even close." They have both been dead now for many years, and his words ring truer the longer I walk this earth. My other siblings feel as I do, and we are all grateful and unworthy to have been their children. To Mom and Dad, just know how much we all love you, now and forever. Love, Tim, Harv, Laura, Matt, Joel and Ben.

My feelings for my siblings are much the same. I love them all, and they each have played a large part in who I am. A very large part of my favorite characters was influenced by them, in ways they probably don't even realize.

Then there is my wife, my beautiful Farzaneh, who is the smartest and most capable woman I have ever known. I can humbly say, she is a far better person than I, in every way. Just as I didn't deserve the parents or siblings I was generously given, I don't deserve her either, and yet she chose me. She is the love of my life, and without her I would never have completed this work.

It was my nephew Adam that contributed a great amount in the development of this story. I wrote the first 9 chapters with him in mind when he was around ten, and he loved the story and helped write portions of the first draft of what is now books 1 and 2. Though many of the details have changed since then, the basic story remains the same. Thank you Adam for motivating me in keeping the story alive through the years and finally completing it.

To my oldest friend Tony, it was from the make-believe worlds we created when we were children that this story sprang to life. Without those fun-filled days of youth, Arax would never have been created. It was from those days that we created the characters that came to populate Arax, Cronus, Terin, Raven, Zem and Tyro, and many more that came to mind as we played. Thank you, Tony for your imagination and friendship. It is the friends we make in childhood that live with us forever.

Having spent most of my career traveling the world, it was the countless interactions with so many people that shaped many of the characters in my writing, from taxi drivers in Las Vegas to bar tenders in Frankfurt, and so many in between, but the most impactful were my friends such as Damian, Jim, Steve and Tony, and so many others. I can't leave out my children, each proving every day they are smarter than me, which I attribute to their mother.

I also thank Col. Wes Martin, US Army (Retired). Wes has been a dear friend of mine for more than 34 years. It was from him I learned much of the tactics and strategies I used throughout this epic, as well as the inspiration for many of the great commanders that fill these pages. He is a man of incredible honor, integrity and competence, and the finest officer the US Army has ever produced.

I have also drawn inspiration for this story from countless movies, books, television shows, music, poetry, art, history and philosophy, and countless other mediums, each playing a part in the narrative.

I would like to give a special thanks to those that have read it, and provided encouragement and vital feedback, which is the life-blood of any writer, especially an amateur one as myself. My brothers Harv, Tim and Joel. My sister-in-law Pat, who gave the most detailed feedback, looking at characters in a way I hadn't considered. My niece Jill, who seemed to cry at so many parts. My nieces Katie and Nichole. My uncle Dave, who always shared my love for science fiction, and said he cried in book five, though I won't say which part.

And last, is Sayde, who helped me shape the ending and bring the story fully together. To all of you, thank you, I love you all.

DEDICATION

I originally meant to include this last person in the acknowledgements, but recent events changed that. When I finished the first book in the series, I struggled to find the right artist to do the cover, wanting someone who could fully capture the essence of the story. My friend Jim Curry mentioned that his cousin, Karl Moline, was an artist, who had done incredible work on many projects, including Marvel Comics. We spoke on the phone, and he agreed to do each of the covers. After completing the first six, he tragically died this summer. He was a decent and kind-hearted man, who I never met in person, but spent countless hours on the phone discussing a myriad of topics, and especially pop culture and the stories that inspired our respective works. He managed to draw the cover for book seven, but hadn't colored it when he passed. The artist from my publishing company managed to finish Karl's work.

I cannot think of a more deserving person to dedicate this project to than the one who created the images my words described. To Karl Modine, an incredible artist, and a better person. May you rest in peace, my friend, and thank you.

RESTORATION PART ONE

NODDEGAMRA

BENOTORIS
FEDERATION OF THE SISTERHOOD
ANDLER RIVER
LAYCROM
MORGA RIVER
TINSAY
GORGA RIVER
FERA
MOTE MOUNTAINS
TUSS RIVER
COT RIVER
VORUN GAP
FELA
BANSOCH
TENIN
TELFER
TENIA RIVER
RULON GAP
REGO
NILA
STLEN RIVER
PEI
YATIN
MUVA RIVER
FAUST
MOSAR
EMPIRE
CENTRAL CITY
TURLIS
YAGAN MARSHES
ZULON
RIVER
TESO
LAKE MONATA
TUK NILA
TORRY SOUTH
CAGAN
MONATA RIVER
SAWYER
FLEACE
MACON
CLEV RIVER
CESA
NULL
EMPIRE
CHIHAN ISLE

EMPIRE
PAGAN
TUR RIVER
BEDO
CORPI
TERSE
NISIN
REGUN RIVER
LAKE VENEBA
ARTE MTS.
CROF
BACEL
TRO
BESOS
NOTSU
CORELL
KREGARIN ISLE
TORRY
LONE HILLS
NORTH
TALON PASS
APE
TORN
GREGOK
EMPIRE
EL ORVA
JENAII
BARBEIRO
NAIBA RIVER
ELARIS RIVER
NON
PLOU
NAYBORIA
ENORUCTA
EL TOVA
MIKUS
VARABIS
LINKORTIS
ROCKY SHORE
CASIAN SEA
MILITO
TERIS
COVEN
PORT WEST
CASIAN LEAGUE

CHAPTER 1

They stood there for an eternal moment, neither saying a word, the village matching their silence with nary a sound in the air. The late day sun hung low in the west, symbolic of their setting friendship. There were no questions asked nor answers given. There were no excuses for what transpired to bring them to this point. What more was there to say but goodbye. With that, Ben went for the draw, and Raven followed, flashes of blue laser streaming through the air as Tosha screamed.

ZIP! ZIP! ZIP!

Laser flashed through the air in a dizzying array, streams of blue light racing across that narrow space. Tosha froze in place, her disobedient limbs betraying her, as if the fates deigned her presence to only bear witness to the unfolding scene. Raven's first blast took Ben full in the chest, Thorton's return fire striking the ground at Raven's feet. Zelo never cleared leather, his winged form succumbing to numerous blasts, the first from Argos, standing at Raven's left, the others from somewhere behind them, where stood Zem and Orlom with rifles drawn down upon the gargoyle. Unbeknownst to Raven, they had followed them on the second ski, taking up position in the distance where the first ski rested. A woman's scream drew Tosha's attention as she rushed from the same structure Thorton had emerged just moments before. The woman ran to Ben as he dropped to the ground, kneeling at his side with tears running down her cheeks.

"Damn him!" Raven growled, stomping forward with his pistol drawn, closing on his fallen friend, signaling Tosha to join him.

ZIP! ZIP!

Raven sent two more blasts into Zelo's thrashing corpse, the creature's body convulsing under the strain of his mortal blows, laser blasts tearing apart his torso and another punching through his skull. Raven didn't break stride, closing on Ben before holstering his pistol, pushing Ella aside as she tried to take Ben's head into her arms.

"Damn fool!" Raven growled, with Ben looking back at him with a twisted smile on his lips. The last thing Ben heard was Raven's voice calling out to Tosha before his world went dark.

* * *

Ben Thorton felt himself lifting through the air, the world below fading from his vision, his senses dulled in a formless void. He lingered there, lost in time and place, his thoughts a maelstrom of disjointed memories and futures unrealized. Visions swept over him, one after another, building in intensity, each more momentous than the last, some glorious but many more terrible to behold. Was this a portal to the future, or a punishment for his sins? Amid all the chaos one voice called out to him... Promise me, Texas.

"Jen," he called out to her, feeling her near. He found himself amid a swirling mist, as if caught in the clouds, before a slender sliver of light took shape before him, its blurry image solidifying into her familiar form. Jennifer appeared as he remembered, her vibrant brown eyes sparkling with so much life to convince him she was real, though her ethereal visage gave him pause. Her raiment shifted with the light before taking a loose form, wearing a white gown that melded with their surroundings.

"Yes, it is me, my love." She smiled at him, reaching out her hand to his face, caressing his cheek with fingers that were half flesh and half spirit. It was soothing and tantalizing, drawing him further from the mortal realm to wherever she dwelt.

"You were dead," he said, his voice breaking with emotion.

"Perhaps, in a way, but life is deathless, true life and true love." She smiled, her gentle eyes filling his empty heart.

"Then I am home, finally home with you." He almost wept with joy before she again broke his heart with her next utterance.

"It is not your time, my love. Not yet."

"No! I have no desire to live."

"You made a promise," she reminded him, keeping her hand to his cheek.

"I kept my promise. I let him kill me, so we might be together."

"That was not what you promised, Texas, not in spirit. I must go," she said, drawing her hand from his cheek, her form drawing away from his desperate grasp.

"No, bring me with you!" he called out as she drew further away, his own body frozen in place.

"It is not your time, my love." Her voice grew faint, her visage disappearing into the murky void.

"No!" he cried out to her, feeling his body leaning back before falling freely, the world passing before his eyes.

"No!" he growled, his eyes springing open.

"You kept your promise by letting me kill you?" Raven growled in English, having overheard his fevered ramblings.

Ben turned his head, finding Raven sitting upon the opposite bunk, staring at him with a deathly scowl. He found himself in the 1st crew cabin on the 1st deck of the *Stenox*, laying abed, with a loose sheet covering his naked chest. He still wore his thick trousers and socks, his boots resting on the floor beside his bunk, with his shirt, jacket, Stetson and holster resting atop them. Looking at Raven brought only one question to mind.

"Why am I alive?" Ben growled back, speaking in their native tongue as well.

"Because I aimed for your gun arm, and when you leaned into it, I hit near your heart. Tosha brought the regenerator, and we managed to save your life. That's why you are alive."

"Why bother? There will never be peace between us, not after everything that's happened. Just finish me and be done with it!" he growled back.

"Was that your plan, to have me kill you so you can leave this world?"

Ben's silence was all the confirmation he needed.

"You wanted me to kill you, instead of doing it yourself? Coward!" Raven came off the bunk, standing over him with his fists balled.

"Coward? I'm the one who killed Kato, allied with Tyro and gave them the weapon to attack this ship, and even then, you couldn't finish me? What more do you need?" Ben growled back, coming up to a sitting position, staring up at him angrily.

"You aren't the only one who made a promise, fool!"

"What use was your promise when you let her die?" Ben said, coming to his feet, his nose pressed to Raven's.

And there it was, the terrible truth that lay between them, laid bare.

"You're not the only one that loved her. How was I supposed to feel? I lost her and I lost you that day. My sister dead, and my best friend gone. Oh, you are here physically, but your mind sure as hell ain't. If you want to die so damn much, do it!" Raven drew his pistol, offering it to him.

Ben just glared at him, a loss for words.

"Take it! Put it to your head and pull the trigger and spare the rest of us your self-pity!"

There they stood, staring one another down, neither saying a word for the longest time. What more was there to say? Ben was too proud to offer any excuse for Kato's death, willing to let Raven think the worst. He simply didn't care. He wouldn't be judged for what he did, though he regretted their friend's death. He was the first to choose sides in this war when Raven and the others didn't care, selling their services for gold they didn't even want or need.

"Nothing to say for yourself? Too weak to put it to your head and finish what's left of your sorry excuse for a life?" Raven goaded.

"I don't need lectures from you of all people, Rav."

"I'm not the one who killed our friend."

"I aimed for his shoulder, the same as you did for me, and he shifted into it, exposing his heart. I returned the favor with you, but for some stupid reason you decide to bring me back, and here I am."

"You blaming me for saving your life again? Unbelievable."

"I never asked you to save it, not now and certainly not then. I asked only one thing from you back on Cragnellon, and you couldn't do it, or wouldn't do it."

"Even I couldn't save her at that point, and you would have died too. And maybe I didn't want to make my nephew an orphan. Did you ever think about that? And despite all that, you still didn't recuse yourself from the *Eden Expedition*. You shouldn't even be here. You should have been home taking care of your son."

"That was her place, not mine. A boy needs his mother, and you took that away, and for what? Me." Ben's voice trailed, his ire easing into more self-pity.

"You came along on this expedition hoping to die, didn't you?" Raven suddenly realized, the look on Ben's face confirming it.

It was then he realized how hopeless Ben Thorton was, and for some inexplicable reason, he couldn't bring himself to kill him.

"No, Rav. I was already dead."

* * *

"Why don't we just kill him and be done with it?" Kendra asked, looking at Raven and Thorton's exchange from the viewscreen in the weapon's room with Brokov. Since she was trained by the ship's neural link to learn English, she understood every word they spoke.

"I don't know. If you asked me a few months back, that would have been an easy choice, but now? Something feels off, and I can't put my finger on it." Brokov shook his head.

Kendra spent enough time with him to understand most of his strange references, but *a finger on it* was a new one. By their interrogation of Alen and the woman Ella, they discovered Ben's recent activities, including his ignorance of the attack on the *Stenox* and his not meaning to kill Kato. It didn't absolve him fully of these crimes, but it did put them in perspective. There was also his protection of Alen, and Brokov felt there was more to it than merely using the former palace slave as bait to lure Raven to Near Point. From all they learned of the attack on Tro, it was originally supposed to commence with the broken laser rifle destroying the ruling forum, followed by an attack on the city fleet, leaving the apes unscathed, leaving the blame for the attack on them for failing to protect the city. That plan was modified by Morac, who wanted to attack the apes directly, and then by Hossen Grell who wanted to attack the *Stenox*. Most troubling was the fact that the heir of House Maiyan was involved with the plot, and Tyro planned for him to be the only surviving member of the ruling families, raising him up as regent of the city and Tyro's vassal. That information was best kept quiet as House Maiyan was now among the staunchest supporters of the war. If the other ruling families ever learned the truth, it wouldn't be from the Earthers.

"Then what do we do with him? We can't let him go." Kendra asked the most obvious question.

"That, my dear, is the trillion-dollar question."

"Why is it I know what that means?" She shook her head.

* * *

Alen sat at the table in the dining cabin, stretching his repaired knee as Ular looked on, observing his range of motion. Ella sat across from him while Tosha lingered at the door with her arms crossed.

"It is fully healed. Thank you, Ular," Alen said, giving Tosha a wary look from across the cabin. He didn't know what to think of her presence, considering their history, but she didn't appear dangerous. He wondered at that. Brokov gave him a brief narrative of events since they last parted, but much was left out considering their time constraints. His description of the events at Bansoch were very brief, omitting much of what happened there, but her presence suggested her and Raven coming to an accord. Her wearing Earth garb and carrying herself like the others portended an extreme change from the woman he knew before.

"Though your wound was crippling, it appeared to have been impressively attended," Ular observed, his watery voice taking Alen aback. It was another strange sight he was growing accustomed to. Of course, every moment with the Earthers brought about strange occurrences that were difficult to grasp.

"Thorton treated it as well as he could and then had the matrons at Nisin attend it daily," Ella interjected on Ben's behalf.

"That was kind of him," Tosha said, trying to gauge Ella's opinion on one Ben Thorton.

"He has shown mercy when he has been able." Ella sighed, lowering her gaze to the table, fearing she said too much.

"Except for poor Kato." Tosha shook her head.

Ella opened her mouth as if to refute that but relented. She simply sighed and lowered her head.

Alen was torn by the grim tidings. He learned of Kato's death only through others during his captivity at Nisin, wondering how Thorton could have slain his friend and former comrade, though Ben never spoke of it. The more he learned of what transpired between them, the more tragic it seemed. He didn't truly know what to think of Thorton, the man's behavior as unpredictable as the sea. One moment he performed terrible acts, and the next was strangely merciful.

"Kato was a good friend," Alen sighed, recalling their journey to Corell so long ago.

"It seems you have made many good friends since we last parted," Tosha said.

"Yes, and many of them died fighting at my side here in the north." Alen gave her a hard look, wondering her motive for probing so blatantly.

"You seem to have found success as well if the tidings from Gostovar are true," Tosha said, bringing to mind Alen's greatest victory in their revolt, the sacking of the vital trading hub southeast of Pagan.

"Yes, we razed the city and freed their slaves." He looked at her sternly, wondering why she seemed so unmoved by the tidings.

"You were quite effective in drawing out my father's garrisons to combat your uprising. Take heart in that, Alen," Tosha said with an impressed tone.

"It was all for naught. Most of my people were slaughtered, many by Thorton's hand. I only survived by Thorton's strange motive, which I do not understand."

"It was not for naught, Alen. Your revolt contributed much to our cause, in ways you do not see," Ular said with his watery voice.

"How so?" Alen asked.

"By keeping Thorton in the north to put down the uprising, Raven had a free hand at Corell, once he determined that Thorton was not there. He and Orlom slew many of Tyro's soldiers before the walls of Corell and struck down twenty thousand when Prince Lorn arrived with his army. Had you not kept Thorton's eyes in the north, that would not have transpired so impressively," Ular sagely pointed out.

Alen hadn't considered that. For so long he thought of his many friends who died fighting here in the north, thinking their sacrifice was for nothing. Perhaps their sacrifice did have purpose.

"You contributed much to Lorn's victory, Alen, and can contribute even more to our cause now," Tosha said.

"Our cause?" Alen was taken aback by her eagerness to overthrow her father.

"Our cause. My mother has called for war with my father, and the Sisterhood has answered. They are moving against him as we speak. I am oathbound to obey and shall join our Torry allies gathering at Nisin. Where you can contribute is in rallying your rebels to our banners."

"That shall be difficult as they are scattered, and you are so few."

"There are more of us than you realize, and many of your rebels are still active along the Tur River Valley. They can reach here rather quickly if summoned," she pointed out.

He had heard little of the rebellion in this region since he departed for lands in the west, but if true, they still might not heed his summons, and he voiced why that was so.

"It is little secret that your armies will soon march for Nisin, leaving Pagan weakly held. Why would the rebels risk coming here and having the Benotrist garrison attack them?" he pointed out.

"Because Regent Galenta has declared his loyalty for Terin and established a ruling council to seek out and rally other Benotrist lands to do so. The garrison has sworn oaths to Terin as well," she said.

"Terin? Why would they do so?" Alen made a face.

"Because he is my father's rightful heir." Tosha smirked, enjoying the confused look on Alen's poor face all too much. She let him linger for a painful moment before explaining everything.

* * *

It was late in the evening when Matuzak joined Raven upon the 3rd deck of the *Stenox*, looking out across the bay with moonlight reflecting off its tranquil surface. Raven was weary of arguing with Ben, the two venting years of pent-up rage in the matter of two hours. Raven couldn't bring himself to kill him, and Ben wouldn't kill Raven or himself, which left them at an impasse.

"I don't know who suffered more this day, my boy, you with your friend down below, or me dealing with the politics in Regent Galenta's palace," the ape president chuckled in good humor, setting his furry forearms on the low wall of the lookout deck.

"I'd wager on my misery. I should have killed him back at Near Point, but something held me back. Talking to him was useless and looking him in the eyes is even worse. It sort of takes away the need for killing a man when he wants you to do it." Raven sighed, resting his forearms upon the wall, matching Matuzak's.

"War does strange things to an ape, or a man in your friend's situation. I once knew a young warrior not much older than Orlom who was a quiet lad, kept to himself and barely spoke a word. One day he took a blow to the head and began singing bawdy songs and reciting off-putting puns which we all found to our liking. We found the new version of him an improvement, but reason suggests it could have easily been done in reverse, making an entertaining ape dull, but there you have it. It was the oddest thing I have seen, other than when you rascals arrived on our little world upsetting the nature of things." Matuzak slapped him on the back.

"I've heard of such things too, but Ben wasn't hit on the head," Raven pointed out.

"Aye, but losing someone you love more than yourself can do something to you. Have you thought on what you will do with him?"

"No. I can't kill him, but we can't let him go, not while we have a war to finish, though by the look of him he doesn't have any desire to fight us either. It's all so stupid."

"Well, we plan on marching for Nisin in the coming days, and I suspect you'll be coming along," Matuzak rightly guessed.

"That's the plan, but I don't know how I can leave him behind, all things considered."

"Bringing him along might be worse. Perhaps you could find a lonely isle to drop him off on. Maybe that girl will go with him. She's a right pretty lass."

"I've considered that, and Tosha thinks the girl is fond of him, but Ben doesn't share those feelings."

"He doesn't?"

"No."

"Then why did he take her?"

"From what Tosha determined, it was her voice, and to save her from the occupying forces of Tenin."

"Her voice?" Matuzak made a face.

"It reminded him of his wife. She would sing for him. Of all the insane things he has done, that about sums it all up. It reminds me of what my dad used to say…"

"*Everyone around here is nuts but you and me, and you're a little bit off*," Matuzak chuckled, repeating it before Raven could.

"I guess you know me too well." He shook his head.

"Aye, my boy, you're as predictable as the sunrise."

"Probably," he conceded.

"Aye, but predictable is good. It lets others know where you stand and if they can depend on you. Isn't that why you are friends with Cronus, Ular and all the rest of them?"

"True. I trust them all."

"Aye, and trust is the greatest of virtues, for if one doesn't have that, his words are worth nothing."

Words, Raven thought, recalling the words he and Ben both promised to his sister. In many ways, Ben was volatile and unpredictable, but when it came to keeping his promises, he was as trustworthy as anyone. If he left him behind, he would extract his oath to not interfere.

"I am curious of one thing," Matuzak said before stepping away.

"Just one thing?" Raven could think of a dozen off the top of his head.

"Why did Thorton join with Tyro? For a man committed to his own destruction, it seems a waste of effort traipsing across Arax at the behest of a man like Tyro. He claimed no interest in gold or wealth of any kind for his troubles, or even power or position. Why did he even bother?" Matuzak wondered.

Raven just shook his head, knowing the absurdity of the truth.

"For the greater good," he sighed.

"Greater good?" The old ape warrior made a face.

"He believed Arax needed to be united and that Tyro was the only one strong enough to do it."

"United for what reason?"

"In the event people from my world found us. He rambled on about evil bureaucrats or bankers, or something like that. It was all confusing, which about sums up Ben Thorton in his current state."

"Hmph. Why did he think we could ever unite with gargoyles?"

"Good question. He's spent enough time with them by now to realize the only good gargoyle is a dead one."

"Aye, my boy, that is the right of it."

* * *

The following days saw the harbor abuzz with activity as the ships unloaded supplies, and the armies prepared to march. Regent Galenta offered up two telnics of the garrison's best soldiers for the expedition, while his agents reached out to the rebel groups still operating along the Tur River Valley, calling upon them to gather at Pagan, offering local pardons and promises of alliance should they join in the march upon Nisin. Alen went about organizing the rebels that filtered in, preparing them to spread the word throughout the eastern half of the empire, calling upon their fellows to gather at Nisin, joining their new allies for the battles ahead. It was the rebels influence across the vast countryside of the realm that would be most beneficial to their armies as they advanced through heart of the empire, fortifying their lines of communication.

Tosha used her position as the Princess of the realm to reach out to other Benotrist strongholds that lay between Pagan and Nisin, convincing several to join them in cause. Most would rebuff her outreach until their armies were at their doorstep. For that reason, above any other, she would join the march upon Nisin, forgoing her Earth garb for her martial uniform. Most of the holdfasts of the eastern half of the empire were populated with non-Benotrists, their loyalty to the crown tethered by the thinnest of strings.

As for the others in the crew, it was decided that one ski would depart with the armies, leaving the other with the *Stenox*, allowing anyone to return or join the armies with relative ease. Raven, Zem and Argos would join the march, each taking turns flying the ski. Ular would stay with the ship as his countrymen remained with the fleet. Orlom was most disappointed when Raven asked him to remain and help safeguard the ship and help train their newest recruits, Gorbad and Darpak.

Brokov produced an additional eight comms that he distributed to their allies, including two to the Casian army, one to Kaly, two to the Ape army, with the three others spread evenly to their armada. He also produced three more regenerators, sending two with the armies and the other as a gift to the harbor matrons' guild. If they won this war, he planned to have every major municipality on Arax given a regenerator within a year. It was but one of many ideas Brokov had for improving the lives of the inhabitants of Arax.

Thorton stood upon the 3rd deck, resting his forearms upon its low wall, observing the activity on the wharfs below. He spied the long columns of infantry parading forth, moving toward the west gate of the city, joining the others already enroute for Nisin. He noted the sizable number of garrison troops joining them, adding their strength to their former enemy. They matched the impressive number of Benotrist warships dotting the harbor, now bearing the sigil of the Torry Champion, a blue glowing sword upon a field of silver. They were what remained of the 3rd, 4th, and 6th Benotrist Fleets, with Admiral Silniw the only surviving admiral of the three, the old mariner having sworn to Terin just yester morn. He could hardly blame the man for his treason considering the state of things and the bedeviling dreams he and every other Benotrist shared of late. Was he the only one not to suffer such visions? In the grand scheme of things, it didn't truly matter, for Tyro's empire was doomed. The fatal blow was delivered at Tro and then Corell. Once the Earthers were brought into the war it was decided, with the crushing of Tyro's legions at Corell ending the matter for good.

The Benotrist Empire was now subject to a painfully drawn-out death, its fate sealed. It reminded him of the ancient wreck of the Titanic, where the doomed ship struck an iceberg, but took more than two and half hours to sink. Tyro was like one of those unfortunate passengers watching the last lifeboat draw away while still having to wait a while for death to take him. Most men face death as it comes at them quickly, especially in battle, or have an unusual amount of time with illness in worlds without regenerators. The people on that fated ship had the torturous fate of knowing they would die in a short period, but not quickly. He hoped Tyro saw the truth of it. Unfortunately, his defeat would only doom this planet to more endless years of war and backwardness. The very suffering that the Torries and their allies decried would only continue with their victory. Once they defeated Tyro they would make peace for a time, pat each other on the back and go their separate ways. Eventually their descendants would rise, not sharing the friendship that bound them together, and they would wage war upon each other again, all in an endless circle.

It's not my problem anymore, he thought, wearing a mask of indifference as Raven cleared the ladder, joining him upon the lookout deck.

"Up here again, I see," Raven quipped, stepping to his side, resting his arms on the wall as well.

"Yep." Ben didn't turn to look at him, maintaining the icy wall between them.

"I'll be leaving soon."

"Bye" was all Ben said.

"When I return, you need to decide where you want to be dropped off. I don't care where, just as long as we don't see each other again after. You go your way, and we'll go ours."

"Yep."

"And I have your word you won't pull anything while I'm gone?"

"I keep my word, Rav, I always have." Ben finally looked at him.

"I know. You can use the time while I'm gone to decide if you want Ella to come with you. She seems to want to go with you."

"She is free to go where she wants. I was only protecting her. As for me, wherever I go, I will go alone."

Raven just shook his head, knowing his friend was truly dead. He stepped away before stopping at the ladder.

"Maybe it's time to finally look at this once I leave," Raven handed him a glowing green disc the size of his thumbnail.

Ben reluctantly took it, looking down at the small object that promised him nothing but pain. Perhaps Raven was right. He needed closure on that final strand connecting him to his humanity.

"Very well," Ben sighed, tucking it his jacket pocket.

"You were my best friend, Ben, and I loved you more than my brothers." Raven shook his head sadly and descended the ladder, leaving Ben Thorton standing alone upon the deck.

CHAPTER 2

South Bank of the Cot River.
Between the Mote and Plate Mountains.

Terin knelt at the river's edge, filling his water satchel while keeping a wary eye to the opposite bank where a large gargoyle host was once camped. He could still see the parapets lining the far shore made of soil and rock, with pointed timbers jutting prominently southward. The defensive works were built by the remnants of the 15th Gargoyle Legion, the only survivors of the Battle of Tuft's Mountain, who fortified the northern banks of both the Tuss and Cot Rivers, guarding these approaches from Torry incursions. Whatever became of the creatures was anyone's guess. All they knew was that they were not here. Finishing, he gained his feet, scanning the far bank and the forest beyond, which obscured the distant foothills of the Mote Mountains, resting to their northwest. Scores of others emerged from the forest behind him, stepping over the wet matted grass that lined the riverbank, filling their satchels as he did.

Terin took three steps before the lacing on his left sandalled boot gave out, snapping behind his left calf. He continued on toward the tree line, where sat his pack and gear. He would have to see to its repair, hoping to do so before they continued their march. The entire column remained here much of the morn as Lorn awaited Deva's guidance before continuing. Most thought they would cross the river, aiming to skirt the southern face of the Mote Mountains before breaking north along the gap separating the Mote and Cress Mountains. The other possibility was to continue northeast along the Cot River, before breaking north between the Mote and Plate gap. That route would bring them out far east of Fera, if the Black Castle was their final destination.

Terin put such worries from his mind as he made his way through the scores of others sitting amongst the trees between the forest edge and where his pack rested up ahead. His pack rested against the smooth trunk of a Topac, with vines winding around its thick base. A smiling Squid Antillius greeted him, sitting upon his pack across from his, the elder statesman seeming to enjoy their foray into the wild a little too much.

"The water is quite refreshing, I assure you, Terin." Squid smiled, lifting his satchel to his lips, partaking the surprisingly pure liquid, having topped off his just before Terin.

"Another fortunate boon considering the many foul rivers I have passed in all my journeys," Terin said, recalling the muddy creeks and streams he encountered in his flight from Fera.

"Aye, but this is mountain runoff, probably from the winter snow caps of the Mote or Plate ranges. Drinking pure mountain water brings back memories, my boy." Squid happily sighed, recalling his times traveling with Jonas during the Sadden War, so long ago.

"You are enjoying this journey." Terin smiled, setting his satchel down and fishing repair straps and gear from his pack before sitting down. He quickly removed his left sandal, unthreading the leather cords that wound through its workings.

"Perhaps. After so many years attending court and dwelling in great castles and holdfasts, it is a pleasant change to camp again beneath the stars for more than just a few nights. It does something for the soul," he wistfully sighed.

"Sleeping beneath the stars is fine if you have means of shelter and time to hunt game. This seems more hardship than pleasure," Terin said, working the leather straps free of his sandal.

"I believe that is the purpose of this journey, Terin, to cleanse our appetites of pleasure and our minds of unimportant thoughts. Think of those who have joined us on this journey, men of renown and men of little note, all now equal before Yah's eyes. We have forsaken the trappings of position and privilege, venturing forth to an unknown fate, following his will and his will alone," Squid said, easing his leg out in front of him, the coarse hem of his wool undertunic rubbing against the back of his thigh. Even their clothing was a means of hardening their bodies and sharpening their minds, each donning a woolen undertunic with a brown or tan leather overtunic, to endure the harsh use of their travels. Their mail was simple, with no individual adornments or lavish trappings. The only thing setting them apart was their weapons, each bearing their own swords, axes or bows. They were all afoot, with nary a mount of ocran or magantor among their company.

Terin thought on what Squid had said as the old man continued.

"Yah is emptying our hearts and bodies of everything that would distract us from his purpose."

"For what reason?" Terin asked.

"Is it not obvious, my boy? To fill us with something new."

* * *

"What do you see?" Lorn asked, standing over Deva where she knelt upon the forest floor, her hands outstretched to her sides and her head thrown back. King Mortus and Elos stood farther back, giving her room as if they expected the heavens to open, sending lightning and fire to consume them all, while Lucas stood dutifully behind her, her ever vigilant guardian.

Deva's mind swirled with visions of a great battle where gathered the nations, with faces both strange and familiar. Men fought men amidst the clash of shield walls and flames, slaying each other in great numbers in the shadow of the dark vale, where crimson eyes observed the carnage from afar with gleeful delight. The skies above twisted in swirls of black and gray, pregnant clouds straining to burst amid howling winds. She saw the face of friend and foe falling in battle, their blood soaking the ground, turning soil to rivers of red sludge. She saw Lorn take a blow to his chest, falling under a golden blade alit with a fiery crimson glow. King Mortus cleaved a man's sword arm before a hammer found purchase in his skull, the Macon King collapsing in a torrent of blood and cracking bone. Aldo and Squid fought desperately under a barrage of arrows, succumbing to the endless torrent. The land was beset in horror and bloodshed, the armies wasting themselves in mutual slaughter before the horns sounded in the distance. There, issuing from the bowels of their subterranean realm, came the combined might of the gargoyle race, black winged juveniles, joining their kin in the darkening skies, while countless thousands of gargoyle maidens swept over the land below, sightless eyes driven unnaturally upon the armies of men.

Thousands of Jenaii coursed above, contesting the gargoyles for dominion of the sky, their scant numbers overwhelmed in the dark multitude. 'Twas if the fountains of the deep were cast open, spilling forth untold legions of gargoyles upon the mortal realms. She looked to her left and right, seeing her fellows fall under the rising tide, apes, Jenaii and men of all realms succumbing. The Sisterhood was there, gathered at their side on this final day, centuries of conserving their strength for that final battle counting for naught. She saw several of the Earthers firing their terrible weapons with abandon, slaying thousands before they were overwhelmed. Elos was beset, dark winged forms striking from all directions, taking him piecemeal before his bloodied corpse fell from the heavens. She saw Terin fighting to the end, until even he succumbed. And she saw Lucas fighting by her side, protecting her until his last measure was spent. She wept at the sight, before the world grew dark.

The color returned to her eyes, vibrant hazel replacing clouded white, suddenly blinking to gather her senses.

"Deva?" Lorn asked, taking a knee beside her, concern etched on his face.

"We were not at Fera this time," she said.

"Where then?" he asked, for her visons were shifting, as if the future was fluid, every action triggering another result.

"I do not know the place, but the direction. We must continue along the Cot and break north five days journey from now."

"Can you describe what you saw?" he asked.

She hesitated, her silence sending tendrils of fear across his spine, before steeling himself. He belayed his request, touching a hand gently to her shoulder.

"Do not speak of it, Deva. I have had terrible visions, which changed with time and heeding Yah's will. Let us trust in that." Lorn smiled, his kindness setting her at ease.

"So, we continue in this direction," Mortus said, receiving a confirming nod from Lorn, before bellowing orders. The word quickly spread along the forest trail behind them, signaling everyone to their feet to begin their march.

"Thank you," Deva said as Lorn and Lucas helped her to her feet.

"Thank you, Deva." Lorn smiled, nodding to Lucas, trusting her again to his care.

"Let me fetch your pack," Lucas said, stepping briefly away where sat their gear at the base of a nearby Topac, sunlight breaking through its swaying boughs above.

She was thankful for his attentive care, almost feeling as a young child again with her father doting upon her. *Her father*, she thought sadly, missing his kind smile and gentle touch. She knew he was odious to poor Terin and suffered Corry's wrath for his transgressions, but she would always remember that he loved her. She could place the blame of his demise at her mother's feet, having spent a lifetime of belittling him, relegating him to a mere servant in their household. With his death there was no one who truly loved her other than her brother Guilen. She wondered where he was, resigning herself to never seeing him again. Though she held a great role among her current company, she would always be an outsider, the former cruel mistress who abused their champion and hero. She could see the mistrust and hatred in their eyes, though they kept their tongues. She could hardly blame them, but it still filled her with shame and regret. She knew her place among them was merely a gift from Yah, appointing her this task, while he could just as easily have chosen another. There was nothing special about her in that regard. In fact, it proved how un special she truly was, for she was chosen because she was evil. By granting her mercy, Yah demonstrated his power of redemption for all to see. It was for this reason she was thankful for Lucas' company. Though he was ordered by Lorn to protect her, he was not required to be kind, but he was. He took her aside whenever they stopped for the night, sparring with her and improving her sword-handling. He was a powerful warrior, and clever.

"Thank you, Lucas," she said as he helped her hoist her pack.

"If it is too heavy, allow me to carry it," he generously offered.

"You have your own pack to bear. I can manage," she said, grateful for his offer.

"As you wish, my lady." He waved his hand to the way ahead, following in step behind her.

* * *

It was late in the day as the column continued their steady pace, skirting the southeastern bank of the Cot, before the forest gave way to open ground, revealing the foothills of the Plate Mountains to their right and the Mote Mountains to their left, their distant peaks kissing the horizon. King Mortus paused before stepping clear of the forest, wary of them being exposed on open ground. His concern turned to shame as he caught sight of Tessa the seamstress up ahead, marching forth with no sense of fear.

So be it, he sighed, marching forth to reach her.

"You are faring well for a woman of your years, my dear lady Tessa," Mortus said, drawing alongside her.

"Your Majesty." She paused, bobbing a curtsy to the Macon monarch before continuing her pace as he waved off such formality. It seemed a silly thing considering their current path, the trappings of power placing no claim upon his heart anymore.

"My dear lady Tessa, you need not curtsy throughout this journey. I am simply one of many, the same as you, my brave lady," he reminded her.

"I may share your company, oh great king, but you are still a KING, and I am honored to march beside you. Also, I am but a simple seamstress, and not a lady, though it is kind of you to say such." She smiled back at him, her vibrant eyes staring through the curls of her silvered hair.

"Oh, you are a lady, my dear Tessa, one who has sacrificed everything to our cause. I am proud to be in your company."

"Thank you, Your Majesty." Tessa was touched by his words. After the death of her husband and sons to this awful war, she thought she had no reason to live, but fate interceded. She labored without rest, working in the bowels of Corell throughout both sieges, doing whatever she could to aid their cause, no matter how feeble her contribution was. When Galen the minstrel penned a ballad honoring her, he proclaimed to the realm all that she had sacrificed, and the realm embraced her with such love to make her old eyes weep. And here she marched, willing to sacrifice again for their cause, and she accepted this fate as an honor. There was little left to live for, and if her death could spare the lives of countless others, as Yah promised, then she offered it gladly. She only wished her feeble hands could better wield a sword, though she took up practice every night at the end of their march with the short blade riding her left hip and the spear she held in her right hand. King Lorn had taken it upon himself to train her in their use, emphasizing the spear over the sword, for it was often the superior weapon in battle.

"You have improved your martial skills, dear Tessa," he quipped, having observed her recent sessions with Lorn.

"It takes little to improve on nothing, and that was where I began, Your Majesty. My only hope is that I might take one of those foul creatures with me before I meet my end." She smiled at the thought.

"That should be possible if you keep practicing. Perhaps I shall spar with you this night once we set camp," he offered.

"I would be most honored."

With that, they continued on, each member of their esteemed company growing closer with each passing day. At times Terin walked with Squid, and others with Elos or Aldo. Lorn shared much of the journey with Mortus, but also matron Dresila. The four gorillas each marched with all of them, and the Jenaii as well. The few warriors of the Sisterhood forged bonds with their Yatin comrades, especially Telnic Commander Yarlo Gilian, as well as the many Macons and Torries marching beside them. Perhaps it was knowing they shared the same fate that drew them together, or it helped them forgot those they left behind, but march forth they did, loyally into the unknown.

34

CHAPTER 3

Fera. The Black Castle.

Jonas sat at the edge of their bed unable to sleep and not wanting to wake his dear Valera, who rested behind him, their daughter nestled near her breast. Starlight shone through the open window across the room, affording him a generous view of the night sky. A gentle breeze swept through the chamber, a welcome respite from the stifling air. He could ill imagine the suffering of those dwelling in the lower levels of the large palace, despite its impressive design. Such trivial musings failed to take his mind off his troubles. Foremost of his concerns was protecting his wife and child. Only his father's authority shielded them from the greater threat that surrounded them. The lives of Cronus' men stood next in his priorities, along with Valera's handmaids. He could not escape this place without them, not without insuring their deaths. He was worried for his son, wherever he was, and the Torry people and realm. He needed to trust their victory to Yah, as the deity led him here, leaving Terin in his place to lead them in battle. And last, he needed to save his father, despite his many sins, but how? This question plagued his dreams, tormenting him without relent.

"You should be sleeping," Valera gently whispered.

"I cannot," he sighed, turning so as to look at her, running his fingers through her hair, smoothing it behind her ear.

"More troubling dreams, or too many worries?" she asked.

"Both, but mostly worries. We have no shortage of those."

"There is danger everywhere, my love, and we are no less safe here than elsewhere."

"Our safety here is false. We are standing upon a cliff with loose sand beneath our feet, one step and it shall all give way."

"Then be sure to hold my hand and we shall go together." She smiled, disarming him with her gentle humor.

He laughed, presenting his hand for her to take, which she did.

* * *

Eastern approaches of Fera.

General Gavis drew his ocran to a halt alongside his standard bearer, gazing in the distance as the towers of Fera broke the horizon. Behind him marched fifty-three telnics of his reconstituted 10th Legion. Beyond the forty telnics he brought from Notsu, others joined his growing ranks from throughout the holdfasts of the empire, especially Nisin. Men were forsaking their garrisons ahead of the approaching enemy, joining with General Gavis, who hastened to Fera at the behest of the emperor.

"Your orders, general?" his nearest aide asked, holding position upon his opposite flank.

"Bring the men forward and prepare camp, while I seek audience with our emperor," Gavis ordered, galloping forth with his small entourage.

* * *

Castellon Larus Braxus received General Gavis in the courtyard of the palace, before escorting him to the emperor's council chambers, forgoing the protocols of the throne room. Gavis tossed the reins to his mount to his subordinates, ordering his guards to wait for him there as he followed Castellon Braxus.

"The emperor would hear your account of the events at Corell,"

Larus quietly said, his emotionless tone contrasting the outspoken general's.

"Does he desire an honest assessment?" Gavis asked, knowing the emperor's affinity for *Lord* Morac.

"Candor is a wise choice, general. The emperor does not suffer fools or liars, as you well know."

"Good, for I am neither."

They continued along wide lit passageways giving way to winding narrow corridors, imperial guards saluting with their spears over their shields as they passed, before coming upon the emperor's council chambers. Braxus' guards remained in the outer corridor as they entered the austere chamber. Gavis was surprised to find only the emperor waiting for them, standing over an elaborate map table centered in the room, its rich detail contrasting the plain, barren chamber, with torches set upon their black stone walls. Gavis remembered himself, beginning to kneel when Tyro waved off the protocol, again taking the general aback, before dismissing Braxus. The Castellon waited for Gavis in the outer corridor, leaving the general alone with the emperor. Tyro was always strict on the protocols of court, and for him to disregard them gave the general reason to pause.

Gavis greatly respected the emperor, who earned his trust and confidence during the revolution over their Menotrist foes. This was no small thing considering Gavis' fierce reputation and ornery disposition. He was equally surprised to see the emperor martially attired with light mail and twin swords upon his hips. It had been years since the emperor wore such things outside the training arena. Was this sudden change a sign that the war was coming to their doorstep? Or did it portend the emperor taking an active part in the battles ahead?

"Gavis, you have brought your legion safely home," the emperor stated. Whether he was impressed by this or not, his even tone would not reveal.

"Aye. I assembled over 40 telnics from the remnants of the 8th, 9th and 10th Legions before departing Notsu. I gathered another 13 after departing Nisin in accordance with your instructions. I have yet to order a full muster for an accurate number. They are setting camp outside these walls as we speak, my emperor. Do with us as you command," Gavis stated firmly, his chin held high. His declaration established his loyalty, waiting for Tyro to speak before continuing.

"I sent six legions to seize Corell last summer and three more this spring, and all that remain are your legion and the gargoyles Kriton has returned with. Those numbers combine for less than two full legions. I would hear from your lips what transpired at Corell and Notsu, other than what is written here." Tyro lifted the parchment that Gavis sent during their retreat from Corell, calling upon the emperor to name him commander of what remained of the 8th and 9th Legions.

"I know you are fond of Lord Morac, my emperor, but I will speak the hard truth of his failings," Gavis began.

"Speak freely, general."

And so, Gavis detailed all that he had witnessed throughout the campaign, from his arrival at Notsu, and the invasion of Torry North, and the defeats that followed.

"…Once the Earther revealed himself, we should have fully withdrawn from Corell. I advised sending three legions west to ravage the Torry countryside, with the rest of our legions returning to Notsu. That would have permanently crippled the Torry logistical position for many years, while keeping us firmly in control of the crossroads. Instead, he sent half a legion west, which was equally matched by Fonis' 2nd Army, while the rest of us remained at Corell. Once Prince Lorn arrived with the might of the south at his back, the Earther unleashed his ultimate horror upon our legions, slaying twenty thousand in a moment's time. Even at Notsu, Morac refused to see reason, insisting on remaining while the enemy closed in. Had you not granted me command of the legions when you did, they too would have been lost. Madness." Gavis shook his head.

Tyro's silence gave him pause, wondering if he spoke too freely. Gavis threw caution to the wind and pressed on, needing the emperor to see clearly and act accordingly if they were to win this war.

"He does not deserve to wield the *Sword of the Sun*, my emperor.

Only a warrior who is worthy can face the Torry champion, and that is you."

Tyro knew the truth of that, but did not reveal the true reason only he could defeat Terin.

"Perhaps. Morac preceded you, and I have sent him to Laycrom, where he is to gather the 13th Legion and a significant portion of the garrison and to bring them here," Tyro redirected Gavis' attention to the military question at hand. He would decide Morac's fate another time. He went on to explain their current situation, with the enemy closing upon Tinsay to their west and Nisin to their east.

"It is wise to consolidate our forces, though there lies a risk in forsaking so much territory to the enemy," Gavis conceded.

"Yes, though if we prevail, all those lands can be swiftly recovered. Only victory can restore our realm, and for that, I would draw out the enemy while we consolidate, and then…"

"Then we strike, like a coiled serpent, destroying whichever enemy draws near first." Gavis nodded with approval.

"Yes. The only question is which one it shall be."

"The eastern armies will come first, once Nisin succumbs. They will seize the crop lands along the Reguh and Morga River valleys before they can be harvested. That will feed their armies. The western coalition will have no such benefit as the crops along the Gorga and Andler River Valleys have had their first harvest," Tyro pointed out. The crops along the Gorga and Andler Valleys were astian, the fast-growing starch that matured under one hundred days, allowing two harvests a year. The crops along the Morga and Reguh Valleys were traditional ottein, which was harvested only in the autumn and was more suited for the harder climate of the Araxan interior.

"I assume we are well stocked?"

"Either stocked or soon to be."

"Should we destroy the crops to our east before the enemy can make use of them?" Gavis said, for that was what he would do.

"No. They may slow their advance to secure those lands, allowing us time to deal with the armies in the west. It is a risk, but one I think is a worthy one. Besides, the peasants working the lands along the Reguh and Morga will not be endeared to our visitors once their food is stolen from them. When we are victorious, perhaps those populations will look upon us more favorably."

Gavis nodded in agreement, wishing Morac had displayed a portion of the emperor's political astuteness. Despite his harsh treatment of the Menotrists and to a lesser degree the Venotrists, Tyro had cultivated good relations with most of the lands he absorbed into his empire, especially in the east.

"I plan to reconstitute our remaining forces into three legions, which I appoint you to oversee. You are to use the soldiers that have been stripped from the garrisons to fill out the third legion. Morac is to bring fifteen telnics from the Laycrom garrison along with General Trinapolis' 13th Legion. I have sent Nels Draken to oversee the Tinsan campaign, ordering most of the garrison to withdraw, leaving behind a small force to delay the enemy."

"I thought you desired the enemy advance first from the west so we might destroy them here. Why delay them?" Gavis thought that odd.

"They are not fools, Gavis. My wife leads them, and she will suspect if we give ground too readily."

"With Trinapolis and myself, along with the new legion, that gives us three legions and the gargoyles. Any tidings of their status?"

"I have sent Lord Regula to oversee their reorganization and to prepare them for battle."

"And where has he gone to do so?" Gavis asked, wondering where Kriton had taken their vast host.

"Here, where sits their sacred nesting grounds." Tyro swept his hand over the map, where rested the gargoyles' ancestral lands north of the Nameless Mountains, whose foothills rested at the headwaters of the Morga River.

* * *

Laycrom. Capital city of the Benotrist Empire.

Morac stood upon the veranda of the imperial palace, looking out at the sea of rooftops that spread to the city walls in the distance and points beyond. Laycrom was the jewel of the empire, its imperial center, where resided the officials that oversaw its vast holdings. Said officials were now in a state of panic with the enemy upon their doorstep. Most were preparing to flee to the countryside should the enemy come this way.

Fools. Morac shook his head, knowing if they lost there was nowhere to run. He gazed across the city, admiring the grand structures that dotted its landscape, from the towering pillars of the forum to the amphitheater that seated thousands, its marble columns rising imperiously across its entrance. Standing upon the imperial palace denied him a clear view of its majestic beauty, with towering citadels spiraling into the heavens behind him.

Laycrom, formerly Laycoris, was founded by the ancient traitor kingdom of Corvar after the death of King Kal, if the legends were to be believed. Its current name arose after the rise of the Northern Kingdom, when the Warlord Clorvis Cal became the first king of that Tarelian realm. It was rumored that Laycrom was renamed to honor the conqueror's dead son, who fell in battle, Crom Cal.

Morac snickered at such sentimental weakness. If he was to rename a city, it wouldn't be of a dead son, but after his own triumphs.

Lore's Bane or Kregmarin? He pondered which was most fitting. Perhaps he would rename Laycrom with one of those inviting options if he could not claim a realm of his own. A realm of his own? That dream was likely gone, unless…

No. He shook away the temptation. They were beset by enemies, and unity was their only recourse.

"Wine, master?" a comely slave girl called out to him. He turned, appraising her inviting form as she knelt within the archway of his private chamber, her brief tunic riding unseemly high upon her legs. He admired her rich black hair that shone in the sunlight and her alluring green eyes that were currently cast downward as she held the wine pitcher and goblet in her small hands. She was gifted to him upon his arrival by Darom Croon, Regent of Laycrom, in whose palace he was currently residing.

Morac strolled casually toward the girl, keeping her on her knees while lifting the pitcher and goblet from her hands, filling the goblet before handing the pitcher back to her. He slowly sipped his drink, looking down at her as she stared at his sandaled feet peeking from the hem of his robe. He enjoyed this respite, forgoing his warrior's garb for the comforts of palace life while awaiting General Trinapolis, whose legion was completing its muster outside the city walls. Only his sword rode his hip, forsaking his armor and helm for soft robes and a loose tunic. He savored partaking luxurious foods and wine, and of course the flesh of the slave girl kneeling at his feet.

"Look up, Corry," he ordered, savoring the frightened look upon her face.

"Yes, master," she said, addressing him as he demanded, recalling the beating she received the night before for daring to ask why he changed her name to Corry.

"You learn quickly, Corry. That is a valued trait in a slave. Go, prepare yourself," he ordered as she gained her feet and hurried to his bedchamber to await him.

Morac watched her retreating form, imagining the day the real Corry would hurry to please him.

"One day." He smiled, downing his goblet before tossing it aside and following her.

* * *

It was late in the evening when General Trinapolis presented himself to Morac, meeting him in his private quarters. The aged general was a thin man with silvered hair and discerning gray eyes. He was the eldest commander of legion at the start of the war and held that distinction with only himself and Gavis the only surviving members of that rank. He was dressed in the uniform red mail and tunic of the 13th Legion, holding his crimson helm in his left hand as he entered the lavish chamber.

"General, welcome." Morac received him leaning back on a large settee, with a fresh goblet in his hand, the slave girl Corry standing at his side.

"Lord Morac." Trinapolis bowed stiffly.

"Corry, a drink for our esteemed general." Morac snapped his fingers as she hurried to obey before Morac dismissed her.

"A fetching lass," Trinapolis said, taking a sip from his goblet, turning to see her retreating form disappearing through the archway.

"A fine gift from our dear Regent Croon, one that I have gladly partaken."

"The pleasures of palace life. It is a welcome respite from your journeys as of late," the general quipped.

"Yes, it has been far too long since I partook a comely wench. I look to our final victory before adding many Torry prizes to my collection."

"Victory? The tidings I have heard of late would dampen such optimism," Trinapolis said.

"Have you not heard, general, the enemy is coming to us, and that portends many possibilities, or opportunities if one knows where to look?"

"I would lean toward caution, Lord Morac, for the enemy would not extend their necks without strength to back their play."

"Strength or desperation? I have seen them in battle, general, and their strength, as you call it, is but a brittle collection of mismatched allies that will shatter if strongly met."

"Yes, strongly met, but according to your orders, I am to withdraw."

"The emperor plans to consolidate our legions and armies, and draw out the enemy before smashing them," Morac explained, though his tone proved he did not favor the strategy, something Trinapolis keenly observed.

"From the tidings I have heard from court, our emperor has been distracted." He decided to gauge Morac's loyalty.

"Distracted?"

"Yes. There was a strange visitor to Fera some time ago, a Torry elite, no less, who is now a guest of our emperor."

"A Torry?" Morac's lips curled, disguising the fact that he already knew of a Torry guest of the emperor. If the general believed he was ignorant of the fact, he would divulge more than he intended to apprise him of the fact.

"Yes, very peculiar, and even more intriguing is the name that has been associated with the man… Joriah."

"Joriah? I have not heard of any man so named."

"Not unexpected, considering so few have borne that name. In fact, I have only known of one man by that name, a boy actually, who, if he lived, would be of an age to our emperor's guest." Trinapolis offered up the information like dangling fruit, waiting for Morac to inquire with the next obvious question, like a skilled debater leading someone to a desired conclusion.

"And who was the boy? He must be of some importance for you to offer up this information."

"As you know, I am very old and have served our cause long before our emperor joined our fledgling ranks, when your father still commanded us."

"I am aware." Morac knew Trinapolis served in the earliest days of their revolution and was a loyal lieutenant to his father, Morca.

"Our emperor once had a son…" the general began, relaying the tale as he knew it to Morac, though he was ignorant of Jonas' Kalinian bloodline.

Morac stopped drinking from his goblet at one point in the story, his appetite for it quickly fading. Was this tale true? Who was this Joriah, and why did he wear the uniform of a Torry elite? It made little sense.

"Did you happen upon a Joriah during your battles at Corell?" the general asked.

"No, but I didn't stop to ask their names," Morac sneered at the absurdity of it.

"Indeed, but you might have heard the mention of a Torry warrior named Jonas."

"Jonas?" Morac shook his head, unfamiliar with the name as well.

"Jonas Caleph, a Torry warrior of great renown and the father of Terin Caleph." Trinapolis enjoyed the look that came over Morac's face of intense shock and bewilderment.

"That cannot be." He shook his head, realizing if true, the emperor and Terin were direct kin, that Terin was his heir. If true, where did that place Morac?

"There is much to think on during our march to Fera, Lord Morac. I believe I shall enjoy your company. Now, if you will forgive me, I must see to our legion." He gained his feet, departing the chamber, leaving Morac to his million thoughts.

CHAPTER 4

East of Nisin Palace.

Corry stood upon a low rise, staring at Nisin palace in the distance. Wind Racer stood beside her, the morning sun casting his shadow far afield as she removed her silver helm, freeing her golden tresses in the late summer breeze. From here, she could clearly see the imperial sigil blowing above the highest citadel of Nisin's inner keep, a black tower upon a field of red, the large standard billowing in the wind. The palace was of a similar design to Corell, though smaller by the slightest of margins. Its only gate rested along its north face, matching Corell in its orientation. She wondered if its internal layout was equally similar as the archives indicated. That would help in the planning of any attack if they were forced to storm the palace. She could make out the heads of Benotrist soldiers peaking above the parapets of the east wall, sunlight playing off their helms whenever they shifted.

"Packaww!"

She looked up, watching her escort circling above before setting down beside her. Just as they dismounted, a small contingent of cavalry drew nigh, closing from the south, bearing the standard of the Torry-Macon alliance, a golden crown upon a field of white and black. Corry quickly recognized Torg Vantel leading the small procession, breaking ahead of the others before coming to halt before her, his ocran's hooves kicking up soil as it slid to a stop.

"Master Vantel," she greeted Torg as he dismounted in a flourish one would not expect for a man of his years.

"Princess," he said with a rare smile, pleased to see that she had arrived safely from their previous encampment, where a third of their army was still in place, preparing to join them in the coming days.

"Any activity from the enemy?" she asked, stealing a glance to the castle in the distance.

"None. They have withdrawn to the safety of their walls," Torg said, giving the castle a disagreeable stare.

"Strange. They have yielded ground so easily it gives me doubt of our plan." Corry's eyes narrowed severely, trying to guess the enemy's intent. Other than skirmishes with local holdfasts and enemy scouts, they met no resistance since crossing the Kregmarin. The latest reports from Brokov showed no Benotrist forces of significance east of the Reguh River. What remained of Benotrist power was now holed up within the walls of Nisin. With Thorton now removed, their great fear of him targeting their soldiers from the high walls of Nisin was eliminated. If Thorton was to be believed, Morac was not present either, and the garrison reduced to a mere few thousand defenders. It appeared all too easy, and that bothered Corry deeply, for nothing was ever this easy.

"The enemy here appears spent, but that is a two-edged blade. As much as I favor an easy fight, it defeats our true objective of drawing Tyro's strength away from the Chosen," Torg said, as if reading her thoughts.

"Do you think he has discovered our plan?" she wondered.

"It is possible, but that doesn't fit with what Yah revealed. And that is what worries me more, that Yah is denying our plan to draw Tyro's gaze away from Lorn and Terin. Yah has set the stage, and we cannot change our place upon it."

She had no answer to that, at least not one she wanted to consider.

"Bah, don't listen to the ramblings of a cantankerous old man, Corry. All we can do is focus on the task before us, and that task is taking this castle." Torg refuted his own misgivings, bringing a gentle smile to her lips. Oh, how she loved this old man. If she had to endure this journey, she was grateful to be sharing it with him.

"And take it we shall. What is the position of our forces?" she asked.

"Our Jenaii friends are covering the western flank, holding at a farther distance than we are here," he said, pointing out General Lewins' 1st Torry Army positioned to their direct front. Lewins' soldiers were preparing defensive works, the sound of their spades echoing dully in the morning air.

"General Ciyon's troops arrived yester morn and are digging siege works along the northern perimeter, facing the main gate," Torg added, removing the comm Lorken gifted him from his satchel.

Corry lifted a curious brow, still taken aback by the sight of Torg Vantel using the Earthers' device.

"General Ciyon, this is Torg. Report!" Torg barked into the comm.

"*Not so loud, Master Vantel. I can hear you,*" Dadeus' voice answered back. Corry could envision poor Dadeus on the other end wincing from Torg's loud voice.

"Is this more to your liking?" Torg spoke much lower, which for him was still louder than Corry shouting.

"*Fine,*" Dadeus answered back, knowing that was as good as he could expect from the Torry Master of Arms.

"What tidings from your position?" Torg asked.

"*I am staring at a closed gate and lowered porticus. They have considerable ballista positioned upon the north-facing turrets and the adjoining causeways but do not seem to be manned. My men are well occupied preparing their siege works, both forward and rear, should an enemy relief force appear behind us,*" Dadeus detailed his operations.

"Very good. The Princess is here, and we shall be establishing a command pavilion along the eastern perimeter. Raise us if trouble stirs," Torg said.

Corry looked on as Torg next contacted El Anthar, the Jenaii king responding in kind. She wondered the effect of on-time communications between their armies during battle. In her studies of military history, she understood the difficulty in coordinating different flax, units and telnic-sized elements, let alone entire armies spread out over vast areas. The Earthers comms made that task far simpler. It was another tool they considered a small thing that would dramatically change Araxan warfare.

King El Anthar reported no sign of enemy activity to the west. The Jenaii were the first to arrive three days past, along with Lorken, who scouted freely around the castle once word of Thorton's fall reached them. Raven and the others retrieved Kato's lost pistol, which they recovered from the gargoyle elite named Zelo, who was slain at Near Point. That left no weapons in the enemy's hands that could target Lorken's air ski, unless he unwisely swept low over the palace.

"When our ape friends arrive, I shall place them along the southern perimeter." Torg pointed in that far-off direction, where stretched a long expanse of flat ground skirting the southern face of the palace.

"Would it not be wiser to place General Vecious and the 2nd Macon Army there, and the ape 3rd Army north, alongside Ciyon?" she advised.

"I thought of that, considering their rumbustious nature. One could well imagine the fear the palace garrison would feel seeing the apes aligned in front of their main gate."

"Then why not do so? I would much like our enemies to have a healthy measure of fear when we negotiate their surrender," she reasoned.

"Because preparing for a direct assault will take some time, and do you truly want to place the apes across from the main gate for that long?"

She conceded him that point, knowing how eager their ape friends were to attack. Staring at the gate day after day without attacking would drive the apes insane.

"I will move them into position there on the eve of our assault," Torg added, heeding her advice.

"Fair enough," she said. She thought of how wonderfully they complemented each other in command, each willing to listen to the other's points before making a final decision. It helped that he was the better tactician and she the better strategist, each strength shaping their decisions.

"I have sent matrons to the western and northern perimeters along with the regenerators. The others have yet to arrive. When they do, I shall place them accordingly," he said.

"Lady Ilesa should arrive by nightfall and the others in the coming days as they are still at our base camp," she said, having passed over the column of troops escorting Ilesa on her journey here.

"Havis!" Corry called out to one of her escort, who hurried forth.

"Princess." Havis Darm saluted with his fist to his chest. He was one of her favored guardians after being named to the elite for saving her life during the first siege of Corell. He and Dalin Vors were both so named, each saving her life after being saved by Terin earlier in the siege. It was another irony, where Terin felt driven to intercede on their behalf, as if some internal sense knew they would in turn save the woman he loved.

"Havis, please find General Connly and have him send a sizable escort to bring lady Ilesa forward."

"As you command, Princess." He bowed and withdrew.

"She should be at Corell until her child comes, not traipsing across battlefields like a mad woman," Torg snorted, recalling what happened to poor Leanna.

"Ilesa insists upon staying with the army, Torg, and I will not deny her her rightful place. Besides, should any problem arise, we now have plenty of regenerators to protect her," Corry said, watching Havis gain his mount and take to the sky.

"Just another stubborn fool, and I should know." He guiltily shrugged.

"Are you speaking of me or yourself?" She smiled.

"We are not the only ones," he said, watching another stubborn fool draw closer as the air ski appeared to their south, sweeping over the perimeter before setting down beside them, bearing Cronus and Lorken.

"Welcome to the party, Corry. It won't be long before your standard is flying above this castle," Lorken said as Cronus dismounted.

"Your optimism is always reassuring, Lorken, if not misplaced," she reminded him.

"Just stating the facts, Corry. We got a nice encirclement going and plenty of reinforcements on the way," Lorken said.

"It will take many more days to bring up the rest of our army, and many will have to be detached to secure our ever-lengthening supply trains," Torg reminded him.

"We can establish new sources of supply and shorter lines of communication, thanks to our new friends," Lorken said.

"New friends?" Corry asked, wondering what he was talking about.

"Haven't you heard? Ever since Tosha negotiated with Pagan, dozens of holdfasts have sworn to the new alliance, swearing loyalty to the emperor's true heir."

"True heir?" Corry made a face.

"And who would that be?" Torg asked.

"Terin. They have sworn to him and raised his banner," Lorken said.

"His banner?" Corry and Torg asked at the same moment.

"A glowing blue sword on a field of silver. Sounds pretty awesome if you ask me," Lorken said.

"Awesome?" Torg wondered the use of that word in such a context.

"Just another of their expressions, Master Vantel." Corry shook her head, trying to make sense of Benotrist warlords swearing fealty to Terin.

"Whatever gave them the notion to swear to Terin of all people?" Torg asked.

"Actually, it was Raven's idea," Lorken said.

"Raven?" Corry asked.

"Yes. When Tosha was trying to convince the regent of Pagan to surrender, Raven suggested he swear to Terin and form an alliance with us rather than die when we stormed his city. He explained Terin's lineage and that he was Tyro's true heir, which would not force them to violate their oath to the empire since Terin is of the royal bloodline."

"This is madness!" Torg made a face.

"But Terin is the Torry Champion and their sworn enemy," Corry pointed out.

"That's one way to look at it, but another is that he is fighting to free his people from the gargoyle curse," Lorken said.

"His people?" Torg asked.

"The Benotrists. They are his kin as much as anyone else."

Corry and Torg stood there, stupefied by the insanity of it all. Had the world truly lost its mind?

"It didn't hurt that the Benotrists have been having terrible dreams as well, helping them come around to Raven's suggestion," Lorken added.

"Dreams? Of what nature?" Corry asked.

"Gargoyles, what else? They have been having nightmares of the creatures turning on them. As far as they see it, Terin is trying to save his grandfather and his people from them."

Again, they were struck dumb, wondering how this could be.

"And Raven thought of all this?" Corry asked, not expecting such a thing from the man.

"He just got the ball rolling but lucked out with the dreams they were having. It certainly wasn't his master plan," Lorken said.

"You are claiming he simply stumbled into a great idea," Cronus said.

"Well, yeah. It's not like he could have thought all this on his own. Even a blind squirrel finds a nut every now and then."

"A blind squirrel?" Corry asked.

"Never mind." Lorken didn't bother explaining the reference.

"There is still one important detail you have overlooked. Terin is not with us. In fact, he is not expected to survive as Yah's visions have shown," Torg pointed out.

"We'll worry about that later. For now, we need to move General Horzak's army northeast along the road to Pagan," Lorken advised.

"Horzak? For what purpose?" Corry asked. General Horzak commanded the small ape army cobbled together from the crews of the sunken 1st Ape Fleet. They suffered heavy casualties storming Notsu, reducing their force to 3,300. Since the arrival of the 3rd

Ape Army prior to the advance across the Kregmarin, Horzak's small force was overshadowed by the larger force.

"Horzak's troops will be here shortly, and who better to greet President Matuzak when he comes marching up the road in the coming days?" Lorken pointed out.

"Coming days? He is that close?" Torg asked.

"Yep, and has a large army with him. Casians, Troans, rebels and even a few telnics of Benotrists who we hope can talk some sense to the fellas holding out in the castle. If they don't persuade them, I'm sure Rav, Argos and Zem will convince them otherwise." Lorken grinned.

"Raven is with them?" Torg asked. He became quite fond of the large Earther during their time at Corell.

"Yep. Hopefully between Arg and Zem they can keep him out of trouble, but I doubt it. You know what Raven is like." Lorken chuckled.

"You shall finally meet the legendary General Zem, Master Vantel." Cronus smiled at that, imagining the look on Torg's face when the insufferable Zem presented himself.

"If he is anything like this one and Raven, I shall be most entertained." Torg snorted, pointing a thumb toward Lorken.

"Probably. Just don't let him start in with one of his stories or you'll spend half a day listening to him before he puts you to sleep," Lorken warned.

"Don't listen to such drivel, Torg. Zem is an exemplary warrior and a true friend of our people," Corry said.

"I was just warning you, Torg, but you know what they say, experience is the best educator. I best get going. Don't worry too much about the siege, Corry. Once our northern forces arrive, the castle will strike their colors in a day," Lorken boasted.

"That is a mite presumptuous," she said.

"They don't have Ben, and Morac is nowhere in sight. One day. You can take that to the bank," Lorken said before speeding off.

"One day? He doesn't lack for confidence." Torg sighed.

"In all my time with the Earthers, they rarely boast what they are not capable off," Cronus opined.

"Despite our advantages, we shall suffer many casualties if we have to storm that castle," Torg warned.

"Only if we take it from the bottom up," Cronus said, giving Torg and Corry something to consider.

Corry's thought went from that to Terin, guarding the optimism taking hold in her thinking. If what Raven started bore greater fruit, perhaps many of the Benotrists Terin would be facing might switch to his side. Could that truly be? She so desperately wanted it to be true that she couldn't help but consider it. It gave her hope, and what more could she cling to but hope, no matter how desperate it was.

* * *

Twenty leagues southeast of Nisin.

"Can I fetch you more water, my lady?" Dougar asked, riding at Ilesa's side as she lowered her empty water satchel from her lips.

"I can wait for our next stop, but thank you, Dougar, for your concern." She gifted the boy a smile. He had been her ever-vigilant companion since crossing the Veneba.

"You should not suffer thirst, Lady Ilesa. King's Elite Kenti tasked me to protect you in his place, even lending me his mount to do so," Dougar said, leaning forward in the saddle to pat the ocran's neck.

Ilesa stifled a laugh, finding the young child's adherence to duty adorable. He stood vigilant watch over her day and night, stepping away only when relived by Cronus or Lorken when they returned to their campsite. Both men took the boy underwing, teaching him skills he never learned growing up in the streets of Fleace. She wondered what would have become of Dougar if King Lorn hadn't plucked him from the street on that momentous day when he wed Queen Deliea? She imagined the suffering the poor child endured as a homeless orphan, surviving on his own for so long. It made her think of her unborn child's fate should she die. Would her babe be returned to her kin? Would he or she be lost somewhere along the way? She was in the middle of a war, and anything could happen. She needed to live for the child's sake, lest it die, or live and suffer as Dougar had.

No, she promised herself, she would live and see her child kept safe.

I promise you, Kato, she told herself.

"How fare you this fine day, Matron Ilesa?" Galen called out, riding back from the front of the column. The minstrel had taken on the role of a message runner throughout the march, usually with the trailing elements, which rotated between each encampment. Today he ferried messages between General Bram Vecious' 2nd Macon Army and General Vorklit's 3rd Ape Army, which was the trailing army on the last leg of their journey to Nisin. The other armies were already laying siege to the castle, and Vecious and Vorklit were eager to join them.

"The weather is perfect and the company superb, Minstrel Galen," she greeted him, giving Dougar a flirtatious wink, causing the poor boy to blush as Galen circled about, coming alongside them.

"That will please our dear friends Cronus and Lorken and Princess Corry. She has sent an impressive escort to bring you on ahead. Two flax of General Connly's riders await you at the head of the column. If you would both come with me," Galen said, leading them forth.

* * *

Nisin Castle. Jenaii encampment.
Western perimeter of siege lines.

"Hold!" Criose said, placing his hand on the barrel of Culn's rifle, lowering it as a Benotrist magantor passed overhead, heading west over the Nisin Plain.

"We can kill it," Culn Davorin pleaded, watching helplessly as the enemy warbird passed behind them before disappearing over the horizon.

"We could, but Princess Corry said not to unless they attack first," Criose said. The two of them were selected to wield the Earthers' laser rifles and spent most of the campaign under Lorken's tutelage. They took a lead role in assailing the bridges over the Greater Veneba and found themselves in several skirmishes since, which were quickly decided, in no small part to their advanced weapons. Wielding the rifles was almost intoxicating, their power incredible to behold. They could only imagine using them against enemy soldiers in close ranks. They could fire with impunity, even with poor aim, and slay countless thousands.

"Very well." Culn sighed, obeying the orders of the Princess. He was selected for this important role for his adherence to duty and his integrity and candor, attributes essential for wielding such power. He and Criose spent the previous day along the northern perimeter with General Ciyon, watching the skies for any threat that might emerge. This morning they were moved to the Jenaii encampments along the western perimeter, again tasked with protecting their allies from enemy magantor threats. They knew their role would change once their armies attacked the castle. It didn't take a cunning mind to guess how they would be used. They would likely ride upon Lorken's air ski or upon a magantor, flying high above the castle's ballista range while firing at will upon the palace defenders. If they could clear the palace rooftops and upper battlements of their defenders, the Jenaii could set down unopposed, greatly hastening Nisin's downfall. They could also be used in multiple ways, many that they were unaware of, limited only by Lorken's creativity.

As midday gave way to late afternoon, a stirring of activity atop the inner keep of the palace drew their attention. Criose lifted the scope of his rifle, sweeping the red stone surface of the palace walls through the lens, catching sight of a Benotrist magantor springing from the southeast magantor platform. The warbird dipped briefly before climbing, circling the towering citadels, ascending higher into the firmament with each pass before sweeping over the palace walls in their direction. The warbird was followed by two more magantors, each with a single rider and bearing fire munitions dangling far below the bird's necks.

"Here is what you were waiting for," Criose said, taking aim at the lead mount as Culn trained his sights on the second.

The surrounding encampments came alive with activity, Jenaii moving into defensive positions with fluid grace, nary a soul shouting in excitement as was common among their human comrades. Criose admired the Jenaii stoic indifference, facing battle with an unnatural calmness. They would not cry out or shout in panic but simply hold their ground and do their duty. Criose was glad that these brave warriors would not have to suffer death or harm this day because Lorken placed one of his terrible weapons in his unworthy hand.

"Packaww!"

The lead magantor screamed its war cry, sweeping over the outer battlements of Nisin's west wall before pressing on, driving toward the Jenaii siege lines that lay well beyond the palace ballista range. The lead warbird grew ominously large in Criose's scope, dark brown feathers filling the end of his lens. The Benotrist rider swept over the open ground separating the west wall and the Jenaii army to his west, his gaze sweeping the enemy siege lines for any sign of Jenaii taking flight to oppose him, wary of their ability to attain these airy heights. He held tight to the reins and the cords holding the fire munitions dangling below, waiting to release them upon the enemy. If this attack proved successful, they would send all their warbirds to assail the Jenaii, knowing they were their greatest threat.

ZIP!

The lead rider nearly spilled from the saddle as his warbird dipped severely, a flash of blue light striking its breast. He could barely tug on the reins before another blast tore into his mount, the avian dipping left before falling from the sky, its rider's screams dying in the wind.

ZIP! ZIP!

Culn dropped the second mount as Criose shifted aim to the third, riddling the warbirds with multiple blasts, sending them crashing to the open ground between their lines and the palace walls, flames erupting wherever they dropped their munitions, their large bodies crashing into the unforgiving soil. Criose scanned afield for other threats before lowering his rifle. After several moments he looked around him, finding hundreds of Jenaii staring back at him, many thrusting their fists to their hearts, saluting their accomplishment.

It was at that moment that Criose thought of Jentra, wishing he were here to see him. He slung his rifle over his shoulder, returning the Jenaii their salute.

* * *

Two days hence.
Twenty-one leagues northeast of Nisin.

General Horzak held the northeastern approaches of Nisin along a narrow ridgeline where the road to Pagan passed over, positioning his ape warriors along its length, straddling either side of the prominent causeway. He was joined by the several hundred men of Tro that fought at his side at Gotto, Notsu and across the Kregmarin. They were further bolstered by the men of Teso and Zulon, along with the Zulon King Sargov. The small ridgeline overlooked open farmland to the north and east, with homesteads and large manor estates stretching to the horizon. The peasants working the fields were either hiding or fled in the face of the armies converging upon their lands.

The men of Tro, Teso and Zulon began preparing defensive works in the event their friends pushed hostile Benotrist elements inadvertently into their path, though the last sightings from Brokov waylaid those fears. Their ape friends didn't bother themselves with such precautions, facing northeast with swords or axes in hand, slapping them against their shields every so often when not sating their voracious appetite at the various cook fires they prepared. A nearby forest to their direct west provided ample supply of wood for their fires, while hundreds were sent out daily to hunt game or pilfer local food stores or livestock.

General Horzak stood in the center of the ridge, beside the causeway, staring northeast with his furry arms crossed, flanked by King Sargov and General Velen of Teso. The midday sun shone down overhead as they waited, their patience finally rewarded when Lorken's air ski cleared the horizon, moving quickly in their direction.

Their sense of relief turned to excited curiosity as another ski drew alongside of Lorken, following him to their position. Their excitement spread through the surrounding ranks until the familiar riders of the second ski came fully into view, causing thunderous cheers to echo along the ridge.

Raven drove the ski with Zem seated behind him, the ground passing swiftly below as they kept pace with Lorken. The ridgeline ahead was lined with apes in the center and human soldiers upon their flanks. They appeared to be cheering their arrival, though he could barely make anything out until they drew closer, his curiosity turning to disappointment as their shouting grew louder and clear.

"General Zem!" they shouted as the air skis drew in range, heralding the hero of Tro and Gotto with thunderous cheers.

They came to stop short of General Horzak, hovering in place as Zem dismounted, stepping forth as the apes swarmed around him, embracing their hero, leaving Raven and Lorken astride their skis, shaking their heads.

"Unbelievable," Raven growled.

"Forget general, Zem would make a better politician. They love him." Lorken was enjoying Raven's pained look, leaning forward and resting his arms on the top of his view shield.

"Don't give him any ideas," Raven said as General Horzak and King Sargov pushed their way through the crowd to speak with them, leaving Zem to his crowd of admirers.

"General, King Sargov," Raven greeted them as they cleared the crowd, stepping near.

"Captain Raven, again we meet," King Sargov said, his personal guard emerging through the crowd, taking up position behind him.

"The last time you were part of the army coming to help us at Corell, now the roles are reversed. We got a large army just up the road coming to help you, not that you need it," Raven said, referencing the size and capability of the forces already gathered at Nisin.

"Perhaps, but your presence might make the regent of Nisin see reason," King Sargov said.

"There are no enemy between our armies as far as we have seen, so you can stop breaking your backs digging defensive works. Might want to let your men know President Matuzak and the others will be here by nightfall, so don't get jumpy when you see forty thousand men and apes clearing the horizon," Lorken informed them.

"Nightfall?" Horzak asked excitedly.

"Yep, at least the vanguard. Might want to clear an area for their campsites. They won't have time to pitch tents or pavilions tonight. They'll probably bed down wherever they can and continue on for Nisin come sunup," Raven added.

Horzak quickly relayed the information to his soldiers, setting them to work to prepare for their president's arrival as King Sargov did likewise.

* * *

Two days hence.
Eastern perimeter of Nisin siege lines.

Corry stood before her command pavilion, where gathered King El Anthar, Torg Vantel and Generals Valen, Ciyon, Lewins, Connly, Vorklit and Vecious. Looking east they awaited the arrival of their allies, with columns of infantry aligned to their flanks in ordered ranks. Horns sounded to their north and east since midday, heralding the arrival of Matuzak, leading the vast host of apes, Casians, Troans, rebels and even Benotrists now sworn to their cause. The grand army approached along the Pagan road before skirting the eastern face of the palace as if in a grand review, impressing upon the defenders the futility of their cause. They continued across the eastern face of the perimeter, where the leaders broke off from their ranks to join Corry and the others at the command pavilion.

When she was first told of the armies landed along the northern coast, Corry imagined a small contingent limited by the capacity of their ships. What marched before her was far grander, an impressive host drawn from the might of the east. Her gaze was drawn to the familiar figure making his way across the open ground before the pavilion… Matuzak. The ape leader was clad in boiled leather armor, over thick dark shirt and trousers with a mix of axes and swords hanging from his broad belt or strapped across his back. Dark eyes stared through the slits of his heavy helm, projecting a fearsome visage that would've taken her aback if she did not know him and the fondness he had for her people. Beside him marched General Motchi, commander of the Casian 2nd Army, wearing bright mail over a black tunic, his dark cape lifting in the summer breeze. Upon Matuzak's other flank marched General Mocvoran, commander of the 2nd Ape Army, his martial attire as austere and frightening as Matuzak's. They were followed by Kaly, commander of the Troan contingent, Alen, representing the rebel faction, and a Benotrist commander of telnic who led three telnics gathered from the garrison of Pagan and several of its surrounding holdfasts.

Lorken sped around the entourage, sharing his ski with Argos, stopping before Corry and the others, allowing his gorilla friend to dismount before speeding off to the side where Cronus stood. He was followed by Raven, bearing Tosha and Zem, who each dismounted before he too sped off, joining Lorken along the side, where they looked on, neither bothering to dismount. Corry stepped forth, embracing her cousin, Tosha returning the gesture as the others looked on.

"Welcome, cousin." Corry smiled as they drew apart.

"A most warm welcome, Corry. How fares your army?" Tosha asked, noticing Lucella Sarelis standing behind the assembled generals, sharing a look with her mother's captain of the guard. Lucella had recently arrived herself, along with General Valen, keeping her magantors away from Nisin until called for, which was now.

"Our alliance grows stronger each day," Corry said, the steel in her voice trying to conceal the pain of Terin's absence.

"We must talk after," Tosha said, sensing her anguish, gently squeezing her hands before backing a step as President Matuzak drew nigh.

The ape leader took the onlookers aback as he lifted Corry off the ground, swinging her about in a fearsome hug like she was a wee tot. The Torry elite were set on edge with Matuzak and Corry's familiar exchange, though she had warned them of the apes' aversion to proper protocol and decorum.

Think of Raven, but many times worse, she had warned them, though their interactions with the apes to this point prepared them.

"Aye, look at you, lass. Your legend has spread throughout our republic, inspiring all our ape lasses to emulate the brave Torry princess who led her people though the two greatest sieges in Araxan history," Matuzak bellowed, causing Corry to blush.

"We welcome your friendship and the mighty armies you have brought to our aid, President Matuzak," she proclaimed loudly for all to hear, before kissing his furry cheek after he removed his heavy helm. She then introduced him to Torg, the two warriors clasping forearms like two old friends.

"Aye, the mighty Torg Vantel, grandfather of the Torry Champion and a dear friend to Orlom, as he boldly tells it." Matuzak grinned, the mention of Orlom bringing a smile to Corry and Tosha as they looked on.

"Aye, a fine lad he is." Torg shook his head, half expecting the ape leader to refer to him as *Coach,* but thankfully he didn't.

Matuzak moved along, introducing himself to the generals gathered about, giving his own commander of 3rd Army a strong slap on the back. General Vorklit grinned proudly, the gesture a sign of admiration from his president. It wasn't thought possible for an army of his size to march from the Talon Pass guarding the Ape Hills to Notsu, but they did, much to Vorklit's stubborn leadership and keen mind for logistics. Between Vorklit's 3rd Army, Mocvoran's 2nd and Horzak's smaller contingent, Matuzak's apes boasted 31 telnics, with two dispatched to fortify Pagan Harbor.

Tosha then went about the other introductions, starting with the Casian General Motchi, who Corry warmly received, espousing her deep gratitude for their aid. Next Corry received Kaly, recalling their time together at Tro and expressing her gratitude to him and Klen for the Troans that had rallied to their cause. Next came Alen, who Corry took into her embrace, thankful he returned to them alive.

"I so feared for you." She smiled as they parted, combing his hair from his eyes. Though part of him appeared older and wiser, there was still the boy she remembered who helped them through the first siege.

"Thank you, Your Highness. I am grateful for your coming to this land to free my people from Tyro, and if we can help Terin wherever he is, I am proud to offer what help I can."

"Thank you," she mouthed wordlessly, imagining the suffering he endured.

Alen looked past her shoulder, regarding King El Anthar and wondering where Elos stood, still unaware that his friend was with Terin, which he would later learn.

Of all the new arrivals, it was Zem that drew the most curious stares. Though all had heard tell of his unique nature and impressive deeds, seeing him with their own eyes was something altogether different. He quickly ingratiated himself, greeting El Anthar and Torg with hardy handshakes which they returned, having come to understand the Earther greeting. By the looks on their faces, one had to wonder if they feared he might crush their hands in his powerful grasp. He went on to espouse his gratitude for their company in the coming endeavor before them, greeting the other commanders with equal pomp, lauding them with ridiculous praise that caused Raven and Lorken to shake their heads in disgust.

"Of all the things I expected Zem to become, a slimy politician was never on the list," Raven snorted, he and Lorken looking on out of earshot.

"Not so loud, or he might hear you," Cronus whispered.

"Who would ever vote for him?" Lorken tried to put that notion to rest, ignoring Cronus' warning.

"They would, because people are morons." Raven lifted his hands to the gathered crowd.

"I heard that," Zem shouted back, causing everyone to stare in their direction.

"I told you." Cronus smiled.

"Never mind those idiots, let us commence with our planning," Zem said, urging the leaders and commanders to gather in the pavilion.

"Should we go?" Lorken asked Raven, watching as the others started to file into the pavilion to plan their way forward.

"Yes, or they might all agree with one of Zem's stupid plans."

* * *

The command pavilion was more aptly named a Grand pavilion, for it stretched some eighteen meters abreast, allowing ample space for all the generals, commanders and leaders to gather about the large map table erected in its center. So great was the assemblage that one could barely stand without being pressed on either shoulder. Torry, Macon, Jenaii, Casian and Ape Generals joined groups of Teso, Zulon, Tro, rebels and Benotrists. Tosha, Corry, Torg, Lucella and several prominent members of the Torry elite took their respective places while the Earthers looked on, with Zem, Argos and Lorken flanking Raven at one end of the table.

Though Corry presided over this grand assembly, it was Matuzak who began, his booming voice carrying through the walls of the pavilion with thunderous resolve.

"Never in the annals of history has an army of apes ventured this far from our sacred homeland. Tyro will regret his attack upon our fleet and the murder of our warriors. Our armies will shake the walls of Nisin and then Fera with the sound of our roars and blows of our hammers, axes and swords. Whatever we decide this day, the might of our republic stands with you all!"

"My people are honored to fight beside yours once again, Matuzak, great warrior and friend," King El Anthar declared from his place opposite Matuzak.

The others meant to voice their agreement but paused, taken aback by the enormity of the scene before them, the unity of the ape and Jenaii realms, brought together for this grand purpose. In truth, they were all a part of this grand alliance, hoping to accomplish what King Kal attempted so long ago. Unlike Kal, they were not alone, for they had each other, and so many others that were not presently here, each striving to that one overriding objective.

"We shall begin," Corry finally said, breaking the serenity of the moment, drawing all eyes to her, where she indicated Brokov to commence with his scouting report.

Upon her signal the hovering device ascended from ceiling, coming to rest above the table, spinning slowly as those who had not yet witnessed its wondrous ability stared in awe.

"*The combined ape, Troan and Casian armada sits anchored at Pagan, joined by the remnants of the Benotrist eastern fleets. They shall move west upon confirmation of Nisin's fall, shadowing your advance along the coastline.*" Brokov's voice echoed from the large disc, a small beam of light issuing below it, illuminating the map, outlining the places he indicated.

"*The lands along the Tur are currently yielding to the rebel and Benotrist factions sworn to Terin. This process is continuing apace westward, up to fifty leagues west of Nisin. These forces are securing food sources and safeguarding our lines of communication. The most recent scouting sweep west of Nisin, which I completed this morning, finds no enemy force larger than a unit this side of the Reguh River Valley. Advanced analysis of Nisin places its garrison strength between 4300 and 4420,*" Brokov added.

"And your scouting can verify the integrity of our new Benotrist allies?" General Lewins, commander of the 1st Torry Army, asked, regarding the Benotrist commander warily, his question foremost in the minds of many of those gathered by the looks they also sent the commander's direction.

Tosha interjected, for it was her initiative that sought out common ground with her father's people.

"It was I that reached accord with Regent Galenta of Pagan. For those Benotrists willing to align with us we offer full pardon and agree to property rights other than slave holdings. In return they will fight by our side and secure all lines of communication as we advance, swearing loyalty to a new realm to be established in these lands, one ruled by Terin."

"Why would they so easily change allegiances? What of the vows they swore to Tyro? Can we trust men that forsake their oaths?" General Bram Vecious, commander of the Macon 2nd Army, asked.

"Terin is my father's true heir and Benotrist by blood. But there is another reason why Regent Galenta and many others have agreed to our terms. Commander Dalomos should speak of it in his own words." Tosha looked to the Benotrist commander, revealing his name.

"Common folk might change allegiances, those of low position who have not sworn formal oaths to our emperor, but men of the legions and garrisons of the empire would not do so without great cause. The people of the eastern empire are not native Benotrist or even Menotrist, but come from a collage of tribes, small kingdoms and freeholds. As Tyro's empire advanced eastward, these various entities were absorbed into Tyro's growing realm, some under duress, but many joining freely. The emperor wisely forced marital unions between high-ranking Benotrists and the former kings, chieftains and warlords of the east, politically unifying the realm and strengthening his tenuous hold on his easternmost lands. This mixing of our bloodlines has only reached the upper ranks of our people, though in time, Tyro intended it to be extended to the middle and lower positions of the populace in the coming generations," Commander Dalomos began.

"Are you Benotrist?" General Valen asked.

"My mother. She wed a commander of rank of the garrison of Pagan," Dalomos answered, establishing his heritage.

"But you took an oath and are now breaking it," Torg said, wanting him to expound on that.

"As I first stated, men of the legions and garrisons of the empire swore oaths to our emperor and would not forsake them without cause." Dalomos' voice trailed, his eyes fixed to the table, lost in his thoughts.

"And what cause brought this about?" General Lewins asked.

"Dreams." Dalomos sighed, hardly believing it himself.

"What sort of dreams?" Torg asked, not at all surprised, considering they were all visited by them as of late.

"Before your armies crossed into our lands, our people have had visions, terrible visions of gargoyles and men fighting in a great battle, the fate of mankind resting upon the outcome, or at least the fate of my people resting upon it. We did not know what to do, considering the armies of man were led by our enemies, many who now stand before me. The army of gargoyles were clearly aligned to our destruction, and yet they are currently the servants of the empire. When Princess Tosha appeared at the court of Pagan offering terms, our regent found a way to reconcile our oaths with the survival of our people. By swearing to Tyro's true heir, we can hold to our vows while fighting for our future," Dalomos concluded, receiving a mix of responses and a healthy dose of mistrust from Alen and his fellow rebel leaders standing across the table from the Benotrist.

"Have all your people had these visions?" King EL Anthar asked.

"All that I have spoken with. If Regent Gorel has had them, perhaps he shall surrender Nisin peacefully," Dalomos said, hoping these visions spread far and wide.

"Once he sees the army that now surrounds him, he would be wise to do so, visions or not," Corry said.

"If not, then we take the castle tomorrow night," Raven said, the others no longer doubting such a boast after all the miracles the Earthers seemed to bring about with such ease.

"Before we discuss our plans to do so, I would hear from Alen on his efforts." Corry looked to the former slave and rebel leader.

And so, Alen relayed his tale, beginning at Corell after the first siege was lifted, and his journey north alongside Elos. He explained the revolt Elos helped him ignite near the Plate Foothills, and spreading north into the heart of the surrounding regions where they now stood, including his slaughtering the garrison of Nivek and the sacking of Gostovar before his capture along the Reguh. He detailed the process by which they spread revolt throughout the eastern empire, and where they presently stood, by his recent contact with the current leadership along the Tur.

"I have contacted the larger rebel factions east of Nisin, and they have agreed to cease hostilities with the Benotrists swearing to Terin and will help escort supplies to your army," Alen concluded.

"Between your rebels and Dalomos' people, our supply trains should be well secure," Torg reasoned.

"That only leaves Nisin between our armies and the west. Before we review our plans to take it, a brief strategic overview of happenings to the west should be discussed. General Valen." Corry directed the magantor commander to present his findings.

"We received word three days ago of allied movement along the western coast. The Sisterhood has disembarked two armies upon the Benotrist shoreline near the Yatin border, as a combined Yatin-Macon-Torry armada is skirting the coast to join them, while a Torry-Yatin Army marches north from Tenin. They will soon advance upon Tinsay Harbor," Dar Valen said, piquing the interest of those who had not learned of this before this day.

"That should draw the eye of the 13th legion to their direction," General Motchi, commander of the Casian 2nd Army said, eyeing the northwestern corner of the map. He was familiar with the placement of all enemy forces, having studied their latest movements throughout their march from Pagan.

"Perhaps, but there is still General Gavis' 10th Legion sitting somewhere between us and Fera, and the question of where the gargoyles have fled to," General Lewins, commander of the Torry 1st Army said.

"Can Brokov scan farther west and put eyes upon the enemy?" General Valen asked of Raven.

"I don't know, but you can ask him yourself." Raven directed him to the disc still hovering above the table.

"*I heard him. The problem is the more discs I deploy, the more my attention is diluted. Right now, I have six discs covering vast stretches of territory this side of the Reguh River Valley, prioritizing your armies' campaign at Nisin. I am still using a primitive iteration of discs with limited range. Once we move west along the coast, I will begin scouting beyond the Reguh and Morga Rivers and the approaches of Fera. I am currently limited in the time I can commit to this considering I am also running most of the ship's functions while many of our crew are with you,*" Brokov answered, his voice echoing through the comms on the hovering disc.

"Might I ask a question?" Dalomos regarded Corry respectfully.

"You may," she said.

"My people have sworn to Terin Caleph, your champion, as our rightful king, but I do not see him among you. Nor do I see King

Lorn, or even King Mortus. Should they not be here among this esteemed gathering?"

And there it was, the question hanging above their heads, and the great unknown plaguing their advance. Should she lie? Could she inform this Benotrist commander that the boy they swore fealty to, Tyro's true heir, was likely to die, sacrificing himself to save them all? What would that portend for their fragile alliance? No, she couldn't lie, but she wouldn't give him the full truth, at least not brutally.

"They are elsewhere, commander, attending a vital duty to our collective realms," she said, her words doing little to placate his concern.

"Let us conclude that the quicker we take Nisin, the quicker we can aid our king and yours in the role appointed them," Torg said.

"Then let's get on with it. We've talked enough as it is, and most of us haven't eaten yet," Raven growled, his mention of food causing the apes to snort in agreement.

"General Zem, perhaps you should begin," President Matuzak said, causing Zem to perk up at the mention of his esteemed rank.

And so, General Zem began to detail the most efficient means of assailing the castle, starting with the air skis clearing the uppermost battlements and allowing the Jenaii to secure them with ease, while the apes would be aligned before the north gate, keeping the enemies' eyes in that direction.

* * *

It was dusk when the arriving armies finally set camp for the night, most erecting temporary bivouacs along the eastern perimeter of the siege lines before repositioning the following morn. The nearby forests provided ample wood for their cookfires, which was a welcome respite from the privations crossing the Kregmarin, or the hasty advance from Pagan. Though the Casians and Troans were exhausted from their arduous trek and had only enough strength to eat and fall fast asleep, the apes were possessed with lively spirit, gathering about their fires partaking drink and song. They raided nearby holdfasts, carrying off generous supplies of ale, distributing the casks among their ranks. Matuzak limited them to three drinks per soldier, not wanting his armies hung over and helpless should the enemy prevail themselves from their castle. They generously offered their wares to their allies, with the humans reluctantly accepting the inviting spirits, and the Jenaii refusing, as was their nature.

The Benotrists manning the battlements of the castle observed the merriment below with despairing sadness, knowing their fate was sealed, so much so that their enemy celebrated with no concern of retribution. There were no legions marching to their relief, leaving them friendless and alone. The entire countryside seemed to turn upon them, adding their strength to the enemy. Thorton was un-heard from and Morac long gone, leaving them no swords of light or Earther weapons to contest those held by the enemy. They could only stand there, trapped within the walls of the palace, listening to the cheers and song of their foes.

Raven stood along the eastern siege lines, scanning the battle-ments through the lens of his rifle's scope, looking for any sign of activity in the closing dark. He had ample targets to shoot at, but the poor wretches looked too pitiful to brain. He didn't really want to kill men that might surrender tomorrow, and if he started shooting, he would only kill a few before the rest all went into hiding. His primary concern was them planning an attack while his friends were downing their casks, but that didn't look likely from what he was seeing.

"I thought you would be with the others." Cronus's voice caused him to lower the rifle, turning as his friend closed in the dark.

"Just checking on our friends up there," he said, jerking a thumb toward the palace. They stood between two large cookfires where scores of apes and men were gathered about, their silhouettes visible in the firelight, casting their shadows on the ground between them.

"We haven't had time to speak much this day, but I am glad to see you, old friend." Cronus smiled, placing a hand to Raven's shoulder.

"Yeah, we haven't had a moment's quiet since we arrived, until now, if you can call this quiet," Raven said just as the apes to their left broke out into another drinking song about a three-legged moglo, their raucous laughter echoing through the night air.

"They are a spirited bunch, that I can concede." Cronus kept his smile, looking briefly to the source of the distraction, where stood scores of apes and men with their arms about each other's shoulders, swaying to the music.

"You missed out on their celebrations when we were at Torn and Gregok, before the attack at Tro. I lost count of how many casks they downed. Must have been a thousand. You could imagine the smell of their latrine sheds the days after. I have to say the smell of your waste ditches here isn't much better. I can hardly wait until I have to drop a shit." Raven made a face, missing the privacy of the *Stenox* when the call of nature occurred.

"Welcome to the smell of an army in the field," Cronus japed, recalling Raven's distaste of the facilities at Corell, as well as their trek after escaping Fera. If he was being fair, he too could barely stomach the stench of the waste pits resting far behind their siege lines, the noxious fumes drifting painfully through their encampment whenever the wind leaned in this direction.

"It's something I never thought of at Corell, what Morac's legions endured during that long siege."

"And that was before you started shooting, sending them hiding in their trenches. I still recall the stench of those siege works after the siege was lifted." Cronus made a face as well, recalling the awful experience.

"At least we can end this siege quicker than that one. Tosha and Corry are writing up the terms of surrender they intend to deliver to the palace come sunup," Raven said, looking off to the east, where sat the command pavilion with scores of guards standing post around it, ample firelight playing off their armor and helms.

"Let us hope Regent Gorel sees reason," Cronus sighed.

"Doesn't matter if he does or not, because we can take the castle tomorrow. I don't know why those girls are taking so long. They've been in there for half the day writing. What's there to say but give up or we kill you?" Raven shook his head, his blunt remark causing Cronus to laugh.

"Only you would refer to the princesses of the Sisterhood and the Torry realm as *girls*." Had anyone else been so crude they would have been severely punished, perhaps even slain, but that set Raven and the Earthers apart, for who would enforce such an edict? Besides, Raven merely treated them the same as anyone else, and both Tosha and Corry had grown accustomed to their crude manner of speech. He almost forgot how much he missed Raven and was thankful for his company, even if his opinion on the siege was overly optimistic. Of course, there was still the matter of his terrible visions weighing upon him, preventing any smile to remain on his lips for long.

"Don't worry about Corry and my wife over there, they give as good as I dish out to them," Raven snorted.

Cronus smiled again, having heard Raven use that term more than once. He might be the only Araxan that could converse with the Earthers and understand what they were saying more than half the time.

"Now that we are mostly alone, why don't you tell me why you were so insistent that I remain on the *Stenox*?" Raven asked.

"I can't say." Cronus' smile quickly faltered, taken aback by the sudden change of topic.

"You can't or you won't?"

"I won't, and before you ask, understand that I cannot explain it to you at this time. But I implore you to return to your ship once we take the castle."

"I'm not going anywhere but with you, Cronus. We are almost at the end here, and I will help you see it through. Tyro doesn't have Ben helping him anymore, and he has one sword to… I don't know how many of yours, was it four or five now? So, don't worry about whatever it is that's… well, whatever it is that's got you worried."

Cronus knew there was no point in turning his friend back now. If you didn't want Raven to do something, the last thing you could do was tell him not to do it.

"I know you feel differently, Rav, but the way ahead is fraught with unknown peril," he said, trying to shake the visions from his mind.

"Relax, buddy. We are taking this castle, and then we're heading west and finish Tyro and rescue Lorn and Terin from whatever stupid mess they've gotten themselves into." Raven slapped him on the shoulder, his infectious optimism bringing a smile to his laden heart.

Cronus meant to ask of Thorton and what transpired between them when young Dougar rushed up to them, panting heavily after searching to find them in the dark.

"King's Elite Kenti, come quick!" Dougar half shouted, half coughed, trying to catch his breath.

"What troubles you, Dougar?" Cronus bent down, gently gripping his small shoulders to steady him.

"It is Lady Ilesa. Her baby is coming!"

* * *

"Agghh!" Ilesa's screams rang out from inside the matrons' pavilion as Raven, Dougar and Cronus approached, finding Galen standing outside awaiting them. Dozens of others lingered about, listening to the painful screams mixed with the euphoric moans of pleasure that normally accompanied childbirth, wondering what to make of it.

"How fares Lady Ilesa?" Cronus asked, recalling the painful memory of Leanna dying after birthing their child.

"The matrons are attending her most zealously, and Princess Tosha and Princess Corry are at her bedside, offering encouragement," Galen explained, giving Dougar a pat on the head for fetching Cronus.

"What ails her?" Cronus asked as another scream issued from the pavilion.

"A most troubling affliction due to the child's paternal lineage, we surmise," Galen said, exchanging a look with Raven.

"Oh." Cronus recalled what the others told him of Tosha's and Jenna's troubled birthing, each suffering the same as Earth women with their pained labor. Thankfully they also retained the pleasure an Araxan woman feels during birth, strangely afflicting them with erotic pleasure and intense pain simultaneously.

"Lorken, meet us at the matrons' pavilion along the eastern perimeter," Raven said into his comm.

"*Be there in a minute*," Lorken answered back. He was currently along the western perimeter, checking with Criose and Culn, making sure they charged their rifles before sunset and then giving them further instructions on scanning the castle's battlements through the night optics on their lenses.

Raven sent the same message to Argos and Zem, who quickly joined them, keeping outside the pavilion through much of the night awaiting the birth. It was Lorken who was first to enter, called upon to ensure the regenerator was ready if needed, though the other matrons were quite handy with the devices by this point. He remained nearby if needed as they attended Ilesa. She lay upon the narrow cot used for the wounded, placed in the corner of the large field tent. The matrons erected a makeshift wall of linens surrounding the cot, giving her as much privacy as possible. Corry stood at her head, wiping the sweat from her forehead while smoothing her hair, trying her best to comfort her. Tosha sat at her bedside, holding her left hand, while the matrons waited at the end of the cot, examining her womb as the baby's head began to emerge.

"You are almost there," Tosha said soothingly, holding her left hand, remembering the painful birth she endured, wondering how Earther women tolerated such agony. It was a wonder how the Earthers didn't go extinct, for she could not imagine their women-folk being much enthused to partake of this torture.

"Agghh!" Ilesa moaned again, pushing with all her might, tucking her right hand between her teeth, bracing for the pain.

Tosha and Corry noticed the parchment clenched in her right hand, which she removed from her bosom at the outset, clinging to it dearly throughout.

"Would you like me to hold this for you?' Tosha asked as Ilesa caught her breath to try again, waves of pleasure and pain flowing from her womb in uneven torrents.

She regarded Tosha for the longest moment, reluctant to give over her dearest possession, as if her life itself was bound to its written script.

"We shall keep it safe for you, Ilesa, you have our word," Corry whispered in her ear, stroking her hair.

She relented, tearfully handing it over before the next wave passed over her. Tosha carefully smoothed the soiled parchment, placing it in her lap after adjusting her sword belt, her scabbard scraping across the dirt floor as she shifted it further back. She hadn't removed her breastplate or greaves as yet, the stiff armor growing heavy by this point. It was times such as these she wished she wore her Earther garb, though she would never admit such to Raven, for he would be insufferable. Despite the image they presented, the Earthers' clothes were very comfortable.

With great effort the child finally came, the matrons presenting a baby girl to Ilesa's tired eyes. Her heart melted as they placed her in her arms, having her suckle her breast as soon as she was able. Corry and Tosha looked on, pleased she survived this ancient battlefield that every mother had to brave. The matrons quickly applied the regenerator to thoroughly mend the slight tearing she endured and to be certain no other complications arose, before pulling it away and covering her up. By the time they were finished, Ilesa succumbed to exhaustion. The matrons repositioned the child in her arms so she would not slip, placing several bundles of supplies beneath her arms to support her. Corry and Tosha drew away, giving Ilesa peace and quiet when the parchment fell from Tosha's lap, unfolding as it landed. She quickly retrieved it. There was no place to safely store it, so she brought it with her as they stepped away into the open area of the pavilion where Lorken, Raven and the others were gathered around waiting. With no other patients to tend, the matrons allowed them all to enter but warned they would have to leave should a number of wounded suddenly appear.

"Well?" Raven asked impatiently.

"A girl," Tosha bluntly answered, pushing back on his rudeness.

"Are they healthy?" he asked.

"Yes, and lower your voice, they are sleeping," Tosha scolded him as Zem slapped him on the back of his head to drive the point home.

"Let us give her some peace. We shall come back in the morning," Cronus said, urging the others to follow him out.

"That would be best. Corry and I shall stay with her this night," Tosha said, pushing Raven out the door when Ilesa's parchment slipped from her grasp.

"What's this?" Raven asked, reaching down to pick it up, the parchment unfolding as it dropped. He hesitated to hand it back upon noticing Kato's name on the bottom.

"What is it, Rav?" Lorken asked, leaning in around his shoulder to see for himself.

"It belongs to Ilesa, and we must return it when she wakes," Tosha implored.

"What does it say?" Corry asked, watching Raven's face fall as he read.

Raven paused, looking up as the others formed a circle around him, all curious of its contents.

"Read it aloud, you're better at this sort of thing." Raven handed it to Lorken.

"My dearest Ilesa, I hoped this letter to never find your hand…" Lorken began, speaking only high enough for them to hear, and no louder. They were taken aback by Kato's moving words and prose as he wrote of his love for Ilesa and the dreams they shared. Corry and Tosha wiped their eyes as Lorken finished, Kato's words breaking their hearts. The others fared little better, with Zem sadly shaking his head and Raven wanting to kick something. Cronus took the parchment gently from Lorken's hand, folding it back to its original shape, handing it to Tosha.

"We should not speak of this. These were Kato's words intended for Ilesa's eyes only. Let us remember our friend as we last saw him," Cronus said. Kato's words could just as easily be the same as his or Leanna's. Hearing them tore him apart for that very reason.

* * *

None of them got much sleep that night, each thinking about their friend, reminding them of so many other friends they lost in this war. Fortunately, the weather was clear, allowing them to lay their bedrolls out beneath the stars without consequence. Raven shared a small cookfire with his fellow crewmates and Cronus and Dougar, the young boy fast asleep upon his bedroll beside him as he sat on his pack, looking into the dying flames of their fire. The others slowly succumbed one after the other, leaving him and Zem the last holdouts, his large friend sitting on a large wooden block he managed to find, though Raven couldn't fathom where from.

"You ready for tomorrow, big fella?" Raven asked, twisting a stick into the fading embers to stir their fire awake.

"I have prepared my assault team for every conceivable contingency should the parlay fail in its objective," Zem bluntly stated.

"I never say it much, but I owe you a lot, Zem. Thanks for saving our bacon more times than I can count."

"Is that a compliment? That has to be a first," Zem said in disbelief.

"Don't let it go to your head, but yes, it's a compliment," Raven sighed.

"Very well. The appropriate response is to say you are welcome, so you are welcome."

"Thanks, but you could say thanks as well."

"For what?" Zem asked.

"Never mind." Raven shook his head.

"Thanks," Zem said.

"For what?"

"Because you must have done something I'm not aware of, so whatever it is, thanks. Do you feel better now?"

"Sure." He shook his head, knowing that was about all the acknowledgement he would get from Zem when all of sudden the large android surprised him.

"You ever wonder if there is a reason for us coming here?" Zem asked.

"Yeah," he said, recalling what Lorn had said to him back at Corell on the roof of the palace that night so long ago.

"When you consider the probabilities of passing through that strange anomaly and being deposited on the only non-terraformed Class T planet other than Earth we have ever discovered, it is beyond calculation. There has to be a presence behind it, something far beyond our comprehension," Zem said in a faraway voice. His tone was so eerie it sounded almost human.

"Lorn has an answer for that, if you want to know."

"And that is?"

"Yah, the God he claims has guided him through all of this. He claims he saw our coming long before we ever did, if you can believe him, and for some reason, I do."

"It seems logical to believe such," Zem said.

"You believe in their God?" Raven didn't expect that from an artificial life form.

"It is not without consideration if one looks deep enough. There are only two possibilities to the great question of the origin of the universe. It is either happenstance, with the miracle of life springing from a series of chemical interactions, or it is the result of intelligent design. The intelligent design answer could be of the result of countless thousands if not millions of sources and possibilities. It is understandable for one to adhere to either possibility when the universe itself functions with both a sense of order and chaos, each seeming to operate within the same space. Much of it depends on one's preconceived notions, where each discovery reinforces one's own belief. I find it interesting that you humans always find the answer you are looking for, even if it is incorrect."

"Then what's your answer, Mr. smart guy?"

"I just told you."

"No, you didn't. You rambled on about a bunch of nonsense like Professor Milton back in the academy," Raven said, recalling his instructor in Astro-Philosophy during his first unit of learning at the Space Fleet academy.

"I shall summarize. The probabilities of either answer border on impossibility, so much so that only a fool would claim full understanding. I would lean upon your ancient philosopher, the Greek Stoic Socrates, who claimed to be wiser than his contemporaries because he was aware of his own ignorance, where they were not."

"You call that summarizing? That was as clear as mud."

Zem looked at him as if he were a moron, deciding to simplify his answer so even Raven could understand.

"I don't know, and no one else does either."

Finally, a straight answer, Raven thought.

"That still leaves Lorn's God, and I have to say he knows things about us that no one could know unless his God is real."

"Then what is your issue?" Zem asked.

"What do you mean my issue? What do you make out of it? Just wondered your opinion since you're a well of information with that perfect memory of yours."

"This is not about the vast knowledge stored in my memory banks that you can access for an answer. The collective knowledge of the universe cannot do that, let alone what I have stored. You must rely on what you believe, Raven. Do you believe in Yah?"

Raven never expected Zem to be so openminded on the subject, but considering everything they experienced the last few years, nothing should surprise him anymore.

"Well, if you put a gun to my head, I would have to say… yes."

"Then there is your answer, and everything that happens going forward will only reinforce that belief," Zem stated bluntly.

Raven sat there for the longest moment, trying to sort it all in his head.

"That leads to a whole bunch of questions that don't make much sense." Raven scratched his head.

"Such as?"

"Well for one thing, why would Yah need us to come here? Couldn't he have helped the Torries to topple Tyro without dragging us across the universe? And aren't we a little overkill? Let's be honest, Zem, without Ben helping them, we are going to win this war pretty easy, unless I'm missing something. Hell, we could drop you off on the palace roof and have you storm through the halls slaying everyone in your path, and there ain't a damn thing they can do about it."

"True, and that would be a detriment to Yah if his goal is to gather converts to his faith, as the people would see us as their deliverer and not him. The same could be said of Terin and the others wielding their powerful swords. It takes a deeper intellect to praise the one who summoned great warriors to their cause, then praising the warriors themselves."

"There has to be more to this then we can see. There has to be some greater reason for us to be here, some greater force for us to contest than what's left of Tyro's legions and a bunch of gargoyles."

"Well, Raven, it's like they used to say back in the academy, *there has to be someone that needs some killing*, and if there is, who better than us? You should get some rest, it's been a long day."

"You're right on one thing, killing is what we're good at," Raven said, easing himself in position to sleep. That would prove difficult with Argos' snoring echoing from the other side of their cookfire.

"If you truly want to know what I think, Rav, Kato didn't come here and die for nothing," Zem added, leaving him with that last thought before bidding him goodnight.

* * *

The following morn found Regent Gorel sitting his throne, his mind a maelstrom of bitterness, fear and dread. He contemplated his sorry state, surrounded by an enemy host that grew larger each day, while half his garrison abandoned him. He held Nisin with a mere five telnics, with no help forthcoming. He was abandoned by half his men and the empire as well. Morac did not even deign to visit him on his return journey, bypassing Nisin for Fera, while Thorton wandered off to face his former friends, his fate as yet unknown to Gorel. The enemy was certain to have a Sword of Light at their disposal and several Earthers, with one of them buzzing about the castle in the past several days on their flying machine, while decimating his magantors, many of his warbirds slaughtered beyond his western battlements. His lookouts spotted several others arriving yesterday with a great host of apes and men. They spotted sigils of Torries, Macons, Casians, Jenaii, Apes, and numerous lesser realms and city states among the enemy. He guessed their strength to be as high as a hundred thousand, and with no Earther or magic sword to fend them off, he was doomed.

"My Lord Gorel, the enemy calls for parlay," his steward again said, waiting upon his response, standing patiently at the base of the dais.

"There is nothing to say," Davin Gorel said with a dead voice, his eyes vacant, forlorn of hope.

His steward remained statue still, needing his regent to offer more than that, the silence in the chamber sending bumps across his flesh.

"That is my answer. Be gone!" Gorel's eyes came briefly alive, forcing the steward to lift his robes and make for the door, leaving a disordered Gorel sitting upon the throne, his mind bordering on madness.

* * *

Command pavilion. Eastern perimeter of Nisin siege lines.

"He refuses parlay," Torg said, reading the missive just delivered to the commanders gathered about.

"Very well. Are your soldiers ready, Your Majesty?" Corry asked, looking to King El Anthar, who stood stoically at her side, his silver eyes studying the layout of the palace detailed on the map upon the table.

"Yes. We shall commence immediately upon their signal." El Anthar looked to Raven and Lorken, who stood opposite them.

"No time like the present. You got Zem, and I'll take Arg," Raven said to Lorken before making for the door.

"I am coming with you," Tosha said.

"We already discussed this, and you should stay here," he refuted, trying to move past her, but she stepped again in his path.

"Cronus and I have our swords to protect us, and Zem and Argos will need us before the others can join them. And we didn't agree to anything, you just assumed we did." She poked him in the chest.

"Oh, for crying out loud, come on," he growled, knowing when there was little point in arguing with her.

* * *

They lifted into the air, the campsites below shrinking as they ascended, men and apes looking up, saluting their friends as they pulled away. They lifted higher and higher, drawing level with the outer walls of the palace that rested in the distance to their west.

"You both ready back there?" Raven asked over his shoulder as Tosha clung to his back with Argos sitting behind her.

"Just don't turn sideways and we'll be fine," Argos growled, testing the weight of his rifle, which would occupy his hands throughout this maneuver.

"I got you covered, big fella, and the faster you clear a path, the faster I set you both down. Here goes," Raven said as Lorken sped off to the north with Cronus and Zem sitting behind him. Raven eased the accelerator, following close behind.

Lorken angled higher before banking left, circling the north face of the castle, sparing a glance to the upper battlements of the inner keep where several heads peeked above the parapets. He rose even higher before banking left again, skirting the western face of the palace, Raven drawing close behind, as he drew level to the uppermost platforms of the palace citadels.

"What's your latest, Brokov?" Lorken said into his comm as Zem readied his first shot, fixing a lookout upon the Tower of Netso in his sights.

"*Spotted only a handful of sentries in each tower, and only three upon the upper platforms. Another dozen upon the upper roof of the inner keep and a hundred more waiting in the three levels below,*" Brokov said, having slipped three observation discs into the palace in the days prior, detailing the location of the enemy in position to oppose what they were planning.

"Alright, keep us informed," Lorken said, drawing closer as Zem took his first shot.

Blue laser streamed from Zem's rifle, striking the lookout who was caught staring in their direction, struck with wonder at what he was seeing, the blast taking him by surprise. Zem shifted aim as the lookout dropped where he stood, finding the next target standing upon the Tower of Fire, its crimson walls cast in a brighter hue than its sisters. That lookout already dove for cover, dropping below his line of sight behind the thick parapet that circled that level of the tower. Zem sent a volley of blasts through the wall where he ducked, moving on before Brokov confirmed the kill.

"Target the roof below!" Raven ordered Argos as they kept close to Lorken, speeding around the upper keep, Zem's laser blasts spewing from his rifle up ahead.

"Aye," Argos snorted, lowering his aim below where the four towers of Nisin rose from the roof of the inner keep, the Benotrists manning the platform scrambling for cover.

ZIP! ZIP! ZIP!

Argos strafed the rooftop with several blasts, managing to strike one soldier in the hip, the rest missing altogether. Raven angled lower, his air ski dropping below Lorken's, giving Argos an easier angle.

ZIP! ZIP! ZIP!

Argos spread a volley to the base of the Tower of Vatar, where several soldiers struggled to clear the stairwell and escape below. His blasts struck several, killing one and wounding three. More laser blasts swept overhead, striking soldiers gathering at the base of the Tower of Netso, trying to form a shield wall. Argos looked up, finding Lorken sweeping down from above, Zem firing with deadly accuracy from the back of the ski. The two skis swept around the inner keep twice over, dispatching the enemy from wherever they gathered before lowering to the red stone surface, hovering briefly while Zem, Argos, Cronus and Tosha dismounted.

The skis lifted into the air, Raven looking down as his comrades swept over the battlements of the inner keep, dispatching the enemy that remained. The flash of laser and the golden glow of their swords shone in the late morning air, the enemy fleeing before them. He caught sight of Tosha splitting an upraised blade, her follow strike taking the man's sword arm at the elbow. Argos drew alongside her, sending a volley into the soldiers retreating to the nearest stairwell. Zem lowered his rifle, catching a fleeing soldier by the scruff of his neck, tossing him over the nearest parapet, the poor wretch's arms flailing as he fell, smashing on the causeway below. Raven winced at the sight, the body splattering as it struck.

Raven followed Lorken into the sky, passing high above the inner walls that circled the inner keep and then the outer walls beyond, Benotrist ballista falling short of them as they sped off to the north.

* * *

ZIP! ZIP!

Zem dropped the last soldiers still standing upon the roof, before shifting his aim skyward, scanning the towers above for sign of any lookouts they might have missed, while Argos and the others cleared the nearest stairwell. Cronus peered through the opening, wary of a blade striking out at them from the shadows.

"Brokov, what do you see?" Tosha said into the comm, trailing Argos and Cronus who were standing fully in the stairwell.

"*That tower is clear every point higher. The nearest soldiers are still two levels below, making their way up.*" Brokov relayed what the discs revealed.

They held position, waiting upon the enemy as Zem remained in the open behind them, clearing any threats to emerge along the roof.

ZIP! ZIP!

Argos blasted the first heads to appear along the circled stairwell below. The clang of metal echoed off the stone steps following his blast, where their dislodged helms tumbled below. His blasts must have struck true, for the enemy held where they were, none braving that deadly space. They lost all track of time, surprised by how swiftly Raven and Lorken returned, bringing Criose and Culn with them, along with two ape warriors, dropping them off beside Zem, before speeding off to bring more soldiers to the roof. Argos directed Criose and Culn to cover the stairwells of two of the other towers, and Tosha and Cronus to a third, while he remained where he was. Zem continued clearing the upper platforms of the surrounding towers before stealing a glance over the parapet, overlooking the inner battlements of the north wall below.

ZIP! ZIP!

Zem blasted the crews of two ballista positioned along the outer battlements of the north wall beyond, before strafing the inner walls behind them, sending soldiers scrambling for cover.

ZIP! ZIP!

He shifted aim to the ballista along the east wall, sweeping away the defenders as Raven and Lorken returned from the north, gliding past him, each bearing two ape warriors, who jumped onto the roof of the inner keep beside Zem. Zem quickly ordered them into position, joining the other two who already arrived, reinforcing each opening of the tower stairwells, and the large stairway in the center of the roof leading to the keep below. Zem continued along the perimeter of the roof, aiming his rifle over the parapets, striking targets along the east, south and west walls as he moved, while Raven and Lorken ferried more ape warriors to reinforce them. Once they had enough warriors in place, he ordered Criose, Argos and Culn to different positions along the roof of the inner keep, freeing them to target the outer and inner walls below, keeping them under constant fire. Zem himself returned to the northern edge of the roof, targeting any soldier peaking above the parapets below.

Tosha stepped away from the stairwell she guarded, removing the comm from her satchel, raising King El Anthar, signaling him to commence stage two of the attack.

Within moments hundreds of Jenaii filled the western sky, ascending high above the palace battlements as they drew nigh, keeping out of range of ballista and archer fire, though few if any could respond with the laser fire striking them down from the inner keep behind them. The Benotrists could only look on from behind their ramparts as the Jenaii approached unchallenged, their gray-white wings casting hundreds of shadows while passing overhead, setting down upon the inner keep in the hundreds.

King El Anthar led his warriors to the roof of the inner keep, sunlight playing off his blue helm and armor as he set down. His commanders quickly ordered their warriors to sweep the upper levels of the surrounding towers, placing their own garrisons in all four of them, while hundreds of others barricaded the stairwells from counterattacks coming from below.

"Hail, King El!" Cronus greeted the Jenaii king in the middle of the roof of the inner keep, quickly orienting him to where their forces were positioned.

The apes were all moved to guard the central stair leading to the keep below, while the Jenaii took control of the towers. They currently had a laser rifle on each wall, providing enfilading fire on the outer and inner battlements below, while Raven and Lorken continued to ferry reinforcements to them. Tosha stood in the center of the roof, relaying to Corry that the roof of the inner keep was secure.

"We have enough space to bring three more telnics of my warriors forward," the Jenaii king said, sparing a glance to their surroundings, standing in the center of the large flat roof, with the four towers rising imperiously around them.

"Yes, and I would hold off any more than that until we decide to advance deeper into the palace. Hopefully Regent Gorel will see reason before that is necessary," Cronus said.

"Even he must the know the futility of his position, though crazed men rarely see reason," El Anthar said.

The enemy stopped all activity, their remaining archers and ballista standing down, awaiting word from their regent while Zem gave the order to cease fire.

Raven drew alongside Lorken, hovering in place above the outer battlements of the north wall.

"What are they doing?" he asked, wondering if they were about to give up.

"Probably talking it over since their position is hopeless. From this point we can destroy them at our leisure, and there ain't a damn thing they do about it," Lorken said.

His words proved prescient as they raised a blue flag after a painfully long time had passed, asking for parlay.

* * *

Davin Gorel received the emissaries of the surrounding armies in the throne room, expecting them to meet him beyond the palace gate, or upon the roof. Instead, they agreed to convene in the throne room, much to his surprise, though any notion that their appearance put them at a disadvantage was quickly waylaid when he set eyes upon them. He recognized Princess Tosha leading the strangely diverse group into the storied chamber, her golden eyes fixed sternly upon him as she led them across the mirrored stone floor, clad in her golden armor and black tunic, with her helm resting in her left arm. Her presence would normally be received with pomp and ceremony but was now one of treasonous betrayal. If she was conflicted by her actions, she showed it not. He noted the uniform of the Benotrist commander of telnic among her assembly, though his face was unfamiliar, wondering how far this treason spread. It was her other comrades that took him aback, removing any notion on his part of killing them outright, the protocols of parlay be damned. He recognized the Earth garb and large stature of the man upon her right, guessing he was the villainous Captain Raven, the man's countenance frightening to behold. He noted an ape warrior, several Torry and Macon commanders and a Jenaii among them, but it was the other Earther that sent a ripple of fear down his spine, for he wasn't a man at all, but a metallic creature of some foul nature.

"Regent Gorel," Tosha addressed him as she came to halt before the dais, the others stopping beside her, displaying no fear of their surroundings, as if privy to every detail of the throne room.

"Your Highness. I would formally welcome you to the eastern capital of your mighty sire's empire, but I find you standing among our enemies and would inquire why?" Davin asked, curious of her intentions.

"Though I am Benotrist by blood, and my father's daughter, I am first sworn to my mother's realm, as all daughters of the Sisterhood are raised to be. My mother's realm has declared war upon the Benotrist-Gargoyle empire and moves upon the western coast as we speak," she began.

This was news to Davin, adding greatly to their troubles.

"It must trouble you to be so torn between loyalties to father and mother, forcing you to painfully choose," he said, gauging the conflict in her mind.

"Perhaps it would if certain events had not transpired, Regent Gorel," she retorted.

"And what events are those?"

"The first is that my father arranged an assault upon my mother's palace, which portended dire consequence if things turned differently. The second, and more pertinent, was the visions invoked upon my mother's court through the personage of Terin Caleph," she said, seeing Davin's mouth curl at the mention of the Torry Champion.

"What visions could be trusted from the likes of our people's greatest enemy?" Davin asked, his trained indifference dropping with his obvious disgust.

"Visions of Yah, invoked through the power of his ancient blood, powerful enough to take many from their feet, bathing the throne room in its omnipotent authority!" she declared.

"Convenient for the enemy to claim a god speaks for them, and that we should embrace said deity for our own. Why should I lend credence to such drivel?"

"Have you not had visions of late, of gargoyles swarming over the land, devouring all in their path?" she asked, knowing the truth by the taken aback look passing his eyes.

His silence was damning.

"Would you care to know the truth of your visions, Regent Gorel, and the truth of Terin Caleph?" she asked, pressing her advantage.

"I assume you shall speak of it regardless, princess, so illuminate my ignorance," he growled, leaning back on his throne, unimpressed with her discourse to this juncture.

And so, she told him, revealing Terin's heritage and his connection to her father and their people, as well as the greater threat the gargoyles posed to mankind if humanity would not unite to expunge them fully, condemning Arax to thousands of years of continuous bloodshed. Tosha finished, lifting her chin to receive his answer, her iron countenance projecting the strength of her will.

"Well, what's your answer, Gorel?" Raven finally spoke, tired of these silly games. As far as he was concerned, they gave this idiot too much respect as it was.

Gorel regarded him briefly, wary of his mercurial reputation. It was all too much, presenting a version of events and history that turned his world upon its head. The princess provided him a recourse to forsaking his sacred oath, by claiming Terin Caleph as Tyro's true heir, even over her own sons. That last fact gave steel to her outlandish claims, for why would she disinherit her own sons for a stranger, unless that stranger was no stranger at all, but her nephew.

"We ain't got all day, Gorel. Make your mind up. If you want to hold out, all you'll do is delay us a day or so, while we wipe the floor with your tiny garrison," Raven added, receiving a disapproving look from Tosha for his crudeness.

To drive Raven's point home, Zem stepped forth, sending Gorel's heart racing by his towering presence.

"Captain Raven's threats might be boorish and obtuse, but not without merit. A more eloquent interpretation could be simply stated that any resistance will be forcefully met. To expand on what that portends, know that we shall decimate your garrison with little to no loss of life on our part. Also know that I shall lead the forward ranks into these lower dwellings of the palace and remove you from your throne where I shall dismember your flesh most brutally. This shall be done at the outset, and there is no recourse to prevent it. We know where you are at every moment, by means you are unaware, and I shall find you, and find you rather quickly. You cannot hide, or feign a disguise to escape this fate," Zem said with his deep metallic voice, sending tendrils of fear across Davin's pimpled flesh. Davin shrank back as he stared into Zem's narrow luminous blue eyes, his black silver metallic flesh swallowing the dim torchlight of the chamber. To stare at Zem was akin to staring down death itself, terrible and awesome with equal measure.

Tosha meant to speak, to quell the terror rising in Davin's eyes, but King El Anthar interceded, stepping to Zem's side.

"Peace to you, Oh Regent Gorel. We come not to destroy you but to light the way forward, for your people and ours. There is no other choice but to join with us, preserving your people from certain destruction. Your emperor will look favorably upon your decision should we win the day, for his current path is folly. Swear to Terin. Name him your champion and king, and he shall protect and lead your people to greatness, standing equally among the nations," El Anthar stated, his serene aura calming Gorel's heart.

"I…I shall relent." He sighed, the weight of the decision deflating his spirit. He could not ask his men to fight under such duress. Even if they were on equal ground as the enemy, which they were not, there was still the dreams they were suffering, dreams Princess Tosha and her fellows were fully aware.

"A wise choice," King El Anthar said.

"Bring forth Terin Caleph and I shall swear my allegiance," Davin Gorel conceded.

"Terin Caleph is currently elsewhere," Tosha carefully said.

"Then who shall I swear to?" Davin scowled suspiciously; his question met with silence before Tosha again spoke.

"While Terin Caleph is elsewhere, his queen is present."

"Queen?" Davin asked.

"Queen Corry, the former princess of the Torry Realm, and now Queen of Pagan and its surrounding tributaries."

"Very well," Davin relented.

* * *

The following morn found Corry and Tosha upon the upper battlements of the inner keep, overlooking the surrounding lands where their armies were still encamped. With the siege lifted, the armies went about filing their trenches, reordering their ranks and consolidating their hold on the surrounding region. General Vecious oversaw the regarrisoning of Nisin, using his 2nd Macon Army along with a telnic of the current garrison, with the remaining garrison soldiers joining commander Dalomos' Pagan contingent outside the palace walls. Though some of the surrendering Benotrist soldiers reacted poorly to their submission, most were strangely subdued, or visibly relieved as if waking from a terrible dream. Corry and Tosha knew the last group endured their visions longer than the others, plagued by what they saw… gargoyles.

"You should have warned me before announcing that I am to be Queen of this fictitious realm you have created," Corry said, looking out to the west, with the morning sun at her back, recalling the awkward moment they informed her of the surrender arrangements after treating with Davin Gorel. She had waited beyond the north wall when the gate was opened and the herald rode forth, bearing the terms. It was late in the day when Regent Gorel bestirred from the palace and knelt before her, proclaiming loyalty to his new king.

"And what fun is there in that, dear cousin. Besides, he did ask for Terin, and who better to represent his majesty than his beloved queen?" Tosha smiled mischievously, enjoying this all too much.

"And what shall become of it should Terin perish?" Corry asked, cringing at the thought of him dying.

"We shall address that if the situation arises, but for now it gives us a means of uniting our peoples, a means I intend to fully exploit. Besides, I find the new imperial sigil quite fetching," Tosha said, sparing a glance behind and above, where the new standard waved above the Tower of Vatar, a glowing azure blade upon a field of silver.

"Even if Terin survives, he will refuse the crown."

"Even if it serves the greater good?" Tosha asked.

"You do not know him as I do. He desires nothing of power and position. You should see how he shyly receives the praise of our people. He cringes with their adulation, feeling it unearned, claiming it is the power of his blood generously given from Yah, by no merit of his own. Terin has many admirable traits, and I love him dearly, more than my own flesh, but he is not a king. He has not even held command of any sort, acting in accordance with his nature. He is a loyal soldier and warrior, perhaps the greatest to have ever lived, but a leader he is not. He would hate it." Corry wiped a tear from her eye, speaking of Terin so intently reminding her how much she missed him, fearing she would never look into his beautiful eyes ever again.

"Terin might surprise you, Corry. Besides, he doesn't need to be a great leader. All that is required is his handsome smile and charming demeanor while his beautiful queen rules the realm, as she has proven repeatedly without fault." Tosha gave her an infectious smile, causing Corry to roll her eyes before smiling herself.

Their lighthearted moment quickly passed as the frown returned to Corry's face, her gaze returning to the west, where Terin awaited somewhere countless leagues away.

"What are we to do?" Corry lamented.

"What do you mean?"

"We came here to draw your father's eye in this direction, to clear the way for Lorn and the Chosen to accomplish what Yah has asked them to do, and yet, Tyro has withdrawn his strength, making their task more difficult."

"We have taken half the empire, my father must respond or risk losing the rest," Tosha said, though even she began to doubt that.

"Your highness!" One of their guards announced as a large flock of magantors drew nigh from the southeast, silver-white wings indicating their Jenaii origin.

"What now?" Tosha wondered aloud.

CHAPTER 5

Nisin Palace. Throne room.

The last thing Corry expected this day was to already be seated upon the throne of Nisin, and holding court. It was entirely absurd, and if someone told her this was to unfold, she would have called them mad, but here she sat as the Jenaii escorted King Lichu, King of Nayboria into the grand chamber, flanked by ten of his imperial elite, each armed and arrayed for battle. Gone were the bright golden mail and ostentatious uniforms they were known for. In their place were the austere gray mail and tunics of simple warriors, practical yet subdued. The king himself was similarly attired, his helm resting in his left hand, freeing his once vibrant red hair that was matted and heavily tainted with silver, denoting his years.

King El Anthar stood upon her right, as if expecting their guests, though his stoic countenance betrayed no such notion. Cronus and Tosha stood upon her left; their swords ready should she have need. She wondered why their enemy was allowed to be so heavy armed, but they displayed no sense of aggression. If anything, King Lichu looked more a defeated man than a great monarch, and she wondered his purpose for being here. The answer to that question was soon explained with the Naybin King's first utterance.

"I have come at your behest, King El Anthar. My realm stands defeated and broken asunder. My family and kin are at your mercy, and yet I stand before you with my sword upon my hip, making me question my purpose here." King Lichu addressed El Anthar, his eyes shifting between Corry and the Jenaii king.

"You are here by Yah's will, Oh King. You and your men shall join us in battle should the need arise," El Anthar proclaimed.

"It appears your battle has ended," Lichu said, sparing a glance around the vast chamber.

"The battle of Nisin is ended, but the war continues," El Anthar answered.

"We have been enemies since the days my people claimed our homeland, Oh King Anthar. You have defeated us at last, aided by this grand alliance, my people beset from all directions. Despite this, you have spared my line, and ask that I join you here, myself and only ten of my bravest. No conqueror would show such mercy when he could merely quash his enemy for all time. Therein lies my distrust, for this action is madness, unless I have overlooked something," Lichu said warily.

"When my people first set ashore at the mouth of the Elaris, nearly two full millennia ago, we brought forth the sacred gift, delivering it into the hands of those loyal to King Kal, the Tarelians. From this gift they forged the Swords of Light, gifting them to their warlords and generals, sending them forth to establish kingdoms to push back the gargoyles, liberating the land from their scourge. The Southern Kingdom was the nearest to our own realm, and our loyal friends when the Nayborian tribes crossed the Naiba, throwing down that Tarelian Kingdom, replacing it with your own. Few remain of the ancient peoples of the Southern Kingdom, their descendants scattered and diluted throughout your realm. It was my intention to see your people removed from Arax, destroyed for all time, root and stem, but Yah demands mercy for your people, a mercy you wisely accepted," El Anthar said, those gathered throughout the chamber hanging upon his every word, most ignorant of this ancient history.

"And why is this deity inclined to grant us mercy?" Lichu asked warily.

"He grants you a chance, despite your blindness to the gargoyle threat through the ages, a chance to amend this failing. You shall remain and fight beside us until that threat is removed. Your kingdom will then be returned to you when the blood of Tarelia is joined to your heirs, and the heirs of your vassals," El Anthar declared.

"And should I perish here in the north?" Lichu asked.

"Then you perish, your fate no more ensured then our own."

"I ask again, why is Yah offering this mercy?"

"It was always his intent that all men stand as one against the gargoyles. By joining us in battle, you shall represent your people and see with your own eyes the evil we face."

"But you are not men, Oh King EL Anthar. Where is your place in this great conflict?"

"The Jenaii are the devout servants of the most high, placed upon Arax to contest the gargoyles and guide mankind in this task. The apes and Enoructans were so placed to be friends of men, joining them in battle. Only now, after so many thousands of years, have all the nations joined in purpose. Now is the time of choosing, Oh King Lichu. Yah would see all peoples partake in this final conflagration."

King Lichu released a guarded sigh, torn by what he felt and what he must do. These were his age-old enemies, the villainous Jenaii, the hated Torries and the traitor Maconians, but he too was beset with terrible visions as of late, revealing the greater peril. There was truly no choice but one. With that, he took a knee, drawing his sword and placing it upon the mirrored stone floor.

"You have my sword, my life, and those of my men. I fight beside you until the gargoyles are destroyed or death takes me. This I so avow!" Lichu declared, before gaining his feet, sliding his sword back into its sheath.

* * *

The following days continued with the reorganization of their armies and gathering of provisions, which were now augmented by sources throughout the newly conquered lands. Corry was anxious for every report Brokov provided as his probes moved farther west, looking for sign of enemy movement. Whatever Tyro planned, marching a force to meet them did not appear his intention. Since their purpose assailing Nisin was to draw Tyro's eye east and away from the Chosen, they failed in doing so. Though they conquered vast tracks of territory, the danger to their friends was now even greater, with Tyro's strength now concentrated where they intended to march. Further confounding was the fact they were not to follow the Chosen, placing an imaginary line somewhere between Nisin and Fera that they dare not cross, though that sentiment was not shared by all the members of their diverse alliance.

It was late in the evening two days after King Lichu's arrival that found Raven, Lorken and Argos seated at a table in the great hall, partaking their supper, with young Dougar seated between them, listening to their stories. The young boy was a constant shadow, following after them whenever Cronus was elsewhere. He listened with his jaw agape as they told of their adventures, most so fantastical even he would doubt them if they were spoken by others, but their mere appearance was more fantastical than their stories. He first befriended Raven at Corell, the large Earther and Cronus inviting him into their circle of friends. Lorken, he came to know upon his arrival at Notsu, he and Cronus taking him underwing after Jentra died.

Raven had just finished the tale of the rescue at Molten Isle, emphasizing the part where he jumped through the hole in the fortress wall and into the sea, holding Tosha while he did so.

"You weren't actually holding her. From what I heard, you tried to toss her first, but she wouldn't let go, biting you as you both dropped," Lorken corrected him, causing Argos to chuckle.

"How would you know? You were on the other side of the island!" Raven growled.

"I was there, and he speaks the truth of it!" Argos bellowed, causing Dougar to grin. He loved when they argued, for they always made funny faces that made him giggle. He enjoyed their stories and their friendship, feeling a part of something special. He was ever thankful for King Lorn for drawing him into his world after so much suffering living upon the streets of Fleace, a homeless orphan. Argos reached over and ruffled his hair, the gentle gesture shaking the poor child's head more than Argos intended.

"What about Coach O'Brien? Can you tell that story again?" Dougar asked, recalling the first time at Corell when Raven told it.

"Coach O'Brien? The man is a relic. He belongs in a museum, not coaching football." Lorken shook his head.

"Ease up, Lorken, the poor man did the best he could with limited talent at Quarterback," Raven said.

"And a lousy Middle Linebacker," Lorken added, receiving a sour look from Raven with that insult.

"I have better adventures to share than these idiots' grand delusions," Zem's metallic voice boomed.

Dougar looked up, finding Zem looming behind him, having overheard their conversation. Of all the Earthers, Dougar found Zem the most fascinating, his eyes drawn wide with wonder with his every utterance.

"Don't bore the kid with your stories, Zem," Raven said, his words falling on deaf ears as Zem began to tell of their assault on the mercenary army at Bansoch, with Argos adding his version, detailing how they smashed skulls, and tore limbs from their hapless victims. It was the stuff of nightmares, but Zem spoke of it with such technicality to remove all the horror of it. It was like Raven always said, the worst killers always talked like librarians.

"How many did you kill that night?" Dougar asked.

"Just Zem and I killed two hundred, maybe more," Argos said, trying to recall the total.

"That many?" The boy asked.

"It was truly an insignificant achievement, at least for Argos and I. Now my academic exploits deserve far greater accolades, young Dougar. Let me explain my first dissertation on the variations of climate on terraformed worlds within the parameters of lunar influence. It was widely received by the international council of..." Zem began, causing poor Dougar trying to understand what he was babbling about. To his credit, the boy listened attentively, spellbound by Zem's unique prose, while Argos stared blankly, as if he was struck on the head.

Raven and Lorken thought to say something to refute their friend's nonsense, but relented, shaking their heads. Sometimes others needed to see for themselves, and that was poor Dougar, who would suffer Zem's longwinded narration, which led to nowhere.

It was Tosha who rescued them, coming to their table.

"You should be abed, Dougar, it is growing late," she said, touching a hand to his shoulder before finding a seat beside her husband.

"Bah, the lad seems to be enjoying himself," President Matuzak said, joining them as well, with a small crowd gathering about, many calling upon Zem to continue.

Zem agreed, pleased to expound on his narrative, continuing with his long-winded explanation of things the Araxans had no concept of understanding. Zem's inane lecture didn't seem to bother his Araxan audience, who were more mesmerized by his prose and voice than the content of what he was saying. As soon as there was a lull in his speech, Raven quickly changed the topic, calling on Matuzak to tell one of his stories.

"When I was a youngster, not much older than Argos here, I found myself on a patrol along the low hill lands near the headwaters of the Torn…" Matuzak began.

And so it went, with one after another sharing stories of their adventures. A Macon commander of Unit told of their journey marching from Fleace to the relief of Corell, and the many skirmishes he fought from Corell to Notsu. A Torry magantor rider spoke of dueling a Benotrist warbird along the Eastern Plate after the first siege of Corell. Guilen and Dadeus found their way into the growing crowd, where the Macon General told of Guilen saving King Lorn before the walls of Corell. Guilen blushed with embarrassment as many lauded him with praise. And so, it continued, the soldiers telling one story after another with Dougar in the center of it all, his little face looking up from his seat in one direction and then another. Eventually Galen made his way into their midst, offering to teach Dougar a song. The men and apes dragged the poor boy to his feet to stand upon the long table, joining Galen to look over the crowd.

"My dear Dougar, might you have heard the ode of *The Crossed Eyed Moglo*?" Galen asked.

Dougar simply nodded that he hadn't.

"Well, then lend a voice, and I shall teach you this tale." Galen began, starting slow as the boy repeated each line, before increasing the tempo the third time through. Eventually many of the others joined in, especially the Torries, who knew the song well.

Alen and Cronus were late to the revelry, observing the others from the entrance to the great hall. It was well into the night and most of the soldiers should have been asleep, but here they found so many deep into their cups, sharing stories and song, reminding Cronus so much of their victory after the second siege of Corell. Though he needed to speak with Tosha, Cronus couldn't help but enjoy this simple moment. He couldn't partake the celebration at Corell, for he mourned Leanna, and though that wound still weighed upon his heart, he could at least savor a measure of friendly banter. He sensed Alen's unease standing beside him, his young friend still tormented by his experiences.

"You will not disgrace your friends' memory if you join in the festivities," Cronus reminded him.

"I know, but… I find no favor in it. It all seems so pointless," Alen sighed.

"Celebrating?"

"No, the war."

"The war? Don't you want to see Tyro's empire brought down?"

"Is that what we are doing?" He gave Cronus a sideways look.

"Yes. If you venture upon the battlements, you will see a new standard raised above the castle."

"True, but is it truly different? We have named a new emperor to lead us, and though Terin is my friend, he is still the blood of Tyro. The Benotrists will still rule this land, for all we will accomplish is replacing the grandfather for the grandson."

"I doubt Terin or Tyro would agree with your assessment. There are no two men more different than them."

"I know, and I do not mean to disparage Terin, for I know his good heart, but the fact remains, he will seek common cause with the Benotrists to gain peace, and they will remain the true rulers of this land."

"They will have a part to play but will place no higher than your people. Terin will honor his Menotrist kin as he honors his Benotrist, as well as his Torry and Kalinian blood. For true peace, those old rivalries must be put aside. You have to learn to live in peace."

"I don't know if I can." Alen sighed, looking to the opposite wall from the others, where stood a handful of Benotrists, looking as apprehensive and out of place as he did.

"Isn't that what we have done so many times in this war, coming to terms with age-old foes, making friends of enemies? I can give many examples of this, but you need only one. You see that man clad in silver armor standing beside General Ciyon?" Cronus pointed to Guilen who stood beside the long table where Raven and the others were gathered.

"I do," Alen sighed.

"When Terin was captured at Carapis, he was taken by pirates and sold as a slave at Bansoch. That man you see is Guilen Estaran, the brother of his former mistress. Terin suffered greatly in her keeping, and yet he befriended Guilen and helped him escape, and when Deva, his mistress, was brought low and at Terin's mercy, he forgave her. With that one act, the power of Yah filled the throne room of Bansoch, converting the Sisterhood to our cause. Deva now marches with our king, devoted to Terin, Lorn and especially Yah. If Terin can forgive his tormentor so can Alen. Your wounds are still fresh, the wounds of your heart, but patience and time can mend all wounds, my friend." Cronus smiled wanly, placing a hand to his shoulder.

Alen lowered his head, his heart so broken with loss that he struggled feeling anything good. The one thing he was certain of was the loyalty of his friends.

"We have traveled far together, Cronus, and you are my good friend. If you say it must be so, I shall give an honest effort. That is the least I can do for what all of you have done for me and my people. If anyone can close the divide between Benotrist and Menotrist, it is Terin," Alen sighed.

"If he is to succeed, he will need men like you at his side," Cronus said.

"Aye, I can do that."

Cronus smiled at that, hoping Yah would deliver Terin so he

might accomplish what they had just committed him to. It was then he was again drawn to the revelry, with Matuzak leading a thunderous chorus of his favorite refrain.

> *"In the halls of the apes*
> *Where we raise our tankards high*
> *Cheering our place*
> *Beneath the southern sky…"*

"Come, Alen, let us join our friends." Cronus urged him along, joining the others.

* * *

It was late in the night when the crowd finally dispersed, men and apes emptying out of the great hall. Most were bone weary after so many days of marching and preparing siege works, that they would fall fast asleep wherever they set down. Before Tosha slipped away with Raven, Cronus drew her aside, asking her to meet him upon the battlements, the concern upon his face sending tendrils of fear along her spine. The look on his friend's face didn't sit well with Raven either. He knew Cronus well enough to know something was amiss and joined them upon the roof of the inner keep. There was little privacy there either, with soldiers milling about and lookouts constantly rotating out through each of the surrounding towers that jutted prominently into the night sky. It didn't help that all three of them drew crowds of onlookers wherever they went, but Cronus managed to find a somewhat remote corner of the vast platform to speak with them without eavesdroppers overhearing him.

"What's this all about?" Raven asked, stealing a glance around as if they were part of a conspiracy, and worried about someone listening in.

"It would be easier if I show you," Cronus said, drawing his Sword of Light from its scabbard, the once-vibrant bronze-hued blade strangely subdued, its golden glow cast in shadow, as if afflicted.

"What's wrong with it?" Raven asked.

"It still retains its unique power to cleave anything it strikes, but its luster has been removed," Cronus said.

"It looks like Terin's blade after his power was altered," Tosha remarked, eyeing the blade closely.

"It does, and I do not know why. You should see if yours is similarly afflicted," Cronus said.

Tosha backed a step before drawing her own carefully from its sheath, releasing a gasp as it appeared the same as Cronus', its blade dull, and glow abated.

"That can't be good." Raven stated the obvious.

"It is similar to Terin's. His was dull when he grasped it, growing murky and darker as he used it in battle," Cronus said.

"Did it ever shine again?" Tosha asked.

"It would whenever it drew close to my blade or Elos'," Cronus recalled.

"It shined pretty bright during Lorn's coronation, when you and he raised your swords in the air," Raven reminded him.

"We didn't cross blades at that time, but it shone all the brighter. I once asked Terin why this was so, and he only shrugged and said he was happy at that moment," Cronus said.

"His joy fueled the power of the sword?" Tosha asked.

"Yes, but only its brilliance. It still retained its same function. Otherwise, it grew dull, and very dark when used in battle, as if violence swallowed its light," Cronus explained.

"And when it drew to another blade?" Tosha asked, moving the point of her blade toward Cronus', light flickering wherever they drew near. They tested it again, drawing their blades apart before pressing them together, flashes of gold merging with green and purple, joining with other hues in a cacophony of light.

They drew their swords away, their light extinguishing as they did so, returning them to their sheaths.

"What does this mean?" Tosha asked.

"I don't know." Cronus shook his head.

"You don't think..." Tosha began to say, the awful thought hanging on the tip of her tongue.

"What?" Raven asked.

"Do you think something has happened to Terin? Is that why the power of the swords is corrupted?" she asked.

Cronus hadn't thought of that. He turned briefly away, scrubbing his hand over his face.

"Better have Brokov send out his discs further and have a look," Raven said as Cronus turned back, nodding his agreement.

"Corry needs to know," Tosha said, hating what that might mean to her cousin.

"Alright, but just remember we don't really know anything. It's all speculation at this point. We should wait until morning. No point in interrupting her sleep; the poor kid hasn't had much of that lately," Raven said.

"I agree. We have our commanders call on the morrow anyway. It is time to decide," Cronus said.

"Decide?" Tosha asked.

"Yes, to decide just how far we are willing to go."

* * *

The following morn they Gathered in the council chambers of the palace, generals, kings and those of renown. Cronus and Tosha began, revealing what had become of their swords, their grim tidings drawing a pall over the assemblage. Neither of them offered speculation on its meaning, letting those gathered to decide for themselves what it portended. The chamber erupted in debate, with the greatest misgivings shared by the rebels and the Benotrists who recently joined their cause, the source of their concern surrounding Terin.

"We have sworn to the grandson of Tyro, and now he might be dead?" A Benotrist commander of telnic protested after Corry revealed the path of the Chosen and their fated journey. It was necessary to finally speak of it with the changing situation. She couldn't keep this from them while deciding their own path forward.

"Without Terin, how can we ever bridge our differences?" Alen asked, torn between mourning his friend and fearing for his people.

"You dare bemoan your plight in my presence!" Torg growled, his harsh rebuke taking them aback. "You swore your vows to Terin, raising him up as pillar between you, as the only way you could make peace. He and the others are marching to certain death, for no other reason than to spare all of us that same fate. If he does die, and I will not accept that he will, then you owe it to him to come to an accord."

A long silence followed, most shamed for their selfishness when the Chosen sacrificed all in their stead.

"Should they live, we shall move to help them, and should they perish, we shall honor their sacrifice," King EL Anthar stated firmly.

"Aye, I agree, but what path should we follow?" King Sargov of Zulon wondered.

"King Lorn told us not to follow him. Invading the east and taking this castle did not violate that order in truth, though it did in spirit. Should we advance west, we will surely violate his wishes," General Lewins, commander of the 1st Torry Army pointed out.

"Bah, I came here to kill gargoyles and will continue marching until they are all dead!" Matuzak said, pounding his furry fist upon the table.

"Yah was specific in his instructions, my friend. The Chosen are to face Tyro without our interference," King El Anthar countered.

"Our Jenaii friends speak true. We came here to draw the enemy's strength from the west, which they have not done. Should we march west, they will further consolidate their armies. This is folly," General Lewins pointed out.

"Stand in place or march off to engage the enemy, when doing so might cause untold harm to the Chosen, those are the choices before us. The correct path escapes me." General Vecious sighed, explaining their dilemma.

"You all can do whatever the hell you want, but I'm going west with President Matuzak," Raven said, leaning against the far wall as if he hadn't a care in the world.

Corry looked over to him, her eyes moist with unshed tears. She never loved the big Earther more than that moment. As the overseer of this assembly, she had to appear neutral in the debate, hoping others would head the call to march west. While Anthar, Vecious and Lewins calmy weighed the merits of what they should do, Matuzak and Raven threw down the gauntlet. They did not offer debate. They simply said they were going, no matter what the others decided, and the next utterance showed they were not alone.

"I too will march west, for my people, my kings and my friends," Dadeus Ciyon declared.

"And I with you," Guilen Estaran said, standing at his general's side.

"Raven's not going without me," Lorken said.

"Or me." Zem's metallic voice echoed strongly off the chamber's walls.

"And Me!" Argos growled, with the rest of the apes joining him.

"I'll be damned if I stay here. If Yah demands our Chosen to sacrifice themselves, then he can sacrifice me too," Torg said, his sentiment shared by most of them.

"We all go, every one of us. I would rather die upon the field of battle with those I love than grow old without them," Tosha said, looking first to Raven, before her eyes rested on Corry, regarding her with a reassuring nod.

"What of your sword? What if its power continues to wane?" General Lewins asked.

"If my sword is corrupted, then so is Morac's. Either way, I march to war," she said.

"What of you, Cronus, you have been quiet to this point?' Corry asked, looking across the chamber where Cronus stood alone.

"I was always going west, no matter what was decided here. It was Terin that gifted me this sword. Terin once ventured to Fera to rescue me, and I shall return the favor. I would know his fate, whatever that might be," Cronus said, looking to Raven briefly before turning his gaze to Corry.

"Is there anyone opposed?" Corry asked, those who once thought to stay now agreeing to march. She thought to call upon Alen, but he simply gave her a knowing look. He and the Benotrist commanders agreed to join them.

"It is settled then, we march west," Corry said, her eyes sweeping around the table, each returning her gaze in agreement.

"*Now that you decided that, are you ready for my latest scouting report?*" Brokov's voice echoed from the disc floating above the table.

* * *

The armies gathered themselves over the coming days, preparing to march west. Corry detached General Vecious and the 2nd Macon Army to strongly garrison Nisin and secure their lines of communication to all points east. He would also coordinate with the local Benotrist holdfasts and rebel held territories, consolidating their hold on the region. The soldiers were busy breaking down their pavilions and field tents, preparing them for the march ahead. The main road was clear through to the port of Mordicay, allowing their wagons to easily advance over the stone causeway that ran the length of the empire.

"Packaww!"

Cronus looked up as a magantor patrol passed overhead, departing the castle for the west. He found himself beyond the palace walls among the column readying for march. His ocran shifted slightly at the sound of the warbirds, its natural instinct to be wary of their ancient predator, as wild magantors favored the flesh of moglo and ocran.

"Easy." Cronus stroked his mount's neck, calming the beast. The last thing he needed was to die of a broken neck from being thrown from the saddle. He wasn't afraid of death, but had too much to do before it could take him, namely helping his friends survive this war, if he could help it. It was truly the only thing that drove him now, the one thing he could cling to, the one thing that gave him honor.

Cronus spared a glance to the heavens, thankful for the clear morning sky above that would ease their travel. He wasn't one for prayer, or to seek Lorn's God, but something touched him this day, as he sought the answer above.

"If you are up there somewhere, whoever you are, show me the way to save him, to save them. I don't know what you expect me to say, or how to say it, just... well, just help me do this, and should I die, protect my daughter. Give her love, and let her know that we loved her," Cronus whispered, his throat growing tight with his words. A gentle breeze swept over his face, bringing him back from where his thoughts had taken him. He lowered his gaze, catching sight of Ilesa settling in the matrons' wagon, cradling her baby in her arms. He kicked his heels, urging his mount along the column, skirting the lines of infantry waiting to begin their march.

"Ilesa!" he called out, drawing alongside her, where she sat in the back of the open wagon among the matrons' provisions and pavilion equipment, while her sister healers marched alongside the men.

"Cronus," she greeted him, lowering her head respectfully.

"Where are you going?"

"With the army, as my duty demands," she said, regarding him carefully.

"You have fulfilled your duty, many times over. You have come far enough. General Vecious shall need your help here at Nisin, where you and your daughter will be safe. The battlefield is no place for an infant," he pleaded with her.

"My place is with the army, and I shall follow this through to the end," she insisted.

"Ilesa, please don't do this. Please, for the sake of…"

"You are a good man, Cronus Kenti. I am very fond of you and your friends, and I see why Kato so loved each of you. I appreciate your concern, and your friendship, but I MUST do this." She smiled wanly.

He sat there for a long moment, fear taking his heart for the dangers that awaited them, that awaited her and the child.

"I shall guard her, King's Elite Kenti," a small voice echoed from his right, where Dougar stood alongside the wagon, wearing his mail and helm, thrusting his little fist to his heart, saluting him.

"Dougar, you are supposed to remain here. General Vecious will need a trusted attendant," Cronus said. Cronus already arranged this assignment for him. Having the boy march with the army to this point was one thing, but to certain death was beyond all decency.

Dougar stared at him with watery eyes, his lips clenched tightly as if he might break. It was the saddest thing he ever saw, and nearly broke his heart.

"Pl…please, King's Elite Kenti," he began before his voice broke with emotion, unable to speak.

Cronus dismounted, taking a knee before the child, lifting Dougar's helm off his head to clearly see his face.

"Dougar, it is dangerous where we are going, and I might not be able to keep you safe. Stay here and wait for us. Can you do that?"

"What if you die? What if all of you die? I will be alone again, and I don't want to be alone. I would rather die beside you then live alone without you," Dougar said, tears running down his checks. Ilesa was crying also, looking down at the boy from her place in the wagon, imagining her own child alone in the world should she perish.

Cronus closed his eyes, overcome with the decision he was about to make, but Dougar was right, what was life without those you love?

"Alright, you may come," Cronus conceded, opening his eyes as Dougar rushed into his arms, hugging him fiercely.

Cronus wondered if he would regret this decision, until the fates intervened as Lorken drew his air ski alongside them, the object hovering silently in the air, causing Cronus' ocran to shift uncomfortably.

"What is with all the crying?" Lorken asked, looking at all three of them.

"Dougar is coming with us," Cronus said, gaining his feet, placing a hand to the boy's shoulder.

"Of course he is, or he'd miss all the action. Climb on, Dougar, and I'll show you how to fly this thing," Lorken said.

"Can I?" Dougar looked up to Cronus, seeing if he would agree.

"Go on." Cronus smiled as Lorken dragged him aboard, setting him in front of him.

"Pull back on that lever real slow," Lorken said, showing him the accelerator, and off they went, gliding to the front of the column, disappearing in the crowd ahead as Cronus shook his head.

CHAPTER 6

Fall of Tinsay.

Queen Letha sat astride her spirited mount, gazing north where the towers of Tinsay peaked above the high walls of the port. Her ocran stood upon a shallow rise skirting the southern approaches of the Benotrist port city, which rested in the distance, much of it obscured by the high gray wall that ran from the coast to her immediate west to the vast open farmland to the east. The city was built upon both banks of the Gorga River, where it emptied into the Tinsan Bay, its high walls running the north and south sides of the city, before meeting upstream. A series of lesser walls ran along the coast, circling the watchtowers of the city, which guarded the mouth of the bay, before continuing along the shore upstream for some distance. Another series of lesser walls lined the riverbanks of the city, guarding the flanks of the many circled docking piers that jutted into the bay nearer the river's mouth, which housed the Benotrist Fleets. Said fleets had fled the city for points north, fearing destruction against the vast armada that now blocked the mouth of the bay, waiting just beyond the breakwaters that crisscrossed the harbor between the watchtowers to the north and south.

Letha was struck by a memory, recalling her first visit to this ancient port upon her marriage to Taleron. They paraded through the broad avenues of the city, with throngs of people gathering along the streets, throwing voli petals into the air, greeting her warmly. She recalled her youthful spirit, naïve and blinded by love, thinking she could turn him from his dalliance with the gargoyles, converting him to their cause. Instead, he attempted to subvert her, bringing her realm into his empire, fueling his expansionist bent. Only her mother's cunning and insight prevented that disaster, opening her eyes to his subterfuge. Her mother purged their ranks of traitors, but passed not long after, leaving Letha alone upon the throne with her infant daughter her only immediate kin, save for her brother, who was far away with a kingdom of his own to oversee.

"Taleron, oh what might have been." She sighed, her mind wandering to a far-off place, a realm of possibilities that was never realized.

"My Queen?" General Jani asked, overhearing her strange utterance.

"Never mind me, General, just the musings of a weary mind." She looked over to the commander of her armies, the stern Elise Jani whose mount stood beside hers.

"Perhaps, but a mind as sharp as the sword you carry, Oh Queen," the general snorted, regarding the sword of light riding Letha's left hip, and a source of confidence to their cause.

"Yes, but a sword that grows dim of late." She sighed, regarding the change that recently overtook her blade, its luster much subdued.

"It still cuts as before, does it not?" Elise asked, knowing the answer.

"Yes, but it begs that I ask why? Why has its luster drawn dim. It feels heavier as of late, something I hadn't noticed until yester morn. What this portends I cannot say."

"Could something have befallen our champion?" Elise asked, said champion so named by the queen herself, and agreed upon by the ruling forum, designating that esteemed title to Terin, the heir of the Kalinian bloodline.

"That is a possibility, though a dark one I dare not contemplate." Letha gave her a look.

They each knew of the march of the Chosen, and the perilous path they trod. If Terin had fallen, then what of their own fate? Was there still a reason for this campaign?

"If something befell Terin and the others with him, I sense we would know," Letha reasoned.

"And how would we know?" Elise asked the obvious question.

"Was not the purpose of the Chosen to sacrifice themselves in place of everyone else? If they fell, I would think it would cause the undoing of the enemy, and yet Tyro's standard still graces the walls of Tinsay." Letha lifted her chin toward the city, where the imperial Benotrist standard graced the highest minaret, a black tower upon a field of red.

"We were not told the nature of their sacrifice, or if the enemy would be destroyed outright, or suffer a long decline thereafter. The mystery of Yah and what he intends is beyond our simple comprehension. That leads me to conclude the enemy before us is well entrenched and prepared to give battle," General Jani stated.

"True, general, as any commander worthy of the rank plans for the worst, and acts in accordance. Keeping with that perspective, we have a commanders' call to attend," Letha said before they drew away, skirting the line of soldiers of their advance element. Said soldiers were the 2nd telnic of the 1st Sisterhood Army, each standing along the shallow ridge with their shields lowered and spears planted beside them, held loosely in their strong hand, facing the port in the distance. The soldiers were simply standing along the imaginary line where the army intended to break ground for its first line of siege works, holding position as the rest of the army drew from the south, long columns of infantry snaking across the open ground behind them.

The queen's pavilion was already placed halfway between the shallow ridge and the advancing columns, hastily erected to receive the commanders of the allied armies and navies gathered at Tinsay. Much of its furnishings were still leagues south with the baggage train, with only the barest of essentials to facilitate the meet. Letha and Elise passed within the folds draping the entrance, finding the commanders therein circling the table with the map of Tinsan province unfurled across its surface.

"Queen Letha." Grand Admiral Kilan greeted her with a deep bow, standing across from her as she took her place at the table. Kilan brought the entirety of the Torry Navy to this campaign, the masts of their five fleets dotting the sea. He was joined by admiral Goren of the 1st Macon Fleet, Admiral Vulet of the 2nd Macon Fleet and Admiral Horician, commander of the Yatin 3rd Fleet.

"Admiral, you are acquainted with Admiral Nyla, commander of the Sisterhood 1st Fleet. She holds overall command of the Federation Navy." Letha regarded the stern-faced admiral standing off her right. Her sister admirals Carel and Daila were currently with their respective fleets, holding position north of the Torry armada.

"Yes, she commands an impressive armada, Oh Queen," the Torry Grand Admiral said, regarding Nyla respectfully.

"Oh Queen," General Yoria next greeted her, standing off her left, the Yatin General standing beside his fellow Yatin commander, Yitia, both men bowing deeply as she looked to their direction. She noted Yoria's missing sword hand, the stump of his right wrist scarred from its cauterization. She learned of his maiming in the dungeons of Mosar, suffering his emperor's addled delusions and torture at the hands of the cruel Minister Shatero. Thankfully both men were dead now, burned alive at the hands of their people. How much suffering could have been prevented had the Yatin emperor been just and of sound mind?

"Generals, your armies are most welcomed," she greeted, pleased of their swift advance from Tenin, the Yatin port liberated by their 1st and 2nd Yatin Armies, along with General Farro's 4th Torry Army, who stood beside them. All three armies marched swiftly along the coast, joining her armies on their march upon Tinsay.

"We are pleased to join you in taking Tinsay, Oh Queen," General Farro said. His army had marched from Cagan to Mosar to lift the siege upon the Yatin capital, before advancing to Maeii, and then returning to Torry South, before marching again for Yatin, taking Tenin Harbor and advancing here. His soldiers were battle-hardened, and weary, but their spirits were high with the opportunity to invade the Benotrist homeland.

"And we are pleased to have you, General Farro. You fought beside your King throughout the Yatin campaign, and I am honored to have you fight beside me in taking Tinsay. As most of our cavalry and magantors are busy scouting the approaches of Tinsay, we must lean upon your recent information, General Valen," Letha said, regarding the Torry Magantor commander of the Cagan contingent, one Denton Valen, kin of Dar Valen who was currently at Nisin.

"I have yet to hear from our scouts aboard our magantor carriers, but as for my contingent, we have scouted as far east as Teculah," Denton began, indicating the Benotrist holdfast forty leagues southeast of Tinsay, home to vast iron mines that supplied the region.

"Did the enemy contest the air?' Queen Letha inquired.

"No, Queen Letha. There were no signs of Benotrist warbirds," Denton said.

"Continue," she said, her gaze fixed upon the map.

"General Cornyana's cavalry are sweeping the south bank of the Gorga, and are currently ten leagues upstream, somewhere in this vicinity." He pointed out the position, before continuing.

"Your magantors are currently scouting the northern approaches of Tinsay, while the Macon warbirds are scouting the road east. They are planning to scout as far as the confluence of the Gorga and Andler before returning," Denton said.

"That could take several days for the Macon scouts to return," General Jani pointed out, sweeping her hand along the map from Tinsay to the confluence.

"Any sign of reinforcements making their way to reinforce Tinsay?" General Farro asked.

"The opposite," Denton said, drawing curious stares from the others.

"Explain," Letha ordered.

"We spotted columns of infantry at several points along the river road, marching east."

"East?" More than one asked at the same time. Their main objective was to draw Tyro's forces away from the Chosen. If they were withdrawing toward Fera, that plan was foiled.

"Yes, they appear to be soldiers of the harbor garrison withdrawing, though the walls of Tinsay still appear strongly held."

"That goes against all sense," General Yoria said.

"We are missing something," General Jani said, her eyes narrowed severely searching for the answer.

"Where is the nearest fording point along the Gorga?" General Yitia asked.

"Gadena, at least three days ride east, but it is not a ford. There is a bridge there," Elise Jani said.

"The Gorga is a deep and navigable waterway from Tinsay to the confluence with the Andler. Its course east from that point crosses many shallows and natural fords. The Andler, however, is deep and navigable as far as Laycrom," Queen Letha further expounded, which explained the natural trading routes that ran between the two cities.

"What are your suggestions, Oh Queen?" Grand Admiral Kilan asked.

"For now, we should concentrate our armies along the southern approaches of the city. From there we can send one army to secure the bridge at Gadena, before advancing forces to the north side of the port," Letha explained.

"Might more of the enemy escape if we tarry in isolating the city?" General Yoria asked.

"Perhaps, but we shall move with method and purpose, and avoid risking our soldiers by blindly assuming the enemy will not bestir themselves from their walls, or send another force to attack us from behind. Once we commit armies to the north, they cannot be easily reinforced should the enemy strike," Letha explained.

"Then we move to this juncture and begin our siege works," General Farro said.

"Yes. How far south are your troops now, General Farro?" General Jani asked.

"Ten leagues. I can have them in place by tomorrow morn."

"And you, General Yoria?" she asked.

"Five leagues, marching north along the coastal road," he said.

"Three leagues," General Yitia added, his van already within sight of the Sisterhood armies.

"Very good. By tomorrow we shall begin the siege of Tinsay," Letha said, dismissing them to see to their armies, the commanders filing out one by one before she called upon General Yoria to remain.

"Oh Queen." Yoria bowed deeply as the others stepped without, wondering her purpose for delaying him.

"Before you return to your men, general, I would have you call upon our head matron. Her pavilion rests at the center of our southern encampment, which is just half a league south. I will have one of my guards show you the way," she said.

"Might I inquire as to why, Oh Queen?" he asked, wondering what aid a matron might lend him.

"The Earthers gifted us a healing device of incredible power. The matrons can use it to restore you," she said, looking down to the stump of his right hand.

"Truly?" he said, recalling Kato's device that he used to heal so many of their soldiers at Mosar. He didn't expect them to have another so close by.

"Truly, and you would better serve our cause with two hands than one," she said.

He saluted her, pressing the stump of his right arm to his chest before stepping without.

* * *

Imperial palace. Tinsay.

Regent Jetar Slars stood upon the veranda of his imperial palace overlooking the Tinsan Bay, his voluminous robes swirling in the breeze. He stared bitterly beyond the harbor entrance where rested the enemy armada. He spied the sigils of Macon, Yatin, Torry and Sisterhood fleets gracing the masts of the vast assembly, a host so great that the entirety of the Benotrist navy could not avail it. His gaze shifted to the now empty piers lining the shores of the harbor, and the empty circle shaped docking facilities of the Benotrist Navy, grim reminders of their absence. What remained of the Benotrist navy was now sailing for points north and east, lest they were caught up by the enemy's growing strength or trapped within Tinsay.

He looked across the bay where sat the *Sea Maiden* of Tinsay, the massive sculpture cast in the visage of a nymph with its arms pressed into the ground as if lifting her from the sea. The nymph's head was arched back, with her black hair cascading below her shoulders, plated in obsidian, sunlight playing off her midnight tresses. He observed the fist sized emeralds embedded in her eye sockets, casting her wanton gaze across the bay and the sea beyond. The Sea Maiden was built long ago during the days of the old Northern Kingdom, another realm now relegated to the faded pages of history, much like his own.

Jetar contemplated his sorry position, surrounded by the large armada blocking his escape to the sea, and the massive armies drawing from the south, who were certain to envelope the city from the north and east, cutting all escape routes. Much of the garrison was sent to Laycrom, their current ranks now filled with pitiful conscripts, most barely able to hold a spear properly, let alone wield a sword. Said recruits now manned much of the city walls, giving an appearance of strength. He wondered how it all came to this, the might of their empire stripped away, with the strength of the south arrayed against them?

He considered his precarious position, not wishing to fall into Queen Letha's hands considering the fate of his fellow conspirators at Bansoch who joined in Guardian Darna's coup. The survivors were sold at market, most gelded and whipped, their days now measured by the lash and toil. He was only given leave to return home by his position as ambassador, and his participation in the plot not coming to light. He was sent to Bansoch to retrieve the emperor's heir but was poorly received at Queen Letha's court. That preceded the coup, and the decimation of their hired swords. He journeyed to Bansoch with the famed swordman Guise Valeyan of the imperial elite, and the master sage Colbo Tailen. He never saw them after that fateful night, wondering their fate. The only member of his company to return to their homeland was Nels Draken of the imperial elite, who now oversaw the defense of the city at the behest of the emperor. It was Nels Draken he waited upon, who soon joined him upon the veranda.

"A fine day," Nels said, stepping through the archway behind him, with a panoramic view of the southern, western and northern approaches of the port, the late day sun settling in the western sky, its light reflecting off the sea.

"A fine day to meet our end," Jetar snorted.

"Oh come, my dear regent, where there is life there are endless possibilities," Nels said almost musically, as if he hadn't a care in the world.

"Waning possibilities perhaps, or have you not opened your eyes to what surrounds us?" Jetar waved his arms over the mouth of the bay and the southern approaches of the harbor where countless thousands of soldiers took up position, with many more to follow.

"Yes, most unfortunate, but not unexpected."

"Expected and yet we have no plan to counter them." Jetar scowled.

"Caution, my friend. You have been apprised of the emperor's plan, a plan he trusts you to carry out."

"I was spared Queen Letha's wrath once; I doubt she will be as merciful this time."

"Trust in the emperor's wisdom, my friend. The enemy is like water, flowing along the easiest path. Your task is simply to provide that path, and once we achieve victory, everything you treasure will be restored, many times over." Nels faux smile did little to assuage Jetar's misgivings.

"And if our guests are less magnanimous than our emperor believes?" Jetar asked doubtfully.

"The Sisterhood are not barbarians, my friend. And if any should know their queen's mind it is our emperor," Nels said before stepping away.

"It is simple for you to say," Jetar whispered as Nels disappeared through the archway, before taking his leave of Tinsay. After nightfall he would lead his small cavalry contingent through the north gate of the city, leaving Jetar to his fate.

* * *

Two days hence.

Queen Letha awaited Jetar Sars mid distance between her forward siege works and the south gate of Tinsay under the blue flag. She was surprised by Regent Sars asking for parlay when her armies barely broke ground for the siege, and her allies had not begun the full encirclement of the harbor. She was joined by Grand Admiral Kilan and General Farro representing the Torry contingent, and General Yoria and Admiral Horician representing The Yatin forces, and Admiral Goren standing on behalf the Macon fleets.

They waited with their escort forming a half circle behind them, while Regent Sars approached, his own escort halting short of their position, allowing him to gallop forth of his own volition. Regent Sars was as she remembered him, his silvered hair tied in loose braids draping his shoulder, wearing an ill-fitting cuirass with the morning sun playing off his steel helm. Though richly adorned with a bright cape and polished greaves, he was clearly a pampered bureaucrat donning the vestment of a warrior, trying to project strength and failing.

"Hail, Regent Sars, we meet again," Queen Letha greeted him as his ocran drew to a halt, its hooves clopping the matted grass as he came to stop.

"Queen Letha," he greeted curtly, warily regarding her comrades.

"Regent, my allies," she said, answering his unspoken question, before introducing each in kind.

"You called upon us to parlay. Speak to your intention," she added, cutting to the point.

"Yes, things have progressed since we last parted, Oh Queen, the tides of war losing favor for our cause," Jetar began.

"A generous summation of your emperor's current plight, but go on," Letha said, letting Jetar know she was fully apprised of their sorry state.

"Yes. Our empire is beset, attacked from without and pressured from within. The disastrous affair at Corell has struck a great blow to our strength, perhaps fatally so. The emperor asks that we hold

Tinsay to the last but offers no course for its relief. Should I do so, I fear for my people, people I have sworn to protect."

"You have also sworn to Tyro, vows that precede those to your people," she pointed out.

"So many vows and so little choice but choose I must. What assurance do you give if I open my gates?" he asked.

She wasn't expecting him to be so direct so quickly. He certainly did not wish to be here, shifting nervously in the saddle.

"Assurances? None! Open your gates and disarm your soldiers and I will decide your fate," Letha insisted, her icy veneer brokering no compromise.

"If I refuse, you will lose much time moving your armies to the north side of the city and lose many thousands storming our walls. Sparing you such trouble should earn us some concession," Jetar pointed out.

"Oh, it shall Regent Sars, but I and I alone will determine what concession shall be given. You can earn my good graces by opening your gates and throwing down your weapons."

The others didn't expect the Tinsan regent to relent, but he did.

"So be it." Jetar bowed his head, before dismounting and kneeling before Queen Letha.

* * *

Two days hence.

The masts of the Torry, Sisterhood, Macon and Yatin fleets filled the bay, occupying the circled docking facilities, and the piers lining either bank of the Gorga. The 3rd Sisterhood Army oversaw garrisoning the city walls, while the remaining allied armies swept the city dwelling by dwelling, gathering up every male between fifteen and fifty years of age. Queen Letha ordered all male captives to be gathered and removed from the port, most taken to Bansoch, their fate to be determined, including Jetar Slars, who vehemently protested such treatment. Letha could only guess what game Tyro was playing, but doubted Regent Slars undertook the surrender on his volition. She voiced her doubts with General Jani, the two finding themselves upon the steps of the city forum, looking on as a column of Yatin soldiers paraded in the streets below.

"You think it a ruse, My Queen?" Elise Jani asked, her steely gaze drifting from the soldiers to the Sea Maiden, the massive statue towering above the opposite shore of the bay. One could hardly look across the harbor without being drawn to its beguiling beauty.

"I know Taleron too well. He is no fool and would not place a garrison of such importance in the hands of a cowering fool."

"Unless he is no fool," Elise surmised.

"Yes. I have known Jetar Slars for many years, as far back as my nuptials, and he is no fool, or disloyal to Taleron," Letha said.

"I have inspected the garrison soldiers after their surrender. There are fewer than twelve thousand, and most can barely stand to post, let alone wield a blade properly. Even their spear handling is suspect," Elise said.

"The full garrison should be twenty telnics, and they drill relentlessly," Letha said.

"That can only mean these are false soldiers."

"Apparently, but not all. I would guess five or six telnics to be true, the rest dregs gathered to fill the ranks."

"Then where are the other fifteen thousand men?" Elise wondered.

"Perhaps drawn off to fill the empty ranks of the legions or withdrawn for some other purpose."

"Or to draw us farther from the coast, and extend our lines of communication," Elise surmised.

"That would be my guess, unless…"

Elise gave her a sideways look, waiting for her to continue.

"…Unless they are truly this weak." Letha only recently learned the extent of Morac's losses at Corell, losses that might drain the garrisons of the empire if they were tapped. Of all the garrisons to deplete, Tinsay should be one of the last, for it guarded the empire's western flank.

"It is my rule to assume the enemy is strong, and act accordingly," Elise snorted.

"A rule every commander should follow, General, and a rule we shall keep in mind as we march east."

"Resuming our original objective," Elise remarked. Their original plan of invasion involved taking Tinsay and advance into the continental interior to press Tyro. That plan was altered upon conferring with their allies concerning the Chosen. That plan involved them taking Tinsay and drawing the enemy to them. With the surrender of Tinsay, that plan was now useless, as they enemy was drawing away from them, not advancing to engage them. The only means of forcing the enemy to battle was to move upon them. The other commanders agreed to this change upon taking the city so easily.

"Yes, and hopefully draw Taleron in our direction, and away from the Chosen," Letha said, confounded by the fluidity of their situation. If Tyro intended to draw them away from the coast to counterattack them where they would be weaker, that would still accomplish their objective of drawing his strength away from the Chosen. But what if they advanced and enemy still refused to meet them? How far should they advance? Should they march all the way to Fera? Would that not defeat the purpose of protecting the Chosen? Were they spoiling Yah's plan by attacking at all? So many questions and so few answers.

"Something troubles you, My Queen?" Elise sensed her unease.

"Many things, old friend. First among them is that somewhere out there my nephew and our champion, and many others are walking blindly into the heart of Taleron's realm, and I fear no matter what we do, we cannot change their fate."

Elise considered that for the longest moment, before shaking her head.

"We cannot worry about what lies beyond our control. All we can do is act with reason and logic and press on."

"That simplifies the matter, general. We press on," Letha sighed.

"I advise we strongly garrison Tinsay before advancing."

"Our allies agree. I suggest the 3rd Sisterhood Army be delegated that task."

"I shall inform General Mial."

"Inform her that every unwed soldier may take a mate of her

choosing from the captives, and every soldier in the 1st or 3rd Army who is under her period of indenture will be redeemed at the end of this campaign," Letha ordered.

"That shall enhance morale. I would add that any mate chosen be taken to Bansoch and set aside until our return."

"A wise concession."

And so, the coming days saw the allied armies consolidating their hold on Tinsay and the surrounding region. They were pleased to discover the food stores of Tinsay fully stocked, aiding their invasion. With the 3rd Sisterhood Army detached to fortify Tinsay, Letha led the rest of their vast host east, including the 1st Sisterhood Army, The Yatin 1st and 2nd Armies, and the Torry 4th Army, nearly eighty telnics in strength. The road east skirted the north bank of the Gorga, with their armies stretched over many leagues along the vital causeway. Their magantor contingents swept the lands ahead, keeping a vigilant eye upon any sign of the enemy.

* * *

Nine days hence.
Gelih.

The city of Gelih rested at the confluence of the Gorga and Andler Rivers, built along the three bridges passing over each branch, with a main thoroughfare connecting each bridge in a large circle. The city was lightly protected by a series of low walls and archer towers, suitable in resisting small raids, but not armies, which explained its empty streets when Letha and her allies approached its open gates. The unique geology of the rivers rested in the lesser Andler jutting northeast in the direction of Laycrom, the Benotrist capital, and the greater Gorga continuing directly east. The unique nature rested in the smaller Andler being navigable and the upper Gorga unnavigable by boats larger than a raft. This disparity caused the trading routes along the Andler to prosper, and the Upper Gorga to linger, though each passed through rich farmlands.

It was here where Letha and her allies were confronted with

another decision, to hold in place, advance to Laycrom, or to march east toward Fera. Their magantor scouts discovered that many of the garrison troops from Tinsay withdrew to Laycrom, further fortifying the Benotrist capital. Should they continue east, the garrison of Laycrom could advance upon their rear. Fortunately, they also received word that large elements from Laycrom, including the 13th Legion were spotted marching east, likely toward Fera. Unfortunately, that meant the strength of the enemy was moving toward the path of the Chosen. Letha and the others decided the only way to remain relevant in the entire affair was to continue their march east. It was decided to fortify Gelih before marching east, leaving the Yatin 1st Army that vital task.

Thus Queen Letha continued her march with sixty telnics, the fate of her people, army and her many allies linked to the great battle ahead.

CHAPTER 7

SPLIT!

The rock split, Elos' blade cleaving it in half, his silver eyes running the length of his dull blade. He sighed internally, maintaining his stoic resolve, but inwardly relieved that his sword retained its fell power. The sword no longer glowed, its once emerald luster wanning to its current dull state. Every passing day it grew darker, lending him to believe it might turn cold black before disappearing altogether. What this portended, he could only surmise.

"It is nearly as murky as mine," Terin said, standing at his side, holding his own darkened blade, the two swords sharing the same turbid property.

They stood upon the forest floor, thick boughs high above shielding the midday sky. They lost count of the days, marching from the headwaters of the Cot River westward, skirting the foothills of the Mote Mountains before breaking north, finding themselves somewhere in the thick forests that spanned much of the lands between Fera and Nisin. Their company stopped to rest, with their comrades strung out in a long column, the forest obscuring their view to anything beyond a few dozen meters in either direction. They were fortunate to come upon a weathered trail running a northerly direction through the thick forest of Topac trees, with vines circling their smooth trunks. With higher set branches and thick foliage above, there was little light for undergrowth, sparing them to suffer brambles and underbrush.

With no set order of march, every member of their company rotated throughout their journey, coming to know many of their comrades, if not all. No one instructed them to do so, but each felt something else guiding them in this, most accepting it as Yah's will. They came to disregard their differences, becoming as one with every passing day. They were no longer Torry, Macon, ape, Jenaii or any of the many other realms or cities they called home. They were simply the Chosen, the precious few given this task, willing to sacrifice themselves if necessary to spare everyone else. For some strange reason, their fear seemed to abate the further they marched, replaced with overwhelming love for one another. Despite all of this, not one of them had the faintest idea of what was expected of them, other than to march north, following Lorn and Deva's guidance, though even they seemed as ignorant as the rest.

It was in recent days that Elos discovered the change coming over his sword, its emerald luster abating, replaced with its now murky and dull appearance, matching the affliction that came over any of the swords of light that Terin touched. By splitting the head sized rock that rested upon the ground, he was reassured that the sword retained its impressive ability to cut anything, but its other powers were becoming impaired, if not removed. The sword felt heavier as of late. It was still much lighter than a sword of its length and size should be, but it now possessed a noticeable heft it lacked before. The sword was always weightless in his hand, allowing him to wield it in battle without respite. Its current weight would limit him in battle unless another power emerged from the blade that he could not see.

Elos felt a sudden urge to press his sword toward Terin's, as if drawn by an otherworldly power. No sooner had the blades drawn within a breath, light flickered wherever they were closest. He drew the sword away, the blade's surface returning to a murky dullness, before again pressing it toward Terin's. Light again flickered as they drew nigh before venting in a cacophony of bright hues as they touched, flashes of red, green and blue erupting along their length, followed by bright yellow, orange and purple, all swirling into one another. They held the swords in place for what felt an eternity, the others standing near gathering about to witness the strange sight. They finally relented, withdrawing the blades, struggling to return them to their sheaths, each breathing heavily as if taxed.

"Wh…What does… it mean?" Terin asked, leaning over to catch his breath, his hands resting upon his knees.

"I do not know. The swords were forged from the divine gift, given to the Smiths of Tarelia long ago. They were intended for the blood of Kal, the very blood that flows in you, Terin. They were a gift from Yah, and their purpose is linked to you and this journey we are undertaking."

"But if they grow much heavier, they will do us little good in battle considering how outnumbered we shall be. The swords are our only hope of matching the enemy," Terin lamented, feeling their only hope slipping away.

"We were never intended to fight our way to victory. Such vain hopes are now fully set aside, Terin. We must place our faith in whatever plan Yah intends."

Terin hated the unknown, and the helplessness it sent through him. He wanted to control something, focusing his strength on whatever kernel of hope he could cling to and fight for, to fight and live to see Corry again. This too he must surrender, placing everything in Yah's hand, and in Yah's plan.

* * *

It was past sundown when they again stopped for the night, the weary travelers resting on their packs wherever they sat down. Some propped themselves against the smooth trunks of the towering Topacs, others lay sprawled upon the forest floor. It was two days since they came upon a creek to refill their water satchels, with most running low. Whenever this problem arose, they somehow found another, Yah providing for their base essentials. They trusted he would again soon deliver. Their food stores were also running thin, though every portion they ate lightened their pack.

Deva set down somewhere near the front of the column, spent

by another day's march. She was too weary to eat, falling fast asleep where she stopped. Even her sleep was no respite, her every dream turning to nightmares, or visions as she came to know them, and this night was no different.

Again, she ascended into the heavens, rising through the thick branches and heavy boughs above before breaking into the clear. She rose higher still, the midnight sky turning to day, the sun illuminating the surrounding lands. The forest below shrank as she ascended, before speeding north, caried upon the wind, passing over endless forest, then open ground, crossing rivers and farmlands, then jagged canyons. Her eyes drew wider as the Nameless Mountains came boldly into view off her right, white snowcaps covering their misshapen peaks. She rose higher still, floating above their unforgiving slopes and jagged foothills that no mortal could attain, skirting their western face before coming upon the northern approaches. There at the base of their northern foothills gathered a terrible host, countless thousands of gargoyles crowding the heights of a great vale that stretched wide and open to the north. Rock and discolored grass covered the Valley floor, carpeting the large open expanse in a morbid pall. Jagged ridgelines ran northward along either flank, fueling the vale's ghastly aura. It was a land of bones and death, the very heart of darkness where the kindest soul would shrivel and die if stepping upon its cursed soil.

"Kai-Shorum!" Gargoyle chants began, their low echoes building into a crescendo, rising through the fetid air to torture her ears.

She winced painfully, her ears pained by their sound, before gazing to where they stood, swarming the southern end of the vale, guarding the face of the twisting foothills beyond. Her gaze drew her to them, passing through the vale and into their midst, clawed hands reached to grab her as she flew, their black digits passing through her as if she were a spirit. They could see her, but not touch her, venting their fury by screaming all the louder.

"Kai-Shorum!" they shouted as she continued through their ranks, before breaking higher, passing above the forward slopes of jagged and twisted rock. There, beyond the first foothills, and below the Nameless Mountains rested an open canyon with caverns cut into its base, burrowing under the mountains themselves. She lifted briefly before descend-

ing, sweeping over the sheer vertical drop into the canyon, before passing through the entrance of the nearest cave.

She was greeted with complete darkness as she entered the subterranean realm, before it suddenly illuminated as if for her benefit. She had seen this before, but not in this detail, the cavern expanding endlessly in all directions, the floor of the chasm covered with pure white flesh of sightless female gargoyles, reaching out to her with their clawed hands, their white cloudy eyes haunting her vision as they chanted. She drew higher beyond their grasping reach, her gaze drawn to the greater threat rising along the cavern walls. There, cut from the cavern walls, were countless more caves, with untold thousands of gargoyle juveniles standing at their openings, half wingless females, the rest black winged males, all staring at her with blood red eyes, hissing demonically.

"Kai-Shorum!" The gargoyles screeched, the sound nearly taking her before she closed her eyes.

The sound stopped. She clenched her eyes tightly shut, daring not to open them, lest the terrible scene fill her vision. An eternal moment passed, time losing all relevance, before she dared to see again. She opened her eyes, finding herself standing upon the valley floor, where gathered another host, but of men, wearing the livery of Benotrists. Standing at the head of their great company stood a man dark of hair, an evil smirk twisting his fell lips, and wielding a Sword of Light, its crimson luster dimming before the midday sun. She knew this man, though had never seen his face. He was Morac, son of Morca, and the Bane of Lore. He stood upon the open ground, turning his head, his terrible gaze finding her across that deadly space.

"No!" she gasped, crying out in the dark as she stirred.

"It is well, Deva. You are safe," she heard Lucas say in a soothing voice. She opened her eyes, finding herself cradled in his arms. It was still the dark of night, and she sensed no one else nearby in their place in the column, thankful to have not made a spectacle, but even that vanity seemed pointless after what she saw. She meant to tell Lucas she was well and that he could loosen his hold, but part of her didn't want to. She wanted to be held, to be protected, to be… loved. She wanted nothing more than to complete what Yah sent her to accomplish, but would she even have a life after? No, not after what she saw.

"Did I say anything?" she asked him, wondering what caused him to draw her into his arms.

"Just moans, and the terrible shaking. I didn't want you to hurt yourself with your thrashing about. You didn't cry out until the end," he said in the kindest voice.

"Thank you, Lucas. I didn't mean for you to hear that."

"It is my place to protect you, Deva. What did you see to vex you so?"

She grew suddenly quiet, stubborn tears squeezing from her eyes.

"Deva?" Lucas cradled her in his lap, looking down into her eyes.

"I…I saw them. Oh, Lucas, I saw where we must go, and…" She couldn't speak, her voice caught in her narrowing throat.

"What did you see?"

"The gargoyle nesting grounds and the armies they have gathered there. I know why Yah sent only us, for all our armies would die defeating them."

"What are we to do?"

"I do not know, Lucas. I only see what Yah deigns to reveal. We must go to that awful place, but I see no hope that we shall survive," she lamented, hating the thought of her friends suffering such a fate. She had come to love her fellow travelers, so much so that she could not reconcile the creature she was with who she was now. She hated the thought of them dying, especially Lucas, who held her so protectively. She liked to believe it was more than duty that drove him to do so. It was strange that such a fearsome warrior could be so gentle.

"We knew undertaking this journey likely meant our deaths. I can accept that if it means the others live." He smiled gently, his calmness giving her strength.

"How can you be so brave?" she asked.

"I am not brave, Deva. I am as scared as everyone. I simply hide it."

"Fear is not the absence of courage, Lucas. Courage is marching forth despite your fear."

"Then you are braver than I, Deva, for you have seen what awaits us, and yet you march on."

"You are a good man, Lucas," she sighed.

He held her in his arms until she fell asleep, gently rocking her to assuage her anguish. She would talk of her brother in her sleep, wishing to see him again, and hoping he lived. It was then that he let go all his misgivings of Deva Estaran, truly forgiving the person she was, and coming to respect the woman she is. He eased her to her bedroll, placing a tender kiss to her forehead.

* * *

Three days hence.

Their company finally reached the edge of the forest, with a vast open land stretching endlessly before them. Lorn and Mortus stood within the tree line, staring north at the rolling farmlands and open ground before them. They stood at the head of the column; the rest gathered behind them waiting upon their decision. This was the moment when everything would change. Their advance into the heart of Tyro's realm brought them to this juncture. They came this far undetected, shielded by the forests and rough terrain they carefully traversed. Despite their caution, the enemy should have seen them at some point in their journey. They assigned their good fortune to dumb luck or the hand of Yah. Going forward, even dumb luck couldn't conceal their movement on that open ground. As for Yah, wasn't this the point of their journey, to deliver them into the enemy's hand?

"What think you?" Lorn asked of his father by marriage, his gaze sweeping the length of the horizon, and the many homesteads spread out for as far as he could see.

"Deva's latest vison was quite direct. We must go north, straight through these lands," Mortus said as firmly as he could, trying desperately to hide his own fear.

"Aye, that seems the heart of it. It should not take long now for them to discover us and arrange our destruction." Lorn hated sounding so grim but could see no other future.

"If that is Yah's will, then so it shall it be," Mortus said, placing a hand to Lorn's shoulder.

"Your courage shames me." Lorn looked over to him, encouraged by his steely presence.

"Shames you? You are the bravest man I have ever known, Lorn, and I am proud to march beside you. You have shown this old fool the meaning of courage, loyalty and honor, and I would follow you to the gates of damnation."

"If I have shown you these things, you have now returned the kindness, filling my cowardly heart with the courage to step from the shelter of this forest. A very large part of me died with Jentra, and I miss him terribly, but I am ever thankful for your company. Without you I would have despaired. You have given me the strength I needed to come this far, and perhaps Yah brought us together for that very purpose."

"Aye, together then." Mortus smiled.

"Together," Lorn said before giving the order to advance.

The column advanced from the shelter of the forest, stepping onto the open ground, before continuing north, passing farms and homesteads, with the locals hiding, or looking on at the strangers marching past. It was late in the day when a magantor circled overhead before flying off to the west.

CHAPTER 8

Fera. The Black Castle.

The late evening again found Jonas sitting at his bedside, with Valera asleep beside him, lost in thought. This was becoming habit, each night finding himself awaking in the middle of the night, beset with visions, each more intense than the last. They began as disjointed images, of old friends and loved ones, both living and dead, before advancing to scenes without connection. He saw King Lore fall in battle, with Morac hoisting his head in view of the Torries gathered upon the hillsides at Kregmarin, taunting them with his grisly trophy. He saw the first time he set eyes upon Valera upon the battlements of Corell, so long ago. There was his mother's deathbed, and his son's birth, and so many other momentous events that shaped his life. He saw Corry and Torg leading a great host, but he could not see where, and Queen Letha leading another, her destination clouded in his vision. Lastly, he saw Terin marching across the Benotrist heartland among a sizable company, though too few to be considered an army. It was this last vision that woke him from his slumber, sending tendrils of terror coursing his flesh.

"Where are you going, my son?" Jonas whispered.

* * *

The following morn.

Tyro stared at the map of his realm, his pounding heart matching the sorry state of his empire. All his plans and dreams had gone to ash. Only victory could preserve some portion of his once grand empire, a mere shadow of its former glory. If he could preserve but one portion, he could renew his strength, and then plan accordingly. If he could defeat the armies arrayed against him, the survivors would flee in shame to their homelands, never to return, or not return with this united front. And therein lay the danger to his foes, if they could not defeat him with all their strength combined, then they never would. In this coming fight he still held the advantage in numbers with his Benotrists and gargoyles combined.

His gaze drifted to the Northern foothills of the Nameless Mountains, where the gargoyle nesting grounds lay. It was there where they now gathered, summoned by their calling, which was curious as their calling was not for many years from now. And yet, there they were, gathered for some purpose he could only guess. He sent Lord Regula to investigate. As their ranking chieftain, his word was law among the gargoyles. He was to explain to them the coming battle and prepare them to meet the enemy. As yet, he heard nothing on that front, and he doubted he could win without his stalwart allies.

He heard General Gavis shift across from him, the craggy commander too polite to interrupt his thoughts as they surveyed the map. They were joined in this war council with the garrison commander of Fera Dev Faran, and Castellan Larus Braxus, both men among his most loyal confidants.

"You have words, General Gavis?" Tyro asked, his gaze still fixed on the map table between them.

"Queen Letha and her Yatin and Torry allies are fast approaching Fera. Lord Morac and the 13th Legion currently sit at Plateres," he began. Plateres was the main stronghold of the Benotrist Magantor forces, resting almost due north of Fera, positioned equal distance between Laycrom and the Nameless Mountains. Gavis pointed out Nels Draken's position just west of Fera. With fifteen telnics of the Tinsay garrison.

"And you would have us converge upon Letha with our combined might," Tyro said, scanning the placement of each force upon the map.

"It would be my choice, My Emperor, to strike this force before shifting east to meet the other." Gavis waved his hand over the regions west of Nisin, where the large army of Torries, Macons, apes and Jenaii were fast approaching Mordicay. The port city might have already fallen for all he knew, for their most recent sightings were ten days old.

"It is wise to destroy one threat before facing them simultaneously, but there are other considerations, general. One, Morac and Draken are bringing over thirty garrison telnics from Tinsay and Laycrom. They are inexperienced in fighting on open ground. Since they will form the heart of our third legion, they will need to converge and have time to organize themselves. Two, the further we stretch Letha's lines of communication, the weaker her force shall become. Three, I have yet to learn the reason of the gargoyles' summoning. When we meet the enemy, we must have them beside us," Tyro pointed out.

"If we delay, might the enemy armies converge, doubling their strength? And if the gargoyles will not bestir themselves, what other course is open to us?" Commander Faran asked.

"The Torry coalition in the east is still far off. There is still time to hear from Lord Regula on the state of our gargoyle cohorts," Tyro reasoned.

"That time is narrow, My Emperor. If the gargoyles begin their march today, it will still be seven days for all of our legions to converge on Queen Letha," Gavis said.

"You speak to what I already know, General Gavis. Though time is limited, it is not yet gone. Lord Regula still has a few days to inform me of his status," Tyro said just as an attendant appeared at the door.

"We were not to be disturbed!" Castellan Braxus admonished his young attendant, the man fidgeting nervously, for only the brave and foolish interrupted the emperor's private council. The fact that he did so made Tyro realize the importance of his missive.

"Speak!" Tyro said, ordering him hither.

"My Emperor, our scouts have spotted the enemy." the attendant bowed deeply.

"They have been spotting the enemy for days now, what sets this discovery apart from the others?" Gavis asked harshly.

"It is not from the previous armies we have followed, My Emperor. Our magantor scouts spied a column of enemy afoot to our direct east, emerging from the northern forest. They appear to be heading north. Their numbers appear quite small, counting fewer than four telnics, perhaps even less."

The chamber grew deathly quiet, the unsettling tidings throwing their plans to the wind.

"There is more," Tyro said, knowing when an attendant was holding something back.

"There were Jenaii and apes among them, not more than a hundred Jenaii, and only a handful of apes, but their presence was noted, My Emperor."

Tyro pondered this, wondering why such a small force would dare venture into his realm. There must be more hidden within the northern forest, or they were intended as a diversion.

"You said they were marching… north?" Castellan Braxus asked curiously.

"Yes. If not slightly north and east," the attendant answered nervously.

BEHOLD!

A voice rang in Tyro's mind, his eyes clouding over as he swayed, nearly taking him from his feet.

He could not hear the other's voices, or the alarm in their tone, his mind taken to another place. He stood upon open ground as the column approached, a collage of men from different realms, along with a handful of women, Jenaii and even fewer apes. There at the head of this small army was a face he found familiar… Terin. He waited upon the column as they drew nigh, wondering why they did not respond to his presence. His feet were affixed in place, unable to move as they drew closer. He could see Terin's face so clearly, it took him aback. The boy looked older than he remembered, his youthful aura replaced with a warrior's carriage. He could see both his mother and father in his handsome face, a perfect blend of their two bloodlines. He couldn't help but wonder what might have been in a different life. He lost track of the time as the boy drew closer, until he was upon him. Tyro's feet still would not move as the boy passed through him as if he were a spirit, oblivious to his presence. His vision faded before growing fully dark. He strained to open his eyes, feeling the weight of the world pressing them closed, until it lifted. His eyes sprang open, finding himself on the floor of a desolate vale, a place he recalled, having seen it but once. His gaze swept the surrounding landscape, finding the gargoyles gathered along the foothills to his south, and Terin's small army gathered to the north, at the end of the wide valley.

"Your eminence?" Tyro heard Castellan Braxus say as his eyes returned to their normal luster. He found himself still standing where he remembered, with the others looking on, each spellbound by his strange affliction. By this time, all were aware of the visons afflicting many of their people and soldiers, visons of gargoyles and men fighting in an epic battle, though the nature and makeup of the human army varied with each vision. They could see in the emperor's eyes that he suffered a vison, the nature of which they were curious to learn.

"I saw them," Tyro said.

They shared a look, knowing he meant the newly sighted enemy.

"The Torry Champion is among them," he said, that revelation drawing the expected reaction.

"They would send him here with so few warriors? They must have many more waiting in the forest," Castellan Braxus said.

"I am not certain. Slipping four telnics across the frontier and through the northern forest unseen is one thing, but an army sized force, or larger? No forest could hide a host so large," Gavis said.

"Then what is their objective? Do they intend to catch us unaware as we are drawn off by their armies to the east and west?" Larus Braxus wondered.

"I know where they are going," Tyro said, jabbing his finger upon the map, along the foothills of the Nameless Mountains.

"That is madness," Gavis said, knowing what waited them there.

"The Valley of Oddigem?" Braxus asked, leaning over the map

to read the fabled locale, the place the source of cautionary tales the people of the Northern Kingdom once told their children.

"The gargoyle nesting grounds. If this is true, it could be a boon for our efforts. They are drawing closer to our most unreliable vassals. If that does not bestir them, nothing shall," Gavis reasoned.

Tyro didn't want that. He needed to intercede before they got that far. Nor could he trust this to anyone unless he was present. He needed to capture Terin before he was killed or before he destroyed the gargoyles, either possibility ruinous to his plans. If he could take the boy, it would solidify his hold over Joriah, and Valera as well. It would also remove the Torries greatest asset.

"Send word, General. No one is to attack them without me. Observe them from afar and shadow their advance. I will soon join you," Tyro ordered.

"As you command, My Emperor."

"Larus, I have an important task for you," Tyro said to his castellan as the others filed out of the chamber.

* * *

"What did you see?" Valera asked, cupping Jonas' cheeks with her hands. He was struck with another vision, this one in the light of day, the midday sun shining through their open window. Cordela was fast asleep behind her as they sat on the edge of their bed. His visions were progressively vivid and expansive in their scope, this one the worst he suffered yet. He sat in place, his iris' clouded for the longest time, before it relented, the luster returning in his eyes.

"I saw him again," he whispered.

"Terin?"

"Yes, and I know where he is going."

"Where?" Valera asked, her heart beating faster with every revelation.

"The Valley of Oddigem," he said, his voice softer than a whisper, the very name of that fell place sending tendrils of terror across her pimpled flesh.

"For what purpose?" she asked, fearing the answer.

"He…he was chosen, he and the others."

"Chosen? Chosen for what purpose?"

And, so he told her, revealing all that Yah had shown him, his every word tearing at her heart. When he was done, she was in tears.

"No, he can't die, not after all that he has endured. Speak to your father, make him see reason!" she pleaded, willing to risk everything they managed to secure to this point for the safety of their precious son.

"Valera, this is beyond my father now. He cannot stop what is about to occur."

"Whatever are you saying? There must be a way. What use is his authority if he cannot call back his armies?"

"There is more at play than that, my love. There is only one way to save our son, and even that might fail."

"What?"

"Lorn must have my sword."

"Lorn? How can you give it to him if you are here?"

They shared a look for the longest time, reconciling what must be done.

"I would not leave you here, but there is no safe place to run," he said, his voice breaking with emotion.

"I will endure. Save Terin. Promise me!"

"I will do all that I can, I so avow with my very life."

"I want both of you. Promise me that!" she insisted.

"I promise." He smiled, his eyes softening as they beheld her beauty.

Before he could plant a gentle kiss, the guard announced his presence at the door.

"Enter!" Jonas ordered as the guard stepped within.

"Castellan Braxus," the guard proclaimed as Larus Braxus entered, his robes swirling at his ankles before bowing deeply.

"Princess Cordela's presence is required in the throne room," Larus proclaimed, summoning them to follow.

* * *

Valera cradled Cordela in her arms as she and Jonas were escorted to the throne room, passing before the face of the grotesque sculpture of a gargoyle and man merging into one united form. She refused to look up, not wishing to gaze upon the abomination, wondering how a man who shared blood with her Jonas could create such a thing. Jonas kept close to her side, her ever vigilant guardian. She felt safe in his presence, dreading when he would have to leave her to save their son.

They circled the sculpture, before passing through the large open doors of the throne room. Her breath caught in her throat, pausing at the entrance as hundreds of court officials, commanders of rank and countless others were gathered along either side of the chamber, all their eyes drawn to her and Cordela.

"Courage," Jonas whispered in her ear, guiding her forth between the multitude of faces. She kept her gaze forward, where the dais awaited, and the massive golden throne that rested atop of it. She felt the eyes of Tyro boring into her as he stood before the throne, adorned in his regal attire, forgoing his warrior garb for this grand ceremony. At least she believed it to be ceremony by the size and status of the assembly.

Larus Braxus led them to the dais, before stopping at its lowest step, bowing deeply to the emperor.

"Rise, Castellan Braxus!" Tyro ordered.

"My Emperor, I present the Princess Valera, and the Princess Cordela!" Braxus declared loudly for the entire assemblage to hear. Few understood Valera's connection to Tyro, or her daughter's, listening now with rapt attention to ascertain the truth.

Valera's heart raced as Tyro ordered her forth, leaving Jonas where he stood as she approached the dais, and ascended the steps to the throne above. Tyro reached out, taking her hand in his, helping her up the final step, directing her to stand beside the throne before taking Cordela from her arms.

"With war upon us on all fronts, my heirs through my daughter, the Princess Tosha, are now in the hands of our enemies. I would be remiss to risk our unity should I fall in battle, and thus I must declare a new heir, one of my direct line. I present my granddaughter, the

Princess Cordela, *Heir to the Empire!*" Tyro proclaimed, raising her into the air.

Jonas looked on, horrified with his father's decision, watching helplessly as one commander and court official after another ascended the dais, knelt before his daughter and swore vows of loyalty and affirmation. Larus Braxus was first, followed by General Gavis, and then the rest, each swearing fealty to the child.

* * *

Following the ceremony, the palace was abuzz with activity, with Tyro preparing to depart, leaving Dev Faran, Commander of the garrison in command of Fera's defense. Jonas struggled to gain audience with his father, Tyro busying himself with matters of state and the coordination of his armies. Tyro sent word for Nels Draken to bring the garrison troops he brought from Tinsay to reinforce Fera. Once accomplished, Nels was to join with Tyro and General Gavis, who would lead the 10th Legion north to the Vale of Oddigem.

Jonas finally caught up with his sire in the corridor outside his personal chambers, Tyro now wearing his warrior's garb, with his twin blades riding each hip. His steel helm graced his head, its simple design symbolic of the austere carriage he now projected. He meant for his men to see him focused upon the enemy and battle ahead, rather than the pampered trappings of his regal station. Jonas wondered if this was what his father was like during the revolution, a focused and deadly warrior, rather than the distant figurehead he projected during the later years of his reign. Tyro's guards yielded as Jonas approached, having grown accustomed to his proximity to the emperor. All knew the emperor favored him, many guessing the nature of their kinship.

"Did you plan to speak with me before departing, or did you simply wish to ride off without a word or explanation?" Jonas asked, falling in step beside his father as he strode boldly along the corridor, eager to make haste.

"Do not presume to question my actions, boy," Tyro bluntly stated.

"I will since you crowned my daughter. You had no right to do that."

Tyro stopped midstride, turning to face Jonas, his golden eyes ablaze.

"I have every right to do that! She is my heir and will sit my throne since you are too weak to claim it."

"You know why I do not, and that she will suffer if this is forced upon her."

"Then you had better guard her well, boy. I gave you that sword for a reason. See that it serves you as I intended," Tyro said, regarding the *Sword of Light* riding Jonas' left hip.

And there it was, the true reason Tyro so armed him, forcing him to remain at Cordela's side, guarding her with his life. It was a means to keep him here forever.

"And if you die?"

"Then Cordela shall be empress. Castellan Braxus shall guide and help you protect her."

"If you die, your empire is gone. And what of Terin?" Jonas whispered that last part, lest the guards overhear.

"What of him?"

"I know where you are going, and who you shall see there."

"Hmph, if I see the boy, I shall administer the correction you failed to instill. Since he knows who I truly am, then he suffers the same hinderance as you when facing me."

"You would use that against him?" Jonas growled.

"I will use everything at my disposal to bring him back to you, even if I must shave parts of him to do so."

"It shall not end well, not for either of you. Only death awaits you and him at Noddegamra," Jonas warned.

"What did you say?" Tyro growled.

"Noddegamra," Jonas repeated, the name associated with the final battle of the ages, a source of speculation and fabled lore. To associate it with the valley of Oddigem reflected either a deep understanding by Jonas, or the fevered ramblings of a madman, and Jonas was not mad.

"I will secure the boy, defeat his friends and then face the other armies marching against me in detail. Then this war will be ended, now and forever."

"Only destruction awaits you there, and I would not see any of you perish. It is not too late to call for peace," Jonas pleaded.

"See to your wife and daughter, Joriah. Keep them safe."

"Only one thing can save you," Jonas said.

"And what would that be?" Tyro asked, stepping close, his nose nearly touching Jonas'.

"Love."

Tyro stood there for an eternal moment, a loss for words and understanding. Jonas might as well have spoken a different tongue, for what could Tyro know of such.

With that, Tyro turned and left, making his way to the stables before riding forth to war.

* * *

The days that followed were maddening for Jonas, knowing his father and son were marching to face each other under the shadow of that far off valley. Fera was strongly garrisoned with its complement of twenty-nine telnics, which were further reinforced with the telnics Nels Draken brought from Tinsay, making the fortress nigh invincible from the army Queen Letha was bringing from the west. Tyro's original plan to join the garrisons of Tinsay and Laycrom into a third legion set aside to reinforce Fera with the telnics Draken brought from the port city. Draken spent less than a day at the palace before departing upon a magantor to join the emperor enroute to Oddigem. Jonas spent each night standing at his window, brooding on the sorry state of things. He needed to depart soon but struggled leaving Valera here without him. Should something happen to her or Cordela, he would never forgive himself, and neither would his father.

His father, he thought miserably, wondering how he could save him. His life was one thing, but his father's soul was what truly mattered, and the man was hopelessly lost, blinded by his pride, and fueled by revenge.

"Revenge," Jonas whispered, the very word tearing at his heart.

Hadn't his father gotten his revenge a thousand-fold? What more did he seek? Must the whole world burn to sate his ire? The men who wronged him were long dead, most slain by Tyro's hand.

He needed to leave soon if he harbored any hope to save Terin, but wondered if there was a way to save his father as well?

"Show me the way forward," he whispered, staring at the night sky, beseeching Yah's guidance.

He briefly drew his sword of light from its scabbard, testing its strength, its once vibrant luster replaced with murky darkness. He wondered what afflicted the blade, and if the others were similarly struck. He quietly pushed it back into the scabbard, gazing again at the night sky through his open window.

He stood there in silence for the longest time, before he was drawn to the outer corridor, where Larus Braxus awaited him. The castellan stood before his chambers with his hands tucked into the billowy sleeves of his robes. The man's usually nondescript face looked out of sorts, as if troubled. The fact that he called upon Jonas in the middle of the night bespoke the urgency of his audience. Jonas crept from the chamber, not wishing to wake Valera, who rested upon their bed with Cordela nestled near her breast.

"Joriah," Larus greeted him guardedly as he stepped into the corridor.

"Castellan Braxus, this is a strange time to call upon me," he said, noticing the troubled look upon his face.

"I would have words and could not wait for the morrow," Larus said as Jonas looked left and right, noticing the guards were positioned out of earshot.

"Speak freely," Jonas said, his voice but a whisper.

"I know who you are, who you truly are."

"Did my father reveal this to you?" Jonas asked warily, feeling as if he was standing on a thin branch about to give way.

"Partially, but not your Kalinian blood. That was revealed by the visions that have plagued me since the emperor departed."

The mention of visions was enough to cause Jonas to draw away.

"You have them as well, I see. Tell me, Joriah, what have you seen?"

Jonas paused, knowing he shouldn't trust this man, a servant of the enemy, but something felt off. Was it the hand of Yah, or the inert desire to confide his troubled visions with another fellow traveler?

"I must leave if we are to have any hope."

"I know. Yah has revealed to me what you must do." Larus sighed, looking away, troubled by this contradiction of all that he believed to this point.

"I can't leave unless I know she is safe," Jonas added, looking back to his bedchamber.

"I will guard her with my life, both Valera and Cordela, I so avow," Larus Braxus affirmed.

"I will need a magantor, and driver."

"It shall be provided. How soon until you can leave?"

"Two days. I'll need to bring one of my servants with me," Jonas added, trying to determine which of Cronus' men to bring with him.

"Very well, Joriah. Speed well, and good fortune."

CHAPTER 9

Vateris. At the confluence of the Reguh and Morga Rivers.

Corry guided Wind Racer overhead, the large magantor circling above Vateris, the vital trading city straddling the northern road connecting Nisin and Fera. A less traveled southern road was built nearer the Plate foothills, that would take them directly to Fera, but the northern approach skirted the northern face of the Nameless Mountains, bringing them down upon Tyro's armies from the opposite direction of the Chosen. At least that was the plan as it currently stood, but their plans seemed to change with every report Brokov provided.

The news of their advance spread like fire on dry grass, hastening the city's fall, with their advancing armies finding it mostly abandoned. Nearly half of their forces already passed over its massive bridge, emerging on the west side of the city. Corry looked east where the rest of their forces were strung out in an endless column along the east-west road that meandered the rich farmlands and rolling hills of the Benotrist heartland. A dozen of General Valen's warbirds patrolled the skies of Vateris, the rest scouting north and west, though most of their intelligence was now provided by Brokov, who constantly kept Torg apprised of his findings.

Torg. Her thoughts shifted to her dearest friend and surrogate father. She spotted his gray ocran in the city square below, resting near the east end of the bridge. He looked like a statue carved from granite, observing the columns of infantry parading by, likely cohorts of General Ciyon's Macon-Torry Army. She looked east where General Lewins' 1st Torry Army was approaching the city's east gate, following their standard, a blue hammer and ax upon a field of white. Beyond them marched the men of Teso and Zulon, along with numerous auxiliaries drawn from dozens of Benotrist holdfasts that swore fealty to Terin.

Terin, her thoughts again shifted to her beloved husband, wondering where he was amidst all this chaos. Was he safe, was he injured or captured? Was he starving, lost somewhere in the northern forest? His fate could be any of a thousand possibilities, and few of them good. She shook such thoughts from her mind, for they served no one but the enemy. She needed to keep her focus on the tasks at hand, moving their armies ever westward where they might help him in some way. Most of Ciyon's army was already beyond the west gate of the city, where the Jenaii 1st and 2nd Battlegroups awaited them. She could see King El Anthar's magantor circling above his armies, its gray-white wings soaring majestically through the autumn air. Lowering her gaze to the Jenaii armies below, she was struck by how many of them had already given their lives to their cause, especially the 1st Battlegroup who now numbered only seven telnics, while the 2nd suffered greatly at Corell and Notsu. Somewhere in their great host marched King Lichu and his ten Nayborian warriors, representing their people in this final campaign.

Final campaign, her thoughts shifted to that very thing that hung ominously above their heads, before gazing westward, where the road bled into the horizon. It looked so peaceful from this airy height, but that road led to destruction, either their own or the enemy, or both.

From there she shifted her gaze north, where somewhere beyond the horizon, their ape allies and Raven fast approached the port of Mordicay, securing the harbor for their advancing fleet. Much of the harbor garrison had fled, leaving it ripe for the taking. She hoped they completed the task quickly and joined them on their march. Their help was needed should Tyro send his legions in their direction. She wanted to meet the enemy with their full might and ordered their van to slow their pace for their ape friends to catch up. It was not just their ape friends marching upon Mordicay in the north, but the Sisterhood magantors, led by Lucella Sarelis, Queen Letha's captain of her guard. Tosha was also with them, sharing a place upon Raven's air ski. They also sent half of their new Benotrist allies, and a sizable portion of their rebel counterparts to negotiate with whoever commanded Mordicay. The situation in the port was mostly unknown, with Brokov's last report indicating a chaotic scene of street riots and open rebellion in large parts of the northern port.

Not all the Earthers went north, as she spotted Lorken upon his air ski returning from the west, where he scouted ahead of their van. Seeking Zem amongst their host was difficult to miss, finding him approaching Torg in the middle of the city square, preparing to converse with the craggy commander of the elite.

Poor Torg. She shook her head, imagining the tedious conversation Zem was having with him. Zem had many admirable qualities but was insufferably boring when he droned on. Unfortunately for Torg, Zem saw him as an eager recipient of his stories. Whatever gave Zem such a notion, she could only guess. It was probably Raven's doing, if she were to guess, using Zem to torture Torg. By this point, Torg was probably missing Orlom's company.

* * *

"...As I was saying, I will prioritize a thorough geological analysis of your world's surface once we conclude our current activities. The tectonic similarities to Earth are quite astounding and require a detailed assessment before I can ascertain risks. Intelligent planning in advance can mitigate loss of life and prepare multiple contingencies." Zem rambled on, giving Torg a list of his post war priorities, including a geological study of the planet's surface.

"You appear to have thought about this to great lengths," Torg snorted, easing his ocran across the bridge as Zem kept pace beside him afoot.

"It is not a deeply intelligent endeavor, I assure you, Master Vantel, just one of many small tasks I can perform that you will find useful," Zem said.

"Why me?" Torg asked, though he shouldn't have, for any question would give Zem reason to ramble on further.

"With your king's absence, you represent the authority on matters of the realm, particularly assessing threats both natural and martial," Zem explained.

"Who gave you that notion?"

"Raven. He spoke quite approvingly of you and mentioned your authority on such matters."

"That was kind of him." Torg shook his head, making certain to *thank* him personally when he returned from Mordicay.

"Now, as I was about to say, we need to discuss…" Zem began, causing Torg to inwardly groan, cursing Raven under his breath.

* * *

Mordicay. The Northern Coast.

Raven set down upon a hilltop overlooking the harbor in the distance, with the Reguh River running north off his left, running directly into the port, feeding into the Mord Bay. Paved thoroughfares ran along either bank of the Reguh, connecting the vital port city to points south, particularly Vateris. Tosha sat behind him with his rifle in hand, lifting its scope to scan the city gates and walls in the distance.

"Packaww!"

Raven ignored the screech of the Sisterhood magantor circling overhead, where their entire contingent dominated the skies around Mordicay. He drew his pistol, taking a look for himself at the state of the city. The southeast gate was drawn open, as well as both river gates that flanked the riverbanks of the Reguh. They noticed a steady stream of people and wagons exiting one of the western gates, fleeing the city for one of many reasons they could only guess. Brokov's last message indicated that Mordicay was an open city, with the harbor garrison withdrawn to the central district, sheltering within its protective inner wall. Tosha observed one small structure engulfed in flames along the western river front, with only a small crowd attempting to douse the flames. Thankfully most of Mordicay's structures were stone and brick, limiting the spread of fires, though half the dwellings had thatched rooves, rather than slate.

"What a mess," Raven grunted, eying the chaos from afar.

"No, it appears manageable, all things considered," she said, lifting the scope further north, where their fleets dotted the bay. She could see the familiar hull of the *Stenox* in the center of the flotilla, holding position. There were no signs of Benotrist warships in the harbor to contest their fleets, another indication of the weakness of the empire. The only Benotrist ships of note were their own, taking up position within their armada, all bearing Terin's sigil. She hoped whoever held regency of Mordicay was reasonable and joined their coalition. Dacer Coflis held that title the last she was aware of, but regional potentates were changing with every moon as of late.

"We'll see how manageable it is when we offer to talk and they see the army we're bringing to their doorstep," Raven said.

"A position of strength is the greatest motivation to bring an adversary to terms," she pointed out, sweeping the rifle's scope across the breadth of the bay.

"That's not the problem. The problem is the city looks to be divided. Who knows how many people are in charge, or even worse, if no one is."

"To use one of my husband's stupid phrases, *there's only one way to find out.*"

* * *

Dacer Coflis, regent of Mordicay, stood upon the terrace of his palace, looking out across the Mord Bay at the grand armada arrayed against him. He was without hope, having watched a massive ape army approach from the south, blocking any escape by land, while their fleets blocked the sea. They left him only the narrow northwest road that ran along the coast for his withdraw, a route exposed to the foul weapons of the Earthers' ship. They already demonstrated its fell power in recent days, leveling several watchtowers guarding the mouth of the harbor. It was a needless and cruel gesture, one meant to demonstrate their capabilities, which any fool fully understood at this juncture. His troubles began when the emperor ordered half his garrison to be withdrawn to Plateres, leaving him with only five telnics to hold the city when tidings of Pagan's fall reached them. Those grim tidings were merely the prelude to even a greater calamity, with the fall of Nisin to a massive coalition of apes, Torries, Jenaii, Casians and Macons. That was followed with the fall of Vateris and the arrival of the enemy armada. Sight of the Earthers' vessel alone would set the city to panic, let alone the forces that currently surrounded them. He forsook holding the outer city, leaving it to its own devices while he concentrated his remaining soldiers holding the inner walls that protected the central district and his palace.

Amidst this chaos and despair, he was surprised to see the Earther Raven appear before his southern gate bearing a flag of truce, accompanied by her highness, Princess Tosha. Their request for parlay preceded the arrival of the ape armies, and to his further surprise, a large contingent of Benotrist warriors who were strangely allied to this enemy coalition. He reluctantly agreed to treat with them, and the time of that parlay was at hand.

"Regent Coflis," his aide greeted, stepping upon the terrace, before bowing deeply.

"Is my escort ready, Kayless?" Dacer asked without turning, his eyes still upon the sea, where the late day sun reflected off its tranquil surface.

"Yes, Regent, as you requested."

"Then let us not keep our visitors waiting."

It was before the walls of his city that Regent Coflis treated with President Matuzak, Tosha and Raven, as well as Commander Dalomos, a Benotrist telnic commander now sworn to Terin. Had Tosha not revealed Terin's true lineage, Coflis would not have believed their outlandish yarn, but her doing so meant she forsook her sons' birthright, lending credence to her claim. As a regent of a great port, Coflis was so named by the emperor himself for his ability, local connections and most especially his loyalty. His loyalty was not given cheaply, and only the direst of situations could bring it into doubt. Unfortunately, his plight was dire. Most of his city was in the hands of unruly mobs, and his provisions were inadequate for a lengthy siege. Beyond this, he was hopelessly surrounded, and the Earthers could decimate his position without risking any of their many troops. Most troubling of all were his dreams of late, dreams so terrible he dare not voice them with any of his subordinates or confidants.

When Princess Tosha offered generous terms, he was taken aback. His men would be spared, and he would retain his regency of Mordicay, though every slave would be given manumission, especially those of Menotrist origin. Revealing Terin's true lineage and asking that he swear loyalty to Tyro's *True* heir dulled the sting of his disloyalty, but in fact rather than spirit, and the spirit of an oath meant more to a man of Coflis' character than order of fact. He might have held firm in this, condemning himself and his garrison to certain death had Princess Tosha not asked if he had dreams of late.

And so it was, that the city of Mordicay lowered the standard of the Benotrist Empire, before raising the sigil of a glowing blue sword upon a field of silver, swearing oath to Terin Caleph, grandson of their emperor.

Regent Coflis agreed to send half his garrison with the coalition army led by his eldest son, while Matuzak ordered General Horzak and his contingent of ape warriors to remain at Mordicay to help Coflis restore order to the port city. Horzak's apes had fought at Tro, Gotto, Notsu and the campaign in the north, earning their president's gratitude for their bravery. They were formed form the surviving crews of the 1st Ape Fleet, forsaking their place as sailors for the role of soldiers. They voiced their displeasure of missing out on the battle ahead but resigned themselves to their duty. Such was the price of their rapid advancement across the Benotrist Empire, having to thin their ranks by dispatching forces to secure their lines of advance.

Once the port was secure, President Matuzak quickly turned his armies about, marching south to catch up with Torg and the others who were many leagues past Vateris by this juncture. Commander Dalomos split his command, ordering half to remain and help General Horzak secure the city, while leading the rest alongside Matuzak.

* * *

Ben Thorton stood upon the lookout deck of the *Stenox*, resting his forearms on its low wall as he stared out across the Mord Bay. He was lost in thought, seeing nothing wherever he looked, his mind elsewhere. His return to the *Stenox* changed nothing in his outlook, cursing Raven for not killing him in their duel. He tried to kill himself several times since they departed Pagan, holding his pistol to his head, but failing to pull the trigger.

Coward, he recalled Raven's words. He couldn't disagree. He was a coward, too weak or frightened to end himself and spare the others his miserable presence. Whenever he put the gun to his head, he couldn't help but see Jennifer's face, her gentle eyes breaking with disappointment. Every time he saw her, and every time he lowered the gun, such was the power she held over him, even in death. Why Raven and the others allowed him his gun was beyond him. Was he so pathetic that they no longer saw him as a threat?

No, he gave his word to not interfere, and his word was his bond, something Raven knew all too well. He thought briefly on where he might go once this war was over. Raven said they would drop him off wherever he wanted as long as they never saw each other again, but where could he go? Wherever he went Jennifer would not be there. Only death could reunite them, and she denied him that option, demanding he continue to live this foul existence. Perhaps a deserted isle with no one around. He could live out his days looking out across the sea, alone. If Jennifer wanted him to live, then that is how he would live, like the miserable wretch he was. He would almost cry if he was human, but the human part of him died with her. Of course, Ella would be distraught. He suspected she harbored feelings for him, though why was beyond him. He was not kind to her, but he did protect her. As she came to realize that, her feelings toward him softened, before blossoming into outright affection. Unfortunately, he did not share her sentiment. He loved only one woman, and she was dead. Ella was still aboard, helping Brokov and Kendra with the ship, along with their new ape crewmates, who seemed more trouble than they were worth. Thankfully they had Ular to help them, but even he was leaving, joining Raven on his return to their army, somewhere south of here marching for Fera. He wasn't the only

Enoructan going by the look of things, as Ben counted nearly five hundred of them gathered along the wharves of the harbor, preparing to march, leaving their remaining doruns with just one rider apiece. They would join with Matuzak's army, which was still just south of the city. Ular was the only crewmember to speak with him in recent days, the others giving him a wide berth. Even these encounters were little more than acknowledgements as they passed each other.

He could hear Raven and Ular speaking on the deck below, discussing their upcoming journey by the nature of the conversation. Raven and Tosha set down on the 1st deck about an hour before, gathering Ular and speaking with Brokov before rejoining the march on Fera. Raven didn't even look at him, the two ignoring each other as he remained upon the lookout deck, lost in his morbid thoughts.

Ben didn't turn to look as Tosha cleared the ladder, stepping to his side, placing a hand on the low wall, looking out across the bay, pretending to see whatever he was staring at. They both stood there in silence for the longest time, each daring the other to speak first. Tosha snorted in frustration, obviously annoyed that he wouldn't speak.

"If you want to say something, then say it," Ben said, refusing to look at her.

"He cares about you. You should know that. He will never say that, and I doubt you will either, but there it is," she blurted, hating the way she sounded.

She waited for a response, but nothing.

"Do you wish to speak, or simply stand there as I do all the talking?" she growled.

"Talk away."

"It finally happened," she snarled.

He just gave her a look, refusing to ask what she meant.

"I have found a man more stubborn and frustrating than Raven."

Still nothing.

"You can stand here and brood until you die and your eyeballs fall from your skull, but what shall that accomplish? You must reconcile with him," she insisted.

"That can never happen, not now," he said dryly, still refusing to look at her, his gaze fixed to the bay.

"Why can it not happen? What is holding you back?"

"I killed Kato, Tosha. There is no going back from that."

"Raven….Raven can forgive you," she reasoned.

"I don't want his forgiveness. I didn't mean for him to die, but that is war, and he drew the same as me, and stepped into my shot. I wished he hadn't died, but he did. Forgiveness won't bring him back, and if I had to do it all over again, I would still have shot him. Raven will never overlook that, and I don't blame him."

"You don't blame him for being angry at you?" She made a face, trying to understand the most difficult man she ever met, and considering who her husband was, that was quite a feat.

"I don't blame him for that. There is only one thing I blame him for, and that will never be reconciled," he said with a dead voice.

"Your wife." She sighed, knowing that to be the source of all their grief and regret. It would forever be a wall between them. "She must have been a great woman."

"She was."

"What would she say to you if she were here now?" Tosha asked, before turning to step away. She paused, leaning in to kiss him upon his cheek.

He finally looked at her, wondering what that was for.

"That was from your Jennifer. Remember that she loved you. Farewell, Ben Thorton," she said before stepping away, sensing she would never see him again.

He watched silently as they departed, only sharing the briefest of glances with Raven as he, Tosha and Ular climbed aboard the air ski and lifted off, speeding across the bay, circumventing the city walls, before disappearing altogether. He thought on what she said, before fishing the glowing green disc from his jacket pocket. He hadn't seen it yet, putting it off to this point. It would bring him pain, and as he came to realize, he was a coward in that regard. He closed his eyes, resigning himself to finally face his grief.

* * *

Thorton made his way to the engineering room, finding it empty, before taking a seat at one of the consoles. He pressed the disc into the intake mount, causing a familiar image to appear on the viewscreen. It was Jennifer, wearing a beautiful silver gown, holding their infant son in her arms. It was the last message she sent him before joining him aboard the *Stalingrad*. It was sent from her parents' home in Colorado, and didn't reach him until after her death, for some strange reason. Raven handed it to him before they departed on the *Eden Expedition*, but he refused it, knowing it would rend his heart seeing her, and knowing she was gone.

"Hello, Texas, we miss you so much. Your son is getting so big, just like his daddy. Say hi to daddy, Mike," she whispered into the child's ear.

His son just stared blankly at the screen, drool escaping his lips, coating his wife's hand.

"He misses you, Texas." She smiled, wiping the fluid from her hand on the lap of her dress, the small gesture causing her to roll her eyes. Her mother warned her that infants never did what you wanted them to. Any moments of cuteness were sporadic, never planned.

He could see the weariness in her eyes, despite the efforts she put in concealing it for his sake. Her maternity time was nearing its end, and she would return to duty at the Earth based fighter wing she was recently assigned.

"Let me take him," Jennifer's mother said, stepping in front of the screen, lifting the child in her arms, before waving to Ben.

It was almost as if it was happening at this moment, as if it was happening across the universe, and all he needed was to find a way home to live his life with them. Alas, it was but a memory, like a letter stored in a box and only read to relive a time long gone.

"I am sorry about that, Texas. He was so lively all morning, and now... well, he probably wants a nap. He is wonderful though, and I wish you were here to see him. I hope this message reaches you before your next engagement. News of your fleet's activities is quite limited, even for us with the highest clearance, but I trust you are safe, and Nanouk also. Tell him mother is asking if he has found a girl yet. She wants more grandchildren, and right now we are the ones doing all the work. Of course, the idea of Nanouk finding a girl is ridiculous, especially when

he uses the name Raven. You just keep him out of trouble. Father and grandfather still hear from their contacts in the academy about all the antics he was up to as a cadet during those years." She smiled and rolled her eyes, knowing Ben was also involved, but didn't mention it.

"I shouldn't be too upset with his antics though, for if it wasn't for him, I would never have met you. I will never forget the day he brought you home during your first leave from the academy. I came down the stairs and found you standing in the foyer shaking hands with grandfather. I knew then I would marry you. You are the handsomest man I ever knew, Benjamin Thorton, and I miss you terribly." She wiped a stubborn tear from her eye, pausing to check her emotions.

"I don't mean to cry, Texas. I should be stronger. What sort of Space Fleet pilot weeps like a little girl? I just miss you, and I worry about you. I've heard too many stories of our pilots dying in deep space, so far from home. Promise me you will be safe. And keep Nanouk safe as well. We have to depend on you for you are the responsible one."

"I found a song in the archive that reminded me of what your coming into my life has done for me. Please do not laugh or roll your eyes at my foolishness. I hope I don't sound like a silly girl singing this. I do warn you, it is quite ancient, but not as ancient as your Yellow Rose of Texas. Here goes," she began, reciting the lyrics to Top of the World, originally sung by the Carpenters in the late 20th century.

He had never heard it before, and it wasn't the sort of song he would listen to, but her voice was so femininely perfect it soothed his racing heart. The song spoke of the happiness a woman's lover brought to her life, changing her outlook, and helping her see all the wonders the world offered. By the time Jennifer finished, her tears were gone, replaced with a joyous smile.

"When I first heard that melody, I thought of the joy you brought in my life. Everything I see holds a deeper meaning now, as if I am seeing its beauty for the first time. I wondered how that could be, how my whole outlook could brighten to such extent? Then I knew. It was Love. Love cures so many ills in our life, Ben. Genuine love. True love. No matter what happens in our life, always keep that truth close to your heart. All I want is to reach through this screen and hold you, to kiss you and never let go. We have so much to look forward to together, so much life worth

living, but should something happen, know that I love you, now and forever. There will never be another, so be sure to return to me safely, or I will die an old woman, alone and widowed, for there is only one man I will ever love, and he is Benjamin Thorton. I love you, Texas." She smiled, pressing a kiss to her hand and placing it on the screen before it faded to black.

There in the engineering room of the *Stenox*, Ben Thorton's cold heart melted.

CHAPTER 10

The Chosen camped within the shadow of the Nameless Mountains, their western foothills resting to the east, with their towering peaks silhouetted against the eastern sky, the setting sun shining off their jagged slopes. They settled down along the banks of a shallow stream, filling their water satchels and partaking their dwindling rations, before discovering it was teaming with fish. Most had less than a day's food left, some not even that. Those with some shared with those with none, their collective bond growing throughout their travels, each willing to sacrifice for the others. When King Mortus discovered Tessa's food satchel empty, he gave her his last ration, unbeknownst to the old seamstress. When Aldo's pack grew heavy, Lucas carried it for him. When Terin despaired, thinking of Corry and all she meant to him, Lorn drew him into his embrace, sharing his grief for his dear Deliea. And so it went, with a thousand small acts of kindness they each gave and received every day of their journey, giving them the courage and strength to continue on. With the discovery of so many fish, Lorn and Mortus decided upon an early encampment. Many brought nets for their journey for scooping fish, an easy means of preserving their dwindling stores. As they were followed since emerging from the forest, and under constant surveillance every day after, there was little risk in starting cookfires to prepare their catches. Lorn surmised this might be the last decent meal any of them would have before the issue was decided.

Lorn topped off his satchel after generously partaking the cold mountain water, before stretching his sore back. He lived a soldier's life, especially in recent years, enduring countless nights sleeping under the stars, or marching from one end of Arax to the other, yet, this was different. This journey was all on foot, traveling unknown wilderness, guided by visions, faith and luck. It was difficult on the body, and the spirit. It forced them to empty their bodies and minds of needless distractions, purifying them for the task ahead. Whatever task that was, he could only guess. Despite the harsh nature of their journey, it felt easy much of the time, almost like a stroll through the countryside with your dearest friends. It was that sense of belonging and friendship that eased their journey. His father often said the harshest task is made easy when sharing it with your dearest friend. Conversely, the simplest task is made painful if shared with a difficult person.

"Our friends are here," Squid said, squinting as he stared west, where several riders held at a distance, Benotrists no doubt. Various cavalry elements had followed them in recent days, always at a distance. Their mounts rested below the setting sun, an obvious attempt to mask their position.

"This location offers no concealment," Lorn said, the ground where they stood nothing but matted grass along the meandering stream, with a few clusters of trees interspersed, which they made use of for their fires. It would take little effort on the Benotrists part to surround and slay them. Why they hadn't, he could only guess.

"We have undertaken this journey at Yah's behest, for a purpose only he knows, but I can't help but wonder why they have not attacked?" Squid asked.

"They seem willing to allow us to continue. Considering we are so few and hopelessly alone in their realm, perhaps Tyro is curious of our destination. We certainly are no threat to them," Lorn said.

"We are nearly three thousand armed warriors in the heart of their realm. We are a threat, and they have not yet attacked us. It is both curious and troubling."

"If they attack, then we shall fight, likely to our death, but we shall fight all the same. Yah did not say we are to surrender ourselves, and I care not to be captured and subjected to their mercy," Lorn said.

"Yah did not reveal that intention… yet. But we were sent here for a purpose, and it wasn't to defeat the enemy in battle."

"We do not know that, Squid. Perhaps he sent so few of us to demonstrate his power. I do not wish to offer false hope, but it is a possibility."

"I hadn't considered that, perhaps I have grown dour with our future. Perhaps we might survive after all," Squid reflected.

"We might indeed, and if not, we shall account well of ourselves." Lorn smiled, placing a hand to his friend's shoulder.

"Packaww!"

The sound of a passing magantor drew their gaze skyward, its rider circling overhead several times before passing on. It was the third pass over this day and was a regular occurrence since they emerged from the Northern Forrest.

"Perhaps it shall be tonight," Squid mussed, regarding an enemy attack.

"If so, we shall fight with our bellies full," Lorn said, looking forward to the bounty of fish that was cooking over their fires.

* * *

They rotated those standing watch with regularity, affording the others time to partake the food and merriment that permeated the camp. Lorn and Mortus decided a celebration was in order, one last pleasure before the plunge. They were aware the enemy might assail them at any moment, but nothing they did could prevent that now. And, so it was that they gathered about their cookfires and shared stories, and generously partook their meal. Most doubted they would have such a feast ever again, the path ahead filled with many unknowns, and one ominous known that weighed upon them in the form of the towering peaks that they camped in the shadow of to their east.

Deva sat upon her pack, staring at the towering peaks of the Nameless Mountains as their dreary slopes seemed to swallow the light of the setting sun. The mountains filled her with dread, their jagged slopes and misshapen summits reflecting their foreboding aura, their morbid air contrasting the merriment circulating in their camp. She stood apart from the others, drawing her cloak about her shoulders as she gazed upon the source of her fear, thankful that the ominous peaks were still far afield, at least for now.

"You haven't eaten," Lucas said, bringing her a generous portion of fish he just retrieved from a cook fire, offering it to her.

"I don't feel like eating." She smiled wanly as he presented the inviting meal.

"You need your strength, Deva, and I know you are hungry," he said, not taking no for an answer.

"I don't deserve…"

"That again? Deva, we have forgiven you. The person you were before is no more."

"How can you know my heart? Truly know it, Lucas?"

"I know by your actions."

"Kind and good acts can mask an evil heart."

"Are we born righteous and kind? I don't believe we are, and neither does King Lorn as he claims time and again. A wise man once said, if you want to be kind, then practice kindness. If you want to be good, practice good acts. These behaviors shall forge your path anew. Your every action since Bansoch has proven this. We are following this path much because of you, because Yah has chosen you, the same as he chose Lorn and Terin. Each has their part in this grand play. Your part is to lead us to where we must go, and my part is to guard you."

She lowered her head, overcome with gratitude for his kindness. She could not imagine enduring this journey without Lucas beside her, giving her encouragement that she so desperately needed. She reluctantly took the food, eating it while he looked on, making sure she fully partook.

"You are my ever-vigilant guardian." She smiled softly, eating the last morsel.

"You do a fair part watching over me as well," he said, looking east, where the mountains loomed.

"We guard each other, just as all have done during this journey, but I am thankful for your special attention."

"It is my pleasure, Deva. So that is where we are going, it doesn't appear so terrible," he said, still looking at the towering peaks in the distance.

Her silence gave him pause as she nearly trembled, her visions playing cruelly in her mind. She couldn't bear to tell him what awaited them upon the northern side of the mountains, in the dreadful valley she saw in her dreams. She nearly wept thinking of that awful place, the very place she was leading them. What hope had they once they reached it? None. Nothing but death awaited them there, and she cursed herself for such despair. He could see the hurt in her eyes, the torment of things she could not say.

"Would you hold me, Lucas?" she dared ask, fearing he might refuse, but she so desperately needed.

He said not a word, but merely drew her into his arms, holding her tightly as she closed her eyes, pressing her head to his chest.

* * *

Terin shared his cookfire with Elos and a few men from Yatin, listening to their tales of events that happened after he departed Mosar, much of it harrowing. They spoke of the atrocities committed by their mad emperor, and his grisly end. They each shared their gratitude for his intervention in saving their city, and his slaying of General Yonig upon the north wall of Mosar. It seemed so long ago to Terin, as if it were a different lifetime. He spared a glance to his left where Carbanc, son of Hukok, was instructing Aldo how to use his ax, the powerful ape swinging it with great effect. It was but one of many odd pairings that repeated itself every day throughout their journey. He had come to know so many of his new comrades, nearly all of them if he were to guess, though many names still escaped him. Unfortunately, everyone knew his name, and he hated to disappoint them when he couldn't reciprocate when they greeted him. None held a grudge if he forgot or never knew their names, though he took it to heart. Everyone in their company was worthy of remembrance, and he hoped their names were recorded for posterity, so they might be honored through the ages. It was the least they should expect for sacrificing their lives for the sake of everyone else.

Sacrifice. The word tore at him as he looked around, knowing every face he saw was doomed to perish. These were good men and women, and Apes and Jenaii, the kindest of souls, if he were to rightly guess. He looked to the stars above, beseeching Yah to spare them.

Take me, Oh Yah! he silently prayed, willing to offer himself for the rest if Yah would agree. He came to love them, all of them, so much so that he nearly wept.

Elos sensed his thoughts, sharing a look with his friend. The two of them grew exceptionally close as of late. Their swords were growing heavier throughout their trek, nearly the weight of a common blade now. They were both completely subdued, their blades growing darker as they drew closer to the Nameless Mountains, the foreboding peaks looming ominously nigh. Another strange observance was the swords flickering in shades of blue and green whenever they drew close to one another. They felt lighter as well whenever they were near, almost as if they were meant to be used in concert. In fact, it was the only way they retained much of their power. What this meant, he did not know.

I don't know, he sighed, realizing how little he truly did know, if anything. Why were they marching to the heart of gargoyle power? Why did their swords grower weaker as they drew closer to their destination? Weren't the swords created to slay gargoyles? Why would they fail as they neared their ancestral nesting grounds? Why were those chosen, chosen at all? Why was he chosen? There was nothing special about him, other than his Kalinian blood, and that was by no merit of his own. Who was he that destiny ordained such a prestigious role? All he truly wanted was Corry, to live a quiet life with her away from the pomp and ceremony of court, to live out their days in peace. He loved her so much it hurt, and longed to see her again, but alas, it was not to be. He asked Yah to send her another, someone to share her life with once he perished. He didn't want his sacrifice to mean nothing to her, and if she lived out her days alone until old age took her, then his sacrifice was for everyone else, and not for her.

It was Gorzak who drew Terin from his melancholy, the ape warrior joining them at their cook fire, noticing their dour faces.

"Aye, my lads, how about a spirited ape song to lift your spirits?" Gorzak bellowed, slapping Elos on the shoulder, nearly knocking him from his feet. To Elos' credit he took no offense, knowing the apes' affinity for such familiar gestures.

"That would be agreeable, friend Gorzak," Elos said, sharing a look with Terin.

"Aye, that's the spirit, my Jenaii friend. How about the *Last Keg of Ardar*?" he suggested, wishing they had real ale to drink whilst they sang.

"I never heard that one," one of the Yatins said.

"Well, gather round and lend a voice, and I'll learn you the words!" Gorzak bellowed.

"Ardar was a chieftain
An ape of many years
He took a wife who scowled
And sent the tribe to tears…"

Terin laughed as the other apes gathered about, joining in the bawdy song, soon joined by the Yatins and others gathering about. It was a welcome respite from their troubles, a precious moment in time to savor.

* * *

Benotrist encampment. 10ᵗʰ Legion.
Twelve leagues west of the Chosen.

Nels Draken made his way to the emperor's pavilion, having just arrived from Fera, where he left the garrison telnics he brought from Tinsay. The camp was bustling with activity, soldiers moving to and fro, attending a myriad of tasks as he moved briskly around their cook fires. Most of these men were veterans of the Torry Campaign, where most of their comrades fell in battle. They were seasoned soldiers who no longer rushed headlong into battle but moved with calm precision. He heard the rumors of what they endured during their long retreat, dispirited and starving, held together by the tenacity and experience of their general, the famed Gavis. Whispers swirled through the ranks of their hatred for Morac, most blaming their defeat on his actions throughout the campaign, likely encouraged by their general's dislike for the son of Morca. The men's spirit seemed to lift with the arrival of the emperor, who would fight beside them in the battle ahead. They were further motivated by the defense of their homeland, where the stakes could not be graver.

He passed through the inner perimeter, displaying his sigil of the emperor's elite before entering, and then again at the pavilion, before entering. He was struck by how few elite he encountered as of late, many having perished in the battles at Corell. He wondered where Thorton and Zelo were, hoping to see them at the emperor's side, but alas, that was not to be.

"My Emperor." Nels bowed deeply upon entering, finding Tyro standing across from him with a table between them, where gathered Gavis and his commanders of rank.

"Draken, I assume you have delivered the reinforcements to Fera?" Tyro asked.

"I have. The palace is well fortified should Queen Letha and her alliance test its walls," Nels said, taking his place on the opposite side of the table. With the Tinsay garrison positioned at Fera, Tyro decided against consolidating them with the Laycrom garrison into a third legion. With the sudden appearance of the Chosen, those plans were now set aside.

"Very good. Continue General Naruv," Tyro ordered his magantor commander, who was is in the middle of his report to the emperor when Nels appeared.

"As per your last order, Lord Morac is leading the 13th Legion due east from Plateres. They are currently forty leagues northeast of our position, and shall soon attain the Oddigem valley," General Naruv stated, pointing out the northern approaches of the wide valley, where the enemy was likely to enter.

"Lord Morac understands his orders?" Tyro asked.

"Yes, My Emperor. He is to enter the valley from the north, moving south through the vale and position the 13th Legion… here," General Naruv said, indicating the Nasser Pass, the narrow passageway along the vale's eastern ridge. It was the only direct route to enter the vale from the east. It was a dangerous, winding causeway, that narrowed to the width of ten men standing abreast at several critical points. Any army attempting to cross through it, could be bottled up by a much smaller force.

"And the latest sightings on the enemy to our east?" Tyro asked, his gaze sweeping the regions surrounding Mordicay, where Corry's host was last sighted.

"We lost two magantors patrolling the western approaches of Mordicay in the last day. Before then we spotted a large host marching west, the force including Macons, Torries, Casians and Jenaii. We placed their number from forty to sixty telnics," Naruv said, the size of the host drawing a chorus of moans from the telnic commanders gathered around the table. A stern look from General Gavis put an end to such weakness.

"They will likely enter the Oddigem Valley from the north, and will first seize Darcol, using it to support their lines of communication," Gavis said, pointing out Darcol on the map, the key trading hub north of the Oddigem Valley.

"Shall we meet them in battle at Darcol?" General Naruv asked, looking to Gavis and then to the emperor.

"No. The path to Oddigem shall remain open. Let them fully enter, along with the armies Queen Letha is bringing from the west," Tyro said, his words taking the others aback, save Gavis, who was apprised of the emperor's change in strategy.

"Your Majesty?" General Naruv asked.

"We move as one. We shall follow these few cohorts that are led by the Torry Champion northward. You are not to engage them. By the direction of travel of the other armies, it appears they are all heading for the same place… Oddigem. For what reason, I can only surmise, but I would guess it to be the destruction of the gargoyle breeding grounds." Tyro's words sent a chorus of whispers around the table, before they were silenced by Gavis' stern look.

Tyro's gaze fixed sternly on the marker representing Terin and his companions, their location invitingly close on the map. His plan to sweep him up along with the others was set aside for a new strategy, allowing them to enter Oddigem. He feared allowing Terin to draw near the gargoyle nesting grounds, knowing he could not control the creatures' bloodlust once the battle was joined. Such fear was overtaken by his dreams of late, the fate of his realm now resting on the valley floor in the shadow of the Nameless Mountains, with one word whispering over and again in his mind… *Noddegamra*. It was the fabled battle marking the end of days, a tale told to frighten children when they misbehaved or cater to the addled minds of doomsayers. No matter the reason of its purpose, it was where his fate was to be decided, and Terin needed to be there for that to happen, not bound in the chains he would clap him in. He wanted nothing more than to seize the boy and send him off somewhere safe to secure Joriah's compliance, but that was beyond him now. Terin needed to lead his pitiful band of malcontents to Oddigem, setting the stage for the final battle. Why this was so, he did not know, but there it was, and he could not change that now.

And so it is, he mentally whispered, relenting to his fate, and following his destiny.

"And our legion?" one commander of telnic asked, wondering their course of travel.

"We follow the Torry Champion and his group to Oddigem, where we wait upon his comrades," General Gavis said, moving the marker representing the 10th Legion to the Oddigem Valley, before setting Queen Letha's army and Princess Corry's army there as well.

* * *

Nels Draken remained at the behest of Tyro as the others filed out, the emperor waiting for the last to exit before ordering him closer.

"One trait I value over any other in my commanders, and especially my elite, is loyalty. Having led our armies in battle since the earliest days of our revolution, I have been a good judge of character, knowing who I can trust and who I must manage. Some questioned my wisdom when I recruited free swords into the elite. Of course, such criticism was never spoken in my presence, but I have ears that know," Tyro said, regarding Draken with a discerning look.

"I hope I have proven my loyalty, My Emperor," Nels said evenly, unable to think of any disloyalty on his part. One could never know if they had enemies at court that might manufacture false evidence to condemn you.

"If I doubted your loyalty at this time, you would already be dead. No, you have proven loyal, Draken. You have demonstrated both martial and political acumen, and as you know, both skills are required in a high elite. One might question your success rate, or lack thereof, but considering most of your failures came at the hand of my daughter's insufferable husband, I cannot hold you to account." Tyro sighed, pouring them both a drink of wine in two goblets set upon the table.

"You are most merciful, My Emperor," Nels said, receiving the drink from Tyro and partaking.

"Aye, I expect this war might have gone differently had the Earthers crashed on a different world, sparing us their interference," Tyro snorted.

"Such is fate. Do you wish to hear of my actions at Tinsay?" Nels asked.

"I have read your missives. You delivered the city garrison to Fera. That should convince Letha to forgo an attack there."

"Leaving open the path to Oddigem, if she does what you expect," Nels said, wondering at that.

"A woman never does what you expect, but I see no other choice for her to exploit, not when every other army seems headed in that direction. The fate of the war shall be decided there, and that is why I wished to speak with you. I will have need of loyal men at my side in the coming battle. I count you among them."

"I am honored by your trust, My Emperor."

"Very good. A place has been prepared for you to sleep this night. We have another long march ahead of us on the morrow."

With that, Nels Draken bowed and withdrew, leaving Tyro alone in his command pavilion. He stood there for a time, the light of the basin torches illuminating his face in a ghastly pall, reflecting his tortured soul. He carefully drew his swords from their scabbards, holding them apart, their once vibrant blades now murky and dull. They felt heavier now, nearly the weight of a common blade. He wondered the cause. It could portend a myriad of possibilities, and none of them to his benefit. He wondered if his swords were afflicted, were the others similarly corrupted? He felt the pull of the swords drawing themselves together, touching the point of one blade to the other, shoots of gold flickering along their length wherever they touched. He noticed they felt lighter the closer they were near one another, pondering the meaning of this as well. He expected no answer this night, wondering when such questions would be revealed.

Oddigem, he reminded himself. It was Oddigem where all truths would be laid bare.

* * *

West of Fera.

The eastern sky was ablaze with the morning sun as Queen Letha narrowed her eyes against the horizon. The Yatin outriders scouting the terrain ahead returned with strange tidings, causing her to ride to the head of the column, where the Torry 4th Army formed the vanguard of their combined host. There she was joined by General Farro of the Torry 4th Army, and General Yitia, commander of the Yatin 2nd Army. They waited upon a low rise overlooking the east-west road that passed below its northern face, where their column halted, awaiting their decision. The way east was clear, the road running over flat barren terrain, before disappearing between the hills ahead. To her trained eye, the way ahead looked like a trap, where they would be set upon once crossing between the hills. She traveled this road once before, during her courtship with Taleron, visiting his imperial fortress, and recalling the unforgiving countryside that surrounded the palace. Just beyond the hills ahead, the road split, the southern branch leading to Fera, the northern branch skirting the Black Castle, leading north of the Nameless Mountains toward Mordicay.

She listened attentively as the Yatin scouts relayed their findings, revealing the path ahead to be clear along either route of travel. Their magantors earlier discovered the 13th Benotrist Legion marching east, approaching the Nameless Mountains from the north, while the 10th Legion skirted the western foothills of said mountains.

"We believe Fera to have been reinforced by the telnics of the Tinsay garrison, Oh Queen," one outrider said, confirming her suspicions. Fera was already heavily garrisoned before the new arrivals. Tyro obviously wanted her to remove any possibility of laying siege, leaving only the northern route open to her. The scouts found no enemy waiting for them in the hills ahead, especially with all of Tyro's strength now moving north and east, but to where?

"We know where they are going," General Yitia snorted, recalling his dreams of late, dreams that they all have shared.

"Oddigem," General Farro added, emphasizing the source of all their visions.

Letha sighed, feeling the weight of her sword upon her hip, even in the saddle, as if the ancient blade was growing heavier with every step they drew closer to their destination. Weighing heavier than her sword was the decision that lay before them. Assailing Fera was impossible considering their numbers and those of the garrison. That left only to remain in place in order to draw the enemy from the Chosen's path, or to march for Oddigem. The enemy showed no interest in coming to them, and if they remained here, the enemy would gladly let them.

No, there was only one choice left to them, the very choice that was made for everyone taking part in this grand game.

"We march for Oddigem." Letha relented, the others strangely agreeing, no one raising the slightest objection. It was as if they were becoming of one mind on the matter.

* * *

One day hence.

Morac drew alongside General Trinapolis. His lathered mount panting in the warm autumn air. The 13th Legion and the men of the Laycrom garrison were stretched out in long columns to their rear, marching apace through the mouth of the Oddigem Valley. The valley floor stretched endlessly before them, a sea of discolored grass and dark rocks strewn across their morbid surface. Aligned to either flank were the jagged slopes forming the valley ridgelines, each running almost straight north, one east and one west, stretching north in a continuous unbroken line, both foreboding and unforgiving, save for the narrow passage along the eastern ridge, the Nasser Pass. Other than that dangerous route, both ridgelines were impassable by human armies. Only Jenaii and gargoyles could attain their perilous slopes. A narrow stream meandered the center of the vale, its turbid waters fouled upon passing through the gargoyle nesting grounds resting to their south, along the base of the foothills skirting the northern face of the Nameless Mountains.

"General, advance to the Nasser Pass, and position the Laycrom garrison to guard it. Then camp your army just west of them," Morac ordered, the Nasser Pass resting nearly halfway south along the eastern ridge of the valley.

"Aye, in accordance with the emperor's wishes," General Trinapolis said, gauging Morac's disagreement with this strategy.

"Yes, just as the emperor has ordered," Morac said, his gaze fixed southward, where the foothills rested in the distance, and the towering peaks of the Nameless Mountains loomed ominously behind them.

"I sense you would have chosen otherwise, if the decision was yours, my Lord Morac," Trinapolis said.

"I would have destroyed the small band of interlopers as soon as they appeared, and then moved in unison upon Queen Letha, before gathering the gargoyles to attack the enemy drawing from the east, destroying each in detail. Now we are all gathering to this one point, the fate of everything decided at this dreary place."

"The emperor must have a reason for choosing this battlefield, but I agree with your assessment. I too would have destroyed the enemy in detail than risk them coming together."

"Your loyalty to my father and his house is noted, General."

"I shall follow the son of Morca wherever he leads," Trinapolis said.

"And do your subordinates share your leanings?" Morac asked.

"Every commander of Unit and above, for I have so placed them," the general answered.

Morac nodded, he and the general sharing one mind on many things, particularly their concerns of a certain Torry warrior that held favor in the emperor's eye. His spies reported nothing new in this regard, still unaware of Tyro's naming the Princess Cordela his heir.

"Lead the men to their encampment while I attend another matter," Morac ordered, riding alone south through the valley floor.

* * *

It was midday when Morac reached the northern foothills of the Nameless Mountains, where gathered untold thousands of gargoyle warriors along their weathered slopes. From here he could make out the long line of fortifications built atop the hillsides, stretching across the breadth of a dozen hills, forged of stone cut from the mountains. The structures were simply built, but sturdy, able to weather the harsh environs of this cruel landscape. Stone towers the height of three men dotted the hilltops, connected by a lower wall between them, stretching from hillside to hillside, the heads of gargoyles peaking above their crude ramparts.

He eased his ocran to slow canter before halting at a distance, as his presence was detected. A hush fell over the grand assembly, each creature upon the hillsides stopping in place, staring at him in eerie silence. From afar they appeared as insects, their dark wings silhouetted against the backdrop of the gray slopes of the foreboding Mountains behind them. He knew what awaited below the reverse slopes of those foothills, the fabled nesting grounds of the gargoyles. 'Twas a place only one man had ever trod in the last thirty years, the one man to have forged an alliance with the creatures, the very creatures that turned the tide of their revolution so long ago.

He briefly questioned the wisdom of coming here, considering the state of their uneasy alliance. The last time he saw gargoyles was at Notsu, where Kriton betrayed him, forsaking him and fleeing the battlefield, to come here. Since that fateful night, gargoyles from across the empire abandoned their posts, heeding a mysterious spirit calling them home.

Home. He pondered the greater meaning of these nesting grounds to the gargoyles. They were the fabled place of origin of their kind, where a thousand generations were spawned from these ancient hills long before the days of Kal. Even that great king of old could not drive them from this fell place. Only the Tarelians of old achieved that, their first king Clorvis Cal founding the Northern Kingdom, constructing Fera and driving the gargoyles from this Valley. Those were the days of woe for the gargoyles, cursing the Tarelian King and the fiery golden sword he wielded to achieve that aim. Their ancestral lands were not returned to them until Tyro led them to victory over the hated Menotrists, restoring the gargoyles' birthright.

Now the sword of Clorvis Cal was his, the very bane of the gargoyles in the hand of their ally, but would they see him as such? Would they forsake the emperor if he favored another, the very enemy of their kind, the Torry warrior he harbored at Fera? He took a great risk coming here, stepping on dangerous ground. He took a deep breath before advancing.

* * *

"We follow the Nordhenz. We must answer his call!" Lord Regula proclaimed before the assembly of chieftains gathered in the great hall, a crudely built chamber cut from the base of the hillside ages past. The gargoyles of old built a series of structures, all cut from the rocky terrain at the base along the reverse slopes of the foothills, and the forward slopes of the hills to their south, with a stream running between them before breaking north between two of the lower hills and continuing north through the Oddigem Vale.

The hall of chieftains was squarish in shape, cut crudely from the rocky hillside, with simple block columns liberally spaced to reinforce its unstable ceiling. There were no fine adornments carved into the ceiling, or smooth stone floor to denote its grand importance. It was large and boasted simple torches bracketed into its uneven, rocky walls. It was here where the chieftains assembled day after day since the summoning gathered the gargoyles to their ancestral home. Greatest among them was Regula, Tyro's second, and chief minister of the empire. He was the grand chieftain, whose word was law to their brethren, their loyalty to him equal to his loyalty to Tyro. The Nordhenz was the human foretold to restore the gargoyles to prominence among the nations, to raise them to their rightful place upon Arax. Tyro was so named, receiving the appellation of Nordhenz upon his victory over the hated Menotrists, and returning these nesting grounds to the gargoyle tribes.

"The Nordhenz has fulfilled his quest. He has returned us to our ancestral grounds, these hallowed temples forged by our ancestors. We must now look to our own future, our own path, our own destiny," Kriton countered, his voice clear and void of any guttural hiss. He stood apart from the chieftains, wearing his blood red tunic and gray mail, his pointed ears arcing from the sides of his steel helm. The chieftains stood in contrast, wearing robes of human skin, layer upon layer, trophies taken in battle from their kills. Regula's raiment was further apart, adorned in the vestment of his imperial station, calnesian robes of crimson and cape of black, his rich attire meant to impress upon them his regal authority.

"Your words are treasonous, Kriton. You shall not ascend the council of chieftains until your generation of guardians comes of age. You stand here among the chieftains as a guest, nothing more," Regula admonished.

Kriton snarled, his lips retracting ever briefly, baring his fangs. He was invited to this council for leading their beleaguered remnants from Notsu, saving them from certain destruction, gaining their loyalty. Those telnics represented a large portion of the warriors that answered the summoning, joining the guardians of the nesting grounds, who numbered twenty telnics in their own right. Their swelling ranks now boasted one hundred and forty telnics, gathered from Notsu, Yatin and every part of the realm, drawn from the visions that plagued them without cease.

"I wouldsss hearsss his words, Grand Chieftain," Chief Snarzak hissed, his eyes aglow.

"I have seen where we must go. There is a land beyond our northern shores, a land we can escape to and build an empire unrivaled, far beyond the reach of man. From there we can renew our strength and one day return and conquer Arax with numbers so great that no human army can contend," Kriton managed to say without hissing, succeeding in calming his ire.

They debated the meaning of Kriton's vision, weighing the possibilities of new nesting grounds, ones he claimed are many fold grander than their own. Some favored the advantage of their own continent, a place to husband their strength unmolested by human interference. Others questioned where they might find enough ships to take them there, or the mariners to man them. They were aware of the sorry state of the imperial navy, rumors spreading of their losses to the east and west.

"Our place is here, our time is now. We cannot flee and hope for a better time to return to these shores, even if we could find the ships to take us there, which we cannot. And what shall the humans do in our absence? What great power might they gather without our interference? They might finally unite under one banner, as they almost achieved in the days of Kal. No, we must keep our alliance with Tyro, and forge an empire unrivaled, gargoyles and men united forever, just as Tyro and I have sworn oaths of brotherhood," Lord Regula proclaimed, his words finding purchase with most of the chieftains.

Kriton thought how to refute this, struggling to find the words when fate intervened.

"A human approaches!" a warrior hissed, entering the great hall.

* * *

It was as Morac foresaw in his visions as he passed through the wall linking two of the hills. He followed his escort, a unit of gargoyle guardians clad in heavy mail, armed with spears with short straight swords sheathed upon their left hips. These were deadly, well-trained warriors, the strongest of their kind, chosen to guard their sacred grounds. Once beyond the gate, they turned left, passing between two lines of foothills, one to the north and one to the south, with an onrushing stream passing between them. The path was covered with fat stones embedded into the soil, easing travel during the rainy season. At the base of each hill facing the path were large openings cut from the rocky slopes, many leading to larger caverns within. He spared a glance to his right, where stood two juvenile gargoyles at the mouth of a cave, brandishing spears, watching him pass with keen interest.

Before he passed the first series of hills, thousands of gargoyles emerged along the opposing hillsides, many spilling out of the caverns that lined their slopes. Many were warriors, similar to his escort in their weapons and carriage. Many others were veterans of his Torry campaign, wearing the red tunics and gray helms of their legions, each bearing a scimitar rather than the straight swords and spears of the guardians. He noticed the stark difference between them, with the guardians' superior carriage and weapons. He recalled what he knew of their customs, where the strongest of their warriors were ranked as guardians and given breeding privilege with their females. The greatest of the guardians were chosen as chieftains, and some placed to lead legions. He wrongly believed common gargoyles could earn ascension to guardians through battle, rising to the rank of general. But the darker truth he did not know was the guardians were the survivors of the previous summoning. With every generation, the adult male gargoyles return to their nesting grounds and fight to the death until twenty thousand remain, who are selected as guardians. Upon their ascension, the previous guardians would lead their spawn into the world, the greatest among them named chieftains. It was during his days leading his warriors in battle that Regula was waylaid by a Menotrist warlord and taken captive, before he was saved and set free by Tyro. It was at that moment the two formed their bond, joining their strength to overthrow the Menotrists.

He knew Kriton was also unique as he was the champion of the guardians before his placement in Tyro's elite, the greatest of their kind. Every generation of summoning had one champion, though said champion was not named a chieftain until he led his spawn from their nesting grounds. Kriton was swiftly placed in Tyro's elite two years after surviving his summoning, leaving his breeding duties and guardianship for imperial service. Had he remained, he would be among the current guardians waiting for their sons to reach maturity before leading them into battle. Only then could he attain the rank of chieftain.

Kriton's place among Tyro's elite afforded him greater privilege and power than most chieftains, who mostly formed the commanding ranks of the gargoyle legions, setting hm apart from his elders, and a source of animosity from the chieftains. Only Regula superseded him as the emperor's second, and as the grand chieftain.

Kriton, Morac bitterly recalled his betrayal at Notsu but had to relent of it, for he needed his help for the grim work ahead. Morac had dreams of late, dreams of his sword and how to reawaken its waning power. If he drew his blade from its scabbard, it would betray its now dull state to the thousands of eyes watching him ride through their sacred grounds. His dream was implicit, revealing the only path to restoring his sword to its former glory. He needed the other Swords of Light. Only by bringing them together could he restore his own. He would have the heads of those who wielded them and their swords to have as his own. He also saw in his vision the swords converging upon this valley, before these very hills.

Most convenient, he mused wickedly, amused that his enemies might be kind enough to bring themselves within the shadow of the Nameless Mountains, where he could easily destroy them. Of course, he needed the gargoyles to play their part in this. While his foes were occupied with the gargoyles, he would be free to dispatch them in detail, taking one sword after another.

He was so lost in his musings he nearly forgot where he trod, noticing the great multitudes emerge from the caverns to his right and left, winged warriors and juveniles and…

Of all the unsettling sights Morac had ever beheld, seeing a gargoyle lass was most disturbing of all. There along the opposite side of the stream stood several of the creatures, smaller than their male counterparts, wingless, with pasty white flesh, leathery and taut. Their eyes were vacant, pure white as they stared at him. No, they were only staring in his direction, following the sound of his ocran's hooves as he passed. They were blind, seeing only through sound, their heads turning as he passed. They were slight of stature, wearing simple black tunics that barely covered their upper thighs. Their fangs were less prominent than their brothers' but viciously sharp, as were their clawed digits. He thought they might rend a man with their bare hands.

He came upon more and more of the strange creatures as he advanced, hundreds now emerging from their subterranean holdfasts, drawn by his presence. He found their sightless eyes unnerving as they stared at him, as if they could see him, their senses attuned to any change in their foul environment. Despite the hundreds of females, tens of thousands of male gargoyles now lined the slopes of the foothills as if summoned from every crevice and crack in the hellish landscape, each staring intently as Morac trod. He wondered where they found the food to feed these untold masses. He stole a glance skyward where the late day sun broke through the dark clouds above, eerily reflecting the fell nature of these fabled grounds. His nostrils twisted with the foul air, thankful whenever a strong breeze swept down from the mountains to clear the stench. He thought no human could long endure the odor, quickly succumbing if exposed.

At last his journey bore fruit as he caught sight of Kriton and Regula and many others of great renown emerging from an impressive structure cut from the stony slope of the hillside off his left.

"What brings you to our sacred grounds, Morac, son of Morca?" Regula asked, standing forward of the others, regarding him suspiciously.

"I have foreseen our future and the danger that threatens us all, Lord Regula. I offer parlay to discuss these most urgent affairs." Morac smiled, looking past Regula to Kriton, knowing what the gargoyle warrior sought and where he could find them… ships, and the crews to man them. He could arrange that in return for a favor.

"Are you here by the emperor's command?" Regula asked harshly, doubting it was so.

"These are matters that have come recently to my attention, my Lord Regula. But I assure your eminence, the emperor shall soon learn of them."

* * *

The Northern Coast, due north of the Nameless Mountains.

The masts of six thousand ships covered the horizon, their dark sails full with the wind, driving them toward the barren shore. The images of gargoyle maidens carved upon their bows broke the surf, waves crashing upon their naked breasts. Upon their serried decks stood untold legions, their crimson eyes ablaze for war and bloodlust, staring hungrily to the lands ahead, the promise of slaughter and death waiting enticingly nigh. They waited upon their decks in eerie silence, waiting expectantly as the rocky coastline filled the horizon, thousands of years of planning coming swiftly upon them. Upon the lead ship their great war chief stood, their ancient war chant repeating on his lips, before his followers picked up the morbid refrain. Their voices sounded above the waves, drifting ship to ship, until the entire armada joined in the dreary mantra, their guttural chants echoing hauntingly in the salty air.

> *The time of our reckoning has drawn near*
> *The time of our ascension has drawn nigh*
> *Vengeance, mutilation, death chants cry*
> *Flesh of man, flesh of Jenaii*
> *Devour the favored sons of Yah*
> *Slay them child, lass and all*

There upon the Northern Coast of Arax, the great horde set ashore, spilling from the holds of their fell armada to wage war upon the realms of men.

* * *

The following morn found Corry and her coalition arriving at Darcol, the small trading hub twelve leagues north of the Oddigem Valley, straddling the road connecting Fera and Mordicay, and all points between. Wind Racer set down along the outskirts of the village, where Torg and a flax of General Connly's cavalry awaited her. She swiftly dismounted, growing accustomed to doing so since bonding with the great avian. She softly rubbed his feathered neck, the warbird gently nudging her with his massive beak, before she stepped away to treat with Torg.

"You have made a friend, I see." Torg gave her a rare smile.

"A very good friend." Corry returned his smile, regarding the powerful avian as Torg dismounted in turn.

Corry spared a glance to their surroundings, where their armies continued to move through the village to their immediate south. The lands surrounding Darcol were a collage of grassy fields and forests, with several rocky, uneven grounds interspersed between them. Their leading elements already passed through the village, taking up positions west and south of Darcol. The brisk autumn weather made for pleasant travel in recent days, neither cold nor hot, a welcome respite to the summer heat that plagued them at the outset of the campaign.

"What is the latest from Brokov?" she asked. They were surprised to learn of the vast numbers of gargoyles dwelling along the northern foothills of the Nameless Mountains, which Brokov's reconnaissance discovered in recent days. His following reports detailed the extent of the gargoyle presence, describing wingless white creatures that he surmised to be females of the species. His most recent finding was the arrival of the Benotrist 13th Legion, which took up position along the western edge of the Oddigem Valley, guarding the narrow pass there. Dar Valen's magantors spotted another legion advancing north along the western face of the Nameless Mountains. Brokov investigated these movements as well, marking the advance of the 10th Benotrist Legion, the very legion that escaped them at Notsu.

"The 10th Legion is just south of us and appear to be entering the valley to join the 13th," Torg said.

"Are they blind? Why do they not engage us?" she growled. That was the purpose of their advance, to draw Tyro's eye, and yet the further they marched, the further Tyro withdrew.

"They are not blind to us. Their magantors have spied our advance long before we reached Vateris. They seem to think we shall enter the Oddigem and fight them there," Torg said, unable to think of any other reason for their strange behavior.

"We might have exposed our neck for them to strike, but they must know we are not foolish enough to do so, so brazenly. Why should we march to them when we can cut their supply routes to the Oddigem and let them starve? I doubt they have enough provisions there for their army," she pointed out.

"Perhaps they are having dreams of that fell place as we are." Torg scrubbed his chin with his hand.

Corry wondered at that, recalling the awful visions now plaguing them all, of a great battle in a dreary place, a place many now believed to be Oddigem. Brokov's discovery of gargoyles there only fueled such beliefs.

"Can any of this be real? What madness has overcome the world?"

"Aye, but that is where they are concentrating, and for some reason another great host is heading there as well," Torg said.

"Who?"

"Queen Letha. She is leading nearly sixty telnics of Yatins, Torries and Sisterhood troops. They are close on the heels of the 10th Legion, just to our southwest. Our magantors have come across their scouts. We have two of them in Darcol, waiting for an audience."

"Are they Sisterhood or Torry?" she curiously asked.

"Sisterhood. Lucella is with them now," he said, referencing Captain Lucella Sarelis of Queen Letha's personal guard, and leader of the Sisterhood magantors that had fought by their side since Corell.

"Take me to them."

* * *

Corry made her way to the village square, maneuvering through the river of soldiers swarming the causeways of Darcol, before coming upon the merchant exchange in the center of the trading hub. Torry warriors were posted around the impressive structure, saluting with their fists to their chests as she entered. Torg preceded her, he and his escort clearing the way. The main floor of the exchange was a large open chamber with a stone floor and sturdy timber walls and ceiling, with a large hearth upon the far wall. There she was greeted by two magantor scouts wearing the livery of the sisterhood, each taking a knee as she drew nigh, before she ordered them to stand. They were joined by King El Anthar, and Zem, who seemed to be everywhere as of late. The other Earthers were elsewhere, with Lorken patrolling their perimeter, and Raven away to the east with General Matuzak.

"Princess Corry, we bring salutations from Queen Letha. She is presently to your southwest, trailing the 10th Legion and strongly reinforced with the 4th Torry Army and the Yatin 2nd," the magantor rider said.

Upon that revelation, Torg ordered a table to be brought forth, unfurling a map of the region across it as Corry and the others gathered round.

"We have outriders here, here and there," Torg said, pointing out locations several leagues southeast to southwest, covering the northern approaches of the Oddigem Valley.

"And they have seen no sign of enemy movement," one of Torg's aides added.

"Not a one. But that doesn't mean they are not there, but it does give us a good view up to six leagues south. The Oddigem is a very wide and flat valley with severe ridgelines running north from their foothills. You can only enter from the north, save for a small passageway through the east ridgeline, situated nearly two thirds distance southward right… here." Torg pointed out the Nasser Pass, which their new Benotrist allies revealed to him, and Brokov confirmed through his reconnaissance.

"How large is that passage?" Corry asked.

"It narrows to a width of five meters in three separate places, greatly hindering large movements through its confines," Zem pointed out, having reviewed Brokov's live feed from the discs that scouted the region.

"That would make the enemy trapped within the vale?" Corry asked.

"Perhaps, but we do not know the state of their provisions, or the preparations they have made before marching there," Zem pointed out.

"Then why should we oblige them by entering the vale?" Corry shuddered to think of facing two Benotrist legions within the shadow of the gargoyle nesting grounds, where they could be set upon by hundreds of thousands of the creatures taking flight from the heights of the foothills.

"That decision can wait if we first consolidate our forces," Torg advised.

"That would be the wiser choice. Queen Letha should join us here while we fully assess the enemy's strength and disposition," Corry suggested.

"We shall inform her upon our return, Your Highness." The Sisterhood rider again bowed.

"I shall return with you. I need to apprise our queen of all that has transpired since our departure," Lucella added.

"Should Tosha go with you? I am certain Queen Letha would be thankful to see her," Corry advised.

"That should wait as she is still to our east," Torg said, tapping the map where Matuzak's armies rested, a day's march to their east. Matuzak's armies trailed them since he broke off to seize Mordicay. Though Tosha and Raven could race ahead on their air ski, the magantor riders needed to leave now to hasten Queen Letha's movement.

"True," Corry conceded, knowing the urgency of communicating with Queen Letha of their intentions.

"I strongly suggest you send one of our comms with your riders, Captain Sarelis," Zem said, the others agreeing with his logic.

"I will have the one Lorken gave me and will demonstrate its function to our queen," Lucella said.

"Very well, go with all haste, and we shall apprise Tosha of her mother's arrival," Corry said, her gaze returning to the map, wondering where Terin was in all this confusion? Was he already captured? Was he dea… no, she would not contemplate that. Part of her wondered if Yah might punish Terin and the Chosen for her disobedience for interfering. She intended to draw Tyro away from the Chosen, nothing more, but her every advance was met with Benotrist withdrawal, forcing her to continue into Tyro's realm. Then again, perhaps she had finally accomplished what she desired, bringing Tyro to battle, freeing the Chosen to do whatever Yah intended them to do. She smiled internally at that, hopeful that she might have saved them by leading these armies to face Tyro. Perhaps it was not the Chosen's place to die for all of them, but for them to die for the Chosen. If that were so, she would gladly suffer it. She would die for him if the price were required. All of her fanciful thoughts were quickly thrown to chaos with Brokov's sudden utterance just as Lucella was about to depart.

"*Torg, I've found them.*" Brokov's voice echoed through the comm.

"Found who?" Torg made a face, raising the comm to his lips.

"*Your Chosen.*"

CHAPTER 11

"The Chosen."

Brokov's words took her breath, freezing time as Corry's voice failed her. Her initial shock quickly gave way to a thousand questions, so many she didn't know where to begin.

"Are they alive?" Torg asked before she could.

"They look pretty alive to me, though I don't know for how much longer." Brokov's cryptic answer swiftly focused Corry's thoughts.

"What do you mean? Where are they?" Corry sharply asked.

"They are close by, marching south through the middle of the Odd-igem Valley."

"What!" Corry exploded.

"Marching through the Oddigem? Were they captured?" Torg asked, unable to think of any way they could be on that open ground without being seen, especially with two full legions of Benotrists close by and untold numbers of gargoyles waiting along the foothills further south.

"That's the strange thing, Torg. They are simply marching through the middle of the valley unopposed. The Benotrists know they are there. The 10th Legion is following them into the valley, while the 13th awaits them near the Nasser Pass. Don't forget the thousands of gargoyles crowding the foothills farther ahead."

Brokov's bleak report cast a pall over the chamber.

Corry's heart sank, all her plans gone for naught. All their advance had accomplished was to push the enemy's strength into this forsaken valley where the Chosen happened to wander. What hope had they now? What course could she take to save them?

The others had no immediate answer, no one saying a word, each bereft of advice.

"We should gather our commanders and plan accordingly," Torg finally said.

"There is no time." Corry shook her head.

"Then we make time," Torg countered.

"No, Torg, there is no time. I cannot speak for the others, but as for our armies, Lewins' 1st and Farro's 4th, give the order to march," Corry said.

"To march where?" Lucella asked.

"To the valley of death. We march into oblivion to fight beside our friends and kin, to live or die by the mercy of Yah. They will not stand alone," Corry declared, sharing a look with Torg, who gazed upon her proudly.

"My battlegroups are with you," King El Anthar proclaimed.

"We are with you as well, Princess Corry. You are truly a daughter of the Sisterhood," Lucella said, thrusting her fist to her breast, saluting the Torry princess.

"*Corry, Raven and Tosha are on their way, but Matuzak, the apes and Enoructans are too far away to make it on time.*" Brokov's voice echoed through the comm.

"Tell them to hurry, for we cannot wait," Corry said, making her way for the door.

* * *

Word quickly spread, with every warrior sharing Corry's zeal for battle. General Ciyon immediately gave the order to advance, Guilen eager to join him, determined to save his sister. Lorken quickly returned from his patrol, before taking off again to meet Raven, who was fast approaching from the east. Alen gathered his rebel cohorts, now numbering eight telnics, their numbers swelling throughout their advance from Nisin, marching forth, eager to give battle. Their new Benotrist allies marched beside them under the banner of a glowing azure sword upon a field of silver, the sigil heralding Terin as their king, though half of their telnics were currently enroute with Matuzak. King Lichu honored his vows, marching south without protest, eager to fulfill his duty and return home or die with honor battling the scourge of mankind. And so it went, with their entire host turning sharply south, marching with all haste to reach the battlefield in time. Lucella joined her sister magantor riders, hurrying off to seek Queen Letha, relaying Corry's intentions.

Corry ordered a small detachment to remain and secure their baggage, knowing they would slow down their advance, though no one wished that duty, each eager to give battle. Cronus drew Dougar aside as soldiers hurried to and fro in nearly every direction, marching off as soon as they formed into columns. The narrow streets of Darcol were serried with wagons and men moving through them like a river cresting its banks, giving Cronus little space or quiet to speak with his young charge. He drew him into the nearest dwelling, a small thatched home abandoned by its owners in recent days.

"I would have you remain with our supply caravans and help guard them. Can you do that for me, Dougar?" Cronus asked, taking a knee before the boy, looking at him at eye level.

"But my place is beside you. Please let me fight?" the boy pleaded, his eyes welling with tears.

"Dougar, I…I don't know if many of us will survive this. I could not bear seeing another person I care for perish. You have a full life ahead of you, a life worth living."

"But life without you is terrible also. I don't wanna be alone anymore, Cronus. I would rather die with my friends than live long without them. Please let me come with you?" Dougar begged, tears running down his small cheeks, his sad voice breaking Cronus' heart.

"I…" Cronus was a loss for words before Ilesa passed through the door, having seen them enter from her place across the way.

Cronus looked up as she stopped beside them, carrying her baby in her arms.

"Dougar, would you watch over her for me? I must go south

with the others, and I trust no one more than you to safeguard my baby," Ilesa asked.

"But you cannot go, Lady Ilesa. Your baby…" Dougar pleaded, but she shook her head.

"I must go, Dougar. There will be many wounded that will require my help," Ilesa said, holding back tears of her own as she knelt beside them, passing the baby into Dougar's arms.

"Ilesa, there is no reason for you to do this. Others can operate the regenerator. Your baby…" Cronus began to argue, but she refused.

"I MUST go, Cronus," she insisted, before looking back to Dougar, cupping his cheeks with her trembling hands. "I trust no one more than you with her life, Dougar, my brave warrior. I do not know if any of us shall survive where we are going, but should we fall, the enemy will surely come here. If they do, you must run. Do you understand? You must take her and run! Run first to one of the forests, before fleeing east. Nowhere here shall be safe, so you must keep moving," she said, setting her water satchel around his neck. She filled it with her milk and hoped it would last the day. Anything after that and he would have to improvise. It was all too much for a young boy, but what choice had she? These were the end of days, and chaos ruled their fragile lives.

Cronus thought to demand that she stay, but something held him back. There was a determination in her voice, as if there was something more at play that he could not see.

"Will you protect her, Dougar, will you be my brave warrior?" Ilesa asked, her voice breaking with emotion.

"I…I will, Lady Ilesa, I so avow," Dougar said, lifting his chin proudly, his unrelenting tears flooding his cheeks.

Ilesa smiled softly, pressing a kiss to his forehead.

* * *

Dougar stood upon a small rise east of the village, standing among a detachment of warriors and provisioners, holding the baby in his arms while watching his friends depart. There were no main roads passing south, forcing their armies to traverse the collage of grassy fields and clusters of trees that dotted the landscape. He watched as Cronus' ocran slipped from sight, taking a weathered trail crossing over the open grassy fields skirting Darcol's southern approaches. Ilesa rode beside him, each looking back one last time before passing from sight. He didn't see the Earthers, as Lorken headed due south upon meeting Raven to their east, while Zem marched alongside the Torry 1st Army. General Connly's cavalry were the first to depart, racing ahead of the infantry at the behest of the Princess. They were quickly followed by General Valen's magantors, the great avian swarming the skies above before disappearing over the horizon. Then the armies slipped from sight, the Torry 1st, General Ciyon's Macon-Torry Army, followed by the Jenaii battlegroups and the men of Teso and Zulon, and their rebel and Benotrist cohorts. He saw Criose and Culn riding alongside Torg, brandishing the rifles given them by the Earthers, weapons he was most thankful for.

Dougar sadly looked on as all his new friends passed from sight, wondering if he would ever see them again. Galen was the last to say goodbye, handing him his mandolin, asking that he watch over it, before ruffling his hair and riding off to join the others. The minstrel had two belts of daggers strapped across his shoulders, and brandished a long spear and sword, though Dougar doubted his skill in using them.

"Farewell, Dougar, my brave fellow." Galen saluted him before riding on.

"Farewell, my friend." Dougar sniffled, his voice choked with emotion as the baby fussed in his arms. Thankfully one of the washerwomen who worked with the armies' supply caravan helped him with the child, showing him how to feed her with the milk satchel Ilesa left for him. Most of the provisioners set camp just east of the village, where there was ample space for their endless train of wagons.

Dougar looked south one last time as the last of their soldiers passed from sight.

* * *

Oddigem.

Terin stood upon the valley floor, gazing south where the foothills of the Nameless Mountains loomed ominously ahead, presiding over this tortured landscape like corrupted spirits. From afar he could make out winged forms circling above the battlements lining their weathered summits, a mere trickling of the vast host waiting beyond. What untold numbers were hidden within those foothills? No less than the entirety of their fell kind, coiled to strike like a cornered serpent.

"Packaww!"

The sound of a Benotrist magantor echoed overhead, its dark wings coursing across the face of their uneven ranks, before passing to the east, where rested the might of the 13th Legion. The sky above shone bright and clear, with not a cloud in sight, a strangely beautiful day to die, but what other path awaited them but certain death as his gaze drifted to his immediate east, where stood the might of the 13th Legion, its standards lifting in the morning breeze. They stood in ordered ranks before the Nasser Pass, stretching along the eastern ridge of the valley. They silently stood there, not voicing their contempt, or throwing insults upon their hated foes. Perhaps the Benotrists thought so little of them, that such taunts seemed joyless. If he were them, he would think little of their small band as well. What threat could less than three telnics be against fifty? And the Benotrists had many more than fifty. He need only gaze in the opposite direction, where stood the might of the 10th Legion, arrayed for battle along the western ridge of the vale, their standard rippling in the wind, a black cloven shield upon a field of red. The 10th legion was arrayed in gray mail and black tunics, their large rectangular shields covering their front from chin to knee, more than a match for the paltry armor afforded the Chosen, whose austere mail and small circled shields paled in compare. Resting between the Chosen and the 10th Legion ran the foul river, its slow current and shallow stream making it easy to crossover along its impressive length.

Enemies to the east, enemies to the west, and enemies to the south, Terin bitterly reflected. There was no deliverance from the might that surrounded them, 2,734 brave souls against the might of Tyro's realm. They were weakly armed, and formed into a loose formation, brandishing mismatched weapons against the disciplined ranks of the enemy.

Why hadn't they attacked them before this? he wondered, for Tyro had every opportunity to do so. They were followed since crossing into the Benotrist heartland, Benotrist magantors and cavalry maintaining contact ever since. Every time they bedded down, they were watched. Every time they awoke and marched, they were followed. Once they neared the Oddigem, they decided to march through the night, only stopping at this place, in full view of the foothills where the gargoyles had gathered, and the 13th Legion was already waiting for them to their east. The 10th Legion followed them into the vale, shifting to their immediate west.

But why? he wondered. Why did they expend such effort pursuing them, wasting time and provisions just to confront their meager host? Was this simply to amuse them? Or were they simply playing with them, like a lincor toying with its prey? Were they allowed to come here to be a spectacle, or serve as a sacrifice upon this grand altar? He could think of no place more fitting for their sacrifice than the Oddigem Valley. The ground beneath their feet was a collage of cracked hard soil and discolored grass, with the foulest river coursing its length, despoiled by gargoyle feces polluting it, giving off a noxious odor to match the desolate landscape. This was a place of death, a foul land conjured from the darkest of inclinations, and yet it was all too real. Here they would meet their end, in this he had no doubt.

He stood between Squid and Elos, their presence a needed comfort to him now. He could see King Lorn further to his left, standing alongside King Mortus, facing their grim reality with stalwart resolve. He would marvel at his courage if not for the bravery he saw in all their company. Tessa and Dresila stood behind them, facing the might of Tyro's realm with arms weakened with age, and little skill, but they stood all the same. He could see Lucas beside Deva, her ever vigilant guardian. Deva herself stood unmoved, resigned to the fate Yah had consigned her. She brought them to this place, her visions stopping before the foothills waiting beyond, visions that offered no instruction beyond this place and time. Whatever Yah intended of them from here forward, they could only guess. Everything was beyond their power now, their fate hanging upon the will of the enemy.

He turned one last time to Squid, resting his hand upon his shoulder.

"I am honored to fight beside you this day, Squid," he said, wanting to say so much more, but the words escaped him.

"Aye, Terin. It is only fitting that I fight beside a Caleph in my final battle. I wonder what your father would say if he could see us now?" Squid smiled.

"I think he would be proud, and I hope he somehow survives all this, though I cannot see how."

"Have faith, Terin. Yah did not have us come here without purpose. Though we are offered up to the mercy of the enemy, the others shall be spared, just as Yah promised."

Doubts started to creep upon Terin's mind. He looked south again, where hundreds of gargoyles began to emerge from their fortifications, spilling out from their gates, or descending from their high walls. Were they gathering into formations, or simply sending scouts to observe the spectacle? He could feel the apprehension taking root in those around him, even Elos, whose stoic demeanor never broke with emotion. He could see his winged friend's shoulders sag, as if he was preparing to die. This grim fate was what they all thought about throughout their journey, but now it was upon them. They marched without food for two days now, and the last of their water was about gone. They used all they had to reach this point with no plan for anything after. Even Gorzak and his fellow apes looked despondent, standing off to his right, staring ahead with grim determination, while lacking their usual lighthearted vigor. They were likely preparing themselves for the inevitable, much like the rest of them. The apes must have noticed him staring, when Carbanc, son of Hukok, broke out in a toothy grin and began to sing the apes' favorite drinking song.

"In the halls of the apes
Where we raise our tankards high

Cheering our place
Beneath the southern sky..."

Carbanc's deep voice boomed in the still air, his fellow gorillas joining in the bawdy refrain. Others took up the song, joining in their growing chorus. The lighthearted melody eased the tension, if only for a moment, and Terin was thankful for the respite. The song ended all too soon, and he wished it would go on forever. It was Aldo who sang next, the young scribe's voice echoing though the autumn air, calling upon the memory of Terin's ancient kin.

"Kal, Kal, Oh ancient king
That bards write and poets sing..."

Terin recalled when Galen sang the storied ballad on the eve of Morac's final assault upon Corell during the first siege. He remembered Galen's rendition as he stood upon Zar Crest while Torg revealed that he was his grandfather. He didn't know then that Kal was his ancient kin, though the melody always touched a part of his soul that he could not comprehend. That was secondary now to what the ballad reminded him of, Torg's revelation that he was his grandsire. How he missed the old man, wondering where he was at this moment? He was drawn from his musings as others began to sing, adding their voices to Aldo's. The ballad spread throughout their assembly, over two thousand voices joined in unison, their song growing louder with each verse, honoring the ancient king.

The Benotrists stirred uncomfortably as the melody reached their ears, as if its very words might rend them where they stood. The song drifted higher and farther afield, reaching the growing gargoyle host, causing the creatures to scream and screech as if daggers were driven into their skulls. Terin felt his skin pimple, the melody sending tendrils of euphoria across his flesh, as if their small host was brought to this place and time for this very purpose, to speak the truth of Kal's glory to his hated foes. No matter what happened, he would have the satisfaction of their displeasure in hearing it.

No, it was not Kal's glory they were singing, but Kal's faithfulness.

Kal was faithful, his power given him by Yah, and he was slain facing the gargoyles in those long-ago days. Here stood the Chosen, offering themselves up to the same enemy on faith alone. Their sword arms could not deliver them now. His *Sword of Light* could not deliver them from the enemy, not now. It rested upon his hip, its once vibrant blade dulled, and its weight now heavier than a common sword. Elos' blade was similarly afflicted, rendering their only significant weapons useless against the masses arrayed against them. They might still break other swords they meet, but their power was but a candle to the raging fire they invoked before. He wondered the cause of it, deciding it was Yah removing every strength they might lean upon other than him. They had no choice but to trust in Yah, trust in his hand to deliver them, or in his mercy for a quick end.

He wondered how their sacrifice might unfold. Would they be slaughtered here upon this valley floor, before the ground opens fully up, devouring the enemy in turn? Might a star fall from the heavens, consuming them all in a fiery blaze? Perhaps a pestilence might spill out from their slain corpses, infecting the enemy host. Before he could conjure another possible fate, the song ended, a hush falling over their brave assembly, which the enemy answered in kind with grim silence. The gargoyle host continued to build, thousands of the creatures now spilling over the battlements while countless others poured through the gates. He could barely make out the strange mix of white and black flesh of the gargoyle masses, or the multitude of smaller winged creatures barely able to take flight from the hilltops. The larger male creatures gathered into their formations, while the remaining of their foul kind gathered behind in a disordered mass, filling the valley floor before the foothills. Their mighty host covered the ground from the base of the east ridge to the jagged slopes of the west, the sound of their drums summoning them from their subterranean holdfasts. It was as if the bowels of the world opened up and spewed their grotesque hordes from its broken fissures.

While the gargoyles still held at a distance, a column of riders drew from the west, parading before the might of the 10th Legion, before breaking east, easily fording the shallow stream, riding for the open ground before the Chosen, stopping between their small host and the gargoyles to the south, and equal distance between the 13th Legion to the east and the 10th to the west. One of them bore a large standard bearing the sigil of the empire, a black tower upon a field of red. The standard bearer broke ahead of the others, stopping a short distance before them, heralding the arrival of his fellows, who followed close after. They formed a semi-circle, facing the Chosen as one broke forward of the others, a sturdily built figure upon a majestic mount, wearing an austere helm and mail. A plume of dark feathers ran the length of his helm, ending at the back of his neck. Terin sensed a kinship with the man, wondering their connection, as if the two were somehow linked by unseen bonds. Another fellow drew ahead of this warrior, bearing a blue flag of truce, his voice calling out to them.

"The emperor offers parlay to the leader of this host. Come forth and hear his generous terms!"

The ranks of the Chosen stood unmoved, wondering if Lorn would assume the mantle of their leader, or if another would stake such claim. They never abided such formality through their travels, driven by their mutual understanding of their purpose. And yet they all knew that Lorn was their unspoken leader. Deva was their guide, but she deferred to him in all things. Mortus was his father by marriage, but he looked to Lorn to direct their path. Terin was the blood of Kal and ordained for a great purpose, but he was never their leader, as he also deferred to Lorn.

With that, Lorn stepped forth, beckoning Mortus, Deva and finally Terin to join him. The four of them came together before marching forth while their comrades looked on, wondering what fate awaited them.

* * *

Morac looked on from his place at the head of the 13th Legion, watching from afar as the emperor waited upon the leaders of this pathetic rabble, honoring them with his time, which he felt beneath his esteemed position. Who were these fools who dared invade their realm with so few and so weakly armed? He did know one who stood among them worthy of interest… the Torry champion. This was the grand test of the emperor, if he had the temerity to strike down their most dangerous enemy. If he failed to do so, then the rumors of their kinship were true.

"We shall now truly see where his heart lies," General Trinapolis dryly observed, his ocran shifting slightly beside his own steady mount.

"Yes," Morac said, his eyes narrowing severely as he watched the emissaries of the Chosen draw nigh. Trinapolis had whispered his poisonous words in his ear throughout their journey from Laycrom, fueling Morac's anger and distrust. A more discerning mind might question the general's motives, but Morac was lost to his delusions, seeing traitors in every direction and plots in every shadow. Here he sat astride his mount, waiting for the emperor to slay his hated foe, who offered himself up so foolishly. He wondered if Terin's sword was afflicted as his own. He recalled their last duel upon the battlements of Corell, noting the shadow that overtook Terin's blade, its once vibrant azure glow replaced with murky darkness. He recalled how difficult it was for his legions to see the Torry Champion, as if the sword rendered him invisible. He suffered no such weakness, his own sword protecting him from such beguilement, though he did note the shadow that consumed Terin. His own sword now suffered the murky affliction but was growing heavy, its weightless nature altered to its current state. It could still destroy anything it touched, but its other beneficial attributes were impaired. Had Terin's sword's impairment infected his sword as well? Were the other *Swords of Light* affected? He would be certain to inspect Terin's sword once the emperor slew him.

He spared a glance to his left, where his grisly trophy rested atop the pike driven into the ground, tar coating the rotting flesh, preserving its visage to those who knew him. It was but one of many trophies he would claim this day. Perhaps Terin would be the second. For that he looked keenly on the events unfolding in the center of the valley floor.

Finish him, he mentally growled, watching the scene unfold in the distance with expectant glee.

* * *

Terin knew who sat astride the powerful ocran standing forward of the others, golden eyes fixed intently upon him through the eye slits in his austere helm. Gone were the richly adorned trappings that defined his reign. This was Tyro the warrior, the man of legend that forged an empire through battle, toil and blood. Terin and the others came to stop several paces before the herald, who reposted behind his royal liege, leaving none between Tyro and them.

Lorn removed his helm, freeing his dark mane in the autumn wind, his companions following in kind, baring their heads to the Benotrist emperor, whose eyes remained fixed upon Terin.

"You called for parlay, Emperor Tyro. We have come," Lorn said, drawing Tyro's eyes to his.

"I called for parlay with your leader, and you send four." Tyro raised a skeptical brow, hidden beneath his helm.

"We each play a great role in our company, and each of our ears should hear your words."

"And you are?" Tyro asked.

Lorn paused before answering, sharing a look with the others before offering it up.

"I am Lorn, King of the Torry Realms."

If Tyro was surprised by this revelation, he hid it well, his face a mask of indifference, though his helm helped in that regard.

"I am Mortus, King of Maconia." Mortus followed, drawing Tyro's curious gaze.

"I am Deva of House Estaran, former Guardian of the Sisterhood," Deva said, lifting her chin, preparing for whatever invective Tyro might cast.

Tyro regarded her evenly, recalling that she was the one who enslaved Terin, if she spoke true of her identity. He motioned Nels Draken forward, the former free sword's ocran cantering to a halt beside his emperor.

"Do you recognize this woman?" Tyro asked.

Nels struggled briefly before recalling her face.

"She is the daughter of Darna. We were briefly acquainted at her mother's estate. I am surprised she still lives considering her treason," Nels said, lifting his helm to regard her better.

Tyro raised his open palm, silencing Draken before pointing at Terin.

"You I know, Terin Caleph, son of Joriah."

"Emperor Tyro." Terin thought to address him with his true name, but decided politeness was the better approach at this juncture. Whatever Yah intended of their coming here, this was not what he expected, but things could easily sour at any moment.

"What did your father tell you of me?" Tyro asked, his eyes narrowing severely, waiting upon his answer.

"The truth," Terin said.

"And when did you learn this truth?"

"After the first siege of Corell. My father explained his heritage to me before I departed for Yatin."

"Unfortunate that I did not know when we last met. Things might have turned differently."

Terin thought to ask what could possibly have changed, considering the complexities involved, but again decided it best not to irritate his grandsire.

"Why is your former mistress in your company? I thought you would strike her dead for her affront?" Tyro asked curiously, his gaze shifting again to Deva.

"Yah asked that I forgive her, and I have obeyed his will."

"Yah?" Tyro asked, recalling the god of his dear Cordela and Joriah. It seemed they passed their faith to Terin.

"Yes. It was Yah that asked that I show Deva mercy, and he in turn has chosen her for his purpose."

"And what purpose would that be?" Tyro asked, regarding Deva evenly.

"I...I have been shown visions," Deva said.

"Many have visions, especially of late. Is there more to your purpose than that?" he asked, unimpressed.

"Deva's visions are far more detailed, and all encompassing. It was her guidance that led us here, we chosen few, selected specifically by Yah for this purpose." Terin spoke to her defense.

"Purpose? Was it Yah's intention that you offer yourselves up so pitifully? Upon my signal I can order you slain, every one of you, with little cost to my legions. Even your mighty sword will not avail you, Terin," Tyro warned. There had to be more to this than he could see. He knew their armies were not far off, but what madness would have them send their kings and champion forward of the others, where they might be easily slain? And to come here of all places, in the shadow of the gargoyles' might.

"If that is your will, then so be it, emperor of the north," Lorn said.

"My will? You speak so easily as if it holds no consequence, King Lorn. You and King Mortus stand naked without your armies. What madness drove you here? Did your God wish you to perish in the shadow of these mountains?" Tyro waved his gauntleted hand toward the foothills behind him, where the gargoyles began to march north to meet them.

"I do not know. I only know that he asked us to come here. Our visions reveal nothing beyond this point. If we are to die by your order, then so be it, but we shall account of ourselves, and will not die alone," Lorn answered.

"You may not die alone, but not many of my men will join you in death, of that you can be certain. It will be a poor exchange on your part and will account for little in the grander scale. Once it is done, I shall meet your armies all the same, your deaths serving little benefit to your cause," Tyro warned.

"Our armies are far away, and you will not survive long to meet them," Lorn countered.

Far away? Tyro made a face at that. Did Lorn truly think he would believe such a lie?

"As your visions offer no guidance beyond reaching this point, I shall lay the choices at your feet. You are to surrender your arms and order your armies to return to their proper realms, never to set foot upon Benotrist lands again. Once they comply, you are free to join them, save for Terin. He shall remain in my keeping in perpetuity as my *guest*." Tyro looked possessively into Terin's eyes.

Lorn looked to Mortus, wondering why Tyro would be so lenient considering they were helplessly in his grasp. And why mention their armies? Their armies were already in the south unless… no, it made little sense.

"Why were you chosen and not the others?" Tyro asked, trying to make sense of their ramblings. There had to be more to this.

"Deva was told which of us were chosen to undertake this journey, but the choice was still freely made. Not one that was chosen refused the call," Terin said proudly, regarding Deva with admiration, the small gesture touching her heart.

"And what are you given for agreeing to this?" Tyro asked, still not understanding their point.

None of them quickly answered, each sharing a look. It was Mortus who spoke for the group.

"We were offered the most precious of gifts, that everyone else would be spared should we undertake this quest. We come here of our own free will so that those we love survive."

If everyone else would survive, then why are they at my doorstep? Tyro thought miserably. Was this a deception, or were they ignorant of the movement of their armies?

"We came so those we love might live, though each of us would likely perish in doing so. Our fate now rests with you, Grandfather. You hold the power of life or death, to choose your blood or side with creatures bent on our destruction," Terin pleaded. He struggled reconciling the fact this monster was his grandfather, wondering how a man that sired his own father could be this evil tyrant. He placed his hope in appealing to the man that sired Jonas Caleph. It was that man that he needed to see reason. He could see the conflict in Tyro's eyes, torn between his loyalty to his kin and his allies, or was it something else?

"Fool boy. I make my own choices, not the feeble options you offer. I am loyal to those loyal to me, and I am loyal to my kin, but that loyalty only demands that I keep them safe. Protecting your friends is not my concern. I will spare them to end the feud between us, and then you will take your proper place, though considering the nature of your blood, your place will have many walls around it, where you will live out your days. That should ensure your father and mother's obedience," Tyro growled, his intense gaze nearly driving Terin to his knees.

"The gargoyles must die. Every last one. There is no compromise on this. It is the will of Yah and our sacred duty," Lorn calmly stated, drawing Tyro's ire.

"And how do you intend to do that, King Lorn? Not with this rabble you have brought here," Tyro growled.

"I too once defied Yah, Oh great emperor. He is not to be denied. We freely offer our lives to his divine will," Deva proclaimed, looking past Tyro, where the gargoyle horde drew ever closer, the beat of their war drums echoing dully in the autumn air. She steeled her heart, denying the fear rising to claim her. This was the place of her visions, and the horrible events that were about to unfold, unless something changed.

Tyro sneered at their naivety. Were these the kings and warriors that waylaid his legions at Corell? They were either delusional, arrogant or raving mad. He was about to order his men forth when Terin's words tore through his shields.

"I would give anything to save my father's life, even my own in exchange. A friend of ours who is no longer with us once said that there was no greater love than one willing to give up one's life for another. My father once said something similar when I was a boy. He said he would gladly give up his life for those he loved, his son, his wife, his mother, and… his father."

Tyro froze, tormented by Terin's words just at the others looked skyward. He followed their gaze where one of his magantors swept overhead before circling about, bearing three riders, one standing out from the others arrayed in the silver armor and blue tunic of a Torry Elite… Joriah.

* * *

Morac held in place at the head of the 13th Legion, looking on as the magantor circled above the emperor before angling lower, heading for a patch of ground between the parlay and his own position, wondering which of their riders could be so brazen.

"A truer test of our suspicion," General Trinapolis sneered, pointing out the Torry clad warrior seated between the other two riders.

"Caleph!" Morac ground his teeth. He watched in muted rage as Jonas and the second rider dismounted from the avian, before its driver took to the sky, leaving the two men standing between him and the emperor's parlay. Jonas appeared to give the second man implicit instructions, handing him a long, bundled object and directing him toward the parlay, while he remained in place, turning his gaze toward… him. Jonas removed his helm, freeing his dark mane in the autumn breeze, staring directly at Morac as if the distance between them were but a breath. Morac scowled severely, receiving Jonas' gaze for what it was, a challenge. His mind was consumed with unfettered rage, Jonas' stare stripping away all reason and judgement.

"AGGHH!" Morac howled, screaming like a wounded animal, venting his fury. He leaned in the saddle, snatching the pike bearing his trophy in hand before kicking his heels, driving his mount across the valley floor.

"Lord Morac?" Trinapolis called after him, wondering what he might do.

* * *

Terin froze in place as his father revealed himself, tossing his helm aside, looking briefly toward them before looking again to the east, where a Benotrist rider burst from the ranks of the 13th Legion, raising dust across the valley floor. His heart soared, seeing his father in all his glory, alive and well, and arrayed for battle. He was so enraptured he barely noticed the others' reaction, or the man his father sent running in their direction, or the rider galloping from the east, where the 13th Legion began to stir, its forward ranks marshalling forth.

Tyro's eyes were now fully drawn to the east, ignoring the parlay as he looked upon his son staring down Morac as he rode apace to meet him. He paled, watching the scene unfold in horrific wonder.

He forsook his parlay, turning his own mount about, racing forth to intercede, but knew in his heart he was too far afield.

"No!" Lorn heard Terin shout, the Torry Champion running after Tyro, his frantic gaze fixed to the happenings to their east. He knew the Torry clad warrior to be Jonas, his heart pounding as he beheld Morac draw nearer by the moment while Tyro closed from the opposite direction, his imperial guards following in his wake, with Draken riding at their head.

Jonas kept his gaze upon Morac, drawing his full ire, drawing his attention solely upon him and nothing else. His challenge achieved its purpose, drawing Morac from the shadow of his subterfuge into the open. He thought of his dear Valera, wishing to hold her in his arms one last time, to kiss her tenderly and never let go. He thought of his daughter and trusted her fate to Yah and the promises of Castellan Braxus. He wished to run his fingers over her small face and to see her beautiful eyes staring up at him with all their wonder. He wished there was another way for this to end, another way to save his father and his son, whom he loved with all his heart. He closed his eyes briefly, steeling his heart for what he must do. He opened them, turning slowly in the opposite direction where rode his father, riding fast to meet him. Just beyond him rode his imperial guard, and beyond them ran Terin, partly obscured by the rising dust. He looked first to Terin, his son's handsome face contorted with the effort of his charge. How he loved that boy. He wished he could tell him how proud he was of him and how much he loved him. Alas, it was not to be.

I love you, my son. He smiled wanly before looking to his father, his visage growing clearer as he drew nigh, his lathered mount struggling under the strain of his desperate charge, a vain hope to attain him before Morac. His father's effort would go for naught, for he set down on this spot for this purpose, just as Yah had shown him. He needn't look past his father where his comrade ran afoot, bearing the precious gift for King Lorn, just as Yah had instructed. He kept his gaze on his father, pressing his fist to his heart, saluting him before turning again to face Morac. This was his father's only hope, his last reprieve before Yah's judgement, though Jonas would not be there to see it.

Jonas stared down Morac as he drew nigh, outstretching his arms to receive him, weaponless, his empty hands spread wide. The defenseless gesture only fueled Morac's rage, blinding him to all else, his eyes ablaze with hatred. He drew forth the *Sword of the Sun*, its once vibrant blade dull and murky. It now felt heavy in his hand but retained its fell power to smash everything it touched. He closed upon Jonas, tossing the pike bearing his trophy in the dirt as he sprang from his mount, his armored boots imprinting in the cracked soil.

Jonas lowered his arms, staring at Morac with apparent indifference, as if unimpressed. He thought to say something but decided against it. There was truly nothing to say. He need only remain as he was, receiving the hate and anger of this flawed and spiteful creature. He lifted his gaze to the heavens as Morac stepped nigh.

"I have obeyed your will, Oh Yah," he said, smiling wanly as he beheld the clear blue sky above. He closed his eyes, waiting upon the blow as Morac's blade drove deep into his chest.

There in the Vale of Oddigem Jonas died, struck down by Morac's blade as the drums of war drew from every direction.

Thus began the Battle of Noddegamra.

CHAPTER 12

NODDEGAMRA.

"No!" Terin screamed as he beheld Morac strike down his father, too far afield to save him. He was running desperately to reach him, but he was too late, watching helplessly as Morac's blade punched through Jonas' heart before driving him to the ground and twisting his sword free.

There stood Morac, his murky blade alit as if restored, bright crimson erupting along its length, fueled by the blood of Kal anointing its surface. The bright sheen quickly waned, returning to its turbid state. A brief silence overtook the vale, the legions of men and gargoyles holding in place, watching as the scene unfolded before them.

Morac removed his helm, standing triumphantly over Jonas, his dark eyes alit with unfettered glee. His moment of triumph was short lived. He felt the ground shake, looking up as the emperor's ocran drew nigh, its powerful hooves clopping the soil like thunderclaps. Morac backed a step as Tyro came to a halt, dismounting in a flourish.

"I have slain our hated foe, My Emperor." Morac pointed the tip of his blade to Jonas' still form, wondering what Tyro might do. His addled mind began to clear, realizing his folly. He wanted the emperor to destroy the Chosen and perish facing the enemy drawing from the north, but seeing Jonas kindled his ire in a way he could not understand. Now his treason was exposed. He had no choice but to slay Tyro now and be done with it, though doing so in full view of their legions might turn many against him. His feeble attempt to placate the emperor went for naught as Tyro drew his blades, closing upon Morac with forceful strides.

"Very well," Morac sneered. He had the golden blade, and despite its lack of luster, no other could match it. He closed the distance between them, bringing his sword down upon the emperor's upraised blade, expecting to rend it in half and then do for the other, which Tyro held back in his right hand. Morac's blade came down upon Tyro's as ten thousand pairs of eyes looked on. He wondered what madness took the emperor to believe he could defeat him, common steel against the *Sword of the Sun*? He would take his head, just as he did King Lore's. He would claim Fera as his own and have imperial artists decorate the throne room with frescos of his twin victories, with Lore's head held in his left hand while his right held Tyro's, both raised to the heavens in immortal triumph. He smiled at the delusion as his blade finally met Tyro's, his smile falling as they stuck.

NOTHING.

Morac's eyes bulged as he failed to split Tyro's blade, flashes of color erupting along the length of each sword.

How? His muted voice echoed before realizing his folly as Tyro's second blade swept across his knees. Morac screamed, his thighs sliding off his severed legs, falling upon his back. Tyro pinned his sword arm back, while his second blade took it above the wrist, and then took the other at the elbow. Tyro looked down upon his traitorous champion with contempt, his twin *Swords of Light* trained upon Morac's flailing, limbless body.

"I trusted the *Sword of the Sun* to your hand but held these swords should you ever betray me, son of Morca. Die well or die poorly, but you shall die all the same," Tyro said in a dead voice before driving his sword through Morac's groin, pleased with the anguish fueling his screams.

Tyro backed a step, savoring his vengeance for an eternal moment before looking to his son, who lay several paces beyond, his vacant eyes staring skyward with a strange smile upon his lips. He felt his heart rent, his own grief coming upon him in waves. All his plans were in ruin, his empire sundered, his son dead. He was so lost in his thoughts he didn't notice his imperial guards flooding around him. Looking up he saw Draken shouting something, but his ears were not hearing, His eyes drifted to the pike Morac had tossed aside, stepping closer to see what it beheld. There upon the ground was the head of Lord Regula, his oldest friend and loyal comrade, the great chieftain of the gargoyles. His death at Morac's hand meant only one thing. The gargoyles had their own civil war, the winners aligning with his traitorous champion. Looking east he beheld the great wall of infantry drawing near, the 13th Legion, whose commander was surely part of Morac's conspiracy. It then dawned upon him. Joriah knew what they had planned and offered himself up to draw them out before he waged war upon Lorn and the others. But why did he allow himself to be struck down? Why not fight and slay Morac outright as he was certainly able to?

No! Tyro's thoughts screamed, the truth rending his heart. Only seeing his son die would force him to clearly choose which side he would align. His son gave his life to force his hand, and here he stood, his world crumbling around him.

"Your Majesty!" Draken's voice now rang clear.

He looked up as Nels Draken pointed out the approaching danger to their immediate east and south. From the east marched the might of the 13th Benotrist Legion, their new standard lifting in the autumn breeze, a golden sword impaling a severed head upon a field of black. The new sigil was an obvious reference to Morac's victory over King Lore and a sign of the legion's loyalty to the son of Morca.

The greater danger drew from the south, where the vast host of the gargoyle species marshalled forth from their last nesting grounds. The number of their adult warriors was a mere shadow of the ranks that once filled his legions, but behind them came the next generation, several hundred thousand juveniles, and untold numbers of gargoyle lasses, their blind eyes staring hauntingly forward. Their lasses relied on sound and the smell of human blood to guide them, following on the heels of their males and juveniles, each bearing daggers, spears or merely their sharp clawed digits and voracious fangs.

"Hold!" Tyro heard one of his guardians shout. He turned as Terin drew to a halt several paces away, the boy's eyes fixed to Joriah's body.

"Let him pass!" Tyro commanded, the guards lifting their spears as Terin ran to Joriah, pressing his lips to his father's forehead as he knelt beside him. Tyro stepped toward the boy, finally noticing Joriah's empty scabbard, wondering where his sword was.

Terin looked up to his grandfather towering over him, at a loss for words. What could either of them say? They were mortal enemies bound by blood but now sharing the same foes.

"Get up, boy. We have a battle to win!" Tyro growled, turning on his heel, marching off to retrieve his mount, which one of his men had already gathered its reins.

Terin stood, reluctant to leave his father's body, but there was no time to save it.

"Fetch Morac's sword and come with us!" Tyro ordered, mounting his ocran, the beast shifting as he did so.

"Be quick about it before we all die here!" Draken said as arrows began falling, striking the broken soil a hundred paces to their east.

Terin's eyes quickly found the *Sword of the Sun* lying beside an anguished Morac, whose eyes were growing dim from the blood issuing from his severed limbs. Terin thought to make sure of him but left him to rot. He wrapped his right hand about the hilt of the golden sword, lifting it off the ground, a sudden tremor coursing his flesh, followed by a burst of crimson light igniting along its blade, flashing brightly, causing the others to look away, before fading altogether. With the *Sword of the Moon* sheathed upon his left and the sword Torg had forged for him riding upon his right, he had no place to store the weapon, keeping it in hand as Draken reached out his hand, drawing him onto his saddle.

With that, their small band raced back across the valley floor as the 13th Legion gave chase.

Morac's last breath escaped him, his unconscious body expiring as Carka birds circled above, waiting for the others to clear so to claim their first prize of the day.

* * *

Safed Corlen raced across the valley floor, having evaded Terin and Tyro and all those that rushed to confront Morac, keeping his eyes upon the Chosen. Jonas pointed out those he was to reach, delivering the sword he carried into their hands. Thankfully he was ignored by those rushing toward Morac, whose fate he didn't spare a glance behind him to witness. He simply fixed on the three figures standing forward of the Chosen, struggling to keep his feet along the uneven, cracked soil. He could barely believe he was almost free of his bondage, having suffered unbearable torment since his capture at Tuft's Mountain. Of Cronus' men, only he and two others still lived, their recent fortune a tribute to Jonas' mercy and protection. While his comrades guarded Lady Valera at Fera, he joined Jonas on this desperate quest, a quest that meant certain death to his benefactor. Had he the time for tears, he would shed them for Jonas, who was certainly dead by now. He continued apace, rushing toward the men in question, before realizing one was a woman. He stumbled upon his approach, barely keeping his feet before reaching them.

"King Lorn," he gasped, trying to catch his breath. "I seek King Lorn."

"I am he," Lorn said, regarding the man guardedly, Safed's eyes drawing wide in disbelief that the man he sought was the first he came upon.

"I bring a gift from Jonas Caleph, of the Torry King's high elite," Safed said, removing the *Sword of the Stars* from its bundle, offering it to his king.

"…" Lorn was at a loss for words. Where had Jonas found this while captive at Fera? And why did he not use it to defend himself from Morac? Watching Tyro slay the son of Morca gave him pause, the truth of Jonas' sacrifice now dawning upon him.

"He asked that I deliver it to your hand, Your Majesty. Do with it what you will," Safed said.

Lorn felt the will of Yah move him as he gifted the blade in turn to King Mortus.

"You should wield it, my son. You will have need of it this day." Mortus tried to refuse it, but Lorn insisted.

"It is Yah's will that you should have it, my friend." Lorn handed it to him, a slight flicker running the length of its turbid blade before returning to its murky state.

"Who are you?" Deva asked of Safed, her question drawing Lorn and Mortus' attention.

"I am Safed Corlen," he said, before explaining that he was of Cronus' fated unit, and that he knew Terin from his time in their company.

Speaking of Terin caused them to look on as Tyro's escort returned, raising dust as the 13th Legion lumbered forth in the distance. Lorn was relieved to see Terin returning with them, sharing a saddle with Nels Draken. It wasn't lost on them, the strangeness of it all, this temporary truce that so quickly came between Tyro and the Chosen. Sparing a glance to the 13th Legion drawing from the east, and the greater host of gargoyles approaching from the south, likely made their alliance all the briefer. None expected to live long against the numbers arrayed against them, even if Tyro brought the 10th Legion to their fledgling cause.

Tyro rode at the head of his small party, drawing to a halt in front of the Torry King, the two men leaving much unsaid, more to that lack of time than politeness. Lorn could see the fire in Tyro's eyes, his sudden turn to their cause more of practicality than a true change of heart. He knew this too was the will of Yah, and whatever differences they shared would have to be resolved latter.

"Send your people across the river and position along my left. The 13th Legion will be upon us before the gargoyles. I've returned your champion. I trust you will put him to good use," Tyro said, before kicking his heels, continuing west toward the 10th Legion.

Terin dismounted before Draken rode off, following the emperor across the shallow stream. He quickly approached Lorn, offering him the *Sword of the Sun*.

"Take the sword, Your Majesty. It is the sword of a king." Terin offered it freely.

"It is the greatest of the *Swords of Light*, Terin. It was meant for the blood of Kal to wield, and you are the only one left to carry it. Yah has appointed you this task, my friend. You are his champion as well as ours." Lorn refused the gesture, pushing the sword back to its rightful master. The blood of Kal was meant to wield its fell power, and he was eager to see the greatest of the swords in Terin's hand.

Terin paused briefly before realizing what must be done.

"If you shall not accept the *Sword of the Sun*, My King, please take the *Sword of the Moon*," Terin said, drawing the silver blade with his free hand, offering it to Lorn.

Lorn sighed, taking the weapon, though feeling unworthy to wield it. It felt wrong in a way. The *Sword of the Moon* would always be Terin's birthright. It would be forever linked to the son of Jonas through all the great deeds he achieved wielding it in battle. There was no time to argue the point, for the enemy would soon be upon them.

"I shall wield it with great honor, my friend." Lorn smiled before they all returned to their comrades, ordering them across the stream. Strangely, not one voiced a protest over their joining with Tyro's 10th Legion. It was but one of a million ironies that would visit them this day, a day like no other.

* * *

"We have been betrayed. The 13th Legion is marching upon us, and the greater might of the gargoyles are drawing from the south!" Tyro proclaimed before General Gavis and his subordinate commanders, who stood forward of their ordered ranks, and General Naruv, commander of his magantors.

"And *Lord* Morac?" Gavis nearly spat the name.

"Dead," Tyro answered, his blunt response bringing a smile to Gavis' scarred face.

"Your orders, My Emperor?" Gavis asked, sitting higher in the saddle with the news of Morac's demise.

"We hold the 13th Legion at the river and align half our strength to the south, joining the end of the river line at a right angle. The Torry Champion and his rabble will position to our left along the river's

211

edge," Tyro said, this strange tiding causing a myriad of reactions on his commanders' faces. If any thought to question, they decided against it with time now pressing.

"I will see it done, My Emperor!" Gavis thrust his fist to his chest before bellowing orders to his telnic commanders, the legion moving soon after upon his command.

"Nels, you will see to King Lorn's men and guide them to their proper position. Remember what I said about the gargoyles. Inform them," Tyro ordered.

"Aye, My Emperor." Draken saluted before riding off north along the river to meet the Chosen.

"General Naruv, concentrate your magantors along the ridgeline behind us. The gargoyles will certainly attempt to flank us by sending a large cohort up those slopes to our south and spring upon us from above. Stop them where you can, or delay them if you can't," Tyro ordered his magantor commander.

"Aye, My Emperor."

"And, Naruv, I have one other task for you to attend," Tyro said.

* * *

Nels Draken aided King Lorn as he moved his people into position to the west side of the shallow stream, hurrying into some semblance of ordered ranks as the 13th legion pressed their advance from the east. They formed up along the left wing of the 10th Legion just as the first arrows filled the sky, many dropping short of their position on the far riverbank. The Chosen were in no means prepared for pitched battle against seasoned warriors trained to fight as one. They were a collection of individuals and warriors thrown together without time to work in cohesion, most poorly equipped with small circular shields and half helms that barely covered their skulls, compared to the men of the 13th Legion, who wore full helms, breastplates, greaves and large shields that could easily interlock, covering neck to knee. But they did have many great warriors in their mismatched ranks, and now four *Swords of Light*, though the blades were growing heavier as the day wore on. Once positioned, Nels returned to his emperor, riding with all haste behind their lines.

Lorn held position in their center, standing among the forward wall of infantry, surprised to see Tessa standing behind the man to his right.

"You should be with Dresila, Lady Tessa," Lorn said, fearing for her safety. Dresila was set in the rear of their ranks with several attendants prepared to treat the wounded.

"Matron Dresila has enough helpers, My King. Yah chose me to accompany you all this way, and here I shall fight," she said, shaking her spear to show her mettle.

Lorn smiled at her courage. Of all those that followed him to this fell place, she was the bravest. She had lost her husband and sons to this awful war and gladly offered her own life to see it ended. Galen was right to pen a ballad of her, a ballad that would live in their people's memory long after their own names were forgotten.

"Here they come!" more than one voice shouted as the enemy drew nigh, long columns of infantry drawing from the east, their forward rows aligned across the shallow stream, arrows spewing overhead. Most were aligned across from the 10th Legion, whose interlocked shields and battle-tested ranks prepared to receive them. Unlike the 10th Legion, the 13th Legion had yet to fight a battle in the war, spending most of it safely at Laycrom.

Lorn could see the enemy right wing strongly reinforced with extra telnics sweeping around to the north to envelop them, planning to turn their flank. He placed both Terin and Elos on his extreme left with their four apes and a hundred of their finest warriors, an odd collection of Macons and Torries. Horns sounded to their south, heralding the enemy's advance along the entire front. The sky was thick with arrows as walls of infantry forded the stream, bearing long spears to drive the 10th Legion from the river's edge. Hundreds of Carka birds circled the sky above, waiting to feast on the promised carrion. Gazing farther afield one could see many thousand more coursing the breadth of the Oddigem Valley, their morbid gathering a portent of the coming slaughter. Lorn held tight to the *Sword of the Moon*, keeping it behind his shield, waiting for the enemy to draw near. It felt the same weight as a common blade, perhaps even more, its once vibrant luster turned murky and turbid, like swirling black clouds shifting along its surface. Despite its changing nature, he felt the power of the blade coursing up his arm, fueling his courage and resolve. This was the blade of his ancient kin, first wielded by the first king of the Middle Kingdom, King Zar. It was only fitting that it was now wielded by him, the descendant King of Zar, completing his legacy. His worthiness was further ordained by Terin placing it in his hand, the blood of Kal anointing him with this privilege.

"Kai-Shorum!" the men of the 13th Legion shouted as they advanced across the stream, their long spears leveled upon the Chosen's center.

Lorn lost sight of happenings to his south and north, the enemy before him filling his line of sight. He waited upon the bank of the shallow stream, meeting the leveled spears of the enemy, blocking the first to draw near with his shield while he struck at the shaft with his sword.

SPLIT!

The blow snapped the shaft where it struck.

SPLIT!

His follow strike severed the one to his right. He struck again to his left, before working his way forward, striking the man to his front.

SPLIT!

The blow rent the man's shield, a spout of blood spraying above its sundered metal. The terrible scream that followed indicated the severity of the blow. He didn't have time to gauge its effect, cutting left and right in rapid succession, severing spears, swords and limbs, blood and shards of wood and metal flying off his blade.

* * *

Lucas was just south of Lorn, blocking a Benotrist spear intended for Deva, stepping into its path, its tip glancing off his shield. Deva moved to his side, jabbing fiercely at the offending Benotrist, driving him back as Lucas struck true, piercing the man's elbow above his vambrace. A Yatin guarding his right cried out, taking a spear to his hip, driving him back into the ranks behind them, his void quickly filled by a Macon commander of flax. Lucas shifted, dodging an errant blade from his left, his riposte nearly disarming his attacker before Deva struck his side. He gave her an appreciative look, the two fighting in unison, their bond strengthening as the battle waged.

The Benotrist shield wall faltered upon ascending the riverbank, their ranks briefly parting as they drove into the Chosen. The Chosen didn't grant them time to reconfigure their formations, driving into them as they emerged from the stream. The tactic was desperate and necessary, evening the odds, if only for a brief respite. Men were falling to each side, stomachs ripped open and limbs severed. Fingers and blood flew from clashing blades. The cries of the dead and dying rent the morbid air as the waters of the foul stream turned red with blood.

South of Lucas, King Mortus drove into the enemy, wielding Jonas' gift with determined skill. He cut men down like stalks of grain, rending shields and limbs with cruel efficiency. Despite the sword's fell power, it was not weightless, its heft beginning to strain the king's aged arm.

SPLIT! SLASH! THRUST!

He cut down several pressing his front, caving a small section in the enemy ranks. The cry of the dead and dying rang numbly in his ears as Mortus felled one after another, the blade following his will as if they were one. Despite his efforts, the enemy pushed the Chosen back, their numbers too great to hold. He found himself forward of his comrades, the Benotrists flooding around him like water around a rock protruding in a river. He carefully backed away, withdrawing to the safety of the others, mindful of the bodies of friend and foe alike littering his retreat.

* * *

Nels Draken rode south behind the ranks of the 10th Legion, watching the battle unfold off his left where the 13th Legion pressed their front, walls of shields slamming into one another along the length of the shallow stream. He was thankful for the natural obstacle to slow the 13th Legion's advance, as only half the 10th was aligned to face them, the rest lining from the stream to the western ridgeline to block the advancing gargoyles.

"Packaww!"

He looked skyward as a pair of magantors swept overhead, before angling southwest, joining the rest of the Benotrist magantor contingent guarding the slopes of the western ridge. Gazing south he could see the great mass of the gargoyle host drawing ominously nigh, covering the valley floor like a dark tide approaching the shore. His mount shifted, an arrow striking the soil off his left. He swerved right and left, dodging several more shafts passing over their ranks, most falling amidst their formations. He passed before a line of their own archers returning the favor, sending their volleys into the enemy ranks massed east of the shallow stream.

Up ahead was the right angle, where the legion was split and where the emperor placed his standard, overseeing the battle beside General Gavis. Said general could be seen atop his ocran, moving along their ranks, directing reinforcements where needed, though most he kept in reserve. His reserve would be needed along the south-facing formation where the might of the gargoyle horde was soon to strike.

"My Emperor!" Nels saluted, drawing alongside Tyro, whose golden eyes were fixed southward, eying the gargoyle mass drawing ominously nigh.

"Did you relay what I told you?" Tyro asked, keeping his eyes forward.

"Aye. They were told of the unique nature of the gargoyle juveniles and lasses," Nels said, having told Lorn and Mortus all that Tyro had told him. Tyro was the only human to have visited the gargoyles' hallowed nesting grounds to their immediate south, where he was anointed the sacred title of Nordhenz, the prophetic figure promised to bring about the gargoyles' ascension upon Arax. That anointing was now desecrated by Morac's foul treachery and whatever gargoyles he recruited to join in his treason.

"Very good," Tyro said evenly.

"Your orders, My Emperor?'

"Fight well or die," Tyro snorted, looking on as the lead gargoyle telnics drew within archer range, hundreds of feathered shafts rising to meet them.

Nels Draken looked on as thousands of winged forms sprang into the air along their front, soaring into the sky, dozens succumbing to feathered shafts. The archers increased their rate of fire as they drew nigh, dozens more dropping, working their crippled wings through their descent or dropping quickly, dead or mortally wounded.

"Shields!" The order went out throughout their ranks, soldiers interlocking their shields forward and overhead as the gargoyles slammed into their formation from above and aground, their curved scimitars glancing off upraised steel. Benotrist short swords jabbed furiously between the seams, piercing poorly armed flesh.

From above, the battlelines took the shape of a giant L, with the 13th Legion pressing from the east and the gargoyles from the south. Just as Tyro expected, thousands of gargoyles broke west, scaling the rocky heights of the valley's western ridge. General Naruv's magantors swept down from above, snatching creatures in their talons, before flying off, crushing their wings in their powerful grasp before releasing them to their deaths.

Draken raced behind their southern flank, cutting down any stray gargoyles that managed to fly over their forward ranks. He leaned in the saddle, lopping the head of a creature standing over a dazed warrior he struck from above, killing the gargoyle before it could finish its prey. He swerved as another dropped unexpectedly in his path, dodging a group of camp attendants hurrying to and fro. He turned about, racing his mount back east toward the angle of their lines where the emperor held position. His return path was more chaotic than when he first traversed it, bodies of men and gargoyles strewn everywhere. The scene off his right was far more horrible, with gargoyles swarming the entire front, slamming into their shield walls, while thousands more took flight, flying above their spear thrusts, before setting down beyond, many landing in Draken's path. He passed scores of other riders patrolling the rear area as he was, cutting down gargoyles wherever they found them. He saw more than one empty saddle, their riders missing to whatever fate he could imagine. He slew a handful before the angle was in sight far ahead.

Draken caught sight of Tyro afoot, cutting down gargoyles dropping in his midst with pitiful ease, his twin swords moving in unison, golden light flickering along their murky blades whenever they drew near each other. He was easy to spot from afar, moving about the battlefield in a golden blur illuminating his path. He had never seen Tyro like this, like the warrior that forged his empire so long ago. Years sitting the throne caused men to forget how dangerous a warrior he truly is. The death of his son further fueled his determined rage.

Despite their strongly held position and Tyro's deadly power, they could not hold for long, with the 13th legion pressing them along the river's edge, and the gargoyles swarming from the south. The adult male gargoyles were still not fully arrived, their combined might over one hundred thousand, perhaps more. Beyond them came the male juveniles, numbering in the hundreds of thousands, and beyond them the gargoyle lasses, numbering hundreds of thousands more. It was all hopeless, unless they were reinforced.

CRASH!

He turned sharply, looking on as a massive section of their forward ranks gave way off his right, gargoyles pouring through the fissure. Draken turned in the direction of the break, as General Gavis ordered fresh reserves toward the breach.

* * *

The left flank of the Chosen.

Terin waited as the enemy moved around their flank, crossing over the shallow stream to their north before attempting to envelop them. He stood among the finest warriors from among the Chosen, nearly a hundred in total, along with the four ape warriors, Elos and Squid, the aged minister standing at his side, facing north with the river to their right. He held tight to the Sword of the Sun, seeing a slight shimmer of fiery light flicker across its blade before abating. He raised it before his eyes, looking to see if the light would return.

Nothing.

He sighed, hoping it would ignite, but alas, it was not to be. He gazed skyward, beseeching Yah to intervene.

You led us here, Oh Yah. We have come of our own accord, obedient to your will. You struck away my power to ignite these blades for my sin of pride and disobedience during my enslavement. Please restore it so I might save my friends. You may take it away again after, if it pleases you, Oh Yah, but let me have use of it to save these brave people. Take my life if you must as payment for this favor, Oh Yah. I freely give it. Please help us! Terin prayed, a tear squeezing from his eye, running along his cheek as the enemy drew nigh. He thought of the many times when all hope seemed lost, when some miracle occurred to deliver him from ruin. How many times must Yah intervene before he fully trusted him?

He scolded himself for his self-pity. It was never their place to win this battle, but to offer themselves up freely for everyone else. That sacrifice required all of those gathered here, not just him. Somehow if they fought to their utmost, the gargoyle species would die here this day, delivering mankind from their curse. For such a thing to come to pass, they all must fight and likely die. With that, he resigned himself to that fate.

"I am proud to fight beside you, my boy. Let us give our full measure," Squid encouraged, standing beside him.

Terin regarded him, sharing his sentiment, each leaving unsaid what that truly meant. They would likely die here this day, along with their fellow Chosen, and gladly gave of them selves to do so. He truly loved Squid, never more so than now. And with that thought the enemy drew nigh, a wall of shields drawing forth to meet them.

"Shields!" the command went out, the Chosen raising their small circular shields to their best effort, a poor match to the enemy's heavily protected ranks.

Like hammer striking clay, the Benotrist shield wall met the Chosen's left flank, cutting down dozens as they drove them back. Only Terin and Elos held position, their swords cutting through spears and shields like wet parchment. Terin's sword retained its fell power, but was growing heavy in his arms, the same for Elos, though the burden eased whenever they drew near each other, light flickering along their blades whenever they did so. Where their swords in recent days grew heavier in proximity, they now felt lighter, but they had little time to investigate what that meant. Terin swung in a wide arc, cleaving several shields with his forceful blow, blood and shards of metal flying off his blade, before returning it to a guard position. Elos kept to his side, cutting down a soldier breaking free from formation where the shield wall was compromised. Elos cut him in half, cleaving him shoulder to chest before freeing his blade just as another came upon him. Terin interceded, lopping the man's head before shifting right, meeting another errant charge.

Crunch!

Elos turned, finding a Benotrist collapsing off his left, a hammer caving his helm, with a grinning Carbanc, son of Hukok standing over him. The stocky gorilla gave Elos a toothy grin, his fellow apes sweeping past him. Terin and Elos collected themselves, following the four apes into the fissure they carved with their swords, feeling a dozen others joining their maddened charge.

From above their plight looked hopeless, their brief victory a mere pinprick as the greater Benotrist host swept around them, driving the Chosen far to their rear. Terin surrendered himself to the blade, cutting and slashing with abandon. He moved apace through the enemy, slaying one foe after another, the weight of the blade growing with every step he was separated from Elos. His winged friend closed the distance between them, feeding off each other's strength. They would not last much longer, especially if they were again separated, their proximity renewing their strength.

"Agghh!" Huto, son of Hutoq cried out from their left, impaled on a Benotrist spear, his blade stained with the blood of many foes before he went to his knees. His fellow apes roared in anger, pressing their advance, cutting down his killer, Carbanc caving the man's chest, while Gorzak planted his axe in his face. Krink soon followed, sharing Huto's fate, a Benotrist sword impaling his neck. He struggled briefly, tearing free of the blade, driving his own into his attacker's face, before collapsing to his knees. Terin winced at the painful roars of Carbanc and Gorzak, mourning for their fallen friends. He moved ahead of the two ape warriors, cutting a swath through the enemy to their front, Elos guarding his flank as he went. Carbanc rushed to guard his other flank while Gorzak followed on their heels, spinning his axes with abandon, blood spraying off their sharped edges as he went.

Elos stumbled at his side, an arrow piercing his right wing, blood pooling along his gray-white feathers. Terin spared only the briefest glance, knowing the swords no longer shielded them from errant strikes and happenstance. They were vulnerable now, and death was drawing nigh. He threw himself into the madness of the blade, a madness now restricted by his mortal limits.

ZIP!

Terin paused, staring in disbelief as the familiar light flashed before his eyes.

ZIP! ZIP! ZIP!

More flashes swept the enemy formation ahead, the cries of the wounded and dying following soon after.

"PACKAWW!" The sound of magantors roared above. He looked skyward as scores of the warbirds passed overhead, driving southwest across the sky.

They were Torry warbirds. They were followed by Sisterhood, Macon and Benotrist magantors. It made little sense, and Terin thought he was dreaming until a strange but familiar object circled overhead, an air ski, with Lorken seated upon it, and Ular with him, each firing their pistols, clearing a path around him.

ZIP! ZIP! ZIP!

The men of the 13th Legion started falling away like the tide receding from the shore, their initial shock giving way to panicked retreat. They never suffered the Earthers' weapons before, learning quickly their devastating power. Lorken lowered his ski to the ground, hovering beside Terin as the enemy pulled away, leaving them oddly alone, their own ranks now far to their rear. Ular didn't speak a word, springing from the back of the ski with a regenerator in hand, ordering Elos to his back so he could treat him.

"Lorken?" Terin gasped, taken aback by his presence.

"Looks like you could use some help," Lorken said dryly.

"Packaww!" Another pack of magantors passed overhead, briefly distracting Terin, who stared up with his eyes drawn wide.

"We brought some friends." Lorken gave him a smile.

"WE? Who else is here?" Terin managed to ask, trying to sort it all out in his brain.

Who is here? It would be easier to say who wasn't, Lorken smiled. He just gave Terin an infectious grin before lifting into the air.

"Your King needs help, but Ular will lend you boys a hand while I'm away." Lorken gave him an Earther salute before lifting higher and speeding off to the south.

No sooner had Lorken departed another familiar sight emerged from the heavens, a large white magantor setting down before him… Wind Racer.

If seeing Wind Racer took him aback, the person riding him nearly took his heart. Corry lifted her helm, freeing her golden tresses in the late autumn breeze, her gaze fixed to his sea blue eyes as she sat high in the saddle. She nearly wept looking at him, her heart leaping in her throat as they shared this brief and eternal moment.

"Corry, why…" he tried to ask, too many questions flooding his mind at once.

"We live or die together, Terin Caleph. If I had time I would jump from this saddle and kiss you, but we have a war to win," she said, drawing her helm over her head, preparing for battle.

"Corry, wait, the Benotrist 10th Legion is with us, Tyro…" he began to explain but she raised her palm, silencing him.

"We know. Brokov told us what happened. I am pleased Morac is dead by your grandfather's hand, though I wanted to finish him myself. He saw your father die as well, Terin. For that I am very sorry. I loved him dearly, and so did Torg." She shook her head sadly, preparing to lift into the air.

"Torg, is he here also?" Terin asked as Elos and Squid appeared at his side.

"He and so many others. You Chosen have many friends. Rally your men and chase the enemy from your flank," Corry ordered,

Wind Racer lifting into the air but not before nudging Terin with his large beak, the small affection causing him to cry happy tears, his heart bursting with unending joy. He looked on as his true love swept into the heavens, following the other magantors into battle.

Terin froze in place, wondering what he should do next when Carbanc and Gorzak roared their war cries, rushing past him.

"Onward!" he heard Squid shout, calling more of their men forward, while Ular stood at his side, firing several blasts into the retreating enemy before following Terin and Elos into the fray.

* * *

Center of the Chosen line.

Lorn struck down another foe, his blade splitting a shield and the arm that held it, his follow strike finishing him. He was lost in maelstrom of clashing steel and blood, shards of flesh and metal flying off his murky blade. Lucas and Deva were at his side for a time, but he hadn't seen them for what felt an eternity. Others came into view, if ever briefly, like ships passing in a storm. He was lost to the blade, fueled by its awesome power. Though it grew heavier as he went, it still drove him beyond his human endurance. Even that power started to wane, and he found himself surrounded by walls of shields closing around him as the enemy drove the Chosen from the river's edge. He lost track of how far he retreated, or the number of men he slew throughout his withdraw. It was all pointless now, the enemy drawing upon him, his life measured in moments.

ZIP! ZIP! ZIP!

Lorn looked up as laser fire swept around him, dropping his enemies like ripened stalks.

ZIP! ZIP! ZIP!

He looked up as Lorken circled overhead, clearing the enemy all around him. Men cried out in anguish, others simply dying where they stood.

HARROOM!

The sound of horns echoed above the din. They sounded again, giving him a semblance of direction, placing them north and east, somewhere beyond the stream and behind the 13th Legion.

ZIP! ZIP! ZIP!

Lorken fired blindly into the Benotrists' serried ranks, driving them further away from Lorn, before lowering his ski to the ground, hovering beside the Torry King, as the other Chosen far to the rear gathered themselves and advanced to their position.

"Lorn, we finally meet," Lorken said, keeping a steady rate of fire into the retreating Benotrists, who drew away like a receding tide, revealing scores of bodies in their wake, many wounded and many dead.

"Lorken, you are a welcome sight, a magnificent welcome sight." Lorn surprised him by knowing his name, though if half the things Raven said of Lorn were true, it was little wonder he knew who all of them were.

"Can't talk long, I got another king to help. Rally your people and keep driving the enemy back. The horns you just heard are Connly's Cavalry hitting their right flank," Lorken said, sending a few more blasts into the enemy before holstering his pistol.

"Connly is here?" Lorn asked in disbelief. He had seen the magantors flying overhead but couldn't spare a moment to identify them considering the enemy that were all about.

"Yes, and the rest of your armies are close behind. Rally your troops for another go at it because help is on the way." Lorken leaned over, slapping Lorn on the shoulder before lifting in the air.

Lucas and Deva quickly reached the Torry King, looking on as Lorken sped southward.

* * *

Mortus slashed through another shield, feeling his blade pass through soft flesh somewhere along its arc, gore and blood splattering as it cut free. He shifted left, lopping a spear tip thrusting between two shields before turning right and cutting through a sword slipping around another.

"Agghh!" Tessa cried out.

Mortus looked behind him where she lay upon the ground, knocked off her feet by a shield smashing her own, the Benotrist wielding it looming over her, preparing to finish her with his sword. Mortus shifted, striking the fellow from the flank, his blow tearing through the man's shield arm, before pivoting back to the front, where others filled the vacuum he left, splitting another blade driving for his gut. He parried another strike from his right and then his left, chopping whatever he could, fighting desperately to live another moment. He hoped his blow to Tessa's attacker was enough to spare her. If he was able, he could have seen her dodge the blow intended for her, her attacker's thrust weakened by his severed shield before he too stumbled into the dirt for the loss of blood.

ZIP! ZIP! ZIP!

Lorken sent his deadly volley into the Benotrists below, carving a swath around the Macon king, finding Mortus amid the chaos by Brokov's guidance, his observation disc hovering higher overhead, directing Lorken throughout.

Mortus lowered his blade, recognizing the Earthers' weapon cutting down his foes from above, wondering which of them came to his aid as Lorken lowered his ski beside him.

"King Mortus, gather your people and push on past the river. The enemy right wing is in full retreat. We have forces converging on their flank, so you needn't worry about them countering your charge," Lorken said before lifting again into the air.

"Aye" was all Mortus managed to say, finding the entire episode surreal. He soon collected his bearings as Tessa and several others made their way to his side.

"Your orders, King Mortus?" one soldier asked, a Yatin by the hue of his faded tunic.

"To me! Rally to me! Forward!" Mortus bellowed, pointing his *Sword of Light* toward the retreating Benotrists of the 13th Legion, who now flooded back across the shallow stream.

* * *

Southern flank of the 10th Legion.

Gargoyles massed along the southern face of the 10th Legion, pressing upon the forward ranks, while thousands more clambered overhead, stepping and clawing their way over their comrades, falling upon the Benotrists several rows from the front. Overhead many more took flight, flying above spear thrusts, succumbing to archer fire before falling upon the rearmost ranks. Farther west, many thousands more ascended the heights of the western ridge, preparing to assail the 10th Legion's right flank, crushing them under the weight of their numbers.

Another massive breach caved their lines near the angle where those aligned along the river met the southern formations facing the gargoyles, hundreds of the creatures pouring through the fissure. Tyro led a small host into the breach, his swords cutting down his foes with pitiful ease, his fell power strengthening the resolve of his men as they turned the tide. He severed a clawed hand reaching for the fellow off his right, his second blade lopping the creature's head above the nose, its carcass dropping at his feet. He moved around the thrashing corpse, cutting down another, his two blades moving in unison, hues of golden light flickering whenever they touched, their weight also shifting with their proximity. He noticed the gargoyles avoiding him as if he were poison, or wary of him for some reason. He lacked the time to consider the reason for their odd behavior, desperate to drive them back. The creatures flooded around him, pressing their advance. His men started to succumb, falling to the gargoyle numbers while he advanced, cutting a swath through their center. If he could see the carnage from above, he would see his entire front about to collapse, tens of thousands of gargoyle warriors swarming his forward ranks.

ZIP! ZIP! ZIP!

Laser fire swept behind the gargoyle front from above as Raven sped across the battlefield, firing blindly into their serried ranks where no Benotrist rested in his line of fire. He couldn't miss firing into the dark mass, each blast passing through several of the creatures crowding atop of each other. He kept a steady rate of fire while Tosha scanned below for a sign of her father, finding him alone amidst a stream of creatures swarming past him, like a boulder breaking the current of a stream.

"There!" she shouted in Raven's ear, pointing out her father below.

"I'm not setting you down there!" he growled, seeing the tide of gargoyles flooding around him and the many thousands more swarming across the valley floor.

"I must save him!" she shouted above the din, desperate to intervene before he was overcome. She knew this was his chance for redemption despite all his sins. Without his intervention the Chosen would have already perished, and without their intervention, the Chosen and the 10th Legion would soon expire.

"Ah hell." Raven shook his head, relenting to her request, maintaining his rate of fire as he descended, one hand on his outstretched pistol and the other steering the ski.

ZIP! ZIP! ZIP!

He cleared a swath near Tyro before sweeping around him, stopping at his side while Tosha sprang from the ski.

"Take care of her," Raven said before lifting into the air, his laser flashing into the growing horde gathering to their south.

Tyro stared blankly at her for the longest moment, at a loss for words, a thousand emotions swirling in his brain.

"You will not die alone," Tosha said, drawing her sword before her, turning to guard his flank as the enemy drew nigh. She lopped a creature's head passing by, almost as of it couldn't see her.

Tyro gathered his senses, cutting down another pressing near while Raven circled above firing with abandon. Tyro concluded that the gargoyles either couldn't see them or were avoiding them altogether, wondering if it were the swords or their blood that invoked this odd behavior. Either way, they fought on, their efforts closing the fissure as reinforcements began to fill the breach.

"PACKAWW!"

Magantor war cries echoed above, where scores of the mighty warbirds filled the sky. The beleaguered men of the 10th Legion gazed skyward, their spirits lifting at the glorious sight as Torry, Yatin

Sisterhood, Macon and Benotrist magantors swept overhead, driving for the gargoyles ascending the western ridge.

* * *

Wind Racer sped forth, his gray-white wings pounding the air in effortless grace. Corry sat his saddle, scanning the battlefield below where the 10th Legion formed an L shape, running south along the foul stream that divided the valley floor, holding off the might of the 13th Legion, before breaking sharply west, where the gargoyle masses were converging upon their winnowing ranks. Flashes of laser fire pointed out Lorken and Raven's location on the battlefield, their deadly volleys tearing chunks from the enemy as they circled safely above the fray. She made out Tosha's position, watching briefly as she aided her father in closing the break in the Benotrist line to her south. She still couldn't reconcile that Tyro was now fighting on their side and that he slew Morac just as she was leading their armies to help him in turn. It was madness. She shook such thoughts from her mind, fixing her attention to the western ridge where a massive host of gargoyles attained the jagged slopes to her immediate southwest. She was trailing the leading cohorts by a fair distance, watching General Dar Valen's warbirds leading the vanguard of their winged formations.

The Torry magantors swept over the ridge, diving upon the creatures serried along its high slopes, snatching dozens in their talons as they passed. She looked on with satisfaction as they ascended, appearing unscathed, dropping crippled or dead gargoyles from their grasp through their ascent. They were followed by another cohort of Dar Valen's riders, and then a flock of Yatin warbirds. Captain Sarelis led the Sisterhood magantors soon after, followed by General Naruv's great host of Benotrist riders. A fair number of Macon and Jenaii warbirds followed after, each claiming many kills as they swept over the gargoyle ranks. Eventually the gargoyles succeeded in bringing one down, several of the creatures managing to cling to its wings and breast, hacking viciously with their scimitars or driving daggers between the avian's feathers. It appeared to be a Yatin magantor, if she were to guess, watching sadly as it tumbled from the sky, hitting the near slope of the ridge. It would not be the last of their brave warbirds to perish this day.

Corry girded herself for her first pass, Wind Racer rising higher into the air before his rapid descent. She peered over his white-feathered head, the ridgeline below coming at her, her golden tresses trailing in the wind beneath the back of her steel helm as she held tight. She wanted to close her eyes but kept them trained on the creatures gathered below, most scattering, fearing Wind Racer's outstretched talons, others sending arrows to greet them.

WHOOSH!

Wind Racer swept over their serried ranks, snatching creatures in each talon before speeding away, ascending with arrows zipping left and right, one grazing his left wing, causing him to shift. Another creature almost managed to grab hold of his breast but missed by a claw's length, grabbing at empty air as the grand avian ascended into the heavens. Corry looked back, seeing the disorder in the gargoyle ranks gathered upon the ridge below. Their tactic proved effective, delaying the gargoyles' eventual assault upon the 10th Legion's flank.

"Tosha, you better get them moving. I don't know how long we can hold them back, up here," Corry said through the comm she kept at her side.

"*I already told him. It is easier spoken than executed,*" Tosha answered back after a lengthy pause. She told Tyro the plan for his withdraw northward where their relief was marching to join them.

"Very well. Do your best while we buy you time," Corry said before raising General Valen, informing him of the situation. He circled about, leading his formation back to the ridge for his second run, their allies following his lead.

* * *

Right flank of the 13th Legion.

HARROOM!

The sound of horns heralded the arrival of the allied cavalry, over a thousand mounts trotting briskly through the valley's center. Torry, Yatin, Sisterhood and Macon riders formed into unified wall of lances drawing toward the 13th Legion.

HARROOM!

A second blast of their horns signaled their charge, their hooves pounding the cracked and broken soil like distant thunder, growing in a deafening storm as they drew nigh. They lowered their lances as they approached the right flank of the 13th Legion, billowing clouds of dust lifting in their wake. The Benotrists guarding the flank raised pikes to blunt the onslaught before flashes of laser spewed from the lead mounts, Criose and Culn Davorin riddling the forward pikemen while seated behind the Generals Connly and Cornyana, sharing their mounts and directing their fire where they were ordered. Their fire was enough to break up the hastily erected pikes, as the Cavalry spilt, General Connly leading the left wing around the Benotrist rear while General Cornyana led his Yatin cavalry through the enemy center, their lances tearing through the 13th Legion's faltering ranks.

The 13th legion was hard pressed from the west with the Chosen and half the 10th Legion pushing them back across the shallow stream, aided by Lorken's laser fire and the swords wielded by Lorn, Mortus Elos, and Terin, each cutting men down as they advanced, preventing the men of the 13th Legion to exploit the Chosen's poor armor and disordered ranks. The Chosen constituted a small portion of the line, guarding the 10th Legion's left flank, but they advanced with the fierceness of ten times their number, collapsing the 13th Legion's right flank as the cavalry struck from the north. The 13th Legion's crumbling flank quickly spread south where the 10th Legion joined the maddened charge, driving their former comrades back across the length of the shallow stream while Lorken circled overhead, breaking up strongpoints in the enemy line.

* * *

Cronus drew his mount alongside Torg Vantel, the two stopping just ahead of their vast host. Behind them marched the might of their alliance, the convergence of Queen Letha's combined Sisterhood,

Torry and Yatin armies from the west with Corry's alliance of Torry, Macon, Benotrist, rebel, Casian and Jenaii host from the east, along with contingents of Zulon, Teso and Nayboria. The two forces combined upon entering the vale, marching south through the wide, flat and barren valley.

Gazing south, they beheld the battle take shape, with the 13th Legion falling back from the bank of the shallow stream that divided the vale, while pressed by half the 10th Legion driving them east, aided by the Chosen and the cavalry they sent to aid them. Farther south and west, the other half of the 10th Legion was desperately holding on against the vanguard of the gargoyle masses, suffering untold casualties, their forward ranks obscured by the creatures swarming their front.

"They won't be able to withdraw from that position to join us," Torg snorted, his steel gray eyes scanning the sorry state of the Benotrist lines running from the river to the western ridge where their magantors were desperately fending off another gargoyle host from flanking them. Flashes of laser disappeared into the gathering mass of creatures being fed into the battle. Scanning farther south and east, Torg could see the greater host of the gargoyles carpeting the valley floor. It was as if the gates of damnation were opened, spewing their foul spirits upon the world in an unending stream.

Cronus followed his gaze, looking over the sea of black and white flesh stretching the breadth of the vale and endlessly south. It was the entirety of the gargoyle race, prepared to give battle, here at the end of all things. He now understood the role of the Chosen, seeing that their willingness to sacrifice themselves somehow turned Tyro to their side, but even with his 10th Legion, they were still outnumbered. He felt they could yet win, considering they held the *Swords of Light* and the Earthers' weapons, but many if not most of them would perish in the attempt. He could see where Torg was referring, the Benotrist 10th Legion's defiant stand, where they held back the might of the gargoyle masses. They could hardly withdraw to join their lines. No, there was only one choice now.

"If they cannot retreat to join us, then we must go to them."

"Then what are we waiting for?" Torg growled, raising the comm to his lips, giving the order.

His order was followed by a blast of horns, their walls of infantry lumbering forth like the advent of a tsunami preparing to break upon an empty coast. Aligned to the far west was the Yatin 2nd Army, led by General Yitia, numbering nearly twenty telnics. To his east marched the 4th Torry Army, their once winnowed ranks restored with garrison soldiers, conscripts, and men of Maconia added to their number while at Cagan. Their general, Farro, stood ahead of his men upon a spirited gray mount, drawing his sword upon the enemy host to the south, urging his men onward.

Next came the 1st Sisterhood Army, led by their General Na, nearly twenty telnics strong. She was joined by General Jani, commander of all Sisterhood armies, and their Queen, who sat astride her fiery ocran. Like Cronus, she carried a *Sword of Light*, its unusual constitution strangely shifting with every passing moment now. It was light to wield one moment and heavy the next, light now flickering intermittently. She looked in Cronus' direction across that distant space separating them, each feeling a strange connection, a bond growing stronger by the moment.

Next came King Sargov, leading the small contingents of Teso and Zulon, riding forth before his brave men, waving his sword toward the distant foe. Joining King Sargov was King Lichu and his ten Nayborian warriors. It was here where his oaths would be upheld, to fight the gargoyles to their death or his own.

Beside them marched the growing ranks of Benotrists sworn to Terin, led by Commander Dalomos, who Raven brought forth on his air ski earlier in their march while more of his men marched with the apes far to their west. Their present numbers exceeded ten telnics. Had they time, they could have gathered even more. Tidings of their new alliance spread across the breadth of the fading empire. They marched forth, determined to save their new king who was currently somewhere in the heart of the fighting ahead.

To their immediate east marched the 1st Torry Army, led by General Lewins, his army numbering twelve telnics, a near-even split between native Torries and Macons. Beside him marched General

Ciyon, leading the Macon-Torry army, riding before his twelve telnics with Guilen at his side, his young friend eager to save his sister Deva, who also was among the Chosen, her fate unknown amidst the chaos before them.

East of Ciyon's army marched Alen and his rebel cohorts, fighting under the same standard as their new Benotrist allies, each sworn to Terin. Beyond them marched the 2nd Casian Army led by General Motchi, with ten of his twelve telnics aligned behind him in ordered ranks.

On the far Eastern end of their line was the 1st and 2nd Battlegroups of the Jenaii, their generals standing forward of their rows of warriors, with King El Anthar circling above upon his great warbird. It would fall to the Jenaii to clear the Nasser Pass, where stood the Laycrom garrison guarding the vital passageway, resting along the eastern ridge of the Oddigem, just to their south. It was by this pass their ape allies would soon arrive from the east, allowing them a direct path to the vale and saving half a day's march that their original route would have taken them. Since Matuzak led over thirty telnics of ape warriors and ten telnics of Benotrists, along with 500 Encructans, clearing the Nasser Pass of adversaries would greatly hasten their arrival and might be enough to win the battle.

The armies hastened forth, eager to join the battle unfolding before them. Cronus and Torg held in place, waiting to melt into their approaching ranks where Galen and Ilesa rode beside their new Benotrist allies with Zem marching afoot behind them. Cronus regarded the Benotrists' new standard lifting in the late autumn breeze at the head of their army, a glowing azure blade upon a field of silver, the sigil denoting Terin as their king.

"You should be at the rear with the other matrons to receive our wounded," Cronus said as Ilesa approached, scowling his disapproval.

"My place is here, King's Elite Kenti," Ilesa said drawing alongside him.

"You should know not to question our fair Lady Ilesa, my friend," Galen quipped, drawing along his opposite side.

"Once we reach their lines, I need each of you to draw back, at least several rows," Cronus ordered.

"That is without debate!" Torg growled, riding at Ilesa's opposite flank.

"Very well, Master Vantel," she acquiesced, her thoughts divided between the task at hand and the welfare of her baby, trusting her safety to young Dougar. Like so many others, she wondered if she would survive this day. Gazing south, she could see the vast gargoyle host drawing ominously nigh, a savage wall of fangs, claws and flesh, driven by blood-red eyes that found her across that fell space. With dark, jagged ridgelines to their left and right, and a flat expanse of despoiled, barren soil between, it was a place of death and dread, threatening to devour her spirit.

HARROOM!

A sound of war horns signaled the Jenaii forth, their battlegroups drawing far ahead off their left, angling to the Nasser Pass, where the cohorts of the Laycrom Garrison guarded its entrance to the southeast.

"It is time!" Zem's metallic voice boomed, running alongside them before breaking ahead, firing his pistol into the approaching hordes still a distance off.

* * *

Raven hovered above the forward ranks of the 10th Legion, keeping a steady fire into the gargoyles crowding their front. He didn't even need to aim, each blast of his pistol cutting through their serried throngs. Despite the carnage they continued to charge, feeding untold thousands into the fray. Lorken hovered off his left, joining his fire to his own, now that the 13th Legion was withdrawn into the valley's center, where their relief armies were soon to arrive. If he could spare a glance, he would see them drawing close, with Zem leading the charge in the center of that vast host. A few of the creatures swarming below attempted to reach him, but he simply blasted them if they drew near, sending them twisting through the air, dropping into the masses below.

ZIP! ZIP! ZIP!

He fired into a massive bulge forming in the Benotrist line, tearing into chunks of the gargoyles pressing the advance. He kept a close eye on Tosha below, never letting her from his sight. She and her father worked in unison, fueled by the swords' synergy, cutting down any foe that drew close, leathery wings and limbs flying off their blades, the creatures funneling around them, moving to easier game beyond.

"This is like throwing toothpicks against a tidal wave!" Lorken grunted through his comm, hovering nearly two hundred feet to his east.

"Tidal wave? Looks more like the entire ocean!" Raven answered back, looking to the mass of creatures now carpeting the valley floor. The forward ranks were populated with the remaining full-grown male gargoyles, whose numbers were now drawing thin, but behind them came a multitude of juveniles, their weaker wings limiting their flight distance. Beyond them came their wingless females. Raven managed to scan their ranks with his scope, curious to see them close up. It was the thing of nightmares.

"If these were humans, our fire would have least slowed them down, if not sent them off in panic, but these things are like rabid dogs," Lorken said.

"With them crawling over the forward ranks, we have to fire far behind their lines so we don't hit our own people," Raven added, still struggling thinking of Benotrists as their *people.*

"A whole lot of these people are going to die before this thing is over, unless you got a better idea," Lorken snorted, blasting a creature through the skull attempting to reach him, its desperate wings working futilely to attain his height before he shot him. Lorken shifted aim as the creature dropped like a stone into the masses below.

"There is only one thing I can think of. Cover me," Raven said, holstering his pistol while drawing his rifle, which was slung over his back, before lowering his ski.

"You sure about this?" Lorken asked, watching Raven drift half his distance to the ground, exposing himself to the gargoyles attempting to reach him.

Raven knew they needed to buy time for their armies to move in position and draw alongside them. He tucked the rifle tight to his shoulder, fixing his aim just beyond the Benotrist front ranks, shifting his start point east of the river. With that, he pulled back on the trigger, holding it tight as a continuous stream of blue light erupted from the barrel, before bleeding into a beam of pure white. Gargoyle screams rent the air, the laser cutting hundreds in half as it passed east to west, carving a swath through their serried throngs. Raven shifted all the way to the western ridge before raising his aim, passing again to the east, just as he did at Corell. Each pass cut down several rows of gargoyles, cutting skulls and chests with the front group, the intense beam passing through to the rank behind them, cutting across their waists and hips, before severing the legs of the next row, and the feet of the fourth, each pass of the laser dropping four to five rows of gargoyles. Raven lowered the rifle as it went dead, its core now burnt and useless. He tossed it aside, lifting into the air before any creature could reach him.

Lorken looked briefly at his handiwork. Beyond the 10th Legion's front lay a jumbled mass of dead and dying gargoyles, fifty to seventy paces wide, running half the breadth of the valley, east of the river to the western ridge.

"My turn!" Lorken barked into the comm, lowering his ski, taking aim to the ranks beyond as Raven covered him. It was a costly exchange, ruining their rifles but killing many in return, while buying their friends time to join their armies. After he was done, he and Raven would only have their pistols, and staring at the mass of creatures swarming the valley floor, that would not be enough.

* * *

Terin chased the retreating men of the 13th Legion beyond the river, racing across its shallow stream and up the opposite bank, bringing his sword down upon the back of a sandaled heel. The man ahead of him face planted in the ground, losing his sword as he fell.

ZIP!

Ular brained the man, following close behind as Terin left him his kills. Men of the Chosen rushed to join him, filling in along either flank. They could see the Yatin cavalry up ahead, moving swiftly through the disordered ranks of the 13th Legion. Elos set down beside Ular, having flown across the shallow stream before advancing to Terin's side, shoots of emerald light flickering across his blade as he drew nearer to Terin.

"AGGHH!"

A Benotrist warrior screamed off their left, where Gorzak buried his ax in the man's back, driving him to the ground before Carbanc brained him with his hammer. The two gorillas worked in tandem through the enemy ranks, their rage fueled by their fallen comrades. Ular kept the regenerator strapped over his shoulder, preparing to use it where necessary, but the chaos of battle would not relent. He hoped to find Matron Dresila somewhere among the Chosen but could not. For all he knew she might be dead or be anywhere in the crowd. There was no order to the Chosen's ranks. They were more mob than a disciplined military unit. Thankfully they were but a small part of the forces aligning to their cause. Already horns sounded across the valley floor, heralding the advent of the armies drawing from the north end of the vale. If he could rise above the chaos, he would see flashes of Zem's pistol just to their east, drawing even with their ranks, with the 2nd Yatin, 4th Torry, and 1st Sisterhood Armies aligning between them. Even now Ular could see the standards of the 2nd Yatin Army to his direct west, just beyond the Yatin cavalry.

He followed Terin into the retreating enemy ranks, the 13th Legion now fleeing south and east, desperate to find ground to regroup. They were now caught between the Chosen and the 10th legion pressing them from the west, and the cavalry and allied armies arriving in force from the north. This forced them south and east, where the gargoyle hordes now covered the valley floor, driving north.

General Trinapolis managed to withdraw to his rear, struggling to issue orders amidst the chaos. His only salvation rested in the arrival of the gargoyle hordes drawing from the south, hoping they would not turn upon them amidst the madness of the situation, unable to discern friend from foe. Only now did he regret his betraying his emperor for the fool Morac, knowing if the 10th Legion had joined with his own it might have won the day, along with their gargoyle allies. The gargoyles were unreliable assets that only Tyro could direct to their desired aims. Without him, it was folly. He only hoped their alliance of convenience might hold until the battle was won.

Trinapolis sighed in relief as his men passed south of the southernmost arm of the 10th Legion, which was entangled with the gargoyle host, managing to turn upon their pursuers just as Raven and Lorken decimated the gargoyle ranks to his immediate west, leaving row upon row of dead creatures. This bold tactic gave pause to the creatures following after, and time for the alliance armies to fall into position across Trinapolis' front, while other gargoyles drawing from his southeast filled in along his right flank.

It was there, across the middle of the Oddigem Valley the two great hosts faced one another over a small deadly space. It was but a moment in time, the two forces divided by the narrowest of margins before they slammed into one another. From the eastern ridge to the western ridge, the armies clashed, walls of shields and spears meeting the horde of leathery flesh and fangs. Amid the chaos the alliance cavalry managed to withdraw to the rear of their armies, their place along the front closed between the Benotrist 10th Legion and the Yatin 2nd Army, with the Chosen intermingling between the two.

Zem fell back behind Torg, blasting gargoyles one by one as they swarmed their front. Torg and Cronus fought side by side, having dismounted and sending their mounts to the rear. Galen stood beside Zem, brandishing a spear, the minstrel managing to impale a gargoyle juvenile dropping into their midst. Ilesa kept just farther behind, healing soldiers wherever she could, while keeping close to her comrades. They were fighting beside men of Teso and Zulon, losing sight of the battle beyond their proximity.

King Lichu found his first gargoyle kill, cutting down an adult warrior, the creature attempting to sweep down from overhead, before he rent its right wing. The blow caused it to drop beyond his feet, where he finished it with a blow to the back of its neck. The Nayborian monarch turned just as another came upon him, one of his men stepping between them, blocking the creature's scimitar with his shied, jabbing blindly around its curved steel. A ghastly shriek proved he struck true, the gargoyle dropping beyond, gore and blood spilling on the ground at Lichu's feet. The king finished the creature for his second kill, and it would not be his last.

* * *

General Gavis moved laterally along his lines, directing reserves forward where needed, and rotating fresh troops into the front ranks. Men could only fight for so long before their arms grew weak with exhaustion. His right wing struggled doing so with the gargoyles swarming their front, caving holes throughout his lines, and giving them no time to recover. Raven and Lorken's deadly volley gutted the gargoyle ranks nearest his front, giving him time to restore the line and rotate much needed reserves to the fore. This happened almost simultaneously with his left wing driving the 13th Legion from the river, pushing them south and east, just as the alliance armies arrived from the north. The end result was his two wings now running in a straight line from the western ridge to beyond the shallow river, where his extreme left joined with the 2nd Yatin Army's right, with the Chosen mingled between.

The emperor was somewhere off his right, his fell blades flashing hues of gold whenever they touched. He and Tosha moved in concert, as if their blades fed off one another. Off Gavis left, he spotted the Torry and Macon kings now fighting beside each other, moving in unison as well, pushing back the 13th Legion wherever they threatened their lines. Somewhere beyond them, where Gavis could not see, was the Torry champion, now fighting beside the freshly arrived Yatin 2nd Army. Nor could he see Elos at Terin's side, working in natural unison like the others, as if their swords were joined by an unseen bond. Gavis was still reconciling that his former enemies were now his allies, and his former comrades were now his foe. The world had truly gone mad.

He spared a glance to the west, where another magantor succumbed above the ridge, its dying body relenting along its steep slope, throwing its Torry riders as it struck. It was the tenth warbird they lost so far, though their brave attacks kept the gargoyles there occupied, preventing them from smashing their right flank. He noticed a few of the warbirds break off, sweeping east over the battlefield, snatching gargoyles flying over the front ranks from the air, crushing them in their talons. One was particularly large, a white feathered avian with black beak and talons. It broke off from the others, circling above the Chosen, its rider keeping a watchful eye on events below.

* * *

Corry circled above, finding Terin below, his sword flickering to life, its once murky luster giving way to crimson brilliance, before fading again. She watched as he moved forward of the 10th Legion's shield wall, cutting through the fore ranks of the 13th Legion.

"Foolish boy!" she growled as he moved farther ahead of his comrades, now surrounded by the enemy. Only his swift and deadly strikes kept them off balance, preventing them from closing in unison. It appeared his enemies could see him now, and she wondered at that. Perhaps it was the sword's power returning that fueled this change, though its glow was still weak and sporadic. She sighed in relief as Elos suddenly appeared again at his side, the two carving a hole through the enemy formation. Flashes of Ular's pistol soon followed as he moved behind them, spraying laser fire left and right, expanding their breach.

She caught sight of a gargoyle taking flight, soaring over the heads of the 13th Legion, appearing on course for Terin. She doubted he could see it from his vantage point. She directed Wind Racer into a steep dive, sweeping down upon the creature from the east, snatching it in his outstretched claws. The great avian crushed the juvenile in its grasp before releasing it into the serried ranks below, before ascending, catching sight of dozens of Jenaii taking to the air from the scattered ranks of the Chosen. They were what remained of the Jenaii named to the Chosen. They were armed with bows, circling above the carnage, loosing their arrows into the ranks of gargoyles and the men of the 13th Legion, whichever they passed over.

ZOOM!

Corry shifted, feeling the air of Lorken's passing air ski upon her left leg, looking on as he sped off to the east.

* * *

"Lend them a hand and I'll hold down the fort," Raven's voice said through Lorken's comm as he sped toward the Nasser Pass, passing over the massive throngs below. From the 10th Legion in the west to the Casian 2nd Army to the east, their armies were aligned across the valley floor, a sea of humanity against an ocean of gargoyles. All along that vast front their soldiers held bravely against the onslaught, steel and discipline meeting maddened bloodlust. They slew many times their own losses, but the gargoyles would not relent, fueled by a savagery no human army could summon. The gargoyles very existence was in the balance, and they had no choice but to fight to the last. Their adult warriors were running desperately thin, but were replaced with juveniles many times their number, though weakly trained and diminutive. Beyond them came the greater host of wingless gargoyles, whose ghostly white flesh seemed to despise the sunlight, but they came at them all the same.

"Don't do anything stupid while I'm gone," Lorken said, knowing that request was certainly to be ignored. He continued on, following Brokov's direction to aid the Jenaii assailing the Laycrom garrison guarding the Nasser Pass, needing it cleared for Matuzak's armies drawing from the east, though the battle might well be over by that time.

* * *

Cronus split a gargoyle warrior's scimitar, his blade passing through its shoulder as it swept down upon him, sending it tumbling behind him.

ZIP!

Zem brained the creature before it could rise, quickly shifting his aim to the creatures crowding Torg's front, the Torry master of arms holding many at bay, driving his sword around the side of his shield with practiced grace. Torg was light on his feet, never giving the creatures repeated looks as he jabbed low then high, or not at all. They were now fighting beside a flax of Teso soldiers, each man fighting desperately, several of their comrades succumbing. Ilesa followed close behind, heeling two of the fallen before they perished. She struggled finding space to work, often having to fight herself, fending off gargoyles before her friends interceded. She lost count of the times Zem, Torg or Cronus saved her. Even Galen accounted well for himself.

Cronus and Torg closed another breach in their lines, their swords and Zem's deadly fire carrying the burden. It was the same across the breadth of their lines, gargoyles throwing themselves against their walls of shields, where they were cut down in the thousands, while many more clambered overtop of their fallen, springing upon the second and third ranks, or taking flight, setting down further beyond. Men struggled under the weight of the creatures. Even if their shields were raised overhead, the weight of descending gargoyles could break limbs or necks before the creatures were slain. The juvenile gargoyles were easier to resist but came in numbers too great to imagine.

"Agghh!" Torg growled in pain, finding a gargoyle lass trying to chew his ankle. He looked down, finding her clawed digits gripping his left leg, snarling as she planted her fangs through his calf, her head tucked around his knee. He struck her back, severing her spine. The creature fell back, staring up at him with milky white eyes, her fangs snapping violently before he drove his sword through her throat, kicking her off his blade.

"Where did it come from?" Cronus managed to ask, guarding his flank.

"Cursed thing crawled through his legs." Torg pointed to the soldier off his left, a Teso warrior occupied with another creature jabbing at him with a spear.

Cronus thought the gargoyle lass was the most hideous thing he ever beheld, a creature of nightmares brought to life. It was the first he saw up close this day but would not be the last. A vast host of the wingless creatures trailed the juveniles. Their eyes appeared sightless, cloudy and haunted, but looked in their direction as if guided by other means. Perhaps it was their larger ears that pointed severely or their flaring, slender nostrils that twitched rapidly as if attuned to the scent of their prey.

Cronus moved to aid their comrade, splitting the gargoyle's spear as the Tesoan drove his sword into its gut. This bought them no respite with another wave coming upon them. Cronus wanted Zem or Torg to hail Raven on their comm, anxious of his friend's whereabouts but there was no time to breathe. Torg blocked an errant shaft intended for Cronus' side, ignoring the pain shooting up his now bleeding calf where the gargoyle lass bit him. The battle was devolving into maddened chaos, their lines wavering from the east ridge to the west. Even if they won the day, many of them would perish. Victory would mean the end of the gargoyle threat for all time, but the cost would be exceedingly high. He knew why Yah called upon the Chosen to spare the rest of them, but had they not intervened, the Chosen would have perished along with the 10th Legion, and the gargoyle threat might still remain. Perhaps that was the point of this, having the Chosen appear vulnerable as they did brought Jonas to intervene, his death bringing Tyro to their side. If they had to fight both the 10th and 13th Legions, along with the gargoyles, he doubted any of them would survive this battle.

ZIP! ZIP! ZIP!

Zem again cleared out the area to their immediate front, allowing those around them to reform their shield wall as the gargoyles again pressed close.

* * *

The center of the Sisterhood 1st Army.

Letha made her way to the fore, driven by the power of her sword, light again flickering along its ancient blade. The heaviness that afflicted the sword leading up to his battle began to wane, though would return at times as the conflict progressed. The light emitting along its blade flickered and waned, sometimes exploding in brilliance before relenting. She felt it pulling her as if beguiled, urging her westward along their lines. Her brave guardians tried to keep pace, working their way through the rows of soldiers waiting behind their shield walls, thousands of gargoyles pressing their front.

Letha shifted, her upraised blade meeting a gargoyle juvenile that swept over their ranks, her blow cutting it shoulder to opposite hip, its two halves dropping to either side.

* * *

Lucas fought his way closer to Terin and Elos, trying his utmost to protect them as they again advanced into the shield wall of the 13th Legion, tearing another chunk from their formation. To the 13th's credit, they still remained engaged, fighting on with *Swords of Light* cutting into their front, and laser fire riddling them throughout. They held their ground stubbornly, driven by courage or desperation. He divided his attention between Terin to his front, and Deva, who trailed close behind him, guarding his back. They came to fight in unison, her skill with a sword nearly his equal. They had each saved the other's life several times this day, so much so, that he lost count.

ZIP!

The flash of Ular's pistol caught his eye, his friend following Terin and Elos into the fray. He was delighted to see him but had to get close enough to speak with a sea of warriors still between them. Lucas fought beside King Lorn for a time, but the flow of battle carried him closer to Terin, who was still up ahead. There was a brief respite from the enemy, the walls of soldiers separating him from Terin and Ular as the others suddenly moved, clearing his path.

He ran apace with Deva close behind, coming upon his friend, Ular regarding him with a slight smile, to which Lucas grinned widely. The distinct gesture was alien to Ular's kind, but his time with Lucas and the Earthers had changed the Enoructan in so many ways. Lucas smiled, pleased to fight once again by his side. He recalled their parting at Notsu, when he was Chosen and Ular was not, but here they were, fighting together in the great battle of the ages.

His elation turned to dread as Deva cried out behind him.

* * *

After she cried out, Deva felt the world spinning, falling on her back, her eyes clouding over, struck with another vision. Lucas and Ular came to her side, each knowing her visions took priority over the battle around them. For it to happen now portended a greater message. They waited patiently for her to finish, her body shaking violently while they stood guard over her, Ular's eyes shifting left and right, his pistol at the ready, while Lucas held her, cradling her head in his arms. After an eternal moment her eyes sprang open, coming into focus, shifting frantically before settling upon Lucas.

"What did you see, Deva?" Lucas asked.

"The… the swords." She coughed.

"The swords? What swords?" he asked.

"*The Swords of Light*!" she said, gripping his shoulders.

"What…" he began to ask, but she stopped him.

"I know what we must do!" she nearly shouted, the revelation blooming in her eyes. It was all so clear it nearly took her breath.

* * *

"What for?" Raven asked, sending another volley into the gargoyle ranks below, hovering a hundred feet above Tosha and her father. They stood below surrounded by the bodies of men and gargoyles, blunting another break in their line. The 10th Legion was forced back several times as the bodies piled up before them, creating growing mounds which the gargoyles used to launch themselves upon them. Most of the adult warriors were slain, giving way to the hundreds of thousands of juveniles that followed. Thankfully, most of the gargoyle archers were elsewhere, limiting any danger to Raven hovering above. He kept a watchful eye on any threats they might pose to Tosha, his blasts breaking up any concentrations forming nearby.

"*We need all the swords together*," Brokov's voice echoed through the comm.

"You already said that, but why?"

"*Because Deva said so*," Brokov growled.

"Why are we listening to her?"

"*They say she sees things. Just do it!*" Brokov growled, knowing they didn't have time for a full explanation.

"Aren't we all seeing things?" Raven mumbled, closing his comm.

Wonder what the exterminators back on Earth would charge for a job this big? he asked himself, looking south to the sea of gargoyles covering the valley floor. He simply shook his head, lowering the ski to the ground beside Tosha, firing a few blasts to clear away any nearby danger.

"Grab dear old dad and climb on board!" he shouted over the din.

"I can't leave. There are too many. The Legion might break if we do." She grunted, the weight of the sword taking its toll, growing heavier again.

"Tell that to Deva when you see her, but we have to go."

"Deva?" Tosha asked, before realizing what this portended. She gathered her father, who glared daggers at Raven before complying, joining Tosha on the back of the air ski.

* * *

The Nasser Pass.

Lorken passed along the length of the jagged pass that wound through the eastern ridge of the Oddigem, firing into the crowded ranks of soldiers guarding the vital passageway. The pass was more a narrow canyon that cut through the ridge, with steep slopes to either side throughout much of its course. The men of Laycrom retreated deeper into the pass at the outset of the battle, confounded by the battle where their emperor was battling the 13th Legion. They thought to ride out the battle remaining in place before they were beset with the arriving Jenaii who took up position on the slopes to either side of the pass, their archers firing into their midst, fueling panic among them.

Lorken swept back and forth along the pass, his laser fire adding to the chaos, driving the men trapped there west through the gap, where they escaped through its western end. Once free of the pass, the men of Laycrom scattered into the open countryside beyond, a collage of rolling hills, forests and farmlands. Upon his second pass through the pass, Lorken was hailed by Brokov, calling him back into the vale to help bring Cronus and Queen Letha to Terin.

* * *

Alen brought his shield before his face, blocking a spear bouncing off its curved front. He stood amidst the ranks of his fellow rebels, who were crowded between the Casians on one side and General Ciyon upon the other. Their forward ranks were decimated several times now, meeting each bloody gargoyle attack with savage desperation. Thousands of dead gargoyle juveniles were piled upon heaps to their direct front, forcing them to withdraw and dress their ranks. The maneuver was difficult to execute, especially for men not trained to do so, costing the lives of so many. The tactic had to be repeated once the next pile began to build, thousands dying all around them. It was the same problem each of their allies suffered, though their ranks were well drilled in withdrawing, unlike Alen's men. There was little chance of his men breaking, though, for there was no place to run where the gargoyles could not find them. This was the final battle of the age, a battle to the death, man against gargoyle.

"Kai-Shorum!" A demonic hiss echoed above the din, heralding the advent of the gargoyle lasses, their hideous chants sending tendrils of disgust and terror through the ranks as they came upon them, climbing over the piles of corpses to their front like serpents sliding along the ground.

Alen closed shields to the men beside him, preparing to battle the newcomers. He kept his shield tight, jabbing his sword around its side, the blade sinking into soft tissue of some sort. He drew back, feeling something at his feet, looking down to see one of the white-skinned creatures trying to bite his ankle, having crawled under his shield. He lopped its neck, lowering his shield while crouching, closing the exposed area between his shield and the ground. All around him men were beset by the newcomers, the creatures throwing themselves into their shield walls, or climbing overhead, or crawling underneath, driven by the scent and sound of their prey.

"Agghh!"

A man cried out off his left, a gargoyles lass gouging his eyes with her clawed fingers, sinking her fangs into his neck, driving him to the ground.

ZIP! ZIP!! ZIP!

Alen looked skyward as Lorken swept overhead, blunting the creatures' charge to their front, if ever briefly, buying them precious time to close their ranks.

* * *

Kriton crawled through the mounds of dead, his crimson eyes aflame with unfettered rage, fixed upon the enemy lines ahead that always seemed to draw farther away. He suffered laser blasts tearing into the ranks all around him. He saw more than one of the humans bearing the cursed *Swords of Light*, though he couldn't tell which it was, and wondered how many of them the enemy now possessed. He endured rains of arrows, laser strafing all around him, and spear thrusts and shield walls smashing his formations. And yet, he endured, clawing his way among the dead before another group of his minions passed by, joining their maddened charge into the enemy host. The last group was solely juveniles, his adult warriors nearly spent. His hope for victory seemed lost, but he was determined to slay as many of the enemy as he could. With the untold thousands of juveniles and lasses, he doubted many of the enemy would survive this battle.

To the death, he snarled to himself, joining another maddened charge.

* * *

Terin looked up as Lorken set down beside him, bearing Cronus and Ilesa, who quickly jumped to the ground before he sped off to fetch Zem. He already brought Queen Letha, who stood watch at Terin's side, joining Elos, their swords held at the ready, waiting upon the others to arrive. Ular joined Lucas to their front, shooting any Benotrist or gargoyle drawing within sight.

ZIP! ZIP! ZIP!

Raven spewed a deadly volley across their front, beyond their shield wall which formed up to their south, their forward ranks clearing space for them to do whatever Deva had in mind. Raven circled about before setting down beside them, carrying Tosha and Tyro. Terin's paternal grandfather shared a look with him that he could not discern. Perhaps it was regret, pride or quiet hatred, for the man was a mystery. Tyro climbed off, sharing a look with him before looking to Letha.

"Taleron," Letha said evenly, gauging his reaction to seeing her. They hadn't spoken in many years other than bland words on rolled parchment. She couldn't miss the flicker of life that passed his golden eyes, a remnant of the passion they once shared. Here they stood at the end of all things, fighting together beside the one person they each loved… Tosha.

"You must give one of your swords to another, for no one can bear the strain of two," Deva warned Tyro, who gave her a dark look.

"Father, please listen to her," Tosha pleaded.

"You," Tyro called out to Lucas who stood guard to the front.

Lucas turned about as Tyro dropped one of his swords at his feet.

"I will expect that back after this is over," Tyro said as Lucas sheathed his own blade, taking up the powerful sword.

Corry arrived next, landing Wind Racer within the large open space that their men had cleared for them behind their forward shield wall, bearing King Mortus, Tessa and King Lorn. King Mortus refused to leave poor Tessa without his protection, the three of them climbing down.

Ilesa and Ular backed away, each keeping their regenerators at hand, preparing to intervene if needed. Lorken sped overhead, circling about before lowering into their midst with Zem sitting behind him. Zem jumped clear, his heavy boots imprinting in the broken soil as Lorken lifted higher, keeping an eye to their surroundings while Deva prepared what must be done.

"Whatever you're going to do, you better do it soon," Raven told Deva, hovering just above their heads, his gaze fixed to their south, watching their forward shield wall holding the enemy at bay.

"It is time," Deva said, looking to Terin, before backing away, the others forming a loose circle around him.

Terin held the *Sword of the Sun* aloft, a dull crimson glow illuminating its blade. He held it tighter, lifting it higher, its luster growing stronger before bursting to life. The others looked briefly away, shielding their eyes before its ethereal brilliance. A distant moan bellowed from the nearest gargoyles, as if struck by a kinetic pulse, a wave of immense pain coursing their leathery flesh.

Deva directed Elos and Lorn forth, each raising their blades, the two *Swords of the Moon*, touching them to Terin's blade. Emerald and azure light burst along their blades, engulfing their ancient metal in near blinding radiance. The others looked on with wonder as all three swords shared their unique hues, a cacophony of crimson, azure and emerald flowing around their joined blades.

"Queen Letha," Deva said, calling her forth.

Letha stepped between Terin and Lorn, lifting her sword, golden light bursting from its blade before touching its tip toward the others.

"Princess Tosha." Deva called forth her cousin, who followed her mother, stepping between Terin and Elos, pressing her sword to the others.

"Lucas." Deva summoned her protector forth, a golden light bursting from his blade as well once he joined it to the others.

"King Mortus."

"Emperor Tyro."

"Cronus."

They each stepped forth, holding their swords aloft, pressing them to the others, golden light bursting from their blades before melding with the light of the greater swords. They joined in ethereal brilliance, hues of gold, crimson, azure and emerald churning about all the blades, shimmering and swirling with growing strength and speed. The colors were joined with shoots of violet, orange and purple, their glow now engulfing them all as if a cloud of light consumed them. The hues swirled faster, melding together into a single intense light, pure and white.

ZOOM!

Light shot from the tip of Terin's blade, a beam of pure, blinding light. The beam shot skyward, growing stronger as it ascended, intense and white, passing through the firmament into the sky above and the heavens beyond. He held tight to the blade, as if his hands were fused to its hilt, the others joined in kind, frozen in place, engulfed in a thin cloud of mysterious vapor.

Deva collapsed where she stood. Ular fell next, then Ilesa and Tessa.

"What the…" Raven cursed, the power draining from his air ski. He jumped clear as it dropped suddenly to the ground. Lorken wasn't as lucky with his ski much higher as it dropped. He barely jumped clear, breaking his ankle where he landed. Zem took one step before his luminous blue eyes faded, tumbling over, lying there like a still corpse. Wind Racer toppled over where he stood, with Corry slumped over in the saddle.

The men farther afield started dropping like puppets with their strings cut, row by row, spanning out from where Terin and the others stood. The Chosen, the 10th and 13th Legions and the gargoyles nearest them quickly followed. The Yatin 2nd Army dropped next, followed by the Torry 4th. The wave went in each direction, dropping the magantors coursing above the western ridge and the gargoyles gathered below them. It went east, dropping the alliance armies one by one, column by column, before passing the near empty Nasser Pass and the Jenaii serried along the jagged slopes of the east ridge. It went north, sweeping through their cavalry, mount after mount falling into the broken soil, throwing their riders. Criose and Culn's laser rifles went dead, their power drained away as they too succumbed. The wave flowed south through the vale, afflicting the vast gargoyle host, lasses and juveniles tumbling into the dirt upon mounds of their brethren. The last thing Kriton saw before his eyes dimmed was the distant glow of Terin's sword.

The intensity of the beam of light fully blossomed, shooting stronger through the heavens and into the skies beyond. Raven looked away. covering his eyes, the intense light bathing the area in otherworldly brilliance. The beam passed above the terrestrial realm into the heavens beyond. The beam held for what felt like an eternity, before suddenly stopping.

Raven opened his eyes as the light dimmed, finding Terin and the others unconscious upon the ground where they just stood, their swords laying on the ground beside them, each resting where they fell. In every direction he saw nothing but bodies as far as the eye could see. The only sign of life was Lorken wincing in pain some thirty paces east, nursing his broken ankle, cursing up a storm. He tested his pistol, pulling uselessly upon its trigger… nothing. It was as dead as the air ski, and he slammed it angrily into his holster.

"Well, shit," Raven growled, wondering what he was supposed to do now.

* * *

Countless leagues north of the Oddigem.

The great gargoyle host moved across the land, their numbers stretched to the horizon, marching south with strength untold. They came from across the sea, driven by visons of the Oddigem Valley and the final battle of the ages… NODDEGAMRA.

They swept over the land like insects issuing from their nest, chanting their death song, its haunting chorus echoing in the late autumn air.

> *The time of our reckoning has drawn near*
> *The time of our ascension has drawn nigh*
> *Vengeance, mutilation, death chants cry*
> *Flesh of man, flesh of Jenaii*
> *Devour the favored sons of Yah*
> *Slay them child, lass and all*

CHAPTER 13

BANG THE DRUM SLOWLY

Mordicay Harbor.

Ben Thorton stood atop the lookout deck, his forearms resting upon its low wall, staring across the bay lost in his miserable thoughts. He lost count of the days he spent in that place, staring at nothing, recalling Jen's message over and over again. He thought of his destructive self pity, and how she would be ashamed of his actions, ashamed for his giving up. He hated that he failed her in this, just as he failed in keeping her safe. It was easier for him to blame Raven when he needed to blame himself, but hating oneself meant you had to live with the one you hate until death took you. Killing himself was another sin his beloved Jen would lay at his feet in the hereafter. Perhaps that was penance for his crimes, to live a long and lonesome life thinking of her and what he lost.

Maybe I'll slip on the ladder behind me and break my neck, he thought, knowing he wouldn't be granted such mercy.

As he stood there wallowing in his misery, he beheld the beam of light rising above the distant horizon, a pure white beam of intense energy shooting skyward into space. He looked on, wondering the location and origin of the strange sight. He couldn't tell if it was ten leagues away or ten thousand. He stood there spellbound, a thousand emotions sweeping over him, euphoria, dread, wonder, fear, and countless others. No natural power on Arax could manifest such a display. It was beyond imagining, breathtaking and terrible and glorious. It was humbling, for only an omnipotent power could project such a spectacle. It grew in intensity, shooting straight up through the heavens and beyond, and then… nothing.

It stopped as suddenly as it appeared.

With that, Ben descended the ladders to the 1st Deck.

* * *

Ben Thorton found Brokov and Kendra seated at the consoles of the weapon's control room, working feverishly to bring half the screens back online while Orlom stood behind them looking on. He could see nothing but black space filling the screens denoting discs 1, 2, 3, 5, 6 and 8, leaving only 4 and 7 active, their visual feedback filling their screens on the console.

"Let me guess, they all went down with that beam of light I just witnessed?" Ben asked.

"That would be an accurate assessment." Brokov didn't bother turning to address him, too busy moving disc 4 into position, the disc speeding toward the Oddigem from Fera.

"What happened?" Ben asked.

"The beam you saw was caused by their swords. When they brought all nine together, that beam shot out of them, and that's when everything went down," Brokov explained.

"Down?" Ben made a face.

"Everyone near it started dropping, except Raven and Lorken, though they didn't look too good when we last saw them. Take a look," Brokov said, pulling up the observation archive from disc 3 before it went out.

Ben looked at the top screen on the console where the scene unfolded from the point when the last swords were joined. He watched the initial charge where those nearest the event started dropping, including Zem, who toppled over as if his power source was drained. The air skis were similarly affected, with Lorken suffering more since his was higher than Raven's. Then others started dropping as the invisible wave expanded from where the swords joined. He looked on as row after row of friend and foe alike fell over, unsure if they were sleeping or dead, all except Lorken and Raven, who were unaffected for some reason. The wave expanded until reaching disc 3, then the feed cut.

"Have you tried comms?" Ben asked.

"They are dead," Kendra said, having tried raising them as soon as the discs started going down.

"Their lasers are probably out as well," Brokov said.

"How far out was the anomaly?" Ben asked.

"The wave went at least ten kilometers from their location, maybe farther. It didn't reach Matuzak's armies though." Brokov pointed out the ape armies displayed on disc 7 still marching from the east for the Nasser Pass.

"Can you raise them?" Ben asked.

"I just talked with President Matuzak and informed him of what transpired. He is pushing on as fast as he can," Kendra said, having just ended her conversation with Matuzak before Ben entered the room.

That was quick, Ben thought, having raced down here as soon as the beam of light disappeared.

"Do you think they're all dead or just knocked out?" Ben asked.

"I don't think they're dead, but who knows. I just need to get close enough with disc 4 and have a look."

"How long will that take?"

"I am sending it as fast as I can," Brokov said, watching the landscape passing swiftly below disc 4 on the screen between him and Kendra.

Ben went to the gun charging rack behind them, lifting two extra pistols from their stations and a rifle.

"Take this," Ben said, grabbing one of the two remaining regenerators from its charger, pushing it into Orlom's chest.

"What are you doing?" Kendra asked, turning around as Ben pushed Orlom toward the door.

"Give me your comm," Ben said, holding out his empty hand.

Kendra began to protest when Brokov handed over his comm, watching Thorton pass through the door.

"Let's see if we can figure out what's going on," Brokov said, turning back to the console.

"You are not going to trust him, are you?" she asked incredulously.

* * *

"Where we going, Boss?" Orlom asked as they stepped onto the open stern of the 1st deck where their last air ski rested.

"We're taking these to your friends, Orlom. Climb on board," Ben said, handing him the rifle as well before straddling the seat.

A stupid grin spread over Orlom's face, climbing on to the ski as Ella stepped onto the stern.

"Where are you going?" she asked, having overheard the commotion from her crew cabin.

"Away," was all he could think to say, sharing a look with her.

"When shall you return?" she asked, her pounding heart echoing in her ears, a sense of dread washing over her.

"Soon," he lied. He wanted to say more, needed to say more, but the words were not there. He did all he could for her, and hoped one day she might see that. Even that hope was an improvement on his cold heart, proving he was still human after all. The human heart was weak and vulnerable, two traits he could not abide as he wallowed in Jen's loss, but now he was strong enough to suffer it.

"Thank you, Ben Thorton," Ella said, wanting nothing more than to rush into his arms and have him hold her. Instead, she stood there, held back by invisible shields he placed around him.

"Thank me?" he asked, wondering what she should be thankful for, especially from him.

"For saving me from dangers I was too naïve to realize," she said. Had he not taken her at Tenin, she would certainly have been taken slave by one of the slaver factions that roamed the city. As pretty as she was, there was no way for her to escape their lecherous gaze. Somehow Ben Thorton managed to keep her safe and free throughout all their travels. If he were Raven, he would say a flippant remark that would ruin the moment, making sport of her feelings that she laid bare.

"You're welcome, Ella," he said, bidding her farewell.

"Let's see how fast this thing goes," Ben said, removing his Stetson and stuffing it within his jacket, the ski lifting vertically above the deck before easing over the rail. They picked up speed, passing over the gentle waves of the bay before lifting higher as they approached the wharves.

"WHOO HOO!" Orlom shouted deliriously, raising a fist into the air as they soared over the mast of a docked vessel.

"Hang on tight!" Ben growled, moving the accelerator, the ski zooming over the city.

Ella looked on as they disappeared in the afternoon sky, wiping her tears that now ran freely.

* * *

Oddigem Valley.

Raven knelt beside Tosha, checking her vitals, sighing in relief at her gentle breathing as she lay there amidst the other sword wielders.

"Are they dead or alive?" Lorken shouted, sitting a few paces from him, holding his broken ankle, pain shooting up his leg. He was thankful his pain receptors were dulled when he became a space fleet pilot, but they were not gone altogether.

"Alive," Raven said, moving Tosha's head to a more comfortable position, before gaining his feet, looking around at the endless sea of bodies.

"What was that?" Lorken winced.

"Hell if I know."

"Why'd we go through all that work to bring them together just for this to happen?" Lorken wondered.

"Good question. It's the stupidest thing I've ever seen, and considering some of the company we've kept, that's saying something," Raven grunted, kicking at the dirt with his boot before checking on Corry, who lay beside Wind Racer several yards away.

"And why are we the only ones not affected?" Lorken wondered as Raven adjusted her head as well, relieved that she was alive.

"Good question," Raven said looking up in the sky wondering how far that beam of energy went.

"You keep saying that, but do you have any good answers?"

"Yeah, maybe we're just God's special children," Raven said, using the stupid phrase their first line instructors always called their classmates at the academy.

"We're special alright. Why don't you fetch Ilesa's regenerator and see if it's still working?" Lorken pointed to her prone form on the opposite side of the circle from him.

"I doubt it," Raven said before humoring him, walking over, checking on her vitals before snatching the regenerator from the ground. Lorken lowered his head in defeat as Raven started shaking it, as if that would bring it back to life.

"Useless." Raven tossed it back on the ground.

"If our people are still alive, what about the bad guys?" Lorken asked, craning his neck behind him, fearing they might be stirring awake.

"There's one way to find out," Raven said, taking a step in their direction.

"Don't you think you should have a weapon just in case they start waking up while you're standing over them?" Lorken advised.

"Good point." Raven looked around before the obvious object came to mind.

"I'm only borrowing it kid," Raven said to Terin, who lay asleep in the middle of the other sword wielders, retrieving the *Sword of the Sun* that lay beside him. A dull crimson glow ignited along its ancient blade as he took a few practice swings.

"Just don't cut yourself." Lorken shook his head. Watching Raven wield a sword was like watching an elephant trying to play a piano.

Raven just gave him a look before marching off to the nearest pile of enemy soldiers, though couldn't really tell the 13th Legion from the 10th, so marched well past where he thought the forward ranks were engaged. It was more difficult to determine than he thought, considering everyone was piled on the ground in a jumbled mess. He couldn't help but step on them as he went, nearly losing his footing several times, until he noticed an ocran laying on its side with a commander of significant rank resting beside him, with one leg pinned beneath the saddle.

Four braided cords, he thought, marking the man a general of a legion. A quick slice with his right hand and General Trinapolis' head tumbled across the ground.

"That was easy, I can get used to this!" Raven shouted to Lorken.

"At least one of us is having fun!" Lorken growled, twisting his body around to be able to see his friend, the movement sending waves of pain shooting up his leg.

Raven made quick work of a few other Benotrist soldiers while making his way toward the gargoyles just west of them, where a number of adult warriors were concentrated. Once there he didn't waste time with limbs or wings, he simply lopped their heads where they were exposed, while flipping others around with his left hand so he could strike their necks. And so he went, tossing creatures around with one hand while lopping their necks with the other, the *Sword of the Sun* maintaining its dull crimson glow. Its weightless nature was fully restored, easing Raven's task as he went about his slaughter. He lost count of the number he slew, though it wasn't very sporting of him, if he was honest.

* * *

The last thing Brokov expected to find when he moved disc 4 into position above the Oddigem Valley was Raven working his way through the ranks of gargoyles wielding the *Sword of the Sun*.

"What's he doing?" Kendra asked, watching him casually behead another creature, and another after that like he was taking a casual stroll through a village.

"The only thing he can do by the look of things," Brokov said, sweeping the area with the disc's visual, revealing the entire valley in panoramic clarity. Whatever affliction struck the entirety of both armies still did not extend to Raven and Lorken. Only their Earther genetic markers could explain their immunity to whatever affected the others. He zoomed in on Zem's prone form, realizing that the anomaly also affected the power sources of their technology, draining their weapons, air skis, discs, regenerators, comms, and of course, Zem. Zem did have contingencies built into his frame, though he wondered if even they could have withstood what just happened.

"Can we speak with them?" she asked, staring frustrated at the screen.

"No. All of our comm-equipped discs are sitting somewhere in that valley, dead as everything else. We'll have to wait for Ben to reach them."

"How long for that?" she asked.

"ETA 38 standard Earth minutes with his current speed, which is beyond all recommend levels of velocity for an air ski of that type. I'm half expecting Orlom to take a tumble off the back of it any moment now."

"That would hurt," she quipped.

"It would be fatal. Meanwhile, let's see what our new discs are picking up," Brokov said, bringing up a live feed of disc 9, which was halfway toward Matuzak's army, where disc 7 currently stood. Disc 10 was enroute straight for the Oddigem, while 11 was skirting the coast north and west of Mordicay. He launched all three discs after Ben and Orlom departed.

"Nothing but open farmland and rolling hills and vales," Kendra said, watching the live feed of disc 9.

He brought up the feed from disc 10, seeing much the same, the landscape below passing swiftly as it sped forth. He switched to disc 11, expecting nothing but empty ocean and barren coastline before switching back to the other discs when a strange anomaly appeared in the distance.

"What are those?" Kendra asked as the live feed appeared on the center screen between them.

"Ships," Brokov said, his voice suddenly quiet as he pushed the disc forward to its maximum speed, closing the distance as he zoomed in. There upon the Benotrist coastline rested the hulls of thousands of vessels, so many he couldn't count. Many were anchored offshore, their hulls twisting in the surf, exposed to the heavy seas with no natural breakwaters to protect them. Hundreds were capsized or half sunken wrecks, their broken keels jutting from the surf or swirling with the current. Most were beached, their hulls driven onto rocks or loose sand as if on purpose. The ships had no noticeable ballista or trajectory weapons affixed to their decks, which meant they weren't designated warships. Their distinct dark timbers looked like no other Araxan ship they encountered to date. Along the shore he noticed several figures moving about the beached vessels, their dark wings indicating them as gargoyles.

"Is that..." Kendra began to ask as Brokov zoomed in for a closer look.

There upon the beach they could clearly see several hundred creatures scouring the vessels, nearly all of them suffering injuries of sorts, either broken wings or limbs. Two of them were dragging a bound woman behind them, a look of sheer terror transfixing the woman's eyes. The woman's frantic stare bespoke untold suffering they could only imagine. It was a sight that would haunt them for all their days. They seemed to be taking her further up the beach where a larger number of creatures gathered between two wrecks. Zooming in, they discovered scores of remains amidst the macabre gathering, likely human victims of the creatures' voracious appetite. Kendra winced as the visual revealed a ghastly white, wingless creature squatting over a half-eaten corpse, blood staining its pallid lips as its cloudy eyes suddenly looked up in the direction of the disc.

"What is this?" She gasped, taken aback by the grisly sight.

"I don't know. It makes little sense. I scanned this coastline three days ago, and this fleet would not have..." Brokov began to say before a horrible thought entered his brain. He shifted the visual toward the bow of the nearest beached vessel, expanding the image where a gargoyle maiden was carved upon its prow. Why would a human vessel have a gargoyle seductively affixed to its bow unless...

...Unless it wasn't a human vessel.

"What are you doing?" Kendra asked, confused as he sent the disc inland, finding recent sign imprinted on the soil, as if countless thousands of herds had trampled the ground running from the beach southward.

"This is not good," Brokov growled, pushing the disc to maximum velocity, following the path the gargoyle horde made on their way south.

* * *

It was the sweetest of dreams, humans falling to his sword one after the other, his hated foes dying at his feet. To his left and right they fell, some by sword, some by spear, and most by the fangs of his brethren, consuming their waking flesh as they feasted. Gargoyle lasses soon followed, bright red blood staining their pallid lips, a glorious slaughter of humankind. He saw Jenaii taken from the sky, beset by his minions bringing them down, their curved fangs sinking into whatever flesh they could reach. They fell one after the other, great and common, king and soldier, dying in methodic succession. It was almost a ballad of his wicked delight, a symphony of destruction to be sung through the ages of his kind.

Noddegamra. This was the fabled final battle of the ages, the battle foretold in gargoyle lore where they would destroy mankind for all time. A gleeful smile twisted Kriton's cruel lips, humored by his blissful visions playing in his addled mind, unaware of the blade passing through his neck.

SPLIT!

Raven lopped Kriton's head upon finding him amidst a pile of juvenile gargoyles, his unusually large stature and heavier armor standing out from the others, making him easy to find amid the piles of gargoyle flesh. He thought he looked familiar, rightly guessing who it was he killed, though couldn't be completely certain. He grabbed hold of Kriton's head, carrying it back to Lorken for confirmation.

"Is this Kriton?" he asked, holding up the severed head, Kriton's crimson eyes staring dully, and his split tongue draping loosely from his lips.

"Probably." Lorken made a face, wondering why Raven was showing him the disgusting trophy.

"That's close enough," Raven snorted, placing Kriton's head next to Cronus.

"What are you doing?" Lorken asked incredulously.

"It's a gift."

"A gift? It's a HEAD! The last thing Cronus wants to see when he wakes is that thing staring back at him."

"Not if its Kriton's. He's been trying to kill this jerk since Fera."

"Yes, but put it somewhere else," Lorken said. It was enough for him to suffer the throbbing pain in his ankle, but to have to explain common sense to Raven at the same time was a bit much. Alas, Raven never did move Kriton's head as he was soon distracted by the new arrival.

They both looked north and east where an air ski swept over the east ridge, speeding straight for them.

* * *

Ben Thorton eased the accelerator upon clearing the ridge, passing over thousands of Jenaii laying prone upon its unforgiving slopes below before sweeping over the valley floor. There before him lay tens of thousands of soldiers like rows of wheat cut for harvest. To their south rested many times their number in gargoyles, their multitudes covering the valley floor from that point southward. In the center of all this stood Raven, watching as he drew near, holding a sword loosely in his right hand.

"There's Boss!" Orlom shouted excitedly, sitting behind him, the hair on his head sticking out in every direction from their incredible speed.

Ben lowered the air ski as he dropped into the valley floor, speeding just meters above the body strewn ground. He could see countless Carka birds lying amongst the fallen, every living thing suffering the anomaly's effects… everyone but his fellow Earthers. Ben locked eyes with Raven as he drew to a halt before him, the two sharing the longest look.

"You might need this," Ben said, tossing one of the pistols he brought, Raven catching it with his free hand.

Orlom jumped off the air ski, running quickly to Lorken, setting the regenerator beside him, which Lorken quickly put to use.

"We got you a new pistol too, Lorken." Orlom gave him a toothy grin, replacing it with the dead one in his holster.

"You need to wake these people up," Ben said, looking around.

"No shit. I should have thought of that," Raven said, tossing his dead pistol to the ground and sliding the new one in his holster.

A small grin twisted Ben's lips, recalling all the times his friend made him laugh. Of all the things he missed it was this more than any other.

As if the fates heard Ben Thorton's suggestion, a small moan echoed behind him. It was Corry, whose eyes started fluttering. Raven went to her as Ben looked on. Raven set the sword on the ground while kneeling beside her, cradling her head beneath his arm.

"You alright kid?" Raven asked as she forced her eyes open, still struggling to gain her senses.

"I…I had the strangest dream." She coughed, her parched throat desperate for water. Ben already dismounted, fetching her water satchel from Wind Racer's saddle pack, the large avian still resting beside her.

"What was your dream?" Raven asked. He didn't expect it to mean anything, but getting her to talk was the fastest way he could think of to restore her senses.

"Stars."

"Stars?" He made a face.

"Yes. There were stars all around, so many stars and nothing else. They were passing by so quickly…" She stopped, for it made no sense.

"I saw stars once, Corry, when a pulling guard blindsided me and gave me concussion during our opening game my first year at the academy," Raven said.

Ben just looked on wondering why in the world Raven thought she would know what he was talking about.

"I saw them too," another feminine voice uttered.

They turned to see Ilesa rising from where she lay, staggering briefly before righting herself.

"Ilesa, are you alright?" Lorken asked, now standing also, his ankle restored.

Ben frowned at the mention of her name, knowing this was Kato's widow.

"I will endure, Lorken," Ilesa said, looking directly into Ben's dark blue eyes.

They stared at one another for the longest time, each bereft of words. All he knew of her was in Kato's letter, that he loved her deeply, and now was gone. They could hear the moans of several others beginning to wake, though none had yet to gain their feet except Ilesa. Again, the fates interceded at this intense moment when Brokov's voice broke over Ben's comm.

"*Pick up, Ben. I have urgent news!*" Brokov nearly shouted in the comm, causing Raven and Lorken to close around Thorton as he answered.

"*You're about to have unfriendly company. Lots of unfriendly company sometime in the next hour or two by their rate of travel,*" Brokov said.

"Can you expand on that so we can know what you're babbling about?" Raven growled, leaning near the comm.

"*A massive gargoyle armada came ashore sometime in the last couple of days and now several hundred thousand gargoyles are heading straight for you, maybe a million for all I can see.*"

"What? Where are they now?" Raven growled. There were many more questions he needed to ask, but there wasn't time.

"*They're approaching Darcol from the north. They should reach it very soon,*" Brokov hated saying, knowing their small detachment they left there to guard their provisions would be slaughtered.

"Darcol!" Ilesa nearly fainted.

"Ilesa?" Lorken said coming to her side.

"Her baby. She left her with Dougar to keep her safe," Corry said, causing a collective groan from all of them. Everything happened so fast upon their coming here, they forgot about those that were left behind.

"Orlom, come with me," Ben said, walking back toward the ski.

"Where are you going?" Corry asked.

"I'll go," Raven insisted, following Ben to the ski.

"I'll go, Rav. Stay here and take care of your friends. Here, you might need this too," Ben said, handing his comm to Raven while he and Orlom mounted the ski.

There were so many things Raven wanted to say to him, but time would not allow it. He simply extended his hand which Ben shook. Thorton knew Raven was a better friend than he deserved, and should have told him, but the look they shared removed the need. He gave Tyro a passing glance where he lay beside the other sword wielders off his left.

"Send Tyro my regards when he wakes," Ben said before lifting into the air.

"We'll be right back, Boss!" Orlom gave Raven an Earther salute.

"Not if you don't hurry," Raven warned them.

"I'll get him back to you alive," Ben said, sharing one last look with Raven before speeding off.

* * *

Raven and Lorken went about helping those who were first to awake, explaining what was about to happen once they gained their senses. Corry went straight to Terin after Raven handed her his sword. He lay there unresponsive, oblivious to his surroundings. She placed the hilt of the sword in his right hand, squeezing his fingers around it. A faint ripple of crimson light briefly illuminated its blade before waning.

"You must awaken, my love," she begged, pressing her lips to his forehead. Her heart broke as he did not stir, the other sword wielders similarly affected. She saw Lorn and Tosha among them, each lying there unmoving.

"Come, princess, we have much to attend." Ular's watery voice echoed behind her. She turned, seeing the Enoructan warrior fully awake, brandishing a sword, his dead pistol holstered upon his thigh.

Corry gently squeezed Terin's hand before gaining her feet, following Ular's lead. Looking around she could see hundreds now gaining their feet, most staggering as if drunk. She could see Ilesa moving among those nearest them, bearing the regenerator that Thorton brought them, tending the obvious wounds she could see. Many of those that were wounded in the battle before the swords were ignited, succumbed to their blood loss when they were asleep.

Corry saw many Carka birds awakening across the valley, half taking flight, while the rest flopped about, their wings broken when they fell. That brought the Jenaii to mind, knowing many must have suffered in kind across the eastern ridge. She looked off in that direction, seeing a few of the winged warriors standing upon the jagged slopes in the distance, their wings silhouetted against the eastern sky. She looked back in the opposite direction where Wind Racer began to stir, when a thought came to mind.

"Ular, many of the Jenaii are likely injured from their fall. Help ready Wind Racer so we can bring them here where Ilesa can tend them," Corry said, Ular acknowledging with his hypnotic blinking.

Some distance away, Raven was helping men of the 10th Legion to their feet when a strange sensation creeped along his spine. Gazing south he found a lone gargoyle standing amidst a pile of his brethren, staring at him with glowing red eyes, its fangs curving voraciously from its bloodstained lips.

ZIP!

Raven brained the creature, finding another some fifty paces beyond the first.

ZIP!

He dropped that one as the first one fell. Laser flashed behind him where Lorken was striking more of the creatures as they rose from their slumber, like the dead rising from the grave. It was the stuff of nightmares, a tale he would tell his kids if he somehow survived it all.

* * *

Thorton slowed as he drew near to Darcol, stopping along a rise just east of the village. Orlom sat behind him, his hair still standing out in every direction as if he were struck by lightning, the startled look contrasting the stupid grin on his face. The grin faltered upon clearing the rise. Gargoyles were pouring over the land, drawing from the north in endless numbers. They were difficult to spot in places, with clusters of trees and foliage dotting the rolling hills and landscape between them, before emerging from the other side of such obstacles. He could see a few bands of raiders draw ahead of the greater host, breaking off into two columns, one angling southeast, the other southwest, each numbering in the hundreds. Between them came the vanguard of their great host, numbering ten thousand or even more. They were crowded wingtip to wingtip, many flying for short distances ahead of the others before tiring and rejoining the caliginous horde. Others broke into the clear, rushing ahead of the van. He could see men wearing the colors of Torry and Macon soldiers battling with the creatures from his west to his east, clashing desperately, unsure if they should fight or flee. They were obviously caught unaware. These men would soon be overtaken, unable to withdraw with the first creatures now upon them. They slew dozens everywhere he looked, but more came, slaying them one after another.

Ben could make out the men positioned along the encampment to his east where most of their provisions were stored, guarded by five hundred warriors drawn from every faction of their mismatched army. They were joined by many thousands of supporting personnel, a collage of cooks, quarter masters, tanners, leather workers, fletchers, smiths and tradesman and skilled workers of every sort. They were moving about their encampment, struggling to carry off their precious provisions, many forsaking such foolishness, running south or east to escape the slaughter. Scores of gargoyles were already upon them, the clash of steel ringing in the afternoon air. A line of trees north of the camp shielded the gargoyles approach. He could see several leather workers fending off a band of gargoyles with whatever tools they could find. More than one was on the ground, wrestling with the creatures, while others were taken from their feet, gargoyles falling upon them, ripping their guts open, feasting on them while they were still alive. Soldiers hurried to and fro, slaying the creatures as they emerged with little order to their movements, the battle already degenerating into a hundred sperate melees.

To his west rested the village of Darcol, where many of their party took up position, fighting with gargoyles along its narrow streets, smoke billowing from several burning structures.

"You'll find Dougar with the provision depot to your east." Kendra's voice echoed over the air ski's comm, directing him to his target.

He thought they would have been wise enough to keep a few

magantors back for reconnaissance, but they appeared to have sent them all south into battle. He spotted a few outriders loitering along their provision depot, but they hadn't used the ocran for scouting, leaving them unprepared for this disaster.

Fools. Thorton shook his head, easing the ski into the air, turning east toward their provisions, his approach causing a stir in the crowd ahead. He sped into their midst, dozens gathering around as he slowed to a stop, hope filing their eyes at his arrival.

"Where is your commander?" Ben sternly asked when a Macon warrior stepped forth wearing the three braids of a telnic commander upon his shoulders.

"I am he, Commander Juls Filonan," the man answered.

"You don't have much time. There is an even larger horde of gargoyles coming from the north. You have two choices, run or die. If you choose to run you best leave now and head straight east or west. You'll never outrun them if you try going south to join up with the others."

"It will take time to move the provisions. We must…"

"There's no time for that. Leave it!" Ben growled.

"AGGHH!" Voices rang out to their east. They turned to see several tanners on the pathway beset by gargoyles, the creatures tearing into their torsos, blood and innards flying off their fangs.

ZIP! ZIP!

Thorton blasted them with his rifle, giving those gathered around a sense of hope. It was short lived. More gargoyles began to appear nearly everywhere. Commander Filonan ordered the men around him into a shield wall as Ben lifted into the air, with Orlom spraying laser fire into the creatures emerging from the trees. Thorton swept along the pathway, skirting the encampment before circling behind it. There amidst several wagons stood two washerwomen shielding a young boy with a baby in his arms.

"That's Dougar!" Orlom shouted excitedly, causing Ben to drop the ski to ground level, drawing up alongside them.

Dougar's eyes drew wide as they stopped in front of him. He did not recognize Thorton, but his manner of dress and unique light skin and size indicated he was an Earther. Ben saw the look of fear in the women's eyes. They needed to leave but the ski could only hold so many. He quickly dismounted, drawing his hat from inside his jacket, putting it on his head before stepping closer.

"You have to leave," Ben said, ordering Orlom to scoot forward.

The young gorilla gave him a questioning look.

"Can you drive the ski?" Ben asked.

"I drove it twice." Orlom shrugged.

That was good enough for Thorton. He ordered Dougar and the women to climb on and hold tight, with one of the women now holding the infant.

"What about you?" Dougar asked with the saddest voice.

"I'm where I belong, son," he said, taking off his Stetson and placing it on Dougar's head, before running his fingers along the infant's forehead in the woman's arms.

"I will guard her with my life," the woman said.

"You take the high road, little one, for Kato," Ben whispered, pressing a kiss to the baby's forehead.

"Boss?" Orlom gave him a sad look.

"Go, take them to Raven. I'll buy you whatever time I can."

Orlom gave Thorton an Earther salute, easing the air ski into the sky, Dougar and the women weeping as they sped off, rising higher than the gargoyles could soar, one creature springing from atop one of the wagons, reaching out toward the ski, its hands clawing at the air.

ZIP!

Ben blasted the creature, laser passing skyward through its chest as the ski sped away, Dougar looking back one last time.

Ben skirted the wagons and provision shelters, tucking his rifle to his shoulder, dropping every creature emerging overhead. He slung his rifle, drawing his pistol, saving the longer weapon for clearer ground. Circling back to the north side of the makeshift depot, he was met with hundreds of gargoyles now emerging from the trees, and scores of others passing over the thick boughs above, setting down upon the crowd of men desperately fending them off.

ZIP! ZIP! ZIP!

Ben dropped several in quick succession, making his way back west toward the rise, looking for higher ground. He continued to fire, making each shot count, knowing his pistol wouldn't last forever. His deadly volleys gave the small band of gargoyles pause, their bloodlust briefly faltering, giving the men time to cut many of them down. Ben didn't let up, targeting every creature he could get a clear shot on as he moved.

ZIP!

He brained a creature clearing the top of the nearest tree, its corpse falling through the thick boughs, breaking off branches as he dropped. He didn't spend time watching it impact the ground, taking another through the breast as it neared a Macon soldier, the creature releasing a terror squealing cry tumbling to its knees before the Macon finished it.

Looking west, another wave of creatures began to flood the top of the rise where he first arrived upon the air ski.

ZIP! ZIP! ZIP!

He fired into their midst, driving them off the high ground as he moved in that direction. A growing band of soldiers followed him, using the shelter of his laser fire for protection. It was an easy path to follow, but even he could not protect them for long against the massive horde fast approaching. They followed him none the less, their few growing into a small army. They were soon joined by the provisioners, men of all trades grabbing whatever they could find to fight with. Blacksmiths brandished hammers and fletchers carried spears. Tanners and leather workers carried axes and swords taken from the fallen, each following Thorton to the high ground while countless others fled east, hoping to outrun the creatures flooding over the land.

Ben's laser fire temporarily cleared the high ground, slaying many and driving off the rest as he and his followers took up position on the rise. The relief his new followers felt achieving this small success quickly faltered as they could now see the full danger upon them. The entire landscape to their immediate north was carpeted with gargoyles, a caliginous sea of leathery flesh stretching to the horizon. To their west, Darcol was now fully overrun, the last humans slain attempting to flee, creatures setting upon them, devouring the flesh form their bones. To the east, their provision depot was fully beset, fires engulfing the precious stores, black smoke twisting above in tortured spirals. They could see a few stragglers fleeing south and east from the desolation with scores of gargoyles giving chase. They held little hope of escape. Hundreds of creatures already circumvented the high ground, swarming past on their way south.

The men looked on with despair, knowing their fate. They were no longer Torry, Macon, Benotrist or rebel. They were simply men, men united in purpose, fated to die upon this sacred ground. There was no where for them to run, and no mercy promised other than a quick death, if the fates were kind. They closed about, forming a protective circle with Thorton in their center, the large Earther firing away as the creatures regathered all around them, pressing their advance.

ZIP! ZIP!

Ben struck two cresting the rise from the west, shifting aim to a group coming from the south, before returning his attention north.

ZIP! ZIP! ZIP! ZIP!

He dropped several more, their screams drowning in the growing din, countless others swarming over their stricken forms. A clash of steel sounded to his east, where a score of gargoyles met their makeshift shield wall, stalling the creatures advance.

ZIP! ZIP!

Ben blasted several attempting to fly over the others, dropping them upon their comrades below. He continued dropping one after another, keeping the skies above clear for his desperate comrades who fought on foot, their numbers dwindling with every gargoyle charge. He knew it was only matter of time now, a very short time. He kept a wary eye upon the ground to their direct north, where the greater host drew ominously near. He could see their soulless eyes staring at him, his presence the focus of their unfettered rage.

It was time. A slight smile twisted the corners of Thorton's lips as he cleared the area to his north with a few hurried blasts before holstering his pistol and unslinging his rifle.

"Clear away!" he ordered the few that remained, which they hurriedly obeyed, stepping over the bodies cluttering the ground.

Ben tucked the rifle to his shoulder, fixing his aim to a point to his east and squeezed the trigger.

ZIP!

A continuous stream erupted from the rifle, intense blue quickly bleeding into bright white. Thorton shifted aim, sliding the beam west, passing through rank upon row of serried gargoyles, cutting through the heads in the first rank, chests in the second, making its way down with each rank that followed until he reached the western end of his aim. His first pass dropped five to seven rows of gargoyles across the breadth of his vision, his second doing the same as he sent the beam eastward. Thousands of voices cried out, a disjointed symphony of ghastly screams rending the air.

The men about him looked on with wonder, the terrible and glorious sight again sparking hope in their laden hearts. It was again short lived as the beam went west to east and again east before dying at the end of its third pass. With that, Ben lowered the rifle, dropping it in the dirt, drawing his pistol. He already rigged the weapon for his intended purpose, one last parting gift for the foul creatures.

The ground before them was a scarred ruin, as if the hand of God swept through their ranks with a sickle, cutting them down in the thousands. He killed or maimed twenty thousand, perhaps many more. The creatures faltered, their entire horde halting at the carnage, wondering what devilry befell them. Their fear quickly abated, replaced with vengeful lust, their eyes drawn to the source of their affliction. Ben looked on as they began their chant.

> *The time of our reckoning has drawn near*
> *The time of our ascension has drawn nigh*
> *Vengeance, mutilation, death chants cry*
> *Flesh of man, flesh of Jenaii*
> *Devour the favored sons of Yah*
> *Slay them child, lass and all*

The haunting chant echoed through the air, stripping the courage of the men gathered around him. Ben listened with numb indifference; his heart long hardened to such things. The gargoyles closed ranks over the chasm of sundered flesh Ben carved from their masses, trampling over the dead and wounded, before advancing upon them. Others gathered from the east and the west, and those that passed south returned, coming upon them from all sides. Ben spotted a rather large creature in the midst of the charge, adorned in heavier armor than the others, brandishing a large ax, a commander of some import by the deference his brethren showed him.

ZIP!

Ben brained him where he marched, his corpse dropping like a puppet with its strings cut. His brazen act only fueled the creatures' rage, and their rage only fueled his aim, dropping one after another.

As the men started to die all around him, Ben was stuck by a memory, of his sweet Jennifer singing, her voice distant yet growing louder with every passing moment. Was it a memory, or a dream? He couldn't tell, nor did he care. He simply longed to hear her, her voice a balm to his withered spirit, renewing it with her gentle melody.

As I walked out in the streets of Laredo
As I walked out in Laredo one day...

The Streets of Laredo, that was Raven's song, not his, but she had the right of it. No melody better described his wretched existence than the ballad of a dying cowboy reaping the consequences of his actions. He grew deaf to the suffering around him, of men dying, their gut-wrenching screams swallowed by the gargoyle chants. A Casian warrior to his left impaled a gargoyle on his spear before another set down from above, taking him from his feet. He drew a knife as he went to his back, slashing it across the creature's throat, before another dove upon him, sinking its fangs in his gut, ripping it open. A Torry off his right stumbled, a spear embedded in his throat. He fell to his knees before several creatures dragged him away, his silent screams dying in his ruined throat as they devoured him somewhere beyond Ben's line of sight.

ZIP! ZIP! ZIP!

He fired hurriedly into the gargoyles closing around him, every blast passing through several, unable to miss. It was strangely satisfying watching a line of creatures succumb wherever he aimed, laser fire tearing through unguarded flesh. Some would drop dead, others screaming from their wounds.

He felt something trying to bite through his right trouser leg. A sparing glance revealed a white, leathery-fleshed gargoyle at his feet, wingless and blind, its generous breasts indicating its gender. He ignored it, his current targets more valuable than the second he could spare this pathetic creature.

ZIP! ZIP! ZIP!

More rows dropped or stumbled from the blasts he caved through their ranks, every shot striking a dozen creatures. He felt the gargoyle maiden pierce the sturdy material of his trouser leg, her fangs working their way to his exposed flesh. He ignored her.

ZIP! ZIP! ZIP!

More shots flashed from the barrel of his pistol, dropping lines of creatures wherever he aimed. Most of his comrades had fallen, the few that remained succumbing in quick order as the creatures swarmed the rise from every direction. Ben felt another clinging to his back, its fangs tearing through his thick jacket. He ignored it, not even knowing if it were male or maiden of its fell kind.

ZIP! ZIP! ZIP

He fired east, north and west, his maddened blasts doing naught to stem the tide now rushing upon him. He felt them now upon him, a slight smile touching his lips as the time had come. He kept his grip tight upon his pistol, assured that his alteration would work, his finger caressing the lever along its side. He could hear Jennifer's voice again calling to him.

> *Oh, Bang the drum slowly and play the fife lowly*
> *Sing the death march as you bear me along*
> *Take me to the valley, there lay the sod o'er me*
> *For I'm a poor cowboy, and I know I've done wrong*

As her final refrain faded, he could see her now, smiling down upon him from the firmament above, her white raiment as pure as a blinding light. She smiled warmly, outstretching her hand as if to call him home.

"*It is time, Texas,*" her gentle voice called out to him.

"Take me home, Yah." He closed his eyes, his fingers depressing the lever.

BOOM!

There upon the rise above Darcol, Ben Thorton took the low road home.

CHAPTER 14

A massive burst exploded from the overcharged pistol, blasting the small hilltop and the hundreds gathered upon it. The sound expanded, crushing eardrums for a mile distance in each direction, taking many thousands from their feet. A long silence followed, a deathly pall falling over the surrounding landscape, causing the entire horde to freeze in place. The brazen act invoked in the gargoyle host something they had never felt in thousands of years... FEAR.

* * *

Mordicay Harbor.
Weapons room of the Stenox.

Brokov directed the observation disc away from the blast as the creatures gathered around Thorton, rightly guessing what he intended, his visual feed relaying the final moments of his former crewmate's terrible end. He scanned farther afield, gaining a better sense of the effects of the intense pulse wave. The initial burst looked to have killed hundreds if not thousands, their body parts spewed from the blast point in every direction. Beyond this, another thirty thousand were knocked off their feet, suffering from minor discomfort to severe injuries, depending on what they struck when they fell.

By now, Brokov better understood the unique differences between the gargoyle males and lasses. Though the latter greatly trailed the former into battle, a number of the white fleshed lasses were within the outer blast range, suffering damage to their ears. He wondered the effect upon their primitive navigation, since their eyes appeared useless. Were they driven by an internal sonar using their enlarged ears, or by their sense of smell, by their fast-twitching nostrils? If it was ears, he would soon know as they slowly gained their feet, observing their state of disorientation.

"Why?" Kendra asked, sitting the chair beside his, watching his former friend kill himself. He knew what she meant, for he could have kept his place upon the air ski, instead of giving it to the women and child. It was also ironic that Thorton came upon just two women and a child and infant, and not more, just enough for them all to fit upon the seat of the air ski if he gave up his place. If there were more that needed saving at that particular moment, Thorton would have had to decide which to spare and which to leave to die. It was as if the fates decided for him, making his sacrifice a simple choice. The more Brokov thought on it, the more obvious it appeared.

"Yah's mercy," Brokov sighed.

Kendra gave him a look, wondering when he became a devotee of Lorn's God. He looked at her, knowing his answer required explanation.

"What other path of redemption could make up for killing Kato, or reuniting him with his beloved Jennifer? It was too perfect a sacrifice, too simple a choice. Even a skeptic as myself must acknowledge when coincidences are too impossible to be mere chance. something greater is at work. May he be at peace."

"How sad." Kendra sighed, imagining the suffering of Ben and Jennifer, and Kato and Ilesa. It was all so tragic. She looked at Brokov, aching at the thought of losing him, wondering when the powerful woman she grew to be, became so sentimental?

"Sad? Perhaps, in a way, but I think of something a poet from my world once said, a quote Kato would often repeat. It is better to have loved and lost, than to have never loved."

"Do you believe that?"

"Yes. Feeling love is part of life, true love and passion. Without it… well, without it, you never know what being fully alive really means."

They each grew quiet for a time as Brokov further scanned the region, finding the effects of the blast quite devastating for the gargoyle horde, but not fatal. They were soon gathering themselves, pressing on for the Oddigem. He wondered how they knew where to go, ascribing their behavior to a sort of instinctual migration akin to birds on Earth flying north and south with the season. It might not fully explain this strange phenomenon, but he could think of no better explanation. As far as the gargoyle lasses, those effected by the blast looked out of sorts, following the others only by their movements, not by any direction of their own. Perhaps that was something they could use.

Expanding their view, he could fully see their masses drawing from the north in numbers too grand to count. Was it five hundred thousand, or a million? The horde moved across the land like an ancient plague of locust he used to read about on Earth, stripping the land bare, leaving nothing in their wake. Following their path from the coast was easy, and he lost count of the skeletal remains they left behind along that hellish route. Most were human, but many were of every kind of animal they came upon. They devoured the very land itself, stripping vegetation from its roots, leaving naught but barren soil in their wake.

"Does Yah have another miracle for our friends? If not, most if not all are soon to perish." Kendra sighed, looking at the sheer size of the gargoyle horde.

"If he does, I don't know what it could be, even if we could restore all the drained weapons, and all the *Swords of Light* alit with their former strength. I don't favor their chances with only three working pistols and the armies we gathered," Brokov agreed. Time was running out.

* * *

"Come on, buddy, wake up," Raven said, squatting over Zem's prone form, giving his large metallic head a gentle slap. If they ever needed his help, it was now. His internal workings were designed to endure an Aurelian impulse weapon, giving him the ability to reset himself, as he demonstrated during the attack on Tro. That blast was from the overcharged rifle Ben altered, but this? This was something completely different. Whatever the source of the power invoked by the swords it was completely alien to their technology. For all Raven knew, Zem might never recover.

"Come on Zem, old buddy, I take back all the stupid things I ever said to you. You can't die here, not after your promotion to general, can you? You have so much to live for. If you wake up, I even promise to listen to your penguin story again," Raven pleaded.

Nothing.

"I'll let you be captain for a day, how does that sound? You can sit in my chair, and we'll sail wherever you want." Raven upped his bribe, but nothing could stir Zem to move.

"Alright, how about a WHOLE week?" Raven upped his bribe again.

Nothing.

ZIP!

Lorken stood beside him, firing again at a gargoyle rising to its feet to their southeast.

"I don't think he is waking up, Rav. Time to go back to work," Lorken said, targeting another creature gaining its feet, this one farther afield, his blast taking it through the skull.

Raven shook his head, patting Zem on the shoulder before again joining Lorken in the task at hand. He spared Tosha and the other sword wielders a glance. They still lay unmoving where they fell, not one of them stirring even slightly. Ilesa was treating whatever wounded that were brought to her, remaining close by, keeping a watchful eye upon the sword wielders should any of them need the regenerator when they awoke. Their lives took precedent, especially if things grew dim, and by Brokov's last report, they looked pretty dim. He hadn't heard if Ben was successful in extracting Ilesa's baby and Dougar. After her initial shock of the situation, Ilesa kept her emotions in hand, resolving herself to her work. It was an obvious shield against the pain of her potential loss. He could ill imagine what she was truly thinking. She left her baby with their supply depot, thinking it would keep her safe.

So much for safe. He shook his head, realizing there was nowhere safe at this time.

Corry was equally driven in her current tasks, Driving Wind Racer all about the battlefield, bringing wounded Jenaii to Ilesa while ordering those who were awaking into some semblance of order. King El Anthar joined her in this task, flying upon his magantor to every point along their tenuous lines, rallying those who had awoken into some semblance of order. By now, nearly one in four of those affected had awoken, many still struggling to stand. All of them spoke of seeing stars, just as Corry first said, of stars passing rapidly in the night sky, or so they said. He couldn't make sense of it. As for the others, they were coming along slowly. He could only guess how much time they would need for all of them to wake up.

The men of the 13th Legion were a different story, with nearly everyone of them starting to come to. Strangely, they did not seem eager to renew their fight with their brothers in the 10th Legion. They were all babbling about terrible visions of gargoyles, guessing they had nightmares of the horde Brokov told them was coming from the north. Since Raven slew their general, they lacked the single voice that could direct them into action. Most stood there, stupefied without direction, standing with gargoyles laying strewn about to their south and both flanks, while to their north were the human armies arrayed against them, especially the 10th Legion and the Chosen. The worst part for Raven, was that they blocked his view of the gargoyles resting behind them, but there was no shortage of targets to their east and west, which Lorken had been shooting while he checked on Zem. Since the men of the 13th Legion were not moving against the men of the 10th Legion that had awoken, they remained where they were. The men of the 10th didn't see the urgency of engaging them either, considering most of the 13th were awake, while three in four of the 10th were not.

The gargoyles were another matter, with only one in ten gaining consciousness since the incident. As they awoke, they rose staggering to their feet as if drunk before quickly gaining their senses, charging toward the human armies to their north, falling first upon those still affected. Raven and Lorken did what they could, striking them down as they arose, but their pistols wouldn't last forever, and even now needed to start recharging them as the enemy from the north approached. Corry went about ordering the humans and Jenaii that had awoken to reform forward of their stricken, forming a new shield wall between the slowly waking gargoyles and their comrades still slumbering. Of course, these new shield walls were quickly obscuring his line of sight and lacked the cohesion of familiarity that was essential to any trained combat units, but such was the situation.

Ular took it upon himself to gather the pistols Raven and Lorken tossed aside, along with his own and the rifles of Criose and Culn Davorin, bringing them to one place to see if he could get them to recharge. He also sent runners to gather up the drained regenerators, hoping to restore them as well.

To their rear, nearly fifty ocran and their riders had fully recovered, including General Connly, who began ordering the men into formation, preparing to counter any break in their lines. The magantors were similarly affected, with a score of the great avian fully awake. Strangely each rider and mount seemed to recover at the same time, just as they did with the ocran of the cavalry.

Just as Raven began to follow Lorken to reposition for a better field of fire, Brokov's voice broke over the comm.

"*Rav*," Brokov said.

"I hear you. Has Ben found the kids yet? Tell him to hurry up. We're gonna need the extra guns when the rest of these gargoyles start waking up," Raven said before blasting another gaining its feet. If he and Lorken were the only two still awake, he would've kept killing them with a sword, saving his pistol's juice for the bigger battle ahead. As it stood now, there were many of their soldiers doing that very thing, venturing far ahead of their newly formed ranks, slaughtering the gargoyles where they slept.

"*Ben's dead, Rav.*"

A long silence followed, making Brokov wonder if Raven had heard him clearly.

"*Rav?*"

"I heard you. What happened?"

Brokov gave him a quick synopsis of events, reiterating that Orlom was enroute with Dougar and Ilesa's infant. As for Thorton, he simply said that he gave his place for the others and took a number of the creatures with him. Raven didn't have time to consider what just happened, his feelings on Ben Thorton a convoluted mess, all things considered. His old friend had been gone since Jennifer died. When he last saw him before he sped off, was the first time since that fateful day that he saw the old Ben in his eyes. It was as if the fates brought the old Ben back for a brief moment so he could say goodbye.

Lorken stood beside him, overhearing the exchange, his own feelings on the matter as mixed as Raven's.

"He was more use to us alive than dead," Lorken said, shaking his head. Had Ben remained upon the air ski, he could have followed the gargoyle host south, harassing them throughout their march.

"What's done is done. You got an ETA on our new friends?" Raven asked Brokov.

"*At least on hour, maybe two. They are moving pretty fast. You best find a way to wake everyone up. Orlom will be along shortly and give you a hand,*" Brokov said, inwardly cringing at the thought of Orlom being helpful.

"Do you have any *good* news to share?" Lorken asked into the comm, leaning over Raven's shoulder.

"*General Matuzak should be there shortly. He is fast approaching the Nasser Gap.*"

Raven gave that news an approving shrug. The Laycrom garrison apparently abandoned their post, disappearing somewhere north and east, leaving the Nasser Pass open.

"*Unfortunately, it will take time to move his armies through the pass,*" Brokov added, considering the Nasser Pass narrowed severely at several points.

"Alright, keep us informed," Raven said, closing the comm.

They doubled back to where Ilesa, Zem and Ular were, near the still sleeping sword wielders. This was their makeshift command point, since they could think of no place better. They were pleased to see Corry return, accompanied by King El Anthar and a small band of his winged warriors. The Jenaii monarch greeted the Earthers with their own salute, touching his hand to his forehead, which they returned with their own casual salute. If one had time to consider the strangeness of it all, one could only laugh at the sight of the Jenaii king offering such a gesture to these off-worlders as if they were old friends. But as all the Araxans had come to learn, the rules of protocol did not apply to the Earthers. It was revealing that the Jenaii king broke with tradition by offering his salute first, before Raven and Lorken could break it before him. None of this was lost on Corry, who simply shook her head. The small moment quickly passed as Raven apprised them of the situation. El Anthar quickly ordered half his warriors back to the eastern ridge, where their battlegroups currently rested. He would have them clear the way for Matuzak's gorillas.

With only one working comm, which Raven and Lorken passed between them, they became the logical center of command, while Corry coordinated more of their leadership structure through them. She flew Wind Racer to every point along their lines, organizing the soldiers as they awoke, while ferrying whichever wounded she could, back to Ilesa. She desperately sought out Torg, unable to find him amid the numerous slumbering ranks. She could sorely use his guidance with so many issues pressing at once. What to do with the now almost fully awake 13th Legion was the most difficult, considering they simply stood in place, dumbfounded about what to do. Their incoherent ramblings of terrible visions fueled their indecision, weighing who they should attack, the Chosen and their allies, or the gargoyles positioned all around them? For now, they remained just south of the slowly regrouping 10th Legion.

Corry was pleased to see the Casian commander, General Motchi, now fully awake with much of his command. He was now overseeing the left wing of their forces, from the approaches of the Nasser Pass to the left wing of General Ciyon's army, with Alen's rebels jumbled between them.

Ciyon was himself slowly stirring, helped by his aide, Guilen Estaran, Deva's brother issuing commands in his stead. The Torry 1st

Army was in far worse condition, with only one telnic fully recovered, and General Lewins among those still affected.

As Corry passed over the beleaguered ranks of the 1st Torry Army, fast approaching the men of Teso and Zulon, along with Commander Dalomos' Benotrist contingent, her eyes alit, finding a familiar figure staggering to his feet below. There amidst a collage of slumbering warriors below stood Torg Vantel, his gray eyes drawn to Wind Racer and his familiar rider.

* * *

Corry found just enough open space beside Torg for Wind Racer to set down. She remained saddled, unable to spare the time needed to dismount. Torg had more questions than she had time to answer, especially on what transpired to bring about this calamity.

"Come, Torg, I need your help at our command position," she said, urging him to join her in the saddle.

No sooner had she asked him then a wall of gargoyles arose to their immediate south all at once. The creatures' heads turned as one in their direction, as if summoned from the grave, their crimson eyes alit. Beyond them, another wall of gargoyles arose, wingless lasses of their fell kind, their vacant eyes fixed in their direction. Corry felt the blood drain from her face, the creatures taking the heart of her. With a sudden shriek they sprang forth, dark winged juveniles taking flight, while white fleshed lasses ran beneath them, their jowls drawn open, revealing their blood red throats and expanded fangs.

"GO!" Torg growled, stepping between her and the looming threat drawing ever nigh.

"I'll not leave you!" she shouted as he marched forth to battle, joining the handful of others forming a shield wall to their front.

"See to our armies while I deal with this!" Torg shouted back, running south, taking up position among the men of Teso, Zulon and Dalomos' Benotrists, all three groups now intermingled. The men didn't see their differing sigils and colors, only that the one beside them was human.

Wind Racer sprang into the air, climbing high above the ground before sweeping into a steep dive. Torg braced for impact as the line of creatures drew closer when a large white blur passed before his eyes. Wind Racer swept overhead, snatching several creatures in his talons, his powerful wings knocking many others aside.

"Fool girl!" Torg growled as Wind Racer passed to his west, dying gargoyles impaled on its large talons. The bold tactic tore a gash through the gargoyle wall, the others briefly scattering before collecting themselves. Corry circled about, Wind Racer dropping his victims from his talons as she looked below, watching Torg and the others fend off the first gargoyle charge. She could see more men gaining their feet behind them, with others gathering them up, sending them to the front. She circled back to the west, returning to Raven and the others. Off her left, thousands of gargoyles arose all across the valley floor, gaining their senses much quicker than those earlier. Soaring above her own lines, Corry could see their own armies arising as well, but in fewer numbers. She watched from above as the creatures raced north toward their lines all across the valley floor, many skewered upon their shield walls, while others flew overtop, setting down upon those still slumbering behind them. Gargoyles fell upon their helpless prey, ripping throats with their fangs, or gutting men with their scimitars, before the humans' comrades could respond, chasing the creatures off, or killing them where they stood.

* * *

"Can't get a clear shot anymore, might as well start recharging," Raven growled, setting his pistol on the ground where the clear late day sun could shine upon it.

Ilesa knelt behind them, tending the wounded with several other matrons now joining her.

The entire front to their south was now strongly reinforced, with more men awaking and falling into ranks. Ular squatted beside him, looking for any sign of the other weapons able to recharge. Lorken stood opposite him, setting his pistol on the ground as well, before Nels Draken suddenly appeared.

Raven's first instinct was to pick up his pistol and finally kill his old nemesis, before remembering he was still loyal to Tyro.

"Shouldn't you be with your people?" Raven asked, lifting his chin toward the west where most of the 10th Legion rested.

"My comrades are all around you, Raven, especially the emperor, who I am tasked to protect," Nels said, indicating Tyro's still form among the sword wielders behind Raven, none of which had yet arisen.

"As if this day could get any stranger. Alright, dip shit, if you want to help, then post up beside us and keep your eye out for strays," Raven ordered, sparing a look skyward for any gargoyles that flew over their forward ranks.

"Your charm is exceptional as always, Raven." Nels shook his head, moving to his opposite side, inspecting Tyro's still form before drawing his sword and standing watch.

No sooner had Nels arrived, then a great murmur spread through the forward ranks, a response to the massive numbers of gargoyles arising across the valley floor. From their angle, Raven could barely make out what was happening but could well guess.

"Of all the times for our pistols to be running low," Lorken growled, looking south in disgust.

"We better find some swords while we're waiting for these to charge," Raven said, looking around for someone dead to take them from.

"What about the magic ones. No one is using them right now," Lorken pointed out.

"Corry had a point. They need to be ready for when they awaken," Raven said, wishing he could agree with his friend.

"If they awaken," Lorken countered.

"If they don't, then our goose is cooked, considering what's coming from the north," Raven said.

"What's coming from the north?" Nels asked, alarmed by that odd reference. The Earthers had an irritating way of downplaying serious threats, and this was no exception.

"There's about five hundred thousand to a million gargoyles

coming straight for us, if you really want to know." Lorken smiled stupidly, causing poor Nels to pale.

"Truly?"

"Unfortunately. Maybe you should talk to your old buddies in the 13th Legion and try to get them to officially switch sides before we all die together. I don't think our new gargoyle friends will know to separate them from us," Raven advised.

Nels stood there for a long moment, taking that into consideration.

"We ain't got all day, Nels," Lorken goaded as Ular stepped briefly away, attending some task that only he knew.

"Very well." Nels gulped, taking a test swing with his sword before marching toward their forward ranks, disappearing in the crowd.

Ular quickly returned, tossing two short swords at their feet, having overheard their need.

"I bet we look pretty stupid using these," Raven said, taking a practice swing with the blade.

"Speak for yourself," Lorken countered, spinning the blade like a master swordsman.

"When did you learn to do that?" Raven made a face.

"I did some practicing when you were at Corell all that time."

"Practicing with dummies ain't the same as combat, you know," Raven growled.

"I've been practicing with dummies since the academy." He gave Raven a look, earning him a smack in the arm just as the air ski appeared. There to their north came Orlom speeding across the valley floor, closing fast on their position.

* * *

Orlom reached them just as Corry set down, the air ski hovering briefly before lowering fully to the ground. Lorken and Ular helped the women from the ski as Ilesa came running toward them, lifting her baby from the woman who held her. Fresh tears ran Ilesa's cheeks as she held her daughter. Raven and Lorken shared a look, not imagining a worse place for a child than a battlefield, especially this battlefield. Raven noticed Dougar holding tight to Ben's Stetson, sitting the air ski with a devasted look on his little face.

"He… he stayed. He stayed and let us live." Dougar wept, his eyes red with tears. He didn't know Thorton for more than a few moments, but the gift in his hands and the sacrifice he made broke his heart. It reminded him too much of Jentra, and so many others that he loved that perished.

"He did it for you to live, Dougar. Be proud of that. He was my friend, and he knew your life and her life were worth more than his." Raven jerked a thumb toward the baby in Ilesa's arms, his words drawing Ilesa's attention.

"Thank you, Dougar, my brave boy. You kept her safe." Ilesa smiled at him while rocking her daughter against her shoulder.

"I will guard her with my life," Dougar said as Lorken lifted him off the ski, setting him down as Ilesa drew him into her embrace with her free hand.

"I will guard her now, Dougar. I need you to watch over our friends," Ilesa said, directing him toward Cronus and the others. Dougar took one step toward Cronus, his heart racing, fearing the worst.

"They are not dead, Dougar, just asleep," Corry said, dismounting from Wind Racer, as Dougar ran to Cronus, ignoring Kriton's head that Raven placed beside him, before dropping beside him, pressing his head to Cronus' chest, hugging him fiercely.

The others had little time to console him with events unfolding rapidly all around them. Corry was eager to see the state of things before again taking to the air. All around them their armies began to fully waken, men staggering to their feet, disoriented as gargoyles began to course over their fore ranks, setting upon them across the breadth of the valley floor. Nothing could wake men up faster than a gargoyle snapping its fangs trying to take a bite of them. Thankfully, most of the gargoyles were smaller juveniles, far easier to dispatch than their fully grown brethren. Most of the adult warriors were slain by this time, leaving the juveniles and lasses to deal with. Corry knew they needed to finish them before the other gargoyle army arrived, an army with hundreds of thousand of adult warriors. It was this approaching army she yearned to hear of from the lips of those who had seen it, Orlom and the two women he brought back.

"What did you see, Orlom?" Corry asked as the young gorilla remained upon the ski, his hair and fur sticking out in every direction.

"They are so many. They stretched to the horizon, even form the air as we escaped," Orlom explained, his testimony seconded by the women.

"Very well, keep watch on our friends, Raven, while I…" Corry began to say, before the big Earther interrupted.

"You'll do more good trying to wake up Terin than flying around the battlefield, kid."

"I…" she had no answer to that, needing to do something with more apparent use than begging her husband to arise.

"If he doesn't wake up, Corry, we are all gonna die. Our pistols won't last long, and he is the blood of Kal. There has to be reason for all this, and Terin is at the center of it," Lorken added.

She stood frozen in place, torn between her duty to lead, and her duty to Terin.

"If you can't wake him, no one can," Ular said with his watery voice.

She began to falter when Squid suddenly appeared, having just woken, finding them amidst the chaos, Wind Racer's head peaking above the surrounding crowds directing him to their location.

"Go to him, Your Highness, they have the right of it, but only a few words and then return to your duties," Squid said, having over-heard enough of the conversation to know what they were referring.

She wondered at that. Should she say but a few words and then forsake him? Should she remain at his side, leaving their armies without direction? Should she leave now, trusting his recovery to Yah's mercy? She was torn with either decision.

"Speak to him, Highness, and then attend to our armies, and I shall stay in your stead," Squid offered.

"Good enough," Raven agreed, nudging her toward Terin.

She hurried quickly to him, kneeling beside his chest, pressing her lips to his, before whispering in his ear. The others could only guess what she said, her lips hovering enticingly near. With that, she kissed him once more and returned to Wind Racer as Squid took her place at Terin's side, pressing his hand to Terin's chest, speaking gently to his former apprentice.

"Come back to us, my boy. We have need of you," Squid began, urging Terin from his slumber, while comforting him. He continued, while the others went about the pressing tasks at hand.

Corry looked one last time at Terin before taking again to the air.

Raven picked up his and Lorken's pistol's placing them in the air ski's charging station, while having Orlom hand him his own, sliding it into his holster.

"You can have mine when it fishes charging. It should go a lot quicker than relying on the sun," Raven said, before directing Lorken to the ski. Lorken had Orlom back up along the seat, taking his place as the driver, guessing Raven's intent.

"They should be charged once we find them," Lorken said, lifting the ski into the air, speeding off toward the north to find the approaching horde.

Ular gave Raven a look, wondering why he sent away such a valuable asset while the current threat remained to their south.

"We need to slow down whatever is coming for us. Just keep working to restore our other weapons, because we're gonna need 'em," Raven said just as Brokov's voice broke through the comm.

"*Things are looking a little dicey there, by the look of it,*" Brokov began.

"Well, no shit, Einstein, do have any good news for a change?" Raven growled.

"*That's why I called. Help is on the way.*"

"What help is that?"

"*How about 500 Enoructan warriors for starters. They just cleared your side of the Nasser Pass and are taking up position to the Casians' front,*" Brokov said. The Enoructans were the second riders of their Dorun Cavalry who joined Matuzak's armies on the march from Mordicay.

"That will cheer Ular up," Raven shared a look with his reptilian friend.

"If that sounds good, then you'll love this. Matuzak is right behind them, with Argos leading the first units, along with the Benotrists from Mordicay. He's probably listening in since I haled his comm," Brokov said.

"Aye, lad, you have the right of it!" Matuzak's booming voice rang out.

* * *

The western end of the Nasser Pass.

The 2nd and 3rd Ape Armies emerged from the narrow pass, marching six abreast through its winding narrows, spiling out onto the valley floor. Matuzak rode at the head of the lead column, with Argos at his side, their sturdy ocran bearing their immense weight with impressive grit. With the Enoructans and Benotrists supporting the Casian left flank, Matuzak ordered his armies south, skirting the eastern ridge, dispatching the few gargoyles scattered along the route to oppose them, mostly gargoyle lasses aimlessly lost. The 2nd marched first, led by General Mocvoran, followed by the 3rd, led by General Vorklit. They aligned along the base of the eastern ridge, banging their axes gently against their shields, their sound akin to distant thunder.

Matuzak paraded before his armies, outstretching his war hammer toward the valley floor where gathered the last remnants of the gargoyles native to the continent, their masses converging upon the alliance armies across the breadth of the Oddigem. Lines of warriors formed into shield walls to meet them, Jenaii, Torry, Macon, Sisterhood, Benotrist, Menotrist, Yatin, Casian and so many others. All of Arax stood as one, every land represented upon this forsaken landscape. The clear late day sky contrasted the desolate terrain below. The gargoyles pressed into the walls of shields, juveniles throwing themselves into the fray, with their brethren following after, leaping into the sky, their dark wings filling the heavens. Behind them came the gargoyle lasses, following the scent of the men and Jenaii, clawing over their ranks to reach the humans and Jenaii beyond. Many tens of thousands trailed the rest, covering the breadth of the valley floor. Magantors coursed the skies above, diving upon the ranks below whenever gargoyles flew above the fray to land upon the ranks beyond. Magantors swept down from above, snatching them in their talons, slaying them in great numbers.

Bursts of laser fire flashed to the west somewhere in the middle of the alliance armies, revealing Raven's position to Matuzak. He looked to Argos, who rode beside him, directing him to his left, his mighty champion pounding his fist to his broad chest, riding across the face of their armies, before taking position before them. Argos circled his mount about, drawing his laser pistol, preparing to fire upon Matuzak's command.

Matuzak spun his hammer above his head, rearing his ocran into the air as his armies banged their axes louder, their sounds thundering across the Oddigem. Matuzak's ocran settled, its hooves clapping the broken soil, thrusting his hammer toward their ancient foe, a harbinger of the destruction to come. With that, the ape armies charged, thirty thousand gorillas sweeping across the valley floor. Argos rode ahead, laser spitting from his pistol, cutting down gargoyles wherever they turned to meet him.

ZIP! ZIP! ZIP!

He blasted several creatures, hundreds more turning to flee before their approaching doom.

* * *

Corry guided Wind Racer across the breadth of their lines for what felt the hundredth time, watching the desperate battle unfolding beneath her. All across their lines the gargoyles swarmed their forward ranks, throwing themselves upon their spears and swords with abandon, clawing their way to whatever flesh they could sunder. They charged without reason or fear to turn them back, their minds given over to maddened bloodlust. Archers aligned behind the formations released their volleys into the mass of creatures gathering to their front, their shafts arcing over the contested ground without cease. By now, nearly all their armies had awoken, save for the nine wielders of the *Swords of Light*, who lay in slumber, guarded by Raven, Ular, and walls of infantry. Corry was desperate to see the gargoyles turned back before the larger force arrived from the north, squeezing them between the two hordes. Had they time, she would have preferred they move to one ridge or the other, avoiding this open ground, but that was not possible once they were stricken by the power of the swords. Now that they were awake, they were caught up in the battle at hand.

It was then she beheld the apes emerging from the Nasser Pass, marshalling forth into formation. She coursed above the battlefield as they moved into position, the banging of their axes echoing above the din, sending pimples across her flesh as Matuzak paraded before his armies before sending them into battle. It was there, from those airy heights she beheld the wonder of the ape charge. They charged across the valley floor, smashing the gargoyle host from east to west, like an autumn wind sweeping dead leaves from a forest floor. They crushed gargoyle lasses with war hammers or cut them down with axes or swords. Argos rode at the head of their host, firing into the gargoyles' midst, fueling their panic. Behind them came the Enoructans, moving deftly amongst the corpse littered field, keeping their feet as they cut down what their ape friends left them. The apes passed the far end of the Casian line, freeing the men of the league to fall in behind them, slaying all in their path. They cleared away the gargoyles pressing Ciyon's army, freeing him to join them in their advance.

To the east, the skies were filling with the might of the Jenaii, King El Anthar's war bird leading his Battlegroups back into the valley, having cleared the way for the Matuzak's advance through the Nasser Pass. They coursed over the valley, passing above the apes, sweeping any gargoyles braving the skies. Corry circled about, racing back to where Raven and the others guarded Terin, watching the ape advance off her left rolling up the gargoyle flank, clearing the gargoyles from the Torry 1st Army's front, then Dalomos' Benotrists, followed by Torg and the men of Teso, Zulon, and then the 1st Sisterhood Army.

HARROOM!

Horns sounded in the west, where the 13ᵗʰ Benotrist Legion struck their colors, joining with General Gavis' 10ᵗʰ Legion, Nels Draken having succeeded in uniting them. They advanced upon the gargoyles, driving south before turning east, smashing the gargoyles between themselves and the advancing apes drawing westward. The gargoyles were dying in numbers so vast that no mortal could count, their next generation perishing with the last. This was King Kal's dream, his immortal quest to vanquish their fell kind from Arax. Here they fought, all the peoples of Arax, united in purpose to bring this about, and yet it was not the end, for even now an even larger host of gargoyles was fast approaching from the north, as if the fates conspired against them. They succeeded in destroying the gargoyles on their continent only for another land's creatures to be thrown at them. Was every gargoyle of the world brought to this place at this time for a reason? Was this the warning of Deva's vision? Was this why only the Chosen were to be sent, to spare the rest?

Have I doomed all these brave peoples to death to spare my beloved Terin? Corry lamented.

No, she shook her head. Had the Chosen come alone, they and the 10ᵗʰ Legion would have perished, and the gargoyles they had slain here would still have joined with those fast approaching, unified and positioned to destroy the world of mankind. No, they would finish this horde and prepare to battle the next. They were brought here for a reason, unified in purpose. If they fight together here and stand as one against those drawing from the north, they might end the gargoyle curse for all time, slaying warrior and lass alike, though the cost would be high, perhaps very high. Likely, they would all die before the end.

With that, she circled about before setting down beside Raven, looking on as they gargoyles to their south were crushed.

* * *

Time was fleeting. The Araxan Alliance, as they would later be called, struggled reforming their lines as the second gargoyle host broke the horizon. There was little time to resume their former positions, most of their soldiers concentrated where they crushed the first gargoyle host as word spread of the enemy's fast approach. Humans and apes filled in wherever they found themselves, others shifting west and east to balance their new formations. The five hundred Enoructans remained south of the new lines, searching the battlefield for gargoyle strays they might have missed, the reptilian warriors moving across the corpse littered ground with deadly efficiency. They would cut and move before a foe could raise a blade to counter, leaving the stricken to bleed out while seeking their next kill.

The Alliance cavalry shifted south as well, positioning themselves to counter any breaks in the line. King El Anthar ordered his Battlegroups to either ridge, splitting them to deny the enemy the high ground. General Valen reformed their combined magantor units, patrolling the breadth of the vale, providing another counter to any breaks in the line.

The entire formations now faced north, with men of Yatin standing beside Benotrists and Torries, apes aligned beside the Sisterhood soldiers. Casian, Macon, Menotrist rebels, were intermixed with men of Teso and Zulon, their mismatched shields interlocking to an uneven fit, though they made the best of their plight. Torg found himself beside Galen, among a mixed group of Dalomos' Benotrists, Casians and men of Zulon. He stood among the front ranks, his shield interlocked with a young Casian soldier beside him, the lad's eyes staring widely at the great host spilling out across the horizon.

"Keep your spirit up, my lad, they are flesh and blood as you or I. Stick them with your spear and they'll die as any other," Torg advised, the lad nervously acknowledging him.

"Be brave, my young fellow. You stand beside the famed Master Vantel, commander of the Torry Elite, and grandfather of the greatest warrior that has ever lived," Galen assured him, standing directly behind them.

"Master Vantel?" The lad hadn't realized who stood beside him, having only seen him from afar during their march.

"Aye. What is your name, lad?" Torg asked.

"Vencil. Vencil Adorman," the lad said.

"A good name, Vencil. I am proud to fight beside you."

"You are?" The young man could hardly believe it.

"Aye. Are you afraid, Vencil?" Torg asked.

The look in his eyes was all the proof one would need, but Vencil confirmed the truth with a reluctant nod of his head.

"Good," Torg snorted, giving him a rough grin.

"Good?" Vencil made a face.

"It tells me you have brains, lad, and if you are standing here despite your fear, you have courage as well. Every soldier standing among our great host is scared, lad. We are all scared, and yet, here we are," Torg said.

"Let us be scared together," Galen said, leaning in over Vencil's shoulder.

"Aye, and take as many of the wretches with us before we go!" Torg bellowed.

* * *

He was lost in his dream, walking hand in hand with Leanna along a quiet stream, under the shade of swaying paccel trees. It was a tranquil place that he had never been to but felt familiar. He tried to remember if his life before was but a dream, or was this a fevered vision? Which was true? He felt Leanna squeeze his hand tighter, turning to see her look at him with her beautiful blue eyes casting a wanton spell. She took his other hand in hers, holding both as they stood beside the gently flowing stream, the sound of songbirds echoing somewhere above.

"I have missed you." He smiled at her, losing himself in her loving gaze.

"I have always been with you, my love, but our time is waning," she said, her smile faltering.

"What? No!" he protested, drawing her into his arms.

"Your time is not now, Cronus. You have a purpose. You were given a vision. Only you can prevent it." She looked at him with such empathy it broke his heart.

"I…" He had no answer to that, knowing the truth of it.

Her smile fully blossomed again.

"I will do what I must and return to you."

"Your time is not now, my love. Our daughter, you must live for Maura. You are all she has, Cronus. Raise her to be strong like her father, and kind like her father, and so very brave like her father, my beloved Cronus," she said, freeing a hand to caress his cheek, before pressing her lips to his.

They remained in this loving embrace for an eternal moment, joined as one on that ethereal plain, swirling mist gathering about them as if to draw him away.

"You must go back, my love. It is time." She smiled bravely for him, her heart breaking within as she drew away, feeling him reach out, begging her not to leave.

"No, Leanna, please don't go." He wept, his tears feeling all too real, drawing him further from this tranquil place.

"I am letting you go, my love. Our visits must end, for your sake, Cronus. Life is precious, and I would not have you spend your days dreaming of me, wasting the years left to you. You will love again. Live and love… for me," she said, drawing farther away, billowing mist closing about her.

"I can't live without you in my dreams. I'll not forsake the last part of you that I have," he pleaded, outstretching his hand to grasp her.

"You have Maura. She is what remains of me, my love. Now go! Save our friend, the one we both love so very much."

Cronus tried to plead, his voice frozen as she drew away, swallowed by the gathering mist… gone.

He heard the sound of voices, many voices shouting and metal clanging. His eyes began to flutter, feeling the hard ground beneath his back, his head tilted to his side. He struggled opening his eyes, light seeping through his lashes before drawing fully open.

There before him sat a gruesome sight, Kriton's dead eyes staring blankly at him, his split tongue falling loosely from his pallid lips.

"Agghh!" Cronus yelped, jumping to his feet and backing from the awful sight.

"You're awake!" Dougar's excited voice greeted him as he gathered his senses.

All around him lay the other sword wielders, resting as if dead or asleep. He saw Squid sitting beside Terin, his aged hand resting upon his rising chest. He recognized Tessa the Seamstress standing watch over King Mortus, and Ular remaining close to Lucas. They were resting in a small clearing with soldiers standing guard all around them, facing north. Within this small open area rested the sword wielders, and those watching over them, along with Ilesa and several matrons tending the wounded brought to her. Looking to his left stood Wind Racer, his white feathered head towering over the surrounding crowd. Beside the great warbird stood Corry, giving orders to several soldiers gathered about her. And next to her stood Raven, looking back at him with a stupid grin.

Cronus felt Dougar's arms wrap around him, squeezing him tightly. He had no sense of how long he slept, save for the sun hanging low in the west.

Dougar? He wondered where he appeared from, having left him at Darcol with Ilesa's baby. An infant's cry drew his gaze to Ilesa, where sat her baby near her feet, fussing for her attention, attention she could not give with the tasks around her. He embraced Dougar, feeling the boy's relief with his recovery as Raven marched over to him, before slapping him on the back, nearly taking him from his feet.

"You're awake! Welcome back to the land of the living. We don't have much time, so pick up your sword and get ready for round two, though it's more like round ten if you ask me." Raven smiled, happy to see his friend alive and awake.

Cronus didn't bother asking what round 2 meant, Raven managing to use a phrase he hadn't heard yet. There were too many other things he needed to ask, starting with the abomination resting at his feet.

"Is that who I think it is?" Cronus asked, pointing at Kriton's head.

"Pretty sure it's your old friend, Kriton."

Cronus felt quite certain that it was. Most gargoyles looked very similar, but Kriton was different, and he spent enough time in his company to recognize his distinct face.

"How…" he began to ask.

"When you all decided to take a nap, I borrowed Terin's new

sword and went to work. Killed quite a few when I noticed him among all those sleeping beauties. A little chop and here he is. Thought you might like his head," Raven happily explained.

There was a lot there that Cronus couldn't sort, starting with Kriton suffering the same sleep that overtook him, making him wonder just how many were affected? That might be the more pertinent question but could not overtake the grotesque trophy resting at his feet. How did he go from his dream of Leanna to waking with that staring him in the face? Only Raven would think do that, and his next utterance was even more ridiculous.

"Don't lose that head. It will look good hanging on your wall someday."

"Why would I ever want to keep that?" He made a face.

"Something to remember this moment. Never mind, we have more important stuff to worry about. Pick up your magic sword, cause we're gonna need it."

"Kriton's army still stands?" Cronus asked, dislodging Dougar while ruffling his hair, before reaching for his fallen blade.

"Nah, we already killed that army, Ular's people are hunting the stragglers. It's the other army we're worried about."

"Other army?" Cronus made a face.

"Yep. Somehow the gargoyles brought another army from across the sea and are heading straight for us. That's why we're all facing north. If you could work your way to the front, you'd get a good look at them."

"From across the sea?" Cronus asked in alarm.

"Yep, Brokov just discovered them after everyone decided to fall asleep."

"Everyone?"

"Everyone except me and Lorken, and he broke his ankle when his ski fell. Oh, forgot to add that when you put your swords together, it not only knocked you all out, it drained all our equipment too, even poor Zem." Raven pointed out their friend laid out prone behind them.

"That is not good," Cronus said, using one of Raven's figures of speech.

"Yeah, not good at all. Luckily Ben and Orlom showed up and brought us a pair of pistols. I've been using this sparingly, saving the juice for the big fight we got coming," Raven said, patting the grip of his pistol.

Cronus meant to ask of the other sword wielders as he reached for the hilt of his blade, but he could see that he was the first to awaken. No sooner did he grasp the hilt, luminous golden light erupted along its ancient blade.

"It's back! Good, because we're gonna need it." Raven smiled.

Cronus felt euphoria rippling up his arm, filtering throughout his body. He was immediately restored, as if he could float upon the air. The sword felt greater than ever before, weightless and powerful as it danced in his hand.

"Careful where you swing that. We're down to one regenerator unless Ular can get the others working." Raven backed a step as Cronus took several practice swings, with Dougar looking on, a bright smile painting his face.

Cronus lowered the blade, finding more than Dougar looking on, the eyes of all those surrounding them gazing with wonder at the glory emitting from the sword, with no greater smile than Corry's. They shared a look as she leaned into Wind Racer's breast, affectionately stroking the great avian's neck. Her elation was heightened as King Mortus gained his feet, steadied by Tessa as he quickly gained his bearings. He was the second to awake and would not be the last.

"*We got incoming!*" Lorken's voice broke through Raven's comm, disturbing their brief respite.

The final stage of the Battle of Noddegamra had begun.

CHAPTER 15

NODDEGAMRA. Final Phase.

The enemy drew nigh, their multitude covering the breadth of the Oddigem, and extending north, beyond the horizon. They marched apace, with many thousands sprinting ahead, taking flight before tiring and rejoining the trailing host, while others ran ahead, repeating the process. It was a constant buzz of activity, a moving caliginous hive, consuming the very land it crossed, leaving naught in its wake. Trailing this fell host marched the gargoyle lasses, following their brothers to war, drawn to the sacred nesting grounds of their foul kind. Carka birds circled high above, harbingers of coming slaughter, their gauche wings casting lazy shadows to their east, as the sun hung lower in the western sky.

They drew within a league of the alliance host blocking their path, a wall of shields interlocked from the east ridge to the west, with row upon row aligned behind them. Magantors coursed above the mostly human host, preparing to dive upon them as they drew nigh. The gargoyles spotted the Jenaii standing upon either ridge, their ancient foes ready to receive them with spear and blade.

ZIP! ZIP! ZIP!

Lorken sped east across the face of the enemy host, Orlom spewing laser fire into their gathered ranks, each blast passing through several rows, cutting holes in their lines where they dropped. The small fissures were swiftly closed, the dead and wounded trampled underfoot. They hissed at the strange flying machine that tormented them throughout their march from Darcol, thinning their numbers with every pass, while remaining frustratingly out of reach. Lorken and Orlom could do little more than harry their advance, slaying hundreds if not thousands, and still they came, their multitudes covering the valley floor from there to the horizon.

The gargoyles continued on, the front ranks unable to pause before launching their assault, with the weight of those trailing forcing them onward. They began their guttural chants, their morbid refrain echoing hauntingly over the din.

> *The time of our ascension has drawn nigh*
> *Vengeance, mutilation, death chants cry*
> *Flesh of man, flesh of Jenaii*
> *Devour the favored sons of Yah*
> *Slay them child, lass and all*

They drew within two hundred paces, storms of arrows arcing to greet them, each finding purchase in their serried ranks.

ZIP! ZIP! ZIP!

Laser flashed from the east, where stood Argos among the front ranks, standing amidst a group of Benotrists, apes and Casians, their lines hopelessly mixed. The gargoyles hissed, staring hatefully at the fell weapons that tore into them with painful effect. The fore ranks ran ahead of their host, springing into the air, their wings full with the wind. The following ranks ran apace below them, with the next ranks taking flight, staggering their assault, half advancing afoot, and half through the air. Tens of thousands broke left and right, assailing the unforgiving slopes of the east and west ridges, vying with the Jenaii contesting their assault.

The first gargoyles soared over the front ranks of the alliance, arrows thinning their numbers, keeping above the thrusting spears of those clustered below, before setting down, most skewered where they landed. Many crushed men underfoot, their weight snapping necks or breaking limbs with the power of their descent. They were woefully exposed, sans armor of any kind, save for small circled helms. Some passed overhead for clearer ground south, tossing their spears into the enemy below. Magantors swept down upon them, snatching scores of them in their razored talons.

Raven stood over Tosha, shooting anything taking to the air around them, not lacking for targets. Cronus stood off his left, dispatching the first creature to set down in their midst, his first strike taking its arms, his follow strike taking it across the chest, splitting it in half.

ZIP!

Raven blasted a creature trying to set down behind them as Cronus shifted right to counter another, splitting its spear thrusting to strike him. He stepped into its body, his follow strike severing a wing and limb. The creature released a terrible scream, blood spouting from its wounds. Cronus shifted again, his blade lopping another creature's legs, unable to finish his kills as the enemy came upon them one after another.

ZIP! ZIP! ZIP!

Raven dropped three more in quick succession as King Mortus' blade flashed beyond him, the Macon monarch fighting beside Tessa, who was woefully equipped for battle, with no breast armor or greaves, and with only an ill-fitting helm for protection. Ular moved about all around them, dodging spear thrusts and striking down gargoyles everywhere he went. Ular spun and weaved, cutting enemies down from behind, severing spines with impressive precision, or slicing tendons when not landing kill thrusts.

Corry had again taken to the skies at the outset, Wind Racer circling above, diving upon the creatures swarming overhead. Squid stood watch over Terin, his aged arm wielding his sword with the vigor of his lost youth.

Tosha's eyes began to flutter, leaving her dreamy state. She wanted to remain where she was, floating freely in the night sky, watching the stars pass swiftly by before they came to a sudden halt. There she found herself staring at her world from above, a spherical wonder of gray, green and mostly blue. It was breathtaking to see from the heavens above. It was Arax as no one of her world had ever seen, save for the Earthers when they came to her planet. She wanted to remain in that tranquil state, both strangely dreamlike and clear at the same time. The sound of battle drew her back, her eyes drawing fully open, finding Raven standing over her, laser spewing from his pistol, striking targets swarming the sky above. She felt her fingers wrapped about the hilt of her blade, sensing its guidance as she sprang to her feet.

"Welcome back. There are plenty of gargoyles to kill, so have at it," Raven greeted her, keeping a steady aim.

"I have missed you too, idiot." She shook her head, giving him the response he deserved for not greeting her with the affection her ordeal warranted.

"That's my girl." He gave her a half grin, keeping his eye on the next target in his sites.

She gave him a look before stepping to her right, raising her sword as a creature swept overhead, shearing it shoulder to hip, its two halves dropping behind her, blood splashing her helm.

* * *

Zem found himself lost in a memory, again struck down by an intense burst of energy, the shields surrounding his innermost core withstanding the surge that drained the strength from the rest of him. He retained the very essence of his mind, the memories, dreams and values he came to embrace as his own. These were the things that set him apart from the other artificial life forms that preceded him, the very core of his humanity. Since the event at Tro, he further strengthened the shields protecting his innermost self, safeguarding it from the very event that just struck him. He could sense what was going on around him, but required time to restore his full power, focusing his energies on that endeavor. Any length of time in a state of inaction was torturous to his inquisitive mind. He was not a simpleton who could stare blankly at a wall. No, he needed constant stimulation, and the older he got, the more he needed it, whether it was incorporating new knowledge to his internal archives or tapping into those very archives for entertainment.

He recalled his time at Annapolis, engaging in deep discussions with the cadre tasked with his instruction. He found their overall knowledge underwhelming, restricted as they were by their human limitations. He was appreciative of their efforts, however, and constantly found himself in the company of a marine colonel Jorge Santos, a most amiable and adventurous character that took a liking to Zem, for whatever reason some humans are so inclined. It was Colonel Santos that introduced Zem to a broad range of vintage tales that earlier humans partook for entertainment hundreds of years before. They were simple two-dimensional stories they quaintly referred to as… movies. Colonel Santos took a particular liking to one oddly called *Kelly's Heroes*. It was a humorous tale of a group of misfit soldiers robbing a bank behind enemy lines. The story struck a similar chord with Zem, with him finding it oddly invigorating, catering to his quickly developing idiosyncrasies. He stored the movie in his internal archive, along with thousands of others, able to replay them in his mind at his convenience. This ability allowed him to draw upon this source of entertainment while restoring his power, thus quickening the passage of time while he waited.

And thus, Zem spent the better part of the battle of Noddegamra viewing *Kelly's Heroes,* with an internal smile no outside observer could witness. Adding to the film's ancient charm was a lively tune that didn't quite match the tenor of the story, but he couldn't separate one from the other the more he viewed it. The ballad was called *Burning Bridges*, and it played repeatedly in his mind as the story concluded, rivalling his affection for *Anchors Aweigh*. And so, with *Burning Bridges* playing in his brain, he waited for those glorious words to flash before his eyes… System Restore.

* * *

Alen found himself among the second line, standing among a group of his fellow rebels and a collage of Macons, Torries and Benotrists, their mismatched shields and swords struggling to fit as they interlocked. There was a near eight paces between their front rank and the back of the first line, with each line nearly ten deep. Each line stretched the breadth of the vale, with the third line resting behind them, along with a partial fourth. Alen fought without cease, slaying two creatures in the first battle before waking from his strange dream of distant stars, and dispatching several more. After defeating the gargoyles native to the Oddigem, word spread of the second enemy host drawing from the north, forcing them to reform new lines while their old formations were hopelessly disordered. Soldiers filled in wherever they found themselves, with whoever was in their proximity.

They were of one army now, Yatins, Menotrists, Benotrists, Venotrists, Torries, Macons, Casians, The Sisterhood, Apes and Jenaii, with countless others. It was all surreal, a fitting end for their thousands of years of disunity. They were now forced to fight together or perish. Even if they carried the day, he knew most would not live to see it.

He looked on as Gargoyles swarmed over the first line, hundreds impaled upon jutting spears and thrusting swords, most dying at the front of the first shield wall. Hundreds more passed overhead, setting down upon the heads of the center ranks of the first line, caving holes in their formations. Soldiers held shields overhead, jabbing around their seems at the creatures setting down upon them, finding whatever flesh their steel could purchase. Once stabbing the creatures repeatedly, they would twist their shields, letting them drop at their feet, before finishing them with hurried thrusts, returning their shields flat overhead. Some fell victim to the gargoyles' weight, large holes breaking in their formation, others closing the breaks before more creatures followed the opening, spilling into their midst.

Alen braced himself, waiting upon more gargoyles passing over the first line, angling for the second. Scores of creatures swept over the first line across his limited line of sight, driving straight for him, their wings outstretched, and spears leveled, vicious fangs curving menacingly, their eyes glowing as crimson embers. He held tight to his shield, bracing for impact, the Macon soldier to his left keeping his shield close to his own, guarding his back.

THUMP!

The emphatic blow drove him back a step, his feet sliding upon the cracked soil, before thrusting his sword blindly around his shied, jabbing repeatedly, feeling it sink into flesh of some sort, the creature's screams indicating he struck true. He held his ground, jabbing lower, feeling the creature stumbling at his feet. He kept the shield even with his greaves, fearing the creature targeting his legs.

"More coming, lads! Brace yourselves!" someone cried out. Alen kept his grip and dressed his shield to the men beside him, preparing to receive the next wave.

* * *

King Lichu stood among the first line, three rows from the front, somewhere east of Alen, somehow standing among nine of his ten men, the other missing, and the rest keeping beside him throughout the first two engagements. He lost count of the number of gargoyles he slew, driving his sword into the belly of a creature but moments before. More followed, countless creatures passing overhead, while many more pressed their front or fell upon them. The man to his direct front was forced to step forth, replacing the man to his front who fell, a gargoyle spear impaling his neck. The creature twisted the shaft, driving the dying man to his knees, his shield falling from his dying grasp. The man to Lichu's front skewered the gargoyle, snapping its spear, before driving his sword through its middle. Before he could kick the dying creature from his blade, other creature filled the breach, tackling the man, sinking its fangs in his throat. King Lichu stepped forth, the creature lifting its face, hissing at him with gore dripping from its fangs. Lichu lopped its head, stepping carefully over the thrashing carcass, filling the breach, raising his shield as the next creature pressed his front, his comrades filling in behind him, feeling their shields resting above his helm.

* * *

Criose and Culn Davorin had awoken from their star-filled dreams to find their laser rifles missing, with Ular having gathered them, unbeknownst to them. They managed to find swords and shields from the fallen, the flow of battle bringing them to where they now stood, in the center of the second line among a rowdy number of apes, who accounted well of themselves, their ferocity and strength compensating for their lack of shield discipline. Criose skewered a gargoyle crawling over his shield overhead, its hands scratching desperately at the flat iron skin of the shield. He tilted his shield, dropping it at his feet as Culn finished it.

"Hoo!" The gorilla beside them hooted excitedly at their kill, giving them a toothy grin, standing over another gargoyle with his ax planted in its skull.

* * *

Dadeus Ciyon retained command of several units of his Torry-Macon army, holding position in the third line, watching as gargoyles assailed the two lines to his front, with many more passing over them, angling straight for him.

"Brace!" Dadeus shouted, holding tight to his shield as the first creatures struck, the blow backing him a step. He managed to keep his feet, jabbing his sword around the seam of his shield, feeling it sink into soft tissue. He quickly repeated the jab, delivering three quick thrusts. Guilen stood behind him, holding his shield overhead of them both, interlocked with those to either side. Guilen struggled as a great weight pressed down upon it, anchoring his shoulder and ducking his head, the sound of a blunt object scrapping across the metal of the shield echoing painfully in his ears. Dadeus shifted his strokes overhead between the seams of the shields, stabbing fiercely, struggling to find purchase as the shield gave way, the creature dropping between them. Dadeus couldn't turn about without exposing his front as the gargoyle began to rise between them. Guilen dropped his shield, thrusting his sword through the gargoyle's middle, twisting the blade in its innards, driving it to the ground, before kicking it off his blade. He crouched to grab hold of his shield when another creature dropped down upon him, collapsing him under its weight. The men beside him stabbed the creature from either side as he managed to dislodge himself from underneath it.

"Brace!" Others shouted along the line just before their front shield wall buckled, sending Dadeus tripping over the creatures they had slain still lying between them. He fell to his back with two gargoyles falling upon him. He kept his shield between them and him, though it couldn't cover every part of him. He looked over the lip of his shield, a pair of crimson glowing eyes drawing overtop of it, staring hatefully into his.

"No!" Guilen growled, rushing forth, lopping the creature's head, his follow strike driving the second gargoyle back.

Dadeus struggled freeing himself, blind to the happenings where his lower body rested, his view blocked by his shield and the headless creature atop of it. He managed to free himself, slipping to the side, catching sight of Guilen dropping to his knees in front of him, a gargoyle blade protruding from his back.

"No!" he screamed, parroting Guilen's cry but moments before. He stepped forth without his shield, leaving it pinned beneath the headless corpse, stepping around his stricken friend, lopping the head of his attacker. Those behind them moved forward to close the shield wall, advancing a few steps to give him space. He looked down upon Guilen who knelt over two more corpses, fresh kills he claimed to protect Dadeus before suffering his blow.

"Should Deva live, tell her…" Guilen struggled to say, looking into Dadeus' eyes, the words dying in his throat, as Dadeus held him in his arms under the shade of the surrounding shields.

"I will tell her, my friend," Dadeus said, easing him to the ground, his heart breaking.

There upon the battlefield, Guilen Estaran died protecting his friend and commander. He died with honor.

* * *

Elise Jani, supreme commander of all Sisterhood armies, stood among a large contingent of her brave soldiers, joined with an equal number of Benotrists from the 10th and 13th Legions, and their commander, General Gavis, who stood beside her. They stood in the second line, three rows back, under the shadow of the western ridge, whose shadow stretched far to their east. She lost sight of General Na, her subordinate commander of 1ˢᵗ Army, the only army they brought to the Oddigem. She held her shield above her head, interlocked with Gavis', who stood to her immediate right, his scared face a mask of iron will. They began this day as mortal enemies and fought beside each other. Behind them stood Carbanc and Gorzak, the only surviving apes among the Chosen.

She felt another creature fall upon her shield, testing her strength as she held it aloft. She heard a terrible squeal, the weight sliding off the back of her shield, turning to see Gorzak dragging the creature to the ground by its wing with one furry hand, while Carbanc brained it with his hammer, each giving her a toothy grin.

* * *

Raven dropped another creature passing overhead, a fatal shot through its breast. His small victory soured as it fell upon a Torry soldier to his right, taking him from his feet. The poor wretch's screams at least meant he was still alive. Ilesa hurried to the man's side, healing him as fast she could before returning to their perimeter, where they collectively guarded Terin and the others still asleep. Dougar now stood guard over Ilesa's baby, his eyes scanning the sky for threats, wielding his small sword and wearing Ben's hat. Mortus, Tosha and Cronus worked in unison, moving about that large open space, fending off gargoyle attacks as they swarmed overhead, testing them without cease. He noticed none seemed aware of Tosha, easing her kill rate, as if they were blind to her presence, similar to Terin's newfound ability after his rescue from Darna. The three of them were currently drawn to the opposite side of their small perimeter, tearing apart several creatures sweeping into their midst, leaving Tessa and Squid between them, standing watch over the others. He looked in the opposite direction, where Ular took another creature off its feet, his long knife gutting the gargoyle with a dizzying array of quick jabs.

ZIP!

Raven blasted another gargoyle sweeping down from above, its spear aimed for Ular's back, the laser tearing through its chest.

Ular rolled clear, sensing the danger as the creature worked its dying wings, easing its descent, before dropping atop his previous kill.

"Oh!" Tessa cried out in surprise behind Raven. He turned, finding Zem towering over her with a gargoyle in his hands, having snatched it from midair attempting to skewer her with its spear.

Raven winced, watching Zem tear the creature's right wing in half with his bare hands, a terrible scream issuing from its blood red throat, paining their ears. The creature stumbled to its knees as Zem brought his left fist down upon its head, He spent the proceeding moments trying to dislodge his hand from the bloody fragmented skull, eventually tearing it free, blood and bone fragments flying off his fingers.

"Well, that's about the most disgusting thing I ever saw, but it's good to have you back, ole buddy." Raven shook his head.

"It took longer than I planned, but I am here. Besides, now I get to be captain for a week, just as you promised," Zem said before moving to Tessa's other side, shielding her from another creature diving upon them, blocking Raven from getting a clear shot. The gargoyle's savage fury faltered as its spear broke upon Zem's chest, simply tearing a small hole in his jacket, before falling into Zem's grasp.

"Oh my." poor Tessa gasped as Zem tore the creature's left arm from its shoulder, before bashing him in the head with it.

"You heard me promise that?" Raven asked, blasting another creature passing overhead.

"I heard everything," Zem said.

"Me and my big mouth," Raven grumbled. Zem would be certain they won this battle just for the chance to assume command of the *Stenox* for a week. That sounded almost as awful as dying this day.

Cronus moved closer to them, keeping a watchful eye on Raven as he had throughout the battle, when he heard Deva begin to stir. She remained asleep since the swords came together, laying beside the others. He moved closer to her, sparing a glance skyward for threats before kneeling, helping her to a sitting position.

"Deva, are you well?" he asked, wondering what great vision she beheld.

It took her a moment to collect herself, strangely aware of their situation despite being asleep through most of it.

"Time." She coughed, before repeating it, looking desperately into Cronus' eyes.

"Time?" He made a face, Raven and Tosha now standing near, listening in.

"We need time. Whatever we do we must hold a little longer!" she said desperately, looking to each of them.

"Time for what?" Raven asked.

"I...I do not know. I was there, and I heard him say he would help us if we gave him time," Deva said, pointing to the sky, the others looking curiously skyward.

Raven removed his comm from his jacket, raising Brokov.

"What's the situation from up there, Brokov?"

"*Not good*" came the blunt reply.

"Well, no shit, can you elaborate?"

"The entire valley floor is covered with gargoyles running north some distance from your position."

"Do you have a number?"

"At least 380,000 males and even more females trailing them."

"That many?" Raven made a face.

"They started with 500,000, so be grateful," Brokov said.

"How many did Ben kill?"

"At least thirty if I were to guess. He slowed them down a good bit, or else they would have been on top of you while you were fighting the southern force."

At least he died for something, Raven thought of his friend.

Time, that was what was needed, and he could think of only one thing at the moment, at least until Terin awoke.

"Arg and Lorken, are you listening?" Raven asked.

"*Aye!*" Argos' booming voice echoed.

"*I can hear you*," Lorken said, flying somewhere over the battlefield.

"Deva says we need to buy time. Use or it or lose it." Raven gave the contingency order they agreed upon days ago.

"*Alright, we'll find a place to set it up,*" Lorken responded, while Argos acknowledged.

"Use it or lose it?" Tosha gave him a look.

"Yep."

"Are you going to explain what that means or just stand there looking stupid?" she growled.

"I couldn't look stupid if I tried." He gave her that insufferable smile before blasting another creature passing overhead.

* * *

Mordicay Harbor.
Weapons room of the Stenox.

Brokov watched the unfolding drama upon two different screens, each fed by their surviving discs. Their situation was dire, with their armies spread across the valley floor in three and half lines, each narrowly separated by several paces. Despite the gargoyles' numbers, they had enough soldiers to carry the day, numbering somewhere between one and two hundred thousand, but they lacked the cold efficiency and flexibility of most Araxan armies because they were thrown together in a jumbled mess. Moving forward and backward in unison required discipline and training as a cohesive unit. Because of the anomaly and the events that followed, they were forced to reassemble into their current positions wherever and with whoever they found themselves. Commanders were separated from their commands, and soldiers separated from their comrades. It was a total mixing of their armies, with only the Jenaii retaining their unified structure by the nature of their flying ability and congregating along the opposing ridgelines. Their cavalry and magantor contingents also retained their structure by nature of their unique units. He could see their cavalry patrolling behind their lines, slaughtering any gargoyles setting down there. Their magantors accounted well of themselves, scattering any sizable gargoyle group flying over their ranks. He kept a close eye on Wind Racer, who kept vigilant watch over Terin and the others below, diving every few minutes into their midst, snatching gargoyles in his talons.

"You would think we could hold better than we are, considering our large numbers," Kendra said, anxiously watching the battle unfold, seeing the gargoyles swarming over their fore ranks all across the vale.

"It is the unit cohesion that negates our advantages. They should have already withdrawn several times already, but no one can give the order, and every army uses differing signals," Brokov observed.

"They are slaughtering so many, and yet the enemy gains," she lamented.

"That is part of the problem. They have slaughtered so many at the front, the enemy dead are piling higher, which the following attackers use to launch themselves. They need to withdraw and give themselves space to fight," Brokov said.

"Which is why we are doing such a desperate action?" she asked.

"Pretty much. Operation *Use it or lose it*, here it goes," he said, watching Lorken speed across the vale, laser fire erupting from his pistol into the caliginous mass to his north, before circling about, Orlom pointing out something to him below.

* * *

Torg braced himself, the force upon his shield driving him back, his boots retreating in the broken soil as the gargoyles pressed their advance. He tried thrusting his blade around the seam of his shield, unable to gain purchase as it met empty air. The damnable creatures were growing wise to the tactic, keeping lower. He Struck lower, grazing something by the feel of the jab, and the yelp he heard on the other side of the shield.

"Agghh!" the young Casian beside him cried out, a gargoyle spear finding his side, just above his hip.

Torg reached out, splitting the spear as young Vencil dropped to his knees, holding dearly to his shield as the creatures to his front pressed forth, bending it backward down upon him. Galen shifted forward, jabbing his sword tip overtop Vencil's shield, trying desperately to drive them back. Torg reached out, striking a creature crawling over Vencil's shield in a wide arc, severing part of its retracted wing.

"AGHH!"

Men cried out from his opposite shoulder, the entire line giving way. Torg shifted, the gargoyles to his front flooding around either side of him. He cut left and right, lopping heads, arms, and whatever he could take, blood and gore flying off his blade.

ZIP! ZIP! ZIP!

Laser flashed all around him, cutting a swath across his front, stopping the incursion, the men behind him closing ranks to close the fissures.

ZIP! ZIP!

He looked up just as the air ski swept down from above, circling overhead before lowering just above his head, Lorken firing north into the enemy host, keeping the creatures at bay as a familiar face peered over the side, before jumping from the seat, dropping to his feet.

"Need help, Coach?" Orlom greeted him with his toothy grin.

Torg stood there dumbstruck, which for him was a very rare occurrence, before collecting himself.

"Aye, lad," Torg said, as the air ski lifted higher, Lorken speeding away, leaving Orlom below.

Orlom patted the old warrior on the back before stepping to the front where the gargoyles collected themselves from Lorken's laser rife, again advancing upon them. Orlom kept a tight grip on the pistol, aiming it to his left, where approached the gargoyle masses, and squeezed the trigger.

ZIIIIIIIPPPP!

He held the trigger, an intense beam of blue light streaming through the gargoyle horde, before intensifying and transitioning to pure white. He shifted aim to his right, cutting a large swath through their serried ranks, the beam carving a massive hole in their formation. Orlom swept the continuous stream west to east, and back again, lifting aim with each pass, before dying on the third sweep.

He holstered his ruined pistol, the gargoyle host reeling under the assault, thousands upon thousands laying dead, dying and wounded across the valley floor.

It was the second time the gargoyle host experienced the devastation after Thorton's grisly deeds at Darcol. Torg had seen this done at Corell, and again this day with Raven and Lorken decimating tens of thousands at the outset of the battle. It was enough to slow the enemy's assault, as they stood across that deadly space, their once glowing eyes dulling with apprehension. It was only a matter of time before their vigor returned, providing them precious moments to reform their lines.

"Here, lad, you'll have need of this," Torg said, finding a spare sword from one of their fallen, handing it to Orlom, knowing his pistol was now useless. It was a high price to pay, but such was their plight.

"I'm with you, Coach." Orlom gave him his stupid grin. Several others carried Vencil to the rear, blood oozing from his wounded side, Orlom taking his place beside Torg, and Galen holding position behind them.

* * *

Argos took aim, starting east, his continuous laser stream sweeping west across the enemy ranks, dozens of rows dropping as he went, passing east to west and back again, the laser quickly fading. He holstered his dead pistol as President Matuzak placed an ax in his hand, standing beside him. Both apes wanted nothing more then to bend to their natural urges and order a charge across the field of dead and dying gargoyles, taking the fight to those waiting beyond. Alas, they held in place, following Raven's advice. Time… time was what they needed, and this bold act bought them that, but for how long?

* * *

Lorken hovered over the center of the alliance formation, training his pistol to the valley floor where it met the western ridge, squeezing the trigger, sliding it eastward, its continuous stream turning bright white, cutting down several rows of gargoyles as it passed, his angle less advantageous to Orlom and Argos on level ground. His laser went as far as the eastern ridge, turning back west before dying, since it was only half charged.

He holstered his dead pistol, examining his handiwork. Between the three of them, they cut two large swaths in the center and far east, and his longer narrower line further back. In all they slew thirty thousand if he were to guess, and that was all it was, a guess. The bold tactic sent the gargoyles reeling, most lingering beyond the line of decimation. They wouldn't hold for long, and now they were down to one pistol, Raven's, and his was draining rapidly. He would use it to guard Terin, as that seemed to be their last hope.

Lorken noticed the gargoyles again stirring, anger replacing fear as they screamed their war cries. They moved as one, like riding a great wave crashing the shore, hurrying forth across the narrow sea of their dead and dying comrades. Any human army would have given up after suffering such losses, but they were driven by a madness no mortal could comprehend, an instinctive desire to destroy the armies gathered against them, though doing so meant the extinction of their species. He could only guess, but felt what remained of all the gargoyles was gathered here this day. Their warriors crowded the front of their endless multitude, with their lasses following on their heels. They might kill everyone here this day but would certainly die themselves in the attempt. It was mutual destruction, but in the end, the peoples of Arax would be free of the gargoyle threat for all time.

Lorken knew they had one hope to perhaps ensure the survival of at least some of them… Terin.

"Wake up, kid," he whispered under his breath.

* * *

Tyro opened his eyes, greeted by the clear blue sky above, wondering how long he was asleep. His dreams had changed, new visions passing swiftly through his mind, one after another, of things that were, things that are, and things yet to come. It was the latter that troubled him, for the future was fluid, every action sending it awry in a thousand different directions. He no longer dreamed of choosing between his empire and his kin. That choice was now made, if not forced upon him. His son was dead, and his empire but a shadow of its former glory. The future, however, was in flux, a myriad of possibilities playing out before him. The simplest path was death. He could perish here upon the Oddigem, along with so many others. Or, he could live. He could fight and live, and from that point forward the possibilities were as endless as they were varied.

Did he truly even care? His son was dead.

His eyes closed, revisiting the ethereal plain, visions of possible futures again swirling around him, like autumn leaves blowing in the wind. He found himself walking among the clouds, though he felt a solid path beneath his naked feet. The sky was twilight, visions appearing and disappearing as he walked, though none seemed to solidify in any sensical structure. His gaze drew to the pathway ahead, a familiar figure coming into focus, bolder than the passing visions, his face as real as his own... Joriah.

"There is still so much worth fighting for, father, so many worth fighting for," Jonas greeted him, adorned in flowing raiment as white as a billowy cloud.

"You knew. You knew what Morac would do, and you gave yourself up," Tyro growled with his betrayal.

"For you." Jonas smiled, placing a hand to Tyro's shoulder.

"For me? You proved his treason. You didn't need to..."

"Search your heart, father. You know it was the only way for you to quickly choose. Time was fleeting, and the enemy was closing the net around you."

"You are dead, and my empire in ruin. What point is there..."

"Are you truly so blind? Your family still lives. They need you, my sister, and my son, and your grandchildren. Will you not fight for them? It is not your time, for you have much to atone for. Your unrepentant heart clouds your mind. Open it, and you will clearly see the true path before you."

Tyro couldn't answer to that, his heart torn in so many directions.

"Time is again fleeting, and my time with you is at its end. Live,

father," Jonas said, lowering his hand and drawing away, the surrounding clouds taking him.

"No! I will take your place. You are needed more than I. Take my life for yours!" Tyro pleaded, reaching out to his son.

"I have already given my life for you. You cannot exchange it."

"Why?"

"There is no greater love than one willing to lay down their life for another. I love you, father, despite all that you did. I will always love you. I must go now. Live, live for me, and repay my kindness to others."

"No, come back." Tyro wept, falling to his knees as Jonas drew away, his pride crumbling to dust. There upon that ethereal plain all his sins were laid before him, his cruelty, malice and murders, so many that it rent his heart. The weight of his crimes bore down upon him, squeezing the hatred and anger from his mind, leaving him broken. It was too much to bear, too painful to suffer. As he rightly guessed when Jonas died, it was not to save his life, but his soul. Jonas gave his life for the possibility of his redemption, with no more guarantee than that. Would he let his sacrifice be in vain?

His eyes sprang open, gaining his bearings as he sat fully up, finding himself among a host of strangers, and some familiar faces. Letha lay still beside him, along with King Lorn, the Jenaii warrior and Terin, along with the Torry warrior he leant his sword.

"Father!" Tosha called out to him. He looked up as she hurried to his side, with Raven standing watch over them, looking skyward for threats.

He regarded her, looking into her eyes as if for the first time. What could he say in so little time? He had so much to tell her, and so much to ask. He couldn't think of a simple word to utter that felt appropriate without it leading to everything he wanted to say. He gained his feet, pressing his lips to her forehead, before retrieving both of his swords, the second lying beside Lucas, who was beginning to stir, as was Letha.

"Protect her," Tyro said to Raven, testing both blades, spinning them briefly in his hands before stepping away.

"Wait, where are you going?" Tosha pleaded as he disappeared into the forward ranks.

She took a step, attempting to follow when Raven pulled her back by the collar of her cuirass, nearly lifting her off the ground with his free hand.

"Release me!" she demanded.

"We have a job to do, now help your mother to her feet and help keep your nephew alive so he can do whatever the hell he is supposed to do," he said, turning toward her mother who was struggling to her feet.

Tosha went to her, helping her steady herself before reaching down to retrieve her sword, placing it in her hand.

Ular did the same for Lucas, helping him to his feet. Since Tyro took back his sword, Lucas drew his own, the very blade crafted by Torg and given him upon his initiation to the Torry Elite.

"Don't either of you get complacent, its just a lull in the storm. Those flying bats will be back any moment now, so stay close and keep on eye on our sleeping beauties," Raven said to Letha and Lucas, while pointing out Elos, Lorn and Terin who were still resting on the ground.

"Where is Zem?" Cronus wondered, just realizing their friend was nowhere in sight.

* * *

Tyro worked his way through the serried ranks, stepping forward of their shield wall, where a large mound of enemy dead was piled across their front, a growing hindrance as the battle progressed. Looking out across the sea of dead separating the two armies, he could see the gargoyle host renewing their assault, shifting forth, before breaking at a full run, hundreds springing into the air, the rest running apace. He looked into the sea of faces drawing nigh, unable to lock eyes with any of them, as if they were blind to his presence. He stepped forth; his twin swords held at the ready. He would bear no shield, his second blade acting in its place.

Onward they came, hurrying apace, many losing their footing on the piles of dead and dying, others coursing overhead.

"Packaww!"

Magantors sounded above, sweeping down on those taking flight, plucking them from the sky.

SPLIT! SLASH! SPLIT!

He cut through the front rank as they came upon him, and then the next that followed, dispatching gargoyles with cold efficiency, heads and wings flying off his blades. He stepped left, slicing through the legs of two onrushing creatures, catching them unawares, moving on before noticing they hadn't seen him. He cut back to the right, slicing through more ranks, lopping heads and limbs with every arc of his blades.

He heard a murmur pass through the multitudes flooding his left flank, unable to see Zem moving through their masses, smashing skulls with abandon.

* * *

Moments before, Zem pushed his way through their ordered ranks, men calling him back as he stepped forward of their shield wall, fearing how he might fare as he entered that deadly space alone, meeting the thousands charging toward him. He marched forth without pause, his heavy boots crushing gargoyle bones underfoot. He was set upon within moments, gargoyles swarming over him. He snatched the first to approach by the throat, lifting it off its feet, crushing it within his fist. He didn't release it, swinging it around like a club, swatting a whole swath of creatures aside like gnats. One creature raced in from the side after he dropped the corpse, Zem smashing his other fist down upon its skull, driving it into the ground. It lay there unmoving, gibberish spitting from its lips. Zem grabbed the next by its right wing, twisting it across his body, knocking several others aside, before tossing it somewhere to his left, feeling several bones crack where he squeezed it. Others came upon him all at once, grabbing hold wherever they could. He kept his feet, grabbing hold of whatever flesh his hands could reach.

He felt a bone snap as his left hand grabbed hold of something at his side, followed by an audible screech that was muffled by those swarming over him. He lifted whatever it was he held, pulling it higher, moving the pile of gargoyles crowding over him. He used the creature in his grip to sweep away those clinging to the front of his chest, knocking them aside, tossing his victim to his right. He never had time to see just what part of the creature he latched on to, with another gargoyle sitting atop his shoulders, trying to dig its dagger into his right eye, to little effect.

Zem reached over his head, snatching the creature by the arm, snapping it in half while tossing him forward through the air, its body striking another taking flight, sending both to the ground, each breaking more bones in the collision. The gargoyles clinging to his legs held on as he marched forward, stomping several others underfoot. More came upon him from every direction, Zem tossing them off as quickly as they came. He moved through their host like a starving lincor through a herd of tersk, all the while hearing *Burning Bridges* playing in his mind, the catchy tune creating a serene calm in his brain as he slaughtered gargoyles in the hundreds.

* * *

Wind Racer shadowed Tyro's advance, sweeping down upon the creatures taking to the skies above him. Corry leaned into the dive as Wind Racer swept down from above, snatching creatures in his outstretched talons before banking left, rising again into the air. All around her more magantors appeared, tearing gashes through the gargoyles taking flight. Each pass greatly aided their armies, preventing the creatures from concentrating their attacks from above.

Corry circled above, scouting afield before diving again. All across the valley floor the enemy again pressed their advance, driven by instinctive hatred no human could comprehend. The sun was slipping below the horizon, and night would soon be upon them. What then might they suffer fighting in the darkness? Throughout their ranks soldiers were succumbing to fatigue and lack of water as much as enemy blades. Most of their water satchels had long run dry, and there was no means to move the wounded to be treated. Men died where they fell, many trampled with the battle shifting overtop of them.

She spared a glance below, watching as Tyro and Zem moved among the enemy, running almost parallel to each other, tearing through gargoyle ranks like moglos in a pottery shed. Tyro seemed almost immune to the gargoyles' attention, cutting them down with pitiful ease as if they were blind to his presence, whereas Zem drew their attention most zealously, creatures swarming over him like insects crawling over a hive. She couldn't help but hear the gargoyles nearest Tyro chant a familiar word, Nordhenz, and not in the reverent way the gargoyles of his empire referred to him. No, it was more a word spoken in disbelief and horror, almost as if they didn't expect to see him, or sense him.

"Packaww!" She looked to her left, finding a Torry warbird struggling, several arrows piercing its breast, its rider holding on for dear life as the avian drifted lower. Wind Racer turned in its direction, sweeping beneath the stricken mount, snatching a creature closing in from below, dodging arrows shooting skyward all around them. They veered off to the right, circling about as more creatures took to the air to attain them, drawing them away from the wounded magantor.

Wind Racer dipped briefly, taking an arrow in his right wing, then another in his breast, blood issuing from his wounds. Several gargoyles angled higher to reach them, their wings working fervently to attain such height. Corry urged the great avian back to their lines, Wind Racer's strength wanning from his wounds. The land below was a maelstrom of gargoyles flying to and fro, coursing above their brethren forming a caliginous sea of leathery flesh carpeting the valley floor. She felt an odd sensation creeping along her spine, craning her neck to find a gargoyle clinging to Wind Racer's tail, its glowing red eyes staring hatefully at her. She reached for her sword, uneasy about shifting in the saddle at this height.

The creature gained its footing, rising up to stand upon its clawed feet, walking across Wind Racer's back, wielding an odd-shaped sword that bent halfway up its blade. Before she could draw her sword, another blade reached out between them, striking the gargoyle full in the face, sending it tumbling from Wind Racer's back.

Corry looked on as the air ski swept past her in the opposite direction. There rode Lorken, wielding a sword that he retrieved from the ground to replace his ruined pistol, using it to great effect striking down gargoyles braving the greater heights. She briefly watched as he swept around the battlefield, catching gargoyles by surprise, slicing them from behind as he swerved amidst the chaos. She turned back southward, Wind Racer speeding for the small open ground where Raven and Cronus defended Terin and the others. Looking left and right, she was surprised to see the entire gargoyle front unmoving, as if drawn to Tyro and Zem, their bold tactics effectively buying the time they so desperately needed. Their tactic was waning, however, the creatures again moving south, though many continued to be drawn in their direction. The greater host forsook the futile endeavor, advancing again upon their true prize… the armies gathered against them.

They would need another answer to slow the enemy, especially with night fast approaching. This question was foremost in Corry's thoughts when fate threw her another answer.

Her eyes drew wide, catching sight of two luminous swords working their way to the front of their lines as she passed overhead, one blue and the other green… Lorn and Elos.

* * *

Moments before.

Lorn had awoken the same time as Elos, beset with visions of things that were, are and were yet to be. All of his days since embracing Yah had led to this time and place. This was the call of destiny, the very purpose of his life unfolding before him. Now it was shared with all the peoples of Arax, all seeing things as Yah first revealed to him all those years before. Kal once stood here, facing the gargoyle threat alone, betrayed by faithless vassals forsaking him to his doom. Two and half millennia after, Lorn found himself standing against the same threat that consumed Kal, but he was not alone. All of southern Arax had rallied to his cause, and then the Chosen offered themselves up to save everyone else, a selfless act that pleased Yah. The others came anyway, adding their lives to the sacrifice, proving the worthiness of their hearts. And at last, Jonas offered his life, forcing his father to choose between his blood and the creatures he had taken for friends.

Tyro's choice unified all the peoples of Arax to their greater purpose, standing at each other's sides to face the gargoyle threat as one. It was clear to Lorn now Yah's intent, and if he perished on this field of battle, the gargoyles would not survive the day. Their fate was sealed when they entered the Oddigem. They might still slay many if not all of them, but the gargoyle line would end in the Oddigem.

He awoke, knowing what to do, greeted by so many familiar faces, friends and comrades in this great quest. He shared a look with Elos, each knowing the mind of the other in this grave matter.

"Cousin!" Tosha greeted him excitedly, rushing to kneel at his side, helping him to his feet.

"Tosha." He smiled, embracing her before reaching down to grasp the *Sword of the Moon*. A surge of intense power flowed through him, the sword strengthening him, restoring his luster in an instant.

"Deva says we must hold a little longer. I hope..." she began to say but he stopped her with a finger to her lips.

"I know, Tosha. We will purchase her more time, just as Tyro and Zem have just done, and Thorton before them." Lorn gently kissed her forehead, before stepping away, Elos and Mortus following him in step.

"Where are..." she tried to ask.

"Watch over Terin, all of you," Lorn said, looking at each of them surrounding him, Raven, Cronus, Lucas, Ular, Deva, Corry, Letha and especially Squid, who stood constant vigil over his former scribe.

"I will go with you, they have enough here to protect the boy," Queen Letha said adamantly.

"Very well." Lorn smiled, leading the four of them north through their formation, before breaking north of their shield wall.

They stepped forth, climbing atop the mound of corpses piled before their shield wall, just as the gargoyle horde was about to break upon their position, crossing over the sea of dead and dying separating the two armies.

Lorn raised his sword before his face, pressing his lips to its glowing blade.

"Bless us this day, Oh Yah! I commend my life, my spirit and my sacred honor unto you," Lorn avowed, stepping forth to meet the onrushing multitude.

Elos did the same, pledging all to their noble cause, stepping forth into oblivion, his sword alit a bright emerald sheen, shining greater than it ever had before.

"I offer my life, my realm, my all, Oh Yah," King Mortus said proudly and humbly, stepping forth, his blade alit a fiery gold, shining boldly in the din.

"And I offer mine, Oh Yah! By the honor of my Tarelian blood, I offer all," Letha proclaimed, following the others into oblivion, the four of them disappearing into the caliginous sea of hate and malice, their swords lighting the darkness.

* * *

From above Lorken watched as Lorn and his companions crossed into the open, marching into the enemy host, their swords igniting with a terrible fury. He looked further north where Zem and Tyro seemed to be making their way toward them. He saw Zem go under several times, beset with creatures piling upon him, taking him from his feet as he disappeared beneath mounds of flesh, only to emerge, clawing his way free. He tossed gargoyles aside like a grizzly swatting rabbits, crushing others under his heavy boots, or tearing creatures apart with his bare hands. By now his jacket and shirt were torn away, revealing his metallic black-silver chest.

Tyro's movement was far less obvious, cutting down gargoyles with deadly precision, the creatures seemingly oblivious to his presence or frozen in disbelief.

Combined, their actions were drawing much of the enemy unto them, but many more continued on toward their shield walls, clambering overtop, clawing their way through the seams of the interlocked shields, thousands perishing to alliance spears and blades. Archers fired blindly into the encroaching masses, feathering the unprotected gargoyle ranks. By now the gargoyle lasses began to emerge, storming over the shield walls, throwing themselves upon the defenders, sightless eyes staring hauntingly into the defenders' faces, their fangs snapping fiercely.

Torg braced for impact, a dozen white fleshed lasses throwing themselves upon his shield. He jabbed around the seam of his shield, finding flesh, before repeating the thrusts in rapid succession. He retracted the blood-stained blade as another creature peered over top, ghastly white clawed fingers grasping the top of the shield. He brought his blade across its fingers, severing three, its grip failing, dropping upon those gathered below.

"Agghh!"

The man to his left cried out. He turned to find a gargoyle lass atop of him, sinking its fangs into his neck. Galen shifted around behind him, driving his blade into the creature's throat just as it lifted its head, pale eyes meeting his determined gaze, bright red blood dripping from its pallid lips. It died on Galen's blade, its blind eyes staring strangely at Torg.

Could the creature see him? Torg wondered, the ghastly sight matching the awfullest things the craggy master of arms had ever seen.

CRUNCH!

He looked to his right, where Orlom crushed another creature's skull.

"Got another one, Coach!" Orlom grinned stupidly, as if he was having the time of his life.

* * *

Corry set down within the small clearing where Terin still lay, guarded by his friends. Wind Racer bore her without complaint as she dismounted, hurrying to Ilesa and the matrons attending her, grabbing whatever bandages she could find, mostly rags torn from the fallen. She returned to Wind Racer, wadding the material and pressing it around the arrow protruding from his breast, with no means to keep it there if she relented. Ilesa saw her struggle, sending Dougar to help her.

"Might I help, Your Highness?" he asked.

Corry looked to Terin's prone form surrounded by their friends, needing to speak with him, to bring him back from wherever his mind had wandered. She looked up at Wind Racer, her faithful friend who had born her in battle time and again, torn between her loyalties.

The stoic warbird sensed her grief, nudging her toward Terin with his beak, as if to tell her to go to him. She quickly embraced the great avian, hugging his neck before running to Terin as Dougar replaced her, reaching up with his small arms to press the cloth around his wound to stem the bleeding.

ZIP! ZIP!

She passed behind Raven, who was firing into the air as more gargoyles filled the sky, dropping them before they could draw close. Cronus stood watch beside him, while Tosha, Lucas and Ular formed a smaller perimeter around Terin's still form, with Squid at its center, his sword drawn and waiting. Corry rushed to his side, kneeling beside him, pressing her lips to his ear.

"Awake, Terin. Come back to us, come back to me," she pleaded, kissing his forehead, before placing her head upon his chest.

"Stay close to him, me dear. If any can draw him back, it is you." Squid smiled at her, standing vigil, his gaze fixed skyward.

Terin found himself amid a current of memories and visions, passing by him as he walked, mist gathering at his feet, concealing the path beneath him. The scenery around him rested between sunrise and twilight, the features in the distance obscured by his dreamlike state. The visions passed to his left and right, or were they memories? He saw his father and mother bidding him farewell as he began his journey to Rego, seeing now the tears on his mother's face that he was too far afield then to recognize. He Saw Wind Racer when King El Anthar presented him upon the roof of Corell. He saw Arsenc and Yeltor standing bravely upon the hillside at Kregmarin, seeing their courageous and terrifying end. He saw Kato fall at Ben's hand, and Ben dying at Darcol, giving his life for others. He saw his father dying at the outset of the battle, and his grandfather slaying his killer. He saw Raven's sister dying, and the terrible cost that followed. He saw Raven's home world with all its seas and mountains.

He saw visions of events that had not happened and might never come to pass. He saw them all dying here, fighting to the end before succumbing. He saw Raven take a gargoyle spear through his heart, his muted voice shouting to warn him in impotent rage. He saw Cronus falling with a terrible wound, and Corry…

No, he could not look, the awful sight passing him by, another taking its place. He watched each of his friends fall, unable to prevent it, his limbs frozen at his side, unresponsive to his will. He lifted high into the air, drawing over the battlefield before setting down in the gargoyles' midst. He stood as a spirit, the creatures running past him, dark leathery flesh followed by ghastly pale. The wingless, sightless lasses flowed by, like a raging river sweeping around a rock protruding through the surf. They were ghastly to look upon, the things of nightmares, their cloudy eyes staring hauntingly forward as the sun sank below the western sky. He remained in place, unable to depart this vision, looking on, twilight giving way to night as the lasses' eyes drew fully open, their clouded hues giving way to red irises, each staring hungrily at him. It was then he knew, they could see only in the dark, as they made homes in the dark places of the world, their eyes clouding only in sunlight, unlike their winged brothers.

"Time, Terin. You must purchase time to save your friends," his father's voice called to him.

"Father? Where are you?" he pleaded, looking around as the gargoyle lases faded into nothing.

"I am with you, and shall ever be," Jonas said, appearing briefly, clothed in bright white raiment, lifting his hand as to say farewell, his visage drawing away.

"No!" Terin called out to him, begging him to return.

"Terin?" Corry's voice called to him.

He sat upright, his eyes blinking rapidly, taking in his surroundings.

"My boy." Squid smiled, looking down at him as Tosha, Lucas and Deva gathered around.

"What did you see?" Deva asked frantically, her own vision in-complete.

Terin had so many things he wanted to say, but knew there was no time. He needed to move, feeling something pulling him. He started to reach down for his blade when he was stopped, recalling what they needed to know.

"The gargoyle lasses. They are blind in daylight, but can see in the dark, and… at night," Terin said, his words striking Deva with the full weight of their meaning.

Tosha looked to the west, the sun just setting below the ridge-line. The very thought that the enemy might see while they were blinded by the darkness proved their perilous position. They had fought bravely, slaying many times their number, their casualties quite light all things considered. The brutal truth was that there were just too many of the enemy to kill in a day. It would take many days of vigilant slaughter to purge the valley floor of their fell kind, and most of them would perish in the exchange.

"I must join the others. The swords must fight as one. It will buy us time, though I do not know how much time is required, or what deliverance is promised if we do so," Terin said, looking to Tosha and at Cronus, who stood beside Raven just beyond the others.

It was then Lorken's voice broke over Raven's comm, relaying of another impending peril.

"*Heads up, Rav, you got a large number of gargoyles taking to the air coming at you from both sides!*" Lorken said. His air ski hovered above their position, looking north where the glow of Lorn and the other's swords shone amidst the enemy host, drawing much of their strength upon them. The tactic didn't turn all of them, however, with many thousands of gargoyle warriors assailing the length of their shield wall, while ten thousand took to the air, nearly a thousand of which passed just to their east and west, before cutting inward, converging upon the small clearing where they stood.

"I see 'em. Get ready, kids, our lousy neighbors are calling!" Raven growled, his reference lost on all of them, but not its meaning.

A sense of dread washed over Cronus, his terrible vision coming to fruition, the scene around him unfolding with unnatural familiarity. The only change was that he was here in the flesh, and not in spirit. He brought his sword at the ready, gazing west where gargoyles filled the skies, passing over their front ranks, sweeping toward them.

ZIP! ZIP! ZIP!

Raven dropped the three nearest in quick order, making certain of each shot, his pistol quickly wanning. He managed to charge it partially during the battle, but not enough, not nearly enough. Archers behind the rearmost formation loosed their volleys, firing with abandon, every fifth arrow finding purchase, thinning the creature's ranks. Nearly half the gargoyles broke off for inviting targets to the rear as columns of infantry closed ranks around their small clearing.

Wind Racer shifted suddenly, a gargoyle attempting to set down upon his back, the movement sending poor Dougar sprawling to the dirt, the great avian's feet avoiding crushing him underfoot. The gargoyle dropped alongside them, struggling to gain its feet. Dougar rolled onto his stomach, springing to his feet as Wind Racer's head swung around, blasting the creature with his breath. The gargoyle hissed demonically, trying to gain its feet, its eyes lidded from the pressure. Dougar hurried forth, driving his small sword into the creature's gut, the gargoyle swatting him with his clawed digits, blood gurgling from its dying throat. Wind Racer stomped the wretched creature, squishing it into the ground, blood pooling beneath his talons.

More gargoyles set down in their midst, Cronus moving forth to engage them.

SPLIT! THRUST!

Cronus chopped the first one down, moving upon the next without stopping, Ular moving to his left, darting to and fro, cutting tendons and throats with effortless grace. Other soldiers rushed forth, driving their spears into the creatures as they descended, skewering them with prejudice. Raven took careful aim, dropping one after another, keeping to Cronus' right.

Tosha guarded their rear, gazing east where an equal number filled the sky, drawing ominously nigh. Squid stood beside her, his aged arm refusing to yield. Tessa went to guard Ilesa's child, replacing Dougar, as Lucas helped Terin steady himself, his friend's legs still wobbly from his slumber. Deva and Corry stood guard as Terin collected himself, reaching down to grasp the *Sword of the Sun*, the ancient blade bursting in crimson light as he grasped the hilt. He longed for his silver sword, missing its familiar feel but this sword felt as if it was forged especially for him, and in truth, it was. Yah guided the ancient smiths of Tarelia in crafting the blade for this purpose, though he concealed Kal's bloodline from them until a time of his choosing. It was Terin who was meant to wield the *Sword of the Sun*. He was the blood of Kal, the blood of Tyro, and the blood of ancient Tarelia. He was Yah's instrument to fulfill his promise he made to Kal so long ago, guiding his seed in delivering his people from the gargoyle curse.

Terin felt a surge of power coursing his flesh, filtering to every extremity, restoring his strength. It was euphoric, filling him with rapture. He moved with purpose, stepping forward of Tosha, Corry and Deva just as the first creature descended from the east, cutting it shoulder to crotch, rending it in half. He moved left, taking another across the chest, its body dropping beyond him in pieces. Tosha stepped forth, guarding his flank, her blade alit a fiery gold, cutting down creatures in quick order, though she struggled keeping pace. Terin gave himself over to the sword, its fell power feeding his strength and guiding his purpose.

SPLIT! SLASH! THRUST!

He destroyed creatures in quick order, cutting down every one settling in his vicinity. Many more flew on for better prospects elsewhere, others forsaking all reason, their instinctive rage giving way to terror, fleeing whence they came. Terin moved farther and farther east, before stopped by the wall of infantry that formed their perimeter, the men positioned there skewering dozens of creatures during the exchange.

From the west, Cronus, Ular and Raven worked in unison. Cronus cut down every creature he came upon with cold efficiency, often losing himself in the moment, fueled by a deadly calm, before he was brought back. He paused, finding himself standing over a dead gargoyle cut in four pieces, not remembering having done it. Ular was off his left, flipping behind a creature, cutting its knees out from under it. Straight ahead, a flax of soldiers surrounded Wind Racer and Dougar, forming a loose shield wall around them, driving off creatures trying to set upon them. Cronus felt the strangely familiar sense that he had been here before, where time and place were joined.

Actually, he had been here many times, but all were in his dreams. He felt a cold sensation rippling across his flesh, a gripping fear that threatened to take the heart of him. It was playing out just as he saw. He turned, seeing Raven blast another creature from the air, and then another, and another, the sky filled with too many to stop altogether. He killed one after another, all drawing from the west, but the threat was not confined in that direction. Another band of gargoyles circled around from the south, passing between Terin and the others to their east, and them to the west, the creatures breaking off, each half coming upon them from behind.

Cronus turned about, swinging his blade overhead, cleaving the first creature's left wing, sending him tumbling to the ground behind Raven. He moved onward, taking another across the back of its legs as it flew toward Raven, terrible screams following the painful blow.

ZIP! ZIP!

Raven dropped two more to his front, unable to turn upon the threat to his rear, with more coming upon him from the west. Cronus cut down another, losing his footing, as he planted in the blood-soaked soil. He felt something off, his left ankle aflame, looking up as another creature came fast upon them, its wings spread wide, its spear leveled upon his friend. He tried to rise, his left foot giving way, pain shooting up his leg. He didn't have time to look down, seeing it jut at an unnatural angle.

This was his vision, playing out before his very eyes, and he was unable to intercede. All his preparations for this moment were for naught. He could do nothing to save his friend unless he could stand, but time was fleeting. He needed to kill it or turn it somehow. If only he could reach out with his sword, but he was on his hands and knees.

No! he screamed, unwilling to give up. He thrust the tip of his sword into the ground, the blade sinking a good distance before stopping, using it to rise to his good foot. The creature's spear was drawing dangerously nigh, with Raven still firing in the opposite direction, dropping several more at his feet, oblivious of danger behind him. Cronus could not warn him, for there were more threats drawing from the other direction. His sword was too low, and still stuck partially in the ground, and supporting his ruined ankle. The creature ignored his presence, flying just above the level of his shoulder, angling for Raven, its spear level for the killing blow. It was drawing a few feet to his side, with no time to lift his blade to kill it.

Here was his moment of decision, forcing this terrible choice upon him. No blade would save his friend, no laser blast, no arrow, rock or spear. All Cronus had time to do was…

He threw himself in front of the spear, his left hand keeping hold of his sword.

Thrust!

He felt the spear punch through his chest, trying to bring the sword up as it impaled him, swinging it blindly as he fell, his world spinning. He made his choice, resigned to his fate.

No greater love. He thought of Jentra's words, words that came to define all of them gathered here, every soldier in their armies. He would give his life for his friend, one dear to his heart, though it would consign his daughter an orphan.

Please forgive me, Maura, he wept, wondering what life he had condemned her to. He hoped Leanna would forgive him, but recalled his vision, where she told him to save their friend. In that he succeeded.

There in the Valley of Oddigem, Cronus was saved, Ilesa rushing to his side as Raven turned, blasting the gargoyle through the skull, its body dropping somewhere between them. Ilesa set the regenerator upon his chest, ripping the spear free, before initiating. He looked up in disbelief as she shook her head. His wound was mortal, and should have taken him before she could intercede, but he didn't recall seeing her close by. If she stood even a few paces further away it would have doomed him.

"You are not the only one to have visions, Cronus Kenti," she said as his chest healed, a euphoric sensation coursing the repaired tissue. She moved to his ankle, restoring the broken bones and tendons there as well.

He then knew she had come all this way, risking her life and her child's to be here at this very moment to save him, just as he saved Raven.

"My lady," he said, wanting to say more, but there was no time.

"There is time for words later, Cronus Kenti," she said, moving on to help others, the power in the regenerator quickly wanning.

"She's a keeper if you ask me," Raven said, looking at his friend. He knew Cronus had saved him once again, losing count of how many times they had each done that.

Cronus laughed, the reference another he did not recognize, but he could guess the meaning. He gained his feet, guarding Raven's back, waiting for the next wave to come upon them. Scores of gargoyles approached from the west and an equal number from the east, their wings dotting the late day sky, the sun nearly set below the ridgeline.

"*Hold your fire, Rav!*" Brokov said over the comm.

The reason was soon clear with hundreds of Jenaii and magantors closing upon the gargoyles from both sides, slaying many from behind, sending the rest in flight. The air ski emerged from their glorious ranks, Lorken zooming across the sky before setting down in their midst.

* * *

"I can't take all three of you. We need to do two trips," Lorken said, the others gathering around him.

Terin insisted the swords needed to be joined once more. With the others still fighting to their north amidst the enemy host, time was fleeting.

"You sure about this? It didn't work out the first time you did it," Raven pointed out, the blast draining their comms, weapons, regenerators and putting everyone but him and Lorken to sleep.

"It was necessary," Deva insisted.

Raven didn't see the sense in her argument but wouldn't waste the time to debate it. They needed to decide quickly.

"I will take Cronus and Tosha first, and Terin second. I have to warn you, it will be very dangerous, and I don't have a pistol to clear away the danger," Lorken said.

"You can take mine, or better yet, take me and Tosha, and come back for Cronus and Terin," Raven said.

"Why you?" Corry asked.

"In case the whole thing repeats itself," Raven pointed out.

"How much juice does your pistol have left?" Lorken asked.

"Not much, but enough to do the job," Raven shrugged.

* * *

Lorken sped across the battlefield, a score of magantors sweeping the skies before them, led by General Valen. He looked north where Lorn and the others were gathered just beyond their shield wall, surrounded by the enemy host, the light of their swords illuminating the air around them. Raven fired in a circle around them, dropping dozens as Lorken circled overhead before setting down between them. Tosha and Raven dismounted, taking up position, with Raven in their center, the others forming a wall of swords and light, holding back the creatures as Lorken lifted into the air.

Lorn sliced a gargoyle wing, the creature reeling from the blow, while Mortus guarded his right, taking a sword arm at the elbow, followed by the head. Letha severed another's legs above the knee, returning her blade at the ready, guarding Lorn's back. Tosha stood between her and Elos, the gargoyles avoiding her as they had throughout the battle, as if she were poison. Elos' blade shone bright emerald, its light illuminating his face with ethereal light. As the dead began to pile at their feet, they advanced north several paces, giving them space to fight and stand, before repeating the process.

A pair of golden-hued blades drew near from the north, Tyro cutting a path to join them, the swords' instinctively drawn to their sister blades. Lorn shifted as he approached, opening a place for him to stand between he and Elos. Tosha stole a brief glance behind her, pleased to see her father standing beside them. He had done much to hold the enemy at bay, buying them precious time, time that was again fleeting.

ZIP! ZIP!

Raven targeted two gargoyles circling above, keeping the sky clear for Lorken's return. Their magantors were already clearing the area, looking for places to safely set down. Within moments of this, Lorken appeared, circling above before lowering into their midst, gargoyle spears thrown all around him. He stopped a few feet above the ground as Cronus and Terin jumped clear, preparing to lift away.

"Find a spot far to the rear and get on the ground!" Raven said.

"No kidding." Lorken gave him a look before lifting away, not wishing to repeat what transpired the last time.

"It's all you, Terin. Let's hope it goes a little differently, or my arm is gonna get tired lopping all their heads off all by myself," Raven said, slapping him on the back.

"You will have Lorken to help you." Cronus smiled, slapping him on the back in turn.

With that, Terin stood between all of them, raising his sword into the air, crimson light bursting along its golden blade. Elos and Lorn turned about, pressing their blades to his, emerald and azure light melding with crimson.

ZIP! ZIP! ZIP!

Raven fired in the voids left by Elos and Lorn, hoping he had enough energy left in his pistol to get the job done. As if a cosmic answer to a prayer, he saw Zem's familiar face emerge from the sea of leathery flesh, his towering form tossing creatures aside with pitiful ease. He strode forth, entering their protective circle as Queen Letha and King Mortus turned about, pressing their blades to Terin's. Cronus and Tosha went next, leaving Tyro wondering if he should hand one of his blades to Raven, doubting if he should wield two for the process to work.

"Might as well do it. I can't hold a sword and cover you at the same time," Raven urged him, firing all around them now, the creatures threatening to close upon them. Zem moved to the opposite side of their comrades, waiting to crush any creature daring to step forth. The gargoyles seemed to be held back by the power of the swords, and fearful of Tyro, Tosha and especially Terin. It was as if an invisible wall surrounded them, the light of the swords melding into a single stream of purple light.

Tyro stepped forth, pressing both of his blades to the others, feeling a surge of euphoria filter throughout his body, his eyes transfixed as he beheld the intense purple light transform into a brilliant white glow. The light shot skyward, spreading across the breadth of the Oddigem, illuminating the valley floor, sending the gargoyle multitude in panic, shielding their eyes from its intense glow. The creatures that had already passed over their shield walls were now without reinforcements and cut down wherever they settled. The Jenaii and gargoyles battling along the east and west ridges remained engaged, each struggling to control the high ground overlooking the valley.

Lorken and their magantors managed to set down, fearing the swords might repeat what happened earlier. Their fears were waylaid as their armies remained standing, appearing unaffected by the swords' power. Strangely, the gargoyles were unaffected as well, the two armies facing one another across that deadly space, divided by the brilliant light separating them. They loosed arrows at the gargoyles, their feathered shafts dropping upon nearing the veil of light, unable to penetrate it.

Raven and Zem stood guard over their friends, watching the gargoyles surrounding them cower in fear, covering their eyes or ears, hissing hatefully at them, as if the light itself was tearing at their flesh. Their eyes were blood red, revealing the foulest spirits that dwelled within them. They hissed, gnashing their teeth, their jaws snapping at the air about them, poised to launch upon them should the light falter. Raven tried shooting them, his blasts dying in the bubble of light that now surrounded them, shifting in hues of crimson, emerald, azure and gold, thin enough for him to see to the opposite side, where the gargoyles were looking back.

Terin and the others stood frozen in place, engulfed in the swords' light, power surging through them, their eyes clouded with visions, their faces glowing with ethereal brilliance.

"How long is this supposed to last, and what happens when it stops?" Raven asked Zem the obvious question on both their minds. They were buying time, but for what? If the swords didn't strike the enemy dead, then what would? It would take days to kill them all at this rate, and nothing they did here would change that.

"What is it your father used to say? *If we weren't here, we'd just be somewhere else,*" Zem said, enjoying the annoyed look the quote gave Raven.

Raven just shook his head, watching as the minutes rolled by, as if the world was held in suspended animation. The minutes passed painfully slow, but fast at the same moment. At least his pistol wasn't drained by the swords this time, but he didn't have much juice left. He wondered if Brokov could see anything from his vantage point, raising him on the comm.

"*We have fighting still going on along each ridgeline, but everyone else is unmoving all across the valley floor,*" Brokov answered.

"At least we have comms. What do you make of all this?" Raven asked.

"*I don't know, but... wait. There is something odd...*" Brokov's feed cut.

"Brokov?" Raven growled into the comm just as the light dropped all around them, lifting across the valley floor like a curtain drawn from a stage. Terin and the others collapsed where they stood, the gargoyles surrounding them preparing to move upon them, Raven and Zem preparing to intercede when the world around them erupted.

ZIP! ZIP! ZIP!

Blasts of green and blue flashed all round them, carving holes through the gargoyle ranks, row upon row disintegrating into a cloud of vapor.

"A sign has been given," Lorn said, rising to his feet to stand beside Raven.

ZIP! ZIP! ZIP!

Laser flashed to their left and right, spewing from somewhere above, destroying gargoyles in the thousands.

Raven looked up, pimples raising across his flesh as a familiar voice broke over his comm, a voice he never thought to hear ever again.

"*Looks like you could use some help, Captain Mekiana,*" Captain Ahmet Ozturk haled him, commander of blue squadron of Battle Carrier *Stalingrad.*

Raven looked up as his former squadron filled the sky above, strafing the valley floor all around them when the heavens opened up, an intense beam of energy sweeping along the valley from the north, vaporizing the gargoyle host like the hand of God rubbing his finger across the surface of the globe.

"Oz?" Raven said in disbelief, not believing his eyes.

"*Admiral Kruger sends his regards,*" Ahmet said, the young Turkish pilot smiling widely, speeding across the vale.

There in the Vale of Oddigem, the gargoyles were destroyed for all time, removed from the face of Arax.

Thus ended the Battle of Noddegamra.

Restoration Part Two

Restoration

CHAPTER 16

Earlier that day.
Engineering room of Battle Carrier Stalingrad.

Admiral Kruger surveyed the readouts displayed on the terminal, disappointed with the latest results. He spent an unusual amount of time in recent weeks with Commander Pham, the Stalingrad's chief engineer, reviewing the live feeds of the probes they launched, giving them on time analysis of the star systems that appeared most promising. Each planet required in depth analysis, which Commander Pham personally oversaw, using his extensive knowledge of planet formation, makeup, and evolution to produce the most objective data for their success. Of the over 107 star systems within their jump range, they had only enough probes to target the 37 most promising. Of those 37, Commander Pham was limited to analyzing them one at a time, examining the material makeup of each planet and celestial body in each system, before moving on to the next. He completed assessments of 14 star systems, currently reviewing his 15th.

"This is the fourth planet in the Bian System, a solid surfaced type lll planet, with a diameter of 11,000 kilometers," Hao Pham pointed out, the admiral, examining the three-dimensional image projected on the flat area between them.

"A promising find, and resting in the habitable zone," Admiral Kruger conceded.

"Aye, Admiral, and with a molten core and magnetic field," Hao added excitedly.

"But with a ten-day rotation and no moon and lacking in seven of our critical elements. What of the other planets in this system, do they have what we need to sustain ourselves while we terraform this world?"

"The first two each have one, the third has none. The outer planets are all gas giants with 74 moons combined. The odds are much in our favor," Commander Pham explained, almost giddy with the possibilities.

"Complete your assessments. I want a full report on as many systems as you can before I have to choose."

"Of course, Admiral. At least we have this as the base standard going forward," Hao Pham said.

"A very problematic base standard, Commander, and I doubt we will have time for you to complete all 37 star systems before we will have to jump," Helmut said, after they discovered their life support had a mere five days left before they had to jump, far less than they previously believed. At this rate of analysis, Pham might only complete his work on the first 20 systems. Helmut would then have to choose the best prospect of the twenty.

"My team will complete the analysis on this system and the next before day's end, Admiral."

"Very good. Have you completed your daily diagnostic on our long-range drive?" the admiral asked.

"It was completed two solar hours prior to your arrival. That is three days straight since we completed restoration," Commander Pham said.

"And the *Solis*?" Admiral Kruger asked concerning their sister vessel, the fleet destroyer *Javier Solis*, whose long-range drive was equally compromised.

"Their chief engineer transmitted his full diagnostic this morning. All systems are a go, Admiral, at least for one jump for each of us."

"Aye, one jump," Admiral Kruger sighed, his eyes narrowing severely in thought. They had one chance to jump to the correct star system that had all the ingredients they would need to sustain themselves, as well as terraform a planet to support them indefinitely, though such a process would take many years.

"Perhaps we shall find a world or celestial body filled with Rendarium." Commander Pham said hopefully. Rendarium was actually a combination of elements that powered their long-range drives. There was a dozen required to power a drive, and they were all rare, and never found in vicinity to one another. It was almost a certainty, that wherever they jumped to would have only one of the elements at best. That meant wherever they went, it would be their home indefinitely unless a rescue mission from Earth found them. That would be the pinnacle of irony that they were on a rescue mission searching for the *Eden expedition*, and now needed rescuing themselves.

"Keep me informed, Commander, I'll be on the bridge the rest of the day, after I meet with Dr. Chopra," the admiral said, referencing the fleet's psychiatrist, who had urgent information she insisted he would find of interest.

Hao brightened at the mention of the beautiful Aditi Chopra, his attraction to her a poorly kept secret.

"Aye, Admiral. My team should have the results for Bian System completed by the day's end, perhaps sooner. Then we shall commence with the Quyen System," Hao said.

"Bian and Quyen? Where are you finding these names, commander?" the admiral asked curiously.

"It is standard practice in the academy of sciences that all newly discovered systems are named by their discoverer, Admiral. As that currently is myself, I chose…"

"Alright, I get it, Hao, but why Bian and Quyen?"

"Truly, Admiral? They were the greatest female vocalists of the 22nd century, and both native to my home city Da Nang." Hao smiled, proud of his native Vietnam.

"Very well, Commander. I am certain every star system in our new map sequence will be named after a lovely Vietnamese maiden." Helmut Von Kruger shook his head, heading for the door.

"Not all, Admiral. I know of a few lovely Indian names as well," Hao said, referencing the beautiful Aditi Chopra.

* * *

Command Briefing Room.

Captain Masamba Banza (Space fleet rank 0-6), captain of the *Stalingrad*, stood before the viewport, contemplating what the good doctors just revealed. Behind him sat the fleet chief psychiatrist, Commander Aditi Chopra (Space fleet rank 0-5), and the fleet chief physician, Commander Sarah Kensington (0-5).

"Captain?" Aditi asked, the skipper's silence giving her doubt if he fully heard their report.

"Does the admiral know of this, doctor?" the captain asked, his gaze fixed to the stars in the distance, hauntingly displayed through the viewport.

"He shall be, sir. He is on his way as we speak," Dr. Chopra said.

"You are certain there is not a physical explanation for these *Dreams* our crew is experiencing?" Captain Banza asked, turning to face them.

"None that I have discovered, sir. I have run a full physical exam on every crew member Dr. Chopra had asked, and can find no abnormalities," Dr. Kensington explained. A native of Leeds, England, Sarah Kensington was a foremost expert in the field of physiological impacts of deep space travel.

"And as I explained, sir, the dreams our crew are experiencing seem to be interconnected," Dr. Chopra reiterated. In all her years of study, Dr. Chopra had never seen a psychological event of this kind.

"How do you know the crew haven't spoken with each other to coordinate this fairy tale? Or might they have merely influenced each other subliminally by merely mentioning it?" Captain Banza asked.

"No, sir. There is no deception in their claims, and all have only spoken of their dreams during confidential sessions, which I am only privileged to break if they are of urgency to your command," Dr. Chopra said.

348

My command. Captain Banza shook his head at that. Being the captain of a battle carrier was as useless as a fifth leg on a horse. Since every battle carrier was the flagship of its fleet, the fleet admiral was the one truly in command. The skipper of the *Stalingrad* was more of an X/O, overseeing the administrative duties that the admiral delegated.

"These visions, or dreams as you call them, they center around a fair-haired warrior with a complexion similar to your native India?" Banza asked of Aditi.

"He seems to be the central figure in these hallucinations or dreams, but he is of a unique race of humans. Very similar to us, but different in very pronounced ways," Aditi Chopra explained, before expounding on the differences. She further detailed that all those who dreamed did so from differing perspectives, of different characters in this grand drama.

"Terin Caleph." Captain Banza repeated the name, as if he heard it before, his tone giving himself away to the inquisitive Dr. Chopra.

"You have had dreams as well?" she asked, rising up in her chair with her suspicion.

"Captain Banza?" Dr. Kensington pushed, his sudden silence confirming their suspicion.

"I visited this place you speak of, and always through the eyes the same fellow, a warrior. He was named Jentra, and he served at his king's side, giving his life for King Lorn. Upon his death, my spirit lifted so I could see Jentra's face for the first time. He died in Lorn's arms in one of the cities you mentioned… Notsu," he said, his words raising pimples across their flesh. Masamba Banza was no stranger to wild tales of visions and superstitions in his native land, the Congo Federation, which dominated central Africa. He ascribed such things as tourist attractions and idle nonsense, and here he stood, confessing his own wild hallucinations like a fevered fool. But a fool he was not, and knew the ladies were hiding something of their own.

"And who did each of you dream of?" he pushed, his question taking them off guard, the look they shared proving his accusation.

"Well?" he asked again more forcefully.

"I saw their world through the eyes of a princess, Tosha, daughter of Queen Letha and Emperor Tyro," Dr. Kensington sighed.

"And wife of Captain Mekiana, if what you said earlier is truthful," Masamba said.

"Aye, sir, wife of our missing Captain Raven," she conceded.

"But he is not the only one of our wayward crew you have discovered in this fantastical realm our crew has conjured in their delirium," Masamba pointed out.

A painful pause passed between them, revealing the deeper hurt they had yet fully revealed.

"I know of Ensign Nakamura's demise, having heard of his fate through my dreams of Jentra. He dies at the hand of Lt Thorton, is that correct?" Masamba asked.

"He does, or did, though we have no sense of time or even the veracity of what we have seen," Dr. Chopra explained. She had seen their world through the eyes of Ilesa, having wept reading Kato's letter.

"And he in turn dies saving the child of Ensign Nakamura, is that correct?" Masamba asked, trying to make sense of this unbelievable yarn.

"He does," Commander Kensington sighed.

"And that was after their swords came together?" Masamba asked.

"Apparently, though our visions have not run sequentially," Sarah Kensington added.

"There is something else you have not revealed, Dr?" he asked sternly, looking to Sarah.

"I know the fate of most of our missing expedition, Sir, I saw their graves through Tosha's eyes." She lowered her gaze.

"Graves?" Masamba asked.

"Colonel Chang and the entire civilian complement of the *Eden* Expedition. They perished during their arrival upon Arax and are buried near the wreckage of the *Magellan* on a beautiful isle," Sarah said.

That explained why they were not seen in any of the visions. If true, it meant their own expedition was almost a complete failure. The operative word being IF.

With that revelation, Admiral Kruger entered the room.

"As you were," Helmut said, ordering the ladies to remain seated, and directing Masamba to join him at the table.

"Dr, you have information you wish to share, and I assume you have invited Dr. Kensington and Captain Banza into your confidence?" Helmut asked, easing himself into his chair at the head of the large table.

"Dr. Kensington and myself have apprised Captain Banza of our findings, at least partially so, Admiral," Dr. Chopra began.

"Then summarize what I have missed, and then continue. I do hope this is most urgent considering the pressing tasks requiring myself and Captain Banza at this time, Drs," Helmut said.

"We believe it is, Admiral, but shall let you decide where it stands among your priorities."

"Out with it." Helmut sighed, irritated to be distracted from his task of finding the correct system to jump to. That decision outweighed every other concern, since their very lives depended on him being correct.

And so, they relayed all that they told Captain Banza. Throughout their entire narrative, the admiral's expression remained unchanged, as if he was cut from granite.

"I have mapped out the locations that each of our crew has seen in their dreams, as well as the maps they witnessed. I was able to construct this representation, though it is quite crude and elementary," Dr. Chopra apologized, initiating the central view screen, the table flickering to life, with a map of the Araxan main continent revealed across its surface.

There sat the continent in question, with each kingdom and realm depicted in near perfect representation.

"I'll take your crude over my perfection every day of the week, Doctor." Helmut shook his head, causing the good doctor to blush with his complement. Aditi Chopra was a noted perfectionist, leaving no detail overlooked, which bolstered her hypothesis in the admiral's eyes.

"As you can see, most of the activity has centered around the central kingdom of the continent, Torry North, and the battles at

Corell. The story concludes somewhere in this area." Dr. Chopra pointed out the Oddigem Valley northeast of Fera.

"And you believe this is where our missing expedition ended up?" Helmut asked.

"It is a possibility, as are other plausible explanations," Dr. Chopra ventured.

"Speak sense, Commander. I haven't time for you to walk on glass!" Helmut ordered.

"This could be an alien experiment, some unknown entity that is invisible to our sensors toying with our minds." She offered the most plausible explanation.

"For what purpose?" Captain Banza asked.

"An alien entity of such power would find more effective and direct means of destroying us," Admiral Kruger reasoned.

"As we are in unknown space, Admiral, they may be attempting to study us, in the event more of our kind follows us here," Dr. Kensington said.

"That seems a possibility," the admiral conceded. "What other explanation do you have?"

"Well, there is…" Aditi paused, wondering how to begin.

"Oh, out with it, Dr. Chopra!" Helmut pushed, not one to waste words.

"It is possible that everything our crew and ourselves have dreamed is in fact… true."

"I find that…" Helmut began to counter that notion, before pausing, aware of his own bias clouding his judgement. Of all that they spoke of, the most far fetched as he could see was Ben Thorton killing Kato Nakamura in a gun duel on some far-off world. It was not in his nature to do such a thing, but then again, he remembered the state he was in after Jennifer's death. Of all the things to give him doubt it was this, rather than a world similar to their own, with talking apes, flying birdmen, gargoyles and reptilian warriors. Throw in giant flying birds and an epic war set on a primitive planet and it all bordered on the absurd.

Dr. Chopra waited for a time after the admiral paused, before adding another facet she hadn't shared.

"Admiral, perhaps we are suffering the delusions of an unknown entity, but I have to doubt any alien entity would be so attuned to our unique emotions and mental makeup as these dreams have shown. I have seen many of my patients speak of what they saw with such deeply felt emotion it has brought me to tears. What they have seen is all too real, that I must believe it to be true. I can offer no explanation more likely than the deity that has guided these Araxans to this point... Yah. If I am pressed to explain what I have experienced, I would say that their deity is the alien giving us these dreams. All that is lacking is a trigger, some mechanism to bring us to this strange world of Arax."

Helmut Von Kruger leaned back in his chair; his eyes narrowed in concentration. He slowly spun his chair, gaining his feet as he stepped toward the large viewport, looking at the distant stars, each a portal to the past. A long moment passed, the others waiting for him to say what he was thinking.

"If what you believe is true, then what is our role in this?" Helmut asked, not turning around, his gaze fixed upon the distant stars.

"Perhaps to bear witness," Aditi offered, her reason sounding pathetic in her ears once she spoke it.

"Perhaps it is a warning of some nature," Dr. Kensington said.

"Or, a call to help," Captain Banza offered, his answer drawing Helmut's attention.

"Expand!" Helmut ordered.

"It seems a cry for help, Admiral. Have these gargoyles been defeated in any of these dreams?" Masamba looked to Dr. Chopra, who meekly nodded in the negative.

Helmut thought on that for a moment. He had no conception of what any of these things looked like, trying to picture a gargoyle, magantor or any of the characters they described. If half of what they revealed about the gargoyles was true, it would be the stuff of nightmares.

"What of you, Admiral, have you had strange dreams of late?" Captain Banza asked, sensing Helmut was keeping something back, his silence confirming his suspicion.

"Admiral?" Dr. Chopra asked, all of them looking at him intently.

"I have not had visions of this strange world you speak of, but… I have seen something or heard something. Actually both," he said quietly.

"What did you see?" Masamba asked.

"I saw a blinding light, and then a voice."

"What did it say, Admiral?" Sarah Kensington asked.

"*A sign shall be given*," Helmut said, drawing curious stares from the others.

"What does that mean?" Masamba wondered.

"I leave that question to our good doctor here. If you learn anything else, inform me immediately. I have other pressing matters to attend, as does Captain Banza," Helmut ordered Dr. Chopra, just as Lieutenant Commander Bao Chang's voice rang out through his comm.

"*Admiral, we have a strange sighting on one of our probes*," Bao stated, concealing the alarm in her voice.

Helmut considered what Dr. Chopra had revealed, and how Bao would receive news of her uncle's death, seeing as he commanded the *Eden Expedition*. The news struck him personally as well, for Colonel Chang had served as his flight operations officer since he assumed command of the *Stalingrad* so many years ago. There was always the off chance that none of this was true, and just the fevered dreams of his beleaguered crew, but he began to doubt it.

"Send it through, Lieutenant Commander," Helmut ordered, the image from their deep space probe projecting a holographic image above the center of the table.

There above the table a distant star system came into focus, with a beam of concentrated light shooting across the heavens. They followed its source to the second planet in the system.

"Localize the image, Bao!" Admiral Kruger ordered, using her first name, which he never did, that fact lost on the other's minds as they stared transfixed at the image.

"*It will take twenty-three standard Earth minutes to gain a clear image of the planet, Admiral*." Bao relayed the bad news, for their probe could not localize an image beyond the speed of light. Most of the probes could only be maneuvered one at a time with their long-range sensors impaired.

"Initiate general quarters and prepare pre-jump protocols. Contact the *Solis* and repeat the orders. I will be right up!" Helmut ordered, making his way toward the door, with Captain Banza close on his heels.

* * *

The Bridge was bustling with activity as Helmut and Masamba passed through the door, the crew coming to attention.

"As you were!" Helmut ordered, following Masamba to the central raised platform overlooking the surrounding stations in the large open room.

"Captain, Admiral," Bao Chang greeted them, her hands tucked behind her, resplendent in her gold bridge officer's uniform, an impressive feat as she was on her fifteenth straight hour on duty.

"Lieutenant Commander, which probe reported the anomaly?" Captain Banza asked, taking his place in the captain's chair at the center of the platform.

"Probe 23, sir," she said, ordering the technician seated at one of the consoles below to bring it up to the command screens on the central platform.

"Where is the anomaly?" Helmut asked sternly, seeing nothing but the system's star and the empty space between its planets, each barely visible in the vast expanse.

"It just ended, Admiral," Bao reported.

"How long did it last?" Masamba asked.

"Two minutes, fourteen seconds, sir."

"Replay the feed," Masamba ordered.

They watched intently as the scene unfolded, an intense burst of blinding light originating from the second planet, shooting across the star system. It was beautiful and terrifying to behold, and unexplainable. It would require an incredible power source to manifest such an anomaly.

"Admiral?" Masamba swiveled his chair toward Helmut, wondering his orders.

Admiral Helmut Von Kruger contemplated his situation. All his years of command instilled in him an attention to detail, discipline and a slavish adherence to logic and reason, as they did with any good commander. He weighed the options before him, knowing all their lives depended on his decision. Choose poorly, and they would all perish. Commander Pham was only a third of the way through his evaluations. If he jumped to the star system displayed before him, he would ignore Pham's analysis, placing his faith in the ambiguity of what he just witnessed. A wise choice would be to wait, keeping this star system in mind for deeper analysis, but they only had a few days left, and none of the current prospects were promising? What if the visions were true? What if the planet in their dreams was the second planet from the star he was looking at? What if Raven and the other survivors needed their help? Also, weren't they the ones in dire need? They needed to jump to a viable star system, or they would perish.

A sign shall be given, the voice repeated in his mind, a ghostly whisper he thought others might have heard.

A sign has been given, the voice said.

Helmut felt a power overtake him, an impulsiveness alien to his calculated nature. This was his defining moment, the choice of a lifetime. He closed his eyes, feeling a peace fill his heart, placing his faith in something he could not comprehend.

"Prepare the fleet to jump to that star system!" he commanded, his order taking them aback. They knew what that portended, their very lives hanging in the balance. What if they jumped to find nothing of consequence?

"Raise Colonel Smith. I want Blue and Black squadrons ready to launch once we arrive, with Green and Gray on standby," Captain Banza ordered, his subordinates hurrying to obey.

* * *

The fleet emerged from their jump, coming upon the star system of probe 23, just beyond the orbit of the second planet. There before them rested a blue marble, with patches of green and gray. It was an Earth type planet, the only of its kind they had ever discovered without terraforming, and with a comparable moon to Earth's. The bridge crew stared in wonder, not believing their eyes, before Admiral Kruger brought them to their senses.

"Launch fighters, and bring us in closer," Helmut commanded stepping across the bridge, scanning the readouts coming back from the planet's surface.

"Concentrate search on the central continent, along its central northern coast!" Captain Banza ordered, recalling the layout of Dr. Chopra's map.

"Sir, we have lifeforms! The planet is full of them!" Ensign Culver said, sitting at the organic diagnostics station, not believing what his eyes were seeing.

"Sir, we have a trundusium signal coming from the northern coast, a rather large source of it," Ensign Garcia reported, sitting the material diagnostic station beside Culver, zooming in on the position in question, where sat the *Stenox* in Mordicay Harbor.

They watched as the planet grew in focus, their computers mapping the surface as they drew closer.

"Admiral!" Another technician pointed to the central screen that dominated the bridge, watching another intense glowing light emanating from a northern point on the continent, likely the point of origin of the first anomaly.

"Send both squadrons to that point. They are to engage any winged creatures with dark leathery flesh and fangs. Render whatever aid the locals require," Admiral Kruger ordered, the crew wondering if he had gone mad, but they too had experienced dreams of Arax as well. They just couldn't believe what they dreamed was coming to pass before their very eyes.

"Message sent, Admiral," Lt. Maria Lopez said, the ship's comms officer.

"Lieutenant, should they find Captain Mekiana or Lieutenants Borovkov, Umaru, or Zem, send them my regards," Helmut said as their two-ship fleet drew closer.

"Aye, Admiral." Maria Lopez smiled, somehow knowing they would find them there.

"Once we come within range, ready our forward lasers!" Captain Banza ordered. If they found gargoyles gathered in great numbers, they would make quick work of them.

Helmut stood there, his mind a whirlwind of emotions. He pondered what this all meant, realizing the unique destiny or omnipotence guiding their path. Whatever their previous loyalty, Arax was now their home. With that he watched as the screen came alive with a terrible scene, a large valley with two armies facing one another. One was an odd coalition of humans, apes, reptilians and winged men. The other was a vast host of gargoyles, the creatures grossly detailed in Dr. Chopra's report. The gargoyles were being held back by the intense ethereal light emanating from… swords? Beside the swords stood two familiar figures, Raven and Zem, standing watch over the swords' wielders. The light suddenly dropped just before blue squadron reached the outskirts of the valley.

"There is Terin!" Lt. Lopez gasped, recognizing the boy she knew through her dreams of Corry.

Her words swept the bridge like an autumn gale, each crew member realizing it was Terin invoking the full power of the *Sword of the Sun* that lighted their path, bringing them here, and saving their lives. As if he could read their thoughts of praise and gratitude for the fair-haired Araxan youth, Admiral Kruger aptly responded.

"Then let us repay the favor," he said, drawing a host of smiles from his crew.

"Blue Squadron approaching target zone, Admiral," one crewman reported.

"Good hunting," Helmut said as his fighters swept across the vale and his shipboard lasers followed, sweeping the valley floor from the north.

There above Arax, the Battle Carrier *Stalingrad* had arrived.

CHAPTER 17

They all stared in silence at their deliverance, the strange flying machines sweeping the sky, slaying the gargoyles where they stood. Here the peoples of Arax stood, Torry, Benotrist, Menotrist, Sisterhood, Yatin, Casian, Naybin, Macon, Jenaii, Apes, Enoructan, with men of Tro, Rego, Notsu and many others. They fought as one, they fought as Yah had called upon them to do so long ago.

Lorn stood at Raven's side, watching the miracle unfold before them. Never in all his visions did he foresee this. Of all Yah's blessings none were as great as this. He thought they would all perish, either with the Chosen, or during the battle, where every turn their hope of victory seemed a fool's promise. And yet, here they stood, and despite their losses, their casualties were relatively few, all things considered, a fact they would discover in the coming days. Lorn knew then the full glory of what transpired, Yah's invisible hand guiding events to this very moment. It was Yah that gifted Kal's bloodline their unique power, passed down through the ages to Terin. It was Yah that sent the divine gift to the Jenaii, who brought it to ancient Tarelia, who forged the swords of light from its mysterious metals. It was these swords that were brought together, wielded by those Yah intended, for that critical moment, summoning the Earthers' powerful friends to this place, to deliver the finishing blow to the enemy. He felt Yah whisper in his heart, telling him of the dire state the Earthers were in when the signal of the swords brought them here. They saved the

Earthers as much as the Earthers saved them. This fact would be an eternal reminder to all of them that it was Yah that saved them, and not their own devices. It was each of them saving each other, each playing their part, no matter how small, to bring about this victory. Every sacrifice throughout the war, every battle, every friendship forged, every act of forgiveness and redemption was needed for them to triumph.

"I never saw that coming." Raven stated the obvious.

"No, and that is the beautiful part of it all, my friend." Lorn smiled, touching a hand to his shoulder as the others began to stir.

They helped them to their feet as Zem marched off to their south, smashing whatever gargoyles still lingered between them and their now disintegrating shield wall. All across the valley floor their armies lumbered forth, slaying whatever creatures remained, mostly those lingering near their lines where the space fighters did not target for the chance of striking the alliance armies in turn. Men broke from their shield walls, striking down the surviving gargoyles, the wretched creatures stunned witless by the turn of events.

Argos and Matuzak led those around them in one last charge, taking delight in caving the skulls of the few gargoyles left to kill. Torg, Orlom and Galen did likewise, finishing off several lingering before their shield wall, while hundreds of soldiers rushed past them, shouting their war cries, releasing their pent-up anger on whatever creatures escaped destruction to this point.

The Jenaii battled what remained of the creatures along either ridge, with the fighters of Blue Squadron strafing the enemy where practical, without hitting their new allies in the exchange.

With night closing about them, their armies stood victorious, euphoria sweeping through their jumbled ranks, followed by an outpouring of brother and sisterhood. Lorn could feel the overwhelming sense of love for all those in their company. Looking into their eyes, he felt the sentiment returned, especially with his fellow sword wielders. There stood Cronus, Elos, Mortus, Letha and Tosha, each groggily gaining their senses, and finally Tyro joining them, his uncle by marriage sharing a look with him. Could they ever truly come to accord after all that transpired before this day? Time would tell, but he felt Yah's hand in this as well. It was then he realized Terin had not awoken, their friend laying unmoving upon the ground, overcome by the power he invoked in the swords.

* * *

Two days hence.

Was he dead?

Terin lost sense of time, wandering an ethereal pathway, clouds gathering at his feet. The sky was neither day or night, but a tranquil twilight. No worries troubled his heart, as if all his burdens were lifted. There was a figure up ahead, the first he had seen in this endless trek, its murky visage growing in clarity, taking a familiar shape. There before him was his father, clad in the pure white raiment from his last dream, but brighter, his face glowing like a newborn star.

"Father!" He smiled happily, joyous tears running freely along his cheeks.

"You did well, my son." Jonas smiled in turn, his voice rippling like running water, a serene calm permeating his aura.

"Did we win?"

Jonas just smiled at that, leaving the boy to discover the full truth when he woke.

"Am I dead?" Terin asked.

"You are very much alive. You have so much life before you, so many years of friendship, peace and love. You are my great joy, Terin, my brave and loyal son. You are far greater than I could ever be." Jonas smiled, placing his hand upon his shoulder, staring lovingly into his eyes.

"I am nothing compared to you, Father. Everything I am is because of you, your skills, your cunning, your blood."

"Those are fine attributes, my son, but what truly made you great was your heart, your loyalty, and your love. It is these things that carried you through. It is these things your family shall need in these coming years. Your wife, your sister, and your grandfathers."

"Sister?"

"Cordela, she is beautiful, so much like your mother. You must be

strong for her, for both of them." Jonas left unsaid the pain his dear Valera would endure when she learned of his passing.

"I will protect them with my life," he avowed, balancing the pain of his father's loss with the gain of his sister.

"You shall not bear that burden alone, Terin," Jonas said, reminding Terin of his grandfathers' role in that regard.

Terin's face fell with that realization. What common ground could he ever find with Tyro? He could still not reconcile that this man before him was sired by the tyrant. There was no one like his father. Jonas was the finest man he ever knew, and was filled with love and kindness, whereas Tyro was cold and cruel.

"It may seem impossible to reconcile your heart to my father, Terin, but every journey starts with that first step. He is not what he seems. There are men that burn with such passion that only a cold heart can douse their pain. My father was always such a man, his passion for his wife and child all consuming. When he thought we had perished, he placed a wall around that part of him, that very large part of him where dwelt the very things that make us human. What was left was a rotting husk, a grim reminder of what our nature is without the divine spark. That was why I made him choose which part he would serve when I offered myself up to Morac. I saw you there, and I saw him, both of you so intent to save me, and when that failed, my father finally chose his family over his empire, he chose his better nature over the creature that consumed him for so long."

Terin lowered his head, torn over his feelings of the man.

"Remember this, my son. We could not have won without him. His contribution was far more than his legions. It was his blood that aided you during your journey, nearly as much as your Kalinian blood."

"His blood?" Terin made a face.

"He was the Nordhenz, the fabled human in gargoyle legend to bring about their ascension. They were sworn to him, and unbeknownst to them, should they ever betray him, he would be invisible to them in battle, though they could perceive his presence, they could not place him. This gift passed down to his bloodline. Though our Kalinian blood subdued this unique gift, due to its foul origin, Yah allowed it to surface in you once your Kalinian blood was impaired during your enslavement.

It was this ability that carried you through to the choosing, continuing to the battle of the Oddigem, until your true power was reignited through the Swords. Once you wielded the Sword of the Sun, you were able to call the other swords unto it, bringing about their full potency. Only you could do this, and only after the trials you endured purified your heart, and you were willing to sacrifice yourself for all others," Jonas explained.

"So, the swords destroyed the gargoyle host?" Terin asked. The last thing he remembered was the light of the swords holding back most of their terrible host before the world went dark.

"No."

"No?"

"Had the swords done so through your powerful act, then the glory would fall upon you. Yah used the swords' power to cause the gargoyles destruction by other means, leaving the victory in his hand, and his alone," Jonas said, sensing Terin's confusion in the matter.

"He is welcome to the glory. I only wanted my friends to live, and Corry to live. I have no pride left. I know where that led me."

"And that, my son, was why you succeeded where others had failed. You learned the lesson so many in our family line had not. You were forged for this task. We raised you away from court to nurture your innocence and humility, and you never disappointed us. No father could be as proud as I am of their son."

Terin looked at his father with overwhelming love, stepping closer to embrace him.

Jonas held him for an eternal moment, feeling the warmth of Terin's body flowing through his arms. Terin wanted to hold on and never let go as Jonas finally pulled away, holding his hands upon his son's shoulders, looking one last time into his eyes.

"My time is near, Terin. I must leave you now. Always remember that I love you, and please share my love with your mother, your sister, and my father. Love is the true power of this world, our love for each other, rather than mighty castles, armies and glowing swords. I feel it now more than ever, pouring off of me in unending streams." Jonas smiled warmly, his hands withdrawing as he began to fade.

"No, wait!" Terin begged, reaching out to him in vain.

"My time here is finished, son. I must go, and you must return."

Jonas sighed, looking upon his son with heartfelt anguish and joy, his visage fading.

"I love you." Terin wept.

"And I, you," Jonas said, before fading altogether, his hand reaching out toward Terin.

Terin's tears clouded his eyes before darkness overtook him. He struggled opening them, his eyelids feeling as heavy as plated steel. He heard faint voices, as if eavesdropping on idle banter, before forcing his eyes open. He found himself abed upon a cot of some sort, simple and comfortable, with a blanket reaching his naked chest.

"You are awake!"

Terin turned to find Squid sitting at his bedside, trying to make sense of his surroundings. They were in a small pavilion constructed of a strange reflective material in shimmering black and silver. A strange lamp hung from the ceiling, emitting a constant glow, akin to the lights aboard the *Stenox*. He and Squid were alone in the small structure, though it was surrounded by guards along its outer periphery, and a chorus of voices talking somewhere beyond the thin walls.

"Where am I?" he asked, his voice seemingly moist considering he hadn't drunk water since the middle of the battle, and having no idea of how much time had passed.

"We have repositioned west of the Oddigem," Squid said, his vibrant eyes concealing the fatigue that lay beneath. Terin noticed he was still wearing his crude traveling garments, though minus his battle worn mail.

"The battle?" Terin asked.

"Victory, my boy, a glorious victory, though not without cost." Squid smiled sadly.

"How many?"

"We are still counting for an accurate number, but a fair guess is thirty-five thousand dead among all our armies, though many were from the battles between the 10th and 13th Legions when they fought one another," Squid explained, though the number should have been far greater considering the might of the enemy.

"How long have I slept?" Terin asked, before lifting his left arm, noticing a strange metal band wrapped around his bicep, with luminous green lights blinking hypnotically around its circumference. He rightly guessed it was of an Earth origin.

"Two days. That band kept you fed and monitored your well-being in ways I could only guess. Our Earth guests have been most helpful in that regard," Squid said, which explained why he didn't feel hungry considering how long he had been asleep. In fact, he hadn't eaten since the day before the battle commenced, with most of the Chosen marching into the valley on empty stomachs.

"Is this another of Lorken and Brokov's wondrous tools?" He turned his arm, fully examining the strange adornment.

"No, it was placed there by one of their matrons, or doctor as they call them, a lovely woman with skin as fair as Brokov, named Sarah Kensington. She has been a constant presence here and will return shortly now that you have awoken."

"Another Earther? Where did she…" Terin tried to make sense of what he was saying.

"You don't remember, of course, you were overcome by the swords. Perhaps I should begin from there," Squid said, retelling the events that followed that critical moment before the Earthers arrival.

Terin listened with rapt attention, imagining the scene of the Earth squadrons sweeping over the sky, destroying the gargoyle host. Squid described the battle's swift conclusion and the aftermath. The first difficult barrier after their victory was the encroaching night, with tens of thousands of dying and wounded men littering the valley floor. Again, the Earthers were most helpful, with one of their ships hovering above the battlefield, casting a brilliant light, illuminating the valley floor. This was followed with the arrival of transport craft landing in their midst, with dozens of matrons and their attendants, each bearing regenerators, ones far more efficient than the *Stenox* produced. They were accompanied by soldiers wearing strange armor, bearing laser rifles to secure their landing sites. The first Earthers to arrive spoke only their Earth basic language, needing Raven, Zem and Lorken to communicate, before they could use a neural link to learn the Araxan native tongue. Tosha was also instrumental, having learned the Earther tongue aboard the *Stenox* by the same technique.

The alliance armies spent the night reorganizing themselves and coordinating search parties for the wounded, moving those that could be moved to the regeneration locations, while other Earth matrons went about the battlefield to help those that could not be moved. Another problem was water, with many succumbing to dehydration, their water satchels empty by battle's end. The Earthers brought fresh water, though not enough for the multitudes in the alliance armies. This forced them to begin relocating the armies out of the arid valley, using transport craft and magantors, ferrying soldiers across the western ridge to better ground beyond. They were collectively busy attending a myriad of tasks to preserve lives and provision the armies. Many had gone three days without sleep, laboring without respite. Soldiers often dropped where they stood, overcome with exhaustion. Most fell asleep upon the ground, huddled together in their reformed ranks. The Earthers helped construct temporary shelters, watering points and waste facilities while the Araxans organized themselves.

"… And there is the state of things, my boy," Squid said, leaning back on his stool.

"And you have watched over me all this time?" Terin wondered.

"We have taken turns, Terin, though none more than that lovely wife of yours. She has stood vigilant watch over you since we brought you to this place. She has slept on the floor beside you, holding your hand in hers as others stepped in to call upon you. She will be wroth for having not been here when you awoke, but she has other duties to attend."

Terin sighed happily, knowing all his dreams were now possible that he and Corry both lived. He so wished to hold her in his arms and never let go.

"I would be remiss to leave out the others that have taken their turn watching over you. Cronus, Ilesa, Galen, Zem, Orlom, Lorken and Raven, Lucas, Ular and your grandfathers." Squid added the last, placing Torg and Tyro together to lessen the blow, wondering how he might receive that.

"My grandfathers?" Terin made a face.

"Yes, but not together, so you needn't not worry for strife between them. Your aunt was going to stand watch, waiting upon you to awake last evening, but your grandfather took her place," Squid explained without saying Tyro's name.

"Did he do or say anything?" Terin wondered.

"No. He simply sat here beside you and looked at you for the longest time. He said not a word, just staring at you when Orlom took his turn to stand watch."

Terin didn't know what to think. He knew they would have to talk and dreaded it. Tyro was always the enemy, the monster that unified their cause, the source of so much sorrow, and yet... his father had loved him.

Squid could see the conflict in his eyes, regretting having told him.

"There will be time latter to discuss such things. For now, you need rest, my boy." Squid patted his shoulder.

"I am actually quite awake. You should be the one abed." He smiled.

"Do not tempt this old man, my boy. If I lay down, I might not wake until spring." Squid laughed, pleased to see his young friend well, before he recalled the loss they both shared with Jonas' passing.

"Something troubles you?" Terin asked.

"Your father was a good man, and my dearest friend. I had visions of myself dying before this was all over, and yet I was spared, and he was taken. If I could exchange my life..." Squid began to say but Terin was having none of it.

"No. My father would not abide that, Squid. He gave his life freely, and for a great purpose. You still have a duty to fulfill to our people, and our king," Terin said.

"Our king." Squid nodded his agreement, though wondered when he should inform Terin of his own Kingship, since half of Tyro's empire was now sworn to him. He would leave that task to Corry.

"Thank you for all you have done for me, Squid. From my time at Rego before the war, and all of our adventures since. I am proud to call you friend."

"My dear boy, there is no greater honor than to be your friend." Squid placed his hand on Terin's heart.

"Our patient is awake I see," Dr. Sarah Kensington said, passing through the flaps of the tent, with Matron Dresila beside her, the two working in concert these past two days. As soon as Terin awoke, she was alerted through his arm band.

Terin noted the woman's unusually tall stature and form-fitting fleet physician uniform with silver pullover shirt and trousers. Her skin was as pale as Brokov's, yet strikingly beautiful, though in an exotic way.

"You are one of Raven's friends?" Terin asked.

"More of an old acquaintance, but yes, I know Captain Mekiana, or Raven as you refer to him. I assume he has engaged in his usual mischief, if half of what I have heard is true," she said, before leaning close to whisper in Terin's ear. "He can be a bit much," she whispered, giving him a flirtatious wink, before examining the device on his arm.

"Captain Raven is a fine man, but a most difficult patient," Matron Dresila added, recalling his injury at Corell when he attempted to tame a wild ocran.

"Lieutenant Umaru is little better, I assure you," Sarah said while removing the device from Terin's arm.

"Lt Umaru?" Squid inquired.

"It is Lorken's surname," Terin explained, starting to rise when Sarah gently pushed down on his chest, keeping him in place.

"Not so fast, young man, I still need to run this diagnostic before you start running around like a fool. We don't want to anger that princess of yours by letting you hurt yourself," Sarah teased, thumbing through the device in her hands, which drew Terin's curiosity.

"What is that?" he inquired.

"It tells me everything I need to know about you, including your blood, which reveals something very interesting," Sarah said with a cryptic smile.

"Interesting?" Squid asked.

"Perhaps *Special* is a more appropriate word. I sent the results to our med bay for further analysis," Sarah said, finishing his diagnostic.

"The blood of Kal." Squid stated what they were all thinking.

"That explanation is as good as any we have found. We should expect nothing less from our brave hero." She smiled.

"Whatever is in my blood, it has served its use," Terin said.

"I would not be hasty. There might remain a very important reason for your unique blood. We shall have to test your newborn sister to confirm a genetic link, which is likely by all that we know. It is most unusual for a genetic trait to pass down 100% to all offspring, but that appears to be the case. Either way, we have a long time to study it. I am done, so you have permission to dress and go play with your friends," Sarah again teased, speaking to him like a little boy.

The ladies stepped outside, giving him privacy to don his tan worn tunic and sandals, and sword belt, though he found no sign of his mail or helm.

"You'll have no need of it in the coming days, Terin," Squid reminded him, standing at the entrance, waiting upon him to finish.

No need of armor? How the world had changed. He couldn't remember a time when the enemy hadn't held a sword above their heads. Before he could lace up his sandals, Corry burst through the flaps of the tent, tackling him back on his cot.

"I came as soon as I heard. Curse you for always waking when I am elsewhere!" she growled, pinning him to his bed, pressing a ferocious kiss to his lips, while Squid stepped without, giving them their privacy.

He returned her fervor, wrapping his arms around her, holding her tight. How he longed for this, fearing he would never see her again throughout his arduous journey. How many nights did he look up at the stars, begging Yah for one last moment with his beloved, and here he was, holding her in his arms with their whole lifetime ahead returned to them. She lost sense of time as she lay atop of him, kissing his lips, his cheek, his nose, before resting her head upon his chest. There they lay, neither saying a word for the longest time.

"I missed you so. My heart broke every moment we were part-ed, thinking I would never see you again. When I saw you upon the battlefield, I was so overjoyed, and yet fearful you might perish beside me, or even worse," he said, running his fingers through her hair, neither opening their eyes, savoring this serene moment.

"What could be worse than dying, other than torture?" she asked dreamily, not lifting her head, savoring the warmth of his rising chest upon her cheek.

"If you died, and I lived. Anything can happen upon a battlefield, as we both know. I could not bear that after all we have endured." He sighed, thinking of poor Cronus when he fought so bravely at Corell only to have Leanna die in his arms upon the birthing bed.

"I am not dying, my love. No force on Arax can take me from your arms."

"Promise?" he asked.

She lifted her head, resting her chin on his chest, staring into his eyes.

"Listen to me very carefully, Terin Caleph. We are going to live to be very old and die in bed together many, many years from now. You are never parting from me again," she said determinedly, running her fingers along his cheek.

"What of children?"

"We shall have many children, and they will give us many grandchildren, and they will have children also. We will have the largest family that ever lived, and our home will be filled with love and laughter, and most of all peace."

Peace, he smiled at that. No more war, no more killing, and no more friends dying. It all seemed surreal, as if he was in a dream, a dream he never wanted to awake from. He lifted his gaze from her beautiful eyes, staring briefly at the ceiling before noticing its unique texture.

"Wherever did you find such a pavilion?" he wondered.

"Our new Earth friends constructed these out of the ground. How they did it, I could not say. They erected hundreds of them all over this encampment, and the other encampments."

"Other encampments?"

"Yes, all along the western approaches of the Nameless Mountains."

"Just how large is this encampment?"

"Let me show you."

* * *

Following Corry through the flaps of the tent, Terin was met with a surreal sight. They were camped under the shadow of the Nameless Mountains, their towering peaks dominating the eastern horizon. The camp was abuzz with activity, with soldiers and peoples of all sorts hurrying to and fro. The Earthers constructed structures of all sizes and shapes in every direction he looked. Some were as small as a wagon cart, while others as large as a Quadoar warship. Guards surrounded his own pavilion, a mix of Torry, Benotrist and Menotrist rebels, each standing vigil until he stepped into the sunlight.

He was met with hardy cheers, the guards proclaiming his presence, as others gathered about, led by President Matuzak and Galen, the large gorilla shouting his name.

"Caleph!" Matuzak bellowed, passing through his ring of guards, wrapping his furry arms around him, lifting him into the air.

He was soon joined by Galen and a crowd of others pressing nigh. He noticed Commander Connly next, along with General Lewins, the Torry commander of 1st Army giving him an unexpected hug. There were men of Yatin, including General Yoria, and men of Zulon, led by King Sargov. There were Enoructans, men of Macon, Torry, and Tro. He noticed figures clad in strange black armor, with helms covering their heads, made of a reflective material, each brandishing laser rifles, guessing they were Earthers. He noticed one touching his helm, the visor disappearing over his head, revealing a dark-skinned man with a shorn head similar to Raven's. The others soon followed, revealing a broad diversity of faces, denoting the variety of cultures representing Earth. They each raised their rifles into the air, shouting his name.

"Caleph!" They added their voices to the crowd's, many approaching him, slapping him on the back.

Corry remained at his side, watching as the growing assembly praised her husband, one after another hugging him, slapping him on the back, or clasping his arm. Tessa and King Mortus came next, appearing out of nowhere as it seemed, Tessa kissing his cheek and hugging him fiercely, while Mortus placed his kingly hand upon his shoulder.

It was the next face that took him aback as Alen stepped nigh, the two sharing a brief look before Terin drew him into his embrace, holding him tightly. They had not seen one another since Terin departed for the Yatin Campaign so long ago, when Alen departed soon after with Elos to foment rebellion in the far north.

"You are alive! I feared to never see you again." Terin nearly wept, overcome with emotion.

"I felt the same for you, my friend." Alen smiled. There was so much each wanted to say, but that would have to wait for another time as the crowd continued to grow.

Next came Zem, who lifted Terin into the air as if he were a child. Corry bit off her smile, finding the entire scene endearing. Argos followed, repeating the gesture, while Carbanc and Gorzak joined in, the two apes the only surviving gorillas among the Chosen. Terin was well abused by the time Orlom and Torg appeared, the young gorilla squeezing the life out of him before his grandfather had his turn.

"Blast you, boy. You've silvered my hair more than this old man can afford for the worries you caused," Torg said into his ear as they embraced.

"Thank you for helping Corry, Grandfather," he whispered back, squeezing him just as tight, tears streaming down his cheeks.

Corry looked on, wiping the tears from her eyes at the endearing sight. How she loved them both. She loved all of them, she reminded herself, all these strangers who came into their lives and loved them, and they loved them back. Her tears ran freely as Torg moved on to her, lifting her into his arms.

More followed, with the surviving men of Nayboria and their beleaguered king Lichu, who would never have believed he would embrace the Torry Champion, but the Oddigem washed away old rivalries. It was as if the world began anew, a sense of brotherhood sweeping across Arax, as Yah intended since he placed his creation upon these sacred lands.

There were Jenaii and men of Rego, along with rebels of all sorts. Elos and King El Anthar followed, each placing their hands upon his shoulder before Terin broke with protocol, drawing them into his arms. Elos would never admit to it, but Corry saw him smile. She followed that by placing a kiss to the Jenaii champion's forehead.

General Jani followed next, leading a number of her warriors, honoring Terin with a fist to her heart. He ignored the salute and embraced her as he did the others. The Sisterhood no longer filled him with dread, his time as Darna's captive now seeming a lifetime ago. The Federation general shook her head, smiling as she returned the gesture. Seeing the sisterhood warriors reminded Terin of Deva, which he asked of Corry between the hundreds of hugs, shoulder slaps and arms clasps.

"She is mourning her brother," Corry whispered in his ear, the news removing the smile from his lips. Guilen had become another dear friend, and fought valiantly for their cause, rising at General Ciyon's side since the march to Corell where they helped lift the siege. Other than her detestable younger siblings, he was all that Deva had. He should hate Deva, but Yah transformed her vain and cruel heart. Yah had no greater acolyte among the Chosen. He took for granted her sage council throughout their journey, revealing to them Yah's guidance. Though he forgave her for her treatment of him, he never truly forgot, always keeping her at a distance. Corry was far more resolute in her distrust of his former mistress, but even here she seemed to have reassessed her dislike.

"She has earned my respect, if not my love, and I do forgive her. You should speak with her," Corry said.

"I will," Terin said, taken aback by the forgiveness he saw in Corry's eyes. Even she had changed in ways he could not fully comprehend. He loved her so very much, and all those that swarmed him, with hundreds more coming to embrace him, while the rest continued to shout his name. He caught sight of an Earther transport craft coming into view from the direction of the Oddigem Valley, the large vessel setting down somewhere at the edge of their camp, disappearing from sight behind the large structures blocking his view. He marveled at the sight as Corry simply squeezed his hand.

"You shall grow accustomed to it." She smiled, knowing how much their world had changed.

* * *

Oddigem Valley.

Queen Letha stood over Deva, who knelt beside her brother's body, feeling the anguish pouring off of her in waves. Deva wept uncontrollably, all her emotions that she pent up throughout her journeys were now breaking free. She did not expect to survive the march of the Chosen, or the battle at journey's end. Her only solace was those she loved might live in her place, and the only person that she loved died anyway. It was General Dadeus Ciyon who told her of Guilen's bravery in battle, sacrificing his life for his friend. He told her that Guilen marched bravely into battle in the hope to save her. He died not knowing how successful he was in that. Guilen had many plans for his future, and no lack of choices. Squid Antillius desired that he take Terin's place as his apprentice, and one day be a minister to the king. Dadeus wished that he would serve as his second, and one day lead an army. King Lorn offered him a royal commission and a trading ship to build his own merchant fleet. They were all lost dreams now, like the dreams of so many others who perished in this awful war.

She closed her eyes, placing her hands upon his blood-stained chest as she bowed her head.

Letha stood forward of her guards, with only Lucas within earshot of either of them, the Torry warrior standing vigil over Deva as her assigned guardian. She stole a glance north, where lay the ruined masses of the gargoyle horde, most blasted into vapor by the Earthers terrible weapons. The very ground where they once stood was charred and desolate, more so than its previous barren state. Pieces of gargoyle flesh littered the areas between the routes the lasers took, spit up from the lines of death spewing their foul remains on the grounds in between. Nearer their lines, the gargoyle dead resembled their natural form, their bodies mostly intact. She saw the head of one, resting twenty paces to her left front, its sunken eyes staring hauntingly at her, its tongue dangling from its pallid lips. All that remained was the head, its body elsewhere. She wondered how it landed so perfectly, as if to torment her as she stood upon this sacred ground.

Lucas noticed the source of her distaste, marching forth and kicking the creature's skull, sending it rolling in the distance.

"He is a good man, that guardian of yours," Letha said to Deva, before looking south, where their own dead were being gathered, their bodies to be buried in a mass grave, overseen by thousands of their soldiers from every realm.

Deva lifted her gaze to Lucas, thankful for his kindness during their journey. She wondered why he remained at her side, as the purpose was no longer required? Perhaps King Lorn had yet to release him of that duty.

Duty, was that all that she was to him? She had grown fond of the Torry warrior, as any traveling companions on such a journey were apt to do.

"Yes, he is a fine man, and very brave." She sighed, looking at him briefly before gaining her feet.

"You are fond of him." Letha stated the obvious.

"I… Yes, he has been a kind friend, My Queen."

"He would make a good husband for the matriarch of House Estaran," Letha stated, causing Deva's eyes to shift suddenly to hers.

"I…" She had nothing to say to that, her voice failing her.

"You have proven yourself worthy to again wield the sword of your ancestors, Deva, and resume your rightful place as the head of House Estaran," Letha proclaimed, offering her, her sword.

Deva was taken aback, never expecting to fulfill her quest, or to return to lead her house. It was so beyond her expectations, that she had not even considered the possibility. She wondered if she truly ever wanted it before, or was it merely to prove her worth in her mother's eyes? If she were honest, she could only describe the motives of her youth as aimless. Her pitiful infatuation of Terin during his captivity epitomized her childish vanity. She could not reconcile the creature she was with what she now felt. When Terin granted her mercy in the throne room at Bansoch, her heart and mind were emptied of all their vileness, hatred and selfishness, leaving little of the old Deva for her to recognize. She came to like the new Deva, and feared what might befall her if she returned to lead House Estaran. As Queen Letha drew her sword, offering it to her, Deva gently refused.

"Should you find one of my sisters worthy to again wield the sword of our ancestors, then give it to them, My Queen," Deva said, placing her hands upon the proffered blade, directing it toward Letha's scabbard.

"There are no kin of yours more worthy than you, Deva. You have proven my doubts of Terin's mercy false. You are truly filled with Yah's glory, and I am proud to call you cousin," Letha said proudly.

"My gratitude, Oh Queen."

"If not the head of your house, what path would you choose?" Letha wondered.

"I…I do not know. I have not heard Yah's voice since the battle and hold no delusion that I still hold his favor, though I remain faithfully his." Deva sighed, regarding Lucas fondly as he stood nearby, as if cut from stone, her vigilant guardian.

Letha couldn't help notice her fondness for the Torry, and knew Deva was too humble to ever inquire of his affection.

"Perhaps a more suitable path lies before you, Deva. I spoke with King Lorn, and he and I are in agreement in establishing an order of the faith, and naming a chief acolyte to oversee its establishment, a high priest if you will, or… high priestess."

Deva was again taken aback, grateful for their faith in her, but feeling unworthy of such an honor.

Letha sensed her hesitation and pushed a little harder.

"If not you, then who? Only you have spoke so directly with Yah, guiding us to victory with every step."

"There are many who are more favored in his eyes, Queen Letha, Terin and King Lorn chief among them."

"They were his hands, but you were his voice, Deva. The choice is yours, but I cannot think of one better." With that Letha stepped away, pausing only to whisper in Lucas' ear before continuing on. Deva watched as she walked across the battlefield in the direction of Emperor Tyro and King Lorn, who stood together several hundred paces to her southeast, their guards holding at a distance. She shared a look with Lucas, wondering what her queen said to him.

* * *

My son, Tyro lamented, looking down upon Joriah's body at his feet. By a miracle only the adherents of Yah could explain, Joriah's body was found nearly intact, as if the armies that fought all around him managed to not trample him underfoot. It was Nels Draken that found him yester morn, securing his body for him. Draken had proven his loyalty time and again, his most significant contribution bringing the 13th Legion to heel, joining them with the 10th to battle the treacherous gargoyles. Had he failed to do so, their casualties would have been far greater, perhaps too great.

He also learned of Thorton's sacrifice, realizing now what might have happened had he not delayed the northern gargoyle horde. It was another reminder of the many great deeds done by so many to bring them victory. He also knew the man who stood beside him contributed a great deal to that victory, as Lorn told him of his own conversion from a spoilt princeling to a servant of Yah. Had Lorn faltered, Arax would have fallen, fallen by his own machinations, to Tyro's eternal shame.

"Jonas was a brave man. I never had the honor of knowing him, but I did have dreams of him. Yah revealed much concerning your son, and the role he would play in this great war. He loved my people, and he loved his family, and was loyal to both to the very end," Lorn said, feeling the anguish in Tyro's posture. If anyone told him two days before that he would be standing beside the Benotrist Emperor, speaking like old friends, he would have called them mad, and yet here they stood. It was another testament of Yah's mercy and mighty hand.

"Jonas." Tyro tested the name others knew his son by. "I named him Joriah when he was born, my pride and honor. Nothing I ever accomplished was as great as siring him. He was greater than me. Greater as a fighter, and as a man."

"Master Vantel can attest to his skill. He says there is none greater, though I believe Terin might exceed him." Lorn smiled, looking at Jonas's face, which held its luster for some strange reason, where decay robbed all others at this point.

"He could have slain Morac, but he didn't. He offered himself up to him to grant me one last chance to choose the righteous path. His life for a chance for me. He knew. Somehow, he knew what I would choose, and now the world has me, and Joriah is gone. A poor exchange."

"No, a more than fair exchange. Without you, we would have failed. We needed each other, all of us. Remove one piece form the whole and we would have fallen. Yah intended this. I can see that now."

"You are a dreamer. The word is full of cruel and evil men. I spent my youth battling them until I became one. I thought to build an empire to protect my people from ever suffering as they had for so many centuries under the tyrant's boot. I used that fear to push further, securing more lands to protect what I had built. You saw the gargoyles as a threat, and that guided your kingdom's direction. I never saw that. Regula was my good friend, an ally and a brother, whose people suffered at the hands of my enemy. We fought together for the benefit of both our people. This blinded me to their base nature, a nature Regula denied for our friendship. It seems he could not suppress that gargoyle destructive instinct in all his people, and they killed him for it. Now here I stand upon the bones of my empire, all that I thought to be true playing me false," Tyro said, his eyes never leaving Jonas' face.

"You are wrong in one thing. I know men are naturally cruel and wicked, and that is why no one man can be given absolute power, for such power strips away any restraint on his wickedness."

Tyro gave him a long look, recalling what Thorton often spoke of when he feared what might happen to Arax if his people discovered it.

"And how can you prevent one man, woman or being from gaining absolute power?" Tyro asked.

"We dilute power."

"We?" Tyro raised an eyebrow at that.

"We. Your empire still stands, though you have another claimant upon half of it, if what your eastern vassals and rebels attest," Lorn said, referencing the regions to their east naming Terin their king.

"He would have been my heir anyway if I had raised him." Tyro snorted at that.

"True, and he might not even desire it."

"He doesn't know?"

"Not that I am aware. He was with the Chosen when your eastern regions began to break away."

"Why would they name him king without him asking for it?" Tyro asked.

"From what I have learned, it was Raven that first suggested it, but your daughter who brought it to fruition."

Tosha? Tyro shook his head, wondering what madness overtook her. He tried to name her son his heir, but Letha denied him, and now she raises her nephew above herself.

"I have named Terin's sister as my heir. I would have my realm united, and shall name him above her," Tyro reasoned.

"Perhaps you should discuss that with Terin before deciding."

"My people once despised him for being the Torry champion, and now revere him for saving them from the gargoyles. He is the only member of my house the rebels and eastern vassals would follow, especially now. He will do his duty and take my place upon the throne and unite my realm."

"That shall be one of many issues we must negotiate during our grand council," Lorn said, referencing the agreed upon meeting to be held at Fera in the coming days. The monarchs and heads of state of the grand alliance would treat with the emissaries of the Earther fleet to plan their next actions. Much needed to be decided, the political upheaval of what just transpired was certain to alter the course of their world.

"We should conduct a war council first, but it appears our new friends have that well in hand," Tyro said, watching a squadron of space fighters pass overhead, seeking out strays that might still linger to their north, while armored marines from the *Stalingrad* swept the caverns to their south, slaying the few gargoyles that remained hidden within the subterranean holdfast. By last report he heard they had slain over two thousand creatures there, the Earther marines moving methodically about their work. He was impressed with their dark armored helms that appeared like round mirrors, and their armor platted attire, covering them head to foot, all in black, giving them a dangerous aura.

Another transport set down near the western ridge, its ramp lowering upon landing. Another fifty soldiers stood near the strange vessel, waiting their turn to be transported out of the valley to their new campsite on the far side of the ridge. They were men of the 10th Legion, many of them veterans of the sieges of Corell. They were battle worn and weary, and he thought of how many of their comrades perished before the walls of Corell. It all seemed so foolish now.

May they find rest, he thought to himself, wondering if he would ever find it himself considering the life he had led. There were still many thousands of their soldiers in the valley, many helping with the dead, and some awaiting transport. The wounded were already healed, another miracle the Earthers performed with pitiful ease. He thought of Thorton's warning, knowing they would be at the mercy of the Earthers' bureaucracy, but these Earthers were lost just like Raven's crew. What that portended for their future, he could only guess. Their admiral wielded such power to render him a king maker. Was he the only one concerned about this? The Torry king seemed to read his mind.

"The Earther admiral will surprise you. What Thorton feared will not come to pass," Lorn said with a faraway look.

"How do you know this?" Tyro asked doubtfully.

"Yah has shown me. We shall enter our golden age, an age of unity and purpose. We shall receive the Earthers' gifts without their corruption and use them for the betterment of our people… all of our people."

"Without their corruption? What of our own?"

"That burden shall always remain with us, even with the gargoyle threat lifted."

"Which brings us logically to your plan to dilute power, limiting the strength of any one group or man from becoming a tyrant," Tyro snorted, doubting how such a thing could be done.

"There must be a way, and we shall find it together," Lorn sighed.

"We?" Tyro wondered.

"All of us." Lorn smiled, looking over Tyro's shoulder, where Queen Letha approached, her guards holding at a distance as she advanced to treat with them.

Tyro followed his gaze, turning as she drew nigh.

"I believe my dear aunt wishes to speak with you." Lorn thrust his fist to his heart, saluting Tyro before stepping away.

Tyro's guards held at an equal distance as Letha's, giving them privacy to speak freely. It had been many years since they shared words, their feelings for one another a maelstrom of extremes. He regarded her as she came to stop before him, her dark mane lifting in the autumn breeze, and her muscled legs peaking below the hem of her tunic. She returned his gaze with equal fire, regarding his face that defied his age.

"It has been a long time," she offered, using that to begin.

"Yes," he agreed.

A long silence followed, neither knowing where to truly begin.

"I didn't expect things to turn as they did, not back then, and certainly not here," she said, sparing a look to their surroundings.

Perhaps if things had gone differently in the past, they might have endured and remained wed. They might have had many children instead of one. It was another lost chance for happiness that escaped him, as if destiny conspired to steal his joy. Then again, what right did he have for joy and happiness when he was consumed with his empire?

Destiny has a price, he recalled Regula once saying, and that was never clearer than now.

"Perhaps in a different life fate might have treated us kinder," he bitterly said, looking away, staring at nothing.

She thought to say something harsher, to remind him that fate was an excuse for his poor choices, but what would that accomplish but to continue their rift? They were beyond that now after all that transpired in this valley.

"I always knew what the gargoyles were, and their threat to our world. You were ignorant of their true nature. You were naïve in believing in their friendship, just I was naïve in wedding you, hoping to turn you from that folly," she said, sharing the blame between them, knowing it was the best place to begin.

"I never meant to steal your queendom. I only wanted our daughter to receive her full inheritance," he said, recalling his foiled plan in unifying their realms after Tosha's birth.

"It was folly. We are daughters of Tarelia. We are sworn to the gargoyles' destruction, but again, you never knew that, and I never explained it to you. All I did is give you more reasons to distrust the other realms of Arax," she said, placing the greater blame upon herself for their falling out.

"I have been emperor for many years, Letha, and could not have done so without judging character and motives. You are not fooling me with this self sacrifice, falling on your sword to spare my feelings. I knew what I was doing. I wanted your realm joined with mine, not just for our daughter, but to make us stronger. I lost my first wife and child because I lacked the power to keep them safe. I was not going to repeat that mistake with you. Since I was a child, the second unfavored son of a Menotrist warlord, I hungered for power to protect my mother and her kin. That hunger lingered in my heart until two days past," Tyro said, now looking at her, his eyes ablaze like a raging fire.

"And now? Is the hunger still there?" she asked.

"It will always be there, like a part of me, the same as my hands and feet, but it is lessoned now."

"The battle changed many things it seems," she said, watching the transport lift into the air, before passing over the western ridge.

"It wasn't the battle that changed it," he said, his eyes narrowing severely.

"Joriah," she sighed, her eyes following the transport as it disappeared from sight.

"Aye." He sighed also, confessing the pain of his son's passing, the very son who now rested at their feet.

"No greater love," Letha said, her words hitting him like a strong gale.

"Aye, the boy loved me. I don't know why, but he did." He shook his head.

"No, Taleron, it is more than that." She smiled, calling him by his true name.

He looked at her, waiting for her to expound.

"Can you not see? It is the true magic of our world. What power is greater than love? What, but love, could bring all of us together? What but love could lead the Chosen to this valley, giving of themselves for the sake of everyone else? What but love led their comrades here to join their sacrifice? What but love made your son to sacrifice himself for your blind eyes to open? And my dear Taleron, what but love drove you to help us in our desperate fight? Love, true genuine love can only blossom when our pride is expunged, and we can empathize with others. That empathy leads to love, first with our smallest circle before extending to everyone. I feel it now, growing stronger every day. I was always dutiful and loyal to our Tarelian oaths, but it wasn't until that grandson of yours showed mercy to Deva in my throne room that I could see how blind I truly was." She paused before continuing.

"Terin could only do so when he emptied his heart of his hatred and pride, and look what his mercy has wrought? Without Deva, we would have gone astray. She fulfilled a great destiny because Terin forgave her. If he can do that, then Queen Letha can forgive her husband."

"Your husband?" He lifted a curious brow.

"My husband. I have taken no other since we parted," she said.

"Nor have I," he confessed.

There in the Vale of Oddigem, Letha and Taleron began to set right what hatred and division had robbed them of.

* * *

Transport 4.
Approaching Battle Carrier Stalingrad.

Once clearing Arax's upper atmosphere, Raven and Lorken led Tosha, Cronus and Ilesa to the cockpit of the transport craft, where sat Lieutenant Giles and Ensign Galinis in the pilots' seats. There was barely enough room for them to squeeze into the tight compartment, which Lt. Giles rightly pointed out.

"Lighten up, Niles, we're clear of the rough patch." Raven waved off his concerns, slapping the young pilot on the back as he looked over his shoulder at the control panel.

"It is a violation of regulations for passengers to loiter in the cockpit of all Space Fleet transports during transit, Captain," Lt. Giles reminded him.

"Are we not supposed to be here?" Tosha asked, her mouth agape with their surroundings. She looked through the forward viewport, the light of their star illuminating the space around them before Ensign Galinis suppressed the glare, bringing the surrounding space into view, the distant stars now appearing as the night sky.

"Relax, Niles, this is a transport, not a fighter. What's the worst that can happen?" Raven dismissed his concern.

"The admiral will be wroth should anything…" the Lt. protested, but Raven and Lorken wouldn't relent.

"The admiral loves us. Besides, what's the worst that could happen, other than falling on our ass if you jerk the stick?" Lorken said.

"You could break your neck, hitting your head on the ceiling," Lt. Giles snorted.

"You're too good of a pilot to let that happen, Niles," Raven said with as straight a face as he could manage, him and Lorken sharing a look.

"Didn't you once refer to Transport pilots as the fleet rejects? Or that even a chimpanzee could fly one?" Lt. Giles growled, recalling Raven's flippant remarks he was known for.

"Don't get your panties in a bunch, Niles, that's what every branch specialty says about every other. Imagine what we said about the Science Division." Raven chuckled, as that was Brokov's field of assignment.

"Or the Quartermaster Corp," Lorken added.

"Or the Navigators," Raven said.

"Or the garbage brigade." Lorken smiled.

"Garbage brigade?" Tosha made a face.

"Sanitation Collection, Removal and Purification Support. Their work is vital to our fleet operations," Niles snorted.

"You know, Niles, you should have the medical bay run a diagnostic update on you and find out where your sense of humor went," Lorken suggested.

"It can't be a genetic issue. I mean any parent that would name their son Niles Giles must have been fun to be around." Raven chuckled.

"And to think we actually missed you." Niles rolled his eyes, sharing a look with his copilot, the unusually quiet Ensign Galinis.

"Raven missed all of you also, though he will never admit it," Tosha apologized for her husband, slapping him upside the head.

"I like her, Raven." Niles gave her a smile, looking over his shoulder.

Tosha put her hand over Raven's mouth before he could say something stupid.

"And I feared all Earthers were like Raven when we first met. I am thankful that is not true." Tosha returned the lieutenant's smile.

"Princess, you will find not ONE member of our fleet is like Raven. I am thankful that of all the people on your world I could have dreamed of, Raven wasn't it," Niles said.

By now they were made aware that the entire fleet had dreams of different people or events on Arax.

"And who did you dream of, Niles?" Cronus asked, trying not to be distracted by the awesome sight of the surface of Arax from this height.

"A friend of yours, Cronus, Arsenc," Niles said sadly, recalling his noble end.

"How much did you see?" Cronus asked warily, but needing to know.

"It was his blade that wounded Morac at Kregmarin, rendering him lame through much of the first siege of Corell as others have told me," Niles revealed, looking over his shoulder at Cronus, sharing a look before continuing.

"Arsenc was a very brave man, as was Yeltor, who distracted Morac with his life, giving Arsenc time to render the blow. Thought you should know that. That dream has tormented me for months, repeating itself every night until we came here. Now it is gone," Niles revealed, casting a pall over the cabin.

Cronus learned some detail of this event through the prisoners they interrogated after the battle at Notsu, but they were vague and speculative.

"Kato spoke fondly of him," Ilesa said, before hearing her daughter cry from her place in the rear, where the medical staff were watching over her. She quietly excused herself, stepping away.

"She is a brave woman. She risked her life to save you, Cronus," Ensign Galinis said. Recalling her timely intervention after he threw himself between the gargoyle spear and Raven during the battle two days before.

"You took that spear for me." Raven slapped him on the shoulder.

"And she was ready with the regenerator once I fell. She dreamt of it just as I dreamt of you dying. I wondered why she insisted marching with the army when we departed Notsu. It was to save me," Cronus said, recalling the danger Ilesa placed herself and her baby in for his sake.

"She saved you, as you saved Raven. Thank you for that." Tosha leaned over, placing a kiss upon his cheek.

"Thanks, pal," Raven added with another slap to his friend's back.

Cronus smiled wanly, touched by their gratitude. He couldn't bear to see Raven die as he envisioned. He needed to give him a fighting chance, just as Raven did for him by rescuing him from the dungeon of Fera. He only wished he could have spared Arsenc from a similar fate, but such is war. He thought of his men from his unit that fought so bravely at Tuft's Mountain, knowing their cruel end. He was thankful that three survived, though they suffered greatly in captivity. He spoke with Safed after the battle. He accompanied Jonas from Fera and delivered Jonas' sword to King Lorn's hand. He fought beside their armies throughout the battle, finishing somewhere along the left flank under the shadow of the western ridge. He was currently enroute to Fera, joining Nels Draken and a host of others to herald the news of the battle, and prepare the way for the coming emissaries.

Safed would share with his fellow captives that he was now restored, the regenerator reversing his castration. The same would be done for all the slaves held in the Benotrist Empire, and all those held in greater Arax. He looked forward to seeing his men when he visited Fera in the coming days. For now, his attention was drawn to the massive form of the *Stalingrad* coming fully into view.

The skin of the *Stalingrad* shifted in hues of silver and black, blending with space itself, rendering it nearly invisible to the naked eye until one drew close. The superstructure of the vessel was made of pure Trundusium, the powerful hybrid material essential for the skin of any vessel attempting hyper space travel, the very material the Earthers used to forge the *Stenox*. The ship was nearly 6000 feet long, and 1400 feet abreast at its widest point. Its exterior was a collage of rounded bulwarks with powerful laser batteries centered upon them, and a cone shaped nose forming the bow the warship. The lights of the open landing bays contrasted the dark surface of the vessel, growing larger in their viewport as they drew closer. They were cleared to approach the upper portside landing bay, the open hanger one of four running the length of the vessel, two atop and two below the superstructure, two portside and two starboard.

"I never thought I'd see her again," Raven said as they made their final approach.

"It is an impressive sight," Tosha conceded, running her hand along his arm, taken in by the grand spectacle.

Cronus shared her sense of awe. Never in his many travels had he seen anything as wondrous as this, the sheer size of the vessel dominating their viewscreen, and floating above his world as if presiding over creation with terrible authority. That sense of wonder intensified as they closed upon the open door of the landing bay, before passing through. What appeared as a small portal from a distance, the hanger opening was many times wider than the large transport, like the maw of a giant sea beast swallowing them whole.

"Welcome home," Tosha said, kissing Raven's cheek.

* * *

Admiral Helmut Von Kruger waited upon the transport's large circular landing pad, joined by a security detail, and Lieutenant Commander Bao Chang, his dutiful bridge officer and niece of the late Colonel Chang, whose body rested on the isle off the eastern coast of the main continent of Arax. He looked on as the transport was magnetically drawn safely toward the pad, hovering briefly in the air before setting down before him. His transport pilots had been working nonstop for two days now, moving supplies and soldiers to and from the Oddigem. This was the first time they brought visitors to the *Stalingrad*. In fact, he could count on one hand the number of transports that were not currently planet side aiding their new friends. Most of their marines were also deployed on the surface, rooting out the remaining gargoyles from their caverns. He was receiving constant updates of their progress, a grim task, but executed with professional efficiency. The medical team aboard the transport was eager to escort Kato's widow and child to the med bay, and give the child a thorough review. They would also perform genetic and comprehensive DNA testing on their Araxan guests as well as their missing crew. There were risks that Raven and the others might have experienced genetic mutations from their ordeal, though they hadn't observed any irregularities in their own crews.

Raven. Helmut had given up all hope of ever finding him again. As a dutiful commander, he was not supposed to play favorites, but Raven and Thorton held that distinction in his heart. Raven was always the rascal, and Thorton kept him in check, tempering their antics, but together they were quite a team, a team he leaned on whenever a difficult task needed to be done.

Thorton, he thought on all that happened to bring about his ruin, and his redemption. He missed him by mere hours, the man dying to save Kato's child and delay the gargoyle horde.

May he rest in peace, he thought as the transport set down, waiting as the rear ramp lowered.

There atop the ramp stood his missing squadron commander, his towering form stepping down the gradient with Lorken and his Araxan comrades close behind. Helmut stood forward of his detail, expecting Raven to render a salute when the big oaf wrapped him in a large hug, lifting him off the floor.

Bao rolled her eyes, shaking her head as she looked on, sharing a look with Lorken who stood beside Raven. Raven set the admiral down, rendering him a casual salute, with a stupid grin on his face.

"Am I ever glad to see you, Admiral," Raven said as Lorken stepped close to greet Helmut in turn.

"We seemed to have rescued each other. If it wasn't for your friend Terin sending that signal, we would have likely perished in the wrong star system," Helmut said, noticing the attractive woman peaking around Raven's shoulder before stepping fully to his side.

"Admiral, this is…" Raven began to introduce them.

"Your wife." Helmut offered his hand which she shook, familiar with the Earth gesture.

"Raven is very fond of you, Admiral," Tosha said, impressed by his professional carriage. The man was forged for command, with a piercing gaze and sharp facial features. He possessed a large build and dark hair cut nearly as short as Raven's, though his complexion was as pale as Brokov's. She noticed the unique features of the woman standing attention behind him, strikingly similar to Kato's, though her eyes were more downturned than Kato's upward slant. The others gathered behind him were likely his personal guard, each heavily armed and of varying races of Earth, their unique diversity displayed wherever she looked.

"The mighty Raven found a wife. You must be quite the woman, Tosha. I look forward to speaking with you in the coming days. Your unusual courtship is the source of much amusement among our crew." Helmut returned her smile before turning to Lorken.

"You are married as well, and a father to boot. I look forward to meeting her as well once things settle," Helmut said, placing a fatherly hand to Lorken's shoulder.

"She is a beautiful woman, and a better mother, Admiral. Brokov is wed as well. His wife…" Lorken began to explain, but Helmut was well informed.

"Yes, yes, the famed man hunter of Eastern Arax, Kendra Sarn. I've been well apprised of her reputation, and the wedding ceremony conducted by this one over here." Helmut jerked a thumb in Raven's direction.

"I don't know what she saw in him, but they seem happy," Raven added, scratching his head.

"Who are you to judge? You seem to have punched well above your weight." Helmut gave him a look, weighing Tosha's striking beauty against his hulking frame.

"I like him." Tosha smiled, admiring the admiral's charm. She was also enamored finding someone who held actual authority over Raven, though even she couldn't miss Raven's lack of proper reverence for his chain of command as his fellow Earthers did.

"If Raven can find a woman to marry him, there has to be hope for Zem." Lorken chuckled, enjoying the ribbing they were all giving Raven. At least now Raven wouldn't be punching him in the arm after every put down now that they were back aboard the *Stalingrad*.

"And you must be Cronus Kenti." Admiral Kruger shook Cronus' hand.

"I am humbled, Admiral. My king offers his most esteemed gratitude for your intervention. You and your crew saved many of our lives at the Oddigem," Cronus said.

"I see why Raven befriended you, Cronus, you are an honorable and humble man, though your humility is misplaced. I'm the one in your debt for saving Captain Mekiana's neck more than once if everything I heard is true," the admiral said, again jerking his thumb toward Raven.

"And that is a full-time job," Lorken added for good measure, slapping Cronus on the back.

"Indeed. And you are the widow of Ensign Nakumara, I presume," Helmut said, directing Ilesa forward, holding her baby in her arms.

"Admiral," she greeted, bobbing a curtsy.

"You have my condolences, ma'am. Your husband was an excellent officer and navigator, and a better man." Helmut smiled wanly, feeling her grief.

"You are most kind, Admiral," she said, trying not to think of Kato lest she cry.

"Your baby is lovely, ma'am, and as the child of Ensign Naka-mura, you are both welcome to reside aboard the *Stalingrad* as long as you desire," Helmut offered.

"We are most grateful, Admiral." She curtsied again, touched by his warm reception.

"All of you, welcome aboard the *Stalingrad*. Lieutenant Com-mander Chang will see you to your quarters while I speak with Captain Mekiana and Lt. Umaru," Helmut said, directing Raven and Lorken to follow him, the others following Bao.

* * *

Command Briefing Room.

They were joined by Captain Banza, taking their seats at the briefing table. For Lorken and Raven, the entire scene felt surreal, finding themselves aboard the *Stalingrad* as if they never left. The admiral hated needless formalities, but duty demanded otherwise, especially with a situation as strange as this one. They were in uncharted terri-tory, both figuratively and in reality.

"This will be far longer than a standard post operations brief, gentlemen, but for posterity's sake, we must conduct it," Helmut said, sitting at the head of the table, initiating the room's expanded observation features, which would record their testimony in three-dimensional clarity.

"Considering the controversial nature of your activities, most commanders would conduct a formal investigation of your actions by interviewing you separately, but as the admiral and I previous-ly discussed, there will be NO formal inquiry on the events that transpired after your encounter with the deep space anomaly that brought you to the planet now recognized as Arax," Captain Banza said, setting them at ease.

"As this situation presented an unusual level of difficulty to navigate, with no clear guidance to proceed once you were stranded, I have formally waived any question of your conduct on Arax. What

I do need is your honest reiteration of events after encountering said anomaly," Admiral Kruger said.

Raven and Lorken shared a look before beginning. The admiral and captain listened as they told them everything from crashing on Arax to the Battle of the Oddigem, and all the events in between. Much of the story was already known through the work of Dr. Chopra, but much of it was new. Helmut and Masamba betrayed little emotion during the lengthy narrative, but their thoughts were another matter altogether. Had they not witnessed so many unbelievable events in recent days, they would never have believed the simplest of details Raven and Lorken spoke of. At the conclusion, they all sat there in silence for the longest time.

"What happens now, Admiral?" Raven finally asked what was on each of their minds.

"What happens now." Helmut repeated the question, shaking his head. He leaned back in his chair, tucking his hands behind his head as he stared at the ceiling.

"Are we in some sort of trouble?" Lorken asked, not sure how to take the admiral's response.

"Are we in trouble." Helmut again shook his head.

"Admiral?" Masamba asked, wondering what the admiral was thinking.

"Gentlemen, we currently sit in orbit above a planet teaming with alien life, in some uncharted region of space, that I am not certain is even in our home galaxy. We have no means to return to Earth, even if we knew which direction to look. The fact that Arax is almost an identical twin to Earth, eases our life support issues, and negates our need to terra form a planet for our survival. Despite these benefits, we are still lost, the same as you." Helmut began to lay out their situation.

"At least we're now lost together." Raven shrugged.

Helmut shook his head, smiling internally with Raven's optimism.

"We have just begun a geological analysis of the surface and have already found something interesting," Masamba said, bringing up a map of greater Arax upon the table, depicting the main central continent along with multiple others spread across the watery surface.

"So that's what the rest looks like." Lorken whistled, seeing the other continents fully in view before Captain Banza zeroed in on the small landmass resting north of the main continent.

"We traced the northern gargoyle horde that we helped you destroy to this place of origin." Masamba pointed out the large bay where a river emptied into it, surrounded by thick forests and a ring of mountains circling in the distance. At the base of said mountains were a series of subterranean dwellings and caverns. Thousands of human bones littered the sites, likely the remains of older slaves that were taken to the caverns to feed the gargoyle breeding grounds. It was a terrifying place to behold, with hundreds of surrounding settlements that now appeared empty.

"What you are looking at, gentlemen, is the most valuable piece of ground in the known universe, if our initial assessments are correct. Of course, the known universe is limited to those few parts we actually explored, but all the same, this region is as wondrous as finding an Earth like planet, as we did with Arax," Helmut said, leaving unsaid why it was so valuable.

"I guess with a few renovations and cleaning up from the previous residents the place might look like something, but the most valuable piece of ground in the universe? Hey, if you think so admiral, have at it," Raven said, imagining Admiral Kruger building a seaside resort or a mountain villa to retire in.

"You're a knucklehead, you know that, right?" Captain Banza nearly burst out laughing. Of all his squadron commanders, he was the only one to say the stupidest things with a straight face.

"He certainly is, sir." Lorken shook his head as the admiral continued.

"What makes this landmass so valuable, Raven, is that it contains EVERY rare material we need to produce Rendarium, as well as Trundusium. EVERY material," Helmut reiterated. Rendarium was essential for powering interstellar travel, while Trundusium was used in the skin and superstructure of all space vessels. Both were essential for interplanetary travel, exploration and settlement.

"You mean to say the most valuable elements in the universe were sitting under the feet of a bunch of stupid gargoyles for thousands of years?" Raven made a face.

"Apparently. Commander Pham is preparing a team to begin a thorough survey. He is most excited to explore," the admiral said.

"Better take some heavy firepower in case any of the gargoyles are still hanging around," Lorken said.

"He shall have a squadron close by for air support as well as two squads of marines, but all of our sensors show no sign of gargoyles anywhere on the continent. We have found human signatures however along the northern coast, likely bands of runaway slaves that evaded their captors over the years. We will approach them in the coming days and make contact," Helmut explained.

"You could build a whole fleet of battle carriers with that material, for all the good it would do us. We barely have enough people to man the two ships we got," Raven pointed out, though the material would fully repair the *Stalingrad*.

"We have plenty of people, just not enough Earthers," Masamba said.

"You gonna recruit Araxans to man new ships?" Raven asked.

Masamba shook his head at Raven's terrible grammar, cringing with the realization that he had been their primary emissary to the Araxans during his time on the planet.

"More like to man their own ships," Admiral Kruger said, revealing his plan to share their technology with their new friends.

"You sure about that, Admiral?" Lorken questioned.

"We possess incredible military power, gentlemen, but power that is limited by our numbers, and threatened with the passage of time. Our crew is ninety percent male, and even an accelerated breeding program would likely fail to maintain our fleet. We were brought here for a reason; one we cannot deny. The events we have witnessed cannot be happenstance. There is a greater power at work here, a power that intended for us, and only us to come here. I believe the Araxans' God wants us to bring his people into the modern age. We are too few to fully exploit our new discovery, a detail that is again beyond explanation other than my hypotheses. Yah brought us here to help his people. Had we arrived with a capability of contacting

Earth, then these resources would have been seized by our governments to advance Earth's expansion," Helmut said. He was a man of reason and logic trying to apply these principles to the strangeness of their situation.

"You might be right, Admiral, but giving the locals our technology is like handing a chimpanzee a fully charged rifle. A lot of bad things could happen," Raven pointed out. Of course, this came from the man that gave Orlom and Grigg laser rifles.

"We shall proceed carefully and cautiously. We shall first establish sovereignty over the continent in question and establish an official republic of our own. It will be lightly populated, but powerful enough to protect itself while we carefully introduce our technology to the kingdoms of Arax. If we are to bring them forward over three thousand years of advancement, we must tread carefully. Many of their customs are absolutely barbaric," Helmut explained.

"That's funny, that's what they always called me," Raven snorted.

"I wonder how they got that impression?" Masamba asked, shaking his head.

"This will be a central point of conversation tomorrow when we meet with the heads of state at Fera. You are dismissed. Dr. Chopra should be finished speaking with your friends by now. I will expect you at my table tonight," Helmut said, gaining his feet, dismissing them.

* * *

Pilot's Lounge.

Cronus stood along the side of the lounge, feeling out of place among the pilots seated around the room. The small stage rested off his right, with the wide viewport behind it, the surface of Arax centered in its visual field. He had been warmly met by nearly every pilot in the lounge, each recognizing him as Raven's friend. They each thanked him repeatedly for saving Raven. His friend was a legend among these warriors, his fame and exploits a source of pride among their ranks, especially Blue Squadron, whose new commander, Ahmet Ozturk, raised a series of toasts for Cronus.

Raven and Lorken were busy at the bar, ordering another round of drinks for their comrades, before making their way over to him. They all just returned from dinning with the admiral, who was most intent in learning of their world, asking Cronus dozens of questions on his travels, his homeland, and most especially his king. For some strange reason, he held no fear of the Earthers' intentions. If Raven spoke well of them, that was enough for Cronus. Raven was especially fond of Admiral Kruger, and he sensed the admiral felt the same. It was strange, considering Raven's rebellious nature and the admiral's apparent strict adherence to protocol. Of course, it shouldn't be strange at all considering everything else happening in recent days. Cronus' brain hadn't stopped spinning since they departed Notsu so long ago, events unfolding in rapid succession, each more unbelievable than the last.

The ladies were still with Dr. Chopra, who took a keen interest in all of them, especially Ilesa. He learned that she had dreams of her, seeing the events unfolding on Arax through her eyes. It was another strange occurrence he could only ascribe to Yah. It was as if their entire saga was relived through these visions so there would be a thorough accounting of events. Should a chronicler decide to pen their story, it would take a thousand tomes to complete the saga, a saga he would never believe had he not lived through it. It was as strange as the place he currently found himself, standing in a room overlooking the very heavens themselves. This moment should be serene and awe-inspiring but was relegated to a simple matter with the revelry of the room, with a number of the pilots breaking out in songs that would even make Torg blush.

Cronus felt the eyes of the few women in the room constantly upon him, wondering if they found him attractive, or a source of curiosity. Perhaps it was his manner of dress that drew their attention, with simple tunic and sword standing out from their heavy attire.

"Another round of cheers for the man of the hour, Cronus Kenti!" Raven declared, the entire room parroting his adulation.

"Kenti! Kenti!" They heralded his name, as Raven and Lorken came to his side, slapping him on the back and pushing another drink in his hand.

"I think I have had enough." Cronus attempted to push the cup away, but Raven was having none of it.

"We're just getting started, buddy. I always imagined you in my old stomping grounds, and here we are, and what a view." Raven waved his cup toward the viewport where nightfall was closing over the main continent below.

"Cronus might have a point, Rav. We are expected at Fera tomorrow," Lorken reminded him.

"Why are we even going? They don't need us there," Raven snorted.

"Since they will be discussing how we move forward, I would like to be included, and you even more so," Lorken said.

"Why me?"

"Tosha will certainly be a part of it as an official head of state. Do you want her making decisions for you in your absence? Remember, we aren't independent operators anymore now that the fleet arrived. We are back where we started, as pilots assigned to the *Stalingrad*. I wouldn't put it past your wife to have the admiral reassign you to be a liaison to the Sisterhood," Lorken warned, ruining Raven's night.

"She wouldn't dare," he growled.

Lorken and Cronus gave him a look otherwise.

"You are right, she would never do that." Lorken rolled his eyes as Raven started to look around for his wife, forgetting she was currently with Bao Chang, helping put Ilesa's baby to bed.

"I need another drink." Raven downed his cup before storming off toward the bar for a refill.

"I think you just ruined his night." Cronus chuckled.

"Probably." Lorken smiled.

"It wouldn't be the worst thing for him to be there. They are good together, even if he is too stubborn to admit it." Cronus sighed, his gaze drifting to the viewport.

"I guess he is just on edge with what all this means. We've spent the last few years choosing our own path, but those days are now at an end. We each have wives and duties to our people to attend," Lorken said, feeling suddenly morose as well.

"Treasure your time with them, Lorken. Take Jenna and live your life to its fullest, and never look back."

Lorken scolded himself for forgetting Cronus' pain. Leanna's loss hung over his head like a gray cloud, taking his joy.

"Thanks, Cronus, for everything," he said, changing the subject.

"Thanks? It is I who thanks you." Cronus smiled.

"Not for saving our friend's neck more than once, but for being our friend." Lorken regarded him fondly.

"Of course I am your friend. I wouldn't have it any other way." Cronus placed his hand to his shoulder.

"That's not what I mean. When we came here, the men we encountered were not all to receptive to our presence. In all honesty I think we scared them."

"Most assuredly." Cronus smiled, taking a sip from his cup.

"You, however, were the first human who treated us fairly, even risking your life to save Raven, who was only a stranger to you then."

"He was treated dishonestly, and I would not abide that." Cronus recalled the day he and Raven met.

"You could have looked the other way, but you didn't, and that is why Cronus Kenti has been our friend." Lorken patted his back.

"Then I chose my friends wisely." He smiled. He reflected on how that first interaction set in motion a series of events that would shape their world forever.

Raven soon returned as most of the pilots gathered round to hear their adventures. They stayed up well into the night drinking, telling crass jokes and sharing war stories. It was a relief from so much hardship they all endured to this point, with Cronus and the others fighting a desperate war, and the crew of the *Stalingrad* lost in deep space for so long, waiting to die. They referred to Cronus as one of the Sword Wielders, those select few that joined their magical swords, sending the signal that drew them to Arax, saving them from likely death. Tosha was also equally heralded, carrying a *Sword of Light,* the same as Cronus. The men made Cronus feel at home, welcoming him as one of their own.

It was fairly late when Tosha came to collect her husband, dragging him off to their quarters, the other pilots giving him a hard time as he was led away. Ilesa appeared alongside Bao soon after, dressed in a flowing silver gown that shimmered with the light. The men gave her a hearty cheer, welcoming her into their company. Bao stood guard beside her, shooing away the Pilots trying the gather near as Ilesa coyly smiled, her gaze sweeping the room before stopping at Cronus.

The pilots followed her gaze, before egging them on, forcing them closer, while others took up position near the amplifier to start singing, choosing a gentle melody called the *Far-Off Land*. The lights began to dim as Cronus offered his hand, Ilesa receiving it warmly.

They danced across the floor, the lounge growing deathly quiet as the crowd watched. They were more than friends, two broken hearts drawn together through war and suffering. A man could lose himself in her gentle eyes, and Cronus was no different. Cronus was not Kato, but she could see the same kindness in his brave heart.

"If you do not wish to dance, I will not be offended, Ilesa. Our new friends seem quite enthused in bringing us together," he said, sparing a glance to the crowd circling the room, every eye upon them.

"I can think of no one better to dance with, Cronus Kenti." She offered a rare smile, one she hadn't shared in a long time.

"I can think of no one better either." He smiled at that, pleased with her company.

They danced for what felt an eternity, though it was but a brief moment, feeling the warmth in each other's hands as they moved about the floor.

"Have you chosen a name yet?" he asked of her daughter.

"Akira. It was the name of Kato's mother. I think he would like that." She smiled.

"It is beautiful."

"As lovely as Maura." She smiled even wider.

"Perhaps they will be friends," he said, hoping it would be so.

"The best of friends, we must insist upon it," she said.

"I would like that very much," he sighed, wanting to say more.

It was then the music changed, a familiar song beginning to play as a Scottish pilot assumed the vocals, Lt. Ian Macdonald.

"By yon bonnie banks
And by yon bonnie braes
Where the sun shines bright on Loch Lomond…"

Ilesa's breath caught in her throat, the beautiful and mournful ballad kindling memories of Kato. Cronus recalled the ballad, the one Kato had sung for her, the one that so sadly reflected their doomed love. He could see the pain pass her eyes, Kato's shadow lingering ever in her thoughts, just as Leanna's stayed with his.

"My apologies, Cronus. I wish not to be a bore. I fear Kato's loss will always be a part of me," she sighed, insisting they keep dancing, lest anyone see her cry.

"No apologies needed, Ilesa. Leanna will always be with me as well. We cannot unmoor those we loved so strongly, even when death has taken them. They will always live on, if not in our children, then certainly in our hearts."

"Could you love again, even if her heart was so strongly moored to another who is dead? What sort of life would that be? What needless sorrow would you suffer for it?" she asked sadly.

"The same question could be asked of you, Ilesa. My heart will always be Leanna's, but life continues on, and I am so alone, so very alone."

Of all the men in the world, he was the one who truly understood her loss, for it was reflected in his eyes.

"I could, but it would have to be someone special, someone as worthy as Kato," she sighed, gazing into his eyes.

They danced through the song, the words of the ancient ballad tearing at their hearts. They stopped as the song ended, briefly parting when Cronus lifted her arm, his lips kissing the back of her hand.

"If you would allow it, my lady, I would court you," he said, his lips lingering over her hand before lowering it.

"I would allow it." She smiled, her broken heart mending, if by the smallest of measures, but every journey required that first step.

Across the room, Bao Chang and Lorken stood side by side, watching the pair conclude their dance.

"They make a lovely couple, wouldn't you say, Bao?" Lorken smiled with satisfaction, with his arms crossed, enjoying the atmosphere.

"Yes, quite fetching, and that is Lieutenant Commander to you, Lt. Umaru," she said evenly, reminding him of her rank.

"Yes, ma'am." He smiled, knowing she still held a grudge from their previous relationship.

"You're insufferable. I wonder how you managed to wed that poor girl from Tro?" She shook her head.

"Are you jealous, Bao?" He grinned.

"Hardly. I have a whole planet of Araxan men to choose from now, all extremely handsome and wearing the most inviting clothing. Nothing like a pair of handsome legs displayed in a short kilt. I could get used to the view," she said all too smugly, admiring Cronus' apparel.

"Good hunting." Lorken grinned.

* * *

Tosha's plans to lead Raven to their chambers were delayed as he made a detour. She found herself standing on the circled landing pad of a well-used star fighter. She craned her neck, looking up at the tall, arced ceiling of the tubular shaped chamber of the upper starboard side landing hanger. A series of landing pads jutted from the sides of the bay along either side of the floor. The bay ran the length of the ship, its black walls swallowing the light that shone from above and below. It was otherworldly, a sight one could hardly comprehend, unless one was gradually exposed to the Earthers as she was, but even this was too much.

Her gaze finally returned to Raven, who stood beside the fighter for the longest time, running his rough hand along its wing, as if lost in thought. She knew it held a special meaning to him but waited for him to explain its significance.

"My old fighter, fleet designation DSF-47009," he said, stepping under the wing as he circled the fighter.

Tosha remained where she stood, watching as a child like wonder overtook her husband. He stopped several times and stared at the fighter, as if lost in a memory.

"Was this the one you used to destroy the Aurelian Command Ship?" she asked, recalling the visual feed Brokov had showed her at Bansoch, the scene sending her heart to her throat, wondering how he survived such an act.

"Yeah, this is the one. I flew every mission with it. Here it sits like a long-lost friend."

She looked at him with the same wonder as he looked at his fighter. She never considered how far he traveled across the universe before they met. It was beyond all odds that they would ever meet, and yet here they stood. Nothing but destiny could explain their union. To think the fates willed them together sent a thrill of excitement and wonder along her spine. He hadn't moved for the longest time, so she moved to him, running her hand along his thick shoulder, drawing his attention as he stared into her golden eyes.

There was so much she wanted to say, but the words eluded her. She had so many lovely things to say, which sounded perfectly as she rehearsed them, but now were as fleeting as the wind. There was only one thing that summarized all that she felt, and what better thing to say to the simplest man in the universe than the simplest phrase.

"I love you." She looked at him with gentle eyes, failing to cover his lips to stop him from saying something stupid to ruin the moment.

"I love you, too," he surprised her.

There upon the landing bay of the *Stalingrad*, Raven took Tosha into his arms and kissed her, his lover, his wife, his world.

CHAPTER 18

The Grand Council

Valera knew Jonas would not return, her heart breaking at the thought. She remained in her chambers day and night, nursing Cordela, holding her tight to her breast as she wept. Her maids remained close, comforting her as well as they could. Cronus' men remained nearby at her behest, and she took solace in protecting them as Jonas requested. They too were fearful for their friend Safed, who joined Jonas on his fated quest. Hope still remained for Safed, as he was to deliver Jonas' sword to King Lorn, if what Jonas' visions revealed were true.

"I must do this," Jonas insisted, kneeling at her feet as he held her hands, staring lovingly into her eyes.

She wanted to deny him, to use whatever words she could muster to keep him at her side, her selfish heart wanting him to live, the world be damned.

"My father's soul depends upon me, and our son's life and all his comrades," Jonas added, knowing Terin's fate would quell her resistance. It was hardly fair on his part, but such was war and life. He told her of the peril Terin was in, and she begged him to save him, but now he revealed the cost, a price only he could pay.

"There is no other way but certain death? There must be another way," she pleaded.

"It is a choice now, Valera, a simple choice." He smiled sadly, releasing her fingers as he lifted his open hands, mimicking a scale, lifting one higher than the other. It was such a simple gesture, but so profound in its meaning. His life was on the lighter scale, weighing as nothing compared to the rest. It was true, but so very painful.

"You are taking my heart," she said, trying to keep herself from breaking, her eyes betraying her with unwelcome tears.

He looked at her with such sadness that it shamed her. Here he was, willing to sacrifice everything, while she robbed him of their last moments together with her self-pity.

She closed her eyes, steeling her heart for what she must say, before opening them, reaching out her hand, caressing his cheek with her fingers.

"Forgive my weakness, Jonas. I asked that you save Terin, and now that you reveal the cost, I protest. I am so very proud of you. There is no finer man in all the world that I could have wed. Go and save our son, and as many others as your sacrifice might purchase, and know that I love you, now and forever." She smiled before crying as he drew her into his arms.

Those were the last words they shared. She sat there again on the same place upon their bed, reliving the conversation over and again in her mind, holding Cordela, her daughter the only balm to her tortured soul. Castellan Braxus visited her several times each day, seeing to her safety, and that of the emperor's heir, the Princess Cordela. It was during one of his visits two days before that she revealed to him that Jonas was dead.

"How can you know?" Braxus had asked.

"A vision," she said, sharing a look with the stoic castellan, seeing the concern in his eyes for the first time. The man had suffered many visions as well, which he shared with Jonas, knowing the fate of their world depended upon Jonas' quest, a quest that now hung in the balance. Did Jonas achieve what he set out to do before he died? Was he successful, or were they doomed?

That question hung over her heart for the past two days, before one of Castellan Braxus' aides called upon her, summoning her to the throne room. Her fears were eased by the levity of the aide, who seemed most eager to share tidings he was not at liberty to reveal.

"Come, Princess Valera, your company is eagerly desired, as is Princess Cordela's."

* * *

Valera was escorted to the throne room by a flax of imperial elite, each sworn protectors of her and her daughter, a daughter that was quite fussy in her arms, forcing her to pass her to a wet nurse marching behind her. They entered the throne room from the back, avoiding the terrible grotesque statue greeting all visitors at the front entrance, the amalgamation of human and gargoyle forms that unsettled the most stalwart of hearts. She was led through the back entrance, stepping upon the raised dais where sat the emperor's throne, a massive chair platted in gold, with a lesser throne resting below and to the right, where sat Castellan Braxus, acting regent of the realm in the emperor's absence. He would retain that title should the emperor die, until Cordela reached maturity.

Madness, she sighed internally, wondering how it all came to this, with her family fighting to topple the very empire her daughter was set to inherit. The throne of the empire was the last gift she would ever wish upon her infant daughter, but her feelings on the matter were irrelevant. Valera looked out across the throne room, where gathered a growing host of palace officials, soldiers of rank, and a formal escort flanking a smaller group of visitors standing in the center of the red stone floor. She was taken aback by the strange attire of several of the visitors, clad in black from head to foot, with thick black trousers, shirt, boots and jackets, with strange objects hanging from their hips, which she knew to be pistols by her husband's description of Kato. There were four of them in total, each standing behind Nels Draken and Safed Corlen.

Safed locked eyes with her, a profound sadness crossing his face at seeing Jonas' widow. He had returned, meaning he survived the battle, and delivered the sword to King Lorn, or at least she hoped that he did. He looked much different from when he departed, his masculine glow restored, which she could see even from a distance.

She was drawn from her musings by Castellan Braxus, who called her forth to stand before the emperor's throne, with the nursemaid returning Cordela to her arms. Here she represented the line of Tyro, though Braxus spoke on her behalf.

"You may address the assemblage, Emperor's Elite Draken!" Castellan Braxus proclaimed, his voice echoing strongly throughout the cavernous chamber.

Nels Draken stepped forth, ascending halfway up the wide stairs of the dais before turning to address the chamber, opening the scrolled parchment in his hand.

"To the people of the Benotrist Realm, and the garrison of Fera. Let it be known throughout the land that I have come to accord with the lands of the south and have joined them in battle against the gargoyle peoples. The gargoyles native to our realm have betrayed their oaths, slain Lord Regula and those chieftains loyal to the throne, and waged war upon our realm. They were joined in this treason by Lord Morac, who I have slain in battle. With the aid of our new allies, we have destroyed this rebellion and were soon beset by an invasion from the north, a vast gargoyle horde that drew from across the northern sea. Through great sacrifice, and unity, we defeated this vast host, further aided by an Earther Fleet that was drawn to our world by the power invoked in the Swords of Light, which were joined in purpose, led by the Torry Champion, and my grandson, Terin Caleph. We have achieved a great victory for all the peoples of Arax and shall convene in the coming days at Fera to partake in a grand council to oversee this new peace. The Earthers accompanying my emissary have brought devices to heal our wounded, both Benotrist and Menotrist alike, and all others within the palace and its surrounding tributaries. Forthwith, a state of peace shall exist from this time forward, between our armies, and those of the southern alliance, and rebel factions within the realm.

Tyro, Emperor of the Benotrist Empire."

Valera's heart sang, hearing of Terin's fell deed and Tyro's acknowledging their kinship. Had Terin perished, Tyro would have surely mentioned it. Her elation was furthered by overtures of peace. Could such a thing be true? She was again taken aback as the throne room erupted in cheers. She wondered their reception of these tidings, knowing they had been at war with the lands of the south for so long. Now, they rejoiced, celebrating a victory over their true foe, a foe they were unaware of until beset with visions. Those visions had lifted since the battle, a fact they had not fully realized until now.

Amidst the celebration spreading across the chamber and into the outer corridors, Valera asked that Safed approach the throne, Cronus' former comrade taking a respectful knee as he drew nigh under guard, before she ordered him to his feet, weary of such protocols.

"What of Jonas?" she inquired, noticing the pained look passing his face.

"He did what he set out to do, my lady, and turned the emperor to our cause. He died with honor," Safed said before lowering his gaze, not able to bear her mournful gaze.

"Do not be ashamed, my dear Safed. You have done as you were asked, and I am thankful for your safe return. You look much restored, as well," she said, lifting his chin with her gentle fingers, while holding her baby in her other arm.

"The Earthers' magic has restored what the gelders' knife had taken," Safed revealed.

"Then what Jonas said of their power was true." She smiled at that, the noise of celebration drowning each of their voices in the vast chamber.

"He was true to his word, my lady. I look to share this tiding with Tarlan and Geornon," he said, naming his fellow captives who suffered the cruel maiming as he did, a fate shared by most slaves in the Benotrist Empire.

"He was indeed." She smiled, masking her loss with the joy emanating from the crowd.

* * *

It was the next morn when the second transport ship arrived, bringing General Gavis, his scarred face restored by the Earthers' regenerator, and numerous Benotrist Elite and commanders of rank, the large craft setting down upon the largest platform upon the roof of the palace. It took off, only to be followed by another, each ferrying emissaries from the grand alliance, beginning with the Yatin delegation, bringing both Generals Yitia and Yoria. King Lichu and his remaining men arrived next with General Motchi, commander of the Casian 2nd Army. King Sargov and King Mortus followed with their retinues, including General Dadeus Ciyon. King El Anthar and Elos arrived with a number of their warriors, along with President Matuzak, and Generals Mocvoran and Vorklit. Kaly led a contingent from Tro, followed by a group of Enoructans, and many other peoples from Rego, Notsu and Sawyer.

Alen arrived next, along with the rebel leaders and Benotrist commanders from the east now sworn to Terin. He joined the others now gathering in the throne room, feeling pimples raise across his flesh as he returned to this place of so many sorrows. He thought never to return to Fera, and certainly not as a guest. Castellan Braxus reassured him of his safety, as he did with all their guests, and placed him beside the Jenaii king to bolster his sense of security.

King Lorn came next, joined by Torg Vantel, Lucas and Deva, along with Generals Lewins and Farro, and a contingent of his elite. Upon entering the throne room, Torg stopped halfway across the red stone floor, his eyes finding Valera standing upon the dais beside the throne with a baby in her arms. It had been so many years since he last saw her, and her beauty had not changed. She looked so like her mother it made him ache. He broke from the others, who posted beside King Lorn along the left, nearing the steps of the dais. As each of them were announced upon entering the chamber, Castellan Braxus ordered the imperial guards to allow him to approach.

Torg made his way up the steps, stopping before a watery eyed Valera. They stood there for a brief moment, which felt an eternity before he drew her into his arms, careful not to squeeze the baby between them.

"Father." She nearly burst into tears, resting her forehead to his shoulder as he ran his rough fingers through her hair.

The entire assemblage looked on, nary a whisper passing their lips. Everyone knew what this moment meant, for Terin's story and lineage had circled through their camps, fueled by their fevered dreams.

"He died bravely, and your son…" Torg could barely continue, overcome with emotion, a rare affliction for the craggy Commander of the Torry Elite.

"I know. Thank you for watching over him." She smiled as they drew briefly apart so as to look at one another.

"It was he that watched over me. He is quite a boy." Torg smiled in turn. It had been so many years, but she looked the same as the day they last parted, fierce and brave, and so very beautiful.

"Everyone is looking," she said, looking past his thick shoulder, embarrassed by the attention.

"Let them look," he said, pressing a gentle kiss to her forehead, before doing the same for his granddaughter. He smiled even wider as Cordela stopped her fussing, looking into his gray eyes with wonder.

"She likes you." Valera smiled.

"Aye." He sighed happily, running his finger gently along her tiny forehead. With that he backed away, returning to his place beside his king.

* * *

Transport number 4.
Approaching the roof of Fera.

Lt. Giles shook his head at their disobeying of regulations, again standing in the cockpit as he made his final approach. The Black Castle, as it was aptly referred to, towered over the surrounding landscape, its outermost walls jutting sharply skyward, and its inner walls presiding ever higher. Its massive inner keep, with its numerous towers rose higher still, their black stone citadels sharply contrasting the clear blue sky behind them.

"It looks as pleasant as the last time we visited." Raven shook his head, causing Tosha to swat his arm.

"At least it isn't surrounded by two hundred thousand gargoyles like last time," Lorken pointed out, the surrounding Feran plain mostly empty now, its natural soil regaining its luster.

"Hopefully we've seen the last of them," Brokov added. He and Kendra were relieved by a security team, overseeing the *Stenox* while they joined their fellow Earthers for this grand assembly. Zem, Argos, Orlom, Ilesa and Ular waited in the back. They were all summoned to provide their input into the decisions that lay ahead.

"This could be it," Lorken sighed.

"Could be what?" Raven asked.

"Our time together. Everything changed when the fleet showed up," he said.

"Just two ships of the fleet, and we still can't contact Earth. In reality, we are in the same situation as before," Raven pointed out.

"Lorken is right, Rav. There is a big difference between a handful of us trying to scratch out a means to survive on our own and a fully manned battle carrier and a destroyer. We simply made it up as we went, whereas the fleet has rigid command structures and expectations," Brokov said.

"What does that mean?" Tosha asked.

"It means they will likely reassign us. It means the end of our time on the *Stenox*," Lorken said.

"Reassign you to what?" Kendra made a face, standing beside Brokov, her back pressed against the bulwark.

"Wherever the admiral needs us," Lorken said.

"Nobody can make us do anything. In case you guys forgot, our commissions would have expired without a formal renewal, which we haven't done," Raven said.

"Our commissions were suspended in place once we went missing, just as they are with those who die in the line of duty." Brokov couldn't believe Raven was ignorant of that stipulation. It was an Earth custom to honor their war dead by keeping their commissions active. In their case, it meant they were still officially on duty.

"You're awfully quiet, do you know anything about this?" Raven asked, noticing Tosha hadn't said a word, his suspicions from the night before returning.

"Why are you asking me? This is an Earther matter." She shrugged innocently.

"You're not fooling anyone with that stupid look, Tosh. Did you talk with the admiral about us?" Raven growled.

"You really should take your seats," Lt. Giles again suggested, sparing Tosha from answering.

"We have complete faith in you, Niles." Raven slapped the nervous Lt. on the back, keeping his steely gaze on his troublesome wife.

"I am sure you do." Niles rolled his eyes, easing the transport between the castle's towers, lowering to a large flat surface upon the palace roof, where their transports had been landing and taking off from throughout the morn.

"It appears my father's guards have prepared a formal escort for us," Tosha pointed out, seeing two flax of sentries formed up alongside the landing area, attired in copper hued mail over black tunics, with gray helms covering much of their heads.

"Nothing like a visit to the in-laws to make you feel all warm and cozy," Raven snorted, receiving another slap to his head from his beloved wife.

* * *

The *Stenox* crew entered the throne room, feeling every eye upon them. Ilesa broke off from the group, joining the Torry delegation along the side of the vast chamber, where stood King Lorn beside one of the towering pillars that lined the length of the cavernous room.

"We'll be over here," Raven said to Tosha, leading his motley band to the right, finding a place to hide in the crowd, if that was even possible. He knew there was two ways to play this. They could either stand out, reminding everyone of the prominent role they played in this whole affair, or take a step back and hope everyone forgot them, and convince the admiral what they would prefer to do. They chose the latter.

Tosha shook her head at the idiocy of it all, smiling as Raven and the others budged their way to the back of the crowd, Argos and Zem's heads towering over the group of Yatins who now stood in front of them. She continued to the dais, receiving formal bows from the imperial guards positioned along its base.

"Princess Tosha, welcome!" Castellan Braxus bowed reverently after standing from the lesser throne.

"Castellan Braxus!" she greeted, ascending the dais to treat with Valera.

Valera bobbed a curtsy as Tosha drew nigh, lifting Cordela in her arms, turning her little face to her aunt.

Tosha smiled warmly, running her fingers along Cordela's cheek.

"I wished I could have known her father," Tosha whispered, regarding Valera with a knowing look.

"He wished the same." Valera smiled.

"If I cannot have the company of my brother, I shall at least have the company of his wife, my sister by marriage." Tosha smiled in turn.

"I would like that very much." Valera embraced her.

Tosha returned the affection before taking her place beside her on the dais, waiting upon the next entrants to the throne room.

Next came Admiral Helmut Von Kruger, wearing his black fleet uniform, his command presence impressing upon the congregants his authority. He was joined by Dr. Aditi Chopra and Lt. Commander Bao Chang, wearing the red and gold uniforms of their branch specialties. Helmut paused halfway across the chamber, sparing a look at Raven and the others trying to hide.

Some things never change, he chuckled to himself. Helmut continued to the base of the dais, breaking left where his advance team stood, forming a semicircle along the side of the chamber. He stood before them, turning about to face the congregants, with Bao and Aditi posting beside him, standing at parade rest, their hands tucked behind them, their eyes forward and feet shoulder width apart. Like the other Earthers, Bao and Helmut were armed with pistols holstered at their sides, while Aditi carried no weapons. The Araxans present, looked upon them with a myriad of emotions, fear, respect, and most all curiosity. The Admiral and his staff stood in stark contrast to Raven and his motley crew of misfits, so much so, many wondered how they came from the same world, let alone the same command.

General Jani entered after, attended by three of Queen Letha's closest aides, taking her place along the right side of the dais, opposite Admiral Kruger's entourage.

The last to enter were Emperor Tyro and Queen Letha, the congregants watching as they walked side by side. Tosha was taken aback, pleasantly surprised by their united front. At the base of dais, he regarded Letha respectfully before she stepped to the right, joining General Jani and her aides, while Tyro continued up the wide steps of the dais, Valera and Tosha moving to his side as he took his seat upon the throne.

Castellan Braxus looked out to the assemblage, raising an open hand to the onlooking crowd.

"We stand in the court of Emperor Tyro, ruler of the Benotrist Empire!" Larus Braxus proclaimed, bringing the court to commencement, before turning to Tyro, bowing deeply and withdrawing to the side of the dais.

"We are gathered here, the peoples of Arax. Many of us were enemies, and many of us were friends. War has brought us great suffering, loss and tribulation. We have endured endless conflict since the dawn of creation, culminating in the great war we have just waged, a war that ended at the Oddigem, and saw the destruction of the gargoyles for all time. Of all those gathered in this chamber, I bare the greatest responsibility for the state of our world by aligning with the gargoyles in order to save my people. For this bold act, I nearly brought us to ruin, and at the conclusion of this council, I shall abdicate my throne and name Terin Caleph my heir," Tyro proclaimed, a deafening silence filling the chamber.

Nearly every eye looked about the throne room for Terin, who had yet to enter as Tyro continued.

"Some of you know the truth of Terin's lineage, and a few of you know my own, though the visions and rumors have circled amongst you to reveal much that is true and some that is not. Before we begin, I shall lay bare the full truth, of Terin's lineage and my origin." Tyro began, revealing the fate of King Kal and the survival of his direct line, his blood passed down to Tyro's first wife, Cordela. He then told of the events after his own father discovered the Kalinian Vale and the woes that followed, including his wedding Cordela and the betrayal of his brother, who slaughtered Cordela's kin save for Joriah and herself, who fled to Torry North once they learned he had aligned with gargoyles to avenge their supposed deaths. He told of his second wife, Queen Letha, and his plot to annex her realm to his own. He stopped at that juncture in the tale, sharing a look with his wife.

Letha regarded him, bidding him to continue.

He did, though the tale from that point was well known to all those gathered there, save for the final moments of Jonas' life. Once he finished, a long silence filled the chamber. Many there had long seen him as their enemy, their forgiveness offered grudgingly, if at all. But many gathered there were not always aligned with the Torries and were granted mercy from Yah and his followers. If they could be forgiven, then they would be hypocrites if they refused Tyro and the Benotrists the same curtesy.

Tyro then motioned King Lorn forth, the Torry monarch stepping in the middle of the vast chamber to address the assembly.

"Before we continue, you must know my tale of redemption as well," Lorn began, taking many aback as he retold the events of his youth, and the change in his heart after the visions he was given. His confession laid bare his own transgressions. By his own words the only difference between Tyro and himself was the opportunity to do evil, which Tyro was given and Lorn prevented by his early change of heart. They listened as he told of the visions guiding his actions before the war, and through its progression. They learned that it was his many actions that preserved their cause, actions he attributed to Yah, and not himself. If he could be so humble, then they would be hypocrites if they were not.

Lorn called King El Anthar forth to give his account, before stepping back to his place among his entourage. King El Anthar repeated the tale he once told at the Council of Corell, telling of his people that dwelt beyond the southern sea, and of the star that fell from the heavens, striking their ancient temple, a star that contained the divine gift, as they would call it. He told of the great fleet they assembled led by their Prince El Ebiorn, who led them across the sea, coming upon the southern shores of Arax, bringing the divine gift to ancient Tarelia, who used its material to forge the *Swords of Light*.

"We are and always have been the servants of the Yah. It was our place to guide mankind in their war against the gargoyles, and to fulfill Yah's plan for your world," King El Anthar concluded, with a sense of finality to his words, before returning to his place beside Elos. If the Jenaii could be eternally faithful, then so could the assembly.

Queen Letha went next, detailing the founding of the Sisterhood, and how they lost their way, forgetting their true purpose to oppose the gargoyles, before Terin's mercy for Deva reminded them of Yah's glory, and renewed that purpose. If the Sisterhood could be dutiful, then so should the assemblage.

King Mortus followed, detailing his blindness to the gargoyle threat, focusing on his own greed for expansion while the world burned, until Prince Lorn revealed the price of his greed, and the reward of unity with the Torry realm. If Mortus could overcome his greed and blindness to the truth, then so could the assemblage.

And so it went, with each of the peoples of Arax detailing their faults and their triumphs, revealing the lesson each had learned, leaving only the *Stenox* crew and Admiral Kruger left to speak.

Raven's plan to hide in the back of the crowd until the thing was over, was cast aside as Zem and Argos shoved him forward once he was summoned by Tosha.

Traitors, he growled, looking back at his friends who simply shrugged, keeping at the back of the crowd.

"For those who don't know me, I'm Raven, captain of the *Stenox*. Not much to tell. We got stranded on your world and got caught up in this war of yours. We did some killing, some rescuing and, well, here we are," he said, attempting to return to his place before Admiral Kruger called him out.

"You were always lousy with post-op briefings, Raven. Start over, and begin with what happened with Thorton at Cragnellon, and go from there," Helmut ordered, naming the planet where Jennifer died, causing the fallout between Thorton and himself.

"How detailed do you want me to be?"

"Very detailed, so everyone here can understand, including everything that happened up to the Oddigem."

"That would take all day," Raven countered.

"I am sure you can whittle it down," Helmut encouraged.

And so, Raven stepped fully in the open, scratching his head before starting, wondering how to begin. As he told their tale, nearly every ear waited upon his every utterance, from the death of Jennifer to their arrival on Arax and all the great events that followed. He emphasized the day he met Cronus, where his friend saved his life, and ended with Cronus saving his life again, taking a spear meant for him. When he finished it was Helmut's turn. The admiral told of their search for their missing expedition and the dire strait they found themselves, lost in space with only the thinnest hope of survival, before the light of the swords guided them to Arax, saving them all. It was another miracle, a culmination of too many coincidences to be anything other than ordained by a greater power. To further drive this point, he revealed the visions his crew had seen, detailed in the archives of Dr. Chopra. The Earthers' tales were proof that one could believe in the impossible. If the Earthers could believe in the impossible, so could the assemblage.

Helmut had much more to reveal and say, but that could wait until the last entrants arrived. He looked to Deva, who waited until the end to address the assembly.

She stepped forth, taking a deep breath, feeling a hatred that wasn't there, before scolding herself for her self pity. The Deva she remembered was long dead, her spirit renewed by Terin's mercy and Yah's forgiveness. Still, she needed those gathered here to know her tale, to know her transformation from a petulant child to a servant of Yah. And so, she relayed her tale, ending with where she stood now, an acolyte of Yah. The assemblage knew that if she were to be fairly judged for her transgression of enslaving Terin, then so would they all, for every human realm of Arax abided the foul institution.

Deva paused before continuing, letting her tale settle with the congregants, giving them time to consider all she had revealed.

"Emperor Tyro and King Lorn asked that I speak last, allowing the others to share their part in this grand epic. Most, if not all of you, have had visions, each a portal to a part of this tale. These were divine gifts, a tool granted by Yah to draw all of us together. Is there any more unworthy of this gift than I? Yet, here I stand, an instrument of his glory, a voice for his plan," Deva declared, looking to each face in the chamber.

"And what is his plan?" King Sargov of Zulon asked.

"For each of you to make lasting peace. To have each realm not raise its arm against its neighbor. It was Yah's will that Emperor Tyro name Terin his heir and replacement, for him to surrender power of the mightiest realm on Arax. I did not reveal this to him before, the choice coming from his own heart, a sign that Yah has turned him," Deva said, looking to the throne, where sat Tyro, returning her gaze with a knowing look.

It was a test of Tyro, and he passed.

"Terin is yet to be called to enter. He waits without and is ignorant of the eastern half of the realm naming him king, and now his grandfather names him king of all the empire. Once he is told, we are to wait upon him for his answer. Then we must lay the foundation for peace," Deva proclaimed, backing a step as Tyro sent his guards to fetch the Torry Champion.

* * *

"How long must we wait?" Terin moaned, pacing the small antechamber that rested some distance from the throne room.

"Patience. They shall call upon us when ready and not before," Corry said, forcing him to stop as she brushed lint from his shoulder.

"And why was I given this to wear? It is uncomfortable." Terin tugged at the stiff collar of his tunic, a finely woven calnesian garment of pure white with black stitching along its sleeves and hem. He wore a shining silver cuirass and helm with black leather sandals that laced to his bare knees. A jeweled scabbard rode his left hip, where rested the *Sword of the Sun*. It felt wrong for him to wield the ancient blade instead of his silver sword, and he wondered if he should switch swords with Lorn.

"Those should be very comfortable, and you look quite fetching." Corry smiled, running her hand along his cheek.

"You are simply tense, my boy. The difficult part has passed. The enemy is defeated. What is a room full of friends compared to what we have already faced?" Squid reminded him, standing nearer the door, awaiting their summons. He was again attired in the vestment of his station, wearing the deep burgundy robes of a king's minister with its gold stitching along its voluminous sleeves and hem. Corry's attire was even grander, wearing a beautiful silver calnesian gown with its tight bodice and voluminous sleeves and billowing skirt. Her hair was bound atop her head, its golden sheen resplendent in the midday light shining through the room's wide window, affording them a generous view of the outer battlements below and the surrounding lands beyond. Despite Fera's impressive size and majesty, Terin found it depressing and dark, reminding him too much of his first visit to the Black Castle.

"I would be less tense if I knew what was transpiring in the throne room. I am not a foolish boy anymore, Squid, I know when something is afoot. I can feel it," Terin said, looking into Squid and Corry's eyes for a hint of deception. He hadn't missed the coy looks they were passing to each other, or the extreme deference the Benotrists they encountered were giving Corry. As his wife, it would be expected they show her a measure of esteem, as he was the grandson of Tyro, as well as visiting royalty, but it was more than that. They didn't seem to offer the same reverence to Lorn, Mortus or El Anthar. Every time he inquired of this strange behavior, Corry would change the topic or direct him to another task that she found so very important.

"It is understandable, my love. You are meeting your grandfather for the first time in a formal setting where you are both aware of your kinship. Your mother will also be in attendance. You have not seen her since you departed for Rego, so very long ago," Corry said, again directing him from his suspicion. He had to admit, she was very good at misdirection.

Before he could probe further, the door opened, with Cronus peeking his head into the room.

"It is time," Cronus said, himself adorned in the blue tunic and silver armor of a Torry Elite. The garments felt entirely new after the *Stalingrad* crew cleaned and repaired them to their current state. He spent the previous night aboard the Earther vessel, savoring the comfortable bed and rich food they offered. He had returned on an earlier transport then the others, with King Lorn asking that he serve as Terin's escort through the coming proceedings. He was joined in the task with Galen and Dougar, each waiting outside the antechamber alongside him.

With that announcement, Terin took Corry by the hand, before passing through the door, preparing himself for what awaited beyond. Dougar greeted them with a sharp Earther salute, still wearing the hat Thorton had given him, and dressed as a small Earther with matching black trousers, boots, and jacket. Lorken had arranged it, promising to teach the young boy how to use a pistol once time allowed.

Terin returned the salute, Corry smiling, touched by the endearing exchange.

"Show the way," Terin said, waving an open hand down the corridor.

Dougar gave him a sharp grin, turning on his heel to take the lead, though in truth they were surrounded by a small army of his grandfather's guards, the sound of their armored sandals sounding off the stone floor.

"It feels as if an end to a grand adventure," Galen whimsically said, he and Squid trailing them as they traversed the storied corridors of the ancient Tarelian holdfast.

"Perhaps you shall pen a great epic, you lack only a title to match its worth," Squid musically opined.

"Yes, a title worthy of such a tale," Galen mused, touching a finger to his chin, the hem of his long robe swirling about his legs as he walked. Of course, such an epic would take a lifetime to put to parchment. There were many parts of the story he didn't know and would have to research to round out the expansive narrative.

No sooner had they spoke, then they came upon the massive doors of the throne room, noting a darkened circle before the entrance, where once stood the statue of a man and gargoyle melding into one form, the emperor ordering it removed and destroyed. Terin paused before advancing, recalling the last time he stepped upon this place. Cronus came to his side, opposite Corry, each recalling the events of that night so long ago when they escaped Fera.

"Sometimes this seems all a dream." Terin sighed.

Cronus thought on that for a brief moment.

"No, it has seemed a nightmare, but the dream is what lies ahead." Cronus' gentle smile gave him courage. With that they followed Dougar into the throne room.

* * *

Valera stood upon the dais at the side of Tyro's throne, her heart racing as she watched Terin enter the vast chamber, every eye now upon him. She passed Cordela to an attending maid nearby, fearing her arms might fail her as her pulse quickened. She gasped as he approached, walking across the red stone floor, passing between the crowd gathered to either side. He was more handsome than even she remembered; his boyish youth replaced with the man that walked before her. Her eyes found Corry walking beside him, taking her aback with her stunning beauty. She wanted nothing more than to rush into his arms and never let go. His eyes found her upon the dais, a knowing look passing between them, his face breaking with the gentlest smile. Oh, how she loved him.

Terin's heart mended at the sight of her, setting him at ease before tearing his eyes away from her comforting gaze to the man who sat the throne beside her. His smile faltered as he came to a stop below the dais, locking eyes with his paternal grandfather. There he stood and Tyro sat, staring at one another for the longest time.

Should he kneel? Should he stand defiant? What was expected of him? Thankfully his grandfather spoke first, removing his need to choose.

"Terin Caleph. You have been summoned to stand in the court of the Benotrist Emperor," Tyro began, regarding Terin studiously as if looking for something.

"I understand," Terin said, surprising the assembly as he took a knee before drawing his sword, setting it upon the floor before him. He felt the impulse to do so, as if his will was not his own.

Tyro wondered at this odd behavior, taken aback by the gesture.

"I return the sword that is yours by right, Emperor. It has served me well in the time that I held it. I offer it back to you without reservation," Terin said, hearing a chorus of gasps from the lips of those around him.

"You would offer the *Sword of the Sun* freely?" Tyro raised a brow at that.

"It is yours by right, gifted to your hand by my father, its ownership passing from him to you," Terin said, acknowledging Jonas' gifting of the blade.

Tyro stood, descending the dais and stopping before his kneeling grandson, retrieving the blade from the floor. The sword alit with his touch, a fiery crimson glow illuminating its blade as he took a practice swing, the power of the blade coursing his flesh.

"Stand!" he ordered Terin to his feet.

"My son gifted me this blade, the most precious material possession I have ever known. I now repay the debt, gifting this sword to his son," Tyro said, sliding it home in Terin's scabbard.

Terin didn't know how to act, or what to say, the entire scene feeling as a dream.

Tyro regarded Corry with a knowing look, sensing the unease in her carriage, though she masked it well. They were separated by the troubled history of their two realms but united in what they were about to reveal.

"While you were traipsing through the heart of my empire with the Chosen, ignorant of what was transpiring beyond the horizon, or in the far-off lands of my eastern regions, my daughter happened to conspire wresting half my empire from my grasp," Tyro revealed, sparing a look over his shoulder, where stood Tosha upon the dais, her face a mask of indifference, unfazed by his accusation.

Terin wondered what he was referring, feeling the intensity of his golden eyes as they turned sharply back to him.

"Would you care to know how?" Tyro asked.

"I…" Terin was a loss for words, wondering how this involved him.

"She convinced the regents of Pagan, Nisin and Mordicay to join with the rebels plaguing my realm to swear their oaths to a new king, one whose blood made him my rightful heir. They named you their king," Tyro said, enjoying the terrified look in Terin's eyes.

With those words, a dozen Benotrist commanders from the east stepped forth, along with Alen and the rebels joining him at the council. They were aligned to either side of him, before taking a knee to their named king. Terin was horrified by the display, his dread growing as Corry backed several steps away before dropping to her knees as well.

"My King," Corry proclaimed, bowing her head with the deepest reverence.

Before Terin could order her to stand, Tyro continued.

"As the son of my eldest son, and rightful heir to my empire, I name you the emperor of the Benotrist Empire. I shall abdicate as of this day, and you shall take your rightful place upon the throne of Fera!" Tyro declared as general Gavis and Castellan Braxus stepped forth, along with General Naruv and a dozen commanders of rank and court officials, all taking a knee.

"My Emperor!" Braxus proclaimed, the others chorusing his acknowledgment.

"Stand, all of you!" Terin ordered, overwhelmed by the moment, his heart racing.

Terin took Corry by the hand, drawing her to her feet, wondering if she was beguiled, but she only smiled, the love in her eyes tearing through his heart. He urged the others to their feet, wondering if they had lost all sense.

"The realm is yours, Terin. It has to be you. You are the one who led us to victory, all of us. It was you who wielded the blade. It is you that both Benotrists and Menotrists would follow," Corry said.

"It is your duty, Terin. I would have named your sire, had the gargoyle curse not prevented it, so he oft reminded me. That can no longer afflict you, or any of Kalinian blood, such as your sister, who I had first named as my heir, but that title must be yours," Tyro said.

"I have a king, and have sworn my oath to him and cannot break it," Terin said, looking to Lorn who stood off to the side.

"Your birthright takes precedence, Terin, as I told you when we spoke along the banks of the Muva, so long ago. Take up your crown, and lead your people," Lorn ordered.

"But YOU are my king," he protested.

"No, I am your brother, both by marriage and in spirit," Lorn said, a warm smile spreading across his face.

Terin stood there, overcome with emotion, knowing the burden to rule was never to be placed upon the blood of Kal. They were the warriors of Yah, not the monarchs, as Yah had rent the two halves of Kal's destiny upon his death. The burden of crowns was to fall to others.

"The gargoyles are gone, Terin. It is time for the blood of Kal to take up his crown," Deva said with an otherworldly authority.

"You have all sworn to me, first as king of the east, and now emperor of the Benotrist Empire?" Terin asked of those still kneeling around him, though he insisted they stand.

"We have," more than one answered.

Terin paused, giving his mind time to clear, feeling what he must do shaping his thoughts.

"As your emperor, I command you to stand!" he ordered them to their feet.

"From this day forth, no man or woman shall ever kneel again, not to me, and not to each other!" he added with terrible authority.

"Aye," they reluctantly said, looking to each other curiously.

"General Gavis," he called out to the ranking general of the empire.

"Yes, my emperor," Gavis said.

"Are you wed?"

"No, my emperor."

"You shall take a Menotrist bride, joining your blood to hers. I shall name you warden of the west. Laycrom shall be your capital. You shall rule all the lands from the Oddigem to Tinsay. You shall order all Benotrist men within your territory to take Menotrist brides, and all Menotrist men to take Benotrist brides!" Terin ordered.

"Aye, my emperor." Gavis made a face, taken aback by the strange request.

"Good. Castellan Braxus!" Terin called him forth.

"Yes, my emperor?"

"Are you wed?"

"Yes, my emperor."

"Do you have children?"

"I have two sons, and they serve the garrison of Fera, my emperor. They are not wed."

"I name you regent of Fera, second in the west only to General Gavis. Your sons are to take Menotrist brides."

"As you command, my emperor." Braxus bowed and withdrew as Terin called Alen forth.

"My Emperor," Alen said.

"I name you warden of the east, and you shall rule all lands west of the Oddigem. You will take the greater throne of Nisin, and wed the daughter of its current regent, Davin Gorel. Regent Gorel shall retain his position, commanding Nisin Castle and its surrounding territories. My orders to General Gavis are the same for you. You are to order the unwed Benotrist and Menotrist men to take brides of the other. The same applies to all other groups, including Venotrists and those of the former free holds that joined the empire in recent years," Terin ordered.

"Aye, my emperor." Alen thrust his fist to his heart.

Terin felt the questioning gaze of his paternal grandfather, Corry and especially his mother, along with countless others.

"The people of these lands have been at war with one another for thousands of years, killing each other, enslaving each other, and torturing one another without respite. Each cruelty has fed the vengeance of the other, the brutalities growing stronger with each generation. I am the blood of Kal, but also the blood of Menotrists, Benotrists, and old Tarelia. Each of you are of my blood. Each of you are my kin. I would have you joined as one, so that your children's children will one day look upon each other as I look upon you now, as their kin," Terin said, his voice filled with compassion, his words tearing at their hearts.

"I am no king or emperor. I know nothing of such things. I would further my ignorance to believe that I do, simply by the title you have bestowed upon me," Terin protested his appointment.

"You shall have good counsel. We are all here, should you have need of us," Corry said.

"I will help you. You need only ask," Tyro said.

"I know our armies and will instruct you on everything you will need to be their commander," General Gavis said.

"I know each of our imperial ministers, having placed them in their posts. I too shall aid you in every endeavor," Castellan Braxus said.

"And should you need sage advice from beyond your realm, I and my council of minsters will lend you whatever aid you ask of us," Lorn said.

"Aye, the same goes for us, lad," Matuzak bellowed, his fellow apes grunting in agreement.

"Whatever you need from us, kid, you got it," Raven said, his crew agreeing by their shaking heads.

"We offer whatever aid you would ask," General Yoria of Yatin said.

King Mortus, King El Anthar and countless others added their support.

Terin stood in silence for the longest time, again sorting his thoughts before continuing.

"I am honored by your friendship, all of you, and what friendship is stronger than that born in battle. We have shed blood together at the Oddigem, each of us. The people of the northern lands now ask that I take up the title of emperor, but I am cautious to accept. The greatest threat to our race since the dawn of time is the belief that a great warrior would make a great king. Power is a dangerous thing, and total power even more so. No man should wield such power, no matter the goodness of his heart. Our Earth friends have no kings, and they have thrived. Their one attribute that accounts for their success is the layers of checks upon concentrated power. They also choose their leaders through consent of the people, but that is a path that requires years to nurture and prepare. These lands have just endured terrible hardship and war, and such a government cannot be imposed upon them without further suffering, this time from incompetence rather than hostility, but both are equally destructive." He paused, wondering where these words were coming from, for he couldn't fathom conjuring them on his own. Perhaps Yah had again given him strength when he needed it, this time strength of wisdom.

"I would not call upon our people to choose their leader, for a majority might wish to destroy the minority, or choose a leader who speaks well, but is a fool. What I can do is appoint sound leaders from each of the warring factions and name an overlord, a supreme regent if you will. He will be chosen from the masses and shall have authority over regents Gavis and Alen. They will be chosen for their skill as a warrior, and for their wisdom, each to be measured by tests arranged by Gavis, Alen, my grandfather, my queen, and myself," Terin continued, his words not winning many converts to his plan.

"Once selected, the individual will take their place as the overlord of the realm and serve for a period of two years. Their edicts can only be overruled by a majority of a council of judges, whose only purpose is to check the overlord's power. Once they serve two years, they shall join the council of judges, adding to their number, while another is chosen. My grandfather, my mother and Elos shall be named as judges. In two years, Elos may return to his people if he so chooses, once the first named overlord joins the council of judges. Elos, would you accept this post?" Terin asked, looking to his friend.

Elos felt this was Yah's intent and nodded his agreement.

"What say you all?" Terin asked, an eerie silence filling the throne room.

It was Deva who stepped forth, her face alit in an otherworldly light.

"Yah's Champion has spoken. Let it be as he commands!" Deva proclaimed.

"Aye!" Tyro said, first to agree to Terin's plan, recalling Lorn's words about the dangers of unchecked power. If there was a way forward after so many years of war and bloodshed, this appeared to be the most promising.

"Aye!" said Alen, his fellow rebels chorusing his agreement.

"Aye!" said Castellan Braxus, followed by General Gavis, and then the entire assemblage representing the northern factions.

"It is agreed, then!" Terin proclaimed, listening for any voices of dissent, and hearing none.

With that, a sense of relief washed over Terin, a great weight lifting from his shoulders.

"And what shall your role be in this grand experiment, Terin?" Lorn asked the question most were thinking.

"I shall be their champion, should they need me, and after the first overlord is chosen, I shall…" He paused, looking at Corry, taking her hand in his before looking back to his former king…" I shall find a place to build a home and raise a family, a quiet place."

"You would walk away from such power?" General Gavis asked, taken aback.

"Power is fleeting, General. Kings rise and fall with the seasons, but love and family…" He paused again, looking into Corry's eyes. "Love and family are eternal, true love and true love of family. They endure long after we die. They endure until the breaking of the world and beyond. It is love for the one you are promised to and those you call friend. All of you gathered here are my friends, and I love you." He smiled warmly, looking especially to Cronus and then Raven, and then everyone his eyes fell upon.

With that, Terin led Corry up the dais, to embrace his mother, holding her tight before she led them behind the dais and into a private sanctum beyond, leaving the council to plan the ordering of the world.

CHAPTER 19

The late evening found Terin upon the inner battlements of the north wall lost in thought, pale moonlight illuminating the battlements of the inner wall below and the Feran Plain beyond. The crisp autumn air swirled about the ramparts, harbinger of the coming winter. He reflected on the day, and what it portended for the future. He spent much of it with his mother and newborn sister, sharing so many tears, of joy and sorrow, of lives lost and lives preserved. Mostly they just embraced each other. Valera told him of all that happened since she was brought there, and of Jonas' time there as well, and his visions of what he must do. Corry enjoyed her time with Valera, feeling a strong kinship with the woman who was Torg's daughter and Terin's mother, feeling the connection to her through the two men they both dearly loved. Tosha joined them after the council adjourned for the day, wishing to meet her sister by marriage, and her newborn niece. There were a countless number of embraces, tears and kisses, heartfelt and heartbreaking.

Terin finally retired to the palace roof as sunset was upon them, using the cool air to clear his thoughts. The women remained behind, talking late into the night, sharing stories and memories. Terin could make out the silhouettes of the guards standing post on the battlements below, moonlight illuminating their iron helms as they stood watch, staring in the same direction as he was. He wondered what they were thinking. They were his enemies several days before, and now were his countrymen. He could be their king if he wanted, and that thought seemed so surreal. What a strange turn of events. He meant what he said to the council before stepping away. He would help arrange a working command structure, and then step away, retiring to some place remote and quiet to raise a family. He wanted nothing to do with royal position, war and politics. He wanted nothing to do with the ordering of their world. He wanted what his father and mother had had, a quiet life with the one he loved the most.

"I should have guessed to find you here, brooding and nostalgic while others celebrate below," Cronus' voice called out from behind him, his friend stepping to his side, resting his forearms upon the rampart beside him.

"Celebrations? I hadn't heard." He bit off his smile, the noise echoing through the halls of the palace loud enough to wake the dead.

Cronus ignored his playful denial.

"Our ape friends insisted we continue our discussions tomorrow and break for supper. Their not-ungentle request was quickly seconded by Raven. Once that happened, it quickly gained consensus." Cronus shook his head.

"Understandable." Terin smiled, picturing it all in his head.

"Matuzak and Argos dragged our hosts to the great hall and broke out several dozen casks of ale. They dragged along the Earth admiral also," Cronus added.

"Is he drunk yet?"

"He should be, but the man is still on his feet. He looks better than Raven, I can assure you."

"What of the others?" Terin asked.

"Alen is gone, went down after his sixth tankard. Galen is singing off note, slurring the words to whatever ballad he can remember. General Gavis and General Lewins were swaying arm in arm when I left. Orlom was out, sitting on one of the benches with his head on the table, snoring far too loudly. He spent much of the night pushing one tankard after another on Torg, constantly referring to him as *Coach*."

"And how did Torg fare?"

"He is still standing."

"He will never admit to it, but I think he favors Orlom's moniker." Terin laughed.

"I believe so. The two of them make an odd pair."

"They have company in that regard," Terin quipped.

"True. Lucas and Ular, they are both deep in their cups the last I saw them, though with Ular it is difficult to notice. His eyes are always blinking."

"And there is King Mortus and Tessa." Terin recalled their friendship throughout their travels with the Chosen.

"He pulled Tessa to the middle of the floor, starting the first dance. That gave Raven the idea to push General Jani to dance with Admiral Kruger."

"And how did that fair?" Terin smiled, trying to picture it.

"Surprisingly well. You would never guess either of them to lower their guard in that way."

"Raven has that unique ability to convince others to act..." Terin said, thinking of the right words to complete his thought.

"Like fools?" Cronus asked.

Terin shrugged, unable to think of a better way of saying it. There were countless others Cronus had seen in the great hall, such as Dadeus Ciyon, Criose, General Valen, and many others. Kaly, the Troan free sword, was dancing with a Benotrist serving maid, telling her of his adventures, most so outrageous, Cronus thought no one would believe, but the girl listened as if enthralled. Kaly was the sort to have a woman on his arm wherever he traveled. Some men had that gift, he reasoned.

"I wonder what shall become of us, Cronus?" Terin sighed, staring into the gathering night, his mind a thousand other places and none at all, if that were possible.

"How so? You made it very clear your intentions."

"Not that. I mean our friendship."

"Our friendship? I will always be your friend, Terin, you have no worries in that regard," Cronus reassured him, nudging his shoulder.

"I know we shall always be friends, Cronus, and I can think of no one that I am fonder of, but time and distance changes things. My father was great friends with Squid, and when he took my mother and lived in isolation, they never spoke again for twenty years."

"We are not your father and Squid, and even if we were, they were still the best of friends. That speaks to their bond, that even years apart did not dull their friendship, take heart in that. You are my dearest friend, you and Raven and his crew. We will always be great friends, no matter how long we are parted."

"I guess I should be grateful for the war's end, and all the blessings we have been given, but a part of me feels numb, and I cannot explain it."

"You are tired, Terin, just as we all are. The others celebrating below are just as weary, I assure you."

"They don't sound it." Terin looked over his shoulder, the sound of their revelry echoing dully in their ears, even out there.

"That? They are simply releasing the tension. Soldiers can only endure so much before they need a release. You should join them. They would be glad for your company."

"I probably should, but I really just want to sleep." He smiled, sharing a look with Cronus before they both laughed.

"That sounds most inviting," Cronus agreed.

"There they are!" They heard Raven's voice behind them, talking loud enough to wake the countryside.

They turned as he made his way up the adjoining open stair, leaving Lorken and Bao Chang where he left them below, arguing over some trivial matter. Cronus shifted farther left, making room for Raven to stand between them, the smell of ale lingering on his breath.

"I figured I'd find you two up here moping around like Coach O'Brien after he lost a game. Doesn't make much sense since we won, but here you both are," Raven said, causing Cronus to grin at the ridiculous reference.

"We were just reflecting, old friend." Cronus put a hand to Raven's shoulder.

"I know. I was just giving you a hard time. You haven't missed much since you left, Cronus. Zem started talking about penguins again, and how he plans to establish an academy, which Lorn and Mortus agreed to commission. That only encouraged him to keep babbling on with his nonsense. By the way, Terin, your grandfather is looking for you. I think he wants to talk," Raven managed to say before belching.

"Torg?" Terin asked.

"No, the evil one," Raven said, still not forgiving Tyro completely, though he would have to at some point if he wanted to keep his wife happy.

Terin didn't know what to say to that. He knew he would have to speak with him at some point. What would they possibly say to one another?

"You might get lucky, kid. The last I saw of him, Zem was drawing him into his conversation with Lorn and Mortus about redesigning the plumbing in their castles. He might just die of boredom before he ever finds you," Raven slapped him on the back, as if that would make him feel better.

"We were just talking of you, old friend," Cronus smiled.

"All bad, I hope. Don't want to ruin my reputation." Raven nudged him with that stupid grin on his face.

"You have done that yourself. No one is afraid of you anymore, Rav, not after all the good you've done. You are getting quite a following, if I dare say." Cronus chuckled.

"I believe I overheard King Mortus speaking with your admiral about your great deeds, and your suitability for an ambassadorship to his kingdom, representing the new Earth colony," Terin said, his lousy lie good enough to fool Raven.

"I thought it was Queen Letha who requested that assignment for you," Cronus added, enjoying the look on their friend's face.

"We'll see about that. The last place I want to be tied down to is Tosha's island. Luckily the admiral and I go way back," Raven said.

"Perhaps, but if General Jani wins his favor after their dance tonight, who knows what she might request?" Cronus said, enjoying Raven's tortured look all too much, before his friend realized what he was doing.

"Nice try, Cronus. Even the admiral isn't dumb enough to make me the ambassador of anything. Besides, he already said I'll command the *Stenox* for another few months until we sort everything out. Now, what were you two talking about besides little ole me?"

"Terin fears we shall all grow apart once we go our separate ways, but I assured him our bond is stronger than that," Cronus said.

"Why would we grow apart? Weren't you listening down there when the admiral was talking?" Raven made a face.

"If I recall, it was you that kept falling asleep during the discussions, and that is quite a feat considering you were standing the entire time," Cronus reminded him.

"Can't blame me if they were boring me to death, but I caught the important parts, particularly what Admiral Kruger was saying."

Raven went on to explain the discovery of the precious resources on the gargoyles' home continent to their north. The land contained all the materials required to produce both Rendarium and Trundusium, both essential in the construction and long-range operation of space craft. The Earthers were preparing to establish their own homeland there, where they could begin constructing manufacturing pads, and distributing their goods to the other realms of Arax. They needed to proceed slowly, lest they throw Arax into complete chaos, but in time, they would help their new friends skip three thousand years of technological advancement. Healing regenerators were just the beginning. In time they would provide free energy cubes, powering entire cities and realms, as well as smaller ones designed for private dwellings in the countryside. They would implement agricultural advancements to boost food production, as well as clothing and building production. Each home or dwelling would be outfitted with their own smaller production pads, producing a wide array of goods and instruments, using the natural components from their soil.

"From there, your people can expand to larger projects, like constructing your own fighter squadrons. Of course, you'll need help learning to fly them, but we can work that out latter," Raven explained.

"Why didn't you do all this before our people found us?" Cronus wondered, considering the effectiveness of the space fighters in destroying the gargoyle horde.

"For one, we didn't have enough production capacity when we arrived. We had just enough to scrape together the *Stenox*. It wasn't until much latter that Brokov got our manufacturing pad working, which limited what we could produce. The air skis had to be produced in smaller components, and then assembled. The regenerators were able to be made complete, but it took nearly 100 days to produce the first one. Another thing was we hadn't explored your whole world yet. If we had, we could have warned you of the gargoyle homeland and discovered it was full of those resources. With those resources, we could have built nearly anything but would always be limited by our numbers. You can only do so much with a handful of guys," Raven explained.

"Perhaps it is time for an exploratory expedition, to see what lies beyond our coast," Cronus wondered.

"Too late. The *Javier Solis* has been mapping the entire planet the past couple days," Raven said.

"The Javier…" Terin began to ask, wondering the reference.

"The *Javier Solis*. It is the name of the *Stalingrad's* accompanying destroyer. Its laser batteries were the ones that tore the heart out of the gargoyle horde after the fighters made their first pass. Since then, it's been mapping out nearly the entire surface of your planet, and some of their findings are surprising," Raven said, knowing much of these details would be presented to the grand council in the coming days.

"Surprising could entail many possibilities. Are there any particular ones that stood out?" Cronus asked.

"For one, they found the Jenaiis' home island to your southeast. There are still Jenaii dwelling there, but in few numbers. I'm sure Elos and his people will want to send an expedition. I wouldn't be surprised if they already knew about them with how secretive they are. There are even larger continents to your east, mostly uninhabited, except for wildlife. A few have people, though how many are to be determined. Far to your west is another continent, ruled by a matriarchy even more vicious than the Sisterhood, if what the report says are true. We should just stay clear of 'em if you ask me, but I'm sure some nitwit will try and talk sense to them. Beyond them there are a few more good-sized land masses, as well as frozen regions at your poles. Got to say, this place is more like Earth the more we study it. Either way, things are looking pretty good for your future," Raven said, sounding far less drunk than he appeared. Cronus often wondered if his friend pretended to be impaired with drink so others would underestimate him. Raven was far more clever than the others believed, and he had known him long enough to know that.

"A peaceful future is all that I need." Terin sighed, not needing the trappings Raven was speaking so fondly of.

"You know what is better than peace? Peace AND running hot water. Throw in artificial lighting, climate-controlled temperatures and plenty of good food and entertainment and now you're talking," Raven added. He had enough of bathing in cold water and enduring the heat and cold and elements.

"It sounds very nice, Rav," Cronus agreed, appreciating the conveniences of the *Stenox*, and imaging them a thousand-fold more plentiful.

"You're damn right it sounds nice. What good is peace if you have to wipe your ass with…" Raven began to say when Cronus cut him off.

"Alright, Rav, we get the picture," he said, using the phrase Raven often said.

"You're sounding more and more like me every day, Cronus. We'll make an Earther of you yet. You too, nephew." Raven ruffled Terin's hair like he was a child.

"I would be honored, Uncle Raven." Terin gave him a smile, which Raven returned.

The three of them stood there for a time, looking out over the palace walls, thinking of all they endured. It was one of those quiet moments that they would never forget. It was then Terin noticed Tyro along the walkway atop the nearest stair, standing but a few paces from them. Cronus and Raven soon noticed as well, each stepping away, leaving the two of them alone.

"Thank you. Both of you. You are the greatest friends I could have ever hoped to have," Terin called out to them as they stepped away.

"Thank you, Terin. It was our honor." Cronus spoke for both of them, before passing Tyro, descending the stair and joining Lorken and Bao below, and then disappearing into the castle.

Tyro waited for a moment before advancing, resting his hands upon the bulwark, looking out across the gathering dark. Terin mimicked his action, pretending to look as if seeing something, neither of them knowing where to begin.

"I must have stood upon these battlements thousands of times, staring out across the Feran Plain, looking in vain for something I no longer had. So many wasted nights, brooding on what might have been, and blaming everyone and everything except myself. I regret the years that I lost, thinking Joriah was dead, but am thankful for the time I did have with him before he…" Tyro couldn't finish the sentence, though Terin knew what he left unsaid.

"When I was a child, I often asked my father about my grandparents, especially of you." Terin sighed, the pale moon light illuminating his face.

"And what did he say?"

"He said only that you were a good father and that he loved you. He said it with such sadness that I believed you were dead. It was only after the first siege of Corell that he revealed the full truth."

"Had he told you, things might have been different during your first visit here, though I wonder if I could have helped myself from ruining everything that needed to transpire. Our path for victory was a narrow one, requiring many pieces to fall perfectly into place. All I can do now is try to repair what damage my reign has done, though I often feel little remorse, such was the hurt my Menotrist kin prevailed upon me."

"They were cruel, and you returned their cruelty manyfold, and not only to them but everyone."

"Aye, revenge can blind a man to such things. I first sought revenge upon my brother and his evil mother, gaining justice for their crimes, but when he escaped my wrath, he slaughtered everyone in the Vale of Kalin, save for your father and grandmother, leaving me to search in vain for their bodies. All I found were these swords hidden there, but no sign of them. They were the light of my life, the two of them, and when they were removed, I was surrounded by darkness," Tyro said, his voice laced with torment and regret.

"It seems it was pride more than loss that drove you, for I am guilty of that same crime. In that, I am very much your grandson."

"Pride? You?"

"When I was captive to Darna, I escaped with my comrades. All I had to do to complete my escape was run to the ship they were already gathered upon when Darna appeared. I heard Yah whisper to me, urging me to run, but all I could see was my tormentor, and my need for revenge. I couldn't flee and leave her unpunished for her ill treatment. I remember standing there as my comrades called out to me to join them, and Yah whispering in my mind, ordering me to flee, but I refused them. All I wanted was to cut her down where she stood, her and all her soldiers."

Tyro had heard only parts of this story, never fully piecing it all together.

"I raised my blade into the air, preparing to strike her down when lightning struck my blade. When I awoke, I was chained to a bed, with my Kalinian power impaired. I never felt such cold in my life, as if Yah's presence was ripped from my chest. If not for Corry and Raven's crew, I would have remained captive there for all time, as Darna intended to blind me to prevent another escape, planning to use me to sire heirs with Kalinian blood. Only Yah's mercy led them to rescue me, all because of my pride. So, yes, grandfather, I understand what drove you to such madness," Terin turned, looking into Tyro's eyes.

Tyro recalled how he wished Terin remained captive so he might be removed from the Torry cause, while still siring heirs he could claim. He felt such shame for those wicked hopes, shame that washed over him as never before. Yah's mercy had brought him to this, feeling pain again without hatred, feeling human. How could he have wished his grandson to suffer so? Looking at him now reminded him so much of Joriah.

"To want revenge is human, Terin, and I know that well. Unlike me, you have learned to forsake it. You are very much like your father, and I wish he were here to guide you, and to love you."

"You are here," Terin said, his words coming from a place he could not understand. Was he truly saying this to Tyro?

"I am not your father. There is no man finer than him, no one. He should be here, not me."

"He gave his life so you might be redeemed, so you might live as you were intended. You were a great man, and then an evil man, but you can be great again, greater than ever before. That is why I placed you at the head of the tribunal, to help whoever we choose to lead our people," Terin said.

"Our people?" Tyro lifted a brow, surprised to hear Terin claim such kinship to the realm.

"Our people. We are Benotrist and Menotrist. Their blood flows in our veins, both of them. Your father was a cruel man, but he was still your kin, just as you are mine. Let us join both halves of our blood, forging one realm, one tribe, one people," Terin said, repeating his words in the council earlier.

"It shall take a strong leader to oversee this, and you should be that leader."

"No. I have fulfilled my part. I am not a leader. I lack the wisdom, I lack the patience, and I certainly lack the strength. I will help oversee the beginning and then quietly step aside, but should you ever need me, I will always be your champion."

"Aren't you the Torry Champion?"

"Yes, if they will still have me, but I can be yours as well. I also carry the blood of Tarelia, and we can reestablish our unified Menotrist and Benotrist realm into the Northern Kingdom, restoring the Tarelian stronghold of old."

"You are of Tarelia, but our people are not. For this to work, you will need to produce children, children with your blood, who can add their bloodlines to our people."

"My blood has served its purpose. Should Corry and I have children, it will matter little to our realm."

"No, your blood is still special. Even the Earther matron says, claiming your blood is distinct, and must be preserved and expanded through your heirs."

"You are still listening to Earthers?" Terin asked, knowing Tyro had often heeded Thorton's counsel.

"Thorton was far wiser than most know. Most saw him as a powerful brute, but he warned me of what might transpire if his people discovered our world, how their bureaucracy had supplanted their leaders, often ruling from the shadows, unaccountable to all authority. I understood this threat for even I relied upon countless ministers to oversee the empire, for no one man can truly rule without them."

Terin made a face, not realizing that Ben and his grandfather had spoken of such things.

"I often wondered why he joined with you, especially when his friends were so different," Terin said.

"He was a complex man, a man perhaps only I could understand, considering our similar nature and the loss that tormented us, though my loss fueled an inner rage, while his turned his heart cold as winter ice."

"You were fond of him," Terin realized.

"Aye. Other than Regula, he was the only one I could truly speak with as an equal. When you are emperor, others need to submit to your authority. You cannot show favor to one over another, or think any are equal to your station, lest the empire crumbles. With Thorton, it was different. He respected my authority, but joined my cause for intrinsic reasons, reasons beyond gold, women, wealth or power. I had nothing to purchase his obedience or loyalty. Our goals simply aligned for very different reasons, and because of that, I could speak freely with him without undermining my power structure. Our talks were very insightful. He impressed upon me the great power his people wielded, and I am certain my visit to their battle carrier in the coming days will further reinforce in me just how prescient his words were."

"Are you worried?"

"Surprisingly no. We have the good fortune of encountering a mere two of their great warships, warships cut off from the rest of their fleet and civilization. They also appear willing to share their knowledge with us, without their meddlesome bureaucrats undermining our world. Perhaps one day when or if the rest of their people discover our world, we might meet them on equal ground. I believe this was the will of your God, for nothing else explains the unfolding of events in this unique way."

"Raven doesn't speak of him, but I know his loss bothers him deeply." Terin sighed.

Tyro reflected, realizing he lost his two most trusted friends at the Oddigem, along with his son. Surrendering his empire to Terin left him with nothing but his remaining family. In truth, that was more than he had before Valera was brought to Fera. Joriah told him so, that their family would need him now. He regarded Terin for a long quiet moment, feeling a sense of peace he hadn't felt since Cordela. His rage was gone, replaced with a serene calm.

There upon the ramparts of Fera, Tyro and Terin talked late into the night, sharing stories of their adventures, battles, and the man they both loved. From that day forth, Tyro forsook his taken name, resuming his given name… Taleron.

CHAPTER 20

⊰⊱

Corell. 63 days after the Battle of Noddegamra.

The great hall of the palace was alit with the luminous glow of the artificial light, gifted to the people of Torry North from their new Earth friends, in particularly Admiral Kruger. Representatives of the Earthers arrived earlier that morn upon one of their transports, Dr. Aditi Chopra and Captain Banza, commander of the Battle Carrier *Stalingrad*. The arrival and departures of the strange air ships became a regular occurrence since days after the battle, when King Lorn arrived on the first to set down upon the palace roof. The garrison was sent into a frenzy upon its first approach, greeting the Earther craft with leveled spears, nearly half the garrison gathering upon the battlements to face the unknown. They were greatly relieved when the ramp of the strange craft lowered and King Lorn emerged, bearing tidings of victory, followed by the thunderous cheers of the garrison. He was in turn greeted by his queen, holding an infant in her arms.

"Your son, My King," Deliea greeted him upon the palace roof, presenting the child to him.

"A son?" Lorn nearly cried, looking down upon the child with watery eyes, running a finger along the tiny cheek.

"I left his name for you to decide," she said, overjoyed he did not perish with the Chosen.

There were many names worthy of the future king of the Torry-Macon realm, but only one that felt truly right... "Jentra."

His queen smiled at that before he took her in his arms.

Lorn recalled that wondrous moment as he stood upon the dais overlooking the sea of friendly faces. Their Earth guests, the good Dr. Chopra and Captain Banza, stood off to the side, observing the festivities with interest. The Earthers' chief engineer, Commander Pham, would arrive in the coming days to begin overhauling Corell's infrastructure, as he was currently overseeing at Fera. It included running water to all parts of the palace, more artificial lighting, temperature controls, and waste disposal. His advance teams were already at work, beginning the installation of sterilization pads throughout the inner keep. The pads extended a luminous green field above their small surface that cleansed whatever flesh or object that passed through it. It provided a thorough and efficient substitute for bathing. They constructed similar fields above containment cubes, which collected human waste, breaking down the roughage into its base chemical compounds, removing the odor that always permeated such large fortresses during full capacity. These were but the first of many gifts the Earthers were to provide their Araxan hosts in the coming years.

The only other guest that was neither Torry nor Macon was Ular, who was visiting the palace as the first emissary of his people, though Lorn knew it was to visit his good friend Lucas, who was still Deva's constant companion. The three of them stood beside their Earther guests. Deva had recently forsaken her allegiance to the Sisterhood, taking up the calling as the high priestess of Yah. Already plans were being made for a grand temple in ancient Tarelia, the site having been selected by Queen Deliea as the future capital of their new realm.

King Mortus stood at his side, sharing his place upon the dais, while the queen mingled with the guests. He noticed Squid and Torg speaking with one another along the wall to his right. He half expected Orlom to be standing there beside the craggy master of arms, the young gorilla his constant shadow whenever their paths crossed. Orlom visited the palace several times since the Oddigem, finding whatever excuse he could to stowaway on a transport to call upon *Coach,* as he liked to refer to Torg. Torg would never admit to it, but Lorn knew he was very fond of Orlom. He couldn't help but smile, recalling all of their interactions.

"Something amuses you, I see," Mortus said, looking out over the crowd, wondering the source of Lorn's mirth.

"I was hoping Orlom was here. I believe Torg longs for his company."

"Like a rock in his boot, more like." Mortus shook his head.

"He was not the only one to make a friend on our journeys," Lorn reminded him, sparing a glance to Tessa, who was gifted a lovely emerald gown from Deliea. Her hair was beautifully set, the now abundant light in the chamber illuminating her face in all its glory. She was long in years but retained the tranquil beauty that most Araxan women kept in their elder years. Lorn couldn't help noticing Mortus following her with his eyes as she moved about the floor, greeting one guest after another. Since Galen penned the ballad of her after the breaking of the second siege, she had become a legend of sort among the people. Everyone felt a part of her story, for she symbolized complete sacrifice to the greater cause.

"Aye" was all Mortus could manage to say without revealing his heart. Lorn could see it in his eyes, the fondness for her. He was betrothed to the daughter of Vintor Ornovis, Regent of Cagan, as per the treaty they agreed upon outside the walls of Fleace so long ago.

"The intent of our treaty was to bind each of us to a lady of the other realm. We could set aside your betrothal to Lady Illana Ornovis if you find another to your liking," Lorn offered.

"We are both beyond our years, and she could not provide heirs, but I can think of no other I would rather spend my last days with," Mortus said, his eyes fixed upon Tessa.

"Prince Jentra would have to forgo the uncles and aunts you could provide him, but I think he would be pleased to see you happy," Lorn said, sparing a glance to his infant son, who was held in the arms of a nursemaid along the side of the dais. She was accompanied by other maids holding Cronus and Ilesa's infant daughters, the three children behaving quite well among the noisy hall.

"The Lady Illana will be better served with a man nearer her age," Mortus said, giving him a look before descending the dais to seek out Tessa.

Lorn laughed as he watched Mortus approach Tessa, drawing her to the center of the chamber to dance, her eyes brightening with his invite. A small army of musicians positioned in the far corner of the chamber provided the tranquil melodies suited to the occasion. Other couples moved to the center floor, joining the Macon King. Lorn locked eyes with his beloved wife, regarding each other knowingly, before setting out to their intended task. He followed her cue, descending the dais to seek out General Fonis, the aged commander of the Torry 2nd Army. He quickly found him among the guests, accompanied by his lovely daughter, the Lady Enora.

"General," Lorn greeted his stalwart commander, who spent the latter days of the war guarding Central City and the western approaches of the realm.

"My King." Fonis bowed. He attended the gathering at the behest of Lorn, a knowing look passing between them. His daughter stood dutifully at his side, having traveled to Corell long before to serve as a lady-in-waiting to Queen Deliea. It was Lorn that asked the general to keep Enora's betrothal neutral until the war's end, a fact that was unknown to her. Had Lorn perished in the war, then Queen Deliea would have overseen this task without him. Thankfully, he lived and looked forward to playing his small role in what he had long ago planned.

"General, would your daughter accept a dance with her king?" Lorn asked, receiving an enthusiastic response as Enora curtsied and accepted his offered hand.

He drew her toward the center of the floor, joining the growing crowd of couples. He appraised her beauty with a discerning eye, noting her smooth olive complexion and vibrant green eyes, with lush auburn hair framing her lovely face.

"You honor me, My King." She smiled as they moved across the floor.

"We are old friends, Enora. It is I who am honored to share a dance with the daughter of a great commander, as well as a dear friend I have known since we were children."

"Yes, we are old enough friends that I know when you are being mischief. You are about something, which leaves me to question what that is?" She smiled sweetly, masking her racing heart.

"You are far too clever, Enora. I have a friend who I wish to formally introduce if you are agreeable to accept," he said, his request not surprising her in the least.

"A friend? I am to guess he is not one of our many mutual affiliations?"

"He is not. He is Macon, and a general. A general of great ability and renown, and quite charming if you can look past his flamboyant facade, which he often employs," Lorn warned her.

"He sounds interesting and dangerous, or appears to be, is that what you are saying?"

"Only appears to be. He is a very good man who has fought bravely at my side for some time now."

"If you speak highly of him, then how can I judge him poorly? Lead the way, My King." Enora smiled.

"As you command, my dear Enora." Lorn smiled in turn, leading her across the floor where Queen Deliea was dancing, partnered with the man in question.

The two couples paused as Lorn and Deliea stepped away from their respective partners.

"Lady Enora Fonis, I present General Dadeus Ciyon," Deliea introduced them, before taking her husband's hand, letting him lead her in the next dance, leaving the two of them to stare at one another before Dadeus remembered himself.

"My Lady Enora, would you care to dance?" He bowed at the waist, offering his hand.

"It would be my pleasure, General Ciyon."

"Would you agree to address me as Dadeus, my lady?" he asked, leading her across the floor.

"If you are agreeable to refer to me as Enora," she said, admiring his easy charm.

Deliea tried to steal a glance at the couple as Lorn led her away, circling her about the floor as they danced, most in the great hall oblivious to their attempt at matchmaking.

"I believe you are enjoying this more than I, My Queen." Lorn smiled, looking down into her bright eyes, eyes that were constantly looking past his shoulder to see how they were faring.

"I have been anticipating this long before the Oddigem, My King, as you left me this request. It was one of the few distractions I took pleasure in while fearing you would die on your grand *adventure*," she reminded him.

"I have been thinking of this since the treaty of Fleace," Lorn said, referencing the agreement of forced nuptials between their two realms. It was a vital means of uniting their peoples into one homogenous kingdom, which their son would one day rule.

She gave him a look as they danced, shaking her head as a flirtatious smile touched her lips.

"Something amuses, My Queen?"

"The legendary King Lorn, who's renowned throughout the land as a cunning leader and brave warrior, is truly but a simple romantic. How quaint." She smiled.

"Indeed," he confessed, sharing her smile. He couldn't help but wonder if this was a dream, considering all that they endured. What joy awaited them after such sacrifice? What blessings has Yah bestowed upon them, that are too numerous to count? Lorn reflected on this as the music played, and he held his beloved Queen in his arms as they danced. And yet, he almost forgot the true purpose of the night's celebration, the union of Cronus and Ilesa. They were joined in matrimony in the throne room that morn and were the guests of honor in the great hall at the outset, before retiring to their chambers.

He wondered if they were truly happy, considering the loss that plagued each of their hearts. Theirs was not the love of romantic poems and swooning love songs. Theirs was the love of mutual affection and respect, sharing their grief with the only person who truly understood their pain. It was Lorn that placed Ilesa's hand in Cronus', sealing their union before the eyes of the realm, earlier that morn.

"You are thinking again." Deliea's voice drew him from his thoughts.

"Indeed," he again confessed, smiling again into her eyes as they moved across the floor.

"This is a night of celebration. Leave your troubles for tomorrow, my love. Take pleasure in these precious moments," she said, returning his loving gaze.

"I have a wise queen."

"Indeed." She used his own phrase, drawing another smile for the effort.

* * *

As the night grew late, Deva made her way to the battlements, the crisp winter air clearing her thoughts as she tucked her arms beneath her, leaning upon the parapet. The starry sky provided a clear view of the surrounding lands as she stood upon the north wall of the inner keep, moonlight playing off the tower of Celenia off her right, illuminating its white tower with an ethereal glow. The Earthers' artificial lighting had yet to be placed upon the outer sections of the palace. She was thankful, for the unnatural light would interrupt the tranquil serenity she felt standing upon the storied battlements. She felt Lucas' eyes upon her, standing watch over her, as he was wont to do.

"You may join me if you wish," she offered, calling him forth from the shadows.

"It is easier to guard you from where I was standing," Lucas said, stepping to her side.

"The enemy have been destroyed, Lucas. There is little danger now. Why do you stay?" she asked, sparing him a look from the corner of her eyes, her head staring forward as if looking for something in the distance.

"As I have said, King Lorn tasked me to guard you. I shall not relent until he relieves me of that task," he said, using duty to shield his heart.

"I am not a lady of the court who requires your propriety to guard her virtue and station, Lucas. I am a warrior bred and raised, the heir to a great house of the Sisterhood. My mother was a cruel mistress, with many vices, but she instilled in me a harsh candor, to speak forthright and pointed. I shall speak with our king to release you of this duty. If you should remain, it will be of your own volition," she said, looking at him directly, her intention clear as a sunlit sky.

"Do you wish that I remain with you?" he asked.

"I do not require a guard, Lucas, and I desire that you remain by my side." She left unsaid what was obvious, though he was too proper or too naïve to advance.

"Oh, I would like…" he stammered.

"Are all Torry men so blind?" She rolled her eyes, before planting a kiss to his cheek.

"You like me?" he stupidly asked, with an equally stupid grin.

Deva shook her head, her eyes growing frustratingly moist. She had forsaken everything to follow the path Yah set for her. She lost her parents, her title and her brother. She had no one now. She had nothing but her duty and a greater purpose. Here stood the only person who was truly her friend, a friend who was in truth so much more. He was the only one who truly knew the new Deva. He was the only one she knew favored her company. He no longer judged her by her past, something she was never certain of with others. Though Terin forgave her, there would always be a wall between them, as there was with so many. With Lucas, she had journeyed beside him from Notsu to the Oddigem, enduring the hardships of the trail beside one another. He sparred with her, fought beside her, and guarded her with his life. He was everything that she thought she wanted in Terin, but more so, for he returned her ardor freely.

"*Like* is such a small word for what I feel, Lucas." She caressed his cheek, looking deeply into his eyes.

There, upon the battlements of Corell, Lucas took Deva into his arms, kissing the woman who would be his wife.

Unbeknownst to them, another pair watched them from Zar Crest, the observation platform that rose above the inner keep, where General Bode was struck down by Morac during the second siege of Corell.

* * *

"Enemies to lovers, 'tis a tale as old as time," Dr. Aditi Chopra said, watching Lucas embrace Deva below.

"Another story worthy of song, my lady," Galen opined, standing at her side upon Zar Crest, the winter air circling about the platform. He and the good doctor struck up an interesting conversation in the great hall, continuing their discussion as Galen led her to the storied observation platform, giving her a generous view of Corell's surrounding battlements, the source of so many of the visions she chronicled from the crews of the *Solis* and *Stalingrad*.

"You have no lack of stories to tell, Galen. I have compiled a comprehensive narrative of events, if our visions are fully accurate, and I have yet to find a single discrepancy, that lends to the credence that the visions were truly inspired by the entity we accept is Yah. I would like a fresh pair of eyes to look over my data, eyes that are both native to Arax and belong to a skilled orator. I can think of no one better than the legendary Galen the Minstrel," Aditi said.

"I would be deeply honored to review your chronicles, my dear lady. Would this require my presence aboard your primary vessel?" Galen asked, hoping to see the *Stalingrad* with his own eyes.

"It would be easier for us to review my findings, so yes. I will require Captain Banza's approval, but he should allow it."

"Splendid. A full telling of events would greatly serve posterity. I would have to expand upon my original intent of penning ballads of various events. For a task this grand, a comprehensive and sequential chronicle of events would best serve my audience. Even a single play would fail to fully address the volume of events. This could be the work of a lifetime." Galen's eyes shone with a faraway look.

"Perhaps a lifetime is overstated, but a grand endeavor it certainly is. I would be happy to help and can provide the information you require and the means to produce multiple copies," she offered.

"Splendid. Think of it, my lady, bards will sing of this tale long after I am dead using the script I pen." Galen smiled at the thought.

"You need only find a name for this tale, Galen, one that summarizes the story and draws the listener's attention."

"A title worthy of such a work," Galen mused, scratching his chin.

* * *

Ilesa stood at the window of their chamber, staring at the stars, lost in thought, a sense of guilt and failure twisting inside her like iron barbs. She ran her fingers over the small device in her hands, the precious gift Admiral Kruger had given her. Cronus sat on the bed behind her, his heart equally tormented as her own. 'Twas their wedding night, a time of celebration and renewal, but their loss hung over them like a deathly pall. They hoped it would be easier than this, but such was their folly. Their friends gave their blessing to this union, with Raven and his crew gifting them all of Kato's wealth, as well as their archives of Kato and Leanna they had gathered during their times aboard the *Stenox*. They were currently attending other tasks vital to the reordering of their world, but they sent their regards in the days before, visiting them at Corell.

Terin and Corry were also absent, the affairs of state at Fera keeping them there. Corry gifted them her royal quarters for their wedding night, this spacious and cozy chamber feeling nothing like the stone fortress it rested in. If her mind were not elsewhere, she would better appreciate the tranquil setting of the Princess' chamber, with Porian molding casing the windows, and rich furnishings of Paccel and Lupec wood, adorned with silver along their edging. A large, canopied bed centered the chamber with calnesian sheets and thick furs. A large hearth occupied the far wall, with fur carpets breaking up the white stone floor. Corry gifted her several gowns for the ceremony and celebrations that followed, while Terin gifted Cronus a belt of silver daggers from the treasury of Fera, each finely crafted, forged for an ancient king that was long forgotten. Terin could think of no one more worthy to wear it than his friend. Perhaps the greatest gift Cronus received was the freedom and restoration of his three remaining comrades that were held captive in the dungeons of Fera, Safed, Tarlan and Geornon. They each suffered greatly at the Benotrists' hands, enduring hardship, gelding, and humiliation. It was Jonas that secured their release from their hardships and protected them until victory was attained. The Earthers' regenerators restored what the gelders had taken, healing their bodies, though their minds would always bear the scars of their torment.

Despite all these gifts and friendships, Ilesa and Cronus were tortured by the past. They could not consummate their union, stricken with guilt over their lost loves. Ilesa couldn't help but think of Kato, his warm brown eyes staring back at her whenever she tried to embrace Cronus. She knew Cronus was equally afflicted, seeing Leanna whenever he tried to comfort her.

"Forgive my failure, Cronus." Ilesa sighed, unable to turn and look at him.

He wanted to set her at ease, to say there was nothing to forgive, but such words were meaningless to a broken heart. He eased himself off the bed, stepping closer, placing a gentle hand to her shoulder. She turned, staring up into his green eyes, eyes that so easily set her at ease.

"We have time. There is no one here but you and I."

"Time?" she asked.

"It doesn't have to be tonight, or tomorrow, or ever, if you are troubled." He gave her the gentlest smile, one equally torn as she.

"And what sort of marriage would that be? You deserve a woman who can give of herself fully. You are the kindest, most decent man I know, Cronus, and the most handsome."

"No, there are many more handsome than I." He softly grinned.

"Not in my eyes, or any of the ladies of the court, I assure you. You deserve a wife that appreciates all that you offer, not a broken-hearted woman lamenting her dead husband."

"I can make the same argument with you, Ilesa. You deserve a husband that can give to you fully, not a broken-hearted man pining for his dead wife."

She loved him for that, for his understanding and genuine decency. In another world or lifetime, winning his heart would have been her greatest joy. How unfair was life that this should be their fate, each of them losing a great amount of themselves with their lovers' deaths. Kato did say she would love again, asking that she live on after he was gone. She also had a daughter to raise, Kato's daughter, a daughter that needed a father, just as little Maura needed a mother.

To be a mother to Cronus' daughter, then she needed to be a wife to Cronus. Just as she was about to embrace him and consummate her vows, he found a way to surprise her again.

"Allow me," Cronus said, taking the device from her hands, the precious gift she clung to with desperate care. The object was a small oval-shaped device that held a myriad of information, each uniquely tailored to them. He received a similar object from Brokov and Lorken, a collection of images of Leanna during her time upon the *Stenox*. Whenever he desired, a holographic image of his beloved projected from the device. She often stood alone, or interacted with the others, including the brief time they spent together upon his reaching Tro after fleeing Fera. His favorite sequence was her singing, standing upon the stern of the *Stenox* as he held her....

> *He blew a kiss across the still water*
> *He took my hand as we walked along*
> *He vowed to return from war if it took him*
> *He vowed to return and hear my fair song...*

Her words repeated in his memory, the beginning verse in her marital vow, the words she penned for him, expressing her love. It was his fondest memory of Leanna, the memory that always brought him to tears. It was ironic that that memory was captured by the Earthers' device they had gifted him, as if that memory should forever be immortalized. He wondered what memories Ilesa's device had of Kato that caused her to desperately cling to it?

He lifted her device, selecting her most viewed item. An image of an elderly gentlemen who appeared similar to Kato, projected into the middle of the room, his kindly eyes staring back at them, though it was meant for Kato.

"This was the last message Kato received from Earth, but he never received it as he was lost before it could be forwarded from the *Stalingrad*. The man is his grandfather," she said as the man began to sing, his voice retaining a timber that defied his age. The song was a lively tune, a simple melody that reminded her so much of Kato, perhaps more than any visual representation could ever import.

"He loved music," Cronus said, finding the tune strangely inviting.

"The song is called *Sukiyaki*, sung by an ancient musician from Kato's native isle named Kyu Sakamoto. Kato's grandfather loved music, teaching Kato melodies from all around their world, like *Loch Lomond* and *Day Dream Believer*, but this one is from his home, and every time I hear it, I can see Kato as a young boy sitting at his grandfather's side listening attentively as he sang," Ilesa explained, wiping a tear from her eye, hating that she was overcome with emotion for her lost husband while denying her current husband his rightful place. Again, Cronus surprised her, leading her to their bed, holding the device as they climbed under the furs. There he lay, drawing her to rest her head upon his chest as he tucked his arm beneath her, holding her close as they listened.

They lay there all night, falling asleep in each other's arms. They did not consummate their union that night, or the next, but did so in time. They would have three more children between them, two sons and a daughter, while also adopting Dougar, all of them coming together in their new family. Cronus and Ilesa lived a long and wonderful life, often visiting their friends, or receiving them. Torg Vantel would eventually pass his position as Commander of the Torry Elite to Cronus, breaking his familial line's connection to the ancient post. Cronus and Ilesa would never forget Leanna and Kato, sharing their love for them through their children. After years of war and hardship, Cronus lived a life of contentment and peace, wed to a woman that followed him into battle and saved his life after he saved Raven.

CHAPTER 21

The Grand Council of Arax

At the conclusion of the Grand Council, the parties agreed to establishing a permanent Grand Council to oversee the collective defense of Arax, establish fixed geographical areas of control for each council member, and to mitigate all differences that might arise between members. Each member kingdom, republic, plutocracy or city state would provide a representative to the council, whose temporary location was to be at Fera until a permanent site could be established. It was Terin that asked that Squid be appointed as the first named chief of the council. The council would oversee the distribution of the Earthers' technology, particularly power cubes and weapon systems, which required intense training and oversight.

The Earthers explained at the first council their intention to establish a new home on the northern continent where the gargoyle invasion had originated. They detailed their discovery on the continent of the materials vital to the production of Rendarium and Trundusium, which would be first used to build space fighter aircraft and distributed to each member state of the council. The larger realms would be given a full squadron of fighters, and the lesser members given fewer based on their size. Their pilots would require intense training. In the years to follow, more squadrons would be added to each member, and eventually a second or third battle carrier and the construction modules required for their completion. Transport craft, which required few rare materials in their construction, and were easily produced, would be provided first, giving the Araxans experience in flight.

The Earthers also disclosed the discovery of other continents on the planet, many inhabited, including a matriarchal realm across the western sea. The council agreed to leave these lands unexplored for the current time, revisiting the question of first contact for a later date.

The Earthers' detailed plans to terraform and colonize the other planets in the Araxan star system, eventually expanding to neighboring systems, though the process would take many decades or centuries to complete and require the efforts of all members of the Grand Council, whose current loose unity would be a test for the collaboration needed to expand off planet. It was decided to establish academies of science and learning across Arax. The populace needed to be educated on the three thousand years of technological and sociological advancements that separated them from the Earthers, before they could advance into a modern age. They needed to proceed with caution in bringing about such sudden changes to their primitive world. Once knowledge began to be released, it could rapidly spread beyond their control, causing unforeseen complications.

Alen

Following the events of the Grand Council, Alen assumed his post as regent of the eastern half of the Northern Kingdom, wedding the daughter of the regent of Nisin, Davin Gorel. He would serve in that esteemed role well into his fifth decade before relenting, naming a capable successor from among the populace. As Terin's example, he decreed that no future regent could name a successor from their direct line. He sired four daughters, two of which served as pilots in the Northern Kingdom's second fighter squadron. He and Terin remained close friends through the years, with Alen visiting Terin at his home many times, well into his elder days. Despite his humble origin, the people always lauded him as a fierce rebel leader of great renown, and a hero of the realm.

Prince Yanku

Prince Yanku, the eldest son of Emperor Yangu of Yatin, suffered greatly upon his capture after ordering the fateful charge at Salamin Valley in the earlier stages of the great war. He was enslaved and gelded, before being sold to a wealthy Benotrist merchant at Laycrom. After the victory at the Oddigem, all the slaves held in the former Benotrist Empire were freed. Upon learning of his father's fate, the Yatin Emperor having been executed by his own people, Yanku chose to remain in the house of his former mistress, whose husband was slain during the war.

Tro Harbor

Upon his return from the Grand Council, Kaly relayed the details he agreed to on behalf the ruling families. They reluctantly agreed to freeing their slaves in exchange for the Earthers gifts. The lone exception being slaves taken as spouses, as was practiced throughout Arax, especially the Sisterhood. Klen Adine retained his role as magistrate of the harbor for another eight years, before accepting an ambassadorship to the Earthers' home continent, the former holdfast of the gargoyles that came from across the northern sea. Marcus Talana, head of House Talana, and father of Lorken's wife Jenna, reconciled with his daughter. Lorken and Jenna would visit the eastern port over the years, while adding three more children to their growing family. The ruling families power eventually gave way to a more representative ruling council as Tro's territory expanded along the eastern coast. They would hold a post on the Grand Council of Arax, giving their voice to the direction of Arax's collective defense and eventual exploration and expansion.

Nayboria

King Lichu returned from the war to a hero's welcome, with most of his people given visions of what transpired at the Oddigem. As true to his word, he wed his eldest son to the daughter of a great house of Sawyer, joining their Tarelian bloodline to his royal line. After the events of the Oddigem and the Grand Council, the Jenaii decided to withdraw their occupation of Non. Three years after the events of the Oddigem, Cronus returned the *Sword of the Stars* to King Lichu, the very sword he took from Dethine's dead hand. King Lichu renamed Nayboria the Southern Kingdom, reestablishing its Tarelian origin. His coastal lands were returned that were taken by the Casian League, while his eastern borders expanded to the approaches of Barbeario and the Lone Hills.

Casian League

General Motchi, commander of the 2nd Casian Army, returned to Teris, greeted by thunderous cheers. He served as the first delegate to the Grand Council before the ruling forum of the Casian League could appoint a replacement. His army's march across the Benotrist Empire to the Oddigem became a source of pride to their people. The following years saw the Casians abandon their martial means of exploiting trade to adopting a peacemaker role among the realms of Arax. They agreed to return their coastal conquests to Nayboria and fostered peaceful trade among all the cities of the southern coast of Arax. The Earthers provided weapons and training to outfit their first ground and air units armed with the new technology. Like their counterparts, they were forced to free all slaves held within their consortium. Their wooden merchant ships soon gave way to advanced hull design and materials, along with free energy propulsion, revolutionizing their transportation and economy. They eagerly embraced the Earthers objective to terraform and colonize the nearby planets and star systems, establishing multiple academies of science in every major city of their league.

Notsu

The city of Notsu was gradually reborn from the devastation wrought by Morac. In the years that followed, its population blossomed to nearly one hundred thousand, as the Earthers technology brought their surrounding lands to life with agricultural technology. Retaining their geographical position straddling the roads connecting the regions of Nisin, Tro and Corell, Notsu became a powerful city state and member of the Grand Council. In time, they expanded, reestablishing the city of Bacel, raising their sister city from the ashes.

Yatin

The Yatin peoples reorganized their lands into the Western Kingdom, restoring the Tarelian realm of old. The desire of naming a new king died with the death of the emperor Yangu III, whose brutal treatment of his people dispelled the notion that any one man should hold such authority over the people ever again. Generals Yoria and Yitia oversaw the Council of Mosar, where the leaders of the various factions within Yatin agreed upon a new ruling order, deciding upon a governing tribunal, with a separate judiciary to oversee the laws of the realm. In time, Tyro gifted the Western Kingdom one of his *Swords of Light*, returning the *Sword of the Stars* that was lost by King Telfin III in the year 520, which preceded the fall of the Western Kingdom to the invading Yatins. The sword was always wielded by the finest blade master in the land, which served as a source of pride among the people. King Lorn would often visit the realm throughout the years, where he was warmly received by the people, and would always place a voli upon the memorial where Kato was slain in remembrance of his fallen friend. The site became hallowed ground among the people of the realm, a symbol of the ever-lasting friendship of the Torries, Yatins and Earthers.

The Ape Republic

President Matuzak and his warriors returned from battle to a hero's welcome, the streets of Torn filled with throngs of citizens shouting their praises. As agreed upon at the founding of their republic, Matuzak would serve only one term as president, setting the precedent for the peaceful transfer of power from one leader to the next. Upon completing his term, Matuzak established his own brewery, partnering with Admiral Kruger, who provided the ingredients for his favored Bavarian lagers. The small brew house positioned along the wharves of Torn became a favored watering hole for visitors from all over Arax. Eventually **Matuzak's Lagers** became the drink of choice for the pilots and warriors across Arax. New brew houses were established in nearly every city on the continent.

Argos would continue his travels with Raven for a time, before returning home, where he took up coaching football, leading his teams to multiple championships in the growing Araxan League. With humans and Enoructans joining the league, teams spread across Arax. Humans and Enoructans excelled at the skill positions, but only Earth humans could compete with apes along the line. Argos was the first coach to fully integrate the different species into one team, dominating the early years of the league by utilizing the strengths of each group to their specific roles. In a strange twist of fate, posterity would recognize Argos more for his coaching legend than his exploits in the great war.

The apes would remain the only Araxan Republic on the Grand Council for five decades until the other realms began to transition to their form of governance. The apes would enjoy the closest friendship to the new Earth colony, with many of their citizens taking up residence in the Earthers' continent and serving aboard the *Stalingrad*. Though the Earthers offered the same courtesy to the other Araxan realms, the apes represented the greater portion of volunteers. The apes also received the first squadron of space fighters the Earthers produced, with the youngest and most astute warriors selected to pilot them, each undergoing extensive training.

All the crew members of the *Stenox* held a special place in the hearts of the ape republic, each retaining their honorary citizenship among their simian friends. They would each visit the republic through the years, sharing pints of ale and lager over hearty meals, bellowing drinking songs alongside their ape hosts. Lorken, Brokov and Raven's children would all consider Matuzak and Argos their kin, looking to their next visit whenever the current one ended. Cronus and Terin would also visit whenever time allowed, as well as Zem.

Enoructa

Of all the peoples of Arax, the Enoructans remained the most insular, though in the years that followed the events at the Oddigem, they eventually embraced a more prominent role in the coming age. The Earthers advanced technology rapidly changed their tribal society, with on time communications and rapid transportation connecting them to each other as well as all parts of the continent. As Arax progressed into the space faring age, Enoructans were well represented in the crews of the joint Araxan expeditions, with a particular proclivity for navigation. It would be expected to find nearly half the Araxan navigators to be Enoructan.

Of all the Enoructans to participate in the great war, none were as famous or renowned as Ular. His name was known throughout Arax, as well as his many exploits. Despite his many deeds and adventures, it was his friendship with Lucas that defined him in the eyes of the world. He stood as Lucas' second when he eventually wed Deva and visited his friend many times through the years. Their children would even serve together aboard the first Araxan Battle Carrier, the *Noddegamra*, which launched three decades after the Oddigem.

The Jenaii

The Jenaii returned to their kingdom, content that their ancient quest to vanquish the gargoyles had been completed. Elos held to his promise to Terin and served on the overruling tribunal of the Northern Kingdom for the time agreed. He remained close friends with Terin through the years, and visited him frequently, though never for long, as was his nature. He would one day pass on the *Sword of the Moon* to another Jenaii warrior who proved himself most worthy. Upon learning that their native continent was still inhabited by their ancient kin, many Jenaii set off to return. In time, all the Jenaii would eventually return to their ancestral home, though they would retain a place on the Grand Council and offer up volunteers for the collective defense of Arax, and crew members of the ships of the Araxan space fleet as each vessel was commissioned.

Ella

Ella mourned the death of Ben Thorton, remaining aboard the *Stenox* for a time, before she was reunited with her family. Through Dr. Chopra's archives of the dreams she chronicled, she was able to locate Ella's kin in the port city of Tinsay. True to his word, Thorton arranged their safe passage there during the Yatin invasion, where they were given protected status. After the fall of Tinsay to the combined Sisterhood, Torry and Yatin armies, Ella's family remained under the occupation of the 3rd Sisterhood Army, while the others marched east. It was then her eldest brother was taken as a mate by a commander of unit in the Sisterhood Army and transported to Bansoch with thousands of other male captives. Though the Earthers would not bargain with the realms of Arax unless they planned the emancipation of labor slaves, this did not extend to slaves taken as spouses. Ella was able to reunite with her remaining kin, living for a time in the northern port city. Eventually she was invited aboard the *Stalingrad,* where she performed for the pilots of the battle carrier, her prowess as a dancer and singer widely known throughout the fleet, mostly through their visions. It was there she sang in the very lounge that Jennifer sang for Ben Thorton so long ago. It was there she met a pilot from Green Squadron, a Finnish Lieutenant named Onni Hanninen, who asked her to dance. They would eventually wed. She bore him three children and continued with her singing, her fame spreading across Arax as her songs were projected across the mass communications the Earthers introduced and provided to the people of each realm. Her silken voice and gentle face were projected on holo vids in every home of Arax, her fame as a singer eventually exceeding the renown of most of the participants in the great war.

Ella would eventually visit the site where Ben Thorton perished, placing a blue-stemmed voli upon the marker Raven erected for his grave, though no part of his friend remained to be buried there. She spoke a few quiet words over the grave, though no one could hear what she said, nor would she ever reveal what they were.

Dougar

True to their word, Cronus and Ilesa adopted Dougar, formally bringing him into their growing family. When they first asked him if he would be their son, he wept, embracing them so tightly they thought he might never let go. He helped raise both of their daughters, and the children that followed from their union. He became Cronus' shadow, learning the skills of the warrior, while also learning to read and write under Ilesa's loving instruction. Dougar was chosen by King Lorn to be among the first fighter pilots in the newly formed Tarelian squadrons, undergoing years of instruction before the new craft were delivered. He would eventually serve in the joint Araxan defense forces, and later command the first Araxan launched battle carrier, the *Noddegamra*. He kept the Stetson Ben Thorton had placed on his head that fateful day north of the Oddigem and wore it upon the bridge of the *Noddegamra* throughout his years of command. Every day that he lived he fondly recalled the moment when Prince Lorn drew him from the crowd at Fleace, setting him upon his mount and taking him into his world. It was this small act of kindness, small for Lorn, but world-changing for Dougar, that transformed his life in ways no one could have foreseen. He never forgot that kindness, repeating Lorn's generous act ten thousand times over with his every interaction with those around him. One day his grandchildren would lead expeditions, settling on terraformed worlds in the surrounding star systems.

Criose

After the events of the Oddigem, Criose led the first fully trained unit in Earther small arms in the Torry 1st Army. He underwent intense training in the first established space marine academy in New Brussels, the capital of the Earther's home continent. He would be the first of many to pass through its legendary corridors, suffering the tutelage of the Earther marine cadre. He would eventually oversee the establishment of the first academy on the main continent in Cagan Harbor. Like all of Terin's friends, he too would visit him throughout the years, recalling their times in captivity on Darna's estate. He and Terin would always lament the death of Guilen, whose life offered so much promise after all he endured.

Captain Veneva

The slaver captain that sold Terin into bondage at Bansoch continued her miserable trade in human flesh throughout the great war, before discovering the bounty Princess Corry placed upon her head. Once the events of the Oddigem came to be known throughout Arax, Captain Veneva raised her sails, setting off across the western sea, never to be seen again.

Teso and Zulon

The small kingdoms of Teso and Zulon retained their close kinship with the Macon-Torry realm, with the heirs of each realm wedding the younger daughters of King Mortus. With the advance of technology and learning that defined the coming age, the borders of the two realms eventually bled into the new Tarelian nation that arose from the union of Macon and Torry, culminating in formal union five decades after the Battle of the Oddigem.

Nels Draken

Nels Draken remained in the service to the Benotrist Empire and then the new Northern Kingdom, forever forsaking the path of the free sword that defined his existence before he joined with Tyro. He retained his place among the new kingdom's high elite, eventually heading the first units equipped with the Earthers' small arms. He and Raven eventually agreed to an uneasy peace between them, though he would make friends with the many other Earthers he came to know. He went on to wed a Benotrist maiden from Laycrom, who birthed three sons and a daughter. He would later join the first off-planet expedition, joining a team of Araxans and Earthers to explore their hostile sister world Dexos, the celestial body the ancients believed was a wandering star, but was in fact the third planet in their star system.

Safed, Tarlan and Geornon

Cronus' men that were imprisoned, tortured and enslaved upon their capture at Tuft's Mountain, and later protected by Jonas and Valera, were fully restored by the Earthers' regenerators. They briefly returned to their native Torry realm to see to their kin before returning to Fera, where they served as Valera's personal guard for the rest of her days. Safed and Geornon wed two of Valera's handmaids that she also protected during her time as Tyro's captive. Like Cronus, none ever spoke of the suffering they endured in the dungeons of the Black Castle.

Jacin Tomac

Jacin Tomac, the famed Torry cavalry commander of unit, fought in nearly all the great battles of the great war. He was first known for Terin rescuing him when he attempted to reach Corell during the first siege of the fortress, when his ocran was slain, pinning him beneath his mount. Terin earned Corry's ire for risking his life, racing from the north gate of Corell to save Jacin. The daring maneuver earned Terin Jacin's eternal friendship. In later years Jacin served in the Araxan defense forces, commanding the first Araxan Space Marine Division. His youngest daughter would go on to wed Terin's third eldest son, joining their families. Once the first child was born of their union, Corry would realize the impulse in Terin to risk his life saving Jacin that eventful day. It was but further proof that Terin was driven to take actions that served a greater purpose, when it would not appear so at the time.

Ben Thorton's Grave

Every year, Raven would visit his friend's grave alone, always on the anniversary of the battle. There was no body to lay beneath the marker where he fell as nothing remained to place there. Raven would simply stand upon that small hillside, saying a few words that only he would know, refusing to share what he said with anyone. Legend would have it that if one stood upon that hallowed ground in the evening of a late autumn day, one could hear a woman's voice singing the *Streets of Laredo*, a hauntingly beautiful voice that would carry in the wind.

Torg Vantel

Terin's grandfather eventually passed his title of Commander of the Torry Elite to Cronus, removing it from his ancestorial line for all time. He would spend the years after the war visiting his dear Valera at Fera, where she resided as a critical voice in the new Northern Kingdom. He also spent equal time visiting his son at their ancestorial home of Cropus and visiting Terin and Corry at their home. He later helped Criose in the establishment of the first Araxan Marine academy, serving as its first commandant. His unusual friendship with Orlom would continue for the rest of his days, with the young gorilla joining him at the academy for several years. He would eventually pass in his sleep at a very old age. Word of his death was met with great sadness to all the peoples of Arax. As he requested, he was buried at the Oddigem Valley with all the others that had fallen, his brothers and sisters in arms, as he would call them. Everyone who had fought there, gathered upon that day to commemorate their lost friend. As the years went by, nearly everyone that fought there would ask to be buried in that place alongside their comrades.

CHAPTER 22

Bansoch.
Six Earth standard months after the battle of Noddegamra.

An early morning mist hung in the spring air as Lucella Sarelis, captain of Queen Letha's royal guard, surveyed the targets downrange. She was appointed by her queen to lead the first unit of federation warriors equipped with Earther small arms, each equipped with laser rifles and pistols. Gone were their traditional uniform tunics, greaves, mail and swords. They were now outfitted with black space armored suits with black trousers, domed helmets and pistol belts, with holsters riding their strong side. Their new attire looked even more intimidating than Captain Raven and his roguish crew. In all her years in service to the queen, Lucella would never have imagined she would undertake such an assignment. Like all those on Arax, her world was changing faster than she could ever comprehend.

"You have to squeeze the trigger, not jerk it! Do it again, Jara!" 1ˢᵗ Sgt. Hank Simson of the *Stalingrad's* space marines bellowed, kneeling beside the prone form of the warrior in question, Jara Dars of the 3ʳᵈ Flax of the 1ˢᵗ Unit.

Young Jara peered through her scope, firing another blast, striking nearer the mark on the circled target down range, with the slope of the far ridge rising behind the target. The Earthers built the firing range inland of the harbor, keeping downrange clear of any dwellings. Like all warriors of the Sisterhood, Jara was unaccustomed to taking instruction from a male, but 1ˢᵗ Sgt. Simson was unlike any male she ever dealt with, even in the war. The man looked far more intimidating than Captain Raven, Lorken or Brokov, who she encountered many times. Despite his antics, Raven was more comical than intimidating once you got to know him. Sgt Simson, on the other hand, looked as if he was cut from stone, with his large jutting chin and bulging neck.

"Better, now do it again!" Hank ordered, the next shot landing somewhere in between the previous two. He told her to keep shooting until she mastered the process, before gaining his feet as Lucella Sarelis stepped closer, crossing her arms over her chest.

"What is your opinion on our progress?" Lucella asked, her gaze fixed to the targets downfield.

"Give me two more weeks and you'll have as good a strike team as any on the planet, Captain Sarelis," Hank said, before catching sight of Orlom approaching them from the opposite end of the line. For the life of him, he couldn't believe Raven thought it was a good idea to assign the young gorilla to be his assistant on the range. Before he could protest that idiotic idea, the admiral seconded the suggestion. Of all the people he could have had visions of before the Oddigem, Hank had visions of Orlom. He saw too many reckless acts he and Grigg shared on their journeys aboard the *Stenox*. They were a walking violation of every safety protocol in firearms operation. How Raven didn't see that was beyond him. Now this walking violation was his assistant.

"Your assessment is quite generous, Sgt. Simson," Lucella said, doubting her soldiers were near that level.

"Your soldiers take instruction well, and don't give me any grief," he snorted, recalling his first training assignment on Arax, working the last month training the first ape unit at Gregok, where Orlom spent most of the time arguing stupid points with his fellow gorillas. He lost count on the number of fights he had to break up, resulting in more than one bloody nose and a torn rotator cuff. Despite Orlom's antics, the unit performed above expectations, but that only fueled

Orlom's ego, especially when Admiral Kruger suggested he continue being Hank's assistant.

"He is an acquired taste," Lucella said, using the Earther phrase to aptly describe the young gorilla.

"The only question I have is how in the world did he ever survive the war?" Hank shook his head as Orlom approached.

"This group looks good, boss. Should we rotate Flax 5 and 6 to the firing line?" Orlom asked.

"Make it happen," Hank said as Orlom gave him an Earther salute before bringing Flax 3 and 4 to their feet, sending them back to the staging area.

"Are you mated, 1st Sgt?" Lucella asked once Orlom passed beyond earshot.

"Mated?" He made a face.

"Do you have a wife?" she clarified.

"No, I do not." He wasn't sure how to answer.

"Would you accompany me tonight to the Queen's ball?"

"Me?" he asked, taken aback by her boldness.

"Yes. If you disagree, simply say no," she said with an even tone.

"Your answer?" she pressed.

"Yes."

"Very good."

"I'm not used to women being so direct," he said.

"A warrior of the Sisterhood speaks to what she wants." She left unsaid if he was the son of a citizen, she would have asked his mother for his hand. Of course, the idea that she could compare him to the son of a citizen was ridiculous, considering his build and demeanor. There was no taming a man such as him, and the notion that a woman of her station should choose such a consort was frowned upon before the princess chose Raven. Many of her fellow warriors were now looking to the Earthers for their mates, trying to emulate the queens of old who chose warriors over pampered boys for their consorts. Since the Oddigem, nearly two dozen such pairings had been made, but none of those men compared to the powerful Hank Simson.

"If I go with you tonight, perhaps you can return the favor and give me a ride on your warbird," Hank suggested, knowing she commanded a contingent of the Sisterhood's magantors during the war.

"Bargain struck," Lucella said, clasping his forearm to seal the pact.

*　*　*

The Queen's palace. Bansoch Harbor.

Admiral Kruger stood upon the veranda of the Queen's private chamber, looking out across the bay, and the city below. The hooves of plodding ocran echoing dully in the streets would give way to air skis and hovering craft as the years went on. He took in the tranquil sight of Bansoch as it now stood, knowing change was inevitable. Even now the first signs of that change manifested in the form of artificial lighting, with lamps fueled by ever lasting energy cores spreading out across the city. Nearly every dwelling in the city now had sanitation fields to clean flesh, clothing and dispose of waste. Soon central media and communication would be found in every dwelling on Arax, fueling a myriad of changes to their social order. There was much danger in loosing technology on a civilization so quickly, but he knew they were brought here for a reason, and felt they needed to bring Arax up to their standards of knowledge as quickly as practical.

Feelings. He shook his head at such a notion. Never in his years of command did he ever consider feelings over logic and sound judgement, but now his feelings dominated his thinking ever since he decided to jump to this star system. Whatever omnipotence brought them here was now driving him to share their knowledge with these people.

"Something troubles you, Admiral?" Queen Letha asked, standing off his left, sharing the view of the bay with Taleron beside her.

He regarded her briefly, noting the ease with which she suffered her husband's presence. Whatever barriers that stood between Letha and Tyro over the years were now fallen. They seemed content in each other's presence, which was strange considering all that transpired in the intervening years. Their intimacy was not the firestorm of passion that consumed rekindled love, but more the settled and mature companionship of a couple long married. He spoke with Tyro, now Taleron, enough times to know he had changed in dramatic ways, at least a large part of him had. The rest of him was still very much the same. He was the most complex man he had ever known, with a deep love and loyalty for those he held dear, layered above a cauldron of cold anger, an anger that was caged and subdued by his fierce determination. Had Tyro been born on Earth, he could have been the greatest commander their space fleet ever produced. He reminded Helmut so much of Thorton that it often gave him pause. It was Thorton who intended to do what they were now doing, after he unified Arax under a single banner. In a way, Ben's plan was being implemented, though under a looser umbrella of central control. Despite this, there was still that overriding danger in all of this…

"We are on dangerous ground." He voiced that concern.

"How so?" Letha asked.

"The technology we are sharing with you cannot be undone. Knowledge is like a wild beast freed from a cage. Once it is free, it will roam wide and far, its course as unpredictable as a shifting wind." Helmut sighed.

"Was it not your suggestion to proceed thus?" Letha asked.

"Yes, but not without reservation. I am doing so because I feel it is what Yah desires, and making decisions based on feelings is not in my character." Helmut shook his head.

"Do you suggest we slow the process?" she asked.

"It is too late for that now. The love of knowledge is addictive once it is sparked, and my people have perfected the means to spark that interest," Helmut said, referencing the methods used by their artificial intelligence as it evaluated each individual and catered its education to that individual's thought process. It established a base line of a person's intellect and knowledge, charting a course of education that knew when to accelerate or slow as needed. This process was implemented by information orbs given freely to the populace, distributed as rapidly as they could be produced. There were already two thousand such orbs currently given out in Bansoch, and another seven hundred in the other parts of the Sisterhood. A near equal number was given to the other realms at this point. The plan was to bring the populace to a level of knowledge that those on Earth currently possessed. Once that was accomplished with all the population, then the technologies could be shared. Once the populace received both knowledge and technology, they would be empowered in ways no one could fully predict.

Taleron recalled one of his many discussions with Thorton on this very thing. Ben said there would have to be a time when the people were educated and given technology, and that would force a change in the power structure of the government or even the form of the government.

"Monarchies will give way to other forms of authority," Taleron stated flatly.

"Some perhaps, but we Earthers have seen an endless number of forms of governance, and each has its strengths and weakness. Wise monarchies are effective in quickly reacting to crisis but are vulnerable when fools take the throne. Passing authority to someone based upon their birth, rather than merit, will eventually produce a lousy monarch. Even if your heir is sound in leadership, they must also be sound in their ability to nurture that very virtue in their heir. Eventually that process breaks, and the fool becomes king," Helmut explained, and their history was replete with examples of this.

"Then what would you suggest? Should the people select their leaders?" Letha asked.

"Direct democracy can be as dangerous as any tyranny unless there are safeguards to protect the minority. Fools are easily led to vote for tyrants who claim they are not."

"If the people are given knowledge, as you are doing now, then wouldn't they select the wisest to rule?" Letha asked.

"That would be a logical assumption, but our history is replete with examples to the contrary. Throughout our 21st and 22nd centuries, once the world was fully educated to a high standard, they were susceptible to misinformation and groupthink. Knowledge is a wonderful thing, but true wisdom lays in the ability to question generally agreed assumptions. Courage is also a paramount virtue, for it takes courage to speak out when every other voice is against you," Helmut said, his words gaining purchase in their minds.

"My Queen," a voice called out from the archway behind them, where stood Luten, her servant and cup bearer, bearing a tray with three goblets of wine. He was attired in the formal white tunic of a palace attendant, with his long blond hair framing his delicate face.

"Luten, come forth," she ordered kindly as the boy stepped into the open air of the open-roofed veranda, offering each of them a drink, before backing a step with his head bowed.

"Eyes up, Luten. I would see your face." Letha smiled. Luten was the son of her dear friend Mearana and so placed at court to draw the eye of a suitor by his mother.

"Yes, My Queen," he said, looking nervously to the two men standing beside her.

"Tell me, Luten, how fare your lessons?" She inquired of his daily instruction by his assigned orb. It was her intention for all the young men of the realm to have equal access to the knowledge the Earthers were offering. His face visibly brightened with the subject.

"I am currently learning Earther history, My Queen," he said of his most recent lesson that very morning, piquing Helmut's attention.

"Which part are you currently learning, Luten?" the admiral asked.

"The siege and sack of Baghdad in the year 1258 AD. It was rumored the Mongols slaughtered the entire city, stacking hundreds of thousands of heads in towering mounds," Luten explained, causing Taleron and Letha to share a look. They too had begun to study Earth's history, finding it as bloody as their own, and perhaps more so. The Earthers did not have gargoyles plaguing them, removing any excuse for their barbarity.

"That was an interesting time, and very deadly as well, though such carnage continued for some time after. From that time up through the 22nd century, Earth experienced untold bloodshed and technological advancement, rendering the world nearly unrecognizable from the world that existed in the 13th century," Helmut said.

"I thought you were studying the periodic tables?" Letha asked.

"I was, My Queen. I finished them three days ago before starting

Araxan history. I finished that yester morn and began Earther history after," Luten explained. He first began his instruction with a neural link to learn the Earthers basic language, the same link the *Stenox* crew used to learn Araxan when they first arrived. From there he continued with mathematics, geology, geography and advanced grammar. His fellow servants were in various levels of achievement, all learning at their unique pace. With this knowledge, an entire world of possibilities awaited them if they chose to follow them. Letha decreed that any son of the Sisterhood could follow a path outside of the home, as long as that path was beyond their borders. She still had to balance the strict protocols of the matriarchy with the changing times, thus restricting the freedom of the males that chose to remain, while allowing those that wished to depart to do so. The one exception was the Earthers, whose presence in their realm was necessary, and given the status of visiting dignitaries and ambassadors. Then there was her husband, Taleron, who split his time between Bansoch and Fera, aiding Terin in building the structure of the new Northern Kingdom.

"Is there a field or vocation that sparks your interest, Luten?" Helmut asked.

"I love stars and planets, Admiral. I would like to help mapping our galaxy," he said, loving the subject.

"I could speak with Commander Pham and see if we have a place for you, either aboard the *Stalingrad* or one of our ground facilities we are building," Helmut offered.

"Thank you, Admiral," Luten said gratefully before Letha dismissed him.

"Very generous of you Admiral," Taleron said, watching the boy disappear through the archway.

"Yes, though his mother shall be disappointed. She has received inquiries for his consortship, particularly from one of your officers, Admiral," Letha said, taking a sip of her wine.

"One of mine?" Helmut asked.

"Lt. Commander Bao Chang," she said, naming his liaison to her court.

Helmut hadn't considered that. Most of his crew that had taken mates were male. Bao would be the first female of his crew doing the opposite. He should have thought of that possibility when he named her his representative to Queen Letha's court. It was Bao's uncle that led the *Eden Expedition*. He wondered how things might have gone differently had Colonel Chang survived. He might have prevented the falling out with Thorton. Perhaps Kato would still be alive, and perhaps Ben also.

Helmut was suddenly reminded that he was nearing his check in time with Captain Banza and started to excuse himself when Letha recalled what they were discussing before Luten's interruption.

"Which form of governing authority would you suggest?" she asked.

Helmut thought on that for the longest moment.

"That's for you and your people to decide. Whatever you choose, my people and I will stand by you. That goes for all the realms of Arax," Helmut said.

"Then might I ask what form of governance your people shall employ?" she pushed.

With such a small populace as it currently stood, Helmut doubted any republic or democratic union could be possible for some time. There was also their duty to their fleet, meaning military discipline and structure would be needed for the foreseeable future.

"For now, think of my people as guardians of your planet, at least until you can begin to build warships of your own, and contribute to your collective defense. We will help you with that, as best as we are able."

That was the one part neither Letha nor Taleron could understand, why the Earthers would give away their great advantage, gifting the realms of Arax their technology.

"Why would you trust us with your greatest advantage? Why give of your technology so freely, when you know our history?" Taleron asked.

Again, Helmut thought for the longest moment.

"As I said, Yah brought us here for a reason, and I believe it is more than demonstrating his power by using us to destroy the gargoyles as we did. We are powerful, but we are few, and perhaps

Yah intended it that way, for us to bring our technology to you, to teach you and guide you so you might stand on your own should another entity emerge from the anomaly that brought us here." He revealed his greatest fear, that a hostile alien force might threaten a future Arax.

"That is why you are prioritizing the advancement of our military assets," Taleron mused. The Earthers already provided each realm several transport craft and trained their pilots to fly them. In the coming year, they would begin training pilots for the fighter craft they were producing and intended to give to each of the realms. Raven and Lorken were designated the flight trainers for the Sisterhood pilots in the coming months.

"I guess it is. There is an old Earth saying, to plan for the worst and hope for the best. I would rather have your people heavily armed and advanced and face no challenges as you expand off world, then face a threat unprepared," Helmut said.

"For the best then." Letha smiled, raising her goblet to the admiral.

"For the best." He gave her a casual Earther salute, touching his hand to his head before stepping away, leaving Taleron and Letha alone.

Neither said a word for a painfully long moment, each sharing a look before relenting.

"What think you?" she asked.

"It seems whatever shall be has been predestined." He took a generous sip from his goblet.

She regarded him briefly, examining every contour of his face and carriage. His return to her life was as unforeseen as anything that transpired. She recalled those long-ago days when she first treated with him. He was the powerful emperor of an emerging realm, while she was the crown princess of the Sisterhood. Her first intent was to inform him of the gargoyles' nature, and the need to expel them from his empire. She was unprepared for the feelings that stirred her upon meeting him, tearing away her restraints as they were hopelessly drawn to one another. Her plan quickly changed from warning him, to seducing him to her cause. Unbeknownst to her, he also seduced her to bring her realm into his own. The falling out was as predictable as the sunrise. Now, after all those years apart, fate brought them back into each other's arms. Gone was the source of all their division, the gargoyles. They also had many ties binding them together in the form of the grandchildren they shared, and the peace that permeated Arax that was stronger than in the times of Kal.

"Nothing is predestined when hearts are at play," she said.

"Nothing?" He wondered at that.

"Love might be beyond our comprehension, for only the fates can know who shall stir our passions, but to love someone, to truly love someone, is a choice in the end."

"A choice?"

"Yes. In all our years apart, why did you not claim a new wife, or even a concubine to sire you the heirs you needed, or to sate the urges every man must cater?"

"I had two wives in my life. I saw no need for another. What of you? Why did you not wed again?"

"Because I had a husband, even if he was too foolish to know better." She smiled wryly, taking another generous sip. In truth, she also would not risk Tosha's right to the throne by wedding the son of another house, thus impowering that house to undermine her birthright.

"I have wasted much of my life on revenge and hate, angry for what was taken from me. I was blind to what I still had, a second wife that I could have embraced had I forsaken my alliance with the gargoyles," he lamented.

"Could you have forsaken them?" she asked, doubtful that he could have.

"In truth, no. I could not have betrayed Regula. For all the sins of their foul kind, he was my friend." He sighed, turning his gaze to the horizon, looking out to sea but seeing nothing.

"You were loyal, loyal to those you loved. And you loved Regula long before you knew me. I hated you for it but was always proud of you for that as well. Loyalty was your one virtual despite all that you did wrong. In a way, that gave me resolve to remain loyal to you where my bed was concerned. There was no one after we parted," she said as he turned back to face her.

"I am still Tyro, even if I have forsaken the name. The cold anger still dwells in me, though I have placed layers of restraint and regret upon it. I have given away my empire and will one day gift my swords to the Tarelian kingdoms that rise again where their holdfasts once stood. I would hold no power that I might abuse should my restraints fail me. I will spend what days are left to me with my family, my daughter, my grandchildren, and my wife," he said, drawing her into his arms.

"Then let us place another layer upon your heart," she said, pressing her lips to his.

There upon the veranda of her quarters, Letha and Taleron kissed. They would live many years after, sharing in the love of their grandchildren. He would die in bed, holding his wife on a peaceful night twenty-two years after the Battle of the Noddegamra.

* * *

Grand Hall of the queen's palace.

The evening found Raven standing along the east wall of the vast chamber, wondering when the night would mercifully end. The Grand Hall was centered on the west wing of the palace, opposite the feasting hall where Darna's attack commenced during his last visit to Bansoch. Unlike the natural wood and greenery of the feasting hall, the Grand Hall boasted a large open design with white mirrored stone floor and towering pillars supporting its high ceiling. Basin torches were replaced with bright luminous lamps, gifted by the manufacturing teams the admiral lent Queen Letha. Said lamps lined the upper seams of the ceiling and walls, luminating the white surface of the chamber, making it appear even larger than it was.

The sound of musicians plucking their stringed instruments added to his misery, wondering why no one thought to use the musical archives from the *Stalingrad,* or even the *Stenox?* He wasn't alone in his misery, with Lorken and Argos sharing his boredom, having spent the last two weeks at the palace. Lorken was currently in the center of the open floor dancing with his wife, Jenna. Having spent most of the war in the Ape Republic, Jenna enjoyed this time with her husband, making up for lost time. They were already discussing having more children, from what he overheard. Their current children were on the opposite side of the chamber, attended by doting palace staff, the infant boy the spitting image of his father and the girl likewise with her mother. It was an obvious genetic quirk that repeated itself with his and Tosha's children, save for Ujurack, whose skin was scaly black and hardened. Whatever caused the mutation was still unclear. The medical team from the *Stalingrad* were currently investigating the cause. A simple sweep of a regenerator on his reproductive system hopefully prevented it from occurring again. The sweep was conducted on the others as well, particularly Lorken, as one of Jenna's triplets suffered a similar fate, though his was fatal.

Ujurack, or Uju as he preferred to call him, stood alongside his siblings and Lorken's children, barely a year old now and walking without issue. He was already far taller than his brother, with a wide grin plastered on his face nearly all the time, especially whenever he saw Zem. Zem had taken an equal liking to the child, noting Uju's obvious intelligence since he liked Zem. The boy was already fairly strong, the grip of his fingers causing pain if he fully applied it. Little Jake looked just like Raven, and his little Princess, his beautiful Ceana, looked just like her mother, golden eyes and all.

Little Princess. He shook his head, for she truly was a princess. She would be a handful once she got older, he had little doubt. The boys would have to come with him away from this place before some woman got her hooks in them. The last thing he wanted to see was a son of his being reduced to a housewife by one of the locals. It didn't help that the admiral volunteered him and Lorken to oversee the training of the Sisterhood's first fighter pilots' class. That would keep him here for the foreseeable future, at least when it started up in the coming months.

He caught sight of Brokov and Kendra dancing amid the crowd, looking far too happy with each other, by the look of it. The admiral was reassigning Brokov to the bridge staff of the *Stalingrad*, to replace

Bao Chang, who was now assigned as his official liaison to Queen Letha's court. Brokov's assignment would not start for another two months, just as he and Lorken began training the Queen's pilots. The time before then was supposed to be a little R and R, but the admiral said he had a mission he wanted the *Stenox* to undertake, something he would explain to them tonight. The admiral was currently dancing with Councilor Mearana, the palace steward and good friend of the queen. She had to be the tenth or eleventh woman of the court Admiral Kruger had danced with so far, and the night was still young.

Sly old dog. Raven shook his head, never seeing this side of his old friend before. Of course, if he thought about it, the admiral was the most eligible bachelor on Arax, and Captain Banza would be a close second. It was strange behavior by the ladies of the court considering most women of the Sisterhood chose mates that took a secondary role to their own position. *Maybe they want to marry up, like Tosha did*, he thought to himself.

Thinking of Tosha made him find her among the crowd dancing with her father. No matter how much time had passed since the Oddigem, he couldn't wrap his head around that Tyro was a good guy now. Of course, he wasn't called Tyro anymore, but Taleron. He noticed Tosha and Taleron talking as they danced, Tosha's eyes alit with enraptured joy as they moved across the floor. She still took his breath away with her curvaceous form displayed invitingly by the shimmering silver gown she wore, with gold stitching along its sleeves and hem. He wondered what they were talking about. He found himself in Tyro's company more often than not in the recent months, as he helped him and the others on their *special* project. Said project began once Tyro mentioned something in passing. Terin had asked the location of the Vale of Kalin, perhaps wanting to visit his ancestral home once he was able to pass on the leadership of the Northern Kingdom. That was when they got the idea to build Terin a home there, a quiet place to raise a family, just as Terin desired to do. The idea was actually Cronus', but who's keeping score, he reminded himself. By this point, nearly everyone chipped in their time and ideas into the project. He couldn't wait for Terin to see it, and Corry too. The admiral even sent a team to help with the construction and the surrounding layout. It would be unlike any home on Arax, subdued and grand at the same time, if that made any sense. The project was one thing that Raven and Tyro could agree on, and Tosha loved seeing them work together on. Even the apes and the Jenaii lent a hand, adding unique touches here and there.

"I'm hungry!" Argos snorted, standing beside him with his arms crossed, looking around for the second servings that were nowhere in sight.

"You might have to go to the kitchens to find any, big fella," Raven said, looking around to confirm there were none in sight.

"Bah, what sort of party doesn't have food placed throughout!" the large gorilla growled.

"Maybe you can ask the queen," Raven said as Queen Letha drew near, having finished a dance with Orlom, who was now paired with General Jani.

"Mighty Argos, might I have this dance, my dear friend?" Queen Letha asked, giving Raven a flirtatious wink, drawing Argos onto the floor, leaving Raven all alone until Tosha appeared, having left her father to dance with another lady of the court.

"I suppose you want to me to dance with you," he snorted.

"Of course, moron, you are my husband." She took his hand, dragging him onto the floor, smiling with her use of his own language against him. Besides, moron seemed the correct description for the big idiot, one even his dearest friends would agree.

"Remember the last time we danced in your mother's palace?" he said, recalling Darna's attack on the castle.

"How could I forget? It was such a joyous event until you sang your stupid song." She smiled, ignoring the obvious drawback of that evening.

"It was a very good song. Maybe I should sing it again."

"Let's not." She rolled her eyes, using another Earther phrase, cringing at the thought of him singing *Hard to be Humble,* the ancient ballad from his home world that so aptly described him.

"At least the kids are having a good time," he said, watching

Zem lift Uju, tossing him in the air and catching him, with Jake tugging at his trouser leg wanting his turn.

Tosha briefly froze at the sight, worried that their son might fall, but sighed as Zem caught him so easily before tossing him again. The entire scene was in contrast to her father drawing Ceana into his arms, offering her, her first dance.

"Yes, it appears they are," she finally said.

"I was talking about my crew," he said, leaning his head in the opposite direction where Brokov and Kendra, Lorken and Jenna were moving about the floor with far more grace than Raven could manage in a lifetime.

"They appear quite content. They deserve it after all we have endured."

"It's strange really. The rescue party from Earth finally finds us, but they are trapped here the same as us."

"Trapped? This is your home now, Raven," she reminded him, meaning it was their home, hers and his.

"I guess. With the war over and everyone acting so nice and all, it's going to get boring around here."

"You will have enough things to occupy yourself, I have little doubt."

"You mean training your flight squadrons. I wonder who gave the admiral the idea that I should do it?" he asked suspiciously.

"I wonder that myself." She looked away with a smirk.

"Stinker," he said, shaking his head.

"Oh, you will enjoy giving instructions to the warriors that we select for the assignment. It will only boost your ego, as you like to call it, and you are insufferable enough as it is."

"You know Torg called me an ass once." He smiled.

"And he was right to do so."

"I didn't disagree with him."

"You take all the fun out of fighting when you agree so easily." She rolled her eyes.

"Ruining your fun is what I do best."

"You always accuse me of doing the same," she said.

"Because you do. Now you get to have me around for the foreseeable future during this assignment, giving you plenty of chances to ruin any fun in it."

"The war is over, Raven. What excuse can you give me now for not staying here where you belong?"

"I have my own job to do. The *Stenox* needs…"

"The *Stenox*? Your ship is going to be set aside as a museum piece once everything is settled."

"A museum? What are you talking about?" he growled.

"It has served its purpose. It is also the most famous ship on Arax, and the people will want to visit it. One of Admiral Kruger's staff officers suggested that. He also proposed a museum dedicated to the great war, perhaps commissioning a site here at Bansoch. I cannot think of a better place for it." She smiled deviously.

"The *Stenox* is MY ship!" he growled.

"It is the property of the Earth Space Directorate, and as its principal representative on Arax, Admiral Kruger has final authority on its disposition."

"We built that from scraps. The ship is ours."

"Do you think your friends want to sail the seas forever just to humor your sense of adventure? Brokov is replacing Bao aboard the bridge of the *Stalingrad*. Jenna will want Lorken to make a home either at Tro, the Ape republic or at New Brussels, perhaps joining Brokov aboard the *Stalingrad*. Zem is already overseeing the construction of the academies he is planning to direct all across the continent. Argos will have to return home at some point. Time moves on, Raven, and so should you."

"Alright, out with it!" he growled.

"Out with what?" she asked incredulously.

"There is something else going on that you aren't telling me. I know how that devious mind of yours works."

"Very well. Since you will find out soon enough anyway, my mother shall soon abdicate. Father is planning a quiet place for them to live, enjoying what years are left to them."

"Good for them, but what does that have to do with me?"

"It means I will be queen, Raven, and I would like my husband to be at my side."

"We talked about this," he warned.

"No, you talked about it and refused to compromise. We have children to raise, Raven, and they need their father."

"And you?"

"I need my husband. I need you."

For once he didn't know what to say, looking at the ceiling as they danced before she drew his hand in hers, moving it to her belly.

"Our family is growing, and I need you," she added for good measure.

"A baby?"

"Yes." She smiled again, enjoying the stupid look it caused him.

"You never fight fair."

"Nope." She smiled even wider.

"Alright, I'll stay, but there are conditions, and they aren't negotiable."

"Go on," she said, knowing she had him, but considering this was Raven, she could only imagine what he wanted.

"For one thing, I don't do any of that kneeling nonsense, and neither will our boys."

"Very well," she conceded.

"And none of that calling me a consort. If I stay, I will be your husband, and you, my wife. You ain't my queen."

"Go on." She rolled her eyes.

"And whenever I want to go somewhere, I'm not asking your permission. If the boys want to sail the world, then off we go."

That was a big one, but she relented.

"That goes for any missions the admiral wants me to take. The boys get to spend extended periods with the apes, and with my people at New Brussels. And if I want to go fishing anytime I want, I'm going."

"Fishing?" She made a face.

"I like to fish."

"Since when?" She recalled his antics using his pistol to kill the fish in the stream during their long trek to Tro.

"Since I just decided. Also, whenever I want to visit our island getaway, just you and me, we go," he said, regarding the island far east of Tro where the wreck of the *Magellan* lay, and the graves of Colonel Chang and the *Eden Expedition*. The isle was the most tranquil, beautiful place either of them had ever seen.

"Agreed," she said, wanting to go there herself. The isle was already known by all, and Admiral Kruger sent a team to establish a permanent presence. The isle was to be used as an R and R location for all his crew, as well as the peoples of Arax in the coming years.

"And the boys are playing football. No arguments with me on this," he said.

"You can't be serious?" She finally held her ground.

"Deadly serious. You'll warm up to the idea. President Matuzak and the admiral have already discussed establishing a continent-wide league to foster sportsmanship and comradery among all the realms."

"Anything else?' she asked tiredly.

"Yeah, don't ever ask me to wear a tunic or kilt or any of that stuff you people wear."

"Anything else?" she repeated.

"Probably, but I can't think of anymore right now."

"Very well, now here is my list," she said.

"Your list? You don't get a list. I'm staying, and that should be enough."

"I very much do need a list, since you are prone to all sorts of mischief."

Before he could counter that, Queen Letha took her place upon a raised dais along the north end of the chamber, the crowd growing quiet as she began to speak.

"My good people and dear friends…" she began, looking to their many guests.

"…we take this night to celebrate our triumph over the gargoyles. Our Sisterhood was established to further that end, and we can retire that great commission. As for the future, we will look to our new friends from Earth to aid us in that endeavor. The coming years will see much change to our island realm, and all of Arax also. Most of that change will be to our benefit, while some of it shall require our patience. Many old enemies have become friends…" she said, looking to her husband standing alongside the east wall, holding their granddaughter in his arms.

"…and some of those enemies have proven worthy to restore to their proper place. Deva Estaran, head of House Estaran is not here this night. She has earned her redemption, guiding us to our final victory with her visons from Yah. Upon that battlefield, I restored her to her rightful place as the head of her house, but she refused, taking up a different calling as a servant of Yah. She asked that I raise up her sister, Thesta to assume the leadership of House Estaran. Thesta, please step forth and kneel," Letha ordered.

Thesta Estaran approached the dais, taking a knee as Letha descended the platform, drawing forth her sword, and placing it at her feet.

"I return the *Sword of the Stars* that belonged to your house since its founding. Take it, and assume your place as its wielder and the head of your great house," Letha ordered as the young girl retrieved the precious gift and stood to face the crowd.

Polite cheers rang out, heartfelt and sincere, not the raucous bellows that the apes were known to use. Thesta bowed briefly and withdrew as the crowd grew quiet, waiting upon the Queen's next utterance.

"As all of you have witnessed, our dear friend Admiral Kruger has bestowed many gifts to our people," Letha said, waving an open hand to the lights illuminating the chamber from the ceiling above and the walls all around them.

"In the coming seasons and years, many more gifts shall be given, grander and more impressive than these wondrous offerings. We are currently operating four transports, crewed by our own pilots. In the coming moons, we shall commence training our own fighter squadron, a powerful arm of our military, able to destroy entire armies as they were previously arrayed. These weapons of destruction shall be directed to threats beyond our world and will join with those of the other realms of Arax, forming the core of our collective defense. I shall list the names of our pilot candidates in the coming days, each selected for her fitness of both body and mind, as they were screened by the medical team of the *Stalingrad* for this vocation. The first of the names I shall reveal this night, a woman of great renown and ability, who shall be the first squadron leader of the Sisterhood, the Princess Tosha," Letha said, all eyes falling upon her daughter, standing at Raven's side along the west wall.

"Looks like I shall be your first student," Tosha whispered in Raven's ear, giving him a flirtatious wink.

"What about the baby?" he asked, looking at her stomach.

"The babe will come before we commence training." She reminded him of the shorter gestation period for Araxan women.

Raven realized she knew this all along, shaking his head.

"Don't think I'll go easy on you," he warned.

"I am counting on it." She smiled as her mother continued.

"The princess shall assume this esteemed mantel for a brief time before taking her place in my stead. In one year, I shall formally abdicate, leaving the throne in her capable hands. I shall remain in the shadows to guide her, and offer my advice as needed," Letha declared, her proclamation drawing a chorus of gasps, and misgivings, before giving way to acceptance. Tosha's bravery and cunning throughout the war had earned her her people's admiration and respect.

Queen Letha continued, praising all of their efforts in the great war and honoring their fallen. She concluded with calling upon Admiral Kruger to address the assemblage, where he stood in the center of the floor, his iron gaze sweeping the crowd.

"I have spoken with many of you at length in recent days, concerning many of the projects we shall be working on together for the betterment of all. Though much time has passed since the events at the Oddigem, there remains one matter left unresolved. For this, I would call the crew of the *Stenox* forth to reconcile this," Helmut declared as Raven and the others shared a curious look before stepping forward.

There they stood, Raven, Lorken, Brokov, Zem, Argos, Orlom and Kendra, with Tosha taking her place beside her husband as the admiral continued.

"There has been much speculation of late on the fate of the *Stenox*. Some would argue its usefulness has waned, while others would like it preserved for posterity. Either action would be hasty if decided at this time. For now, it still serves a unique role in this rapidly changing world. As very few of you know, our scientists have stored every known lifeform from Earth in a biological archive in the storage banks of each battle carrier, including the *Stalingrad*. These archives are intended to act as an Ark as in the story of Noah, where we can repopulate any planet with our life forms should a catastrophe strike Earth. We have found specific areas of your world where certain Earth based lifeforms would benefit the local environment. Before we commence such an endeavor, we should physically explore said regions with a thorough scientific investigation. This would be an ideal mission for the *Stenox*. It has come to my attention, that a promise was made, a promise that is yet unkept. During the Battle of the Noddegamra, Captain Raven promised Zem he could be Captain of the *Stenox* for a week. I can think of no better time than now for that promise to be fulfilled." Admiral Kruger almost smiled, enjoying the sour look on Raven's face, a look shared by Lorken and Brokov.

"Your wisdom is exceptional as always, Admiral. I will lead the expedition with supreme efficiency and execution," Zem's metallic voice boomed proudly.

"What say you, Raven?" Helmut asked.

"A promise is a promise," he snorted unhappily.

"Admiral, where is this place we are going?" Brokov asked warily.

"Very good question. You are going to explore the northern polar regions, where rests a sizable continent covered in a large ice shelf. Your search will be confined to its coastal regions of course, examining it for species settlement once the stored embryos complete gestation," Helmut explained.

"Not for nothing, Admiral, but just what species are you planning to put there?" Raven asked.

"Very good question, Raven. It is a subclassification of Spheniscidae, Aptenodytes," Helmut said.

"Senicadance aptonotes?" Raven made a face.

"Spheniscidae, Aptenodytes, or as you would call them… Penguins. King Penguins to be precise," Helmut said, breaking the slightest smile.

"Ah, a most excellent choice, Admiral," Zem said happily.

You got to be kidding, Raven thought miserably, Brokov and Lorken sharing his opinion, knowing this was far more than a few days long mission with Zem in charge. Zem was already forming an approved list of activities and songs he intended to implement for their journey, with *Anchors aweigh* and *Burning Bridges* to be played at sunrise and sunset each day of the mission.

"Do not fret, I will go with you," Tosha said, rubbing his arm, unable to hide her mirth, giving Zem a formal Earther salute.

There in the palace of Queen Letha, Zem basked in glow of his crowning achievement, to finally assume his first formal command. He would go on to lead an exemplary career, serving as a professor in each of the academies across Arax, overseeing training directives, joining in advanced research in various topics, leading space exploration expeditions throughout the nearest star systems, serving as captain of the *Stalingrad* and eventually admiral of the joint Arax Space Fleet. Of all these accomplishments, his time as a crewmate aboard the *Stenox* would be his fondest memories and the source of his greatest fame.

CHAPTER 23

Two years after the Battle of Noddegamra.

The ancient ruins of Tarelia had given way to the majesty of the new capital city of the Macon-Torry Realm. Towering structures replaced the broken citadels that dominated the site for a thousand years, with Earther technology lighting their surfaces and interior with spell like wonder. The bay, made impassable over the years with silt and sand, was cleared and cleaned, projecting the tranquil beauty of a tropic port. Long piers circled the harbor, with ships of all sorts moored along their stone wharves.

Two small isles rose forward of the harbor's mouth, constructed by the Earthers' awesome power, each of solid stone foundation, resting above thick bedrock. Rising above each isle arose massive statues cast in the visage of the kings of old, each 300 feet from boot to crown, with their right arms outstretched toward Lake Monata.

The statue on the western isle represented King Mortun, first king of Maconia, arrayed in golden armor over a red tunic, and golden greaves rising to his knees. A massive shield rested in his left hand, and his sword in his right, stretched outward toward the sea, cast in a bronze hue with golden light emitting along its blade, symbolizing the *Sword of the Stars* wielded by Mortus at the Oddigem. Upon his head rested a golden crown with fist-sized jewels embedded along its wide band. His hair was cast in bright obsidian, draping his broad shoulders, with rings of emeralds set in his stone eye sockets, alit from behind with the light of Earther magic, casting his gaze across the surface of the lake. His raiment was colored stone, cast in hues of gold and red for armor and raiment, and deep bronze for flesh.

The statue on the eastern isle represented King Zar, first monarch of the Middle Kingdom, arrayed in silver armor and blue tunic, his austere crown cast in shimmering black, set upon his dark mane. Rings of sapphires set in his stone eye sockets, alit by the same Earther magic, casting an azure light across the surface of the lake. His sword was cast in silver with its blade alit in an ethereal azure glow, symbolizing the *Sword of the Moon* first wielded by King Zar at the founding of his ancient realm.

The statues stood as symbols of the unity of their realms, bound by magic, sacrifice and blood.

A series of structures ringed the bay, rising high into the firmament, with platforms jutting from their sides throughout their impressive ascent, where transport craft and hover sleds set down and took off, their quiet forms filling the sky, going to and fro. Thousands of people lined the streets below, the avenues' surface coated in a gray-white sheen, forged of material that drained rainwater and eased travel afoot. A modest river bisected the city, flowing south from the Arian Hills that ringed the northern approaches of the bay.

A large eight-sided structure dominated the western bank of the stream, with silver-blue walls and roof that shimmered with the shifting sunlight. It was the newly built Academy of Science and Knowledge, the grandest school of its kind in all Arax, where the great thinkers of the continent would gather to instruct the proceeding generations. It would be the gathering place for scientists, researchers, musicians and philosophers, and a diverse array of fields and experts. With the base needs of all the people easily provided for with their new technologies, people were free to pursue their greater purpose. In the spirit of these pursuits, the preamble of the new academy was carved in stone above its entrance, bearing a quote from the ancient Earther philosopher Plato…

Do not teach children learning by force and harshness,

**but direct them to it by what amuses their minds,
so that you may be better able to discover with accuracy
the peculiar bent of the genius of each**

...After thousands of years of intellectual and technological stagnation, the peoples of Arax were set free, seeking knowledge with an insatiable hunger. This transformation would lead Arax into a golden age of learning, wisdom and wonder, which posterity would aptly describe as the great awakening.

Across the river rested the Tower of Celenia, restored to its former glory, rebuilt of gleaming white stone spiraling into the firmament. Above its highest battlement would soon blow the standard of the future king of the Torry-Macon alliance, Jentra the 1st, King of New Tarelia.

Beyond the Tower of Celenia stood the Tower of the Grand Council, rising above the surrounding structures with stately power. Its circled base and superstructure rose seven hundred feet into the air, sunlight playing off its silver surface. A circular observation platform rested atop its apex, with curved windows looking out over the surrounding landscape. Within the covered platform was the circled table where the grand council presided, with representatives of each realm of Arax, along with the nine wielders of the Swords of Light, though the sword wielders only met on the rarest of occasions. It was the symbol of Araxan unity and power, guiding the advance of their collective civilization to the nearest worlds and beyond.

Surrounding the heart of the city were various structures including stores, warehouses, theaters, and amphitheaters, and a large arena hosting sporting events and spectacles. The walls that once circled the ancient city, were fully removed, their need negated by technology and the peace that fell over the land. New Tarelia was the capital of the larger realm that mostly surrounded it, with its only neighbors the allied lands of Sawyer to its west, and the Kingdom of the Jenaii to its east. A wide causeway ran through the heart of the city, skirting the east bank of the river, following its course to the Arian Hills to the north, where sat the newly constructed Tarelian palace.

The palace rested atop the nearest hilltop, overlooking the city below. Its outer walls rose four hundred feet, hued in silverish black, its glossy surface swallowing the sunlight that fell upon it, sending it swirling along its smooth contours. Powerful battlements overlooked the main gate, resting along its south face. The outer walls were connected by twelve turrets, each a hundred feet abreast, and mirrored by those connecting the inner walls, which rose another one hundred feet behind them. Beyond the inner walls rose the inner keep, with several towers rising above its uppermost heights, piercing the firmament above. It was larger than any of the great castles built by the Tarelians of old. Its construction and design were overseen by Commander Pham, the *Stalingrad's* chief engineer, and a small army of his best officers and men, and a larger army of Araxan craftsmen and laborers. The castle and the city below required one and half years of intense work to complete, their construction and majesty a symbol of the golden age to come. The palace was designed with every Earther convenience one could imagine, where even the lowest of servants and soldiers would live in luxuries even a king of old would envy. The palace was the center of the realm's military and communications, garrisoned with a myriad of specialists, its modern interior standing in stark contrast to its martial outer shell.

In the center of the city was an open space where stood an austere structure, a simple flat roof supported by four columns to each corner, and open walls between them. The floor of the structure was covered in flat stones with loose sand filling their seams. In the center of the floor rested an altar, with a torch set upon it. 'Twas the Temple of Yah, where pilgrims would come to offer sacrifices, not offerings of flesh and blood, or even coin, but of pride. As High Priestess, Deva and her acolytes would oversee the temple, ensuring the torch's flame never expired, and counseling its visitors before they entered. They would remind them that the true temple was the heart, the very soul of every being, and the source of all evil. The root of all evil was pride, and it was pride that pilgrims came to surrender, reflecting on their own pride, and giving it over. Visitors would stand upon the simple floor with naked feet before the altar, feeling a sense of relief and joy upon surrendering their pride to Yah. This renewing of their spirit was met with overwhelming love, as if their hearts would lift them into the air. The faith of Yah rested upon the twin pillars of humility and love, essential for a civilization where knowledge and power were spreading to every corner of the world.

In the heart of the bay sailed a royal barge, with golden sails lifting in the morning breeze. Throngs of people lined the wharfs of the harbor as the majestic ship drew nigh, its prow breaking the gentle waves lapping its hull. Upon its foredeck stood King Lorn and Queen Deliea, with Prince Jentra between them, the infant struggling to see over the bulwark, stretching upon his slippered toes before his father drew him into his arms. Deliea smiled at the sight, holding their second son to her chest, gently stroking his tiny back.

"Da! Da!" Jentra shouted, pointing to the crowds gathering to greet them, and the wondrous city ringing the bay.

"This will be your capital city, my son, a gift from your mother and our many friends," Lorn looked over to Deliea, who returned his smile. It was she that selected this sight for their capital, restoring ancient Tarelia to its former glory. In truth, she restored it many times its former majesty, the new crown jewel in their joined realm. It was she who coordinated with the craftsmen form Fleace and Central City, and eventually their Earth friends, to build this city and the palace overlooking it. This was the day they would assume residency.

"Does it meet your expectations, my love?" Deliea asked, gauging her husband's joy by the elation in his eyes. This was the first day he had seen New Tarelia, as she insisted that he not visit the site until it was complete. He faithfully obeyed her wishes, allowing her to surprise him with her choices.

Lorn stared for the longest time, taking in the wonders before him, a perfect blend of restored ancient structures and the modern Earther edifices that intermingled in tranquil harmony. The city was pristine, and new, with stone, wood and shimmering metal surfaces forming a cohesive pattern of order and wonder.

"My queen is a visionary, wise and beautiful." He looked over at her, sharing this heartfelt moment as the ship drew alongside its pier.

Deliea swooned, never loving him more than this moment.

"Your city awaits, my king." She smiled, pointing the way to the portside midship, where the gangplank was lowered.

* * *

Lorn led the procession through the streets of the city, holding Jentra in his arms, his son waving at the crowds gathered along the avenues with Deliea at his side. Behind them marched the royal elite, with Torg and Cronus at their head. They followed the road through the city, continuing north where the gates of the palace were drawn open to receive them.

"Packaww!"

The sound of magantors echoed in the morning air, circling the citadels above, heralding their prince's arrival. Lorn spied the familiar warbird amidst their number, the gray-white wings of Wind Racer, Terin's faithful mount. He could see his friend's golden hair trailing his head as he broke from the others, circling about before passing overhead. He smiled as Terin angled for the platforms jutting form the inner keep, knowing he would meet him in the great hall.

They passed under the gate's raised porticus, following the large tunnel behind it, before it opened into a massive open courtyard. They were met by hundreds of soldiers arrayed in the traditional uniforms of the realm, with mail and helms over white, gray and black tunics, their attire standing in contrast to the royal elite, now wearing the black armor and trousers of the Earther marines, with pistols holstered at their sides, and domed helms that receded behind their heads when not needed. The soldiers thrust their fists to their chests, saluting their king and queen. Lorn returned the gesture, overcome with emotion. Most of these men fought beside him at the Oddigem, and so many battles before. They were his brothers in arms, and his dearest friends.

"My king!" one soldier shouted, drawing his sword and slamming it against his shield.

"My king!" Another followed, causing Lorn to pause in the center of the courtyard, as the others repeated the chant, their shouts of adulation ringing through the air.

Deliea stepped closer to her husband, holding their infant son to her breast, reaching out to him with her free arm, placing her hand in his. She could see a tear run along his cheek. A gentle squeeze of his hand by his wife steadied his emotions. How he loved her.

"My brothers!" Lorn answered them, saying no more than that, saying so much without adding another word. With that, he continued on, leading his party to the great hall.

* * *

Lorn entered the great hall, stopping at the entrance as he beheld the spectacle before him. The great hall seemed more a great cavern, thrice the size of Corell's, its ceiling the height of ten men standing one upon the other. It was one hundred feet abroad and three hundred in length, its broad floor covered with a reflective silver coating, light swirling along its surface wherever it shone. Large paintings and frescos adorned the walls, each detailing events of the great war, from the Battle of Tuft's Mountain upon the east wall, to the Battle of Noddegamra upon the west, with all the others aligned between them. His eye caught the impressive work resting at the far end of the hall, dominating the area behind a raised dais, depicting his father's heroic stand against Morac at Kregmarin. He almost wept at the perfect representation of his father's face, standing in defiance of Morac, meeting his challenge with only a mortal sword. Only through the visions of the Earthers' crew aboard the Stalingrad, could the artist have recreated his face so exact.

His gaze drew wide, watching as his father's image came to life, his silent voice rebuking Morac before their climatic duel. 'Twas more Earther magic, the pictures moving as if they were in the present. Sparing a glance around the chamber, the other images came alive in lifelike wonder.

"If you touch the images, they will emit sound," Deliea whispered, a winsome smile touching her lips. She was privy to every detail in the construction of the palace and the city below, enjoying the childlike wonder in her husband's eyes.

He regarded her briefly, sharing a look. How he loved this woman, who was beautiful and intelligent, and never failed to impress him with her insight and wisdom.

He heard his son speaking gibberish, pointing his finger to the ceiling. He looked up, seeing the black surface of the ceiling with a myriad of constellations displayed in exact detail, with thousands of other stars scattered between them, each alit with varying strength, mimicking their brightness in the Araxan sky. The lighting along the walls didn't seem to interfere with the faux sky of the ceiling, adding to the chamber's majesty.

His gaze then fell on the grand assembly gathered to either side of the chamber, giving him a clear path between them. Here stood the emissaries of the peoples of Arax, many his comrades and dearest friends. President Matuzak and his generals stood along his left, and Elos and the chieftains of the Jenaii beside them. King El Anthar and the rest of the Jenaii stood opposite them upon his right, their silver eyes fixed upon him. King Lichu stood beside them, along with his family, a symbol of the friendship between the former enemies. The men of Notsu, Sawyer, and Rego, stood further along the right side, opposite the men of Yatin, Tro and Casia, with Queen Tosha and the Sisterhood nearer the dais. The Earthers stood opposite her, led by Captain Banza, captain of the *Stalingrad*, and many of its primary officers. Beside them stood the men of the new Northern Kingdom, led by their new over regent, a man selected to replace Terin, named Gais Dorenta, who was former commander of Unit in the 10th Legion. He was joined by General Gavis and Alen.

At the far end of the chamber rested the raised dais, where stood an unassuming throne, an austere chair built of simple sandstone, with no adornments decorating its surface. Behind this throne rested two larger thrones, one black as a midnight sky, and the other white, pure as a newborn star. Before the sandstone throne stood King Mortus, arrayed in his royal vestment, rich burgundy robes over a golden tunic. Upon his head rested the crown of Maconia, with emeralds embedded along its wide band. Behind him upon the dais, stood the princes of Teso and Zulon, with their wives, each a daughter of Mortus, now joined by marriage. Around them stood the high ministers and generals of the Torry and Macon realms. Squid stood directly behind the throne, representing the Grand Council that now oversaw the unity and defense of Arax.

"Go on," Lorn encouraged his son, expecting the child to lead the way, but young Jentra froze in place, taken aback by the sea of faces looking at him. To his credit, he did not hide behind his father's robes.

Very well, Lorn smiled, scooping the boy in his arms, while holding Deliea's hand with his free arm before advancing across the chamber, their procession following in their wake. About the room their march was viewed by live feeds, sending the event to every home on Arax. Their escort stopped below the dais, with Torg and Cronus standing post below the throne as the world watched as Lorn and Deliea ascended the dais. They embraced King Mortus before placing Jentra upon the sandstone throne. It was there Mortus and Lorn placed their crowns upon his head and lap, unifying their realms for all time. It fell upon Lorn to address the assembly as Mortus and Deliea took their places upon the black and white thrones, representing the Torry and Macon realms of the new kingdom.

"We gather this day to formally unite the Torry and Macon realms for all time, placing our crowns upon the head of my son and King Mortus' grandson. When our realms were at war, it was Yah's divine will that we should be as one, revealing his intent through a vision. I revealed that vison to King Mortus before the walls of Fleace, ending our war and uniting us to fight our true foe. King Mortus and I shared many journeys and fought many battles since that day, culminating in our victory at Noddegamra in the valley of Oddigem. We had won the war, but to win the peace, true peace, we needed more than merely uniting our realms. Any future monarch of our union must be clothed in humility and wisdom, lest he bring ruin to our realm," Lorn began, knowing for this to be accomplished, his son would have to be raised in the countryside, ignorant of his birthright, where he would learn hard work, discipline and empathy. Only then would he possess that rare and essential trait any just king required. And so it would be with every successive generation of kings. He and Deliea would dwell in a simple home far from court, while Mortus reigned until Jentra came of age. Once Jentra had an heir, Lorn would rule while Jentra raised his son in seclusion. This was already known by the people, a key factor in ensuring a wise ruler of humble origin would always sit the throne.

"King Mortus and I also agreed that humility and wisdom were not enough to ensure competent and just rule from a monarch. There must be checks upon absolute authority, and a dispersion of power and influence to all reaches of our realm. A king must be powerful enough to protect the realm in crisis, wise enough to guide it to greatness, and limited in all other endeavors. To protect the realm and its people, power is best given to as many citizens as is practical," Lorn added, with the terrible reign of Emperor Yangu reminding everyone of the danger of absolute rule.

"There is one more element one should have in a monarch, one that hasn't been seen in over two and half millennia, the blood of Kal," Lorn said, causing a chorus of whispers to pass through the assembly.

Lorn gave the signal, a blast of a horn echoing through the cavernous hall as a second entourage entered the chamber. The crowd shifted, looking to the entrance where marched Terin, leading his small group toward the dais, passing between the faces of his many friends and comrades. Behind him walked his mother and his paternal grandfather Taleron, once Tyro, and now friend of the peoples gathered here he once fought so bitterly. Between Valera and Tyro walked Cordela, dressed in a shimmering silver gown, her tiny legs marching with purpose, indifferent to the thousand faces watching her pass. Taleron looked down at her, proud of her courage. She was born to be a queen but would never be so in the Northern Kingdom as Terin assumed that mantle before passing it on to his chosen replacement, Gais Dorenta. Terin was now of the north, but his heart would always belong to the Torry realm. With his replacement now in position, Terin and Corry removed themselves from court, residing in the Kalinian Vale, in the shadows of the Plate Mountains, in a home built by his friends. Corry remained there with their young son, watching the ceremony through the holo visual that every dwelling on Arax now possessed.

Terin and his group stopped at the base of the dais, waiting upon Lorn to continue.

Lorn descended the dais, drawing Terin into his embrace, the two friends overcome with emotion. They had fought and suffered at each other's side since Mosar, and so many battles since. They were brothers in marriage and battle, but especially in the spirit of Yah. Terin was one of three comrades Yah sent Lorn to aid him in his quest, the others being Cronus, who stood at their side, and Raven, who was currently elsewhere, leading a long-range patrol to the outer edges of their star system. The world watched as they shared this moment, symbolic of the kinship all the peoples of Arax now felt toward one another.

Lorn drew briefly away, looking past Terin to his infant sister standing between Valera and Taleron. He stepped toward her, taking a knee to look in her tiny eyes.

"Princess, welcome to Tarelia," Lorn said, kissing her hand, before gaining his feet, clasping forearms with Taleron, and offering a kiss to Valera's cheek, and inviting them to ascend the dais.

Once they reached the throne, Lorn directed Cordela to stand beside it, placing her hand on its wide stone arm, while Prince Jentra placed his atop of hers.

There upon the throne of New Tarelia, Lorn proclaimed the betrothal of Prince Jentra and Princess Cordela, uniting the Tarelian throne with the blood of Kal and the Northern Kingdom.

The blood of Kal, Squid marveled, its mysterious properties not fully understood, or properly appreciated, not even now, though the urgency of its proliferation was never so evident. It went beyond its original purpose of sending the gargoyles to flight or invoking the full power of the *Swords of Light*. The Earther chief medical officer, Dr. Sarah Kensington, further revealed the power of Kalinian blood, which was uniquely resistant to cosmic radiation, as she described, affording those with it great advantage in surviving settlement on terra formed worlds, as if they were born to do so. Since this genetic trait was passed fully to each descendant of every Kalinian, in a thousand years nearly every person on Arax would be so gifted. All that was needed was for those with the blood of Kal to sire many children. In truth, Lorn and Mortus agreed that the power of the monarchy would need to give way to a new form of governance, one guided by logic and reason. In that regard, the greater duty of Prince Jentra, when he came of age, was to wed Cordela and sire as many children as possible to expand the Kalinian bloodline as far and wide as they could. Terin and Corry were similarly tasked, and their descendants would wed both commoners and those of renown with equal fervor.

"Let it be known from this day forth that Prince Jentra is crowned the first king of New Tarelia!" Lorn proclaimed,

"When he comes of age, he shall wed Princess Cordela and assume regency of the realm!" Lorn added.

"Hail King Jentra, hail Queen Cordela!" the assembly proclaimed.

Thus began the age of New Tarelia, the restoration of the last holdfast of King Kal loyalists.

EPILOGUE

Seven years after the Battle of Noddegamra.
Vale of Kalin.

Lorken sat the pilot's seat of the basic class transport as the valley came fully into view. Cronus sat at his side, watching the scenic view through the viewport of their vessel. The vale rested under the shadow of the Plate Mountain Range, their towering peaks dominating the southern horizon, the morning sun playing off their snow caps. The vale nestled against the northern foothills, with a sea of lupec trees covering its ridgelines, and a narrow stream meandering its length. Much of the valley floor was open, with low grass spreading from the banks of the river, and a series of rocky formations jutting along its winding course. A number of ruins dominated the lower vale, the graveyard of the village that was the home of Terin's ancient kin. The vale was remote, with only a narrow access point far to the north.

Lorken descended, maneuvering the small transport above the stream that bisected the vale, sweeping over its grassy banks. Cronus looked up ahead, finding the scenic dwelling resting halfway up the western ridge, two miles distance upstream. There upon the uneven slope rested the home of Terin and Corry, a beautifully crafted structure of log and stone, with broad windows covering its eastern face. Its sides were shaded by swaying lupec trees, their needled boughs reminding Lorken of North American pines and evergreens.

The home was alit with the artificial light the Earthers provided to every dwelling on Arax.

Cronus smiled seeing the familiar setting, which he visited many times each year. He lost count of the meals he shared at Terin's table over the years, or the nights he slept at his home. He was but one of many regular visitors to this special place. Lorn and Deliea, Torg, Ular, Deva and Lucas and all the crew of the *Stenox* spent as much time here as himself, as well as Valera, Letha and Tyro, and the high minsters and regents of the Northern Kingdom. Squid would often spend his winter retreat as Terin's guest, reminiscing the adventures he shared with both Terin and Jonas. Even their children spent time here, often for the summer, such as now. Both Cronus' eldest son and Lorken's son were currently here, enjoying their summer trapsing through the woods with their *cousins*, as they referred to Terin and Corry's growing brood. It was but one of the reasons for this visit, to collect their sons.

"Coming here never gets old," Lorken said, circling about the house, before setting down on the landing circle resting just beyond it, the curved silver hull of the craft gliding silently to a halt.

"No, it doesn't." Cronus smiled, trying to recall the times before, when war ravaged the land. Only his memories of Leanna remained fresh, the rest fading with time.

No sooner did the transport set down, then Corry emerged from the home, carrying her youngest in her arms, little Erella, named after Corry's late mother. Corry waited just forward of the large door, dressed in dark trousers and blouse, a pistol holstered on her hip. Rarely did either she or Terin venture from their home unarmed, as the woods were still populated with graggloggs and many other predators. She watched as the ramp of the transport lowered, waiting as Lorken and Cronus exited, each dressed similarly in Earth garb. Cronus had long since returned his *Sword of Light* to the royal family of Nayboria, renamed the Southern Kingdom in honor of its restored Tarelian tradition.

Corry combed her hair from her eyes as the gentle breeze made a nuisance, a bright smile blossoming on her lips at their approach.

No sooner had they reached her, then Lorken took the girl from her arms, tossing her into the air, while Cronus drew her in his embrace.

"You are as lovely as ever," Cronus commented as they drew briefly apart while little Erella giggled, Lorken tossing her a second time, before catching her and twirling her about.

"You are a kind liar, Cronus." Corry shook her head, knowing she looked awful with her unkempt hair and tired eyes, the drain of their seven children taxing both her and Terin.

"I always speak true. I believe country life becomes you now." Cronus smiled, wondering how the former princess of the Torry realm became so humble.

"This is hardly country life when I am blessed with every convenience that springs to mind," she said, referencing the technological wonders built into their home, from climate control, sanitation and lighting to communications with nearly every point on the continent and every form of entertainment available at her fingertips. Beside the home stood a greenery, where they grew any form of fruit and vegetable from either Earth or Arax. She tried to imagine her life before, wondering how she lived without these gifts.

"The convenience of civilization with the peace of the countryside, what better way to live," Cronus said, having spent his years since the Oddigem at court, and now as commander of the Tarelian elite.

"True, and we have each of you to thank for it, along with our many friends," she said, recalling the day she and Terin were brought here and shown their wonderful home. It was a gift from the most eccentric collection of individuals one could imagine, each adding their own ideas to the project, from Raven and the Earthers, to Cronus, Squid, Lorn, the Jenaii and especially Tyro, who revealed this location to the others. There was no place more appropriate for the blood of Kal to propagate than their ancestral home.

"It was our pleasure, and we couldn't think of a gift Terin would treasure more," Cronus said, knowing Terin's desire to shun the public life and the trappings of court. Only he could have set the precedent for the Northern Kingdom to have leaders serve a short time before giving way for others, providing a future of leadership based on meritocracy over nepotism and checks on power to curb tyranny. When needed, his voice was ready to intercede, but he never had to. Every person on Arax knew of Terin Caleph and the role he played in ushering in their new world as the Champion of the Torry Realm, the heir of Kal and the grandson of Tyro. He was the wielder of the *Sword of the Moon* and of the *sun*, and summoner of the Earth armada that delivered the final blow and brought their wondrous gifts to Arax. Now his driving purpose was to propagate his line, spreading the Kalinian bloodline to the world, for which he and Corry accounted well of themselves.

"Speaking of Terin, where is he?" Lorken asked, drawing her into his embrace with his free hand, with Erella in his other.

"He, Argos and Zem took the older children down to the stream." She pointed to the trail off her left which followed between a line of lupec trees shading its path.

"How have you put up with Zem for the past ten days is beyond me." Lorken shook his head, his large metallic friend another of their usual visitors.

"Uju always insists on it. Besides, the children love him and Argos," Corry said, finding it endearing. Both of Raven's eldest sons were also here, with Ujurack's friendship with Zem well known to all.

"I'll fetch them," Cronus said, leaving Lorken with Corry, who drew him into the house, but not before he fetched their things from the transport.

* * *

Cronus made his way along the shaded path, careful not to trip on the raised tree roots that were hidden beneath layers of dead lupec needles that littered parts of the trail. The path meandered its gentle descent down the ridgeline before opening a bit where the river came into view. There he saw Terin and with Raven's eldest son Jake, and Lorken's eldest son John, along with Terin's eldest three children, all standing ankle deep in the water with fishing poles. Some wore tunics, and the others trousers with their pant legs rolled up to their knees.

Further up the bank, Zem sat on an overturned log, with his hands on his knees telling stories to the others, including Cronus' eldest son, little Arsenc, while Argos stood beside him with his arms crossed, thinking of what they would have for lunch. He could overhear his son Arsenc talking, asking Zem another question.

"Can you tell of the day you first met Uncle Terin? I like that story," Arsenc asked, his eyes wide with wonder as he sat cross-legged on the ground beside the other children.

"The part where you crushed the man's head in with your fist," Ujurack added. Cronus marveled at Uju and how much he had grown for a child his age. His flesh was still pure black with scalelike skin. His build was very thick, and he was now able to crush small rocks in his grip. Whatever genetic quirk caused the mutation, no one could guess, not even the medical team aboard the *Stalingrad*. Beside that, the boy looked healthy and was very friendly, especially with *Uncle* Zem.

"Raven and I were meeting with a most unsavory character at the Uxel Tavern when Terin and Cronus entered the establishment..." Zem began, recalling the eventful day at Rego.

Cronus held back, listening to the story so as not to disturb the scene. What better life for a child than to be here in the countryside, hearing stories from Zem or fishing in a cold mountain stream. His presence was soon noted though, when Terin's eldest son, Joriah, pointed him out from his place in the stream, standing beside his father.

"Uncle Cronus!" Joriah shouted, dropping his pole where he stood, splashing through the water as he ran to him.

Cronus laughed, scooping Terin's eldest into his arms as the other children followed, gathering around him. It took a while for him to greet them before he could clasp arms with Terin, drawing him into his embrace.

"I wasn't expecting you so early," Terin said, pleased to see his old friend.

"We finished up in Rego quicker than expected, so here we are," Cronus said.

"How long can you stay?"

"Just tonight, if you will have us."

"Don't be foolish. You are always welcome." Terin touched his shoulder before Zem and Argos greeted him with bone-crushing hugs.

* * *

The afternoon found them in the open living area of the home with a blazing fireplace dominating its far wall, opposite the east wall where large clear windows afforded a breathtaking view of the vale below. Cronus stood at the edge of the room, holding his gift for Terin in his hand, looking out to the east where the encroaching dark colored the distant sky, and the line of towering peaks of the Plate Mountains rested to his right, disappearing in the distant horizon. Behind him the sound of the children filled the air, giving the rustic place the warmest feeling. Terin and Corry busied themselves in the kitchen, preparing their evening meal, with a long wide bar separating them from the great room. Argos and Zem were busy with the children, all gathered about a large table in the center of the room, seated on long couches and chairs pushed closer to play a game laid before them. It was part of their evening ritual whenever Zem stayed with them, playing an old-fashioned board game rather than the holo visuals that usually entertained them.

Cronus turned about, enjoying their happy faces, sparing a glance about the room, impressed with its treated log walls, and open stone floor, blending together with natural warmth, the Earthers' *magic* illuminating the room with minimal presence. Of all the places in the world, this was the most peaceful. If he could, he would bring Ilesa here and dwell beside his friend. Lorken was loitering beside him, placing his hand on the seam where the window met the wood of the wall, testing its strength. The Earthers were the ones to design the structure, their teams erecting the domicile in a matter of days, though the details of the interior took time to decide and coordinate, each of them adding their unique touch. Lorken made his way toward the kitchen, relieving Terin in his duties so he could speak with Cronus.

"It is good to see you, Cronus," Terin said, coming to his side, never growing tired of saying that. Though Cronus visited as often as he could, his duties at court limited such opportunities.

"And I, you, my friend. I wish I could stay longer. You have a wonderful home and family, and you always make me feel a part of it." He placed a hand to Terin's shoulder.

"You are a part of it, and you always will be, ever since that eventful day we met on the road to Central City."

"Where our story began," Cronus recalled, handing the item in his free hand to Terin.

"Is that?"

"The final book. Galen wanted to give you the first copy as usual, before it is officially presented to the public," Cronus said as Terin ran his hand over the intricate cover. Books were a rarity before the Earthers arrived, requiring a scribe to pen each page, copying a text without error. It was a time consuming and expensive process. Now it was simple, though the Earthers hardly had need of books or tomes as they were, relying heavily on their holo feeds for information and entertainment. All of the academies that were established across Arax still emphasized the need to read the written word, an essential skill in the event of technology ever collapsing.

"I thought the cover most appropriate," Cronus said, regarding the design with the nine Swords of Light thrust into the air, their light joining as one. The work was a collaboration between Dr. Chopra, Galen and Aldo, though Galen's prose wove the tale together.

"*Restoration*," Terin said, referencing the title. It was the last in the series Galen aptly called *The Chronicles of Arax*. He had yet to begin Book One, which rested with the other six on the shelf in his study chamber.

"A tepid but appropriate name for ending the tale," Cronus said as Lorken made his way over to them, stuffing a piece of freshly cooked fish in his mouth.

"Raven wanted to add something, so the last line in the book was his," Lorken said after swallowing his food, licking the juice from his fingers.

Terin flipped to the last page, wondering what Raven would say that best described the end of their story.

"...*And they lived happily ever after*," he read aloud.

"That doesn't sound like Raven. He is rarely so sentimental," Cronus said, rather impressed.

"He isn't. That used to be the end of every fairytale on Earth. He was just being stupid." Lorken shook his head.

"I like it." Terin smiled.

"Mentioning Raven brings up another reason for our visit," Cronus said, besides collecting their children.

Lorken took that as his cue to elaborate.

"Admiral Kruger and the Grand Council have decided that it is time to begin contacting the other continents, beginning with the matriarchy resting beyond our western sea. They think using the *Stenox* would be the best approach, powerful but not overwhelmingly so, at least on the surface," Lorken said.

"Raven, of course, wants to resume his captaincy for this mission, and wants the old crew back for this last voyage, and that includes you and I," Cronus added.

"When was the last time it sailed?" Terin asked, recalling that the *Stenox* had been moored at Bansoch for years. It was more of a museum piece now than a working vessel.

"Three years, but the hull is made of trundusium, and the engines and weapons banks are fully operational. It will be one last mission together, all of us," Lorken said.

"Tosha is allowing this?" Terin asked.

"She is coming along. Says he isn't going without her." Lorken chuckled.

"She will be the leading emissary while Raven will command the ship," Cronus explained.

"Which means the rest of us will do all the work while he sits there playing Planet Smasher on his console." Lorken shook his head.

"No. I disabled all those features on the captain's console before I came here," Zem said from his seat, overhearing their conversation.

"Just the captain's or all the consoles?" Lorken asked as Zem gained his feet, making his way over to them.

"Just the captain's. Admiral Kruger informed me of this mission before I came here, but it was still in the planning phase," Zem said, rather pleased with himself at the thought of Raven sitting in his stupid chair with nothing to do other than his job, which brought a chorus of grins form the others.

"What are you boys discussing?" Corry asked from across the room, finishing the last touches on their supper.

"Another mission," Terin said, to which Cronus explained, his declaration causing the children excitement, each wanting to go.

"Do you want to go?" Corry asked of Terin.

He sighed, looking at the children and then her, wondering how he could leave them, if only for a short while.

"The *Stalingrad* will be monitoring our journey and will intercede if we need them to," Lorken said, hoping that would sooth their angst.

"I am coming with you," Corry said, deciding for the both of them.

"What of the children?" Terin asked.

"Your mother and grandfather can watch them," she said.

"Which grandfather?" he asked.

"Both of them. In fact, both of you should leave your children here as well," Corry added, looking to Lorken and Cronus. The thought of Valera, Torg and Tyro watching this horde of children brought a devious smile to her mind.

With all of them now looking to Terin, waiting for his response, he quickly relented. He walked over to the mantel, where rested the *Sword of the Sun*. He took it in hand, drawing it from its plain leather sheath, the blade bursting in luminous crimson light. The children looked on with awe, their eyes filled with wonder. He had not drawn the weapon in years, letting it rest undisturbed upon his mantel.

"Very well, we shall go." he relented, sheathing the blade and placing it back above the fireplace.

"Can we eat first?" Argos growled, the smell of the food drifting from the kitchen torturing his hungry stomach.

* * *

It was late in the evening when Terin retired to their bedroom, having settled the children and made plans with Cronus and Lorken for their departure in the coming days. He changed into his night clothes, pausing at the window of their bedroom, looking out across the beautiful view of the night sky, starlight shining clearly above. He could hear a loud squawk in the distance, looking up to see Wind Racer's shadow passing the face of the nearly full moon. He set the great warbird free when they came here, and his friend made a home in the mountains with his mate. The magantor would visit him from time to time, nudging him with his beak as Terin stroked his feathered neck. The children came to love him, one of Terin's many visitors they came to adore.

He felt Corry come to his side, running her hand along his shoulder before he drew his arm around her as they looked afar, saying so much without saying a word. This was the life he could have only dreamed of, perfect in every way.

"Are you worried about leaving?" she asked, voicing her own concern.

"We shan't be long, and the children will be in good company." He sighed.

"It will do us good to get away, one last adventure before we grow old." She nestled her head against his chest.

"As long as I grow old with you." He smiled wanly, holding her tight.

"Papa!" They heard the sound of their eldest daughter's voice echo behind them, turning to see her in the doorway of their bedroom with a book clenched to her chest, the five-year old's bright blue eyes wide with wonder.

"Leanna, you should be in bed," Corry said, gathering the skirt of her nightgown about her as she stepped from Terin's embrace, kneeling as the girl stepped forth.

"I couldn't sleep, and wanted to ask Papa to read to me," little Leanna said.

"Sure," Terin said before Corry could object, stepping forth to look at what she was holding, seeing the first book in Galen and Dr.

Chopra's series on the great war, wondering how she retrieved it from the high shelf where it sat.

"*The Chronicles of Arax Book One, Of War and Heroes.*" Corry read aloud the cover, running her fingers over its unique design, showing Morac and Terin fighting atop the battlements of Fera, with Raven and Lorken in the background shooting gargoyles.

"If I read it, you have to promise not to be scared," Terin sternly warned.

"I promise, Papa." Leanna beamed proudly as Terin scooped her into the air, tossing her on their bed. She giggled, smoothing her nightdress before sitting between their pillows as her parents took their places on each side of her. She rested her head on her father's shoulder as he flipped to the first chapter.

"Are you ready?" he asked, at which she vehemently nodded.

"Very well, here it begins… *A strong northern gale swept through the trees, drying the sweat building on his forehead. The solace of the early spring wind quickly waned as…*" Terin began reading.

Corry looked on, stroking her daughter's hair, savoring the warmth of her child and the man she loved.

And they lived happily ever after.

Thus concludes the Chronicles of Arax.

Appendix A

Chronology of Araxan History

–502	Fall of Old Kingdom. Deaths of King Kal and Queen Celenia. Rise of the traitor realms. Gargoyles emerge from Mote Mountains and Nameless Hills.
–497	Corvar Dynasty expands from Gorga River to Reguh River.
–493	Verunium Federation conquers upper Veneba and Tur River Valley. Nonn tribes sweep over Lone Hills to Rocky Coast.
–490	Sargoan Kingdom conquers upper Muva; King Sagus builds capital at Faust.
–480	Varabis the Cruel raids southeastern coast and sacks Carig, renaming the port in his namesake.
–471	Remnants of Old Kingdom build settlements along the Lower Nila.
–400	Gargoyles expand to Western Plate and crush Vayon tribes, driving them into the Upper Nila.
–390	Remnants of Old Kingdom are driven from the Lower Nila by Vayon tribes.

-384   Remnants of Old Kingdom settle along the northern shore of Lake Monata and build the sanctuary of Tarelia, sheltered by the Arian Hills.

-314   Ape tribes withdraw to Ape Hills.

-230   Gargoyles expand into Eastern Plate.

-197   Battle of Castara; General Zuvo repels gargoyle invasion along the upper Veneba.

-150   Gargoyles destroy Vayon tribes along the Upper Nila.

-130   Gargoyles expand to Eastern Cress.

-111   Gargoyles defeat Corvar army along the Reguh.

-73   Gargoyles cross the Cress and raid Sargoan settlements along the Muva.

-63   Battle of Tevara.
Gargoyles crush Ionian tribes along the Stlen.

-59   Gargoyles expand to Lone Hills, checked by Nonn tribes.

-43   Gargoyles raid Western Ape Hills, driven off by General Gour.

-31   Tarelian expedition drives gargoyles from the Stlen.
General Pelen crushes gargoyle army at the conjoint of the Stlen and Javo Rivers.
Javo was renamed Pelen.

-23   Fall of Corvar Dynasty.
Death of King Fabis.
Levotrist tribes sack Laycoris.

-15   Gargoyles crush Verunium Army along the Upper Tur.
Verunium Federation fractures.

0   Jenaii fleet reach the mouth of the Elaris and establish port of El-Tova.
El Ebiorn becomes first lord of the birdmen.

5   El Ebiorn leads expedition to Tarelia and presents the divine gift to the Tarelian council.

17   Death of King Sarlat.
War of succession shatters Sargoan Kingdom.

19   Jenaii Kingdom expands from the Elaris to the Clev Rivers.

23   Soch Corsairs seize North Isle, trade exclusively in female slaves, and begin raiding the northwest coast of Arax.

25   Tarelian colonists settle on the Upper Nila.

37   Tarelian colonists settle along the Reguh.

41   Jenaii begin construction of El-Orva, the Blue Castle.

43   Death of El Ebiorn. His son El Ebior ascends the throne.

52   Tarelian colonists settle along the Muva. 53   Nomadic peoples scatter the Nonn tribes and force the remnants across the Elaris and into the Jenaii Kingdom.
Tarelian general Zeitas allies with El Ebior and drives out nomadic invaders across the Elaris.
Jenaii-Tarelian alliance rally Nonn tribes and expel nomadic peoples across the Naiba.
General Zeitas weds Nonn princess Nisa and forge Zeltar Kingdom.
Gargoyle invasion of Zeltar.
Death of King Zeitas.
King El Ebior aids Zeltar king Eustar and drives gargoyles back to the Lone Hills.

90   Gargoyles destroy half of Tarelian settlements along the Reguh.

117   Smiths of Tarelia complete the *Sword of the Sun*. Council gifts the golden sword to General Clorvis Cal. General Cal leads new expedition north of the Mote Mountains.

120   Clorvis Cal founds Northern Kingdom and establishes capital at Laycrom.

122   King Clorvis Cal begins construction of Fera, the Black Castle.

159   Death of Cal. His son Seres Cal assumes the throne.

187   Smiths of Tarelia forge Swords of the Moon and gift the first *Sword of the Moon* to General Zar Zaronan, who leads Tarelian expedition to the Pelen Valley.

197   General Zar expands Tarelian hold along the Pelen and Stlen and founds Middle Kingdom, uniting the tribes and minor kingdoms south of the Plate. He builds the capital city of Central City.

205   Battle of Cular north of the Lone Hills.
King Zar crushes gargoyle army.
Ape tribes drive Kregarins from Torn Valley.
Soch Federation establishes slave ports of Tenin and Tinsay and expands raids along the Gorga, Tenia, and Muva.

237   Smiths of Tarelia forge first *Sword of the Stars*.
Council of Tarelia gifts the sword to General Telfa, who leads expedition to the Upper Muva and establishes Western Kingdom.

242   King Corell assumes throne of Middle Kingdom and begins construction of the White Castle. 243 Jenaii complete El-Orva, the Blue Castle.
Tarelian council gifts second *Sword of the Stars* to Zeltar king Eustice II. Zeltar begins construction of Nonn, the Yellow Castle.

251   Tarelian emissaries and engineers journey to Ape tribes and help begin construction of Gregok, the Green Castle.

253   King Culnar Cal defeats Soch Federation at Tinsan Bay and drives them off the northern coast.

256   The kingdom of Cagia is founded at the mouth of the Nila.

258 King Culnar Cal expands Northern Kingdom to the Reguh.

301 Western Kingdom drives Soch Federation from Tenin.
King Telfer begins construction of the Purple Castle.
Tarelian general Melida and her sister
Telisa are gifted two Swords of the Stars and lead expedition to North Isle.
General Melida slays Soch king
Vagar at the port of Soch.
Fall of Soch Federation.
The port is named the Bane of Soch and eventually shortened to Bansoch.
Melida leads the slave revolt.
Soch Federation is outnumbered by their female slaves by one hundred to one.
Melida establishes the Federation of the Sisterhood.
Massacre of Soch masters throughout the Isle. Melida is named queen and first guardian of the Sisterhood.

331 Tarelian council gifts fifth and sixth *Swords of the Stars* to Generals Vatar and Nisin, who lead an expedition north of Veneba.

337 Battle of Tur Valley.
King Sargos Cal leads Northern Kingdom to aid Generals Vatar and Nisin, and they defeat the gargoyle horde.
General Vatar falls in battle.
General Nisin is named the king of Eastern Kingdom and gifts the sword of Vatar to Prince Sartos Cal of the Northern Kingdom for their aid in battle.

339 King Nisin begins construction of the Red Castle.

351 Fera, the Black Castle, is completed.

380 Nonn, the Yellow Castle, is completed.
It is later named simply Non.

390   Western Kingdom moves its capital to Tenin.

406   Telfer, the Purple Castle, is completed.
        Western Kingdom expands its realm into the Cress foot-
        hills.

415   Gregok, the Green Castle, is completed.
        Ape tribes agree to share command of fortress and form the
        Council of Chieftains.

431   Plague strikes Varabis.

437   Ports of Teris and Coven wage war of control for Casian
        Sea.

441   Corell, the White Castle, is completed.

453   Tarelian colonists build port of Sawyer.
        Naybin tribes cross the Naiba and slay Zeltos king Eustice
        VII at the Battle of Der.
        The *Sword of the Stars* is taken.
        King El Elen leads Jenaii army across the Elaris to aid
        Zeltar.
        Naybin chieftain Plou ambushes Jenaii in the Serren For-
        est. Jenaii withdraw.
        Defenders yield the Fortress of Non.
        Naybins declare Plou the first king of Nayboria.

500   Gargoyle horde sweeps from the Lone Hills, cross the
        Upper Monata, and invade the Jenaii Kingdom. Naybin
        Army, led by Pou II, cross the Elaris. Zar II leads Middle
        Kingdom Army to aid the Jenaii, breaking the siege of El-
        Orva.
        Plou II is slain in battle.
        Sword of the Stars is passed to his son, Prince Plou III.
        Naybins withdraw across the Elaris.
        Gargoyle horde is crushed.

503   Middle Kingdom and Jenaii armies aid local tribes and
        clear gargoyles from the Lone Hills.

Teris and Coven wage second war
for control of Casian Sea. The war ends with a truce and
the Treaty of Casian Alliance.
Gargoyles spill out of the Cress
Mountains and siege Telfer.
Death of King Telfin II.
Prince Telfin III rallies Western Kingdom and breaks siege
of Telfer.
Gargoyles withdraw.

518–
520   Western Kingdom and Northern Kingdom expel gargoyles
from the Cress Mountains and destroy nesting grounds.
Gargoyles withdraw to Mote and Plate Mountains.
King Telfin III is slain in the Vorun Gap.
The *Sword of the Stars* is lost.

525   Plague strikes Tarelia.

522–
526   Tatin, Yatin, and Maltin barbarians swarm southwestern
coast of Arax.
Tatins siege Cagan. Yatins seize Faust and advance up the
Muva. Maltins settle by the lower Monata River and assail
Sawyer.
Tatins are driven off.
Gargoyles invade Middle Kingdom.
Siege of Corell.
King El Evur breaks siege and drives gargoyles back to the
Plate.
Maltin Army crosses Lake Monata and sack Tarelia.
The ancient holdfast is destroyed.
The library of Tarelia is burned.
Maltins siege Sawyer.
King Corell IV and King El Evur lead Middle Kingdom
and Jenaii hosts to lift siege.
The Maltins are crushed.

530   In the Battle of Muva, Yatin king Mosar

slays Western king Telfer V.
Yatins invade upper half of the kingdom.
Fall of Tenin.
Western Kingdom falls.
Yatin general Mosar named first emperor of Yatin.

540   Nisin, the Red Castle, is completed.

543   Kingdom of Cesa allies with Null consortium and fortifies coastal defenses against Maltin barbarians, who still dwell north and east along the Maconan heartland.

551   Ruling families establish Troan city state.

563   Gargoyles siege Nisin.
King Netso II repels invaders.
Gargoyles break upon the ramparts and withdraw to the Plate.

574   King Clorvis V calls for King Corell VI and King Netso to join in alliance to expel gargoyles from their last holdfasts along the Mote and Plate Mountains. Each agree to the Feran Alliance, the last great crusade to expel the gargoyles from Arax.
King Clorvis V and King Corell VI drive gargoyles from the Wid River Valley. King Netso clears the Plate foothills from Veneba to the Reguh.
King El Oberan joins the Feran Alliance and leads Jenaii battlegroups into the Middle Kingdom. Jenaii and the Middle Kingdom drive gargoyles deep into the Plate Mountains.
Prince Clorvis VI is ambushed by Menotrist tribes east of the Mote Mountains. The *Sword of the Stars* gifted by the Eastern Kingdom is lost with him. King Clorvis V abandons Plate Campaign to expel Menotrists from his realm.
Yatin king Mosun II crosses the Rolun Gap and invades the Middle Kingdom.

Siege of Central City. King Corell VI abandons Plate Campaign to lift the siege.

Battle of Turlis ends Yatin invasion.

Death of Mosun II and King Corell VI.

The Sisterhood's fleet sacks Tenin harbor, frees thousands of female slaves, burns Yatin fleet, and seizes the imperial treasury.

Yatins sue for peace with the Middle Kingdom and the Sisterhood.

Nayborians invade Jenaii Kingdom.

Prince Zar V is crowned king of the Middle Kingdom and leads Torry Army to Jenaii's defense. El Oberan abandons Plate Campaign and joins Zar V in Jenaii campaign.

In the Battle of Etavorun, the Naybins are crushed.

Zar V sacks Plou, and the forces of Naybins submit. Jenaii seize Non.

King Netso falls in the battle of the Western Plate.

The *Sword of the Stars* is lost. Gargoyles rout Eastern Kingdom army and swarm the upper Tur Valley.

King Zar V weds Queen Melina of the Sisterhood, the first marriage of the monarchies.

581   Queen Melina III births twins, Prince Zar VI and Princess Melina II. Zar VI is named heir to the Middle Kingdom, and Melina II is named crown princess of the Sisterhood.

583   Tro Harbor is sacked by Venotrist tribes.

Venotrists migrate north along the Veneba.

Gargoyles siege Nisin.

The Eastern Kingdom calls for aid to Northern Kingdom. King Clorvis V ignores their pleas, driven mad by the death of his son, Clorvis VI.

Benotrist tribes seize the Upper Reguh.

Venotrists ambush Nisin's relief army and settle in the Eastern Kingdom. Gargoyles fail to sack Nisin and withdraw to the Upper Plate. The Eastern Kingdom is greatly reduced.

Menotrist tribes invade the Middle Kingdom.
King Zar VI falls in battle.
Prince Cot assumes the throne and drives Menotrists beyond Tuft's Mountain.
King Cot defeats Menotrists at the Winding River. 641
Venotrists sack Nisin. The palace falls in one night through trickery.
Fall of the Eastern Kingdom.

648   Northern Kingdom repels Venotrists at the Reguh.

652   Gargoyles massacre Menotrists near Mote Mountains.

660–   Menotrists migrate into the Northern Kingdom.
663   King Clorvin crushes Menotrist tribes and drives them into the northern Cress Mountains. Clorvin the Cruel slaughters thousands of prisoners, hanging them upon crossed boards along his borders, including women and children.

674   Gargoyles advance to the Nameless Mountains and slaughter thousands of Benotrists, Venotrists, and Menotrists. Clorvin the Cruel ignores their plight, allowing gargoyles to purge inferior peoples.

704   Queen Velima II leads the Sisterhood's fleet into the Bay of Faust and destroys the Yatin fleet.
Yatin prince Yagnar is captured and enslaved by the Council of Guardians. Queen Velima II claims him as slave consort.
Yatins sue for peace.
The Sisterhood's trade routes along the western sea board are secure.

711   The *Sword of the Sun* is stolen. The Northern Kingdom searches the Nameless Mountains and Mote foothills to no avail.
The Northern Kingdom begins to fade.

821   Gargoyles invade the Middle Kingdom. King Corell VI
        and Jenaii king El Enor drive gargoyles back across the
        Plate.
        Naybins seize Non and slaughter Jenaii's garrison.
        Naybin's restoration.
        Jenaii withdraws across the Elaris.

841   King Vanlar is ambushed at Pharna.
        The *Sword of the Moon* is lost.
        The Middle Kingdom begins to fade.
        Menotrists seize Laycrom.
        Garrison of Fera dwindles.
        Death of King Clorvis XII.
        The Northern Kingdom shatters into a dozen separate
        regencies.
        King Vantor II receives great prophecy of the lost sword of
        the Middle Kingdom and gathers the Tarelian faithful from
        the fallen kingdoms to Corell.
        The Middle Kingdom endures.

899   Cagia expands borders.
        King Orvonus weds the princess of Tuk.
        Union of both kingdoms into greater Cagia.

920   Port West joins the Casian League.

931   Bacel and Notsu repel Venotrist invasion. King Vanlar III
        leads the Middle Kingdom to their aid.

1004   Plague sweeps Central City. Sixty percent perish in its
        wake.

1014   Yatins invade Cagia. Storm destroys half of the Yatin
        fleet. Emperor Yagun II sees the storm as an ill omen and
        withdraws.

1036   Menotrists expand westward and seize Tinsay.
        Menotrists name Maglar king of Menot Kingdom and gain

dominion of all lands from the northern coast to the Cress
foothills and Tinsay to Laycrom.

1041 Eastern Menotrists seize Fera.
Last of the Northern Kingdom's regencies falls.
Eastern Menotrists name Malan first King of East
Menot and gain dominion of all lands from Fera to Mor-
dicay and the Reguh and Morga River Valleys. Drive
Benotrists into Plate foothills and eastward into the Vale of
Nisa.

1049– Venotrists repel Benotrist incursion.
1059 Benotrist tribes migrate along the Plate and settle in the
gap between Mote and Plate Mountains, an arduous trek
known as the Trail of Woes.

1099– Gargoyles gather great host in Central Plate and invade the
1101 Middle Kingdom.
Siege of Corell.
King Cot V and King El Evore crush gargoyles at the Battle of Besos.

1115– Naybins seize Barbeario.
1117 Varabin and Casian mercenaries lead revolt.
The bloody streets are heralded in song.
Casian League cuts Naybin sea routes.
Jenaii threatens invasion.
Naybins withdraw claim upon Barbeario.

1241 Menot Armada assails Bansoch. The Sisterhood crushes
invasion. Thousands of Menot sailors are enslaved.

1259 Gargoyles recover strength and sweep across the northern
plains.
Venotrists lose control of Tur Valley.
Pagan is sacked and burned.

1290 Menotrists seize undermanned Nisin.

1305   The Middle Kingdom extends east-west road from Corell to Notsu.

1386   Cesa wars with Fleace.
Battle of Iotia.
Fleace gains control over greater Maconia.

1409–   Gargoyles invade Reguh Valley.
1415   East Menot seeks alliance with West Menot. Union of Fera and Laycrom is sealed with the marriage of Menot crown prince Matan II and East Menot princess Alleria. Greater Menot union drives gargoyles from Reguh Valley.

1425   Matan II ascends the throne of Menot and seeks union with western Menotrist tribes who hold Greater Nisa and the Red Castle.

1431   Union of all Menotrist kingdoms under Matan II.

1440   Gargoyles again invade the Middle Kingdom.
Siege of Corell.
King Toria and El Elon, lord of the birdmen, lift siege and drive gargoyles back to the Plate.

1453   Gargoyles swarm out of Mote and Plate Mountains.
Benotrists flee Gargoyle hordes and enter western Menot at the invite of Menotrist king Matan III to settle lands between Fera and the Nameless Mountains.
Benotrists ae betrayed by Menotrist host. Their leaders are slain, and their people are reduced to serfdom.

1477   Yatins cross the Rolun Gap and seize Turlis.
War of the Middle Kingdom and Yatin.
King Toria II is slain at the Nila.
Turlis ceded to the Yatin Empire.
Prince Torry ascends the throne at the age of twelve.
Yatins cross the Yagan swamps and advance to Cagan Harbor.
King Torry declares war upon Yatin, seizes

Turlis in one night, aligns with the kingdoms of Zulon and Teso, drives Yatins from the Nila Valley, relieves Tuk, and smashes Yatin host before the walls of Cagan.
King Torry weds the princess Galena of Cagia, joining their kingdoms.
Old Cagia becomes Torry South, and the Middle Kingdom is renamed Torry North. Zulon and Teso control Nila between the Torry realms.

1517   Milito, Krakita, and Morito join the Casian League and establish the Plutocratic Federation, controlling trade routes from the Rocky Shores to Linkortus.

1525   Casian Federation seizes Torn and expands control along the Ape Coast.

1542–   Benotrist population swells.
1576   Menotrists relocate one hundred thousand serfs along the northwestern coast. Benotrists revolt over mistreatment. The revolt is put down by Menot king Margos Andler. Five thousand disfigured prisoners perish along the northern branch of the Gorga River, renamed the Andler.

1605–   The Middle Kingdom expands magantor cavalry and
1650   begins clearing lower Plate of gargoyle raiders.

1685   Union of Fleace, Cesa, and Null.
Mortun is named regent of the Macon Empire.
Macons control all lands south of Monata River, between Torry South and the Jenaii kingdoms. Only Sawyer blocks their full access to Lake Monata.

1701   Macons assail Sawyer.
Siege is lifted by King Torry III and Jenaii king El Ellon.

1783   Torry king Lorn I expels gargoyles from Wid River. Colonists flock to the fertile valley.

1830   Birth of Tyro.

1848   Birth of Jonas Caleph

1853–   Benotrist revolution lead by Morca.

1864   Tyro finds the *Sword of the Sun*. He unifies gargoyles and Benotrists. Birth of Morac. Death of Morca.
Tyro overthrows Menotrist kingdom and is named emperor of Benotrist-Gargoyle Empire. Benotrist Empire expands from Tinsay to Nisin.
Gargoyles establish secure nesting grounds across Benotrist Empire and grow in great numbers.
Tyro searches in vain for his wife and child.

1863–   Sadden Wars.

1866   Gargoyles are driven north of the Plate.
Trade routes are secured between Torry North and South.
Yatins are expelled from Nila Valley.
Jonas Caleph finds the *Sword of the Moon* and leads charge of Celti Flats.
Prince Lore assumes throne of Torry realms.
Princess Letha of the Sisterhood weds Tyro.
Birth of Cronus Kenti.
Birth of Lorn II.
Birth of Tosha.
Letha revokes marriage to Tyro.
Birth of Princess Corry.
Birth of Terin Caleph.

1882   Tyro forms alliance with Naybin emperor Lichu.

1887   Earthers arrive on Arax.

1889   Revolution in the Ape Empire.
General Matuzak expels merchant bureaucracy and despot Ape chieftains.

1891   Battle of Tuft's Mountain.
Thus begins the Great War.

Appendix B

Armies of Arax

Torry Armies

Army	Location	Commander	Size
1st	Southeast of Nisin	Lewins	10-12 Telnics
2nd	West of Besos	Fonis	20 Telnics
3rd	Corell	Mastorn	10 Telnics
4th	Tinsay	Farro	12 Telnics
5th	(Destroyed at Kregmarin)		
Torry/Macon army	Southeast of Nisin	Ciyon	10-15 Telnics

LARGE GARRISONS

	Location	Commander	Size
	Cropus	Torgus Vantel	3 Telnics
	Corell	Balka	3 Telnics
	Central City	Torvin	5 Telnics
	Cagan	Telanus	2 Telnics

Cavalry

	Location	Commander	Size
1st	Reconfigured into the 2nd Torry Cavalry		
2nd	Near Nisin	Connly	841

Cavalry (continued)

Army	Location	Commander	Size
3rd	Reconfigured into the 2nd Torry Cavalry		
4th	Tinsay	Avliam	350 mounts

Navy

Fleet	Location	Admiral	Size
1st	South of Tinsay (Includes 3 captured Benotrist warships)	Kilan (Grand Admiral)	29 galleys
2nd	South of Tinsay	Horikor	47 galleys
3rd	South of Tinsay	Liman	21 galleys
4th	South of Tinsay	Nylo	20 galleys
5th	South of Tinsay	Morita	17 galleys

BENOTRIST/GARGOYLE ARMIES

Legion	Location	Commander	Size
1st (gargoyle)	Destroyed		
2nd (gargoyle)	Destroyed and dispersed		
3rd (gargoyle)	Destroyed		
4th (gargoyle)	Surviving telnics absorbed by 5th Legion		
5th (gargoyle)	West of Nisin	Kriton	38-42 Telnics
	(Includes all telnics of 4th, 7th, 12th, and 14th Legions)		
6th (gargoyle)	Destroyed at Corell		
7th (gargoyle)	Surviving telnics absorbed by 5th Legion		
8th (Benotrist)	Surviving telnics joined with 10th Legion		
9th (Benotrist)	Surviving telnics joined with 10th Legion		
10th (Benotrist)	West of Nisin	Gavis	40-41 Telnics
11th (Benotrist)	Destroyed at Notsu		
	(Half of legion surrendered at Besos)		
12th (gargoyle)	Surviving telnics joined with 5th Legion		
13th (Benotrist)	Laycrom	Trinapolis	50 Telnics
14th (gargoyle)	Surviving telnics joined with 5th Legion		
15th (gargoyle)	Dispersed		
16th (gargoyle)	Destroyed at Tuft's Mountain		
17th (gargoyle)	Destroyed at Tuft's Mountain		
18th (gargoyle)	Destroyed at Tuft's Mountain		

BENOTRIST/GARGOYLE ARMIES (continued)

Legion	Location	Commander	Size
GARRISON FORCES			
	Fera		29 T (Benotrist)
	Nisin		10 T (Benotrist)
	Pagan		Surrendered
	Mordicay		10 T (Benotrist)
	Tinsay		20 T (Benotrist)
	Laycrom		20 T (Benotrist)
	Border posts		Dispersed

Benotrist Navy

Fleet	Location	Admiral	Size
1st	Tinsay	Plesnivolk	48 galleys
2nd	Destroyed north of Tenin		
3rd	Destroyed near Terse		
4th	Destroyed near Terse		
5th	Destroyed north of Tenin		
6th	Pagan	Silniw	53 galleys
	(elements of 3rd and 4th fleet joined with 6th, swore loyalty to Terin)		
7th	Destroyed north of Tenin		
8th	Tinsay	Zelitov	50 galleys

YATIN ARMIES

Army	Location	Commander	Size
1st	South of Tinsay	Yoria	18 Telnics
2nd	South of Tinsay	Yitia	20 Telnics
3rd	Destroyed at Mosar (3 surviving telnics joined with 1st Army)		
4th	Tenin	Surrendered to Torab	

GARRISON FORCES

	Mosar	Yakue	3 Telnics
	Telfer	Destroyed in Siege of Telfer	
	Tenin	Surrendered to Torab	

Yatin Cavalry

Army	Location	Commander	Size
1st	Telfer	Destroyed in Battle of Salamin Valley	
2nd	Approaching Tinsay	Cornyana	436 mounts

Yatin Navy

Fleet	Location	Admiral	Size
1st	Tenin	Sunk in Battle of Cull's Arc	
2nd	Tenin	Sunk in Battle of Cull's Arc	
3rd	Approaching Tinsay	Horician	16 galleys

Jenaii Armies

Battle Group	Location	Commander	Size
1st	South of Nisin	El Tuvo	7 Telnics
2nd	South of Nisin	Ev Evorn	12 Telnics
3rd	Non	En Elon	18 Telnics

GARRISON FORCES

	El Orva	El Orta	15 Telnics
	El Tova	En Vor	5 Telnics

Jenaii Navy

Fleet	Location	Admiral	Size
1st	El Tova	En Atar	20 galleys
2nd	El Tova	En Ovir	20 galleys
3rd	El Tova	En Toshin	20 galleys

NAYBIN ARMIES

Army	Location	Commander	Size
1st	Surrendered		
2nd	Surrendered		
3rd	Surrendered		
4th	Surrendered		

GARRISON FORCES

	Plou	Surrendered	
	Non	Surrendered	
	Naiba	Surrendered	
	Border Posts		

Naybin Navy

Fleet	Location	Admiral	Size
1st	Surrendered		
2nd	Surrendered		

MACON EMPIRE ARMIES

Army	Location	Commander	Size
1st	Fleace	Noivi	10 Telnics
2nd	South of Nisin	Vecious	13 Telnics
3rd	Reconstituted into joint Macon-Torry Army		
4th	Null	Farin	8 Telnics

GARRISON FORCES

	Fleace	Novin	3 Telnics
	Cesa	Clyvo	3 Telnics

Macon Navy

Fleet	Location	Admiral	Size
1st	South of Tinsay	Goren	20 galleys
2nd	South of Tinsay	Vulet	20 galleys
3rd	Cesa	Talmet	20 galleys
4th	Destroyed at the straits of Cesa		

APE EMPIRE ARMIES

Army	Location	Commander	Size
1st	Gregok	Cragok	20 Telnics
2nd	Pagan	Mocvoran	20 Telnics
3rd	South of Nisin	Vorklit	10 Telnics
4th	Northern Coast	Matuzon	10 Telnics
5th	Southern Coast	Vonzin	10 Telnics

GARRISON FORCES

	Location		Size
	Gregok		10 Telnics
	Torn		10 Telnics
	Talon Pass		10 Telnics

Ape Navy

Fleet	Location	Admiral	Size
1st	Pagan	Zorgon	9 galleys
2nd	Pagan	Vornam	40 galleys

CASIAN FEDERATION ARMIES

Army	Location	Commander	Size
1st	Naiba River	Gidvia	12 Telnics
2nd	Pagan	Motchi	12 Telnics
3rd	Naiba	Elke	7 Telnics

GARRISON FORCES

	Location		Size
	Milito		3 Telnics
	Coven		4 Telnics
	Port West		3 Telnics
	Teris		3 Telnics

Casian Navy

Fleet	Location	Admiral	Size
1st	Naiba	Voelin	100 galleys
2nd	Pagan	Gylan	80 galleys
3rd	Port West	Gydar	60 galleys
4th	Naiba	Eltar	60 galleys

Federation of the Sisterhood Armies

Army	Location	Commander	Size
1st	South of Tinsay	Na	20 Telnics
2nd	Fela	Vola	20 Telnics
3rd	South of Tinsay	Mial	20 Telnics

GARRISON FORCES

	Location		Size
	Bansoch		10 Telnics
	Fela		10 Telnics

Sisterhood Navy

Fleet	Location	Admiral	Size
1st	South of Tinsay	Nyla	120 galleys
2nd	South of Tinsay	Carel	80 galleys
3rd	South of Tinsay	Daila	50 galleys

Teso Armies

1st Army	Southeastern border	Hovel	4 Telnics
2nd Army	South of Nisin	Velen	1 Telnic

Zulon Armies

1st Army	Northern Border	Zarento	2 Telnics
2nd Army	South of Nisin	Zubarro	1-2 Telnics

City State Armies

Sawyer	5 Telnics	100 Cavalry	
Rego	3 Telnics	100 Cavalry	

(Rego garrison size fluctuates with new conscription)

Notsu	1-2 Telnics	200 Cavalry	

(Notsu's surviving units are joined with Torry forces)

Bacel	Destroyed at Kregmarin and siege of Bacel		
Barbeario	8 Telnics		
Bedo	10 Telnics	100 Cavalry	40 galleys
Tro Harbor	6 Telnics	50 Cavalry	14 galleys
Varabis	5 Telnics		30 galleys

OTHER BOOKS BY THE AUTHOR

Free Born saga

Free Born

Elysia

Dragon Wars (coming soon)

Chronicles of Arax

Book One: Of War and Heroes

Book Two: The Siege of Corell

Book Three: The Battle of Yatin

Book Four: The Making of a King

Book Five: The Battle of Torry North

Book Six: Fall of Empires

Book Seven: Restoration

About the Author

Ben Sanford grew up in Western New York. He spent almost twenty years as an air marshal, traveling across the United States and many parts of the world, meeting people from a broad range of cultures and backgrounds. It was from these thousands of interactions that he drew inspiration for the characters in his books. He currently resides in Maryland with his family.

www.ingramcontent.com/pod-product-compliance
Lightning Source LLC
Chambersburg PA
CBHW020335010826
48970CB00012B/830